I Dig Murder

A story of political intrigue in two times

I0638952

Dean Martin Herr
Roger A. Stacy

Isis, Osiris, and Horus

I DIG MURDER

© 2013 Dean Martin Herr & Roger A. Stacy
ALL RIGHTS RESERVED.

This is a work of fiction. Names, characters, places, and incidents either are the product of the author's imagination or are used fictitiously. Any resemblance to actual persons, living or dead, business establishments, events, or locales is entirely coincidental.

The views expressed in this novel are those of its authors. Hieroglyphic and transliteration errors in this novel are the sole responsibility of the authors.

Cover design by Ron Folsom

ISBN 0-615-77897-6
ISBN-13 978-0-615-77897-6

December 2013
FIRST EDITION

ACKNOWLEDGMENTS

Although the process of writing words on a page is a solitary one, no writer really creates a book alone. A number of people, family and friends, colleagues, other writers, critique groups, editors, publishers, all contribute to a book in one way or another.

ROGER

Special thanks to my wife, Judy, who has patiently waited for this book. To the critique group, Andre, Ralph, Katherine, Erin, Dan and my partner Dean. To Joe Calandra who expanded our horizon. To David Barnes for his editorial assistance and John Leslie for his technical assistance. And to Vicki Tonda.

DEAN

As always, thanks to Connie, wife, BFF, muse, and chief critic. Thanks to my current, furry, four-legged children, Binky and Hershey, who made sure there were cats to be worshiped in this story. Thanks to the Baba Yega critique group, whose members Roger has already mentioned. Finally, thanks to my parents, Martin and Carol, who believed I could do this long before I thought I could, and my sister Sarah, who reads all my stories—even when they aren't very good.

OSIRIS-SETH-ISIS LEGEND

Osiris and his brother, Seth, fought for absolute power over the heavens and Egypt. As much as Osiris was fair and giving, the evil Seth envied his brother and wanted to have all the power he could possess for himself. Seth plotted then killed his brother, Osiris, casting his body into the Mediterranean Sea. Isis, Osiris' beloved wife recovered the body, hiding it, but Seth discovered where Isis hid Osiris. He hacked his brother's body into fourteen pieces, spreading him to the winds. Seth wanted to deny his brother's rebirth.

Isis hunted for Osiris' body in all of its pieces to bring them back together so Osiris could join with the gods. Isis succeeded recovering all of Osiris' body parts with the exception of his organ of procreation which was eaten by a fish in the Nile. Isis prayed to the gods, to the great god Ptah and to Ra, begging their mercy and asking for their help. The great gods, Ptah and Ra, granted her wish. She coupled with Osiris even as he was dead. Osiris passed into the afterlife to be with the great gods, becoming the god of the dead. From her joining with Osiris, Isis bore him a son, naming him Horus.

Horus grew great and powerful, deriving his power from his father. Horus rose up and slew Seth, carving his body as Seth had done to his father. Horus strew Seth's body to the winds with the exception of his heart which he placed with his father's body in his tomb so Osiris could look upon Seth for all time. Seth would travel forever in the nether world between life and the everlasting. Seth would never enter the afterlife across the Nile. To this day Osiris watches over Seth's heart.

THE TOMB

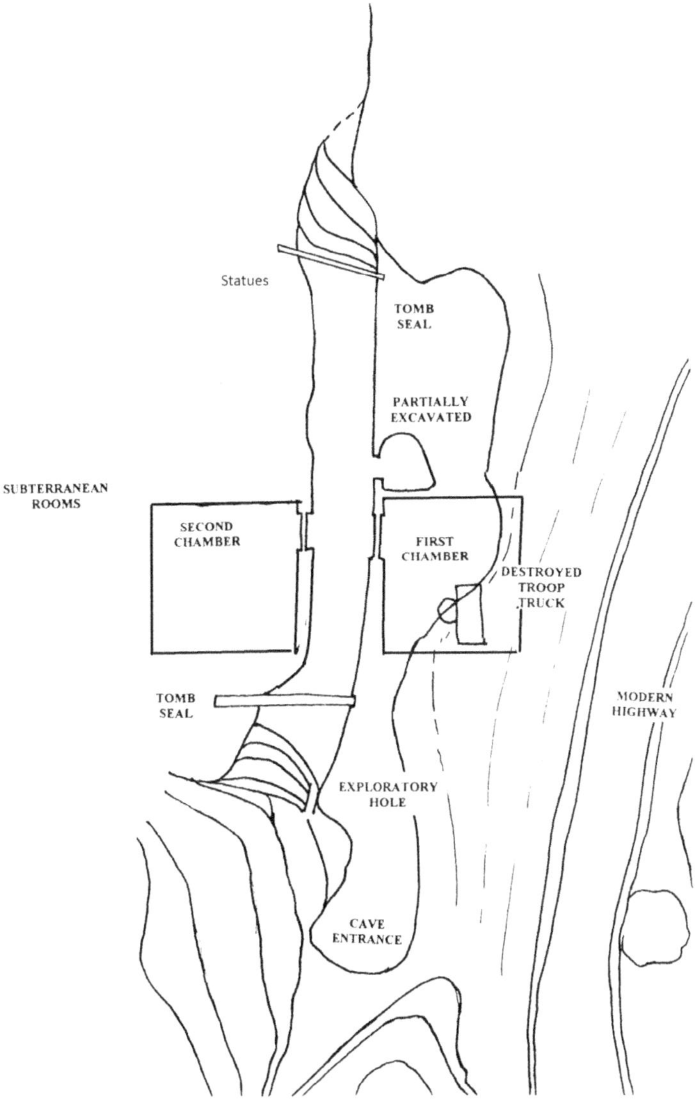

Statues
TOMB SEAL
PARTIALLY EXCAVATED
SUBTERRANEAN ROOMS
SECOND CHAMBER
FIRST CHAMBER
DESTROYED TROOP TRUCK
TOMB SEAL
MODERN HIGHWAY
EXPLORATORY HOLE
CAVE ENTRANCE

ANCIENT CAST

Ạaātchtạ-t — Maid servant to Ḥaāmer and Īset. She is either 12 or 13 years old. Her name means *maiden* or *virgin*.

Ȧamȧam — Woman who lives south of Uas and raises orphans. She raised Ṭeḥuti after his parents died. Her name means *to be strong*.

Āakhu — Youngest of Pharaoh's two daughters. Betrothed originally to Ṭeḥuti she is later married to governor Maaạ. Her name means *a bright and splendid flower.*

Ānukhet — Steerswoman aboard the trading boat Sakhr-Mut, who befriends Ṭeḥuti when he is banished from Uas and joins the crew. Her name means *beautiful and small*.

Ȧri — Friend and companion to Maaạ who accompanies him on a river voyage to see Pharaoh. His name means *to visit*.

Ạsạr — Pharaoh of the 10 provinces of upper (southern) Egypt. Later, after accepting four provinces on his northern border from governor Maaạ, he is Pharaoh of the 14 provinces of Upper Egypt.

Betnu·ȧḥa — Chief of Pharaoh's army. His name means *swift to the fight*.

Baka — Ḥaāmer's cat. His name means *morning* or *sunrise* because of his golden coat.

Gemgem — Governor of the northern province Herui and friend to Pharaoh Ạsạr. His name means *to search out or investigate*.

Ḥaāmer — Oldest of Pharaoh Ạsạr's two daughters. She dies of what comes to be known as tuberculosis. Her name means *the first of our love*.

Ḥenḥen — Fallen priest sent by set to follow and kill Pharaoh Ạsạr. His name means *sickness*.

Hepaba-t — Battered wife who seeks justice from Pharaoh Ạsạr. She is later beaten to death by her husband. Her name means *move toward the light*.

Herti — Son the the caravan leader Khashta. He finds the injured Ṭeḥuti. His name means *child*.

Ḥetep·ḥer — Gifted architect who carves the room used as Ḥaāmer's tomb and a second, secret entrance into the tomb complex. He is the son of Neb-t·ḥe-t's cousin. His name means *peaceful of face*.

Inuaabb – Daughter of Sefher. She lives with her mother along the caravan route. Her name means *desire to see water*.

Īset — Chief and only wife of Pharaoh Ạsạr.

Khashta — Caravan leader. Finds Ṭeḥuti and carries him east. His names means *the foreigner*.

Kefa·ạb — Servant, formerly nurse, to Īset. Her name means *loyal* or *devoted*.

Maaạ — Governor of the province Meḥ, north of Pharaoh Ạsạr's ten provinces. Originally betrothed to Ḥaāmer, he asks for Āakhu as wife after her death. His name means *seer*.

Marmut — The younger of governor Maaạ's two wives. She is pregnant when Āakhu joins them. Her name means *flourishing mother*.

Merakesh — The older of governor Maaạ's two wives. She befriends Āakhu. Her name means *a sprinkling of love*.

Merit — Temple dancer who serves Pharaoh his final meal. Her name means *desire*.

Merptah — Second to caravan leader Khashta. His name means *devotion to Ptah*.

Metiu — Old woman who brings Hepaba-t to Pharaoh and acts as her witness in accusing Neshti, Hepaba-t's husband, of abuse. Her name means *witness*.

Neb-t·ḥe-t — Sister to Īset, married to and now estranged from Set, she talks with the gods and buries the dead.

Neqa — Wife to Gemgem, governor of province Herui. Her name means *to polish*.

Neshti — Husband to Hepaba-t. He beats her to death and is later beheaded by Pharaoh. His name means *cruel* or *violent*.

Rāmạtet — Maid servant to Ḥaāmer and Īset. She is six or seven years old. Her name means *sunlight come to form*.

Sefher — Woman living with her daughter along the caravan route. Friend of caravan leader Khashta. Her name means *long suffering*.

Set — Brother of Pharaoh Ạsạr and husband to Neb-t·ḥe-t. He is also high priest of the Temple of Ptah, charged with guarding and promoting his brother's deity. His name is synonymous with evil.

Shepses — Priest and adviser to Set. His name means *to make splendid*.

Shti-ahk — Priest and adviser to Set. His name means *to tax the land*.

Steppu — Maid servant to Ḥaāmer and Īset. She is 19 years old. Steppu has an extraordinary voice and is an accomplished singer. Her name means *a chosen person*.

Tchefeṭ-t – Maid servant to Ḥaāmer and Īset. She is 15 years old. Tchefeṭ-t is known in a land of dark-eyes women for her unusual and beguiling green eyes. Her name means *pupil of the eye*.

Tehāra — Wife of Teni, governor of province Un, sister to the slain governor of province Atef-peh, and long ago love interest of Ạsạr. She is angry with Ạsạr after the death of her brother. Her name means *the blooming one*.

Ṭeḥuti — Gifted young priest responsible for many of the technical innovations in Pharaoh's land. He is betrothed to Pharaoh's daughter Āakhu.

Temu — Assistant to High Priest Set. His name means *some hard, compact substance*.

Teni — Governor of province Un, husband to Tehāra, friend of Pharaoh Ạsạr. His name means *to reckon or estimate*.

Uāā·t — Orphan girl being raised by Ȧamȧam. She gives Āakhu a small lapis cat on her visit. Her name means *loneliness*.

MODERN CAST

Field Marshal Aaliyah — General Fadi's boss

Minister Saladin Aboud — Minister of the Interior, Egypt's CIA, FBI Homeland Security and police force all rolled into one.

Robert Apus — Lisa Hampton's assistant and doctoral candidate.

Professor Randall Crain — Lisa Hampton's university adviser and professor at Brown University.

Sarah Crain — Randall Crain's wife.

General Abdul Fadi — General in the Egyptian military ordered to clean-up the terrorist problem.

Colonel Fiqar — Terrorist Leader, the ugly one.

Ambassador Jarah Hamimech — Kuwaiti Ambassador to Egypt.

Dr. Lisa Hampton — Egyptologist, Professor of Egyptology at the American University in Cairo.

Dean Hayes — Dean of Archaeology at the American University in Cairo.

Captain Anwar Jagardii — Company commander Egyptian military. Ordered to eradicate the terrorists in the south.

Khidr — A disfigured boy. His name means green.

The Lieutenant — Captain Jagardii's executive officer.

Colonel Mohieddin — General Fadi's aide.

Massouma — Kuwaiti Ambassador Hamimech's wife.

Nefri Mulhan — Omar Mulhan's wife.

Sargeant Omar Mulhan — Captain Jagardii's First Sergeant.

Dr. Stewart Owens — A previous romantic colleague of Lisa Hampton.

Dr. Bill Sanders — Egyptologist, Professor of Egyptology at the University of Chicago.

Snake — The tattooed terrorist.

GENERAL FADI'S STAFF

Colonel Younes — Operations Officer
Colonel Gheit — Intelligence Officer
Colonel Ahmed el-Sa'eidy – Disbursements Officer

for Judy,

for Connie,

with love

Chapter 1

CAIRO, EGYPT, THE GREAT KHAN EL-KHALILI BAZAAR, JUNE 7TH, 8:00 A.M.:

Massouma, wife of Jarah, was wide eyed with excitement. Her gaze swept over the beauty of the great Khan el-Khalili bazaar. The brilliant, panoply of colors, clanging sounds, pushing and shoving, overwhelmed her senses. The discordant symphony of tinkling brass bells countered the low roar of the crowd and the cries of vendors. A door to her left draped with heavy indigo colored beads exuded the sweet smell of incense. What treasures lay in that passage depths?

I have missed this.

She had come to the bazaar with ease. Massouma recognized it as a place for tourists, but she didn't care. Her excitement continued to wash through her. She wanted adventure. Unlike her normal life, she wanted to be with people. The crowd didn't bother her. The bumping and jostling enhanced her lighthearted feelings. She felt like a young girl again.

I remember being here with mother.

Jarah, her husband would not approve. Sometimes he was so stuffy. As much as she loved and respected him, and she did both, she felt he was too protective. He had forbidden this adventure, but she was tired of the suffocating embassy. She was bored. Jarah is the Kuwaiti ambassador to Egypt. Although privately, he was a fun loving, attentive husband; publicly, he was far too forbidding—always the proper diplomat. At a vendor stall, she bent down to look at a bright, sheer cloth. The pure silk caressed her skin. She hoped to wrap it around herself, hiding her non-religious clothes—clothes she wore because of her station.

From the corner of her eye, she saw an embassy escort who must have come after her. He lost her. Not seeing her, he began frantically searching for her.

How did he find me? I confided only with my female assistant. I will have to speak with her.

Amused, she continued to 'hide,' wondering what he would do. With all the jostling, they were soon separated. Now she felt truly free.

Two soldiers pushed through the crowd approaching her. She ignored them. They had no business with her. They grabbed her by the arms, dragging her toward a truck. The crowd separated giving them a path.

"Stop! What are you doing?" she demanded, looking from one to the other. She raised her voice, hoping to get the escort's attention. "You can not do this. Do you not know who I am?"

"You are a hussy–a whore. No respectable woman would be on the street wearing that."

"I am with the embassy," she protested. They ignored her, shoving her into the back of the military truck. She crashed into others, falling down, skinning her knees, tearing her hose.

* * *

"We're supposed to select only people who won't be missed. Now it's too late," he chastised his partner. "If she's with the embassy, you shouldn't have taken her. This will be a serious problem"

"Impossible! They don't come out."

"You don't think. You are stupid," he said back-handing his partner. "You shouldn't have taken her. Now we cannot release her. This will be trouble."

Frantic men were approaching, searching. It was time to go. He ground the truck into gear, easing toward the edge of the crowd.

SOUTHERN EGYPT, THE HIGH ROAD ABOVE ABYDOS, EGYPTIAN MILITARY CONVOY, JUNE 7TH, 8:30 A.M.:

The windshield and the truck windows were down to provide a breeze where otherwise there was none. Heat waves shimmered off the hot road ahead, creating a mirage of standing water. The moving air was a blast furnace in Captain Anwar Jagardii's face, his lips dry and cracked from the heat and the low humidity. Sand pelted him through the absent windshield, kicked up by the jeep ahead, sticking to and chaffing his oily skin under his collar. The sand and grit stung his face and packed into his nose. His wraparound sunglasses limited the debris in his eyes.

Hell and damnation! Shaitan couldn't have designed anything better.

The truck lurched and bounced, hitting bottom with a teeth-gnashing crunch. Anwar bit down hard on his tongue.

"Allah curse this road!"

A cry of pain came from the back.

Gritting his teeth together so he wouldn't bite his tongue again, he pressed his canteen to his lips, wetting his throat and soothing his injured tongue. Three weeks in the field hadn't improved his humor. These minor injuries now became larger than normal for him. His first sergeant glared at him from the wheel. Water rationing was one of Anwar's directives. He was supposed to be an example to his men. The sergeant's expression irritated him. He mentally cursed the heat and First Sergeant Omar Mulhan.

"You'r right, my captain. Satan's at work."

"Since when have you started reading my mind, sergeant?"

His first sergeant gave him a withering glance. Jagardii's mind returned to their mission, dropping his formality with his old friend.

"We support the government against the terrorists," Anwar said.

"We haven't shot any 'em."

"We haven't *seen* any of them."

"Cowardly bastards," the first sergeant started the litany he'd been playing with Anwar for the last week.

Anwar ignored him.

"The nightly views are disgusting. We must figure out what's going on."

"Yes, my captain," Mulhan's sarcasm showed.

"The High Command is all over my ass."

"Fadi? He's never a patient man."

Anwar nodded.

"I can't believe we've pursued the terrorists for three weeks, leaping from one ambush site to the next," Anwar waved his hand in desperation. "Nothing, nothing."

"They'r on the Inta'net. It's the new world order, Anwar—terror."

"Are the men edgy?" asked Anwar.

"We'r spittin' dust but no terrorists. Yeah, the men'r edgy."

"So what are you doing about it?"

"There's no morale, but I do nuthin'. They have'ta suffer. Some say it's *yu'r* 'magination," Omar grinned at his commander.

"They blame me for being here?"

A raised eyebrow from his friend was enough to answer his question.

"Who else can they blame?" sighed Anwar. "You handle it."

"Yes, sar!" Omar said, throwing Anwar a flippant salute.

"The government may be in real trouble with this one," Anwar continued, ignoring Omar's insubordination. "The fundamentalists want the western loving president, the peace broker of the Middle East."

"The fundamentalists bin after 'somethin fur a thousand years."

Anwar turned, staring out the window at the dun-colored, rugged canyon walls. He felt trapped in a tunnel with a beast's claws thrusting inward upon him. He hated being in a box—trapped. The heat and boredom were getting to him.

Omar continued with uncharacteristic slowness. "Can they throw out the president?"

Anwar shook his head negatively.

"They don't have the votes, but it looks bad for him. He's not popular now. The people may rise up like Hosni Mubarak back in 2011. So...the general ordered me to investigate. So I investigate. It's for the president I'm sure."

"It's yu'r duty, Anwar," Omar laughed. "But yu'r always fev'rish."

Anwar turned grinning at his friend.

Two miles away.

Abbas sat cross-legged on the flat stone, having finished cleaning his weapon and making preparations for his final act. Baruti, the only one willing to come, sat facing him. His only friend because the team didn't agree with his mission. Abbas didn't care if they thought him too zealous.

"Abbas, this is wrong. You haven't been ordered. You'll be killed."

"We serve Allah. It is his will."

"Are you sure, my friend?"

"Where's your faith?"

"I'm not sure I have any."

"I've prayed. I'm confident. I'm trained. I will pray for you," Abbas said sliding the bolt of his rifle home with a metallic scrape, testing its proper action and making sure the cup adapter was correctly mounted. He put blanks in the magazine and loaded a grenade.

"I've thought about this moment for a long time."

One and a half miles away.

Anwar's face clouded again, turning away from the depressing cliff walls to look at Omar.

"The government makes me angry, sentencing dissidents to prison and hard labor for speaking out. They're suppressing them to keep control," Anwar shook his head. "The educated, ah, the educated, are once again demonstrating. I could've been one of them."

"The terrorist attacks ul topple the president," Omar brought up his original thought again. "Eel have no chance in the next election."

Anwar smirked.

"He has time if he can hold down the rabble."

Omar nodded. "The Inta'net may get 'im.

"Yes, I watch the damnable murders on my PC," Anwar agreed. "Reporters ask how the president can chase international politics with the domestic violence. His council may have to remove him. Allah in his wisdom be praised!"

"Terrorists claim religion. I'd hate live'n under religious fantics."

One mile away.

"How do you know they will come?"

"The Army has chased us for three weeks. On Internet, we were in Fador last week," Abbas said, "they followed us there and we *appeared* in Baliana yesterday. This is the road between the two. They will come."

"You must leave this path, my friend?"

"I proclaim Allah!"

The whine of a heavy truck engine sounded from the hill on the road behind them.

"Abbas."

"It is time."
Baruti rose, disappearing up the ravine path behind them into the cliffs above.

One half mile away.

"Nothing makes sense."
"We'd go villages, reportin' murd'r 'n terror," Omar said.
"We've seen the brutality on the streaming video, but we've never seen blood let alone a body in the street."
"When we get ta Baliana, a'll seen nothin'," grunted Omar.
Jagardii nodded.
"What'a you reportin'?" asked Omar.
"Reality."
"That's gotta make Fadi happy," Omar laughed.
"Oh, yes. He's questioning whether *you're* going to the right villages."
"I hate High Command, thinkin' they know more'n us. Hell! I kin read'a map. I gotta retire," grumbled Omar his grin fading.
"You're not going to leave me with this pain in the ass. So the men are tiring of this fruitless exercise."
"Most of 'm are babies. They'r in the field without their comforts...their women."
"Bouncing around in trucks can't improve anyone's humor. So the troops think I'm benefiting from this stupidity," Anwar smiled at the thought. "Maybe Shaitan is at work, Omar."
"We not seen a terrorist," Omar mused. "Somethin's strange here."
"In Cairo, I saw people shot on my PC, looked real to me," said Anwar.
"The reporter. I never seen him before, but he's on every news. F'under what rock did da scorpion crawl, and where's he hidin' now? A friend says Fadi's go'n crazy searchin' fur 'im ta lead us ta the terrorists."
Anwar nodded as Mulhan continued, "He's at a landmark 'n each village. I talked da mayor of Fador at ta location on Inta'net". Yet..."
"Nothing. So where are the bodies?" asked Anwar. "This is impossible."
Omar nodded. "Impossible, couldn' happ'n."
First Sergeant Mulhan was remarkably intuitive. Allah frequently revealed to Mulhan truths that remained hidden to others. Anwar snorted at the thought Mulhan talked with God.
"Impossible..." repeated Omar, his eyes defocused as his mind slid back into his thoughts. "Ya know what?"
"Wait a second, old friend," Anwar interrupted. "We'll call a halt when the trucks get down this hill. The men need rest and water."
"Yes, sar," Omar replied.
Anwar lifted the radio phone to tell the lieutenant to look for an appropriate place for the company to halt. The truck rounded a bend in the road, continuing down the incline. Omar slowed, steering left to avoid a rough boulder twice the size of the deuce-and-a-half, standing at the right

edge of the road a hundred meters ahead, weathered, a strange artifact left by the road builders. The lieutenant in the jeep leading the convoy passed the boulder. A man with a black beard and long robe appeared from behind the rock. He raised a weapon to his shoulder, pointing it at Anwar's approaching truck.

"Omar! Look out!"

"Allah, damn da provida' of evil!" Omar swore.

Anwar identified the weapon by instinct, a rifle grenade.

Mulhan stomped on the brakes with all of his strength pitching Anwar forward. Omar swerved right to use the boulder as a shield just as the man fired. The grenade hit the truck above the left front wheel. The explosion ripped away the fender—catapulting it end-over-end above the cab, destroying the steering gear, jamming the front wheels. The tire blew, the broken axle and wheel bent under.

Mulhan hauled on the steering wheel with no effect, the tendons standing out from his neck. The vehicle angled in a skid toward the left. Anwar dropped the phone, grabbing the dashboard for support as the truck plunged off the road and down the embankment, plowing down a narrow ravine, crashing into an ancient landslide halfway down. The sudden stop propelled Anwar through the open windshield over the hood of the truck.

CAIRO, EGYPT, MILITARY HEADQUARTERS JUNE 7TH, 10:47 A.M.:

General Abdul Fadi's staff meetings were usually short and to the point. This one was neither. He was at odds with his staff over the continued military deployment in the South. His operations officer was concluding his report.

"Sir, he's not substantiated a single incident," Colonel Younes glanced at his notes. "This...Captain...."

"Anwar Jagardii," General Fadi supplied. "Is not satisfied with this situation either."

"I was about to say: ...is capable of the task, sir."

General Fadi growled, boring a hole through Younes' forehead with his eyes.

"Jagardii will continue his search," General Fadi said between clenched teeth. "He finds the situation most untenable, and being an excellent officer, he wishes to continue his search."

"He scurries between locations reporting the locals have seen nothing," argued Younes.

"Yet we see the disgusting events through the Internet daily," was Fadi's annoyed response. "I know, I know."

"He's going to the wrong places."

"Let's not argue his competence, but determine how we're going to help him."

"I don't know how to do that," said Younes. "Without replacing him."

"That's not going to happen," replied Fadi. Yet he knew if the carnage continued he wouldn't be able to support Anwar. His friend would become the sacrificial goat.

"It doesn't make sense, general," Colonel Gheit, his intelligence officer, spoke for the first time.

"Correct," agreed Fadi. "The reality doesn't match the evidence. It doesn't make sense. I went to several villages in the past and know many of the leaders. The captain has spoken to them."

"I was raised in Fador. The village has changed some, but I know the well where the reporter stood. I recognize one of the women although I don't think she's from the village," Gheit said with apparent embarrassment.

"That is why we continue," Fadi responded in a soft voice, determined to speak with Gheit later to find out where he had encountered the woman. "That is why I have the captain investigating."

The silent staff absorbed Colonel Gheit's admission.

"Have we found the damnable reporter?" asked the general, changing the subject.

"No, sir," replied Gheit, "but we're following that lead."

"As long as we turn up nothing, it's not much of a lead," concluded Fadi, feeling more comfortable with his field operation than a police investigation. The assembled group sat silently for several moments.

"The expense of this operation is enormous, sir," interjected Colonel Ahmed el-Sa'eidy, the staff disbursements officer. "We're looking like fools."

"The president wishes to step up these actions. I don't believe expense is an issue with him. Do you wish to debate the cost at the Presidential Palace?"

Although el-Sa'eidy disagreed, Fadi could tell that he was unwilling to object with the president.

"As for looking like fools, we will continue *being* fools until this is resolved."

"Yes, sir," nodded el-Sa'eidy.

"We'll continue to investigate," concluded Fadi. "And we'll continue, trying to make sense out this nonsense. We *will* resolve why the evidence doesn't match reality."

The remaining officers shook their heads in disbelief and confusion, but none presented an alternative. A soft tapping at the door interrupted the meeting. The Minister of the Interior, the head of Egypt's intelligence agency, entered. The general rose and walked to the far corner to speak with Minister Aboud.

"Is it your intention to continue pursuing the terrorists, general?"

"Yes, minister."

"How long do you intend to keep your men there?"

"Indefinitely, minister. We wish to catch the murderers of the people."

"I see. But your men haven't found any terrorist activity?"

"That is true, minister," responded Fadi, wondering how the minister knew this detail. "The Internet shows us daily the most explicit acts of these barbarians. I'm disgusted by what I see. The people are disgusted. I'm following the news source, but I've not yet determined his origin. So I'll continue to pursue the terrorists in the desert."

"I understand your determination. May you succeed, general."

"Thank you, minister."

Colonel Mohieddin, Fadi's aide, burst into the room. He saw his aide was agitated, angry.

Disruptions upon disruption, Now what?

"Our convoy has been attacked by the terrorists!" whispered the colonel in a tight, small voice to Fadi.

"What!" responded Aboud. The minister had overheard.

"The executive officer reports Captain Jagardii's truck has been struck by a grenade. It has crashed into a ravine wall. The commander and his driver's conditions are grave."

"Damnation!" spat Fadi. "Where did this happen?"

"On the mountain rode above Abydos."

Fadi looked at the minister. Aboud's rage was evident on his face.

"Have terrorists been captured?" asked Fadi.

"The lieutenant reports a terrorist killed and the others are being pursued."

"Finally, we've made contact. We'll get these bastards!"

Then almost as an afterthought Fadi commiserated, "Jagardii and Mulhan are critically injured? Damn! How many other casualties do we have?"

"I don't know, but the lieutenant reports only the two seriously. We are flying a gunship there," said Mohieddin. Fadi nodded, feeling ill as the reality of the situation settled on him.

"I'll investigate, as well," injected Minister Aboud, moving to the door. "Good work, general."

NORTHERN EGYPT, DELTA SITE, JUNE 7TH, 11:00 A.M.:

Lisa Hampton, Dr. Lisa Hampton, Professor of Egyptology, at the American University in Cairo, stood at the edge of her excavation watching water rushing into the pit. With little satisfaction, she scratched the sticky cake-dried sweat irritating the small of her back, cursing the heat, the University, the Delta and everyone in general. Her mud splashed glasses were a pain, Removing them, her world transformed into her normal myopic fuzz. She pulled her shirttail from her campaign shorts, rubbing a large glop from them, but finally succeeding only in smearing them.

Damn!

She licked them and wiped them again.

As project manager, Lisa led a team of graduate students recovering artifacts from the Cleopatra era in a field outside Alexandria; however, the only things that gave evidence of any worth in the area were a few outcroppings of last dynasty pillars. The area was about three thousand square meters, a little larger than an American football field. Lisa had no doubt this was an area from the Ptolemaic period. She could see several artifacts with inscriptions, showing that fact.

Initially, she walked the area, doing a personal survey, identifying where she wished to explore. The appraisal turned up four possible excavation sites. A few scattered objects that appeared dramatically out of place tickled her curiosity.

She received questions from her graduate labor force about a digging effort. They seemed to feel they were here to read the writing on the pillars, not move dirt, but she soon set them straight. She prioritized the sites, laid out meter squares with markers. She had her team excavate the most promising. She carefully, painstakingly sifted the soil with her graduate student tribe. At the first area, they discovered no artifacts, but they struck water about half a meter down. The incident put her behind her expected time-line.

The second site, the one Lisa had just been sifting, turned out to be more interesting. Lisa discovered a piece of pottery that looked unusual—a painted pot rim, barely showing at the surface.

Robert, her assistant, devised an excavation plan, shoring the sides for safety and hoping to reduce the risk of water. Lisa wished to avoid the risk of water, by pumping away any seepage. She spent the better part of a day brushing away the soil surrounding the artifact until she was about a meter down. Lisa became excited as the rim turned into a large, fired clay pot. She still hadn't reached the bottom of the vessel. With digging being difficult in the gooey soil, she made slow progress on her hands and knees, shoring the sides of the pit with planks to guard against her greatest concern—*flooding.*

This attempt led to the most recent failure with water gushing in at the bottom. Lisa had hauled herself from the swirling mud before the water filled the hole. If she hadn't extracted herself, she would now be underwater struggling for her life. The two graduate students, helping her dig, sprang out first. She glanced in their direction, watching them stomp away in disgust as mud dripped from their clothing. Their dialog couldn't be good. She heard her name disparaged and ridiculed several times.

Now she agonized, as the water filled her work, the pot might be destroyed. After a week of digging, having encountered every form of obstacle, she was going to stop until they had the water problem under control. She couldn't afford to loose promising artifacts.

"Crap!"

Her mind settled on Robert who was supposed to be handling the water problem. She had put him in charge of that function.

Where is he? This flooding is frustrating me. He is frustrating me.

"Damn! Damn! Double Damn!"

Enough water mixed with the soil to liquefy the ground under her feet. The side of the pit sank and she was once again in danger of falling into the hole. Even the walls supported by the pilings crumbled.

Hell and Damnation!

She stepped back and watched a day's work disappear into a brown swirling morass. As the wall gave way, Robert ran to her, pulling her further back from the edge.

"Where have you been?" she snapped.

"Doctor! Careful. You could've fallen into the pit."

"Yes, damn it," she growled. "I hope the pot isn't damaged. I can't deal with the water and soil conditions. Can't you get it stopped?"

"I'm an archaeologist, not an engineer, Doctor," he said irritably.

"You're a doctoral candidate. You're what I say you are."

The expression on Robert's face showed he had not appreciated her remark. Lisa was Robert's advisor and under normal conditions, they had an amicable, working relationship. Lisa now felt badly for what she had said. Robert had actually volunteered for this project.

"I apologize. I shouldn't have said that. My frustration is showing and the wear on me isn't pretty."

He gave her a curt nod.

"I'm sorry I can't get the water stopped, Doctor," he said.

"I think that's an impossible task."

Leaning forward to gaze into the muddy pit, Robert indicated no big deal.

"Which way did the water come in?"

"This side. I can't continue to work until we solve this. Where's it coming from? The government's providing irrigation water, but it should be absorbed."

"We may be excavating in a channel to the river," responded Robert.

"What channel?" disagreed Lisa.

"Over there in the farm field. We may need to bring in a geologist."

"I don't believe that. Getting a geologist will take forever. Then waiting for the report! Ahhh...!"

"Dr. Tu'hut thought it was a good idea."

"Dr. Tu'hut! When did you speak with him?"

"He calls about every day, asking for status."

"Dammit! Why the hell is he talking to you?"

Robert looked at his feet.

"You keep looking for the water source. Tell Tu'hut to talk to me in the future. I'm going to go up to the trailer. I've got to think."

"I'll come with you. I have to get the pump."

"Tu'hut's an ass! There's no way to get along with the bastard! What the hell's he doing, going around me?" asked Lisa rhetorically as they trudged up the slight grade to the trailer.

"I'm sorry ma'am. I should have told you."

"This project is crap. We've recovered nothing to make this study worthwhile."

She wondered if she could or should continue. She certainly didn't want to. At the end of her rope, she hated doing penance for Dr. Tu'hut, the Secretary General of the Ministry of State for Antiquities.

The trailer, that served as the site office, stood atop the highest point in the area where Lisa had placed it in hopes of catching an occasional afternoon breeze. She slept inside because the night, desert air took on a chill. She locked the door, doing the best she could to be safe against intruders. A creepy feeling persisted within her, leaving her feeling insecure,

"Do you want a soda?" she asked as she turned the trailer knob, the loose hanging handle wrapped with a rag to keep everyone from burning their hands. She felt a puff of rank air belch from within. She rummaged through the gas chiller for the drink, imported from Cairo, and always in short supply.

"No, thanks."

Lisa pulled a second camp chair outside into the shade beside the trailer. She collapsed into the chair, pressing the cold can to her aching forehead.

"I've got the pump," said Robert, as he plopped beside her, dropping it beside him.

Lisa looked out to the cultivated area seeing the lush green fields growing in the rich Nile delta soil. The humidity at her location was high. The agriculture of the area and the required irrigation led to the humidity. This was one of her concerns for the artifacts she was trying to locate and identify.

"Damn!" she said, thinking back over what she had accomplished. "We've found two maybe three interesting objects amongst hundreds of pounds of trash and a ton of dirt."

Robert nodded.

"I expect to find a soda can mixed in with the excavation. How are we supposed to sift the wheat from the chaff? This isn't science. Now, I'm dealing with the asshole Tu'hut." Robert remained silent, chewing on his lower lip.

Lisa knew Dr. Tu'hut didn't like educated, professional women.

"Tu'hut told me that women are supposed to stay at home, cook dinner and have sons. He said that once when I was working with him—for him," she said.

Robert twisted his head to the side uncomfortable with her litany.

"I was exploring a more interesting site for the Secretary General, when I butted heads with him over the excavation and the permanent transfer of the ancient artifacts to the museum for his research," she said.

"I know you consider that modern day grave robbing,"

"Right. I called it such. I was no longer welcome at the site. The University intervened for me so I wouldn't be expelled from all work."

"The dean felt you were too valuable to be forced out."

"But now I'm paying the price, digging in this Nile Delta rot-hole."

"At least you didn't openly accuse Dr. Tu'hut of selling the artifacts on the black market. That would have gotten you expelled from the country," he laughed.

"I need to tell the University and the MSA of our progress," she muttered, changing the subject. "I'm confident neither will accept the delay very well. I'm sure the grad students are sending their protests. The MSA is already questioning my accomplishments."

"I'd better start pumping your excavation," Robert said.

"Sorry for the tirade."

A few minutes later, Lisa heard a motor kick off.

Ah, Robert's at it again.

She knew as soon as he quit pumping, the hole would fill in again.

I'm ready for my life to change. Well, I've messed around enough. Back to work.

CAIRO, EGYPT, MINISTER OF THE INTERIOR'S OFFICE, JUNE 7TH, 11:07 A.M.:

The knock on his private door startled Saladin. The minister granted few people access through that entrance. He was not expecting anyone, but he recognized the characteristic knock. Its owner did not make him happy.

"Enter."

Two men came in dressed in combat fatigues. Their unshaven faces and heavy body odor brought distaste to his mouth not unlike the fetid stench of hyenas from the desert.

"I told you not to come here anymore. I will contact you."

One of the beasts, his eyes properly downcast, apologized. Saladin could tell from his brother's angry demeanor he did not approve of this deference.

I tolerate these dogs only so far.

"There has been an incident this morning near Abydos. Abbas died when he attacked an army convoy and damaged a truck."

"Yes, I'm aware of this blunder. The stupid swine! Has anyone else from the group been captured?"

"No, minister. They tried to stop him, but when his piety couldn't be turned, the rest disappeared into the desert. By the time the military began to search, they were gone. All is well."

"How do you know all is well?" demanded Saladin, the tension in his chest causing pain. He brought his fist down upon his desk with a crash. The second man's eyes narrowed to slits. He remained silent.

"Our best stalker followed him."

"Your best stalker should have shot him before he attacked the convoy."

"Abbas did this for Allah," said the insolent brother.

Saladin enunciated his words carefully and harshly to make sure the two understood his warning.

"You know he couldn't have chosen a worse place to attack the military. If he leads the infidel government to us, then Allah will not receive his full measure. This must be done carefully. Inform the men to leave the area, but leave a guard at the cache. Make sure the guard doesn't get captured. Did Abbas carry any information that can implicate us?"

"We follow standard military procedures. None of us carry any papers when we go on a mission. Abbas performed professionally—even if he was too pious."

Saladin doubted this, but kept his feelings to himself. He stared at the two for several seconds before commenting.

"I trust you two with much. I expect much. Your rewards in the new order will be great. If you don't perform well...," He paused significantly. "Go to the desert to clean up the problem then return to the city. Wait for me to contact you. I need you both to leave my office. I cannot be associated with you."

He pointed to the door to indicate the conversation was over. The hate surged through him.

These two were jeopardizing his goal. Saladin stood and paced. He walked tightrope privately showing the president his support while positioning himself to step forward as the logical choice when the president fell. At the appropriate moment, he would show that he supported the muslims in the new order.

His hands balled into fists at his sides. He must control himself. He must control the terrorists.

SOUTHERN EGYPT, HIGH ROAD ABOVE ABYDOS, JUNE 7TH, 11:25 A.M.:

The world reappeared to Captain Jagardii in brief, disconnected flashes, little bits of light falling into his eyes, blinding him, as a face bobbed above him partially blocking the sun. His head throbbed. He recognized his lieutenant's eyes riveted on his, a worried expression painting his face. Jagardii tried to raise his head, but his lieutenant pressed on his shoulder restraining him. Everything swam black.

When he revived, his dull wits were conscious of water being applied to his lips with a rag. His tongue was too thick to speak so he groaned moving his mouth to indicate he wanted more. The rag was squeezed and he swallowed the liquid. His head slowly, painfully cleared. His military sense returned.

"What is our situation?" his voice croaked.

"Lie still, captain. Everything is handled. You've sustained a bad blow to your head and ribs, sir. We examined you while you were unconscious. We did not find any broken bones. You were unconscious for over thirty minutes. We thought at first you might be dead, sir."

"Is everyone all right?" Jagardii gasped as pain shot through his ribs.

"Besides you, one major and several minor injuries. The assassin is dead, sir."

"Who was the major injury?"

The lieutenant did not answer immediately.

"Several men in the back of your truck were injured, sir. Two suffered broken bones and one has a sprained wrist, sir. We'll get you on a stretcher."

"Who was badly hurt?"

"First sergeant, sir."

Jagardii struggled only to have his lieutenant restrain him. A sharp pain in his ribs resulted. His head ached and his consciousness swirled again.

"Allah cast you out! What are you doing for him? Let me see him!"

"The medic says First Sergeant Mulhan has a serious head injury. He may die, sir."

The lieutenant signaled for two soldiers to come forward with a stretcher. They lifted Anwar onto it, pain shooting through Anwar's ribs. Several minutes were required to lower Anwar from the rock pile. He gingerly examined his hands, arms and face. The left side of his head felt sticky with blood. It was tender to the touch and burned. His hands were a mass of open scratches painted with red disinfectant. His forearms ached. He must have taken the brunt of the impact on them jamming his fists into his chest. Perhaps this was why he was still alive.

He thought about what to do. The lieutenant had taken charge well. His first sergeant was badly injured. They had escaped so many times over the past twenty years.

How could this have happened?

They carried Anwar past the driver's side of the smashed truck. He saw Omar lying on his back with the medic working on him. His smashed head hung from the open door.

He understood what had happened. He survived because he went out through the open windshield, taking the brunt of the crash on his forearms while his sergeant's head must have hit the window post.

What if Omar dies? What am I going to tell his wife, Nefri, and his five sons?

"Is help coming?" he rasped.

"A helicopter is ten minutes out, sir," responded the lieutenant, trailing beside the stretcher.

Not quick enough.

They lowered the first sergeant to the ground beside Anwar. The captain struggled to a sitting position and looked down at his friend.

I will kill every one of the damn beasts...those damnable terrorists.

"Lieutenant, you said the assassin is dead?"

"Yes, sir. The troops in the next truck saw the attack. Assuming they would be next, the corporal shot the man as he reloaded his weapon."

"Then we don't have any information from him?"

"No, sir. We searched his body and found nothing."

"When you requested the chopper, you contacted headquarters?"

"Yes, sir. I didn't know when you would regain consciousness so I took command. I called for help and reported the attack, sir. To make sure we were not attacked again, I deployed the company around us. We were unable to find any other terrorists in the area, sir. The medic has treated the injured men from your vehicle. They are out of the sun as you should be, sir.

Captain Jagardii hobbled over to the destroyed truck and lowered himself into its shadow. The lieutenant followed him.

It is cooler out of the sun.

"Lieutenant, you have done well. Use my stretcher to move the first sergeant. Place the terrorist in the truck. We will drive them to a place where the helicopter can land. You are temporarily in command."

"Yes, sir."

Allah! Am I getting careless? I am too old.

His head swam again, but the cool air revived him.

Cool air? My thinking is fuzzy. There it is again, a puff of cool air between the front axle and the rocks.

He rolled over and looked down. There was a fissure cut by the truck. It looked as if it went down two meters.

"Soldier, bring me your flashlight."

He shined the light into the narrow opening that appeared to widen at the bottom. He moved the light around to see if he could get any perspective of depth or a sideways look into the cavern.

No, it it's not a cavern. It's a room. There's furnishings—a box and clay tablets. Maybe the terrorists are hidden underground—no.

As he observed the furnishings, a different idea registered in his mind.

I must keep this secret.

"Sir, we are ready to move out."

"Lieutenant, deploy the company here. Set up a bivouac. Do not move the destroyed truck."

"Yes, sir?"

Chapter 2

wsḫt nt jwsw m wꜣst ḥsbt 18 ꜣbd 1 prt sw 16 ḫr ḥm n wsỉr

The Hall of Balance in Uas,
Year 18, Month 1 of Peret, Day 16 under the Majesty of Ạsạr

A woman's tears watered the smooth stone floor before Pharaoh's throne. She wore a simple, undecorated linen shift, yellowed from many washings in the muddy River. It provided a striking contrast to the jewels and finery of the merchants and governors, the rich land owners and the priests. A single ox spinal bone held her hair together at the base of her neck. Enough had come loose to cover her face. Between sobs she pleaded: "I do not want to die and leave my children alone."

Ạsạr, Pharaoh of the ten provinces of the upper River, glanced at Īset, his chief and only wife. Her throne stood next to his, gold inlaid with lapis. A large ivory moon surrounded her dark head. Her painted face watched from its center. A slight turn of her head, a lifted eyebrow, assured him this was not her doing.

He sought his brother Set, high priest to the great god Ptah. Set claimed a prominent position among those gathered for the day's judgments, chief among the priests and scribes who came to speak, record, and observe Pharaoh. Set—whose attention never stayed long with anyone who was not useful to him—watched in rapt silence.

"Give me your story," Pharaoh said.

She lifted her head. One eye was nearly swollen shut, both were red and wet with tears. A bruise further darkened the already dusky skin of her right cheek from chin to eyebrow. "I failed as wife of my husband's house," she confessed through cracked, purplish lips.

"How have you failed?"

"Does it matter?" Īset interrupted.

Without looking, Pharaoh placed a hand over hers. "In a moment."

"No," Īset said, pulling away, "I will *not* be silent. What could be the justification for this? Women are smaller, we are not as strong—"

"Īset," Pharaoh cautioned. "I did not ask for a debate. I would have her thoughts first."

A nervous sigh went through the crowd. Set and one or two of his councilors smirked. Īset placed her hand back in Pharaoh's. His fingers closed about hers.

"Continue," Pharaoh said.

"My husband Neshti tells me that I am clumsy and slow and too permissive as mother to his children. He finds no favor in the food I prepare. His newborn son will not stop crying."

"What is your name?" asked Pharaoh.

"Hepaba-t."

Pharaoh surveyed the priests, merchants, and minor noblemen assembled in the Hall of Balance. "Is there a witness for Hepaba-t?"

"Here," called an older woman. She limped from the crowd, leaning on a stick of driftwood nearly as twisted and gnarled as herself. She dropped to her knees with a pop of bone and sinew, touching her head to the floor before Pharaoh.

"Your name and witness," Pharaoh said.

She pushed her stick against rock and struggled to rise. A guard to the left of Pharaoh took an unconscious step forward and froze until a word from Pharaoh allowed him to lift both women to their feet.

"I am Metiu," said the old woman with a bow that threatened to topple her. "I brought Hepaba-t here because I fear for her life. Her husband, Neshti is a cruel man who beats her for no other reason than to make himself feel better. He beats his animals, some who have died as a result. He threatens the children who are bold enough to play within sight of his house. Only someone as powerful and wise as yourself, Pharaoh, can save Hepaba-t."

Pharaoh dismissed Metiu. Frowning, he studied the battered wife. "Now what say you, Īset?"

"Captives are treated better than this. The bruises Hepaba-t wears accuse her husband much louder than my outrage."

One of high priest Set's councilors stepped forward. "A clarification, please?"

Pharaoh turned his head. "Yes, Lord Temu?"

The small, dark man, reputed to be one of the intellectuals among Ptah's priests, asked: "Are the men of Egypt no longer allowed to chastise their wives?"

The whispered trades and brokered deals conducted in the shadows of the hall stopped.

"A good question, Temu," Pharaoh said into the unnatural silence. He looked over the hundred people scattered in clusters between the tall stone pillars of the hall. "Is Hepaba-t's husband present or must he be summoned?"

"Neshti is here," said Metiu, pointing to a man further back among the crowd.

Neshti pushed through the audience. He wore the simple skirt of a farmer, dusty from the fields. His black hair, longer than normal and tied by a strip of leather, trailed midway down his back. He frowned at Hepaba-t and Metiu standing together. "They said I would find you two here. Metiu, have you grown so tired of meddling in your own family that you must now meddle in mine?"

"Neshti!" Īset warned. "When you speak, you will address yourself to Pharaoh, unless he bids you otherwise."

Neshti turned to Īset, his expression, for an instant, revealed how rarely he accepted commands from a woman. Before the hardness could linger into defiance, he dropped to one knee and lowered his head. "Yes, Lady. I seek your pardon, Pharaoh."

Pharaoh looked out into the audience with a frown. Silence fell. "Neshti, present yourself."

Neshti rose and came forward. His expression flushed with unease. He went to his knees again and touched his forehead to the cool granite next to his wife's tears.

Pharaoh rose, back straight, sliding from the dais with a deceptive, fluid, lion-like grace. He gazed at everyone, focused on no one. The self-important, craving Pharaoh's favor, shied from him like gazelles from the cold, indifferent glance of a predator. Pharaoh approached Temu, leaving Neshti prostrate before his empty throne.

"Are the men of Egypt no longer allowed to chastise their wives? Seemingly a simple question; but if that were so, it would have been answered by a priest in the temple and not in an open forum before Pharaoh."

Pharaoh frowned at his brother Set before motioning to a guard. "Your whip."

The guard pulled a linen tie releasing the coiled leather whip from his belt. He went down on one knee and presented it hilt-forward to Pharaoh, eyes downcast. Pharaoh accepted it, allowing the coils to unwind to the floor. He tested the whip with quick, short movements of his wrist, sending it slithering across the stone like a performing snake.

"We should start by agreeing on what constitutes a chastisement," Pharaoh said with no trace of amusement. With the sudden, arcing, full extension of his muscled arm, the whip cut the air with a crack.

The audience in the hall jumped as one, surprised by the unexpected action. Neshti gasped and flinched. Within moments, a long red mark appeared across his back.

"I suppose it takes one strike just to get her attention, wouldn't you agree Temu?" Pharaoh said, and the whip cracked again.

Neshti gasped a second time and trembled. His breathing quickened. A second welt appeared. Where it crossed the first, a spot of blood formed.

"To chastise the mate that has left her family to live out her days with you; to physically correct the woman who is under your protection and who has freely chosen to depend on you for her sustenance. It presents a curious ambiguity: hurting the one you have vowed to cherish."

The whip lashed out two more times in quick succession. New streaks of blood appeared on Neshti's back. He groaned and gathered his legs beneath him.

"Don't!" Pharaoh commanded, his voice echoing from the stone walls and columns. "Should I choose to whip you to death you will remain where you are. If you move again my guard will put a spear through you."

A moan from Neshti might have been an affirmation.

Pharaoh scanned the audience. "A man vows to care for his wife. A Pharaoh vows to care for his people. A man chastises his wife when she disobeys. A Pharaoh punishes his people for the same. How much is enough?"

Pharaoh turned back to Temu. "I see disgust and loathing. The gleeful anticipation you earlier had at the thought of imprisoning me with your clever logic and ensnaring words is gone."

Pharaoh turned and approached the audience. He singled out Hepaba-t and stood before her, holding out the whip. "You may continue your husband's chastisement."

Hepaba-t shrunk away from the offered whip and shook her head timidly, tears standing out in her dark, frightened eyes.

The light from the high windows, the warm, orange-yellow glow of the torches and oil pots, softened the marks on Hepaba-t's face. She was nearly the same age as Ạsạr's eldest daughter, Ḥaāmer, who lay alone in a darkened room in the queen's house, dying, an evil spirit stealing more of her breath away each day.

Ạsạr's expression softened, for a moment less aloof and godly. He spoke to Hepaba-t, his face earnest, voice gentle: "I have the authority to dissolve your bond with Neshti. Is there another to whom you would give yourself?"

Hepaba-t looked at Pharaoh's feet and shook her head once more.

"Would you return to your father's house in honor?"

Another quiet sob and head shake.

"Would you be under my protection, a servant in the house of Pharaoh?"

A fourth time: "No."

Ạsạr reached and pushed the hair from Hepaba-t's eyes. Leaning forward, he touched his lips to her forehead.

"So be it," he said, ignoring the whispers stirring about them.

Pharaoh returned to his throne. "She has chosen to stay with you, Neshti," he said to the crimson-streaked back of the man still quivering face down before him. "It is the opinion of Pharaoh that you are not worthy of her."

Pharaoh looked again to Temu, and to Set standing behind him. "I gave Neshti four lashes and evoked your revulsion. Imagine Hepaba-t now. Look at her bruises and see each hand or fist or foot or rod. See her thrown to the floor or against the wall or onto the sharp edges of the furnishings."

"Imagine how long it took to have inflicted that many injuries and how futile her defense must have been. Imagine her children watching this.

"Here is the chance to answer your own question, Temu: Are the men of Egypt no longer allowed to chastise their wives?"

Temu gazed at Pharaoh in silence, bowed his head in respect, and melted back into the ranks of the priests.

"Rise and face Pharaoh, Neshti," Pharaoh said.

Neshti pushed shakily to his feet, wincing as muscles stretched in his lacerated back. He kept his gaze lowered to Pharaoh's feet.

"The eyes of Pharaoh are upon you. What befalls Hepaba-t also befalls you. On the day she dies, if you have not preceded her, you will also die. But if you seek to love her as much as you love yourself, there will be no further trouble between us. Go now. See that we do not meet again."

Neshti turned and stumbled away, clusters of people moving from his path. Hepaba-t waited for him, took his arm, and helped him from the hall. Silence followed their departure and once they were gone, all attention focused once more on Pharaoh.

"Our lives begin, pass, and end in pain: do not make them worse."

Pharaoh scanned the crowd, taking in each face and each expression. He leaned back on his throne, sighed, and added: "The mood here is broken. We will adjourn the judgments until the seventh hour."

The people bowed when Ạsạr and Īset left the Hall of Balance. "May Pharaoh live forever," they chanted in unison, except for his brother Set who, tight lipped, scowled before turning away.

i͗s-nwšt m ꜣbḏw ḥsbt 18 ꜣbd 1 prt sw 16 ḫr ḥm n wsi͗r

The Royal Tomb in Abtu,
Year 18, Month 1 of Peret, Day 16 under the Majesty of Ạsạr

Neb-t·ḥe-t did not like this house. Houses were above ground, built from stone and clay and wood, open to the sunlight and cool breezes from off the River. This house was burrowed into the rock at the back of a cave. Without windows, it was dark and quiet, smelling of dust and sand and smoke. The air did not move. The passages were narrow. It was the house Pharaoh had chosen for his rest once he passed from this life to the next. It was his tomb.

The cave looked like the hungry, gaping mouth of Geb, god of the earth. Neb-t·ḥe-t shivered at the thought of walking into that mouth and being devoured. She took a deep breath and stepped from sunlight into shadow. She located the opening in the small circle of her lamplight.

The priests in Uas still debated whether Ptah, Ra, and Re would find and raise the occupants from this tomb. Underground tombs were rare. For a king or nobleman, the priests excavated a deep shaft, placing the coffin on a ledge fashioned from the side at the bottom or in a small adjacent chamber carved from the base of the shaft into the soft stone. For those without wealth or noble birth, the family dug a small, circular grave high in the hills, lined it with smooth stones, and positioned the body, with a few simple belongings and offerings.

Pharaoh Ạsạr, *may he live forever,* decreed in the first year of his reign that he would rest near his father, and his father's father, in a quiet, remote area near the village Abtu. While examining prospective sites, the priests found the cave and the natural tunnel inside. With Ạsạr's blessing, they widened and extended the tunnel, then carved out the first room. Two inundations ago, on a visit to his northern provinces, Ạsạr came to see the place where his body would rest and await the reviving touch from Ptah. But his satisfaction faded, tempered with the slow, painful realization that his eldest daughter would occupy the tomb before him.

Neb-t·ḥe-t reached the room. A mist of rock dust left from polishing the walls softened the edges and corners and colored the air.

"Are you ready for my inspection?" Neb-t·ḥe-t asked.

Ḥetep·ḥer, the nervous youth waiting inside, answered: "Yes, priestess."

He was sixteen inundations, young for an architect. Stones spoke to him, some said, revealing what was inside them. With a caress of chisel he flaked away all that was unnecessary, leaving behind statues and figures of extraordinary beauty that might any moment take a breath. He touched brush to wall and called forth scenes, poetry, creatures alive and imagined. Those who witnessed, those who yearned for such beauty in their lives, did not care how old he was.

Neb-t·ḥe-t drew a small, soft brush from the sash about her waist. "Have you swept the floor?"

Ḥetep·ḥer nodded. "Yes, priestess."

She bent and buffed the floor to raise the dust. The rock grain sparkled. Ḥetep·ḥer had oiled and polished the rock in addition to sweeping it.

She appraised the room in the soft, uncertain light. She moved close to the wall: step, pause, step, pause, moving from corner to corner. She held the lamp in her left hand, keeping the flame close to the stone at the risk of darkening it with soot. Graceful, rhythmic, she moved as if dancing. At each pause she studied the surface, looking for shadows cast by cracks, divots, or other flaws in the smooth, hewn surface. She found none.

"My water bowl," Neb-t·ḥe-t called into the passageway. A servant appeared, eyes wide and uneasy in the close, underground room. He bowed, presenting it in outstretched hands.

The detailed images of Ptah and Nut and Geb carved along the rim looked like dark smudges. Neb-t·ḥe-t splashed a handful of water to the floor, then lowered her lamp to watch.

If the water moved, preferring a direction, forming a rivulet, the floor sloped and was unacceptable. The water at Neb-t·ḥe-t's feet stayed in a still circular puddle. She nodded, took a step, and tipped the bowl again.

Neb-t·ḥe-t repeated the test, satisfied with the floor long before she emptied the bowl. She continued for the enjoyment of worrying the young architect. She did not want to end his ordeal too soon. It would make a more entertaining story for her cousin, the boy's mother, if she let him worry a little longer for her approval.

She emptied the last of the bowl in the doorway, studying the puddle. She reached her finger to the water, and traced an arc.

"Acceptable," she said, and withdrew a polished wooden cube, each side the length of her finger, from a bag near the doorway. She knelt and wedged the cube into a corner, checking the flush edges for gaps, then twisting it to determine if the corner were truly square.

Neb-t·ḥe-t pushed the cube into each corner and applied pressure with her fingertips. In the third corner the cube rocked from side to side. She frowned, removed and replaced the cube, and reapplied pressure. Again the cube wobbled.

She pulled the cube away and slid the oil pot closer. Searching, she held up a small, flat fragment. Ḥetep·ḥer watched it sparkle in the soft light, and sighed. "I will sweep again before the painters begin."

Neb-t·ḥe-t tested the corner again. The seams between rock and wood vanished—a perfect fit, the wood a part of the rock rather than flush against it. She nodded a grudging approval.

She called for a stool that she might check each of the room's upper corners. Ḥetep·ḥer steadied it. Neb-t·ḥe-t lifted and positioned the cube with one hand, holding the oil pot with the other.

Impressed with the skill and craftsmanship of her young relation and his workmen, she appraised the room a final time. Three double-remen high, four wide, five long: three numbers given by the gods, for three threes, plus four fours were the same as five fives—a perfect, godly sequence.

Four walls, a floor, and a ceiling; like rooms above ground, the rooms of hovels and palaces, warmed by the Aten, cooled by the Aih, where love, light, and living filled the days. But here it was dark and dry and quiet; a place to rest and wait for rebirth.

She turned in a slow, full circle, imagining the placement of the chests, baskets, and tables. In the center, on a small dais of uncut rock, Ḥaāmer's coffin would rest.

Neb-t·ḥe-t imagined the dark days of slumber: one, a hundred, a hundred-hundred. Would Ḥaāmer know or would it be no more than a moment's rest—sleeping and waking into a new and brighter day?

Which god would awaken her? Who would be first to gaze upon her? Who would lead her into the warm light of the Aten?

Inside Neb-t·ḥe-t's tent, part of the makeshift village near the tomb site, papyri were painted with the words and pictures for Ḥaāmer's tomb. Tonight Neb-t·ḥe-t would review them and make her final corrections. Tomorrow the painters would begin the careful process of committing them to the walls in the closeness of the tomb, working the whole day by flickering candlelight.

The words were for the gods, introducing the young woman they came to revive. But they were also for Ḥaāmer, so she might remember who she was, if through long slumber she forgot.

Neb-t·ḥe-t would return to Uas soon to visit her sister, Queen Īset, mother of the dying Ḥaāmer, and console her as she cried. Then she would teach both mother and daughter the duties and responsibilities of dying.

Neb-t·ḥe-t glanced at Ḥetep·ḥer. "You made this special effort for the princess?"

"No," he replied.

His answer surprised her. With a raised eyebrow she asked: "This wasn't your best effort?"

Ḥetep·ḥer shrugged, but did not retreat. "I do my best in each job I am given."

"Ḥaāmer is a royal princess. Surely she deserves special attention."

He watched her calmly. "Each of us is royalty to someone who loves us."

Neb-t·ḥe-t pulled him into a fierce hug. His hands, caught stiffly at his sides, found their way awkwardly to her waist.

"I approve," she said in his ear, "Your work is magnificent."

"Thank you," he whispered in return.

She let him go. His toothy smile glowed. "Modifications?"

"None," she said. "Go tell your men."

Ḥetep·ḥer darted into the corridor. A jubilant shout echoed from the passageway.

Neb-t·ḥe-t raised a hand over her ear and smiled. But with that smile she felt the sting of tears yearning to be shed: tears for her sister, and her sister's daughter who would soon be alone in this room, sealed away in the darkness in her gold-covered coffin, sleeping, until awakened by a kiss from god.

* * *

Workmen in the nearby camp sang an old song about the exploits of a lusty young woman as they sat about the fire, roasting fish taken from the River. Neb-t·ḥe-t tapped a toe to their rhythm and scratched another correction onto the text and pictures for Ḥaāmer's tomb. Two shadows followed the tip of her writing stick, one cast by the nearly full Aih, the other by her lamp.

She focused on a phrase that refused to sound right, scratching and re-scratching the symbols into the papyrus. She did not hear the courier approaching and did not notice him until a larger shadow fell across the skins.

"I come at the bidding of high priest Set from the temple of Ptah in Uas. He wants the tomb drawings."

Neb-t·ḥe-t did not look up. "Temple couriers on temple business do not come stealing into a work camp at night. I know all of my husband's message boys. I do not recognize you."

He was silent while Neb-t·ḥe-t juggled the order of the glyphs in the column once more. With a thud, one of Set's golden seals landed in the middle of her work.

His hard, dark eyes glared at her in the lamplight. She returned the look. "I am sister to the queen. You would do well to remember that before you irritate me further."

She put down the writing stick, lifted the ring, and studied the high priest's signature glyphs in the lamplight. She tossed it back to him. His eyes followed the sparkling arc, and he snatched the ring with the reflexes of a soldier.

"Set has never requested the drawings for a tomb complex before," she said, watching his eyes.

"The high priest has never built a tomb for his brother before."

"I will bring the plans to Uas when the work is complete and they are no longer necessary."

He leaned toward her. Neb-t·ḥe-t held her hand up to the moonlight and twisted a golden ring crowned with a lapis lazuli scarab. "A gift," she said, "from my sister *the queen.*"

"The high priest ordered me to return with the plans," he said, his voice taut.

Neb-t·ḥe-t could argue and perhaps even wrestle with the man, but she could not win. She looked away, into the shadows across an open stretch of sand and sighed. "I will get them."

She rose with a grunt from the table to impress on him the considerable inconvenience he caused. In her tent, she folded the rolls with slow, deliberate motions. He remained where she left him, tall and silent by her table. He watched her emerge from the tent with a warrior's quiet wariness. She nodded at the table. "That contains the pictures and text for Ḥaāmer's room. The workmen need it to begin the work tomorrow. I will make sure Set gets it when I return to Uas. Here are the rest."

He dropped an empty sack from his shoulder, opened it, and arranged the rolls inside.

Walking away in the moonlight, the silhouette of the pack across his back the only deformity in his otherwise perfect physique, he sneered: "I will give your husband your regards."

* * *

Neb-t·ḥe-t called Ḥetep·ḥer to her tent. "This morning I asked about a partially completed storeroom along the passage behind the room for the princess. Do you remember?"

"Yes, priestess," he said, his eyebrows drawn up in puzzlement.

"Why can the room not be completed and used?"

He shifted his weight easily from one foot to the other. "There are seams—cracks—in the rock. Digging through them is dangerous. That is why the previous crew abandoned their work.

"Also, the land above that particular passage slopes. In my opinion," he said, dipping his head in a gesture of humility, "the original shaft in the cave is too shallow. The passage behind Ḥaāmer's room, hewn straight, approaches the surface."

Neb-t·ḥe-t looked past his shoulder, through the linen covering the entrance, and into the night. "How do you know all this?"

"I surveyed the area before beginning the work for the princess."

Neb-t·ḥe-t leaned back and studied her young relation. "Could you create a second entrance to the tomb from the storeroom or the passage beyond it?"

Ḥetep·ḥer frowned. "I must see the drawings again."

"The drawings are gone. A courier has taken them to the high priest in Uas."

"Then I must make another survey."

"How long will that take?"

Ḥetep·ḥer shrugged. "Half a day."

"Be ready to start your survey at dawn," Neb-t·ḥe-t said.

Ḥetep·ḥer bowed and turned away. He took a step toward the linen, hesitated, and stopped.

"A question, priestess?"

She nodded and he returned to stand before her. "I know of no other tomb that has two entrances. And I have never heard of the high priest requesting the plans for a tomb still under construction. Are there problems?"

Neb-t·ḥe-t pushed the hair away from her cheeks with both hands, stirring the beads woven into the long, dark waves. Soon she would cut her hair and weave the beads back into the shortened strands. *Problems,* she mused. *Where do I begin?*

"No," she said. "I will see you at dawn."

ỉs-nwšt m ꜣbḏw ḥsbt 18 ꜣbd 1 prt sw 26 ḫr ḥm n wsỉr

The Royal Tomb in Abtu,
Year 18, Month 1 of Peret, Day 26 under the Majesty of Ạsạr

They completed the second entrance in ten days.

Neb-t·ḥe-t stood shoulder to shoulder with Ḥetep·ḥer and his foreman, looking into the cool darkness. The steps descended into the desert sand as if they had been uncovered rather than cut stoop by stoop from the bedrock. Granite shored the sides of the descent, the pieces diverted from the construction of a small mortuary temple.

On each side of the entrance, Ḥetep·ḥer recreated, in miniature, reliefs of the gods of Uas who sculptors were still chiseling from the cliff face about the main tomb entrance. Those figures were many times the height of a man. Ḥetep·ḥer had created his in the space available.

Neb-t·ḥe-t could not speak. They were regal, but not distant. Their faces showed care and compassion even as the eyes gazed into eternity. They saw all the days of the River but overlooked no single moment. They were perfect in physical characteristics.

Neb-t·ḥe-t saw Ḥetep·ḥer rise before dawn several mornings back, carrying a table stretched with a clean papyrus across the sand to a good vantage point before the cliffs, studying and drawing as the first of Aten's rays warmed the naked stone faces still partly hidden within the rock. He sketched until the rays intensified and the angle changed, losing the lighting he sought. Neb-t·ḥe-t saw him with a sculptor in the late afternoon, discussing as he pointed to the figures above the tomb.

Wiping tears of wonder from her eyes, she said, "I have run out of praise for you. Whatever your price for this, you shall have it."

A sparkle from the rock drew her attention, almost as if Ptah had shed his own glistening tear.

"You have worked magic with the stone. There are but two more things we must do," Neb-t·ḥe-t said.

She put an arm about the youth. She had known him since his birth, remembered celebrating with the rest of his family a new man child.

"Come," she said. "Show me the survey from the tomb markers to the new entrance. I want to record an accurate series of measurements for locating this entrance."

Ḥetep·ḥer frowned but said nothing. He called the men to fetch the stakes and measuring ropes.

They began from marks carved into the stone of the cliff. In a series of swinging, intersecting arcs, they moved steadily across the sand, pacing, driving stakes, stretching ropes. From the final two stakes, two ropes swung in arcs that intersected diagonal corners of the tomb descent.

Neb-t·ḥe-t called for a covering to shade them. She, Ḥetep·ḥer, and the workmen shared cool wine, rough bread, and freshly roasted fish.

"Let's measure it again," she said after they rested.

Returning to the marks on the cliff, the intense mid-afternoon heat slowed their progress. Neb-t·ḥe-t walked with them, asking questions, making notes, checking figures on the drawing. They drank from water skins, planting the stakes and swinging the ropes. Other than instructions and a few words of encouragement, they did not speak.

Midday passed into afternoon, Aten settling close to the cliff peaks separating the river valley from the great western desert, before the measurements satisfied Neb-t·ḥe-t.

She, Ḥetep·ḥer, and his workmen gathered under the linen shade near the second entrance. Caught between the heat of Aten and the heat of sand and rock, they were thirsty, hungry, and tired. Dust stained them in sweaty rivulet patterns deposited on faces, necks, shoulders, and arms.

Neb-t·ḥe-t's hair stuck to her cheeks and the back of her neck, the rest lying limp along her spine. A sweat stain darkened her shift in the hollow between her breasts.

"Is there something else?" Ḥetep·ḥer asked.

"One more thing," Neb-t·ḥe-t said. Her throat closed and she could go no further.

She had not anticipated this, and was not prepared for what she must ask. Ḥetep·ḥer, seeing her sudden distress, unsealed a wine jar, poured a bowl and pushed it into her trembling hands. The tangy, intoxicating juice soothed her throat.

She passed the bowl back to Ḥetep·ḥer, took a deep breath, and said, louder than she intended: "Fill it in."

Ḥetep·ḥer and his men stopped eating and drinking. In the silence, bits of stone slid with raspy cries down the cliff side and settled, a sculptor still tapping at the image of a great god in the distance above the tomb entrance. Neb-t·ḥe-t heard her own painful breathing, felt her own heartbeat.

"Priestess?" Ḥetep·ḥer asked.

"Fill it in, hide it, bury it," Neb-t·ḥe-t said, the words tumbling from her lips. She spoke quickly, so her ka could not stop her. "Wall up the opening underground. No one but those of us standing here must ever know it exists."

"But *why*?" Ḥetep·ḥer asked. His ruddy complexion paled, his eyes grew large in the afternoon light. His shoulders slumped. "I created them to be seen. Why bury them in the ground like refuse to be hidden from sight?"

How could he understand the hate one brother might have for another, hate so deep he might have his brother's body destroyed to prevent him reaching the afterlife? How could she explain the need to have that brother think the tomb forever sealed, his brother's body truly beyond his reach, when, in fact, there was another, secret entrance, known only to those who would never use it for evil?

"I love my Pharaoh," Neb-t·ḥe-t said, "but there are some that do not. There are some who might disturb his tomb and destroy his remains so that he cannot reach Amennt. I will not have that."

"So you created a second entrance," Ḥetep·ḥer said with a shiver.

Neb-t·ḥe-t looked up at him, saw his pain and confusion replaced by a growing understanding. "Yes, I created a second entrance. But even though I have the only measurements giving the exact location, you know it is here. You might be made to tell the very ones I have hidden this knowledge from."

"We will tell no one what we have done here," Ḥetep·ḥer said. Nodded heads and a couple soft affirmations from his men echoed his sentiments.

Neb-t·ḥe-t took Ḥetep·ḥer's hand in hers and looked into his eyes. "There are those who would kill to possess the information you and your men have. They would not just kill you; they would kill your families, your wives, your children. They would use methods that are both slow and cruel."

Ḥetep·ḥer went to his knees before her. "Priestess, I love my Pharaoh too, I am part of his family as are you. I would die before I gave this information to his enemies."

Neb-t·ḥe-t could not see him though her tears. The shiver she felt in her ka found its way into her voice. "You and your men must never give any man reason to think you have this information. Forget what you've done here, forget you have ever been here. One wrong word, one hesitation, and you and everyone you love will die."

"As you wish," Ḥetep·ḥer said. His men stood behind him, quiet, solemn.

The tension in her body subsided, the knot she felt inside loosened. Neb-t·ḥe-t wiped her eyes, looked away to the hills. "After today, I will never speak of this matter again. Do you understand? No messenger of mine will ever seek you out with questions. I will never seek you."

Neb-t·ḥe-t received an assent from Ḥetep·ḥer and each of his men. She looked at each face, into each pair of eyes. She saw fear and bewilderment, but she didn't see disbelief. Ptah would have to see that it was enough.

Word reached Neb-t·ḥe-t the following afternoon that they were done. She watched from her tent while they gathered their tools and trudged away across the sand and rock. Ḥetep·ḥer cast a last, searching look over his shoulder. *I'm sorry,* Neb-t·ḥe-t mouthed, hoping he could see and understand.

Ḥetep·ḥer buried the entrance, no matter what he thought of the request or the requester, with the same skill he demonstrated in creating it. The steps and the extraordinary reliefs were gone, lost except to memory. Neb-t·ḥe-t crisscrossed the sand, looking for a tell-tale sign or imperfection. The fading daylight revealed none.

She hesitated where the first of the steps likely began somewhere beneath her feet, saddened that one brother might strike out at another—even in death—destroying his body before Ptah could rejoin ba and ka and cha and chu. She could now collapse the single known entrance, ending the selfish, evil scheming, leaving the hidden entrance should it ever be necessary to reopen the tomb.

Neb-t·ḥe-t watered the sand, anointing this tomb as she had so many others, with the tears of one left alone and empty. *Have I done well,* she asked the large unfinished relief of Ptah, his face staring serenely from the nearby cliff. *Have I saved him?*

Above the god, circling out over the high desert, a hawk returned a solitary cry.

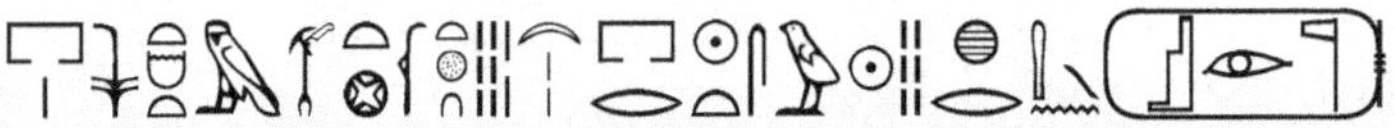

pr ḥmt nwst m wꜣst ḥsbt 18 ꜣbd 2 prt sw 6 ḫr ḥm n wsỉr

The House of Pharaoh's Wife in Uas,
Year 18, Month 2 of Peret, Day 6 under the Majesty of Ạsạr

Īset removed her sandals and slid her toes across the smooth limestone floor. The stones, their roots reaching deep into the earth, remained cool on the hottest days.

A shiver spread upward from the soles of her feet. She sighed and plucked another grape from the bowl beside her. Symbols inscribed around the rim of the bowl read: *Food given by Ptah, for the pleasure of Pharaoh Ạsạr and Īset.*

Her common room was a quiet place in which to revive from the afternoon heat. Īset leaned backward and stretched. Ebony hair fell from her shoulders, hanging freely behind her. The beads in her headdress rustled. The delicate sounds close to her ears soothed her like the whispering of the River.

"You never could keep your sandals on for a whole day," her sister called from the doorway. "I remember the many afternoons mother sent me to find them."

"Neb-t·ḥe-t," she said. Īset looked down. Life drained from her eyes, leaving them lusterless. Her cheeks tensed, pressing her lips into a thin, tight line beneath the mask of kohl and lip-stain.

"I am not death," Neb-t·ḥe-t said, gliding toward Īset one measured step at a time. "I do not bring it with me. That dark god travels where he will."

"I know," said Īset. "But you do not bring a miracle."

"I come to prepare all of you for her journey to Amennt."

Īset nodded. Neb-t·ḥe-t stood by the throne, resting a hand on Īset's shoulder. "I know how hard this is."

"She is sixteen."

"I remember her birth," Neb-t·ḥe-t said. "I remember how happy you and Pharaoh were."

"Pharaoh wonders what he's done to bring this evil on his first-born. I wonder how I failed to prevent it."

"Evil is neither summoned nor hindered," Neb-t·ḥe-t said. "It is like the wind. Pharaoh does nothing but good. You have raised Ḥaāmer with all love and care. Thinking otherwise dishonors you."

Īset nodded and took another grape from the bowl. But it was bitter and difficult to swallow.

"Come see Ḥaāmer's coffin," Neb-t·ḥe-t said. "It is worthy of her."

Īset shook her head. "I could not bear it."

"She should see it and become familiar with it. It will be her resting place until the gods awaken her and carry her to Amennt," Neb-t·ḥe-t said.

"She is ill."

Neb-t·ḥe-t ran her fingers through her sister's hair, pulling it away from her face, tucking it behind Īset's ears as she used to do on many hot afternoons when they were children.

"We have all lost someone, Īset. A child, a husband, a mother, a father. Sometimes it's too easy to lose ourselves. You will have the rest of your days to miss her, but only a precious few in which to love her and say good-bye."

* * *

Baka heard the distant sounds of the coffin makers before either Ḥaāmer or her servant Steppu. The sand-colored cat raised his head, stretched his paws toward the linen covering the window, and opened his amber eyes.

Steppu turned her head to listen.

They worked at the beginning and end of the day, hammers, mallets, and chisels working the wood, because they said, the wood was more relaxed when neither the Aten or the Aih ruled the sky.

Baka, convinced that the sound signaled nothing that needed exploration, yawned, closed his eyes again, and settled his head once more across his paws.

"Is it mine?" Ḥaāmer asked.

The voice startled Steppu who thought her lady asleep. She spoke without thinking. "Your mother said that yours was finished."

Ḥaāmer huddled in her linens like a timid animal in its burrow. Only her large, dark eyes caught a sparkle of stray sunlight. "Is it pretty?"

"I have not seen it, though I am told it is fit for a princess," Steppu said. She wiped at her eyes with the palms of her hands.

"Do not cry for me, I am ready for this journey. I have learned the route. I know the places I must pass through and the gods I will meet. I have memorized the incantations. All my offerings are prepared."

"Do you have an incantation for a maid who will miss her lady?"

"I will be whole and happy there. Share that happiness when you think of me."

They drowsed together through the midday heat, Ḥaāmer feverish and sweating in her bed, Steppu on a bench near the high window. Steppu roused and brought her lady morsels of food or water mixed with honey when Ḥaāmer asked. She called for Tchefeṭ-t or Kefa·ạb and together they lifted and steadied Ḥaāmer over a chamber pot when the withered princess felt the need. Princess and servant were drowsing again in the afternoon when visitors arrived.

"Ḥaāmer?" Īset called from the doorway.

Steppu stood and bowed her head as Queen Īset and her sister Neb-t·ḥe-t entered.

Ḥaāmer stirred and opened her eyes."Mother? Neb-t·ḥe-t?" she rasped.

Īset tried to smile but Steppu saw the strain of holding back tears in the Queen's trembling lips. "How are you?"

"Better, I think this warm day has helped."

Neb-t·ḥe-t knelt by Ḥaāmer, their faces close. "The preparations for your journey are almost complete. I would like for you to come see them."

Ḥaāmer looked at Īset. "Could I?"

Īset nodded. "If I can come too."

"I will arrange for someone to take us to the funerary temple," Neb-t·ḥe-t said.

ḥwt-nṯr nt ptḥ m wȝst ḥsbt 18 ȝbd 2 prt sw 6 ḫr ḥm n wsỉr

The Temple of Ptah in Uas,
Year 18, Month 2 of Peret, Day 6 under the Majesty of Ạsạr

The Temple of Ptah loomed in the near distance at the other end of the Walk of God from the House of Pharaoh. Ḥaāmer's servants lifted and carried her to the litter brought from the temple. They draped brightly dyed linen across the roof to keep the sun from Ḥaāmer and allow her privacy in her suffering.

Īset led the procession, carried in an open chair, a feathered fan draped with linen shading her head. Neb-t·ḥe-t walked between Īset and her daughter, head uncovered, her long hair and interwoven beads hanging loose to shade her shoulders from the sun.

A whisper passed through those with business along the street. Several children found flowers and presented them to Neb-t·ḥe-t. She gathered them and drew aside the linens, placing a bouquet in Ḥaāmer's hand. Ḥaāmer began to cry.

"They honor you the only way they can," Neb-t·ḥe-t said.

The undecorated mortuary buildings stretched along the River side of the temple complex, separated from the main temple and the schools and granaries by a garden and several small reflecting pools.

The litter bearers lowered their burden outside. One, the largest among them, with permission, carried the princess in his arms as if she were no more than a bundle of sticks, following Īset and Neb-t·ḥe-t.

Heat and sand gave way to cool stone and dust. Beneath the mortuary, among bare twisting passages dating to the earliest settlements along the River, Neb-t·ḥe-t had prepared a bare stone chamber once used to hide people and treasure from invaders. It was only a little larger than Ḥaāmer's tomb. Boxes of Ḥaāmer's clothing and jewelry collected from the queen's house arranged in baskets and boxes lined one wall. Baskets for food offerings, empty now, but in time filled with fresh flat breads, fruits, clay jars of wine decorated with date and origin, ordered along another wall. About the center of the room, clay tablets overflowing with tributes, poetry, and praise for Ḥaāmer.

But it was the center of the room, Ḥaāmer's sarcophagus resting on knee-high scaffolds, that drew everyone's attention. Jewels sparked like stars in a sea of gold that shimmered and flowed in the torch light. The gold had been carefully worked into the wood, the jewels swirled about contours and borders. The lid rested beside it, Ḥaāmer's likeness, large dark eyes, jeweled hair and headdress, chaste, enigmatic smile gazing serenely back at them. Prayers and spells, for protection, for godly vigilance, for peace and rest, were inscribed above, below, and beside her image. The symbols danced to the rhythmic flare of the torches.

"Let me sit inside," Ḥaāmer said.

The litter bearer looked to Īset and she nodded. He threaded his way among the possessions and lowered Ḥaāmer into her sarcophagus. Īset slipped a roll of linen beneath to prop her head up. "It's beautiful," Īset said, returning to stand beside Neb-t·ḥe-t.

"It has a wonderful fragrance," Ḥaāmer said, inhaling slowly so that she would not cough.

"That is the wood, and the resins that coat and protect it. There will also be herbs and perfumes so that you might rest comfortably," Neb-t·ḥe-t said.

"My breathing already seems easier."

Neb-t·ḥe-t pointed to a papyrus fastened to the wall. "I brought these from Abtu. They are the words and pictures for safe passage that are painted on the walls of your room. The north and south are your instructions," Neb-t·ḥe-t said, touching the symbols, "to remind you of the challenges you will face and the responses you must make."

Ḥaāmer nodded and coughed, a deep watery sound.

"The east and west walls are for Ra and Ptah. They discuss your life, purity, and goodness. They petition the gods to take you to Amennt."

Īset read the words for each incantation and spell, studied each picture, finally reaching a likeness of Ḥaāmer, cats at her feet, holding up a lotus blossom, the bloom and Ḥaāmer's face touched by rays from Aten.

"What's this?" Īset asked, pointing to another likeness.

"Pharaoh used to swing her up in the air when she was a child. The writer thought it would be a good image for the gods to see."

"Pharaoh will not like such a display of ungodly affection."

Neb-t·ḥe-t shrugged. "It's not for him. What do you think, Ḥaāmer?"

There was no answer.

Both women turned. Ḥaāmer had nestled her head back into the linen and in the confined space folded her arms across her chest. Her eyes were closed, her face pale midst the dark, resinous wood. Īset gasped and choked as tears flooded her eyes. Neb-t·ḥe-t wrapped an arm about her sister. "She is only sleeping. The excitement has tired her."

Īset nodded, trembling. "She looks . . ."

"Peaceful," Neb-t·ḥe-t finished. "She will look the same when the gods awaken her."

* * *

Ḥaāmer was gone, carried gently, still sleeping, back to the waiting litter. Īset could not get the image of her daughter, so still, lying in her coffin, out of her thoughts. Neb-t·ḥe-t had been right. Ḥaāmer looked peaceful, happy, strangely whole, and Īset wanted that for her first daughter almost as much as she wanted to keep her near. So she wanted her daughter to live and die and hated herself for both thoughts.

"How many servants do you plan to send with Ḥaāmer? The traditional four? We need to plan their burials as well." Neb-t·ḥe-t asked when they were alone again in the passage.

Īset regarded her sister with more calm than she felt. "We will not be sending any others with her."

Neb-t·ḥe-t stopped. "You aren't sending anyone to accompany and serve her in Amennt? Who will provide and care for her?"

"I will not deprive other mothers of their children. They die soon enough on their own."

Neb-t·ḥe-t, her face placid like one of her funeral masks, concealed what she might think of Īset's break from royal burial tradition. The moment stretched on, and Īset thought she might have offended her sister by making her a witness to her heretical intentions. Then she saw Neb-t·ḥe-t's shy smile. "Good for you, Īset. Perhaps you will end this brutal practice." she said in a private voice.

Louder, she added: "May I make a suggestion?"

Neb-t·ḥe-t led Īset deeper beneath the mortuary. Stone walls gave way to clay bricks and finally to packed mud. Neb-t·ḥe-t took a torch from the wall and moved into a room that had no door. The air was heavy and still, suffused with dust, but cooler than expected for such a warm day. It was an ancient, undisturbed place where Neb-t·ḥe-t could practice her own heresy.

Shelves filled the room. Hundreds of hand-sized wood and stone figures, servants, cooks, boatmen, soldiers, and workmen, stood row upon row. They were as life-like as human hands could make them. Each was unique in clothing and facial expression. Īset could not recall more remarkable works of art.

"They are ushabtuis, the little servants," Neb-t·ḥe-t said. "They serve the dead who never had the luxury of servants in life. Their families select them. We say prayers over them asking the gods to give them life that they might serve their master or lady."

"Ptah revealed this to you?" Īset asked, touching the ushabtui nearest her, a smiling woman on her knees, grinding grain for bread.

"Compassion revealed this to me. But Ptah will bring them to life as the instructions and prayers direct."

Īset touched another, a man, tilling the ground, a woman beside him, dropping seeds. "They look alive now."

"Take some time. Choose those needed to accompany and serve Ḥaāmer. I will prepare and place them in the tomb."

Īset looked at Neb-t·ḥe-t. "Set does not know about this?"

"No. We give the ushabtuis away, to comfort and prepare the dying—not so we can further fill the temple treasury."

Neb-t·ḥe-t left Īset amid the tiny figures. Glittering eyes watched, faces, expressions, emotions beckoned to her from every direction she looked. The air trembled with their whispers, each wanted to serve. They were not dolls, simple figures of straw, wood, or stone, given only the rough features needed to entertain a child. Nor were they statues, aloof, regal, their faces and poses intended to inspire devotion and worship. Each of these was like a tiny person, captured in a secret moment, turned to stone and clay and wood when he or she thought no one was there, their postures unassuming and graceful, their faces serene and natural in that innocent moment of discovery.

Īset waited and certain faces appealed to her, certain hands reached out. She could not remember picking them up, but realized her arms were full of the tiny figures. They had all volunteered in some magical way.

* * *

"What are you doing?" Īset asked from the doorway to the workshop. She cradled several ushabtuis in her arms.

"Marking it," Neb-t·ḥe-t replied, using the sharp granite chip to score the bottom of the golden figure. "This statue looks remarkably similar to one a priest commissioned for the tomb of a nobleman. The temple treasury assured me it was only a copy, but I've heard stories."

"What stories?" Īset frowned.

"Some say that priests return to a tomb several days after a burial to remove all the valuables—resealing it afterward to hide the theft. They resell the valuables for another burial. By marking these pieces, I will discover the truth."

"Who would defile both the living and the dead this way?"

Neb-t·ḥe-t glanced at her sister.

"Set?" Īset said. "We should take this to Pharaoh."

"Take what?" Neb-t·ḥe-t asked. "A couple scratched gold statues and some whispered accusations? If Pharaoh will not believe that his brother wants to kill him, why would he believe that Set is looting gold from tombs?"

"But if we could persuade someone to witness against Set?"

"Unlikely," Neb-t·ḥe-t said.

Īset brushed her fingers over a small, solid gold statue of Hathor in the form of a cow. "Why are you doing this?"

Neb-t·ḥe-t set the tool and the ushabtui down and wiped her brow. "To end it."

"But if you won't go to Pharaoh?"

Neb-t·ḥe-t ignored the question. "I heard some interesting talk. Are husbands no longer allowed to punish their wives?"

"Is that what people say?"

"It's what Set's priests say," Neb-t·ḥe-t said.

Īset frowned. "Set sent a woman among those seeking the words of Pharaoh," Īset said. "But Pharaoh turned his clever test back on him."

"Did he?" Neb-t·ḥe-t said, looking up to meet her sister's gaze. "Even when playing the fool Set generates sympathy. He doesn't care about the abuse of women. He wants to rule Egypt."

"I will warn Pharaoh again."

"Sure you will. And Pharaoh will ignore you and nothing will change."

Īset frowned. "What would you have me do?"

Neb-t·ḥe-t finished examining a golden image of Ȧpnu and set it on the table. "I'm sorry, Īset, I know you are doing what you can. Pharaoh is stubborn and for some reason the gods want this uneasy balance between him and his brother. I do not understand why they allow Set to continue his plotting and keep Pharaoh ignorant of the danger."

Old words, spoken too often. Nothing more passed between the sisters, except the uncomfortable silence of other memories and regrets that were too familiar to speak of. Īset arranged the ushabtuis she had chosen on the table before Neb-t·ḥe-t.

"I must return and see to Ḥaāmer," Īset said. She bent and kissed her sister on the cheek. When the sound of her sandals on the rough stone floor faded away, Neb-t·ḥe-t wiped the spot away.

Chapter 3

SOUTHERN EGYPT, FLIGHT FROM ABYDOS TO CAIRO, JUNE 7TH, 12:00 P.M.:

Largely unaware of the trip, Anwar flew from the southern region to Cairo. His wounds ached, but his thoughts of visiting Nefri hurt much more. Army medics met them at the Cairo base. Captain Jagardii made sure they handled Omar gently, trying to reduce any further trauma to his friend. Anwar knew the Army's forensic lab would attempt to identify the terrorist. His corpse went into the bed of the Army mortuary vehicle.

CAIRO, EGYPT, BASE HOUSING, OMAR MULHAN'S QUARTERS, JUNE 7TH, 2:30 P.M.:

Dismissing the driver, Anwar took the staff car to Omar's quarters. Remembering the hours of joyful times they had at his sergeant's base housing, he could not go to the door. The sand colored walls and featureless yard seemed somber and drab rather than the normal warm, pleasurable glow he always felt. After several minutes, Nefri came to see who was lingering in front of her home.

"Anwar? Why are you all bloody?"

He did not respond.

"What's wrong?"

"Nefri, we need to go the hospital."

"Oh by the face of Allah," she gasped, putting her hand to her mouth. "What's happened? Is Omar...?"

* * *

Nefri was inconsolable. Her third son called their neighbor to go with her to the hospital. Anwar chose to go by himself. Anwar spoke briefly with the three boys at the house then he went to the university to tell the two adult sons. They handled the news reasonably well, but they were shaken. Omar was a source of strength to his family—a good husband and father. Anwar prayed for his speedy recovery. Not being religious, he prayed anyway. He would make every effort to get to Cairo to visit Omar and his family.

CAIRO, EGYPT, MILITARY HEADQUARTERS, GENERAL FADI'S OFFICE, JUNE 7TH, 3:00 P.M.:

Anwar drove to General Fadi's headquarters.

"Wait over there while I type your report," indicated the staff secretary. "General Fadi wants you to report to him when I complete it."

Moments later, Anwar stood at attention in General Fadi's office.

"You look like hell, captain."

"Yes, sir."

"You don't have to be so pissing agreeable, captain. At ease. You could have been killed."

Perhaps that would have been better.

Anwar didn't respond to the general. A scowl distorted Fadi's face.

"How the hell did you get caught with your ass hanging out?"

"We've been chasing vapor for weeks."

"I expected more from you, captain. What did we learn? How many terrorists attacked your convoy?"

"We have no idea, sir. We never saw any terrorists other than the one we killed."

"Shit! This is as worthless as the rest of your reports," the general pounded his desk with both fists. "Captain, you're dismissed."

Anwar came to attention, saluted and faced the door.

"Captain."

Anwar halted, turning slowly to face General Fadi again. "Yes, sir?"

"I'm sorry about Omar. He's a good man. And a good friend."

"Yes, sir. I will kill every one of the bastards."

"Don't make this a personal vendetta, Anwar."

"No, sir."

"Anwar, I am serious."

"Yes, sir."

CAIRO, EGYPT, MILITARY HEADQUARTERS, GENERAL FADI'S OFFICE, JUNE 7TH, 4:30 P.M.:

After lunch, Fadi stared out his office window at the crystal sky, upset by the interview he had just had with Field Marshall Aaliyah. His boss had ripped him a new one. For obvious reasons, the president was all over the Field Marshall for solutions and Fadi wasn't providing them. Fadi's orders were quite clear: eradicate the problem.

Field Marshall Aaliyah and he had never been on the best of terms. Fadi had risen to his position through his family connections. He assumed that was why he received his current assignment—so he could fail. The Field Marshall never treated Fadi as a brother soldier. Abdul knew he was soon going to be the Field Marshall's excuse. He had become expendable. He could be removed.

Damnation! I need to unravel the threads. What should I do?

Fadi felt exhausted by the problems swirling around him. The terrorists, Jagardii's lack of results, Omar's injury, and now the ancient discovery.

"Shit!"

His aide entered the room from the side.

"May I speak frankly, sir?"

"What is it Mohieddin?"

"It's Jagardii, sir."

"What about Captain Jagardii?"

"He is a common person, sir. I don't understand why you accept him. He hasn't provided you with one terrorist or any leads to them. He's jeopardizing your career, sir."

"I have ultimate faith in Anwar. Although he's not brought this operation to a satisfactory conclusion, *yet*, he's a good soldier. I trust him with my life. He saved both Omar Mulhan and me fifteen years ago."

"Yes, I know, sir. You used your influence to direct commission him to captain, but do you feel that is wise now, sir."

"I will determine that, colonel. You are dismissed."

"Yes, sir."

Damn! I must make a decision about Jagardii.

The jangle of the telephone broke his concentration. He looked down to see who was calling, but did not recognize the number. He waited for the receptionist to buzz him. Fadi lifted the telephone.

"The Kuwaiti Ambassador, sir."

"Please connect us." When the connection was made, Fadi said, "Good afternoon, Your Excellency."

"I understand you're in charge of routing out terrorists."

"Yes, Your Excellency."

Interesting he should know that. I must find the spy.

"I would normally go through diplomatic channels to have discussions with your government, but this is very personal to me. I would like to speak personally with you. My wife has been missing since morning. I am deeply concerned for her. My people are searching for her, but I feel if we had your full cooperation, we could speed her recovery."

"I understand, Your Excellency. I'm at your service. Do you feel the terrorists are the cause of you wife's disappearance?"

"Yes, that is my concern. Do you believe the terrorists are a rogue group within your organization?"

"Your question is most direct, sir. I will answer you directly. No. Early in our investigations of the terrorist activities within my country, this possibility concerned us. Through technology, we verified the location of every commander and his organization. We determined the location of all unaccounted individuals. In other words, were a few individuals from different groups working together to subvert our government? We embarrassed several soldiers who were not performing their duty, but we found no conspiracy. The military isn't behind this scourge, Your Excellency."

"I felt you would say this. My people observed a military truck leaving the bazaar my wife was visiting. I feel it was the terrorists. Please proceed quickly. You have the complete cooperation of my government. I wish to find my wife."

"I understand, Your Excellency. We'll make every attempt to locate your wife and the many others who have been taken."

The connection broke.

Shit! I don't need interference from a foreign power. His communication was highly unusual. Diplomats don't contact people inside foreign governments directly. The ambassador thinks the terrorists kidnapped his wife—I agree. The tests of this day will never end. Has Gheit given the embassy my private number?

Fadi rang his receptionist.

"I need Colonel Gheit here immediately. Have him wait until after my next appointment."

Captain Jagardii's report sat in the center of his desk.

My friend, Omar, is not likely to live. Shit! How could this happen? How can I get control?

His thoughts returned to Jagardii.

He bares watching. His deportment shows he is on a personal mission. That mission could interfere with my sanctioned terrorist pursuit. I don't have any spare officers. Anwar is necessary.

At least Anwar had the sense to keep his mouth shut about the ambush site. It needs to stay shut. I need his attention elsewhere. How can I be sure of that?

An inspiration jumped into Abdul's mind. He tapped the thin folder on his desk. *Stop!* He hated his nervous tic, forcing himself to stop. His tapping was a clear indication of his nervousness over the impending interview.

Now to focus on the immediate problem. The Minister of the Interior will be here momentarily.

Fadi found himself tapping again. The soft knock came at his door.

"Come," he said, picking up the folder and moving from behind his desk.

The Minister of the Interior and another man entered the room. Not expecting to deal with another person, Fadi was on guard. The new person was small of stature. He had a narrow face with a large, beak-like nose making his face pointed and sharp. His protruding lips held a waxed, sharp mustache, standing out straight to each side. He wore a seedy, gray-brown suit jacket. His whole persona brought to Fadi's mind the picture of a rodent, a rat with twitching whiskers. He had never met the Secretary General before, but recognized him from his pictures.

"General, have you met Dr. Jabar Tu'hut? Dr. Tu'hut is the Secretary General of the Ministry of State for Antiquities. He is Egypt's foremost expert on our history. I felt he would be of immense help in judging the new Abydos site. Don't you agree?"

"I've never had the pleasure of Dr. Tu'hut's acquaintance, but I am aware of his prestigious reputation. He certainly would be the most appropriate judge of this find," Fadi said, indicating the sitting area of his office. "Please be comfortable. Would either of you gentlemen desire refreshment? Perhaps some tea?"

Both men accepted. The Secretary General spoke for the first time.

"Yes, tea," said Dr. Tu'hut almost as if he were demanding it.

His voice was high and squeaky in a way General Fadi found irritating. His picture of a rat persisted. They sipped for several minutes. The general, a generous host, offered and poured each man more tea. The minister leaned back in his seat and the Secretary General leaned forward. Fadi began the discussion.

"The military has discovered a new ancient site," said General Fadi. "It's...."

"Really. Where is this find?" asked the Secretary General, interrupting Fadi.

"In the bluffs above Abydos."

"Many of our ancient ancestors were buried in the Abydos valley, but I have never heard of a site in the bluffs. There's nothing up there. No roads. Just a cliff face. How would the ancients get anything there? I'm skeptical of this, general—unbelievable."

Minister Aboud showed no emotion. General Fadi grew uneasy. He forced himself to show no discomfort. His ire with Jagardii rose.

This Secretary General of a Ministry of State for Antiquities is a royal pain in the ass. If Anwar is mistaken, my embarrassment will not show pleasantly on his skin.

"It is underground," continued Fadi, as if unconcerned.

"Underground?" Dr. Tu'hut's eyebrows furled together with a quizzical look. "Are you sure of all this?"

Questioning my factual statement. Definitely a rat.

"My observer is not an archaeologist, Dr. Tu'hut. We, in the military, attempt only to assist our *esteemed* colleagues when a place of interest is discovered. My observer mentioned a wooden sarcophagus surrounded by clay tablets with hieroglyphic writings."

The Secretary General's eyebrows went up. His face grew wistful. His eyes lost focus. Dr. Tu'hut's lips moved as he whispered: "A wooden funerary box? Stelae?"

"Secretary General?" asked Fadi puzzled by the Dr. Tu'hut's change.

"A funerary box, oh, my. The stelae would not be stone if they were early dynastic. If this is so, the site could be ancient, indeed. There are legends about this area. Menes is supposed to have come from there.

"Minister, I would like to travel to this place," said the Secretary General, turning to Minister Aboud.

"Is it safe, general?" Aboud asked.

"I will guarantee your safety, gentlemen," he said, smiling for the first time.

SOUTHERN EGYPT, THE TERRORIST VILLAGE, JUNE 8TH, 8:00 A.M.:

Hours passed. The men moved Massouma from street, to truck, to dark space—from terror, to bruises, to agony—then long, numbing isolation. The foul odor of human waste assaulted her senses.

Where am I? This place is horrible. I never go to the street—why did I?

The Ambassador warned her to stay inside the embassy. He told her Egypt was not safe even for an arab ambassador's wife, but as a child, she went to the bazaar with her parents. She knew her way.

I wanted to go to the bazaar to look and shop. 'Ambassador' will be angry. My back hurts.

Massouma could stand no longer. She sank to the floor, her legs giving out. She sat in the filth forcing her mind away from the smell. She felt dirty. The excreta soaked her clothing. She was hot, thirsty and exhausted.

No sooner had she collapsed than a soldier came, pushing her into a common room with the butt of his rifle. His wrinkled nose indicated her stench did not appeal to his senses. Other women filled the room, common women with whom she did not associate. The others moved away from Massouma. She did not care. They were of a different class.

The soldier who kidnapped me said I am a criminal, a heretic, uncovered—ridiculous.

She now had a piece of dirty cloth around her head and a tattered, bloodstained robe over her embassy clothing. As if on cue, soldiers herded the women together. Some, unused to men touching them, shrieked and were struck.

Be silent, sister!

The soldiers led the group into dazzling sunlight on a village street. Low drab buildings lined one side of the street. They could have been in any outlying village in Egypt. Cables and equipment snaked along in the dust. A dry breeze kicked up sand and gave rise to a soft sound. Only her group of women and the soldiers were there. Forced to sit in the street dirt, Massouma watched as the soldiers gathered behind recording equipment. The scrape of their boots became yet another sound mixed with the whispering wind.

A low wail of agony added to the scrape and the soft wind. The wail, closer and louder, was a voice. The sound was as desolate as the scene, sending chills through Massouma, frightening her. Soldiers led or dragged every form of rejected humanity: male, female, old, young, robed and undressed into the center of the street. Massouma thought one looked like a prostitute. A helicopter appeared over the ridge.

My husband is coming.

It landed behind the equipment, a dust cloud roiling from under it. A liveried chauffeur swung his legs out and turned to assist a distinguished gentleman. A sallow-faced man exited behind them. The trio moved to the row of cameras and waited.

Not my husband. How will I explain?

A middle-aged man stood hesitantly in the adjacent group of men. He made a slight signal to the commanding one. Gathering his courage and drawing a breath, he said, "Minister Aboud?"

The distinguished one stiffened, baring his teeth, making a vicious signal with his hand. A soldier waded into the group of men, clubbing the man into unconsciousness.

Aboud? I have heard that name. What is he doing here? He is a leader. If I dare acknowledge him, will he have me beaten or will he stop this?

A soldier turned from the equipment to face Aboud. When Aboud nodded, the soldier waded into the center of her group, coming to her.

Why am I selected?

She wobbled to her feet. When she was slow to move, he gave her the back of his hand. Having fallen, he wrenched her upright again, dragging her before one of the cameras.

Massouma had a clear view of the lower arm of the soldier holding her. A tattoo of the Arabic crescent and star etched the man's forearm. Below the emblem, a pair of purple and yellow snake eyes stared at her.

The tattooed soldier's other hand appeared gripping a military pistol. She froze in terror. The soldier pulled the trigger.

CAIRO, EGYPT, THE KUWAITI EMBASSY, JUNE 8TH, 9:00 A.M.:

Jarah Hamimech, Senior Kuwaiti Ambassador to Egypt, listened as the Embassy Guard Commander explained how his beautiful wife ignored warnings by the staff and avoided escort outside the embassy. She'd been gone for twenty-four hours.

If she's harmed, by Allah, I will rip them all apart when I find her and have discovered the whole truth.

Massouma requested a peek outside, but he unequivocally denied such insanity. Egypt is unsafe. But she is young and impetuous. She had defied him. Her curiosity was what he loved about her though it often led to trouble. He loved her spunk, her panache. Another time he might have punished her. Now all he wanted was her safe return.

THE SOUTHERN EGYPT, THE ABYDOS FEATURE JUNE 8TH, 3:00 P.M.:

The Minister of the Interior, General Fadi, Dr. Tu'hut and Captain Jagardii went to the new feature by helicopter. Anwar stayed away from the group as much as he could under the cramped travel conditions. He wasn't their social status nor did he feel sociable. His visit with Nefri had been the most difficult task he'd ever performed.

The lieutenant met the helicopter with a jeep and truck. Anwar drove the general's group while the lieutenant followed in the truck with an armed guard. They watched the front, back, sides and cliff tops. The general stopped the convoy on the road above the site, pointing across the plains to Abydos. The Nile, three miles away, flowed through the valley like a slender, silver ribbon, stretching into the distant haze.

As they pulled into the military area, General Fadi gazed up at the ramparts.

"There are sentinels guarding, sir," responded Anwar. Fadi nodded.

Anwar led the Secretary General to the vehicle and he bent to peer into the opening. Anwar lowered a light into the hole to allow the Secretary General to examine the room through a pair of binoculars. The Secretary's excitement increased as he observed the room.

While on leave, Anwar had seen numerous excavations in the Valley of the Kings. Their beauty and age always awed him. He knew this was an ancient place. He didn't need the Secretary General's opinion to know this was an important find.

The Secretary General stood and stretched. "You were wise, captain, not to move the truck. The shifting weight might have dropped rocks on the precious furnishings."

"Thank you, sir."

"General, the MSA must take immediate charge of this site."

"Am I to understand this is a significant find?"

"Yes, general, I don't know what this place is, but the appearance of the objects makes it a significant find."

The general beamed. "With these most recent attacks on my men, I must point out to you this is a dangerous area. I don't know how the MSA can take over the site safely."

Anwar excused himself. His presence wasn't needed while his superiors bickered over who was going to be in charge. After the negotiations, the eminent trio would be in need of refreshment. Anwar went to arrange a sitting area under a tarp and proper food and drink. He wasn't sure he could serve tea, and had no idea where he would get sweet cakes.

Perhaps army biscuits and water would suffice, Anwar snorted at his humor, *I will leave it in the hands of the camp cooks.*

He walked into the bivouac area to find the lieutenant to direct the arrangements.

NORTHERN EGYPT, DELTA SITE, JUNE 8TH, 9:40 P.M.:

"I explored the two pits you created," Robert said, "Watching the water flow, I've tried to locate the source, but water never flows straight point to point."

He paused. Lisa waited, lifting an eyebrow.

"I surveyed our site, looking for slope, but it's hard to see. I used a surveying instrument I picked up at the university. I thought this afternoon I knew where the water was coming from so I went exploring. I found more water when I dug. It's now another water pit."

"So is it the source?"

Robert shrugged. "I don't know. But when I pumped it, your excavations drained. I think I'm close to an ancient channel."

"Let's see the plat map and determine whether your location is on the map. We may be trying to excavate an ancient channel to the Nile."

Robert smiled.

He thinks I've accepted his theory, thought Lisa, having denied it earlier.

"We probably need to talk to the farmer. I sneaked onto his land," added Robert.

"Outside our exploration area? We'll handle that. If it is an ancient water course, we must expand our area."

"Everyone will need to be consulted—the farmer, the government and the university," agreed Robert. "The farmer may appreciate the water."

Lisa nodded as she went to the layout table. She began rapidly turning a stack of prints, searching through the site aerial photos. Robert, looking over her shoulder, indicated a place not in Lisa's survey area. It wasn't farm irrigation either. What he pointed to appeared in the photograph as a fuzzy line, perhaps a trail, half covered by low ground vegetation, extending toward a branch of the Nile a half mile away.

"As faint as it appears in these aerial photos, it can't be recent," he commented.

"Hard to tell age by that."

Lisa went from the trailer across the archaeological site to the adjacent farm field, carrying a flashlight she had grabbed. The small gasoline powered pump was chugging away, water gushing from a canvas hose into a farm furrow. She examined the dirt to make sure Robert had been watching where he was digging. She didn't find any artifacts. Lucky for Robert.

CAIRO, EGYPT, THE KUWAITI EMBASSY, JUNE 8TH, 10:00 P.M.:

Stubbing out his Turkish cigarette in the mounded, overflowing ashtray centered on his leather topped desk, Jarah Hamimech pushed aside the papers requiring his signature.

"I'm not able to do this," he told his aide. "I cannot do it."

When his aide did not respond, Jarah focused on him to find the aide's attention was on the screen behind him. Jarah thought back. They were streaming an Egyptian news source with the sound subdued. Words weren't discernible.

"Your Excellancy!"

Jarah turned to see what his aide was watching. Centered in the screen was his wife's face. The ambassador stopped breathing.

She's been found! Where is she?

Massouma was held among common women—hags. She was dressed in a dirty robe—her skin and clothing stained, filthy. The camera followed a soldier, as he waded into her group. The soldier yanked her standing.

NO! What's happening? Why are they doing this?

Jarah could not process what he was seeing. As he stood, his thoughts tumbled over each other. She stumbled and was back-handed.

The soldier dragged her to the camera. His hand held her by the throat.

I will kill him! thought Jarah.

The soldier's wrist had an Arab crescent and star. A pair of yellow and purple snake eyes gazed unblinking at Jarah. A military pistol appeared and was pressed to Massouma's ear. The weapon discharged.

"No!"

Jarah reeled gripping the corner of the desk to steady his faltering legs. Turning, he cleared the top of his desk with a single swipe of his arm. Paper fluttered in the air. The ashtray, lamp and telephone crashed to the floor. Unintelligible sounds came from the spilled telephone. Ashes and shattered glass scattered over the carpet.

Chapter 4

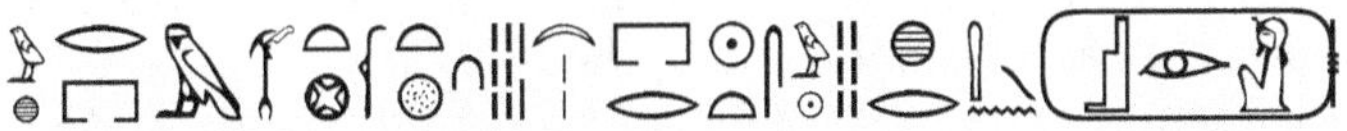

wḫrpr m wꜣst ḥsbt 18 ꜣbd 2 prt sw 6 ḫr ḥm n wsỉr

The Docks in Uas,
Year 18, Month 2 of Peret, Day 6 under the Majesty of Ạsạr

Two boys spilled over a red bluff like whirlwinds, skidding down the side, throwing up a tumble of pebbles and dirt. They raced across a stretch of sand, laughing, before splashing among the reeds at the water's edge. Chasing and being chased, they stumbled through pools cut off from the River flow, falling and laughing again.

Pausing, breathing heavy gasps under the warm sun, they dove into a deeper pool. A moment later two heads emerged; two lithe bodies surged up from the water to watch a boat drift by. One raised a hand and smiled. The other also raised his hand, a fist dripping with black mud, and pelted his friend in the back. Diving, splashing, the chase resumed.

Maaạ watched them, passing on the nondescript cargo boat, pushed by a quiet ripple of air that advanced it against the current no faster than a man could walk. The boys created far more motion along this rocky stretch of the River.

A line of thin clouds stained the sky to the north. The day was warm, the breeze carrying the little cargo boat down the River towards Uas cool and gentle. It was a lazy breeze, little more than a dream of wind, rocking the boat as gently as an infant's cradle.

Red mountains bounded the land on the east, approaching and receding as if they played a child's game of tag with the River along its course from Nubia to the great sea. Ravines and wadis cut between the mountains. Caravans used those that were passable to trade with peoples all the way to the eastern sea and with ships that came from places further away, places with strange names, languages, and customs: Joktan, Arphaxad, Elam.

Red rock and soil spilled from these wadis and spread for great distances.

Where the red rock reached the River, the hilly land remained above the flooding that brought the precious black soil from Nubia to support the year's crops: flax for linen and wheat for bread. Where the red mountains were far from the River, where the land was flat and low, the River could spill over its bank and spread out, slowing, leaving the black dirt behind.

The flooding of the River, the rich soil that remained after it returned to its banks, were the gifts from Hapi who controlled the yearly inundation from his home among the caves at the first of the River's cataracts.

The boat reached a bend where the River turned back to the west, toward the land of forgetting. A boatman mending an old hemp net near Maaạ rose from his crouch, stretched his thin, stiff legs, and swung the linen sail to catch the air from a new direction. The boys were lost from view.

The first of the northern settlements above Uas peeked from around the bend, lining the eastern bank, land of the living.

In this flat area stone or wooden deities, ancestral gods, local gods, gods from the growing temples, marked the field boundaries.

Maaạ recognized some of them. A squat statue of round, fat Geb. Each year his ribs sprout new grain and his back yields the other lush vegetation that appears after the inundations, some of it carried along in the water itself. Geb, providing water, the fertile black soil, and an abundant harvest.

Then a statue with no form, a tall thin obelisk bearing the name Napar, a god with no visible form who begins his life again after death, as the grain seeds taken from dead brown stalks spring forth again in new abundance. Like all life along the River, life arising from death.

Also Andjety, an old and quiet god, who moves in places not seen, remembering his children and their struggles in the valley. He comes to the land in the night, walks the red hills and the yellow sands, stands upon the waters, reminding both the River and the earth to show kindness to his children, to be fertile and bountiful for them.

A scatter of statues with inscriptions to identify both the field's owner and ultimate protector. The fields were empty now, and would be until the next inundation occurred at the beginning of Shemu, still more than a hundred days away.

The men who spent their days tending the fields were off to Uas to haul stones for buildings and monuments. Along the shore, where a rocky spot stuck out, old women gathered pots of water, letting it clear for drinking. They also washed clothes, dipping them in the River, watching for crocodiles and snakes, working the garments with their hands and spreading them on the rocks to dry. Some sang, as accompaniment to their motions, songs of love, songs of friends, children, husbands now lost.

Ȧri knelt to join Maaạ under the linen cover. "There are docks ahead. We could still dispatch a runner to Pharaoh."

"The answer is still no."

"I think this is a mistake. Pharaoh does not like surprises."

Maaạ smiled. "I know. You have said as much each time you broach the subject. All will be well. Wait and see."

Ȧri shook his head and sighed. He looked away, over the bow, over the River to the shore, the sand, the hills and the distant mountains. "You lead a protected life, favored by the gods. Let us hope that favor continues."

The bare land gave way to huts of mud and straw, clusters where extended families lived together for support and protection. Further on, around a bend, past the next finger the red mountains pushed toward the River, a village, the houses clay and stones rather than mud. Simple streets winding among them, houses for craftsmen in addition to simple farmers.

Closer to Uas, larger villages seemed to sprout along the Eastern bank like spring grain after the inundation, towns where the craftsmen lived who were building Pharaoh's city: stone masons, carpenters, architects. Men who worked with ropes and sand and levers to move the cut rocks from the River to their final repose: the walls of the temples in the place where Pharaoh, now god among us, chose to live his days on earth.

The houses were closer together, more regular in their spacing. Streets between them wider, straighter. Clay gave way to cut stones as a building material. The larger houses were decorated, pottery and flowers adorning entrances and roof lines.

In the distance, the heart of Uas shimmered in the afternoon sun.

"More impressive each time I see it," Ȧri called back to Maaạ.

Maaạ nodded his agreement and smiled. There was a beauty to what Pharaoh had done, a balance, a blend of old and new ideas that created a reverence, a sense of accomplishment and belonging, in all who beheld them. Maaạ, as one who governed and built towns and cities and provinces, appreciated the thoughtful planning and careful execution and felt the desire to continue Pharaoh's work.

They were mountains built for the gods, the Temple of Ptah, its carved stone columns and quiet reflecting pools, refreshed daily with water carried from the River. Nearby, the Hall of Balance, where Pharaoh sat and listened to the petitions of his people, where he issued the wisdom and judgment given to him by the gods, and where the priests gathered to listen, to advise, and to record his words.

Set apart, higher, with a view of the growing city, the River, and the western lands beyond, Pharaoh's house and the adjoining house for his wife and their daughters.

The steersman directed the men to reposition the sails in order to push the boat towards the Ukher, the stone docks created to receive and bear the materials used to build Uas, its temples, and its monuments.

When the boat favored that direction, they released the sails, tied them up, and pulled the oars from the rings along the deck. The oars splashed into the water, shattering the smooth rippled surface for a moment. A slow, rowing song started up among the men, the first notes given by the steersman in a clear, deep voice. The oars dipped and rose to the rhythm, guiding the boat serenely towards the shore.

A dock manager in a loose kilt and cloak, head and arms red from his time in the sun, marched to the end of dock and shouted orders. He motioned to a berth along the adjoining pier.

Mid-afternoon produced only light traffic among the docks. Most of the fishing boats would be out until the Aten set. Only a few had given up or filled their nets this early. Merchants departed in the morning, and arrived in the mid-day to unload and take on new cargo. Trading slowed during Peret. The primary commodities, flax and wheat, had been harvested and distributed last season.

A woman waited at their berth. A long, flowing linen dress, its hem drifting about her sandals, a shawl about her shoulders pulled over her head as shelter from the Aten's warmth. Her linens were too fine for a fisherman's wife, not fine enough for a merchant who would decorate her with gold and jewels as sign of his wealth and favor.

She did not move. Maaạ watched her as the boat slipped closer. The men on the dock side of the boat gathered the mooring ropes, while those facing the River waved their oars slowly in the water like fish tails, bringing the boat to a gentle stop.

She watched, her straight, slim form, still as a statue, quiet as a funerary painting on a tomb wall. The shawl shadowed her face. She did not step back when a rope landed at her feet and a youth lifted and secured it to a stone post.

The men jumped to the dock, finished securing the ropes, and wrestled a ramp into place. Maaạ and Ȧri came across first. Ȧri placed a hand on Maaạ's shoulder: "I'll see to our lodging. Should I look for you in the market?"

Maaạ, his mood lighter now that he was back on land, smiled. "I think a bowl of the Uas beer that is praised in Meḥ is exactly what I need. And since I am a boatman today instead of a governor, I may get it at a reasonable price."

Ȧri strode away. Maaạ waited for his legs to lose the feeling that they still lifted and fell gently on the water. He peered down the quiet streets, past buildings of stone and mud brick crowded about the docks. The air smelled of fish mingled with the odors of animals confined in pens and cages waiting to be loaded aboard transport, either out on the River or up into the city and the towns and settlements beyond.

The woman waited. Maaạ passed her without looking.

"Prince Maaạ."

Maaạ stopped. Turning at the shoulders, he looked back. "You seek someone else."

She bowed her head in deference. A line of tiny ankhs stained along the border of the shawl peered at him instead.

"I serve princess Ḥaāmer," she said. "I know who you are."

Her voice made a song of the simple phrases. Maaạ stepped closer. In a near whisper, for privacy, he said: "No one knew I was coming here."

She dared to look up at him. Smooth face, amber skin, burnished eyes. A palace face, protected from hot days toiling in the fields, hidden from the Aten and the wind and sand that made faces so old. Unlike the women washing clothes along the River, too soon turned into dried, withered fruit.

"My princess dreamed you here today. She told me to bring you to her," she said.

She did not beg his indulgence, she did not show him the deference a governor deserved. She turned and moved as graceful as water running over smooth stone down the dock towards the city, not bothering to check if he followed.

She led him along the street that ascended from the Ukher, setting a pace that allowed him to follow and look around without falling behind.

At the entrance to the market, the barter men sat at the tables in front of their shops and stables, taking whatever one had to give, and offering small, inscribed pebbles in return. All the vendors accepted them, and many now found it easier to purchase using a common item of exchange rather than walking around with baskets of eggs or fruit or herds of animals. The pebbles could also be redeemed for whatever the exchangers happened to have. Maaạ knew that the same practice had started in the markets at Meh.

The maidservant, still five paces ahead of him, went to the gate that led to the house of Īset. She paused to whisper something to the guards and slipped past them into the gardens. The guards bowed in honor at Maaạ's approach, offering the usual greeting, ankh and sekhekah, long life and balance. They allowed him to pass.

Maaạ waited for Ḥaāmer in a garden at the entrance to the queen's house, frowning at his appearance in a reflecting pool, arranging a lock of stray hair over his ear. Ȧri would be looking for him in the marketplace and would maybe find a free woman or a good bowl of beer to distract himself awhile.

Maaạ turned at a sound. Four handmaidens, the one from the docks and three others, carried a couch.

Ḥaāmer's bruised, bony face peered from the bed linens. The handmaidens settled her with care, fussed with the corners of the linens, then faded away, back into shadow to await further summons.

"Ḥaāmer," Maaạ said.

Tears grew in her eyes at the sound of her name. They spilled out, carrying dark rivulets of kohl down her painted cheeks.

Maaạ knelt beside her, taking her hand in his. He reached for a linen cloth folded across her feet and touched it to her stained face.

"I'm noting lasts," she said. "The last sunset, the last warm Peret day, and the last time I will see your face."

"Not lasts. Soon you will be well and we will have the rest of our lives together."

She studied him in earnest. Her dark eyes, her gaunt face and shriveled features. She was empty, like a wineskin that had lost its wine. "I will not be your wife. Soon I will close my eyes and the gods will carry me to Amennt."

"It is not too late."

"Yes it is," Ḥaāmer said. "Far too late. And useless. The priests come to cast their healing spells from my doorway, horrified at my appearance and the smell of death that clings to me. They fear coming close enough to touch me. My mother turns from me to hide her tears. My father will not see me at all."

"I am here."

"I dreamed you would come. And hoped you would not."

Maaạ bent closer, dabbed at her eyes again. "You dreamed I would come?"

She turned away from him. "Will you join my father?"

"I will see if that is possible."

The rhythmic tap of sandals drew their attention. Ḥaāmer's younger sister, Āakhu, passed behind the row of columns that led from the gate to the Queen's house. She moved like a stir of air, gentle, calm, her gauzy dress, lit by the setting sun, a mere shred of cloud swirling about her. Movement unhampered, head tilted to the sky, Āakhu passed, unaware of Maaạ and Ḥaāmer nearby.

Maaạ turned back to Ḥaāmer. She peered at him, her eyes again filled with tears.

"She is promised to another," she said, too softly to be anything but earnest.

"I know," he replied.

"Since the day she was born I have been the second-most desirable daughter in the house of Pharaoh. She is young and whole and beautiful—every man she passes must linger to watch and dream. While I have withered away to become ugly and frightening.

"The gods have cursed me with dreams of days not yet born. After cursing my body and taking my life, they must show me all they will do to those I love. I don't know why. My mother says they are jealous and must destroy anything that might otherwise be perfect."

"You dreamed I would come," Maaạ said.

"Yes."

"And what else?"

She shook her head and started coughing. Maaạ hugged her until she stopped and cleaned her lips and cheeks. "What else?"

"You will take Āakhu as your wife, but she will never be yours. My father's kingdom will not continue through her."

"How could that be?"

"Hold me. Kiss me good-bye," she said, sad and frightened. Her wasted limbs struggled beneath the sheet like serpents writhing across the sands. "Go back to your ship and return to Meḥ. Send my father word that you will join him. Have him send his warriors."

Maaạ puzzled. "I will see him while I'm here."

Two dark eyes peered at Maaạ. "I know you will. Oh, Maaạ, leave my sister alone! Join my father. The men gathering on your border will not wait. They will come for your wealth and your land soon, and you will need my father's armies to stop them."

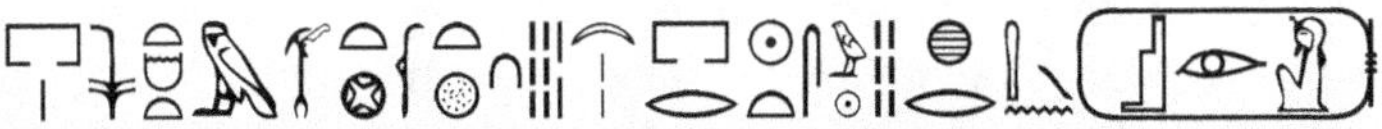

pr ḥmt nswt m wȝst ḥsbt 18 ȝbd 2 prt sw 6 ḫr ḥm n wsỉr

The House of Pharaoh's Wife in Uas,
Year 18, Month 2 of Peret, Day 6 under the Majesty of Ạsạr

Maaạ was gone, back to the inn where his friend Ȧri waited. The Aten was also gone, a violet smudge on the western horizon the last trace of its passing. Ḥaāmer dozed in her room when the tapestry covering her door moved aside and a shadow slipped inside.

"I have come as promised," Set said.

Ḥaāmer stirred, her eyes, two dark pools in the hollows above her cheeks. "Have you brought it?"

Set dropped the door tapestry and stole another step into the room, finger to his lips. His fine, soft robe, his golden bracelets and rings, glowed in the torchlight. "Quietly, princess, I would not have other ears overhear."

Ḥaāmer sighed. "But do you have it?"

Set crept to the bed and lifted a small clay pot from his pouch. "I have it, princess."

She forced a trembling hand out from the sheets and clutched it.

Set looked into the shadows and whispered: "Drink this and you will not see the Aten rise tomorrow. Your pain will be gone and you will wake in Ptah's presence. Is this what you want, princess?"

"I will die anyway. What does it matter whether it be tonight, tomorrow, or next week—except I will no longer be bedridden and in constant pain?"

Set bowed, a dark crescent looming over her. "You will destroy the pot after drinking its contents?"

Ḥaāmer coughed and nodded, wiping her lips.

"Then our business is concluded, daughter of Pharaoh. Is there anything else?"

"Maaạ is here."

Set turned back to her. "Here in Uas? I've had no word of that."

"He came in secret to bargain for what the gods would not grant him."

"Maaa will never be Pharaoh."

"No, he won't."

"Another vision, princess? What have you seen?"

Hearing a sound outside the door, Set drew back into the shadows. But it was only the shuffling of feet and the sad, quiet notes of a song as a servant passed in the corridor. The evening breeze whistling through high windows, a torch sputtering away the last of its pitch, these mournful sounds accompanied the gasp and wheeze, in and out, of Ḥaāmer's labored breathing.

Tears formed in her eyes. They glistened in the torchlight.

"My father is a good man," Ḥaāmer said. "I cannot see what you will do. I've only seen what it will cost. Your name will be known forever, but not for good."

Set's face changed into something else. The eyes sharpened, the lips pressed into a tight, straight line. "I seek only what's mine."

"And you shall have it—for a time."

Set backed towards the door.

"Pray for me," Ḥaāmer whispered.

Set pulled aside the door cover and paused. His throat closed as he spoke. "I will," he said in a hoarse whisper. "Live forever, Ḥaāmer."

pr-nswt m wꜣst ḥsbt 18 ꜣbd 2 prt sw 6 ḫr ḥm n wsỉr

The House of Pharaoh in Uas,
Year 18, Month 2 of Peret, Day 6 under the Majesty of Ạsạr

Pharaoh and Īset shared a late meal of breads, cheeses, and fruits in Pharaoh's private garden, watching the last of the day's traffic crease the slow-moving water.

"I had disturbing news from Neb-t·ḥe-t today," Īset said. "The priests say you no longer permit husbands to correct their wives. Any woman angry with her husband can have him publicly beaten by Pharaoh."

"I would have expected better of them. Set assured me—"

"Set has never forgiven you or your father."

Pharaoh stared at the plate, then lifted a piece of flat round bread and took a bite. "We were not the ones needing forgiveness."

Īset sighed and shook her head. "I don't like this coldness and lack of respect that is growing between you. It serves neither of you well."

She lifted her glass and sipped the tart, fruity wine. "You won't say how it began; that is your right. But Set's power is growing. So is his ambition. My sister does not give her warnings lightly."

"I will talk to him and see if we can finally resolve this."

She placed a hand over his, watching him in the fading light. "You aren't just saying that to quiet me?"

Pharaoh smiled. "Of course I am. But you are right. Set and I need to solve this trouble between us. We must work together if we are to unify this land."

A servant spoke from outside the door tapestry. "May you live forever Pharaoh. I have a message for you."

Ạsạr pulled his hand away from Īset, and growled: "What is it?"

"A message from Ḥaāmer, Pharaoh."

Īset rose. "Is she in pain? Should I go to her?"

"No, Lady. She sends word that prince Maaạ is in Uas and desires an audience with Pharaoh."

"She has seen him?" Īset asked.

"Yes, Lady. This afternoon, in your garden."

"Where is he staying?" Pharaoh asked.

"The inn on the River."

"Why is he here?" asked Īset.

"He did not say."

Pharaoh nodded, frowning. "Send an adviser to him this evening."

pr-nswt m wꜣst ḥsbt 18 ꜣbd 2 prt sw 7 ḫr ḥm n wsỉr

The House of Pharaoh in Uas,
Year 18, Month 2 of Peret, Day 7 under the Majesty of Ạsạr

Maaạ and Ȧri waited outside Pharaoh's private audience room. Pharaoh saw few people here, preferring the Hall of Balance where the priests could attend and listen, where the public might observe. This audience would be private, as Maaạ requested.

Reliefs depicting gods and goddesses colored the walls. They seemed to move in the flickering light from the oil pots. The words of Pharaoh were etched in spaces about the reliefs, as were prayers and praises. They trembled like something alive in the light and the warm smokiness that curled through the air.

A guard opened the wooden door and bid Maaạ to enter alone and bow before Pharaoh.

"Why did you come here unannounced?" Pharaoh asked.

"To speak with you privately and without fanfare."

"What news do you bring me, Prince Maaạ?"

"We need assistance. The provinces to our north are more belligerent and violent. It taxes vital resources to maintain a permanent force there."

"Join me," said Ạsạr.

"May you live forever. But I cannot submit to a Pharaoh who has no heir. Give me your daughter as wife, let me become that heir."

The scribe, recording the conversation on goat skin, stopped in mid-scratch. Silence. He looked up.

"You still bargain your four provinces for Ḥaāmer?" Pharaoh's voice was still, flat, dangerous, like dry air over motionless sand moments before the storm unleashes its fury.

"Not Ḥaāmer. Āakhu."

Silence. Pharaoh's eyes reflected the torchlight. His cheeks tightened, drawing his lips into a thin, straight line. Squares of light, the Aten smiling through the high windows, surrounded his golden throne with radiance.

"No," Pharaoh hissed.

"Egypt may live or die based on who you choose to continue your vision. All of us would be happier if that choice were your own son, born and raised by you and Īset. But I cannot gamble the provinces I control on that hope."

"You question my judgment?"

Maaạ lowered his head. "I honor your judgment, your wisdom, and your courage. I want to be a part of the future you see for this land and its people. I cannot do that from afar."

"I will not trade my daughter for your loyalty."

"Then I cannot join you."

Pharaoh leaned forward, his gaze intent on Maaạ. "What you say shows the respect and deference of a provincial governor for his Pharaoh. But what you do not say, what only speaks from your posture and your face, is that you somehow have the advantage here, that I must eventually give you Āakhu because you are too important for me to do otherwise. Let me correct that error. I will find it no more difficult to deal with the conquerors who hang your severed head from the gates of Meḥ than with you. And they will cost me far less. Think about that. Do not come to Uas again unless I send for you."

Maaạ bowed and rose. He took one step towards the door beyond which Ȧri waited. He turned again, dropped to one knee, and bowed. The scribe gasped. Pharaoh tensed. His guards touched the hilts of their bronze daggers but did not fully draw them.

"I saw two boys playing along the River yesterday," Maaạ said. "Friends. Even as they covered each another in mud and nearly drowned one another, they laughed. Why can we no longer exchange words except in anger?"

"Too much is at stake for this to be a joke."

"Why didn't you tell me Ḥaāmer is dying?"

Silence again for a moment. Pharaoh's voice, softer: "There is nothing you could do."

"I could have married her. It was what we both wanted."

Pharaoh's voice, softer still, the voice of a man, a father, and not a god: "She will spend her last days here."

Maaạ rose and left Pharaoh's private chamber, the guards holding the doors for him as he walked out. He brushed past Ȧri without a word, out of the house, into the street. Ȧri followed and called out to him, but Maaạ said nothing. He marched through the streets of Uas as if a mighty wind forced him along on the clear, still day. Back to the old trading boat. Home to Meh.

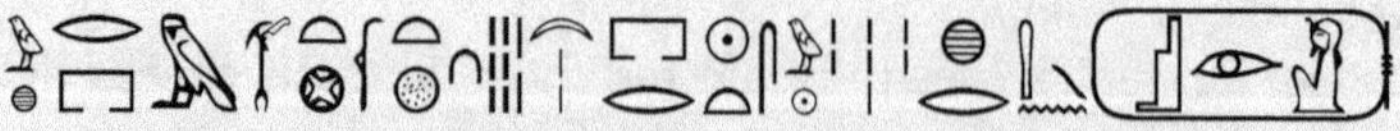

wḫrpr m wꜣst ḥsbt 18 ꜣbd 2 prt sw 7 ḫr ḥm n wsír

The Docks in Uas,

Year 18, Month 2 of Peret, Day 7 under the Majesty of Ạsạr

A priest stood on the ramp leading to Maaạ's boat. Golden bracelets clasped his forearms, a golden circle held a patch of hair on the left side of his otherwise shaved head. It was the sign of an initiate, more than a student, less that a full priest. Arms folded, expression serene, he stared off over the city streets and the haggling traders, over the eastern rise into the Amennt itself.

Maaạ stalked along the dock barely glancing up at the man. "You have the wrong boat," he said.

The priest stepped left, blocking Maaạ's way. He cast a large shadow even in the high sun. "The high priest would like a word with you."

A head emerged from the cover of Maaạ's rooms aboard the boat. Set. A smile appeared, then an amber shoulder, the paw of a leopard skin thrown casually over it.

Set's smile dried away. "I see from your countenance that your discussion did not go well. Did my brother treat you badly?"

Maaạ said nothing rather than the wrong thing. Instead, he glared at the priest blocking his way.

Set continued: "Come, let's talk. I have brought an excellent wine from the temple. I was invited there to witness the harvest. Did you know the local virgins crush the grapes with their feet? It is quite a celebration."

The priest stepped aside. Ȧri and the boatmen stood in an uncomfortable crescent at the foot of the dock. They murmured among themselves, watching and trying not to be noticed.

Maaạ stepped aboard and slipped beneath the linen cover. Set, somehow the host on Maaạ's boat, pointed to a seat and held out a bowl of wine.

Maaạ sipped, letting the flavor roll across his tongue. "Very nice," he said.

"I'm sorry my brother did not give you what you need. Perhaps I can."

"You don't control the army."

Set sipped the wine. He remained standing, closing his eyes a moment. When he opened them again Maaạ saw the hard expression, devoid of expression or emotion or warmth. Set's eyes that seemed carved from stone rather than flesh. "I will send you priests."

Maaạ laughed, drawing a frown from Set. "It's not my people's souls that need saving, it's their homes and their fields."

"These priests are skilled with the knife and bow. A regiment. They will stay in the temples and up in the hills, training and scouting until the day you need them."

"What do you want in return?"

Set took another sip of wine and smiled, but it was only the trace of a smile, a twitch at the corners of his mouth. "Spoken like a governor. These priests will cost you nothing."

Maaạ raised an eyebrow.

"You don't understand so you mistrust me. Here is the truth: I have more priests than I need to serve the gods and staff the temples. I want to teach some of them the warrior arts is case the temples, or the towns to which they belong are ever attacked. I have the men, the wealth, and the weapons. What I lack is space. I need open spaces away from Uas where they can train."

"There is a whole desert in which to train. What is special about Meḥ?"

Set frowned. His voice grew sharper. "For a man in your position, you ask foolish questions. I need land on which to train, you need soldiers to dissuade your northern neighbors from aggression and protect you should they attack anyway. We can do each other a service without incurring obligation. Any more questions?"

Set was condescending and bullying even as he smiled, more than a twitch of the lips this time to soften the sting of his words, then leaned forward, ever the humble servant to the gods, to refill Maaạ's bowl.

"I must think about this," Maaạ said.

"What is there to think about?" Set jeered. "You need soldiers—you came all this way to beg for them. I want to provide those soldiers at no expense to you for their care and provision. I only want for them to camp and train in the hills around Meḥ."

"When a man offers me his house, I wonder what is lurking inside. This is too good to be true and comes at a time when I am sorely pressed to accept. Such a generous offer, but no one I've talked to describes you as generous. So what are these priests going to cost me?"

A fly buzzed about Set, drawn by the scented oil glistening in his hair and across his broad shoulders. He did not bother to swat it away. "Your friendship. Your trust. Your loyalty. My brother is the emotional one. People love him for that. They think he is one of them.

"I am more practical. People see me as cold and distant. I am neither. I have my passions, but I don't parade them through the streets of Uas as he does. I don't make friends easily.

"Your provinces are a gateway. When closed, it prevents the northern tribes from sweeping southward and taking the fields and pastures we all depend on. When open, it will allow us to spread north and bring those regions peace under Pharaoh's leadership. Until we are ready to do so, it is important that the gateway remain closed and secure. You need the strength to dissuade the northern tribes from thoughts of advance."

Set was silent a moment to let Maaạ again consider the offer. Then he revealed the price. "When the time comes, remember who came to your aid and who did not."

Maaạ nodded and leaned forward, finishing his wine. Set raised the jar and poured. "Take the rest, it does not keep once the seal is broken."

"Why does Pharaoh not see this?" Maaạ asked.

"My brother has been Pharaoh for nearly twenty inundations. He is tired. I think he still harbors childhood dreams of traveling the River and the sea beyond. His daughter is dying. His focus is no longer on the days ahead for Egypt. It is for his own concerns and problems. I have priests and temples from one end of the kingdom to the other. I hear things he does not. I do not want this powerful land to falter."

Maaạ shook his head, feeling the heat of the afternoon and the wine keeping truths from him. "There are others I must discuss this with."

Set's expression hardened. Maaạ thought of a cat toying with prey, providing an illusion of freedom, offering the possibility of escape even as it battered and weakened its plaything, finally bringing a final paw down to squash all hope. Maaạ saw that look in Set's eyes. He was growing tired and bored with this meeting, his sense of play, his patience, another word Maaạ had never associated with the High Priest, nearing its end.

"I have asked you twice," Set said. "Do not presume I will ask a third time."

"It seems I have no option other than to accept your offer," Maaạ said.

Set smiled, his lips curled, cheeks tightened. His eyes did not change. "You have made the right decision. When you return home, the chief priest there will advise you."

Set turned and left, bending beneath the cover, across the ramp, down the dock. Ȧri and the boatmen scattered as did merchants there to trade for fish or fruit. They fled like water birds fleeing the path of a hungry crocodile rippling through the water towards them—all except the daughters and maidens who lingered, drawn to the lean, swaggering, powerful figure like flowers to bees, flushing darker with heat when his shifting glances found them, culling them from the others, until fathers or lovers pulled them away to safety inside stores or dwellings.

Ȧri reached the boat first. "What did he want?"

"To save us," Maaạ said. "With priests trained as soldiers."

"Do you believe him?"

"No. But we need help, even if that help has its own purpose. And they are already there. Set was here merely to discover whether I was an ally or an obstacle."

Ȧri shook his head. "He makes me feel like we're holding the wrong end of the snake."

pr-nswt m wȝst ḥsbt 18 ȝbd 2 prt sw 7 ḫr ḥm n wsỉr

The House of Pharaoh in Uas,
Year 18, Month 2 of Peret, Day 7 under the Majesty of Ạsạr

Sleep did not come with the night. Pharaoh and Īset, instead of waiting impatiently for it in their bed, sat hand-in-hand on a terrace of the house of Pharaoh, gazing out over the city.

They found it difficult to watch the stars that wandered the sky overhead. Smoke and glow from the many cook fires in the royal city now hid the more subtle wonders—so much so that the astrologers petitioned Pharaoh for the manpower to build a new observatory temple further up in the hills, upwind of the city.

"Is there anything you can do for Ḥaāmer?" Īset asked in a steady, even voice.

She measured her words, swallowed her tears. Her daughter lay dying, but she tried not to plead with Ạsạr, or beg. She kept the pain from her tone and expression. She would not further burden Pharaoh.

"Ptah is silent about Ḥaāmer."

"You should see her."

Pharaoh drew away from her. "And say what? When she looks at me with frightened, pleading eyes, what should I say? That her all-powerful father, Ptah's hand on earth, protector of the people, can do nothing to save her?"

"Tell her you love her."

She knew that he was brooding from his stiff posture and silent frown. She said: "I have never seen a god walking the streets of Uas—only you. I have not seen Ptah encouraging the farmers, visiting and hailing them in the marketplaces, handing out rewards to the makers of new magics. But you have done all these things. In the eyes of the people, in *my* eyes, you are a god. You are the one walking among us creating miracles with your words and gestures of kindness—not those stone statues hidden away in their dusty temples."

"Being a god has not made Ḥaāmer better."

"All the gods in this land have not made her better. None of them can. She doesn't need gods anymore, she needs a father."

The Aih rose in the East, spilling a pale, bluish light over the terrace and out into the city of Uas. The soft sounds of music and dancing drifted up to them—a party at the house of someone wealthy enough to afford musicians. It was a happy sound, but like many Egyptian songs, was also threaded with notes of sadness and struggle. Fluted instruments could laugh like birds, calling and courting during the inundation. Sweet, tragic chords from the stringed instruments could bring old hurts and forgotten sadness to life once more. That was the way of the River. A promotion, a birth, a marriage balanced by an injury, an illness, a death. When one ascended, one descended. Like the River and the inundation, one season, one generation, washed away, leaving behind a fertile soil for the next.

"What of Maaạ?"

Pharaoh stirred, as if his thoughts were far away. "The betrothal is broken. Maaạ understands that Ḥaāmer will not survive until their wedding day. He is returning to Meḥ."

Īset rubbed her husband's wrist and forearm, feeling the muscles hard beneath the flesh. "Will he and his provinces swear allegiance to you?"

"He thinks that I must bargain with him. Soon he will know the truth."

"Has he asked about Āakhu?"

Pharaoh tensed. "He mentioned her. I said no."

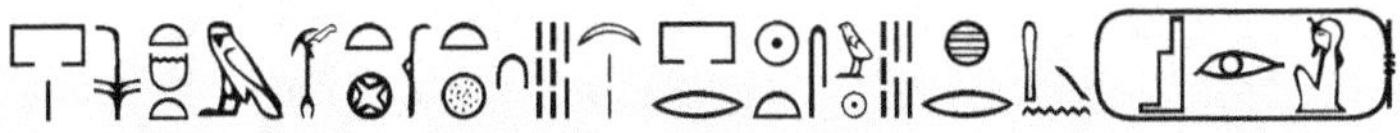

pr ḥmt nswt m wꜣst ḥsbt 18 ꜣbd 2 prt sw 7 ḫr ḥm n wsỉr

The House of Pharaoh's Wife in Uas,
Year 18, Month 2 of Peret, Day 7 under the Majesty of Ạsạr

"You were not waiting at the door of the queen's house this afternoon," Pharaoh said.

Ḥaāmer struggled to lift her head and smile briefly before falling back to the linen-wrapped headrest. Her breath came out in noisy gasps as she replied: "It's been many seasons since I last waited in the doorway for you to come home."

"Yet I still look for you each sunset, ready to catch you and swing you up into the air."

Ḥaāmer coughed, long and watery, before her labored breathing steadied. "Come hold me one last time, father. My season is almost over."

Pharaoh sat on the stool by her bed and took her hand. Her fingers were dry twigs. He held them as if she were newly born, afraid that to do otherwise might crush them.

"Am I a mistake?" she asked, her dark eyes bright with fever. "It is the only reason I have for why Ptah has turned his face from me."

A cat—Ạsạr could only presume it was Baka—stirred and stretched his paws, lying on the linen that covered Ḥaāmer's legs. He lifted his head and focused amber, slitted eyes on Ạsạr.

Ạsạr reached and touched his daughter's dark hair, lifting away a stray strand stuck to her cheek. His fingers lingered at her forehead. The skin was thin and fragile as onionskin stretched across eggshell.

Her possessions loomed in the shadows, stretched along the walls like a great half-seen beast. Boxes of clothing, pairs of sandals differing only in color or the jewels that adorned them, clay tablets written with prayers and praises from her sister, boxes of earrings, bracelets, golden rings—all ready for transport to the royal tomb. Her whole life gathered, waiting only for Ḥaāmer to join them.

Dolls from her childhood, cosmetics, scented oils: Pharaoh could not look at them. He wanted for them not to be there.

"You are no mistake."

"But if I had been a son?"

"A house full of sons could not have been more precious to me than you."

"You have no heir."

"Ptah will send me a successor."

Ḥaāmer closed her eyes. Pharaoh put a hand to her back and raised a bowl of cool water to her lips. She drank with a long, shuddering sigh.

"Mother and Neb-t·ḥe-t took me to the mortuary. I saw my coffin." Ḥaāmer turned her face toward her father. "I want to be well and whole again—even more than I want to stay here."

Ḥaāmer sighed and closed her eyes. She began to whisper something, then stopped. Baka yawned and stretched, tumbling from the bed. He pushed a paw against the door linen, sending a ripple through it, and vanished into the darkened corridor.

Ạsạr looked down at her hand resting in his. After a final caress, he lifted the linen and returned it carefully to her side. Then he drew the linen over her face.

Chapter 5

CAIRO, EGYPT, THE KUWAITI EMBASSY, AMBASSADOR'S OFFICE, JUNE 8TH, 10:05 P.M.:

"Allah rain destruction on them all! Filthy, bastards. Death to them all!"

The ambassador's aide stood. He moved around the desk, approaching his leader.

Jarah faltered, his powerful hands clenched as fists at his waist. Suddenly, Jarah stopped, heaving a huge shudder, tears running down his cheeks.

"Massouma. Oh, Massouma."

Jarah staggered backwards, collapsing into his chair, putting his head on his desk, his arms over his head. The electronic door locks ground as someone worked to gain entry. The massive vault door swung open, banging back on its hinges. The ambassador's three-man security team crashed into the room.

"The telephone is off hook." said the chief of security, scanning the room for threats. He tried to step past the aide, but the aide wouldn't allow it. "What's going on in here? Why is the telephone on the floor?"

"Out! Out!" commanded the aide, waving his hands at the men, his flailing diverting their attention and blocking their vision. "Out! You're not needed."

The aide's authority and aggressive behavior stopped them. The ambassador straightened in his chair, his back to the security team.

"Out," intoned Jarah. They paused, but when they didn't move. He repeated softly, "I said out."

* * *

His aide was his strength, his support. When Jarah wept, his aide came to him, supporting him without comment or judgment, keeping his silence.

He has always been there.

Jarah found himself in the lavatory adjacent to his office—unaware of how he got there. He removed his outer robe, hanging it across his garment rack. Gripping the sink, he forced himself to inhale slow, deep breaths to stop his hyperventilating gasps. He bent, splashing water in his face. He avoided looking at himself in the mirror.

Massouma is dead.

No matter how Jarah ached, he must accept that fact. He no longer could ask why. His anguish washed through him, leeching his soul from him. Purpose replaced the empty hollowness with a crusade to destroy every one of the forsaken dogs.

Allah damn them.

He touched the intercom key to call his aide. Returning to his office, he told him, "Summon the senior embassy intelligence officer."

When his intelligence officer arrived, he commanded: "Identify each of the terrorists in the recording. Determine whether we know anything about the individuals through our sources. Make contact with your Egyptian counterparts and obtain all of the information they have.

"If you locate any of the scum, you are authorized to detain them, transporting them to Kuwait for questioning. When you believe you have all the information you can obtain from them, eliminate the problem."

"Remove them from Egypt, sir?"

"Yes. Once we are rid of them, we will communicate with the Egyptians, our allies. We will apologize, asking for tolerance for our indiscretion. We will assure them that we were merely asking the vermin a few questions. We were assisting them.

"I want everyone on our staff who was involved."

CAIRO, EGYPT, THE KUWAITI EMBASSY, SECURE ROOM JUNE 9TH, 12:23 A.M.:

Later, Jarah sat in the secure room, the information center where the embassy disseminated all intelligence. Massouma's security team was on their way to Kuwait. The sword awaited them.

Jarah forced himself to watch the incident again. He took the front, center seat. The seat on either side was empty. His aide sat behind him, leaning forward whispering encouragement to him. The giant screen flickered and the village street appeared once again. A camera panned over a group of woman sitting in the street.

Strength!

He watched once again the soldier wade into the group, yanking his wife upright. She stumbled—weak and dehydrated—the soldier cuffed her. Unmanly tears formed in his eyes.

Allah, bless her.

"I know this disease. We have seen them before.

"I want these bastards found! Every frame of that recording will be analyzed. All information extracted."

NORTHERN EGYPT, NILE DELTA, A WEEK LATER, JUNE 17TH, 8:45 A.M.:

"So what do you think about the new find?" asked Robert, wiping the sweat from his forehead with the back of his leather glove, leaning on his shovel.

Lisa turned slowly, puzzled by his remark.

"The Egyptians found a new feature," he continued, seeing her confusion.

"Another empty, rock tomb I suppose," she said, placing her hand shovel outside her digging area. She drew a deep breath, shrugging her shoulders, taking a break. Robert and she were working in the farmer's field with his permission for the past hour, creating a channel to redirect the water, replacing the inadequate canvas hose. Not wishing to destroy any artifacts in the process, Lisa hand dug the trench. "Where did you read this?"

"Dr. Tu'hut sent an e-mail to the university."

Lisa scowled. "Damn him!"

"Oh, I'm sorry. I spoke without thinking."

"He's such a pain in the ass. He knew that I'd find out sooner or later," she grumbled. Robert was studying her. "What!"

"I overheard at the University that you're in *big* trouble."

"Oh, damn! The trial just continues."

"I heard Dean Hayes went to bat for you. He asked Tu'hut to give you another chance. Tu'hut agreed to let you come to *this* project."

"I had no idea that my issues with him were that big or that public."

"You were rather vociferous in your comments to him," grinned Robert.

"Oh, you heard about that."

"Yeah, he believes you acted inappropriately for a 'lady' addressing a gentleman."

"Fine. Let's change the subject. Robert, you did a good job locating and excavating the 'well.'"

Her assistant nodded.

"I've concluded that you were right about the water. I think you've found the end of an ancient channel that we'll have to explore independently. In the meantime, we'll use your cistern and this channel to bypass the rest of the site."

* * *

Lisa sat in the trailer contemplating what Robert had told her. Being thirty, she wasn't that much older than Robert. She needed to listen to his opinion about Tu'hut. As Robert's Ph.D. advisor, she understood why he was sympathetic to her.

No matter her situation with Tu'hut, Lisa wanted to learn more about the new find. With the site stabilized, the documenting and cataloging of the artifacts would go forward.

Maybe—just maybe—I can redeem myself and get out of this hell hole. If Robert gets the excavations to drain, we can return to normal shifts. The work will fall on Robert and the grad students.

She would call the University and give the Department the good news. They could explore this Egyptian epoch. If indeed, it were an epoch. As more was understood about the workers who had inhabited this area, for Lisa felt sure it was a worker-based settlement, she would make every effort to preserve it.

Damn! This trailer is hot!

Powering up her laptop, she turned her attention to her e-mail. Having not looked at her account in four days, she found, as she expected, two screens of e-mail. She knew what she would be doing for the rest of the afternoon. She contemplated moving outside even though she knew that wouldn't happen. Her trailer came with an internet router and cable, but Robert hadn't figured out how to hook up WIFI. Lisa understood the apps well, but neither Robert nor she were computer techie savvy.

Buried in all the mess were two e-mails that looked like personal notes. Lisa decided to peek at them first, hoping they would be chatty, a little uplifting.

The first was two days old from Professor Randall Crain. He understood her passion for anything Egyptian. He had been her advisor and first archeology professor at Brown University. She loved Randall because he had an air about him in his wide brimmed, high crowned fedora that spoke of dust and expeditions in the previous century. However, he was particular about the science and artifact preservation. He supported her decision to make a career of archeology, saying it was in her blood. That is why she was so angry with him for not sending her Dr. Tu'hut's e-mail. Lisa figured that he had received it.

lisa: so when are you going south? randall

As she suspected, he knew about the find. Perhaps she was being unfair. He might assume she had already received the information. Randall wasn't normally chatty in their e-mail, but this was a bit cryptic even for him.

I wonder how much he knows?

She decided to read the other e-mail before replying to Randall. The second was from Stewart Owens, an archeologist from Caltech two years older than she, with whom she had become romantically involved. On a professional level, he shared her concern for the preservation of sites, but she really no longer cared. During her sabbatical in the States, they had lived together for six months. She thought their love was real and might go further until one evening, after they had made love, he told her that he had a physical attraction to her, but nothing more. She was devastated. He was a bastard, using her as an object. She moved out.

Lisa decided thereafter to separate her professional and personal lives. Since then, she had made it a policy not to have male relationships. She considered not reading his email, but her curiosity, as to why he suddenly had written her, overrode her intense dislike for him. After all, she did not have to respond to him.

> Lisa: Isn't the new find amazing? Are you going to Egypt? I expect you'll be beating down their door telling them not to move anything. Good luck. LOVE YOU, STEWART.

The asshole is clueless. Yeah, right. Love you too, Stewart!

His e-mail is as cryptic as Randall's. I need to find out why they are leaving annoyances on my doorstep. I know the Egyptians must have made a significant find, but I've nothing more than when I started.

Deciding a little more immediacy than e-mail was needed, she decided to call Randall on her cell.

"Hi, Ran, this is Lisa," she said when he answered on the third ring.

"Lisa! How are you? Where are you?"

"I'm in the Delta and I'm fine. I'm getting dribbles about something in Southern Egypt. What's going on?"

"Wow! All that way from Egypt and you're as clear as a bell. Haven't you heard about the new find?"

"I'm going through my e-mail and haven't seen it yet," she gave a half truth. She'd been going down through her e-mail. She hadn't seen anything about it. "Who sent it out? Tell me about it."

"The Secretary General."

Lisa reordered her e-mail and scanned the ones from Tu'hut. *Nothing.* She continued to listen to Randall.

"The Egyptians have found an undisturbed feature; possibly a tomb, in Southern Egypt. Sarcophagus, stelae, personal belongings—the whole nine yards. They're putting out a rather discreet inquiry for technical help in the United States. I'd say they're keeping this one quiet."

"A complete tomb. Wow! That doesn't happen. I suppose they don't want grave robbers," Lisa's excitement mounted.

"And they don't want their own people knowing the United States is in their country. We're not popular right now with what's going on. Knowing your background, I figured you'd be the one they asked. Aren't you working with Tu'hut?"

"Yeah. Please send me the e-mail."

"I'm logged on over here. I'll do it now. There it's on its way. What are you up to anyway? Do you think you'll go?"

"I'm in the middle of a nasty dig that we just got under control. I'm excavating a late Egyptian Greco-Roman era site that's a water menace, so I don't know if I can go. If it's like you say, I'd give my eyeteeth for such a chance. If we get the water situation under control, my assistant can handle it."

"Lisa, the new one's meant for you."

"Thanks for your confidence in me, Randall."

"Dash! You know my confidence in you is based on your abilities—not on some sentimental sap."

"Thanks, Ran."

"Watch your rear." he continued, without pausing for a breath. "I don't want you getting shot by zealots. There's some rumble they're having internal trouble. The State Department is putting out bulletins."

"I'm not getting bulletins. I haven't heard."

"I'll forward you anything they put out."

"Thanks, Ran"

"I'm serious about your being careful. Talk to you soon, Lisa. Bye."

She heard the connection break. Pressing END on her cell, she stuffed it in her shirt pocket. As she settled back into her chair, she could feel the excitement tingling inside her.

A new find—wow, that's out of the blue. Artifacts, furnishings now that's special. I wonder how they found it? What if it's like Tut in '22? I'm in the doghouse. That's why Tu'hut didn't contact me. Ah, here's the e-mail.

Lisa scanned the multi-paged document to get the gist of the content then reread it for detail. It didn't tell where the site was located. Probably a precaution. She decided to ignore Stewart. She e-mailed thanks to Randall for his words and information. Lisa no longer had any interest in her remaining e-mail. She stood and stretched. She had to get outside; the heat in here was killing her. She grabbed another soda. Lisa threw open the door, stepping out, almost running over Robert.

"Wow! You're moving pretty fast," he said.

"Oh, Robert, I'm sorry. I didn't mean to hit you."

"You missed," he said cheerily. "The way you're gnawing on your lip, I'd say you're pretty upset about something. With the dig stabilized now, did something in your e-mail upset you?"

She stared at him for a long moment.

"Well, yes. I received an e-mail from an old friend who was a professor of mine."

"Is everything, OK?"

"Yes, yes," she broke out into a grin. "No one died. Well, maybe a long time ago."

"What?" His brows knitted with confusion.

She had to make a decision.

"I need to go to Cairo. Since I hope to stay there, could you drive me?" she asked.

"I have to go to the University to get a bigger pump. Our little guy isn't up for continuous use. What's going on?"

"It's more than a three hour drive, and I'd like to get there before the MSA closes today. I'll tell you on the way."

NORTHERN EGYPT, THE ROAD BETWEEN THE DELTA AND CAIRO, JUNE 17TH, 3:45 P.M.:

"You're a worse driver than me," grinned Lisa, gripping the dashboard to avoid being thrown side to side.

Ignoring her jab, he asked. "Is this about the new dig?"

"Yes, the Egyptian government's made a major discovery."

"Really?" His expression changed, as understanding came to him. "Oh, so you've been asked to go."

"No. That's part of the problem. I haven't been asked, but I want to go."

"Oh, Tu'hut. I see your problem. You need to be careful. Don't do anything rash. Tu'hut is looking for a reason to burn you. Is this find that important?"

"Yes, dammit! I get the impression from Dr. Crain that this is a once in a lifetime opportunity."

"You know Crain?"

"Yes. How many times does a find like Tut happen?"

"Tut? Are you sure?" He glanced at her from the wheel. She told him with her expression that she was dead serious.

"Watch the ditch! He and I were reading between the lines, but you saw the e-mail. We read furnishings and stelae to mean a mummy, personal belongings, etc. I need to talk with Tu'hut."

"You know he's pretty immobile." said Robert as they entered the city.

"Yeah, but if I don't try, nothing is going to happen. I want to talk with Dean Hayes. I hope he'll intercede with Dr. Tu'hut on my behalf."

Robert dropped Lisa at the Archeology Department on his way to Engineering for the pump.

"I need to work on my thesis," he raised a speculative eyebrow to Lisa. "If you want a lift back, I'll be sitting at *your* desk until 8 PM."

CAIRO, EGYPT, CAIRO UNIVERSITY, DEAN HAYES' OFFICE, JUNE 17TH, 4:25 P.M.:

"Lisa, please! I've done everything that I can for you. Tu'hut wants you out of the country. I've convinced him that you're too valuable and should be allowed to work on projects. I was barely able to convince him to let you work on the Delta project."

"It's a piece of...."

Dean Hayes held up his hand for her to stop.

"I know it's a piece of crap, but you need to be careful. You'll be out of here in a flash if he has any more issues with you."

"Damn!"

"As to any thoughts about the new feature in Abydos, you'd better forget it. Tu'hut says the site is only an investigation anyway. Go, do you term in purgatory and come back absolved. You might get to be on the opening."

She now knew the site's general location. Tu'hut and Dean Hayes must have discussed the site.

"But I want to lead this project."

"Tu'hut would never allow you to lead the project. Forget it. Besides, I think you're too late. I think he has a man he's sending to the site."

"Damn! I've got to talk with him."

"I'm not sure that's a good idea."

"Well, I've got to try."

* * *

Lisa went to the street to find a taxi to go to the Antiquities Ministry. She knew Tu'hut's office location, 2Shagaret El Dorr St, among the other public buildings in the Zamalek district; however, she had to go through the Muslim sector to get there. At this time of day, it would be a traffic nightmare. If she hurried, she might arrive before the Ministry closed for the afternoon.

She immediately found an English speaking cabby. Rather he found her. After a painful minute of haggling, she negotiated a fare with him and they started toward the center of the city. They moved quickly until they reached the Muslim district where the heavy afternoon traffic slowed to a crawl.

"Effendi, I'm in a great hurry to get to the Ministry before it closes. I'll be more generous if that happens."

"Dear lady," the cabby said, lifting his face to give her a wan smile in the mirror, his eyes never leaving the narrow street. "You Americans are always in a hurry. Your money will do me no good if I am not of this world to enjoy it. We will reach your destination when Allah allows. If you do not arrive before closing, and Allah is willing, there will be another day."

At that moment, a young man darted into the street in front of the cab. With the efforts of the cabby, the brakes and the horn, the man avoided injury. The driver yelled angrily out of the window at the fellow whose hand gestures did not seem appropriate from someone whose life had just been spared. Lisa slumped back into the seat. There were times when she loved Cairo and times when she hated the smog-ridden, over-populated snarl.

She knew there was no hope of her arriving at the Ministry before it closed. She felt this was the critical day. Dean Hayes alluded that Tu'hut had picked his project leader. She'd waited her entire life for an opportunity like this. Suddenly, she recognized the corner building and the shop next to it out the window to her right. The cross street ahead led to the Ministry a half mile away from here.

"Stop!"

Lisa dropped the fare, a tip and a little extra into the front seat next to the driver. She was out of the motionless cab in a flash.

"Lady, we are not there."

Ignoring the cabby, she began jogging up the street toward the intersection. When the driver laid on the horn, yelling at her out the window, she turned to see him shaking his head at her and shrugging his shoulders. Lisa could not make out what he was saying, but got the gist that she should not be out on the streets by herself. She concentrated on her jogging, continuing to run in the roadway. She made better progress than the stationary cars.

She knew the cross street wouldn't lead her into a labyrinth where she would get lost. Occasionally, breaks in the traffic that were too small for an automobile, allowed her to shoot ahead.

This is gaining me some time.

Lisa noted her jogging attracted some unwanted attention. The drivers of the cars gave her surprised looks as she ran past. Muslim woman, completely covered in their burkas, followed her with their eyes. Lisa could not tell their feelings from their eyes.

Just ahead on the other side of the intersection, she saw a group of men, leaning against the building. Their heads came up together, turning in her direction. Their unified expression disturbed her, having lived in the Middle East long enough to know that this could be a problem. Women did not travel by themselves, uncovered, and act in any way like a man. Her running could be interpreted as a male action; however, now was not the time for her to stop. Her appearance identified her as an American. Hatred of Americans was general enough to warrant concern. They pushed off the building, beginning to move toward her.

When Lisa arrived at the intersection, she looked right then left, but the snarled traffic need not have concerned her. She hoped her disappearance around the corner would dissuade the men from following her further. Lisa pulled her cellphone from her shirt pocket, hoping to appear as if she were calling for help just in case they did follow her. As she scanned the street, nothing moved. Up the cross street, leading to the Ministry of State for Antiquities, a soldier hustled a boy, with a disfigured face and a missing ear, into the back of a military truck.

Strange, the military doesn't normally interact with private citizens. Why would they be picking up a boy?

Lisa photographed the pair with her cellphone.

I wonder what happened to the boy?

Dropping out of the front seat of the same truck, a pair of Arab men dressed in Western slacks and shirts caught her attention. They trotted up the street toward her. One looked at the cars as they passed them. He had a bundle under his arm.

Civilians don't ride around in military trucks. Something strange is happening.

The other man cast his attention outward, scanning the streets. When he caught sight of Lisa, his attention focused on her. Lisa's unease increased. She wanted to disappear. The man, looking into the cars, barked something to his partner, as he concentrated on a specific vehicle. The second man looked outward again, scanning the street before responding to his partner. Lisa switched to video recording on her phone, capturing the actions of the pair. The man with the bundle withdrew his hand from inside the bag, dropping it to the pavement and kicking it under the limousine. They sprang forward toward her. Four seconds later, the bundle exploded up through the car, blowing out the windows, doors and driver from the vehicle. The burst gasoline tank exploded. Lisa fell with the shockwave somehow holding onto her phone. She continued to record.

People screamed in terror, shrinking back from the destroyed, burning vehicle, many falling injured from the sprayed shrapnel. The two bombers sprinted towards Lisa, who lay frozen on the pavement. She had to move. She jumped up, jamming her cell into her shirt pocket. She didn't wish to become a hostage. She needed to get to the Ministry. Lisa ran, fear creeping into her.

Running down the street toward the intersection, a police officer flashed past Lisa; his attention focused on the burning vehicle. He would be of no help to her. She wanted to avoid needing him. The man, who originally spotted her, was between Lisa and the Ministry. He angled to intercept her. She needed to be on the other side of the street. She increased her speed, turning directly toward the man. This took him off guard causing him to commit too soon. He turned toward her. Lisa used a break between the two cars to put the cars between them. She hopped onto the back bumper and jumped down on the other side of the car. The car acted as a shield as Lisa pushed to her maximum speed. She passed the would-be pursuer before he could react.

She glanced over her shoulder to see what he was doing. He raised his fingers to his mouth and let out a shrill whistle. She whipped around to see whom he might be signaling. The soldier wrestling the boy looked up. She squeezed past the military truck distracting the soldier allowing the boy to wrench free. The soldier chose to follow the boy who had dashed into an adjoining alley.

I better get to the Ministry and it better be open.

As she turned the corner, Lisa skidded to a stop, almost colliding with a person in the plaza. The entire ministry plaza was filled with chanting protesters. She twisted and turned, threading her way through the crowd, pushing against the shouting people.

What is going on?

From the sounds behind her, her attackers were forcing their way through the crowd after her. Reaching the other side, she sprinted for the Ministry steps. The ministry door was open. She could hear running footsteps, pursuing her.

All I have to do is get up the steps and into the building.

Lisa almost made it. A pair of hands circled her shoulders, pinning her arms to her sides. A flying tackle pounded her shoulder into the pavement. She nearly blacked-out. Her fighting instincts brought her sharply back. She struggled. She wrenched sideways to throw her assailant off her back, but he held on. Someone grabbed at her legs. She brought her knees up to her chest and lashed out with her feet. She caught him on the nose and he went down hard.

She had to free her arms. Her assailant was too strong. She kicked at his shins, but her tennis shoes were ineffective. He grabbed her breast, squeezing hard and pulling her upright. He rifled her blouse for her cell. She screamed. He grabbed her clothes at her throat, twisting. Choking her, he turned, dragging her down the steps.

Chapter 6

ḥwt-nṯr nt ptḥ m wȝst ḥsbt 18 ȝbd 2 prt sw 24 ḫr ḥm n wsỉr

The Temple of Ptah in Uas,
Year 18, Month 2 of Peret, Day 24 under the Majesty of Ạsạr

Each morning for sixteen days Ṭeḥuti sent a request to the queen's house asking to visit Āakhu, having not seen her since Ḥaāmer's death. Each day the request returned, not from Āakhu or from Īset, but from one of Pharaoh's men: *The daughter of Pharaoh is not receiving visitors.* On day seventeen, Ṭeḥuti went to the temple stores and loaded a linen sack with food, gathered some simple toys made by his students, begged two of the little servant ushabtuis from Neb-t·ḥe-t, and went to liberate Āakhu.

The street was quiet, like the day following the year-end festivals. A few people wandered slowly along the way between the temple and the house of Pharaoh, their heads down as if the Aten's brightness were painful. Merchants, the few who opened for the day, sat silent with their wares instead of out-shouting their competitors for each customer. There were many empty places, every fifth merchant had packed his wares and left Uas for better prospects.

Those buyers who stopped did not linger. They found the merchant who offered what they wanted, traded for it, and left. They did not haggle, or browse booth to booth. Each transaction concluded with soft, sober agreement.

This same somber quiet had fallen over all of Uas since Ḥaāmer's death. Ṭeḥuti felt the uneasiness among the people, beneath their greetings, their acquiescence in the markets, their attitudes as they toiled in the fields and on the River. They expected she would live and marry Maaạ and raise many fine sons for him and for Pharaoh. It came as a shock that she would not. There was sadness, for her, for her parents, and in each person's eyes a question: *How could the gods favor me when they did not favor a child of their own.*

So the city mourned Ḥaāmer's death and secretly wrestled with that question, even after sixteen days, as if she had taken a part of the life of the city, a part of each of their individual lives, with her to Amennt.

Ṭeḥuti frowned as he approached the queen's house, squint-eyed like he was walking into a sand wind, a tight-lipped, hollow-cheeked look he hoped would say *I'm on a vital errand for Pharaoh and would enjoy telling him you impeded me* to anyone who got in his way.

"I'm here to see princess Āakhu," he said to the guard standing at the entrance to the queen's house. The guard looked up with tired, dull eyes, as if he had been sitting at his post for a week. He waved Ṭeḥuti through or swatted at a fly, Ṭeḥuti didn't wait to determine which, choosing to pass briskly through the gate and into the corridor that led to Āakhu's rooms.

Servants heard him coming and withdrew into alcoves and dark recesses, supposing he was Pharaoh and choosing to be out of sight.

"Come with me," he called to one who could not disappear quickly enough. She limped back into the light cast by a wall torch. It was Kefa·ạb, Queen Īset's ancient, lifelong servant. "Take me to Āakhu."

Kefa·ạb looked at him once, head to toe, and turned. "It took you long enough," she said.

She led, Ṭeḥuti following in her slow wake. Kefa·ạb wore each year of her service quietly in the fall of her shoulders, the curve of her back. She had been chosen wet nurse for the newborn Īset after her own child died. She had served Īset ever since, neither servant or chief wife able to let the other go. Kefa·ạb stopped at the tapestry covering Āakhu's door and looked back at Ṭeḥuti.

"Announce me," Ṭeḥuti said.

Kefa·ạb slipped through the linen covers and said, "Forgive my intrusion, Lady. The priest Ṭeḥuti waits at the door."

Ṭeḥuti swept aside the cover and entered.

Āakhu cried out his name and covered herself with her arms, though she was not naked. A wrinkled linen dress covered her from neck to ankles, making her look like just another mourner in a city that had seen little else of late. No kohl circled her watery, wounded eyes, no stain brightened her pale lips. There were no rings in her ears or around her wrists. She had cut off most of her hair.

"Walk with me," Ṭeḥuti said.

She could have given many reasons not to go with him. She could have requested an escort or a litter, demanded time to bathe or dress or apply proper cosmetics. She could have dispatched Kefa·ạb to notify her mother or father. She could have just said no, but she didn't.

"Where?" She asked.

"Away from this city and its sadness."

Āakhu motioned to Kefa·ạb who brought her sandals and a cloak. She put them on with slow, deliberate motions, as if her arms and legs pained her. She came to stand before him, the top of her head level with his shoulders. "Okay."

The guard looked up and frowned as they passed through the gate.

"Āakhu is in my care today," Ṭeḥuti said.

He nodded and said nothing, then watched them walk away.

A priest and a woman in mourning attracted little notice among the few people they encountered. Ṭeḥuti led her away from the main buildings along a winding series of paths that crossed one another, passing among a uniform series of mud and brick workers' houses, ascending gradually toward the Eastern hills.

Āakhu stayed at his side, saying nothing. Ṭeḥuti could hear her breathing, the crunch of her sandals on the sand and loose stones. When they passed the last string of the worker houses, each of them a couple of small rooms sheltering an open fire pit, Ṭeḥuti began to sing the Ḥes Ȧturres.

His first soft notes fluttered, reedy and flute-like. To himself, he thought he sounded like a duck in distress.

"Why that?" Āakhu asked after the first small hill beyond the city had passed beneath their feet.

"To remember that death is not an accident or a punishment but a natural consequence of life. It is not something to spend the rest of your life mourning."

Āakhu said nothing, hands on hips, breathing still labored, face tilted up to the cloudless turquoise sky.

Ṭeḥuti resumed the song. They reached the sandy bottom of a small wadi and were starting up the other side when Āakhu added her voice to his. Uncertain, tremulous at first as she matched his notes and rhythm, growing steady as she found her way about his voice and he about hers.

The sounds inside him created pictures. The pictures became memories.

He remembered his parents, tall as mountains in his childish eyes. He remembered the River, his father's boat, struggling with the weight of the nets, and the smile that filled his father's face after Ṭeḥuti's first catch.

He remembered them cold, pale, dead. He remembered Ȧamȧam beside him, her arm around him as she wept. "The gods stole them away and left these dolls in their place," she said to him. "Someday they will steal us too and you will be with them again."

Dolls they were, looking less and less like his parents the more he stared at them that day. He remembered the mourners taking them to the hills, digging the holes, arranging the bodies and a few simple possessions within. He remembered how carefully he placed the first stone, not wanting to disturb or damage the dolls. It was hard work covering the graves, the stones grew heavier throughout the afternoon. He was hungry afterward.

He remembered the first night without them. Ȧamȧam took him in. The sounds were different, as were the smells and the slant of the moonlight through the tiny window. He knew his parents were gone then and would not return. He cried and mourned them alone in his bed the rest of the night. Whether Ȧamȧam woke and heard him, she never said. But she treated him gently the next week, giving him larger portions of food and smaller tasks then she did her other children.

He had not thought of his parents or their deaths in many seasons. The Ḥes Ȧturres was like that. The notes, the rhythm, the voices could get inside you and go where they wished to in your thoughts. Today, it reminded him of something he had known all his life without really knowing or understanding at all: Things that are precious do not linger and are only recognized after they are gone.

He glanced at Āakhu He could not know what the Ḥes Ȧturres had summoned within her, but he could see she was affected.

"What did you see?" he asked.

"Ḥaāmer," she said, her voice turned to cries of grief for her sister. She rushed to Ṭeḥuti and he held her, smoothing what remained of her hair, rubbing her back and shoulders, whispering comfort. A woman's tears could be sweet when you were the cure instead of the cause.

There was no sense of time in the hills except for the movement of the Aten from East to West. Ṭeḥuti did not note that passage, to him there was only Āakhu and his own thoughts and assurances that life was more than a few seasons along the River and though age or accident or evil could change or transform it, it could never end it. Such is what the gods told him and such was what he believed.

When Āakhu shed the last of her tears, emptied finally of all the Ḥes Ȧturres had found and set loose within her, when her arms loosened from around him and she backed away, Ṭeḥuti offered her a linen. She cleaned her face and looked up, then turned slowly around.

They didn't know what to say to each other, how to act. Āakhu had never been outside of Uas before, without proper escort, on foot.

She spent her days in the Queen's house or in the temple, learning the duties of a royal princess. Ceremonies, diplomacy, who was who in politics, religion, and business, memorizing chants and prayers, overseeing the care and maintenance of the house, supervising servants, these were the days and weeks and years of her life. Silent, she looked wide-eyed at the clear, open spaces. No buildings, no people, just hills and sky.

"I come here when too many things in Uas seem too important to me," Ṭeḥuti said. "When I can't sleep for thoughts chasing themselves inside like a litter of kittens, when I think I am too busy to eat, or look up at the night sky, or watch a boat drifting serenely along the River, or pray, I come here to remember what silence sounds like, what the land looks like with no people about, and remember the things that being locked away for so long inside stone rooms has made me forget.

"This is where I come to empty myself of everything that seems so important in Uas so that the gods can fill me with what is true and eternal. They made me, they know how to care for me and how to heal me when I'm hurt and broken. Even if the healing is not what I expect or desire, it is always what I need."

"Is Ḥaāmer in a place like this?"

"I believe so," he said. "Come."

"I want to find this healing you speak of before we return."

"I'm not taking you back to Uas."

"Oh?" She asked.

"Not yet, there is another place I want you to see. We're nearly there."

Āakhu took a last long look and reached for his hand.

The land rose and fell around them, each valley followed by a higher hill. They followed well-trodden paths between Uas and surrounding villages for much of the way, before Ṭeḥuti led them off the path and up a final rise. At its crest was a small, shallow valley that sagged toward a single house.

The house was a ruin, a jumbled collection of different colored bricks, stones, and pieces of wood. Scattered around it, in squares and rectangles marked by stones, children scratched at the soil with rough implements between rows of sparse, bedraggled plants. Two more children came from the direction of the River with poles and oppositely balanced pitchers of water across their shoulders. Midst them all, an old woman hobbled, assisting, showing, encouraging, tousling hair, patting a back, moving from one to the next.

"What is this place?" Āakhu asked, breathless again.

"My past."

She said nothing, but Ṭeḥuti had spent enough days around the royal family to recognize when Āakhu's face became a mask to hide disappointment and irritation. This was not a place she would ever visit on her own and not a place she wanted to be. He had told her of his humble beginnings but like so many things, like the vast, empty spaces beyond the queen's house, his words brought no experience with them—until now.

"Are these your brothers and sisters?" Āakhu asked through the mask of a serene royal face, marred only be recent tears and the absence of royal cosmetics.

"The children are orphans who have no where else to go except the garbage heaps of Uas. Ȧamȧam, the old woman teaching them to raise their own food, raised me after my parents died. I want you to meet them."

Āakhu nodded, her lack of expression, no disagreement or hesitation, announced her hesitation and disagreement to Ṭeḥuti. She was far from her world now, he realized, her sister was dead, it was sunny and hot, and sand coated both of them. He could understand her reluctance.

A child pointed. Ȧamȧam looked up and waved, then started shuffling between the squares of crops toward them. She met them just beyond the last of the squares.

"Ṭeḥuti!" she cried, wrapping him in a fierce hug.

He returned that hug, lifting the gray-haired woman off her feet. "It's only been two weeks," he said.

"Too long," she said.

Ṭeḥuti put her back down and she turned to Āakhu. "I have not seen you before. Are you a new student?"

"This is Āakhu," Ṭeḥuti said.

"God's daughter," Ȧamȧam said and started down to her knees.

Ṭeḥuti caught her beneath her arms and lifted her again. "Only Pharaoh himself is divine and deserves worship. Āakhu will be part of the family soon."

Āakhu presented Ȧamȧam the perfect ceremonial smile, her eyes bright and focused. "My betrothed speaks true. I should do you honor as the one who raised him."

"Your presence honors me," Ȧamȧam said, looking down.

"How is Abuat? Is she better?" Ṭeḥuti asked.

Ȧamȧam said nothing for several heartbeats, looking away and back to Ṭeḥuti's expectant face. All the emotion had worn off her words. "She left us."

"Maybe she returned to her family," Āakhu said.

Ṭeḥuti took Ȧamȧam's hand in his and squeezed. She nodded. "Maybe she did."

Among the small, stony plots of onions and garlic and wheat grasses, Āakhu found the ceremony she could relax into. Ȧamȧam and Ṭeḥuti introduced her to each of the children and she complimented and exchanged a few courteous words with each. It was familiar to her, expected from her, and gave her a chance to practice the duties of a princess among those who would be forever impressed even if she blundered.

Āakhu did relax during the afternoon. Ṭeḥuti was grateful for that. Her bearing lost some of the royal stiffness, her smiles came more frequently and encompassed all her face—not just her lips. She did not shy from touching or being touched. Children can do that. For them, each day is a miracle, meeting a princess is just a small part of that, a small respite from a day's work.

Ȧamȧam, Ṭeḥuti, and Āakhu went inside to prepare the evening's meal. Ṭeḥuti spilled the vegetables and bread from his pack, then sorted and hid the toys in the children's beds. Ȧamȧam brought a few things from the plots outside, a duck, plucked and cleaned, hung in the smoke above the cook fire. Āakhu watched from nearby as Ṭeḥuti built up the fire and Ȧamȧam sorted and cut the vegetables.

"Have any of my students visited?" Ṭeḥuti asked.

Āakhu frowned at him.

"Yes, I appreciate the gifts of food and clothing they bring. But they don't stay long."

Ȧamȧam looked up from her cutting, brushed a stray hair from her face with the back of her forearm. "So young and idealistic, I almost remember what it was like. They are so full of the gods and their goodness, their love and care for men and women. We do not fit into that view and it makes them uncomfortable. The gods have not smiled on these children and your young students cannot explain why. So they nod uneasily, offer a few, small blessings, and return to the temple as soon as they can get away."

"The gods *have* smiled on these children," Ṭeḥuti said. "Sometimes they do so through a single heart and pair of hands."

The old woman actually blushed, but kept on chopping the tough, withered onions. "Priestess Neb-t-ḥe-t has been a blessing for those we have lost. She takes nothing for her service and gives us much to be thankful for."

"Mother's sister?" Āakhu asked.

Ȧamȧam stared in silence for a second until the connection became clear. "Yes," she said.

* * *

They ate dinner outside around a fire. Ṭeḥuti removed the duck from its spit when it showed a brown color on all sides. The aroma of it made small mouths water and undernourished stomachs grumble. Then he unwrapped three fish from the leaves in which they baked.

Ȧamȧam and the children arranged the feast on trays in a circle. They laid mats in a second circle on which the diners would sit. Ṭeḥuti carved slices of steaming meat. The circle was alive with the smell of fresh bread, beer, vegetables, and fruit.

The children contested for the right to sit near Āakhu and Ṭeḥuti, then settled into their places and waited for Ȧamȧam to bring the last of the food and place it in the circle. A son on each side helped her settle on her mat.

Aten touched the western horizon and descended into the earth as they ate. The orange and red of its setting were replaced by the warm yellow of the fire. Ṭeḥuti told stories, imitating the children's voices and expressions to their delight. Āakhu ate with practiced royal grace, taking small portions from each platter and nibbling at them till they were gone, speaking only when Ṭeḥuti asked for her validation of some detail in his story. She smiled once or twice and showed, when asked, the proper way to eat.

The children ate as if they did so only once a year. They picked the duck and several of the bowls clean using their new and proper dining habits.

"I wished I had brought more," Ṭeḥuti said. "What will you feed them tomorrow?"

Ȧamȧam smiled, her eyes glimmering in the soft light. "They won't need very much tomorrow."

Too soon, it seemed, the platters, pots, and jugs were empty or nearly so. The smaller children had already curled up on their mats, eyes closed, breathing slow and steady, while those still upright sat torpid, eyelids fluttering like butterfly wings.

The fire burned down to a warm glow and would soon need replenishing if it were to continue. Above, the moon glowed orange in the southwest just above the horizon. Stars glittered in patterns beyond its glare. Each was a sign that the meal was over, the evening ending for some and just beginning for others.

Ȧamȧam pushed to her feet with a grunt. "The children and I will clear away the meal and put the little ones to bed. Will you join us in song this evening?"

"We will," Ṭeḥuti said.

Ȧamȧam nodded, studying Āakhu. She gathered the children, rousing them, giving orders. They followed her in a single weary line up to the house.

"What's this song?" Āakhu asked.

"The Ḥes Ȧturres. Ȧamȧam and the children sing it some evenings as a remembrance."

"Remembrance of what?"

"Those who have left us," Ṭeḥuti said, softer. He stood and brushed sand from his skirt then bent to offer Āakhu his hand. "Come see."

Āakhu accepted and he drew her to her feet in a strong, smooth, unhurried motion and led her away from the fire and into the moonlight.

"Just to the top of the rise," he said as they passed beyond the house, opposite the direction from which they had arrived in the afternoon.

Āakhu let herself be led, basking in the moonlight, the quiet, the cooling night air. "There are so many new experiences, wonderful experiences beyond the walls of Īset's palace."

"This is only the beginning," Ṭeḥuti replied.

They reached the broad expanse of the rise, the house behind and below them. It looked more inviting with the glow of moonlight spread across it. Before them, the plain was lumpy, piles of rocks and gravel scattered across the otherwise flat land. Sand lay like still water around and between the shadowed humps and made them look like a family of hippos floating serenely in water.

"They're graves," Ṭeḥuti said.

She moved close to him, hip touching hip, leaned her head against him, and circled him with her arms in a silent communion that said much more to him than words.

"I am an important man in Uas," he said. "People seek me out for wisdom and advice. I write as much as I can and gather scrolls and tablets from the ends of the united provinces and from all the known lands beyond. Here I am reminded that I am no one in particular. These children, asleep in their quiet graves, know more about the gods than I do. They are with them."

Āakhu shivered and Ṭeḥuti put his arm about her. "Each has a name. Would you like me to tell you who they are?"

Ṭeḥuti recited the names and gave what he knew of their stories. Neither heard Ȧamȧam and the five older children approaching until they began the first notes of the Ḥes Ȧturres. Āakhu lifted her head from his shoulder, dried her eyes with the linen he passed to her, softly cleared her throat, and found her voice.

The song was different this time, slower, the children's voices higher and quieter. The familiar themes emerged, the distinctive notes of water, sand, and wind. Growing out of this were the melodies and rhythms of prayers offered to the gods. Wordless, but Āakhu heard the words inside. And from the prayers came the songs sometimes used to frame the words spoken for the dead and painted on the walls or on tablets that accompanied them.

In the mist and moonlight, in the voices and the song, something happened. Faces appeared, small bodies formed, one above each mound. Unique themes, haunting phrases, drew them and made them solid. They did not seem sad, but they were silent. Ṭeḥuti watched them move, each acting out some favorite moment from their shortened lives. Playing with a wooden sword or lance, chasing after a pet, planting, harvesting, caring for a doll, skipping stones across the River.

When the song concluded, the children dissolved away. The mounds were once more merely silent graves, the mist merely mist, the moonlight merely a pale light spilling with no particular magic over the land.

Before returning to the house Ȧamȧam, her orphans, Ṭeḥuti, and Āakhu went forward, one by one. Two pots cast egg-like shadows in the moonlight. From the left hand, each took sand and held it up, fingers open, to disappear on the night breeze. From the right, a palm full of water spilled to the ground. Some said a name, some a prayer, some nothing at all. *We come from sand and water, to them we return.*

* * *

"It's late. I must get Āakhu back to the palace," Ṭeḥuti said. "Can I take the boat?"

"The mast is broken," Ȧamȧam replied.

"I will row it."

Āakhu looked at Ṭeḥuti with the frown of a question on her face.

"Pharaoh and Īset will wonder what happened to you."

"My handmaidens knew I went with you."

"But it is *late.*"

"Take it," Ȧamȧam said. "I will send the boys to fetch it in the morning."

"No," Āakhu said. "I will have it repaired and returned, stocked with some things for you."

Ȧamȧam bowed. "Thank you."

Uāā·t wandered in from the other room and tugged on Āakhu's skirt. Her large, dark eyes peered up at the princess: maybe five inundations but already too old. Lines of lighter scars crept across the dark face like cracks in a jar. A finger in her mouth, she said, "Tuck me in."

Āakhu took her hand. Uāā·t led her to a small bed of reeds. Four other beds filled the tight, close space. A window covered with linen shivered from a bit of cool air drifting through. Two of the other girls were turned away, asleep. Two others, Sabi and a younger girl, watched silently in the candle light. Simple, childish drawings covered the mud walls, animals, birds, stick figure people.

Āakhu raised the corner of the yellowed linen blanket, another discard from the temple, and Uāā·t burrowed underneath. As Āakhu tucked the blanket around her, Uāā·t reached beneath a straw pillow and pushed something into Āakhu's hand. A lapis cat the color of the morning sky. A serene, regal pose, sitting, tail curled about it, peering at tomorrow or the day after that. It was missing one paw.

Āakhu tried to return it. "You should keep this."

Uāā·t shook her head. "Mȧu·t wants to live with you now."

Āakhu knelt beside the bed. She remembered nights when the desert wind raged and wailed about the palace like a wild beast, sending breaths of hot dust through the cracks and corners of the window covers. She and Ḥaāmer, Uāā·t's age, held each other under a blanket in Ḥaāmer's room. Mother sat with them, patted their heads, kissed their cheeks, and sang a song to soothe them all. Āakhu sang to Uāā·t:

Close your eyes and float along the starry river.
Rest your sleepy head.
Nut's broad skirt wraps you in warm embrace.
Sleep my child, the day is done.
Dream my child, of a new day to come.

* * *

Ṭeḥuti hugged Ȧamȧam and kissed her forehead.

"She is beautiful, and regal—everything I imagined god's daughter to be," Ȧamȧam said.

Ṭeḥuti leaned away, the old woman still in his arms, and gave her a puzzled smile. "But?"

Ȧamȧam shook her head.

"You are my second mother. Speak your heart."

She looked away and back to his face. "You are from such different lives. Though you live among the royal court, you come from among poor orphans and widows. Āakhu lives in a temple with servants to bathe her and feed her the finest foods. She has seen your world for one evening. She has tolerated it but will never be a part of it. Tomorrow she will be back in her temple with god and will forget us."

"I think you and the children have changed her."

"Perhaps, but how long will that change endure?"

"What are you saying?"

"She is not for you. Yes, you love each other as those finding love for the first time often do. But can that love overcome your different lives? Can it survive when the duties of her royal birth claim her?

"I want you to be happy, Ṭeḥuti. I wish that it might be with your first love, with her. But don't be blind to the possibility that she has a different path before her."

Āakhu returned. Ṭeḥuti took the offered oil lamp, said a subdued goodnight, and led Āakhu down the winding path to the river. He looked back just before the hut disappeared from view. Ȧamȧam was silhouetted in the light of the doorway, one arm balanced on a walking stick, the other raised in farewell.

The sensations of the river strengthened: the sound of night life, the smell of the water. Ȧamȧam's boat appeared at the edge of the lamp light, tied to a small dock at the river's edge. Ṭeḥuti climbed in and hung the lamp from the high bow. Then he took Āakhu's hand, lifted her, and lowered her to a bench near the oars.

He untied the ropes and coiled them into the boat. Then with a shove to the stern, he jumped aboard.

Ṭeḥuti was silent as he found the oars. He dropped them into the guide slots and settled himself. He pulled the boat gently out into the river until he felt the current catch it and guide it toward the palace.

"You seem so far away. Where have your thoughts taken you?" Āakhu asked as he lifted the oars. She sat before him, dark hair, dusky skin. Only her eyes, curious, concerned, sparkled with lamplight.

"Have you seen Maaạ?" Ṭeḥuti asked.

"He was here two weeks ago to visit Ḥaāmer but I did not see him. Why?"

"He arrived without summons and left within a day. It is said he and Pharaoh argued."

"Mother never mentioned it."

"He was going to wed Ḥaāmer. He wanted to be a part of the royal house. He still does."

"My father would never give me to Maaạ," she said, eyes large in the soft light. She leaned forward and touched his knee with her soft fingers. "He will announce our betrothal soon."

Ṭeḥuti nodded and smiled with a confidence he did not feel, and went back to searching the darkness beyond the boat.

Āakhu watched him a moment longer then touched the lapis kitten and held it up. The azure crystal seemed almost alive.

"It is beautiful," Ṭeḥuti remarked.

Āakhu stirred, and sighed. "Ḥaāmer loved her cats. She refused to be rid of them, even when we were surrounded with a couple litters of them. Bast was her matron goddess.

"I remember how they would terrorize the staff, leaping out of dark corners to catch the ankles of passing servants, bumping about in the night, eyes glowing, tails swaying like snakes, knocking things over with their antics. It was the only thing Ḥaāmer and I ever fought over."

"What was?"

"The column decorated with the carving of Bast in the common room. Ḥaāmer and I would fight over who had the right to sit at the base of the column. Our fights angered mother, until she taught us to share the column, a purring kitten in each of our laps to keep us quiet."

The boat drifted down the River. On the horizon, points of lights flickered along the eastern shore, city lights. Ṭeḥuti was content to be with Āakhu under the Aih, carried along through the night.

"Take me to the other side," Āakhu said.

"It is late. You should have been back to the queen's house before the Aten set."

"Please, Ṭeḥuti. The River is not wide here. Seeing the children, seeing them living again, I want to see Ḥaāmer and say good-bye."

"The west side is not a good place at night. Besides the spirits, there are wild animals. There might also be bandits. Pharaoh would never forgive me if something happened to you."

"Ptah will protect us," Āakhu said.

There was no argument the priest could make to that claim. He gave in without further argument and reached for the oars. Āakhu took another seat closer to him. Ṭeḥuti looked at the stars to get his bearing, then dragged one oar while using the other to turn the small boat toward the west.

It was a longer journey than Āakhu thought. Ṭeḥuti pulled at the oars as the Aih preceded them to the west. Āakhu encouraged him each time he lifted the oars to rest. For a priest, he was a lean, strong man. But most of his strength was in his legs, and was due to the walking he did going about his projects and duties. He had not done much work in a boat since childhood—with Ȧamȧam and her husband.

"I see the shore. Slow down, " Āakhu said. The boat grounded with a lurch. Āakhu tumbled into his arms with a small cry. She stayed there a moment longer than she needed. He was about to put his arms around her when she ducked away and reached for his hand.

"Come, Ḥaāmer will be glad to see you."

Ṭeḥuti tossed the anchor at the muddy shore and vaulted from the boat after it. He tugged at the line, pulling the boat through reeds and onto the bank.

"There's some old sail linen," he called. "Toss it to me."

She stood tall and silent at the bow, moonlight and the glow from the oil lamp sparkling from her eyes, like she might refuse. Then she smiled as if it were a grand adventure and searched the deck until she found it, dragged it to the bow, and dropped it to him. Ṭeḥuti quickly spread it open over the mud and reached up for her. She sat and swung her legs over the side and dropped lithely beside him. Ṭeḥuti reached past her for the oil pot and presented it to her by the handle. Her other hand clasped his hand and led him away.

The land was quiet except for the sound of the insects. The sky was high overhead, the milky glow of Nut's skirt stretched from horizon to horizon. The Aih loomed over the hills. The oil lamp that Āakhu carried seemed such a small gesture against the great bowl of the night.

There was solitude on this side of the River, a quiet that brought Ṭeḥuti's reverence and his faith to the surface. All the leaders of Egypt were here, their spirits walking this land at night. He imagined them watching the lights shining from the east bank and wondering what the ones they left behind were doing, and when they might be making their own journey from life to afterlife.

Ṭeḥuti felt them about him as Āakhu led them further up into the hills. He imagined the timeless eyes watching him and Āakhu pass, curious at the young couple who had disturbed their peace. He felt the years they had witnessed with their once-living eyes, the time stretching back in uncounted years.

Āakhu stopped, interrupting Ṭeḥuti's thoughts. They stood at the top of a rise, the edge of the desert sand looming in the distance.

Āakhu handed the lamp to Ṭeḥuti. "Wait here. I won't go far."

She left him, padding silently across the sand. Leaving the glow of the oil lamp, losing substance to the night with each step, she too became only spirit.

Āakhu was silent for a long time before raising her arms to the sky, a shadow on the face of the Aih, and speaking in a strong, clear voice:

I will remember you as seasons pass.
I will watch for you from the east side of the River.
As for any god or mortal who passes by,
I will declare my love for my sister Ḥaāmer.

She continued looking up into the sky, her face surrounded with the Aih's cold light.

"I will never forget you, Ḥaāmer, but I am through mourning. You must live here among the dead and I must return to the living. I will remember you in each face I see. I will work the rest of my life to see that no one suffers as you did."

She waited in silence another moment. Then Ṭeḥuti saw her turn and start back to him. She hugged him. He encircled her with one arm and held out the oil lamp with the other.

"She came to me in a breeze," said Āakhu. "She touched my cheek, dried my tears, and said that she understood. She wished me well, and said she would watch over me."

He took her hand and started back to the boat. Her fingers were warm, soft, a perfect fit for his.

"I am blessed to have such a man as you, Ṭeḥuti."

Ṭeḥuti raised her hand to his lips and kissed it. *If I had all the gold in all the world, I would have nothing if I did not have you.*

wsḫt nt jwsw m wꜣst ḥsbt 18 ꜣbd 2 prt sw 25 ḫr ḥm n wsỉr

The Hall of Balance in Uas,
Year 18, Month 2 of Peret, Day 25 under the Majesty of Ạsạr

A disturbance at the front of the Hall of Balance where it opened onto the street caused Pharaoh to pause and look up.

A woman's voice disturbed the negotiation, but whether the words were angry or remorseful was lost in the expanse and echos of the Hall of Balance.

The noise increased. People around Pharaoh's throne turned to see what was happening. The sound progressed toward the front of the public section of the crowd. People parted and moved back, shying from her as they would shy from a viper or crocodile moving purposefully through the water.

Pharaoh's guards came forward, fingers stretching and flexing, poised near the hilts of their daggers. The woman would not stop.

She broke from the crowd, screaming words no one could make out, sobbing about dying, and ran into the arms of an enormous Cushite guard, who encircled her waist with one arm and lifted her from her feet like a sheaf of flax.

"I must see Pharaoh," she cried, before the guard covered half her face with his hand.

"Wait," commanded Pharaoh, stopping him from carrying her back into the crowd and out of the hall. "Let her down."

He placed the woman back on her feet, and stepped out of her reach.

"I know you," Pharaoh said. "Metiu?"

She dropped to her knees, head down. "Yes," she answered through her tears.

"Approach me."

She rose and shuffled forward, reaching into a bag looped over her shoulder and withdrawing a necklace. An image of Nut carved from amber, strung on a thread with red clay beads. She held it out to Pharaoh.

"What is this?" Pharaoh asked.

Metiu threw the necklace at the first step of the dais. It shattered, scattering bits of red beads before Pharaoh's throne like spatters of blood. Metiu, her cheeks still stained with tears, howled with grief and bitterness.

"It belonged to Hepaba-t," she wailed. "Last night her husband beat her and the son who came to her defense until both were dead. Where is your justice now?"

The only sounds in the Hall of Balance were Metiu's words, a long dying echo spreading through the hall, and the scrape of a few unbroken beads rolling across the stone floor.

Īset choked and raised a hand to her mouth. The color fled from Pharaoh's face. He called to his guards: "Clear the hall. I am done for today. Close and bar the doors."

They pushed forward, herding the people, merchants and priests back to the doors and out. They were silent in the presence of Pharaoh, but he heard the grumbles and protests as they passed into the street.

The doors shut with a thud. "Fetch my sword," Pharaoh said. "Metiu will lead us."

"Is this wise?" Īset asked, laying a hand across his forearm.

"It is necessary," he said.

They left by the side entrance. The disgruntled petitioners still milling about the front saw and several followed, careful not to get too close or voice their opinions too loudly.

Pharaoh was somewhere else, seeming oblivious to the sounds, the buildings, the people that scurried out of his path as he followed, head down in meditation, behind the stumbling form of the old woman. Īset and his guards followed him in silent bewilderment.

Along the street, parallel to the river, out of town towards the bare fields. The midday sun beat down on their heads. A woman ran from a building and presented a shade fan to a guard who brought it to Īset.

Metiu stopped near a cluster of mud houses. "In there," she pointed, panting, her damp shift clinging to her bent, wrinkled body.

Hepaba-t rested in a small room at the back of the house. A single candle burned, illuminating her. Arms folded across her chest concealed some of the bruises. Her son lay next to her, dried blood trailing down his cheek from one closed eye.

Pharaoh entered the room. Īset, and a guard watched from the doorway. Pharaoh knelt by mother and child, touching one finger to the floor to gather dust and sand. With the other, he wiped a tear from the corner of his eye. He rubbed the two fingers together and touched each of the cold, dead foreheads.

"We come from sand and water," he said. "Touched and given life by the gods. I will speak the name Hepaba-t and her son when I reach Amennt. There you will have the life you were never given here."

He held the dead woman's hand. "Where is Neshti?"

"They found him hiding with a neighbor. We are holding him outside."

Pharaoh positioned Hepaba-t's hand back over her heart. He went to the doorway and through, people giving way for him.

"My sword," he said when he was outside.

A soldier marched forward, bowed, and presented the polished bronze sword hilt-first. Pharaoh pointed to a work bench in front of the house. "Put him there, head down."

Neshti's eyes widened. "It was an accident. She fell."

Two guards pushed Neshti toward the table.

"She was just one, stupid woman," Neshti screamed. "The priest said I would not be punished."

"The priest was wrong," Pharaoh said.

The guards forced the struggling Neshti head down across the table. Pharaoh strode forward and brought the sword in a two-handed grip over his head. "I promised that on the day Hepaba-t died you would also die. That day has come by your own hand."

The sword moved in a blur, embedding the edge deep into the wooden tabletop. Neshti's head rolled toward the opposite side and off, taking his last scream with it, pushed by a fountain of blood from his neck.

Pharaoh yanked the sword from the table and said: "Drop the body."

The guards backed away.

Two sword cuts, slicing through Neshti's body and into the dirt, severed his arms. Two more cuts and his legs were severed. The sand turned red.

One final, powerful overhead chop and Pharaoh broke Neshti's torso in two, separating hips from ribs.

Pharaoh paused in the midst of the mutilated farmer, panting, awash with sweat and dust and blood.

A crowd of a hundred now gathered, watching in stunned silence. Sunlight poured down on the rocks and sand, a golden rainfall on the people, warming dried mud rooftops.

The crowd was both entranced and horrified. They had seen in Pharaoh the god of love and hope, appearing without fanfare at a public work, offering blessings and encouragement, adding his hands and shoulders for a moment to a task, handing out rewards, offering gifts of food and wine from his own table. None had ever witnessed the god of justice and vengeance: swift, terrible, and fierce.

Pharaoh presented the bloodstained sword to his bearer. The guards moved the people back from the scene.

A baby cried, held in clumsy embrace by a girl peering from Neshti's doorway. A boy appeared beside her. Eyes wide, they shrank back into the shadows at the sight of blood.

"Who are you?" Pharaoh asked.

They melted away, back into the dark recesses of the house, leaving the doorway empty.

"They are Neshti's children," someone said.

Chapter 7

CAIRO, EGYPT, MINISTRY OF STATE FOR ANTIQUITIES, MINISTRY STEPS, JUNE 17TH 5:00 P.M.:

Lisa's struggles became weak, futile. The terrorist continued to twist her shirt around her throat, cutting off her air, not allowing her to shout for help. She was about to blackout. She would not be getting away. Near the bottom of the ministry steps, the man grunted and went down, landing on top of her. His grip relaxed. Instinctively, Lisa wiggled from under him and rolled sideways. She struggled into a fighting position, yanking her clothing from around her neck. She spun around to face any other attackers as she gasped for air. A familiar old man with a heavy stick raised above his head gestured toward the ministry door, standing open above on the raised porch. She did not hesitate, staggering up the steps into the warren-hole.

Inside the building, she collapsed on the polished, marble floor, her head between her knees, gasping for air. She slid wildly backwards on her rump when the old man entered. She regarded the ministry guard in terror.

Crap!

She knew him well, but in her hysteria she didn't recognize him when he entered. He glanced at her then turned, placing his stick under the security podium.

"You're safe now."

Lisa didn't respond. She continued to gasp for breath, her dizzy brain pounding from her lack of oxygen. Her heart still thumped heavily in her chest. She shuddered. She hurt. She began to cry. She watched him as an energetic shadow, moving through an arched doorway into a vestibule beyond. Lisa tensed, when he returned with a china cup in his hand.

He offered her the drink by lifting his hands several times for her to take the cup. She sipped. It was scalding hot, sweet tea. She took a deep breath and shuddered.

"Thank you," she whispered. Placing the cup on the floor beside her, she settled her jacket from around her shoulders.

"Dr. Hampton! What are you doing out like that? You know better," he said in a stern voice. "Young women should not be out on the streets by themselves."

As he handed her a cloth to wipe her eyes, the ministry guard's tough demeanor turned into a paternal smile. They often had chats when she was in Cairo at the Antiquities Ministry.

"I haven't knocked heads since I was in the army. My trusted cosh did its job," he grinned, pointing at the podium. "I was just closing the door, when I saw you running across the plaza away from those men. Dr. Hampton, I don't understand the chances you take. I must lock for the evening. Recover your breathing then I must call you a cab."

He moved to the door, pulling it open. He immediately thrust it closed again.

"The protesters encroach up the steps," he told her, shaking his head.

"I do not want to go out there. I came to speak with Dr. Tu'hut."

"He's expecting you this late?" He pressed his back against the closed door, as if holding it against the crowd, thrusting sideways the large slide bolt to lock the door with an echoing crash. He shook his head at this errant child with a twinkle in his eye.

"No, he's not expecting you. You'd better hurry if you're going to see him."

"Thank you. Thank you for saving me."

She wanted to hug him, but even with their close friendship, a hug would have been inappropriate with an Arab man. Handing him her rattling cup and saucer, she struggled up from the floor. She lifted her hands in a half shrug cocking her head to the side to thank him. He nodded.

"You're welcome, Dr. Hampton."

She made an unsteady turn toward the back of the lobby. She reached out suddenly gripping his arm to steady herself. The ornate floor pattern made her nauseous. She felt dizzy. Knocking the cup from his hand, it shattered on the floor.

"Are you all right, Dr. Hampton?"

"I will be OK." she gasped. "I am sorry about the cup. I will help you clean it up."

"No, you go. You need to get to Dr. Tu'hut. I'll sweep this up."

Launching herself, she staggered across the lobby to the pointed Persian arch at the back and to the stairwell beyond. Shocked and frightened by the toll the encounter had taken on her, she griped the wrought iron railing, taking several deep breaths.

No, I'm not all right.

Pulling on the handrail, she dragged herself to the between floors landing. Exhaustion and the shakes overcame her. She collapsed on the bottom step of the next riser to consider what had happened. Her attack had been a close-call. These men would have kidnapped then murdered her. In her mind's eye, she saw the man during the bombing. She could see the same man grabbing for her legs on the ministry steps.

Terrorist! Everyone keeps warning me that I shouldn't be traveling alone.

Her mother and she had traveled easily through the city. She would've detected her mother's fear if the streets had been unsafe, but Randall warned her Egypt was having internal problems.

Why don't I know about them? A bombing! Death! Now I'm a witness. Crap! What should I do?

She shook as she forced her breathing back to normal again, placing her fingertips on her temples, pressing to ease the thumping pain.

I have to be more careful. How? Oh, they hurt me.

Concerned about her physical condition, she touched her aching shoulder and chest. She took two deep breaths.

No permanent damage, she assured herself.

She sat for a couple more minutes to regain her strength—her calm. She rose to continue up the stairs.

I want to do archaeology and that's what I'm going to do.

Tu'hut can't know I'm coming. Surprise may get me through the door to talk with the...asshole; however, I have to run the gauntlet of his male assistant, Ali. He's an arrogant, pain in the ass who reflects his employer's demeanor.

Lisa climbed the remaining stairs to the Secretary General's office. She saw Ali, sitting behind his desk.

"You," he said flatly as his eyes traveled her disheveled clothing.

Well at least we share a mutual contempt.

"I am here to see Dr. Tu'hut."

"We're closed for the day."

"I am expected."

"I doubt that. He's seeing his last appointment now. You're not on the list."

"No. I have just arrived from the Delta with information he needs to hear."

"Yes? Well, make an appointment, but as you know, Dr. Tu'hut is very busy. And I'm not sure he's interested in seeing you. Good day."

"What do you mean he is not interested in seeing me," Lisa's voice became angry. "Who do you think you are treating me in such a cavalier fashion?"

She suspected that Ali had overstepped his authority with his last comment unless Tu'hut was making it clear that she wasn't welcome.

A possibility. He may be aware of the fight Tu'hut and I had.

"He doesn't wish to speak with you."

"I said I want to see Dr. Tu'hut." Lisa continued to get louder.

At that moment, the door to Dr. Tu'hut's office opened.

"What is it, Ali?"

"This woman wishes to see you. I told her...."

"I'm here to discuss the new find in the south."

Startled, Dr. Tu'hut's eyebrows lifted as he turned to Lisa. As always with the Secretary General, Lisa reacted impetuously without regard for decorum. This could get her into a lot of trouble or it might get her through the door. Dr. Tu'hut registered genuine surprise.

"Come into my office. How do you know about the new find?" he asked as he closed the door behind them. He was obviously cutting her out, but she had gotten through the door.

"I read your e-mail."

"I sent my letter to a limited list in the United States. I don't remember your name being on the list. Perhaps you didn't come upon the communique legitimately. Are you a computer hacker, Miss Hampton, as well as a troublesome woman?"

"No, I am an archaeologist."

Dr. Tu'hut's dark eyes bore into her—his pointed mustache twitching. His behavior was despicable, showing no regard for a woman. Lisa hated how he referred to her as 'Miss.' He was treating her with the disrespect he attributed to her, not as a fellow Ph.D. of Archaeology. He probably despised the fact she was a foreign, female Egyptologist.

"Miss, I believe you stumbled onto something you weren't privileged to see. I'd like to know how you came upon this information. I thought you were in the Delta."

"As I said, I received your e-mail." Lisa knew that Tu'hut couldn't send e-mail.

He told someone else to send out the notification. Whoever did is going to be in trouble. I hope it is Ali.

"I came to request being appointed as supervisor of the new archaeological feature in the south."

Dr. Tu'hut rocked back and laughed heartily.

"You're impertinent. I'm sorry, but I've already assigned supervision of the site. If you aren't going to tell me how you came upon this information, we've no further business."

The side door to Dr. Tu'hut's office opened. Lisa looked in that direction. A handsome man, her age, entered, wearing a short sleeved khaki shirt and shorts. His well defined, muscular arms and legs were displayed by his clothing. His brown eyes and short, dark hair blended with his deeply tanned skin. He had spent some time in the sun perhaps here in Egypt. Although his head was down reading a packet of papers, his movement was deliberate and self-assured. He looked vaguely familiar, but if Lisa had met him before, she didn't remember where. It hadn't been recently.

"Dr. Tu'hut, I've been studying...? Oh, pardon me; I didn't know you had a guest."

His accent placed him as a fellow American.

"Not a guest. Miss Hampton was just leaving."

The man's expression altered to one of genuine surprise.

"Dr. Hampton, the archaeologist! I thought I recognized you. Do you remember me? My name is Bill Sanders. It's good to see you again."

Sanders walked to her and stuck out his hand. The expression on Dr. Tu'hut's face transformed from perplexed, to surprised. Lisa accepted Sanders' hand without smiling.

"Yes, I remember you, Dr. Sanders. I must assume that you're the archaeologist and project leader that Dr. Tu'hut has chosen to supervise the new find."

Bill Sanders turned to Dr. Tu'hut with an eyebrow lifted. He appeared puzzled as if the topic hadn't been discussed.

"If I cannot supervise the project, I'd like to be included on your site exploration team," Lisa continued to push.

"A thousand pardons, Doctor," Tu'hut was now being gracious. "I have received hundreds of responses from the United States. I do not need you. We can not do that. The area is far too dangerous for a woman."

"Oh?" she said simply, her forehead knotting deeper.

"Yes, the Egyptian Army guards the site. It is a military camp... ah...bivouac area. A man has already been badly injured there."

"You don't seem concerned about Dr. Sanders' welfare."

Sanders, who had been nodding with Tu'hut's comments, met Lisa's eyes giving her a faint smile as she turned to him.

"Dr. Sanders is a *man*. He understands the dangers. Besides, he is only doing a preliminary survey. Our exploration team is small."

"I understand the dangers. I'm willing to take responsibility for my own welfare."

"Even if you are not concerned for your personal safety, the Egyptian government won't be responsible for a woman. Not with Army troops. They are most barbaric."

"You show..." growled Lisa.

Anger painting his face, Tu'hut raised his hand stopping her. He spoke through gritted teeth.

"I will not put up with your disrespect. Your American slang. I will not be called a swine."

"...me one good reason," a puzzled Lisa finished her sentence.

"The Dean of the University told me that you were working in the Delta. Why are you not there? You have caused your last problem. I want you out. You are no longer welcome. I will call the Dean. You are out. The sooner you leave the country the better."

"Dr. Tu'hut...."

"I am tired of dealing with this—you. Miss, you are...are fired. Out. Out!"

Lisa shook with rage.

Damn it!

The result, although not anticipated, was not totally unexpected either. Lisa stormed out the office door, brushing past the receptionist.

What did I say? You show...swine? Oh, crap! Such nonsense! The asshole thouught I was calling him a chauvinist pig. He knows just enough English to be dangerous. He's an idiot!

She turned the wrong direction—away from the stairs, looking up just in time to run into an Egyptian gentleman. He embraced her in a tight hug so neither of them would fall. When they both regained their balance, he released her.

"I am very sorry," Lisa said, knowing the touch would offend him. He had acted as a gentleman.

"Think nothing of it. You seem most agitated." He looked kindly into her eyes, and when she said nothing, he continued. "Is something wrong? Has Dr. Tu'hut been rude?"

"No. We had a misunderstanding. I am sorry I bumped into you. I will not trouble you further."

"You haven't troubled me. Think nothing of it. Perhaps I can help?"

She wondered how he could help her with Tu'hut.

"I'm leaving for the day myself," he continued. "I'll see you safely to your accommodations. Come now. Where's your home, your office?"

Considering his offer, she didn't wish a repeat of her earlier incident. What would the crowds be like when she left the building?

"I am at the Nile Hilton."

"Ah, a fine hotel and not far from here."

"Thank you. I appreciate your offer."

Lisa turned and they walked toward the stairs. Ali jumped to his feet as they approached. Ali looked at her with undisguised disdain. His gaze switched to the gentleman. He bent at the waist, bowing his head in deference. The gentleman waved him to sit down.

"Good evening, minister. I'll call your car."

"Thank you, Ali."

Minister?

Lisa recognized from his title that he was an important person, high in the government, the cabinet. At ground level, Lisa's friend unlocked the door for them, bowing. As the minister passed, Lisa caught the expression on the guard's face behind the minister's back. Although he was bowing to show respect for the minister, he didn't like him.

Waiting at the curb, the driver had the rear passenger door of a limousine open for them. Looking around as the minister waved her into the vehicle, Lisa saw that the plaza was empty, the crowd having been dispersed except for a small group of protesters to the side being hustled away with nightsticks by the police. She slid across and the minister entered behind her.

"The Nile Hilton," he told the driver as they pulled away from the curb. "What's your disagreement with Dr. Tu'hut?"

"He does not want me to go to a new dig."

"Ah, the archaeological site in the south?"

Everyone except me seems to know. She nodded.

He paused, contemplating.

"I can understand his view. Unfortunately, my country has problems with terrorists. We try to control them. Our government can't expose you to these problems. We cannot put you in danger."

"I understood these problems before I left the Delta," she stretched the truth, "And I am willing to accept the dangers."

He shook his head registering surprise.

Lisa continued. "I have studied Egyptian archaeology my entire life. This new feature is an important opportunity."

"I can see you're quite...what is the word...passionate. I'll speak with Dr. Tu'hut tomorrow."

"You are most kind. I certainly do not wish to trouble you."

"It's no trouble. Leave it in my hands, perhaps you'd accompany me to dinner tomorrow evening. We can discuss my success with Dr. Tu'hut. My name is Saladin Aboud. I'll call for you."

"You are most kind."

As they arrived at the hotel, he said, "I'll contact you at the hotel tomorrow evening at eight o'clock. What's your name so I may reach you?"

"Lisa Hampton and thank you, Minister Aboud."

"It's a pleasure to meet you, Dr. Hampton. You're most welcome."

At least Minister Aboud understood she had a doctorate. As Lisa strolled to the entrance of the hotel, she didn't notice the lecherous look the Minister of the Interior gave her.

CAIRO, EGYPT, MILITARY HOSPITAL, JUNE 17TH, 9:50 P.M.:

Anwar felt his life sucked from him as he plodded from the hospital. Omar died within minutes of his arrival, having never regained consciousness. Hate boiled for the bastards who killed his friend. He had no energy for the army, only the hate feeding him. Two duties remained. He turned to Nefri Mulhan to give her what comfort he could. Then he would avenge his friend.

CAIRO, EGYPT, THE NILE HILTON, JUNE 18TH, 7:00 A.M.:

Lisa awoke with a start as the ringing telephone demanded her attention. She reached for the hand-set wishing the noise to cease.

"Good morning, Mademoiselle. It is seven o'clock as you requested."

"Thank you," she mumbled as she replaced the receiver. She didn't want to get up. Her eyes closed. The telephone was ringing again. She lifted the receiver.

"Dr. Hampton? This is Bill Sanders."

The cobwebs cleared.

"Oh, good morning," she said, becoming fully awake, swinging her legs over the side of the bed.

"Do you have a moment to chat?" he asked her. "I felt that our previous conversation ended on a bad note."

"Oh, I must apologize. My upset was directed toward Dr. Tu'hut, not at you," she assured him.

Why is he calling me? Perhaps I've a chance.

"I could desperately use your help."

Lisa's spirits leapt.

"Dr. Tu'hut and I discussed your participation for two hours after you left. He's quite adamantly opposed to your being a part of this exploration."

He wants me out of the country, thought Lisa. *Thanks for talking about me.*

"Unfortunately," he continued, "the old stiff is unmoved. I'm afraid that I wasn't successful at getting you to come. I couldn't change his mind. So I'm sorry for the bad news, but I wanted to tell you that I'll keep working on him."

The bottom fell out of Lisa. She had two men working to get her to the feature, but with no promise at the end. This conversation proved to be worthless. Her despair crushed in upon her.

"Dr. Hampton?"

"Yes," she responded tears running down her face.

"I'm sorry. I didn't mean to upset you, but I want you to know that I hope to work with you soon."

She suppressed her sobs long enough to hang up the phone.

CAIRO, EGYPT, MINISTER OF THE INTERIOR'S OFFICE, JUNE 18TH, 10:27 A.M.:

The private phone on Saladin's desk rang. He picked it up as if it were a dirty thing.

"We have a problem," the voice said.

"You always have a problem."

"It concerns the incident here in Cairo, yesterday. I'm sure you do not wish to discuss it over the telephone."

"Come to our meeting place in one hour," responded Saladin replacing the phone in its cradle without further comment.

I must regain control over these two.

CAIRO, EGYPT, ISLAMIC DISTRICT UNDISCLOSED LOCATION, JUNE 18TH, 11:45 A.M.:

Saladin stepped from his limousine. He walked into a mosque at the edge of the Islamic District without regard to the ornate mosaic nor the calming dark depths. Walking through an ogee archway at the side, he entered a deserted, adjacent building normally used by his ministry for interrogations. In a room at the rear of the building, the two car bombing brothers were talking heatedly as he entered. They turned to face him, their conversation ceasing. The sullen pair waited for him to speak.

"What is *our* problem?" Saladin growled.

"Yesterday, as we were carrying out your holy war, a foreign woman witnessed the incident. We attempted to apprehend her so she would not bear witness against us, but she ran to the steps of the Antiquities Ministry. As we attempted to carry her off, she had some unfortunate luck and was able to disable my stupid brother...."

"She'll die for her insolence!"

"If we ever find her again, brother, before we, ourselves, are brought before a magistrate for trial."

"Stop bickering you stupid dogs."

They turned to Saladin their eyes downcast. Their expressions angry, disrespectful.

"I had her under control when I was clubbed from behind by someone I didn't see. She'd disappeared when I returned to consciousness. We escaped into the crowd. We don't know where the woman went."

Saladin contemplated the two with disgust. He knew where Dr. Hampton had disappeared for he was certain they referred to her, but he didn't intend to inform these ravenous dogs as to her current location. An assassination attempt might lead the police directly to him.

So Dr. Hampton witnessed the bombing? She did not refer to the incident. She's an amazing woman. She was apprehended by these two idiots yet still escaped to carry on with courage. A fine catch...amazing!

"This isn't your *only* problem," began Saladin. "The woman you picked up at the bazaar was the Kuwaiti ambassador's wife."

"We instructed the men to be careful with their choices."

"They're stupid. They put our cause in jeopardy. I want you out! I need to be rid of you!"

The ugly brother stared at Saladin.

Do they contemplate murdering me? Saladin wondered.

"You must disappear. You must go to the desert with the others. Cairo's become unsafe for you. I want you two gone. Attempt nothing further on your own. Go to our village and remain there. I'll make inquiries and find out who this woman is. When we get the proper moment, we'll apprehend her. Now go. I need you both out of Cairo."

"We further the cause."

"If you get us all captured or killed, you fail the cause."

He saw the hatred build in the ugly brother's eyes again.

"Is that the only reason for your concern?" asked the man.

"Out!"

They skulked through the back door into the alley behind. He was loosing control.

I must find a way to be rid of them.

Saladin retraced his steps to his vehicle. He contemplated his next move as he rode back to the ministry.

The two must be out of Cairo. I need them completely out of the picture. My movement will slow for awhile. It's too unsafe to continue.

* * *

Lisa rolled over in bed another time. Her salty tears burned her face, hollow, empty, her frustration and disappointment pouring out of her. Although Sanders was trying to be kind, his words were painful to her. He was working for her, but he hadn't improved her situation.

What am I going to do? I need to talk with someone.

Getting through on long distance back to the States didn't register in her mind. When the phone was answered, she awoke from her trance.

"Randall. This is Lisa."

"Lisa! Good God! It's one o'clock in the morning."

"Oh, Randall, I'm sorry."

"What's wrong? Where are you?"

"I'm in Cairo. They won't let me go to the feature."

"Good Lord, you're moving fast. Wait a second. Let me go downstairs to my office so Sarah can sleep."

The phone went on hold and a long minute later he answered again.

"I'm sorry to wake you. Apologize to Sarah for me."

"That's OK. What do you mean they won't let you go to the feature? Who won't let you go?"

"I've talked with Tu'hut, and a Dr. Sanders, his team leader. They say because of the terrorist business it's too dangerous to go to the feature."

"Both of these men have excellent reputations, Lisa. I told you Egypt's having problems. Maybe they're just being careful."

She'd been trying desperately to downplay the circumstances, but her voice caught. She supressed a sob.

"Lisa, you're holding back. Tell me everything that's happened since you left the Delta."

Lisa didn't want to tell him, but she finally broke down. She told Randall everything that happened, including the attack.

"So they were carting you off, girl?"

"Yes."

"Damn, Lisa, that was close. I told you to be careful? Understanding the situation now, perhaps it would be better if you came home."

In her minds-eye, she could see him shaking his head.

"Ran...," she started with tears running down her face.

"Goodness! Why are you always in the center of the swirl?" he asked.

"I don't know. I try not to be."

"It certainly appears terrorists chased you. I don't see how you are going to be safe. They'll be after you now that you're a witness. Do you know who was killed in the car?"

"No, but I believe it's politically motivated. It was a limo so it had to be someone important. From the way they were looking, it is obvious that they were searching for that car. This business is really scaring me."

"It should. Maybe you should go to the Embassy."

"They'll want to know why I can't just get on a plane. Once they find out that I'm a witness, they'll want to send me to the Egyptian authorities."

"Right. That might not be wise. They could detain you indefinitely."

"If the terrorists are politically connected to someone in the government, I might just disappear."

"From what you're saying, I'm not sure you can safely get on a plane to come home. You probably would be safer if you just disappeared."

"Great, Ran! How am I going to do that?"

"Getting out of Cairo would be a good idea. Hmmm, I've got a wild idea. Would they suspect if you went to the new feature?"

"No, the terrorists can't know I'm an archaeologist."

"I don't know how to get you on the team, but that might be the best way to disappear. You figure out a way. Be resourceful. Follow the trail."

"Oh, professor, I don't know the trail. I don't know what I'm going to do?"

"Can't tell you what to do, but stay calm. Keep your chin up. Be positive. Your thinking will be sharper. Work on getting out of town. Keep me posted. Be safe."

"Thanks for caring, Ran."

"Always have. Goodnight, Lisa."

"Yeah, sorry for the early call."

Lisa hung up the phone. Randall was always a wild, positive force–impossible maybe, but always positive. She came back from her depression. With a deep breath, she felt relief. He echoed her opinion. She needed to get to the feature. He told her to keep plugging. Follow the trail. She wiped her face with the back of her hand, and sat up straight. Her optimism returned. She would continue.

How am I going to get to the site?

She went into the bathroom to wash her face.

CAIRO, EGYPT, AIRPORT CARGO TERMINAL, JUNE 18TH, 11:50 A.M.:

At the airport, Lisa paid the cab driver and went into the cargo shipping and receiving desk. Randall said follow the trail. Sanders might have equipment shipped from the States. A ship would be dreadfully slow. The air cargo clerk summoned his chief.

"I'm an American archaeologist," she told him. "My boss sent me to find out the status of our equipment."

"Do you have the papers?"

"No, he didn't give them to me. It's such a bother. He said all was taken care of, but he wants me to check on the condition of the equipment. He wants to know when it's going to the site."

The inspector eyed Lisa.

"Your request is most difficult. We have hundreds of items here which are being shipped out. Finding specific items without papers will take some time. I do not have such time."

"I will be most happy to do the searching."

"That would not be proper."

The inspector watched Lisa's hand as an Egyptian hundred pound note began to appear.

"Come with me," he said, walking into his office, as the note disappeared into his robe. He peered into his book.

"Where did the shipment come from?"

"From the United States. Chicago, Illinois. Within the last ten days," she told him. Lisa had researched Dr. William R. Sanders on the internet at the hotel.

"I have such equipment with that origin going to Abydos."

"If it belongs to Dr. Sanders, we're in business."

The inspector wrote the number on a slip of paper. He told his assistant to take Lisa back to the particular area where the items were stored. Lisa looked at the crates.

University of Chicago
P O Box 9081
Chicago, Illinois 60611-9081

Attention: W. R. Sanders
Abydos, Egypt
In Care Of: Dr. Jabar Tu'hut
Secretary General
Ministry of State for Antiquities

Bingo!

Even with her excitement, Lisa forced herself to inspect each crate to be sure nothing was damaged. The chief inspector said the shipment was going to Abydos which matched what she knew.

"Chief Inspector. The crates look in good condition. When does the shipment leave for Abydos?"

The inspector consulted his book.

"Early tomorrow morning."

"I'd like to go with it to make sure it's safe."

The inspector nodded. "Be here at 5:00 A.M."

CAIRO, EGYPT, GENERAL FADI'S OFFICE JUNE 18TH, 3:07 P.M.:

"Captain Jagardii is here, sir," said Colonel Mohieddin.

Fadi nodded. Captain Jagardii reported to him.

"Captain, your company's mission will be to guard the archaeological site for the Ministry of State for Antiquities. You will maintain security in the area, insuring no further incidents occur. I stress to you that the safety of the foreign scientist assisting our country be preserved at all costs. Do you understand?"

"Yes, sir."

"No more incidents. Very well, dismissed."

Saluting, Captain Jagardii left the office.

The general grunted with satisfaction after the door closed. A pair of problems solved.

* * *

"All of Fadi's relatives have sex with swine," swore Jagardii. "May Fadi's mother give birth to a...oh, shit. I have been relegated to the damned."

How, this side of Hell, am I ever going to catch these bastards?

CAIRO, EGYPT, THE NILE HILTON, JUNE 18TH, 3:15 P.M.:

Lisa Hampton lay on her hotel bed reading the English newspaper. A half hour of intense reading found no mention of the feature.

This site is under tight wraps. I can't imagine their not requesting help by this time. Maybe I can get a job as digger.

She giggled with wry humor. It ended, when she flipped back to the front of the paper with disgust. She understood why she hadn't known about the terrorism. She hadn't read a paper for ages or followed it on the internet. She originally chose to ignore the ugly picture on the front page. It now reached out and grabbed her. A young man lay on his back on a dirty street, dead from a bullet in his head. His blood darkened the ground under his gore streaked face. The picture's caption screamed:

TERRORISM IN OUR STREETS!

It sickened Lisa to see her Egypt like this. Terrorism didn't occur during her childhood. She felt that her Egypt was a splendid path back through time, connecting with the people of ancient times. They were a powerful and loving people. As an adult, she knew her fantasies were childish. Still, she could not accept this harsh reality. This was not her Egypt.

The next article asked for information about the wife of the Kuwaiti Ambassador. She was killed June 9th. The request was for witnesses to come forward.

An Embassy Protocol and Public Information Officer said that the ambassador's wife left the embassy without a chaperon to visit the Bazaar. The paper read:

> *TUESDAY, June 9th: At 7:50 AM, Massouma–wife of Jarah Hamimech, Kuwaiti Ambassador to Egypt–was shot. She left the Kuwaiti Embassy to shop in the Khan el-Khalili bazaar. Embassy officials attempted to locate her, but she disappeared into the crowd and was not seen further. The ambassador's wife was wearing gray clothing. Anyone having information leading to her assailants is asked to contact the Kuwaiti Embassy, the Cairo police or the Egyptian government.*

A publicity photo of Jarah Hamimech and Massouma, his wife, at the time of their marriage appeared next to the article. She was a beautiful woman, young and vivacious. Her fresh face beamed at Lisa from the newspaper page. She was not dressed in the traditional Arab apparel, but wore a western style suit. That was unusual in their circle. Her husband, the ambassador, was much older. He was very sober faced, very proper looking.

Now she is dead. Amazingly, even an Arab woman is not safe although she probably should not have been out alone. So how did she get lost so quickly? Perhaps this incident was politically motivated.

Lisa doubted the woman was using this as an opportunity to escape from her husband—an event that happened in the Middle East. Everthing she read about the ambassador was positive. He was benevolent, kind and well respected. His wife was young as her picture suggested; a second marriage for him after the passing of his first wife. The news reported that they were happily married.

She turned the page to the next section. There was a picture of the destroyed car she had seen bombed. The paper explained the Minister of State for Antiquities died in the explosion.

Tu'hut's boss!

She saw the two men who carried out the attack. The article said the police had no leads. No one had come forward with an account of the event. She felt guilty about not reporting what she knew, especially with the video recording she had on her cell phone. She hesitated to be involved with Egyptian internal problems. This is Egypt not the United States. If she became involved, the police might not let her leave or move about freely until the incident was resolved.

She saw the bombing. She felt its terror. She turned on the room television, but got only the standard state dribble. Switching to her laptop, she scanned through the streaming channels. One feed showed the latest terrorist pictures from the south. A tall news reporter stood before a village well, talking about the horrors he observed in Gorge. The camera panned away from him, showing several bodies sprawled on the ground. She saw the man with a bullet in his head she had seen in the newspaper. She hated how the foreign correspondents sensationalized the bloody pictures.

She switched feeds. The screen filled with the front of the Ministry of State for Antiquities. It was evening. A commentator was speaking over the scene being shown. Lisa followed his words in the English closed captioning rolling underneath.

...PROTESTERS RALLIED IN FRONT OF THE MINISTRY OF STATE FOR ANTIQUITIES THIS AFTERNOON WHERE IT WAS DISCOVERED THE MINISTER OF THE INTERIOR WAS HOLDING MEETINGS TO DISCUSS THE CONTINUED ACTS OF TERRORISM AND HIS CONTINUED SUPPORT OF THE PRESIDENT....

WHILE THE CROWD WAITED FOR HIS APPEARANCE, WITNESSES SAY TWO MEN ATTACKED A FOREIGN WOMAN ON THE MINISTRY STEPS. A MAN FROM THE MINISTRY STRUCK ONE OF THE ATTACKERS WITH A STICK. HE IS SHOWN RUNNING INTO THE MINISTRY....

The ministry guard dashed through the open ministry door.

My God! I'm the woman. This must be right after I was attacked.

The crowd descended on the terrorists, beating them with signs and their fists. They fought back, kicking and flailing, finally escaping across the plaza. The camera zoomed in on a young man carrying a sign.

SIGN: STOP THE DEATH!

Then to another sign that read:

SIGN: REMOVE THE PRESIDENT!

The video and closed caption coverage continued.

LATER, THE MINISTER OF THE INTERIOR APPEARED WITH THE WOMAN WHO WAS ATTACKED EARLIER....

The streaming video showed Lisa climbing into the Ministry of the Interior's limousine.

I'm in the video! The zealots as well as the terrorists know me.

AS THE FEW REMAINING PROTESTERS ARE BEING FORCIBLY REMOVED BY THE MINISTER'S SECRET POLICE ENFORCERS.

Crap! The minister is in charge of the Egyptian FBI if not worse.

Terrified, she shook, her breathing rapid, as she turned her laptop off. Someone had caught the incident on video. This was up close and personal. They had pictures of her. The phone rang and she jumped as if shot. She stared at the phone for several rings.

"Dr. Hampton?" The quiet voice of Minister Aboud asked. Lisa recognized his voice immediately. "This is Saladin Aboud."

"Hello," she said flatly her trembling becoming worse.

"I will pick you up at 8:00 this evening for dinner."

"Oh," Lisa was startled. She didn't want to have contact with him. In a small part of her mind, she knew this was the Middle East.

Men act differently toward women especially American women. They believe all American women are whores and prostitutes. This will be a problem. He will not appreciate my declining his invitation, summons. He probability expects something more from me than I am willing to give.

"I'm sorry. I will not be able to go to dinner with you this evening" *or any other evening.*

"You refuse?"

"No. I apologize. I'm detained otherwise."

"I see. Good day!"

His tone indicated this was going to be trouble.

* * *

"You are at the village as I requested? Good. I have found the infidel woman. You need to end our problem. She is staying at the Nile Hilton. Take her to the village. When I'm finished with her, you may have her."

"We will apprehend her early tomorrow morning."

"I want her now!"

"We have the latest taping this afternoon. We are setting up now."

"Good. You can add her to the group."

"Then you will not get your time with her."

"Yes. I see. Very well, pick her up tomorrow morning."

"Yes, minister."

CAIRO, EGYPT, AIRPORT CARGO TERMINAL, JUNE 19TH, 4:30 A.M.:

Lisa hefted the kit that she always carried to digs, leaving the remainder of her luggage in the hotel baggage storage. She summoned a cab to go to the airport. At five o'clock, Lisa climbed aboard an old truck weary from its years of labor, taking Dr. Sanders' equipment to Abydos. She carried water and food to make the trip reasonably comfortable. She was not sure whether they would arrive later today or early the next day. Nominally, it was a six hour trip that would get her to Abydos by lunch time, but she didn't know whether the drivers had additional stops. She hoped they would arrive today. She did not wish to spend much time bumping around in the back of the truck. The chief inspector received another hundred pounds for his assistance.

"I have instructed the drivers they will answer to me if any harm comes to you during your journey. If all goes well, you will arrive in Abydos this evening."

"Thank you."

He introduced the drivers to Lisa translating between the members of the group.

"The drivers have instructions where they are to deliver the crates. The truck will be stopped by the military guarding the site. I told the drivers that you are the American professor's assistant and that you are guarding the equipment."

She nodded.

"The military guards will let you through. I told them the American professor will be angry if any of his cargo is damaged."

"That is true and you are kind."

"Safe trip. May Allah go with you most generous lady," he said, touching his robe at his chest.

* * *

The truck headed south out of the city. After two hours, they were free from the modern sprawl and into the Egyptian country. The road was dusty, but the fields to the sides of the road were lush green with agriculture. In the distance, she could see the desert. She lay back against her pack trying to relax for the journey. She soon dozed.

CAIRO, EGYPT, THE NILE HILTON, JUNE 19TH, 6:47 A.M.:

The terrified maid unlocked the American woman's room. The brothers found it empty, but trash indicated that indeed a woman had occupied the space. The desk told them that she had checked out earlier with no forwarding address, but a Dr. Lisa Hampton had been there.

"Where did she go?" they asked the desk clerk who shook his head negatively. He didn't know. This was a dead end.

CAIRO, EGYPT, THE ROAD BETWEEN CAIRO AND ABYDOS, JUNE 19TH, 5:41 P.M.:

In the late afternoon, she passed ancient Abydos where she had visited fourteen years before with her mother. She had explored the Osiris' shrines in the ancient city of Abedju also known as Abtu.

Gosh, has it been that long?

Having slept six hours, she felt refreshed. The verdant fields gave way to rock and sandy plains. Everything took on the yellow, red and tan color of the surrounding hills and desert. The truck turned from the main Nile Road, lurching and bumping along a secondary road. Lisa was sure that the road once had been a natural ravine through the hills carved wider, flatter by modern road builders. She tried to understand why the ancients would have picked this particular place as a burial site. She would have to wait for more information because it did not make sense.

Lisa wondered whether the old vehicle was up to its task for it groaned and squeaked with its exertions. It strained along the poorly maintained road swallowed by the high walled cliffs. Lisa knew the springs were not up to the task for her rump was bruised from the several deep chuckholes that the truck always seemed to find. For twenty minutes, it traveled in the tunnel-like notch. On several occasions the dun colored walls closed in upon them. She worried that the equipment might be smashed by this last leg of its trip. Just when she felt that she could not endure the journey any longer, the truck steered around a large boulder at the right side of the road. Just ahead the road widened looking out over the plains to the Nile. The view appeared to go forever.

It is beautiful.

She understood why the ancients had picked the location. With a sense of forever, they had a view of their daily world beneath their feet.

After clearing the checkpoint, the truck descended into a box canyon to the left of the road containing many Army tents. The military area was surrounded by U-shaped cliffs that rose over a hundred feet above the floor. Deep vertical grooves weathered back into the cliff face gave the appearance of massive columns rising from the base to support the deep blue cloudless sky. A massive rockslide gave a lopsided face between the verticals that ended in a wrecked military truck. The army truck down on its front axle, the left front wheel gone, was jammed into the low rockslide off to the right.

Lisa wondered if a trail led to the top for her eye caught a glint of reflected sunlight from above. She knew that the military must have sentries posted around the semi-circular ridge to protect the people below. A thin dust pall hung over the area churned by the activities of the men working. Lisa worried whether the artifacts were being protected. She knew she was in the right place when the truck slowed turning to the left toward a group of six men whose arm movements indicated a heated discussion. She recognized Sanders.

Suddenly the import of her defiance of authority hit her. She was here against everyone's wishes. Now she had to face Dr. Sanders. Depending on what Sanders did, she could be in deep trouble. She could very well be on her way back to the United States. She felt justified in running from the terrorists *and* Minister Aboud, but she wanted this exploration as well.

ABYDOS, EGYPT, THE FEATURE, JUNE 19TH, 6:51 P.M.:

Bill Sanders spoke slowly and distinctly to the Egyptian interpreter. He read or spoke five languages. Although an Egyptologist, modern Egyptian was not one of them. The Egyptian military commander did not speak English. While he understood that creating a working relationship with the military was essential to the success of his project, he discovered that the company commander was a problem. The captain's lack of cooperation tried Bill's patience. Dr. Tu'hut explained that this man lost his friend, the one killed by the terrorists in the truck accident that led to the site discovery. Sanders endeavored to cut him some slack.

The problems started with simple accommodations. It was late evening. He didn't care whether he slept in a tent or a trailer, but he wanted to know where he could put his things. The captain asked if he had brought a tent or trailer with him. He said no. The captain shrugged.

A message came over the radio to the captain. Sanders wanted to know what was happening. The interpreter said a truck with archaeological equipment for him had arrived from Cairo. He charged after the retreating captain's back to see what had just arrived. A pair of drivers climbed from the truck that pulled into the site's central area. The captain barked a short sentence at them. They babbled at the captain who turned with wrath to Sanders. He didn't understand.

"What's being said?"

"Captain Jagardii wants to know why you did not inform him that your *female* assistant was arriving with your equipment," translated the interpreter.

"What female assistant?"

Lisa climbed from the back bed of the truck. His mouth fell open.

"What are you doing here?"

"Bringing your five crates."

The captain said something. Sanders looked at the interpreter.

"The captain wants to know where you intend to have me stay," said Lisa.

She told the captain that she would sleep under one of the trucks. The interpreter's eyes widened.

"I've brought my own accommodations, captain. I appreciate your concern, but I can handle myself."

Jagardii smiled for Lisa had spoken to him in fluent Egyptian.

"Then you have done better than your boss. He does not know where he is spending the night."

He nodded at Sanders and began to laugh. Lisa looked at Dr. Sanders. He looked very lost. Lisa smiled at him. He took her by the arm, leading her away from the group.

"I need to speak with you."

"OK," Lisa said with trepidation.

"You've just proven that you speak Egyptian. That's a commodity that's going to be important around here."

Lisa nodded.

"But, you've really made me mad. I just don't like your being a loose cannon. From all reports you're a great archaeologist, with problems." Lisa's shoulders tensed, showing her anger. She started to respond. Sanders raised his hand so he wouldn't be interrupted. "I need to know who authorized your being here."

Lisa stared into Sanders' face for several seconds without responding. She drew a deep breath.

"No one sent me."

Sanders looked at her seriously his eyebrows knitting together, his skin turning dark.

"Look, Dr. Hampton...."

"No, Dr. Sanders, you listen. I came here to help you. I want to be included in this exploration. I went to the airport and located your equipment. I determined that it was being shipped to this location. I accompanied it so it would not be damaged or better yet stolen. I want to help."

Dr. Sanders appeared to be digesting her statement.

"I need you back on the truck returning to Cairo."

A frantic Lisa turned to look at the truck that had brought her. Having been unloaded, it was on the road above them lumbering out of camp. When his efforts didn't stop its departure, he went immediately to Jagardii.

"I need Dr. Hampton on the truck that just left," Sanders demanded through the interpreter "You need to recall that truck."

Jagardii didn't seem the least bit interested. The translated battle that followed, was carried on in slow motion through the interpreter. Lisa stayed clear of the argument, but hung close enough to hear what was being said.

"I'm not responsible for getting *your* assistant back to Cairo."

"She's not my assistant."

Jagardii shrugged. The two men were jockeying for authority.

"She's a security issue." Sanders continued. "Do you want a woman on your site?"

"Yes, she's a security risk and no, I don't want her here. Handling her is your problem. Keep her clear of my men. The truck you demanded to return doesn't have a radio that I can call. I tried."

"Damn! Then take one of your trucks and return her."

"I'm in charge of security here. And in matters of security, you won't dictate. I don't have the resources to send her back. You keep *your* people under control."

"Piss!" Sanders turned to Lisa. "You'll be spending the night, but I guess you already know that."

Lisa didn't respond, but wilted under his gaze. Lisa didn't understand the captain's motives, but he refused Sanders' request. She hadn't expected the captain to come down on her side. She was nervous as to her future situation. She didn't want a repeat of the Aboud fiasco. She needed to become invaluable to Sanders.

Quickly!

Chapter 8

**ABYDOS, EGYPT, THE FEATURE,
JUNE 20TH, 5:00 A.M.:**

Lisa awoke at first light. She was snuggled down in her sleeping bag under a truck that Sanders had commandeered from the Egyptian Army as his temporary headquarters. He told her that he was expecting his trailer. She recommended using the truck as his command post until his trailer arrived. She also suggested that the equipment she brought should be guarded. The soldiers loaded it into the back of the military truck. Sanders took the *dangerous* job of sleeping in the truck bed as guard, she thought sarcastically. The fact that Captain Jagardii's company surrounded the truck was overlooked. This turn of events did not make Captain Jagardii happy, but he did yield to common sense.

She could look humorously upon Sanders' plight. She had made several treks into the bush, most recently the Delta. The pain of start up did not bother her. She curled up in her sleeping bag until shelter was available.

After the men's verbal battle the previous evening, Lisa was not surprised at anything that might happen. However, so far all had turned out well for her. Even with Sanders pissed off at her, she succeeded in extending her stay. She didn't know what this day would bring for he told her that he'd be sending her back at the first opportunity. She pointed out that she'd helped him several times.

I must become invaluable.

*　　*　　*

Movement from the truck above her indicated that Sanders was stirring. Lisa wiggled out of the sleeping bag dressed in her field shirt and shorts. He jumped down from the bed of the truck, put his hands straight up in the air, stretched and yawned.

Nice abs.

His bare belly showed beneath his shirt. When he recovered, he pulled his shirt down. His eyes swept over her from head to toe. He looked into her face. His anger with her showed. Lisa was nervous.

"I don't know what to do with you," he growled at her. She knew that he must have spent some of his night thinking about her.

"Are you hungry?" His sudden shift of topic took her off guard. She shook her head, but rummaged in her kit, and tossed him a granola bar. He caught it and smiled for the first time.

"Thanks. You wouldn't have a cup of coffee in there too?"

"I think I smelled that over toward the Egyptian troop area."

"I'm not likely to get any from them."

Holding her thoughts, she asked. "So what's up first, boss?"

Dr. Sander's eyebrow lifted. "I must find my damn trailer. It was supposed to arrive two days ago. If it isn't here today, I'll have to spend time locating it. I'm getting behind. There's a lot of equipment in it. I've a video camera coming, side-looking radar and a robotic rover. Since I have the opportunity, I want to poke a camera down the hole so I have a good idea of what I'm dealing with. I looked down yesterday through a pair of Army field binoculars with a flashlight suspended from a rope."

Lisa nodded following his dialog, but stopped now and looked seriously at him.

"So what did you see?"

"Very darn little. My light source was so poor I couldn't see any detail. Mounds and mounds of gray artifacts. The sheer quantity of the items is overwhelming. Hundreds if not thousands of items."

"Egyptian artifacts?"

"Yes. One never gets an archaeological site like this. It's going to prove amazing."

"Wow!" She had to stay somehow. "You couldn't tell any details?"

"Minimal."

Her eyes roved over the area to familiarize herself with this starting point and its potential problems. She saw the hole covered with a board to keep debris from falling into the chamber below. She appreciated this precaution. She didn't request a light. She would hold her excitement a little longer.

"That rockslide will be a problem," she told him, having formed her conclusion from her cursory survey.

He nodded. "Yes, I'll be moving it so rocks won't tumble into the hole. It's all going to be gone," he waved his arm across the rock slide indicating the entire area.

"You're going to move the whole thing?" she asked startled by the amount of work.

"Yes."

"You were going to request assistance from the military before moving it yourself?"

He nodded. "I didn't think I'd get much help from them. It's a lot of work, but I feel that it's necessary."

"I agree," she said, pleased with his thoroughness, but surprised about his reluctance over enlisting the military's help. Then again....

"Do we have photographs of the surrounding surface area?" she asked.

"I spent yesterday doing that from every direction. I've hundreds by now."

She grunted.

"Is this the truck in which the captain's friend was injured?"

"Killed," he responded seriously. "Yes. Apparently it is lucky the captain isn't dead as well. I understand he ended on top of the rock pile there," he pointed upward.

"His friend's death is probably affecting him."

At that moment, Captain Jagardii walked from behind the truck carrying a cup of coffee in each hand. He handed Sanders one and started drinking the other. Sanders, gritting his teeth, offered the cup to Lisa. The captain shrugged.

"No thanks. I don't drink coffee," Lisa declined. She recognized that Jagardii was giving a peace offering.

"You two are up early this morning." Captain Jagardii opened the discussion. "A truck is coming up the road from the check point. It's pulling a large trailer."

Sanders' humor immediately improved. He slapped his knee with his free hand, slopping the precious fluid from his cup. He gyrated so the liquid wouldn't land on him, dodging and saving the majority of it.

"Great!" he said. "That must be my trailer. Let's go see."

A semi-tractor pulled a modern, oversized trailer into the central area. Lisa was jealous. Her projects never provided creature comforts. She understood Sanders' lack of enthusiasm for camping out.

"Did you fly that over too?" Lisa asked an edge to her voice.

"No, I had it moved from my previous site."

"You certainly have the money to throw around," she said.

Her irritation continued to show. Their eyes met.

"I may have a way of getting you back to Cairo."

Lisa stopped breathing.

Lisa glanced at Captain Jagardii who looked at each of them with apparent amusement. Their flood of English suddenly stopped. Even without understanding English, he seemed to comprehend the edge of their conversation. When his smirk returned, Lisa decided not to bother with a translation. He barked a comment at the driver who had walked to their group. Lisa focused on what they were saying.

"They want to know where to put the trailer."

Sanders stopped. He scanned the area.

"Over there. I want it close, but not in the way. I don't know how the substructure looks."

The captain walked to the other side of the area conversing with the truck driver. He grabbed the driver's sleeve. A heated discussion ensued between them. The truck driver wiped Captain Jagardii's hand off his arm.

"Do you know what that's about?" asked Sanders. "Do I have to wade into another argument?"

The two men separated. Captain Jagardii marched toward the Egyptian military camp. The truck driver climbed into his vehicle maneuvering the trailer into the place Sanders's indicated.

"I couldn't hear," said Lisa, "But I'll find out what's going on."

Lisa jogged after the captain who paused and turned when he heard her approaching. She was not prepared for the explanation. Lisa staggered back to Sanders.

"You look devastated. What happened?"

"The truck I came in was destroyed by terrorists on the way back to Cairo. Burned out by the side of the road. Both drivers are dead."

"What! Shit!"

"I think it may be wiser if I didn't go back in that truck," Lisa suggested. "I'm not just trying to hang on here. I'm afraid."

"Right! You see how foolish it was for you to come," Sanders responded.

Lisa nodded. "Captain Jagardii questioned the driver, but that's all he knew. The driver said he won't be making any more trips from Cairo especially since the captain isn't providing a guard for his return either. That's what they were arguing about."

"Perhaps under these circumstances you can't go back to Cairo."

"I don't think that it would be wise. I prefer not."

Sanders mouth twisted into a grimace.

"Always what you prefer. I must figure out what to do with you. Damn!" he said. "Since you're here, you might as well be useful."

"Why don't I clear the area around the hole so we can drop the camera in? You probably want to work with your trailer."

"You want to work on the rock pile? A great idea if you're up for it."

"You want to clear from the top, right? It's a lot of rock to move."

Sanders nodded. "Right, otherwise the rock will cascade down. OK, Get cracking."

He trudged off toward the trailer, as she raised her hands in resignation.

The two scientists focused on their separate tasks. Sanders spent the morning setting the trailer in the correct position, leveling it. He examined the equipment for damage. Lisa observed that he was excited with his new toys.

Lisa continued to be jealous. She only dreamed of having equipment like that in the field. Granted, in the past not having the equipment forced her to focus on what she selected to send to the laboratory for analysis. She rationalized that she had to use her mind, insight and experience rather than throwing technology at the problem. She felt sometimes keen intellect gave her better results.

Anyway, maybe this project will proceed faster. I'd better hide my jealous feelings from Sanders.

She didn't remove the board, but placed a large stone on it to make sure it didn't move. She cleared the loose rock away from the hole and the axle. She wished the disabled army truck could be moved, but she understood that they didn't know if the ceiling would fall. She cleared everything away from the vehicle.

Starting at the top, she unstacked a few rocks then paused for a short break to enlist the help of Jagardii's soldiers. When she returned to the job, she used the back-breaking manual labor to keep her from thinking about the dead truck drivers with whom she felt a certain amount of kinship.

As the morning wore on, her progress amazed her. The twenty soldiers Jagardii loaned her accomplished wonders. Lisa had the impression this was a disciplinary work detail. A lieutenant watched their work, maintaining discipline. The majority of rocks weren't so large the men couldn't lift them by themselves. There were hundreds of stones, but with the assistance of the soldiers, she cleared the rock pile down to the canyon floor. The soldiers did the heavy lifting. Some of the boulders had to be levered away by prying and rolling them away from the opening. Lisa directed these efforts to be sure nothing moved by accident in the wrong direction. They shoveled the gravel to finish clearing the area.

No artifacts existed at this level so they progressed rapidly. They swept with brooms the smaller rocks. Eventually, she got a vacuum cleaner from Sanders to blow away the particle debris down to the bare stone. By lunch time, she cleared an area ten feet in diameter around the hole and under the truck. Her back ached from the bending and lifting, but she felt good about her accomplishments.

"Lisa, come for lunch."

Interesting.

Sanders had called her by her first name for the first time. He had set chairs and a table covered with sandwich fixings outside the trailer.

"How is it going with clearing around the hole?" he inquired as he began to make a sandwich.

"I cleared a ten foot circle down to solid rock."

"Wow! That's great! I figured it would take me days to clear that area. You're a trooper. How were you able to move the big stuff?"

"I drafted the army," she said as she munched on her food.

"I see. You didn't find any artifacts did you?"

"Oh, you're concerned about that?"

Looking into her eyes, he gave her a steady hard look until he decided that she was kidding and grinned at her. "Right you're the preservationist. I remember."

She nodded. "So how did your work go?"

"I've checked out all of the equipment," he said. "From your work this morning, we can start exploring through the opening in the ceiling this afternoon. The ceiling stability concerns me."

"Yes, me too. Once we move the truck, work inside the opening will be a lot easier," she said.

"I know, but I want to view the ceiling before doing anything. We can tell much more once we get the camera in there."

"How's that?" she asked.

"The probe that the camera is attached to has a laser ranging device mounted in the end. We can tell how far an object is from the camera. We should be able to make good contour maps of the room very soon. We can calculate the thickness of the ceiling."

A disbelieving, Lisa shook her head in wonder.

"You really are high tech," she said as she helped gather the remnants of lunch.

"Sure," he shrugged. "Are you ready? Let's go. By the way, how're your muscles feeling? That's backbreaking work. You really worked hard clearing the rocks. I appreciate your effort and how you coordinated it. Thanks."

"You're welcome. I'm fine. Thanks."

Some recognition. I've got to keep building his dependence on me.

"How I'm working isn't a new concept. As you know," he continued. "Inserting cameras has happened for a long time."

Lisa gave him a knowing nod.

"It's all your other technology that I want to see," she told him.

As simple as his idea might be, several hours passed before they'd made it a reality. It took them both to lift and position the equipment. They assembled a bracket to hold all of the equipment. To a telescoping arm, they added a camera, lights, a laser ranging device, and computer connections.

Idle soldiers gathered, sitting cross-legged a short distance away watching the scientists. They made lurid remarks about Lisa not realizing that she understood what they were saying. She ignored the remarks, but made sure she bent at her knees rather than bending over exposing her backside. Captain Jagardii came to disperse the crowd and check on the scientists. He shook his head at their slow progress.

"Once we get through these preliminary viewings, I want to use GPS readings and stellar observations to get an accurate location for the anchor bracket. For the computer modeling, it is essential we have a good fix on our position as a starting point."

"Computer modeling? Am I hearing GPS, laser distance measurement, HD imaging and 3D modeling?"

"Yes," said Sanders. "Before we crack into the room, I want to know down to the millimeter where every object is. How else are we going to put everything back where we got it?"

"Amazing! I'm very impressed. I respect your scientific thoroughness and concern for the minutiae."

"Thanks," he shrugged, his face reddening with her praise.

Having completed their work at the opening, they headed back to the trailer. Captain Jagardii fell into step with them on the way. Lisa interpreted.

"Are you two done for the day?" Jagardii asked.

Both scientists had learned that Captain Jagardii was responsible for discovering the site.

"No, we're going to see what it looks like inside. Do you want to come along and see?" asked Lisa.

The three entered the trailer. For Lisa and Captain Jagardii, it was for the first time. Lisa's eyes nearly fell from her head.

"Allah preserve us." The captain was obviously impressed as well. The room looked like the bridge of a star-ship.

"You'll never guess where I got the idea for this configuration?"

"I can't imagine," Lisa laughed, shaking her head. "A television show perhaps." Amazed by all the technology, she was careful to avoid the center seat. Facing each of the three seats was a control panel. A one hundred twenty inch flat-panel monitor hung in the center of the opposite wall.

He nodded smiling. "Please take a seat."

Sanders sat in the center seat. His fingers danced over the console. The monitor lit, showing an enlarged, bright area surrounding the opening inches away. The hole was a dark void. Lisa had seen this while standing next to the opening. Within a few seconds, the camera descended into the hole. Everything went black. All of their visual observations to date exceeded the quality of the picture they viewed. Periodically, a brilliant, white light flashed briefly illuminating gray, ghostlike objects ahead of the camera. So confined was the light that nothing appeared in color. In stark contrast to the side, rough rock scrolled past in exaggerated myopic proximity. Columns of numbers rolled on either side of the screen.

"What's the strobe?" Lisa asked.

"The laser ranging device. It works on the light bouncing back from the objects and their interference. I want to see how far I am from what's ahead of the camera," he said. "That's the number decreasing in the upper left corner."

"In meters?" Lisa asked, glancing at Sanders.

Sanders nodded. Lisa decided that the other numbers indicated the position of the camera relative to the bracket. When the camera entered the chamber, everything went black except for the brief flash. The camera descended an additional meter, turned, and faced the ceiling. The circular opening above the camera was a white spot surrounded by black.

"These pictures are not very good," Captain Jagardii said with a disappointed tone.

His voice trailed off as Sanders turned on the powerful camera lights. Lisa did not translate the captain's statment. They observed a bare ceiling carved from the native rock. It was polished to a glistening creamy luster as flat as a modern machine could polish a marble wall. The surfaces of cave-like tombs in the Valley of the Kings were nothing like this.

"Wow!" exclaimed Lisa. "The ceiling is polished stone. This is different from what I've ever seen. I don't see any seams either. Perhaps this is why this site was chosen. For the rock quality."

"Yeah. It takes a certain type of stone to polish like that. Did you notice that the oblique light doesn't cast shadows anywhere across the ceiling except where artifacts touch it," Sanders said. "Ripples in the surface would create shadows."

"That means the polished ceiling must be absolutely flat—that's an amazing feat for the ancient Egyptians working above their heads," she responded. "I'm not pleased with the cracks radiating from the hole."

"Nor am I," he agreed shaking his head negatively. "From the bracket readings, the ceiling is thin."

"Perhaps that's from the Egyptians scraping it flat."

He nodded. His eyes narrowed, looking at her in speculative way.

"The truck has caused considerable damage," he said. "We are lucky the truck isn't sitting on top of the furnishings below."

"I agree. A pile of rubble should be on the floor. May we take a look?"

"I like your conclusions," he told her. Shifting the joystick, Sanders flipped the camera over. The whole room lit for the first time in several millennia.

"Oh, gorgeous!" gasped Lisa. "Unbelievable! Look at all of this!"

Thousands of objects lay scattered, stacked, layer upon layer over the entire room jammed from floor to ceiling. There were chairs, a bed, baskets, and pottery jars containing the everyday needs of the person in the afterlife. A funerary box stood in the center on a raised platform with what might be a canopic cabinet beside it.

"Yes, gorgeous," he said. "Lisa, this is unbelievable. I have seen black and white photographs of Tut's tomb. Everything was piled to the ceiling like this. I never expected to see a find similar to that. And this is in color! Look. We've had our first piece of luck."

A pile of rock debris lay on the floor next to the funerary box. The debris damaged only a small area.

"Oh! How beautiful it all is."

Lisa looked at Captain Jagardii. That was a pretty powerful, emotional statement from the hard, stoic army captain.

"What did he say?"

"He said it's beautiful."

Sanders stared at Captain Jagardii then broke into a grin.

"Yes, it is," he said, nodding his head in agreement.

"I've never seen so many objects in a tomb. How old do you think it is?" an awestruck Captain Jagardii continued in a hushed voice.

"Why are we all whispering?" asked Sanders.

"Because this is so wonderful!" she turned back to Captain Jagardii. "It is hard to tell, but I would say pretty old. Perhaps three thousand years—maybe older. There are no wall paintings. Maybe there weren't any or maybe they faded away with age. Stelae were used before wall plastering allowed the artwork to be preserved over thousands of years. I see hundreds of them. That is a wooden casket with limited metal inlay. Either the person was not wealthy or the tomb is old.

"It appears to belong to a woman whose name is Ḥaāmer," she continued having answered Captain Jagardii's question. She translated her statements to Sanders.

"How do you know her name?" he asked.

"Her serekh is right there," said Lisa as she pointed at the screen. Her finger traced over the hieroglyphs. "Ḥaāmer."

"You may be right. If that is a serekh, than she is very early. She would predate the use of the cartouche in the fourth dynasty as a way for setting off royal names. If that is the case, than she would be closer to four thousand years old, 2000 BCE. Wow, think about that. The Horus falcon is missing so she may not have been royalty. So why would she be buried here in a cave with all the pomp and circumstance? This is strange."

"Unbelievable! We have a woman in a polished stone tomb. A tomb fit for a god, a pharaoh. Four thousand years old. Well we have our first mystery." Lisa responded shaking her head in disbelief. "A fourth dynasty find, this complete, would be incredible. The serekh is probably just a throw back and she must be more recent than four thousand years."

"Yeah, you're probably right. Do you read hieroglyphics like you speak Egyptian?" Bill asked.

Lisa shrugged.

"I'm sure you read hieroglyphics, too," she told Bill.

"I can read hieroglyphics. All Egyptologists do," she said in Egyptian.

Both men contemplated her.

"We can't move the truck. The whole ceiling may cave in. I don't know what we're going to do," Lisa said.

"Why don't you lift the truck with a sky hook and carry it off?" suggested the captain.

Lisa scoffed.

"What did he say?" asked Sanders.

"Now the Egyptians are getting humorous," laughed Lisa. She translated Jagardii's statement.

"No, no," said Sanders. "Let him finish."

Captain Jagardii continued. "A sky hook is a heavy duty helicopter used by the Army to lift heavy equipment like tanks or trucks. I believe you Americans call them a Chinook."

"That's a great idea. Can you request one through the military?" Sanders asked.

"Maybe, I have some friends who owe me a favor."

"Captain, please pursue that," requested Sanders. Nodding, the Egyptian left to make arrangements for the helicopter.

"Dr. Sanders, can we continue to explore the tomb while we are waiting for the truck to be moved?"

Sanders' right eyebrow lifted. "Please call me Bill."

Lisa, nervous about her situation at the site, didn't know if she was comfortable with being informal with him.

"I am not sure that is wise," he continued. "The ceiling looks pretty unstable. When the telescoping arm gets fully extended, it puts a lot of pressure on the bracket. The opening could crumble. Until we remove the truck and stabilize the hole, we run the risk of breaking through. How we're going to stabilize the ceiling is a problem.

"We have a real chicken and egg scenario. We should support the ceiling from below, but we don't want to go in until we've surveyed the room from above."

"If we move the truck," Lisa continued his thought. "The bracket can be stabilized and the telescoping arm won't be a problem."

"I agree, but we need to move the truck without putting more pressure on the ceiling. That's why Captain Jagardii's idea of using a helicopter is such a good one," Sanders rubbed his chin. "I also want to do a complete subterranean radar study of the site. Hopefully, this will show us the original entrance. We may be able to enter the room sooner."

ABYDOS, EGYPT, THE FEATURE, THE CLIFF TOP, JUNE 22ND, 7:55 P.M.:

Lisa found the path up the cliff face that she assumed existed the day before, when she arrived. It started as a fairly gentle incline at the bottom, but halfway up, she was forced to grab rocks as handholds to help her climb. Lisa respected the soldiers who did the trek carrying a heavy pack and a rifle. She wondered if she could navigate the devious path in the dark.

She glanced at the heavens as she climbed. She wanted to avail herself of the night sky. The clear sky turned from a surprising shade of pink, the desert dust at the horizon, to a deep aquamarine at the zenith. The dry air provided no moisture to create the spectacular cloud laden sunsets found at her stateside home or as she had observed in the Delta, but the Egyptian sky provided a solace that had soothed millions over the millennia. As it turned a deep purple, the brilliant canopy of stars appeared.

To guard herself against the expected desert chill, Lisa pulled over her field shirt an old faded olive drab jacket that she purchased in an army surplus store. It made her hot with her exertions, climbing the cliff face path. Across the top, the track ran beside a drop-off that went down a long ways. As she navigated the narrow cliff-top, she was surprised to find another participant. The black wide-shouldered silhouette of a man faced the eastern sky and the Nile valley. She wondered whether she should turn and leave him in peace. So deep was his concentration on the sunset or his own internal thoughts that he jumped when her foot sent a shower of stones down the face of the cliff.

"I didn't hear you approaching," said Captain Jagardii with a chill that was almost as cold as the evening air. His attitude surprised Lisa who thought she'd made progress with the Egyptian.

"I am sorry if I startled you. I did not know you were here until I came close enough to see you against the sky."

Captain Jagardii did not respond, but turned back to the now black sky and the thousands of stars spreading across the celestial dome. Lisa sensed a deep sadness like a dark beast wrapped around the soldier. As she studied him, she detected anger, and perhaps even hatred in his sharp body movements. She shivered as these dark thoughts settled on her mind. Lisa debated whether she should stay, but she had come to absorb the awesome joy of nature not its dark side. She decided she was being silly attributing feelings to her thoughts that might not be there. She moved forward, avoiding contact with him by sitting on a large rock to his left. She focused her attention above her head on the crisp, immobile stars at the zenith. Occasionally, a meteor drew a white streak across the sky. She scanned closer to the horizon, watching the stars shimmer from the heat that rose from the sand.

Several minutes passed with neither speaking. The air became perceptibly cooler. Jagardii shifted his position. Lisa came back from her reverie recalling a similar evening sitting on the Step Pyramid of Djoser at Saqqara with her mother. That had been a pleasant time. Lisa loved spending time with her mother discussing the ancient civilation. Those times seemed to come less frequently now since she had become an adult. She spent much of her time in Egypt by herself or at archeological seminars in the States.

She wondered what kind of man Captain Jagardii was. When dealing with Americans, he acted aloof. When they peeked into Ḥaāmer's tomb, his sense of wonder with things ancient became apparent.

"I sense in you a deep love for your heritage."

He ignored her comment.

"You're a target on that rock," he told her.

She slipped off the boulder, pressing in next to him.

"You speak Egyptian very well. How did you learn our language?" he asked.

"I've lived here since I was sixteen. The only time away was college."

"How was our country then?"

"Quieter, peaceful."

"Yes, we're having bad times. Your government has requested that all U.S. citizens leave the country."

"Really, I had not heard that, but I would still be here. I love your country."

"You'd defy your governments wishes?"

"This exploration is more important than this silly turmoil."

He nodded as if understanding her. "I see. It is not just silly. People are dying. Most recently the Kuwaiti ambassador's wife."

"Oh, I am sorry. I meant no...."

"You have ability with languages. Not every foreign person can speak our language. You speak idiomatically. Many Egyptians speak English. The lieutenant does. I don't."

She sensed almost a bitter pride in his not knowing English. She wondered how that affected his feeling toward Americans. They lapsed back into silence for several minutes. Lisa wished to restart the conversation.

"You have an appreciation for Egyptian antiquities?"

"Ancient Egyptian civilization has greatness and wonder. The clarity of your video pictures amazes me. Does your computer do this for you?"

"No, the video cameras we use have greater resolution than those used for normal television. When we start using the computer to enhance the images you will be even more amazed. The pictures will be in high definition. Dr. Sanders brought software to do what is called virtual reality. The objects will stand out from the rest of the collection. You will have the sensation of touching them even though you are not."

Captain Jagardii simply stared at her as if not comprehending. She explained further.

"We send images from multiple directions so the computer can construct a three-dimensional model. Additionally, the software 'improves' the picture quality."

"I understand what you're saying, Doctor. I'm astounded by your technology. Do you think it possible that I could learn to do these things? Could you teach me?"

"It is Dr. Sanders's technology. We must get his permission first, but I am sure he will appreciate your assistance. We will be terribly short-handed in the near future, but you were telling me about your appreciation for ancient Egypt."

"I contrast what we once were and what we're now. I simply wish we could ascend today into the Second World. I've no illusions that we can compete with a nation as powerful as yours. I'm realistic, but we dip periodically into the depth of the African Third World poverty. Our population grows unbridled. Our economy and government will never catch up. Our president's been educating the masses and now they use their newfound knowledge to speak out. There's no work commensurate with their education. With the threat of this terrorist lowlife, we're on the brink of a national disaster."

Lisa respected his grasp of the political arena. His language was broad. Lisa wondered about his education. She needed to discover more about him later if for no other reason than to satisfy her personal curiosity.

"The terrorists?"

"Yes, Allah, damn them all. The terrorists," cursed Captain Jagardii. "I've pursued them without success for several weeks."

He continued to speak vociferously for several minutes about his failed attempts to stamp them out. He'd exact vengeance on them. Lisa was startled by the depth of his hatred. That could be a security issue at the site.

Was this due to the death of his friend?

"You lost a friend."

Captain Jagardii looked coldly at her. Lisa could see the hard set of his jaw in the pale light. "Yes, I lost my *best* friend."

He began to descend back into his silent depression. Lisa wanted more.

"Tell me about your friend."

"Omar?"

"Yes, Omar."

He paused several seconds, sorting his thoughts. He appeared to be appraising her.

"Omar was a good man. He has...had a wife, Nefri, and five sons. They all live in Cairo. His family and the army were his life. Although not educated, he was shrewd with a great insight into the things around him. I often thought he read my mind. We started out together in the enlisted ranks. We had saved each other's lives more times then I can count. There was a great camaraderie between us. One incident got me promoted to captain. I made him my first sergeant so he could drive for me. He had no great ambition for rank, but seemed content as he was. We would swap old stories or think about what we were trying to do. He approached retirement from the army. I don't think this pleased him, but I cut all of that short."

"You? How did you cause it?"

"I should have captured this vermin that threatens to plunge us into confusion. We scurry like little children from here to there around the southern country, finding nothing, wasting our time. Then that bastard with his damnable weapon murdered my friend. I cut Omar's life short when he was about to resolve the problem."

"You think Omar had the answer?"

"We were just beginning to discuss how fruitless our search was. Omar thought some trickery was at work. He called it the work of Shaitan. I agreed. I know if we had just kept talking, he'd have had an insight. I said we needed to pull off the road for a rest. I stopped the conversation."

"So he did not tell you whom he thought was murdering your countrymen?"

"That is correct."

"Did Omar believe in vengeance upon his enemies?"

Captain Jagardii regarded her. "He was very kind. He didn't believe in allowing the stronger to take advantage of the weak."

"He believed in justice?"

"Yes."

"Omar sounds as if he was a wise and good man." She rose and started across the cliff-top. "Good night, Captain Jagardii."

* * *

He contemplated her retreating silhouette. This American was somehow different. She was smart and a woman, too.

ABYDOS, EGYPT, THE FEATURE, THE NEXT EVENING, JUNE 23RD, 7:15 P.M.:

Bill pulled himself up the switchback path that ascended the ten-story cliff face. The dizzy height made him nervous. His heavy breathing alarmed him. With the workload and trips to Cairo, he had stopped his daily workout routine. Even with his running, this climb was an effort. He wondered how Lisa did it. She never worked out.

She must be in decent condition to make the climb as often as she does. Wasn't she up here yesterday?

He felt at odds with his world. His thoughts drifted over his problems. Bill could not concentrate on the core of his job with all his side issues. Lisa was his biggest concern—Jagardii his second. That left no room for the one thing he should be concerned about, his exploration.

Lisa doesn't take instruction very well. She is capable of running the project, but that's my job. The terrorists hadn't come after her, but how long would that last?

Bill's head broke over the cliff top. He paused gasping for breath.

I need to add this to my workout program. I don't want to die of a heart attack at my age.

Stones clattered away from his feet. He slipped, catching himself with his hands scraping the skin from his palms and bashing his knee.

Damn! I haven't skinned my hands since I was a boy.

He held his injured hand in his other hand squeezing it to subdue the pain. He nodded grudgingly at the army guard, sitting at the juncture of the climbing and upper cliff paths.

"Evening," he said between gasping breaths.

The sentinel's smirk perturbed him.

Yeah, I definitely need to get into shape. My running daily helps, but climbing ten stories takes a different kind of conditioning.

The guard indicated the trail and he nodded, turning to walk across the cliff top.

Wow! That is a drop-off—a hundred feet.

Bill stayed as far away from the edge as he could. Lisa was sitting next to a large boulder at the end of the path. He'd seen her climb the cliff trail earlier this evening. She stared into the distance, east toward the plain and the Nile.

They spoke freely with each other during the day, but that was on a working level. He wanted to 'chat' with her. He wanted to know what motivated her to openly defy Dr. Tu'hut after he had fired her. Or more to the point, he wanted to know her more personally.

What is she about? What drives her?

He knew her slightly by reputation. He'd met her at a symposium which is why he'd recognized her in Cairo. They'd been introduced and shaken hands, but a conflicting session had kept him from attending her presentation.

"Mind if I join you?"

"The sky is free," she added.

He looked at the sky irritated by her smart-assed remark.

"Yeah, it's beautiful. I love the colors."

She nodded sober agreement. He sat on the rock next to her.

"You're a target sitting there," she said flatly. Bill looked at her sourly.

Wow! I guess I invaded her space. She's being a real pain in the rear.

Bill moved off the rock, crowding into the space on the precipice beside her, his legs dangling over the edge. She shuffled sideways, squeezing between the rock and a large outcropping, with obvious, grudging reluctance. Their hips pressed hard against each others. He had seen her climb after the captain on a couple of occasions. Being acutely aware of the Arab phobia for touching, he wondered how they sat together.

"So you like it here?"

"I like to come here for peace and quiet," she remarked dryly.

He decided to let it go. He leaned back against the rock closing his eyes, feeling its warmth and drawing a deep breath. They sat without speaking for several minutes. He felt his tension draining. He was beginning to mellow. He lifted his gaze to sweep over the huge valley lying at his feet, stretching forever into the distance, the silver thread of the Nile crossing the central plain.

Beautiful.

His thoughts circled back to his purpose for climbing here.

How should I approach the question I want to ask her? Maybe I should just say it.

"So why are you so excited about this site?"

"Well, isn't it obvious?" she responded. "How many times in a career does the opportunity come around to explore a pristine and noticeably important find? Once, if then."

"You didn't know that before we began opening the site. Do you just like defying Tu'hut?"

"Of course not."

"Then maybe you don't like following orders—his or mine."

She gasped. Her expression transformed to rage.

"Orders!" she sputtered. "Are you ordering me?"

"If I ordered you to leave, you'd ignore me."

"What!"

"But if Dr. Tu'hut finds out, he'd have Captain Jagardii remove you in an eye blink. Probably from Egypt."

"You're threatening me? You...you," then she caught herself.

He could hear that catch in her voice. He hated when women cried, but then she didn't.

"All I do is help you."

"Your presence has been trouble for me."

"What! Haven't I performed what you needed, what you wanted? Why are you doing this?"

"I'm not doing anything. I'm asking why you're defying everyone."

"I've worked hard."

"Yes, you've worked hard, but you're putting yourself in danger. You're disobeying orders and in general being the person that Dr. Tu'hut warned me about."

"Dammit! Tu'hut's...."

"I don't want to hear about Tu'hut."

"Tu'hut's an asshole...."

"Stop! You are putting my reputation and career in jeopardy," he wasn't going to let her interrupt, his anger rising.

"Is that what you're worrying about? No one knows I'm here."

She stood to leave, swaying in the process. He tried to catch her so she wouldn't tumble over the cliff edge, but she would have none of that. She wrenched her arm free and moved at a determined and unsafe pace along the trail.

That didn't go well. Why's she acting like this? Hell! She's insufferable.

He stood and swayed with vertigo.

Wow!

It took him much longer to descend. The trailer door was locked. He checked.

Damn! I hate having to spend the night in a truck.

ABYDOS, EGYPT, THE FEATURE, THE NEXT MORNING, JUNE 24TH, 6:38 A.M.:

Predictably, Lisa laid awake the remainder of the night staring into the blackness, turning over and over Sanders' cliff top statements. When she struggled out of bed in the morning, she was no closer to a solution than the evening before. She looked in the trailer lavatory mirror.

"I look like hell. No amount of water in my face is going to fix that."

It really galled her to plead for mercy, but that was the best she'd come up with. She decided to find him and get it over with. She dressed and downed two aspirin to quell her pounding headache. Her stomach hurt. She went searching for him, but couldn't find him, eventually, running into Captain Jagardii.

"Your boss went to Cairo," he told her.

Oh, God he's turning me into Dr. Tu'hut.

She felt as if she'd been crushed. She knew this was the end. She was going to have a miserable day with a certain, bad ending.

Chapter 9

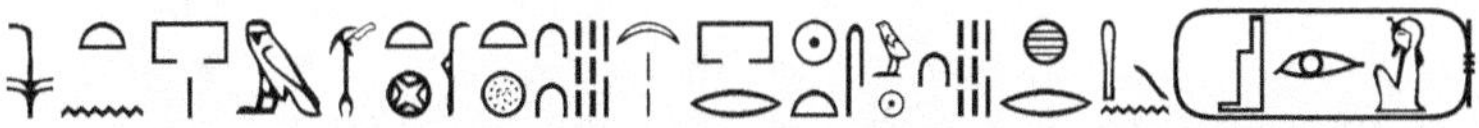

pr-nswt m wꜣst ḥsbt 18 ꜣbd 2 prt sw 28 ḫr ḥm n wsỉr

The House of Pharaoh in Uas,
Year 18, Month 2 of Peret, Day 28 under the Majesty of Ạsạr

The first breath of morning rippled the curtain, revealing pink stains of light on the stones beneath its hem. Īset stirred and rose silently from Pharaoh's bed. Pulling a shift from a stool, she slipped it over her head, the fabric soft against her skin.

She emerged from behind the curtain into his private garden, stretching, taking a deep breath, leaning her elbows on the stone wall.

Cook fires sprang up along the sleepy dawn streets, pushing the last of night's shadows away. Narrow, hazy columns of smoke curled into the sky, bending and drifting overhead to the east. At night, the wind wound down from the ravines and wadis toward the River. During the day, the wind returned, away from the River, through the city, up into the hills toward the great desert, like the land was breathing in and out.

People stirred, preparing for the day. Beyond the city, boats rose and fell as gentle as sighs along the River. Further away to the west, whirlwinds walked along the bluffs, cones of swirling sand light against the purplish sky: restless spirits prowling the empty land, returning to their tombs for the day.

Pharaoh still called her each night from the queen's house. But after a kiss that was no more than a brush of lips across cheek or forehead and a few mumbled words of affection, he lay down at the edge of his bed, facing away, and did not move the rest of the night.

Sometimes he guessed that she was crying, maybe a sound escaping from trembling lips or the shaking of a sob. He sought for and patted her hip in the darkness.

Ḥaāmer's cat, which Īset thought had run away, found its way into the room each night and curled up at his feet. He didn't even bother to push it away.

In three more days she and Pharaoh would bury their first daughter in a tomb in Abtu.

She could not tell Ạsạr why the gods were silent about Ḥaāmer. She could not console him as to why they had not healed her. *I have lost a daughter and a husband.*

He could not admit that he was a vessel used by the gods and not a god himself. He did not possess the power to heal his daughter. He could only draw into himself and assume he had failed and was somehow unworthy.

"I don't believe in you," Īset said to the gods. "I don't believe in your power or your goodness. We are born, we struggle, we die. Where are your hands in this? You demand our worship and give us nothing in return."

Beyond the garden, along a twisted lane that wandered toward the River, a man emerged from a house, stretched and yawned.

The newer houses in Uas were like caves, a straight corridor running from the opening in front to the opening in back, allowing free passage to the freshening breezes. Rooms branched from the corridor; if needed, curtained for privacy. Bedrooms, a store room, an open area at the back with a stone or mud brick oven for cooking.

He was probably one of the laborers building the temples and palaces of Uas. It showed in the stretches he performed: legs, back, arms, in his dark, Aten-stained skin, in his muscular, compact frame, and in his stooped bearing.

He took a rod and stirred the fire, looking for warmth among the ashes. He reached for kindling, tore lengths of dried reeds and arranged them over the glow. Smoke appeared, then flame. He built the embers into a steady cook fire.

A woman came out of the house carrying a bowl of grain. She ground it roughly on a flat rock, returned it to the bowl, and added water from a small cistern. Sitting near the fire, she mixed the grain and water with spices and oil from a decorated jar and poured the mixture into a series of small bread pots.

Īset watched them as she might watch people in the market place or the Hall of Balance. They were unaware of her presence as this was not a public place. Īset could only look down upon their lives by virtue of the height of Pharaoh's garden on a hill above the other houses of Uas.

The man leaned two long sapling poles against the side of the house and bound three cross-members, one in the middle and one at each end, with lengths of animal sinew. His hands moved quickly and precisely between the poles, almost like a servant sewing. He stopped when the woman called him to set the pots into the coals at the edge of the fire to bake.

He said something and she pointed. He went back into the house and returned with squares of linen and animal hide. He strung strips of leather and sinew through holes and secured the linen and hide in the empty spaces between the cross-members. A litter, a simple sled one could pull or two could carry to move objects too heavy or bulky for one to carry alone.

He picked up a charred piece of animal hide and used it to turn the bread pots in the fire. Then he went to sit beside the woman on a bench. She peeled and sliced some fruit that she shared with him. He slipped an arm about her waist in a comfortable, familiar way, their heads lowered and resting together for a moment.

At a nudge, he pulled the bread pots from the fire where they could cool. She went into the house and returned with a box that he secured to the litter with cords.

She put fruit in the box, and something else, wrapped in leaves. She went to the cistern and dipped a jar, stoppered the mouth and added it to the box. She tried one arrangement, then another, placing items within, arranging them, removing them again. Īset watched the frustration grow in her repeated actions, in her rigid posture. She finally snatched everything from the box and hurled it to the ground, collapsed in the middle of it all, and buried her head in her hands.

He left the litter and came to her, stroking her hair, whispering, lifting her gently back to her feet. He gathered the items one by one, brushed them off, refilled the pitcher at the cistern and replaced the stopper. He handed each item to her and she put them back into the box.

He placed a hand close to a bread pot, checking for warmth. Finally he touched one. Assured they were cool, he lifted each one and gave it to her. She filled the last empty corner in the box.

Then they were done. He stood near the fire, she next to the litter. They seemed suddenly awkward, hesitant, uncertain. Neither could look at the other. Neither appeared to speak. She finally shuffled into the house, head down, and returned several heartbeats later laboring under the weight of a large wrapped bundle painted with the image of a child.

Īset jammed the side of her hand into her mouth and bit down until she tasted blood to keep from screaming. Their daughter was dead. They were preparing for her funeral.

Tears filled her eyes. By the time she wiped them away, the couple had already passed through a gate and started up the street. He pulled the litter, she walked beside him. Īset heard the dry, sad sound of the poles dragging across the stones as they walked the uncluttered street.

Īset ran back to Pharaoh's bedroom and slipped quietly behind the curtain. She found her sandals and a robe she could use as a cloak. She looked at Pharaoh before she left. He was a rigid shadow at the far edge of the bed, breathing evenly. The cat raised its head and peered up with uncaring eyes.

She stopped in the garden again to see the couple reach the end of the street and turn the corner. She dashed to the steps and down. A guard stiffened and turned at the sound of her. "Lady?"

"If Pharaoh asks, I've gone out. I will be back," Īset called over her shoulder.

She counted streets, turned and followed. Few people were out this early, fewer still would recognize her in a shift and a cloak. She turned toward the hills.

The streets grew rougher and less straight, the houses further apart. The way was now no more than a trail when she saw the twin lines of the poles cutting through the layers of sandal and animal footprints. Her heart beat faster, her chest ached. She had not walked such a distance in a long time.

Īset struggled up the ravine, following the two scratches left by the litter. Her legs hurt, her feet hurt; dust clung to her arms, her face, her throat. Sun and sand brought tears to her eyes. She wanted to stop, but the scrape and squeak of wood over sand and stone from up ahead drew her on.

No words passed between the parents, no words of comfort or sorrow. Īset needed to know what they felt.

The ground leveled as Īset neared the top, her breathing slowed. She paused to wipe the sweat and tears from her eyes. The sound of the litter ended suddenly, leaving only the moan of the River breeze winding among the hills and wadis.

A few more steps around a worn red rock the size of a hippopotamus and she saw them: man, woman, the small bundle on the litter, and her sister.

"What are you doing here?" Neb-t·ḥe-t asked, startled.

"I am here for the child," Īset said, looking down at the wrapped body.

"Amet," Neb-t·ḥe-t said.

"I saw you this morning from my garden," Īset said to the parents. "I did not realize the child was dead until you brought her to the litter. I had to follow."

"Then join us," Neb-t·ḥe-t said and introduced them.

"Like the queen," the woman said when she heard Īset's name.

"Yes, like the queen." Īset nodded, feeling more like a grieving mother than the wife of a god.

Two young priests sat on a boulder at the other side of the rise, linens thrown over their heads to shield them from the Aten. The baskets and tools they had used to prepare the grave lay strewn about their feet. They passed a pitcher back and forth and spoke in whispers, glancing expectantly at Neb-t·ḥe-t, who, for a moment, studied the depression they had dug, then nodded. They gathered their things in respectful silence and left.

Queen, priestess, man, and wife gathered in a circle around the grave: a circular depression as wide as a man was tall, knee deep, smoothed and lined with rocks. The young priests had left two additional piles of rocks to secure the grave, each rock the size that fits in two hands.

The sun reached its highest point, shrinking their shadows beneath them, reddening their skin. Neb-t·ḥe-t recited the stories, the path through that other land from death back to life.

The man lifted the small wrapped body from the litter and lowered it into the stone-lined depression. The woman laid flowers beside her daughter, sprinkled spices and oil across the wrappings.

Neb-t·ḥe-t knelt and wrote symbols in the loose dirt with her finger. But not in the familiar pattern of words. Something else. She muttered as she wrote, drawing each with care, wiping away with her palm and redrawing any that was not a perfect shape.

They bubbled as if they were boiling. Caught between the red land and the yellow sun, they whispered and glowed orange like the coals of a fire.

She leaned back when she was done, stretching her neck and shoulders, looking away over the River to the West. She reached into a linen sack at her feet and removed a small object wrapped in soft antelope hide. A golden Ȧpnu, resting, paws stretched out before him, obsidian eyes looking into the distance. Neb-t·ḥe-t placed it in the crook formed by the small bent body.

"That statue is more wealth than this family has ever known." Īset said. "We should—"

"Hush," Neb-t·ḥe-t said, rising to stand beside her. "Let the gods teach you."

Īset closed her mouth, glanced at Ȧpnu, and gasped.

Ȧpnu was no longer a golden figure, he was a living god. The short brown fur along his sides gleamed in the midday sun, rising and falling with each breath. The tip of his rough pink tongue peeked out from his jaws. He panted with a soft rush of breath, in and out, resting on the warm rocks. His slender tail, stretching straight behind him, twitched. Large, pointed ears turned from side to side, listening to the wind, the tears and sighs from the child's parents, and other things, things Īset could not hear.

He turned to look at Īset. His eyes were deep and dark like pools of black oil. Īset saw her face reflected in them and felt smaller, more frightened, alone and unworthy than she thought possible. She stepped back and felt Neb-t·ḥe-t's arm at her back to steady her.

"Don't be frightened. Ȧpnu finds her worthy," Neb-t·ḥe-t said. "He will wait with her now until the gods return to awaken her."

Neb-t·ḥe-t reached and placed the first stone on the grave. Man and wife, roused from their sorrow, joined Neb-t·ḥe-t in covering their daughter. Lonely teardrops stained several of the stones she set. The Aten drew them upward; the wind carried them away.

Īset hesitated, looking down to see the shadow of Ȧpnu and his outline dispersing like smoke above a fire or morning fog from off the River. Within, Ȧpnu was just a golden figurine once more.

Solemn, careful, they arranged the rocks over the grave. The child, her dolls and shell necklaces, the golden Ȧpnu all lost from view.

The piles beside the grave diminished, the mound over it grew. When all the rocks had been moved from one to another, father and mother together setting the last one in place, Neb-t·ḥe-t, wiping the sweat from her cheeks and forehead, said: "The sand will do the rest, filling in the cracks. She will sleep. Ȧpnu will protect her."

The parents served a traditional meal, a simple meal: water, coarse bread, and a few small, smoked fish. They poured the tepid water into bowls, arranged bread and fish on trays, serving Īset and Neb-t·ḥe-t. Īset stared at the meal she watched them prepare so long ago this very morning. The man pushed poles into the sand, steadied them with rocks, and secured the litter atop them. The four clustered together in its shadow and ate.

"I work with stones, building the monuments and temples of Uas. I brought fruit and water as a boy to the men who built the Hall of Balance. I have always been good with rope, with lever and wedge—moving the rock, positioning it, lowering it into place." He had a round, honest face, broad, calloused hands, strong shoulders and arms. His hair was becoming gray, but he kept it cut short and the gray could easily be mistaken for dust. Lines deepened his face.

His wife was small, quiet. Her hair was also gray. She had a smaller, oval face that must have been pretty before too many lean years wore away at her spirit. She was polite, but would look neither Neb-t·ḥe-t or Īset in the eye, content to be a servant, a lesser being in their presence.

"We tried for so many years. I thought I was barren. We had resigned ourselves to being childless before she was born. She was our first and only," the woman said. "Our precious Amet. But she got sick and the charms we could afford didn't help. Nothing could help."

She cried and her husband wrapped strong arms about her and drew her close. The wind keened among the rocks. The woman wept against her husband's shoulder.

"I stand in her room and wait for her. But she never returns," Īset said.

"You also lost a daughter?"

Īset nodded. "It is now just an empty, quiet place. I never realized how much she filled it just by standing in its midst, smiling, sighing. I cannot go in there any more."

The woman nodded, looking up at last, her eyes red. "I washed her clothes and put them where she could find them if she needed them. I made her favorite food last night and set a place for her without thinking," the mother said. "I hear noises and see shadows. I turn, thinking it might be her. Just the wind or the shadow of a bird."

"The wind and the birds are her voice now. That is how she tells you she's well and whole," Neb-t·ḥe-t said. "She is with the gods, and also within you, in your thoughts and in the love you still have for her. She will always be young and precious and perfect."

They told stories throughout the afternoon heat while the breeze from the River played with their hair and clothing.

"Her smile was candlelight," her mother said. "It warmed me and made the room brighter. She laughed like a little bird. I will miss that smile, that laughter."

Her father rubbed his large, calloused hand together, uncertain what to do with them. "I would take her out at night to see the Aih," he said, his voice small and soft for such a large man. "Her eyes would glow with its light, as if the spirit of the goddess infused her. She loved watching the Aih in its many faces."

Īset looked up at last and said to the woman: "My daughter loved her father, and he loved the mud. He wanted to travel the River as a youth but other duties drew him and he never got that life. But he has worked hard to help the farmers, with different magics to capture and hold more of the River during the growing season. She always pleaded to go with him, to see some new magic demonstrated, before she became sick and weak. They would return laughing, hand in hand, covered in dirt and mud, looking like two black-skinned Cushites. They couldn't just see, they had to be a part of it, to get in the water and the mud together and splash it all over each other. It was something I never understood and never wanted to be a part of, but now miss for the joy it gave them."

Then there was silence, except for the creak of the litter and its makeshift poles tugged at by the breeze. There were no more stories to tell.

Neb-t·ḥe-t took the woman's hand. "In the Temple of Ptah I keep a record I call the book of remembering those who sleep. I write about those who do not have impressive tombs to announce them into the afterlife. I read from it to the gods each night. I will add Amet's stories to that book."

"I am honored," she replied. Then looking up she added: "And by the gift of your presence, Īset, wife of Ạsạr."

Īset said nothing for a moment. She closed her eyes and opened them again slowly, as if the truth were painful. She drew a single soft breath. "Today I am a mother who has also lost a daughter."

"You have provided comfort to a family of no importance," the mason said.

"I've been told we are all important to someone who loves us. The gods love you. So does your daughter," Neb-t·ḥe-t said.

The mason nodded and stood, brushing the dirt from his skirt. It was time to go. He lowered the litter from the four poles and with a grunt pulled each of the poles from the ground, bound them together, and fastened them to the litter. He squatted to pick up the handles and started towards the edge and over the rise, his wife beside him.

"You will have two more children, a boy and a girl, to become your joy in the years ahead," Neb-t·ḥe-t called.

The couple stopped. The woman turned back and shook her head, looking down. "I am too old to have any more children. And too sad."

"You already carry one," Neb-t·ḥe-t said. She paused and looked past the couple, further west. "The girl, though it is a few days yet before you will know. When you are sure, trust Ptah and believe what he tells you."

She looked up at her husband, then to Neb-t·ḥe-t. "Let it be so."

The mason turned and gave Neb-t·ḥe-t a puzzled nod. Then the couple resumed their trek down the hill, back to Uas, the sound of the litter scraping the rock and dirt, growing fainter until it was gone.

Īset confronted her sister. "That figurine came to life in the child's arms. It looked at me."

"Yes," Neb-t·ḥe-t replied.

"They didn't see it," Īset shook her head, astounded that Neb-t·ḥe-t was not astounded. "You weren't just praying. You were talking to the gods and they were answering you. Did they tell you she was with child?"

"Yes."

Īset waited. Surely Neb-t·ḥe-t was joking and would admit it soon. The silence stretched on. Finally, Īset knew she must ask. "Is Ḥaāmer with them?"

Neb-t·ḥe-t looked away a moment, to the edge of the land, listening. Īset looked also, straining to hear the voices of the gods. Whispers, wind over and around rock and sand. A hawk wheeling over a dusty field.

"She is," Neb-t·ḥe-t said.

"Is she happy? Will I see her again?"

Neb-t·ḥe-t continued to look west, her face relaxed and serene. The Aten stained her cheeks and forehead, illuminating her dark, deep eyes, fine grains of dust at the tips of her eyelashes. "You should live your own life now and think of those you have here."

"Is that their words or yours?" Īset asked.

"Both. You have much ahead of you. Some of it is wonderful, some of it terrible. They want you to be ready."

"Teach me to talk to them."

"I can only teach you to listen. The gods choose who they speak to."

"I am the wife of Pharaoh."

Neb-t·ḥe-t turned to regard Īset but her gaze was still far away, unfocused. "I have known priests and priestesses who have spent their whole lives in worship and prayer without ever hearing a god's voice. I've witnessed farmers with no religious notions at all suddenly called from the midst of a field."

"They called you?"

Neb-t·ḥe-t nodded. "Soon after I left Set's house for the temple."

"Why?"

Neb-t·ḥe-t smiled so sadly that Īset felt tears form in the corners of her eyes. It was the same smile that would cross Ḥaāmer's lips each time Īset reassured her she would be well again in just a few more days.

"I am your little sister and will always be the shadow you cast. I must trail you and be unseen until you are illuminated. The gods wish it to be so."

Īset touched her sister's cheek, tracing its curve, pulling a strand of hair from her forehead, trying to remember the last time she had touched Neb-t·ḥe-t, brushed her hair, laughed with her, shared a secret. Not since they were children.

"I have not been a good sister to you," Īset said.

"We have each taken the path the gods chose for us."

"Yours has been the harder way."

"That will change," Neb-t·ḥe-t whispered.

The two sisters embraced on the plateau beside the grave where the child slept and Ȧpnu watched. The Aten descended, changing from yellow to orange. Each woman cried for the things she had been given, Ḥaāmer's death and Set's cruelty and unfaithfulness, for wishes never granted, for the bonds the gods had forged between them, and in fear of days not yet born.

Wind stirred their skirts, raising and pushing grains of sand. It dried their tears, the Aten warmed them, the lapis sky, like fresh, pure water surrounded and washed them clean.

"Did you find what you were seeking here?" Neb-t·ḥe-t asked at last.

"I don't know. Perhaps. I've never much believed in the gods or their interest and good will toward us. But I saw something here today that I cannot dismiss as too much sun and too little water or as a trick of wind and sand. I want to believe. I want to bury Ḥaāmer with the certainty that she is safe in their care. But I don't know how to stop doubting."

"I'm not sure any of us does," Neb-t·ḥe-t said.

"Will Ȧpnu be there to watch over her?"

"Ȧpnu and many others. A whole host will watch over Ḥaāmer as she sleeps."

Īset sighed, wiped her eyes, and looked at the mound of rocks. "Maybe that will be enough for me. Will they speak to Pharaoh? Heal his heart?"

"Only if he will let them."

Neb-t·ḥe-t lifted her linen sack. Īset took her hand and they started down, following the trail in the sand left by the litter.

Īset looked back one last time to see the words her sister had carefully traced in the sand. They persisted with a faint orange glow, but were no longer in sand. The sand had turned to stone.

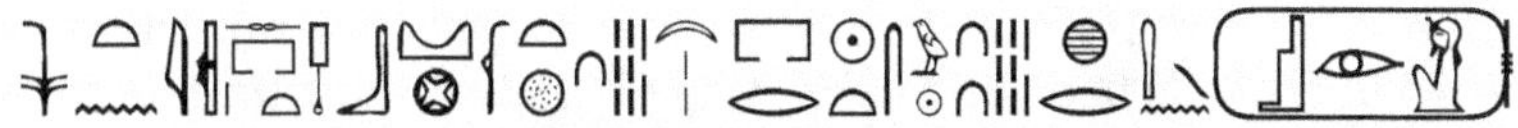

ỉs-nwšt m ꜣbḏw ḥsbt 18 ꜣbd 2 prt sw 28 ḫr ḥm n wsỉr

The Royal Tomb in Abtu,
Year 18, Month 2 of Peret, Day 28 under the Majesty of Ȧsạr

Pharaoh settled into aloof silence again as if it were a familiar robe or a comfortable pair of sandals. He sat in the shade of a linen canopy, lost in the majesty of his gold and ivory throne, a quiet, sad-faced god.

"This is wrong," Īset said.

He struggled not to look as broken and tearful as she. He reached a hand out to her that did not span the gulf between them. She lifted her hand to meet his, to mesh her fingers with his, to bridge their two somber hearts.

"I will say good-bye today," she said, echoing her sister's words, "then I will miss her in the silence she leaves behind."

"As will I," Pharaoh added.

The River held steady, its current bearing the funeral boat with whispers and sighs north from Uas to the royal tomb near Abtu. A sand storm during the night stained the sky the color of tears against cold, dead skin. The last breath of that storm swept down from the western cliffs with an occasional faraway moan. Water splashed against the hull, the boat lifted and fell in creaks and groans. The only other sounds were footsteps, the boatmen moving in respectful silence about the deck.

A servant approached, bowed, and held out a bowl of fresh fruit, but neither Pharaoh nor his wife ate.

The River held very little traffic. No public outpouring, Pharaoh had asked. No spectacle. No legions of mourners, wailing like wounded animals, spread out behind the procession. No procession at all. Just members of the royal family, their servants, and enough priests to see all accomplished properly.

He would not explain his decisions to the perplexed priests who were planning a majestic funeral event, but Īset knew why. He could not rid himself of a sense of failure and had no wish to parade it before the people. Ḥaāmer's death—her tragic. meaningless death—was a shadow that hung over him and which he could not disperse. It was somehow his failing and he had no response but to retreat further into himself, away from those who might console him, but who might also wonder why he hadn't saved her.

Pharaoh was wrong about his people and they came anyway, their boats stretched out behind the formal procession like ducklings following their mother. Many were small boats, with just one or two. Others, bigger, carried families and friends. They did not come to look upon a failure, but to mourn with him, console him, worship with him. They were his people and they would not abandon him.

Īset closed her eyes for just a moment in the heat of the day, to dream, to remember, to flee this moment and this boat and this funeral. The whispering wind in the sails became a voice, a laugh, the soothing sound of water a balm. Then the boat came to a halt at the dock in Abtu and a servant came to awaken her and Pharaoh, their hands still clasped.

* * *

She blinked and took a drink of water. In the western distance the cliffs of Abtu shimmered in the early heat. Off to the right, the mud brick houses of the workers and artisans stood like bleached bones protruding from the rocky soil. The workers had toiled since Ḥaāmer's death to prepare the burial chamber and erect a funerary temple.

The royal crypt was a natural cave whose mouth was sculpted with figures of the gods. On the right side Ra, an imposing man with the head of an orb. He wore a kilt about his waist, and a pectoral collar about his shoulders, each link delicately carved from the cliff side. The pectoral collar was also painted: the yellow of gold, the blue of lapis lazuli, the black of obsidian. In his left hand he carried an ankh. For a crown he wore the sun with a serpent, the uraeus, wrapped about it in a sign of power and protection. His right hand extended over the mouth of the cave where it held the hand of Nut, the goddess of the sky.

Her other hand held an ankh for health and good fortune. A vase holding the moon rested upon her head. Stars decorated her white dress. Bracelets encircled her arms and legs, one white, one red, one yellow, and one unpainted, revealing the natural yellow-brown of the native rock. The bracelets represented the four stars that had no fixed place in the sky, but wandered about as the spirit of Nut willed.

Other gods accompanied them across the cliff face. Behind Nut, Bast with her feline face and Anpu with his jackal's head. Mut stood behind Anpu, but instead of her normal vulture's head, she was portrayed as a woman, with large, almond eyes and a placid smile.

Behind Ra, Ptah with his compassionate gaze, and long whiskers curling from the tip of his chin. Beside Ptah was Hapi, a tilted vase in her arm spilling water—and life—into the Nile.

Hieroglyphics accompanied each god. They offered protection for the cha while it rested inside the tomb, and guidance for the chu, ba, and ka as they explored the mysteries of Amennt.

Set strode in great, pompous steps to the porch at the front of the funerary temple, raised his hands to heaven, and looked out on the people.

"I call upon the gods of sky and water and earth, to attend this gathering today and hear us. We honor you, mighty Ptah, as we celebrate the eternal circle of life: birth, growth, death, and rebirth. You show us your cycle through Hapi, goddess of the Nile, each year destroying and replenishing our fields. You show us in the daily trek of Ra, who is born anew each morning, grows in strength and brightness as he travels to midday, and diminishes and is extinguished as he returns to earth. You show us in the stars that flow from Nut as she strides across the sky, turning and returning each year to their appointed positions.

"Today we confirm the cycle once more as we commend the cha of the princess Ḥaāmer to your care for rebirth in Amennt."

The four servants who had served Ḥaāmer, Steppu, Tchefeṭ-t, Ạaātchṭạ-t, and Rāmạtet, stood apart from the priests and royal family, terrified and trembling, knowing what came next.

"Ḥaāmer's loyal servants will now come forward and take the wine of passage to join and serve their mistress in Amennt," Set said.

Īset stood. "No."

Set stopped speaking, his eyes wide with surprise. He looked at Pharaoh. "I don't understand," he said. "It is a tradition for royal servants to accompany the master or mistress into Amennt. Is this your command?"

Ạsạr returned from his silent distance. He glanced at the four handmaids, silent and alone caught between the line of priests and crowd of people. He stood beside Īset and took her hand, a gesture that made her words his own. "There will be no more deaths today."

The priests, standing with their bowls of poisoned wine, let out an audible gasp.

Pharaoh Ạsạr walked to the funerary temple and ascended the steps. Facing his disquieted audience, he said: "Ptah does not want us to die for him, he wants us to live. We are neither beasts or sacrifices. We are his children; it is time we live as such."

Set edged away, back and off to the side of the temple porch where he could slowly fade from view into the mist and incense that drifted from inside.

Īset looked to Ṭeḥuti to see his reaction. Alone among his fellow priests, Ṭeḥuti sat cross-legged on the sand, his writing stick already in motion, a piece of linen rolled out across his palette as he captured Pharaoh's words.

Pharaoh continued: "The sculptor brings the face of a god from a rock by shaping the rock. He hammers, he chisels, he grinds away; he polishes until the image that was in his thoughts has come forth.

"Does the rock feel pain? No rock has ever spoken. But the sculptor's work transforms the rock into something wonderful, something unique for the enjoyment of men and gods alike—something that could only exist through the sacrifice of the rock."

Wind whispered across the sand, stirring the dust, disturbing the ghostly shimmering of distant hills. Around the mortuary temple, not a soul stirred. Every face watched Pharaoh. *Our god is speaking.*

"The master of wood sacrifices the tree. He removes the bark, he splits the trunk and branches. He cuts until he reaches the heart. From it he crafts a chair fit for a Pharaoh," said Ạsạr, pointing to his own chair, finely carved wood generously inlaid with gold, lapis lazuli, ivory, and precious stones, "or a table or a boat."

Pharaoh brought his hand to his chest, holding it gently over his heart. "The tree is dead but the wood lives on as a table, a chair, a boat; it provides service and comfort and safe passage for generations.

"Egypt is Ptah's workshop. We are his stones and his trees.

"Why do we suffer? Why are so many lives cut short? I cannot say. I cannot say why a sculptor chips away to bring a small face from a large stone then so gently coaxes a large face from a small stone. I cannot say why one piece of wood requires so little curing and carving while another needs so much. Only the craftsman knows.

"Ptah is our craftsman. The changes he makes in our lives—good and bad—are the touch of his hammers and chisels. This is how Ptah makes something beautiful and eternal from us for his delight.

"I *know* it hurts. I do not diminish that. Where once I had my daughter Ḥaāmer I now have nothing. What Ptah has always seen within Ḥaāmer he has brought forth. She sleeps, and when she wakes she will be with him and she will be perfect."

Pharaoh looked again at the handmaids. "We must not send these four with Ḥaāmer to Ptah. The rock does not say to the sculptor: *I am complete.* The tree does not tell the master of wood: *put me on the River, I am a boat.*

"Ptah decides," Ạsạr emphasized. "*Not* me, *not* the priests, not tradition. Ptah chooses the ones he perfects and does so by his own counsel. One day he will draw each of us back to him."

A sigh of wind punctuated his words. As suddenly as the power had come it departed again. Ạsạr surveyed his audience with a sudden shyness. He stepped down from the temple porch and quietly resumed his throne beside Īset.

A visible ripple passed through the crowd, beginning in those closest to the mortuary temple and traveling outward to the edges of the gathered mourners. Īset leaned toward Ạsạr and spoke softly: "Sometimes you frighten me."

Ạsạr raised an eyebrow in question as he turned to regard her.

"In our private time together you are just a man. You laugh, kiss, and talk just like any man. And then, when I am comfortable with you as a man, Ptah takes you for a moment and I feel I should throw myself at your feet and worship you. I am frightened to be on such intimate terms with Ptah."

His face softened. "Ptah is in Amennt with Ḥaāmer. I am here with you. You have nothing to fear from either of us. We both love you very much."

*   *   *

Shepses pushed his way forward to stand beside Set on the steps of the funerary temple and whispered angrily: "What is he going on about? Can't you stop him?"

Set shrugged. "Why?"

"Because he's going to have this rabble believing that Ptah actually *cares* for them. Next he'll be telling them that *Ptah* chooses who goes to Amennt, and that generous donations to the temple make no difference."

"Not for long," Set said with a smile. "Soon he will have other worries."

*   *   *

One by one, the priests holding the pots of poisoned wine turned them over and drained their contents into the dust. The four handmaids embraced, Tchefeṭ-t using the gauzy linen of her skirt to wipe away the tears and smeared kohl from the eyes of little Rāmạtet.

Neb-t·ḥe-t beckoned and an ox rambled forward hauling a dusty cart that had traveled with them from the River. Inside were four rough wooden boxes, each containing a tiny, lifelike figure of one of the maidservants.

Neb-t·ḥe-t removed the ushabtuis from their boxes, cradling each like a child, passing each to a maidservant, oldest to youngest.

"Speak to them," she said. "Tell them who they are and what they must do on your behalf. They will go with Ḥaāmer into Amennt. You will stay here and live out your lives serving Īset. The little servants will quicken and serve Ḥaāmer. Direct them well."

Then she prayed, looking up into the hills, speaking as if the gods stood nearby:

Oh ushabtui, given this day,
If Ḥaāmer be summoned,
If she be required to do any work in Amennt,
If she be given burdens for which you are suited,
Whether putting down or taking up,
Or bearing from one place to another,
'Here am I,' you shall say.

Midday passed, the Aten curled towards the western hills. The priests finished speaking their chants and prayers. Neb-t·ḥe-t took the moment when the meal was prepared and distributed to descend to the cool stillness of the tomb and compose one final prayer for Ḥaāmer.

Retrieving a pot of paint and a reed from the storeroom, she interrupted Set with a temple priestess. The young woman stood quickly, her face flushed in the lamplight. She pulled the strap of her dress over her shoulder and tugged her skirt back into place.

Set rose more slowly, admiring the lithe form. He wiped his mouth with the palm of his hand and seeing Neb-t·ḥe-t, smiled.

"High priest," Neb-t·ḥe-t said, instead of *husband.*

"Nebbe," he said. A name she detested.

The priestess, yearning still in her eyes, traced her fingers tenderly along Set's forearm before slipping away.

"Is she warming your bed now?"

"I need someone to dispel the chill you left behind," Set said.

"None of those who preceded her could do that?"

Set shrugged. "Fires burn low and grow cold. One must kindle them afresh."

He swept an arm in an arc about the chamber. "Is this how you occupy yourself? You have a gift for working with the dead. I had no idea."

Neb-t·ḥe-t's eyes sparkled a moment with a biting reply she did not voice. Instead, she said: "Did you find what you were looking for in the plans for the royal tomb?"

Set frowned. "Plans?"

"The plans you sent a soldier to collect from me."

"Oh, those plans," Set smiled. "A mere formality. My servant was overzealous in retrieving them. I didn't want them lost."

"Don't loot Pharaoh's tomb," Neb-t·ḥe-t said. "Leave Ḥaāmer to her rest."

Set lunged and raised a hand to strike her but held it there, trembling. "How dare you make such an accusation!"

Neb-t·ḥe-t did not shy from the threat, instead coming close enough to smell the expensive scented ointment he used and the stench beneath it. "At first I thought they were copies. Then I marked several as I placed them into the tombs. They returned to the storeroom a month later and were offered to other grieving families."

Set hit her with his fist to the side of her face. Her ear popped, her vision narrowed and filled with stars. A sting bloomed along her cheek and jaw. She staggered against the wall, reaching out to steady herself.

"You worthless, barren crone."

Her sight returned, she regained her bearing, shoulders back, head high, and faced him again. "Beware, high priest. The gods will tire of your excesses one day."

Set sneered. "You still hear voices."

Neb-t·ḥe-t reached up and touched the tender, swelling cheek. She looked at a statue, a shadow against the dark, behind Set. "After all you have done and will do, I pity you, Set. The evil will turn on you."

Set waved her words away, like a bad smell in the air. "Are you so bitter that you would take these mad accusations to Pharaoh as revenge?"

"He would never believe me. He still harbors that innocent, child-like loyalty to his older brother."

Set's voice turned to a taunt. "Then I shall live a long and rich life and die in bed atop a virgin."

Neb-t·ḥe-t nodded, her face sober, her gaze still on the statue behind him. "Yes, you will."

Her words echoed and fled, leaving the room still except for the whispering torch. Set looked about the storeroom, at statues, boxes, ropes—at everything except her.

Set edged toward the doorway, keeping his distance from Neb-t·ḥe-t the way he would a wild animal of uncertain disposition. "Nice seeing you again, Nebbe."

The sound of his steps faded. Neb-t·ḥe-t found the paint and a tray of unused reeds. Bending to choose one, she looked up and said: "I deserve to be there when she cuts his heart out."

*   *   *

Īset found Neb-t·ḥe-t on a mat writing in the last undecorated wall space in Ḥaāmer's tomb. "I missed you at Pharaoh's table. Set said you were here."

Neb-t·ḥe-t drew black paint from the pot and stroked it onto the wall, leaving perfect black glyphs that glowed and etched themselves into the stone. "You shouldn't be here now."

"No, I shouldn't. I should be home and happy, dreaming away the heat of the day with both my daughters alive. But this is where I find myself."

Neb-t·ḥe-t continued to write, saying nothing but the prayer flowing from her wrist and fingers. Statues and boxes threw trembling figures of shadow against the wall beyond her.

"What happened?" Īset asked, touching Neb-t·ḥe-t's puffy, dark cheek.

Neb-t·ḥe-t winced at the touch. "Set."

"He struck you? Pharaoh needs to hear of this."

Neb-t·ḥe-t caught her hand. "No. Set's done much worse and gone unpunished."

"Let me put ointment on it."

Neb-t·ḥe-t looked up. "You haven't offered to minister to me since we were children."

"I'm offering now."

"When I am finished."

Īset studied the letters, rubbing her hands together. The air in the chamber was thick with smoke and sweat. She could hear other workmen moving heavy funerary items into position in a storeroom. She hesitated and asked: "Ȧpnu will watch over her?"

"A different prayer. Watch the statues."

Īset took a step deeper into the burial chamber. "They are still statues."

"From the corner of your eye."

Īset found a statue of Bast. Looking away, she perceived an outline of the lioness reclining in place of the stone carving. The luminous almond eyes regarded her dispassionately. The big cat remained motionless except for a twitch at the very end of her tail and a grumbling purr.

Then Bast's ears turned together. She lowered her head to her paws and looked away to a corner of the room. Īset followed her gaze, remembering to look aside.

"What do you see?" Neb-t·ḥe-t asked.

"A hawk that has the face of a man. A handsome face. What does it mean?"

Neb-t·ḥe-t sighed and placed the reed back into the ink pot. "It is a vision of days to come. That is all I can say."

* * *

Six priests carried Ḥaāmer's coffin into the burial chamber and lowered it gently to the stone platform prepared for it. Neb-t·ḥe-t, Āakhu, Pharaoh and Īset huddled before it. Those bearing the accumulated gifts waited silently in the corridor.

A priestess entered and placed a bowl containing water from the River in Neb-t·ḥe-t's hands. Neb-t·ḥe-t poured the water over the image of Ḥaāmer on the lid.

"Water of Merhyt, who gives us the seasons of the River, once more the seasons of a life are complete. We come from water and from sand. To them we return. All remains in balance."

Water dripped from the coffin and puddled on the stone floor. Pharaoh and Īset viewed their daughter's coffin for the last time.

Neb-t·ḥe-t led them outside to watch as the line of priests brought the gifts into the tomb. Neb-t·ḥe-t stood in the doorway and directed the placement of each gift.

They distributed the ushabtui figures closest to the coffin on its stone platform. Boxes of clothing lined one wall, jewelry another, food a third, and the fourth wall was given to Ḥaāmer's personal items. When it was done, the burial chamber overflowed with gifts.

"Would you do it again?" Pharaoh asked. "Knowing how short her life is and how it ends, would you do it again? Think of all the bright moments, all those precious times, let them push back the darkness and comfort you in the days ahead."

He pulled her into a fierce hug that took the breath and tears from her. "I miss her," he said. "I will always miss her. I wish I could have done something more for her."

"My heart is broken," Īset said, her arms tightening around him. "But if I could relive the days, if I could send the Aten rising in the west and retrace the days, I would do it again. She lived short, but lived well."

Īset began to cry as the masons came forward and laid the first bricks to seal the opening. Ạsạr put an arm around his queen to console her, though Neb-t·ḥe-t could see the grief equally vivid in his face. Īset could not stop and Pharaoh and Āakhu escorted her from the tomb.

Neb-t·ḥe-t stopped the masons just before they placed the last brick. She took a torch from the wall and peered through the opening a final time. The faint, flickering light illuminated an eager, smiling ushabtui at the foot of Ḥaāmer's coffin. Beside her, a stelae with a poem Āakhu had written for Ḥaāmer, the hieroglyphics flowing in Āakhu's delicate hand:

Oh Nut, whose face shines as the moon!
Oh Ra, whose face shines as the sun!
May Ḥaāmer go forth,
May your lights free her,
May Amennt release her when she would see the sky . . .

Chapter 10

ABYDOS, EGYPT, THE FEATURE, JUNE 25TH, 10:15 A.M.:

. . . desires to see the sky,
May she cast her own light on the living,
May her smile warm those who love her.
Oh Ḥaāmer, visit me, your sister, Āakhu,
Dry the tears I shed in you absence.

Lisa's eyes blinked as she read the hieroglyphics on the most prominent stelae. She put her hand to her chest as if it ached with the deep sorrow Āakhu felt at the loss of her sister. She turned from the monitor looking back over her shoulder at Sanders who had moved behind her to hear her translation clearer. His eyes focused on hers with a steady gaze. He gave a solemn nod. Neither spoke for several seconds.

When Sanders returned from Cairo, nothing had happened to her. They did not talk about his trip. She figured retribution would have been quick and final. Now there was an uneasy truce between them. They carried on professionally, but simple friendly conversation was gone, Their non-communication weighed on her.

Lisa's enthusiasm down, the seriousness of the find and the eighteen-hour days had settled upon her, creating a numb professional detachment. She worked as if she were a machine. She worried about Sanders in the back of her mind. Lisa broke the silence wiping behind her glasses with the lapel of her shirt.

"Amazing how reading that stelae makes Ḥaāmer and Āakhu real people," she said. "Not just a chunk of dried flesh. People, who once felt for each other, lived, breathed, thought and then died."

"Yes, a deep emotional statement of sisterly love," he said. "Often, the wall texts are so dry. One never senses another person, but this passage imparts so much love between the sisters."

Lisa murmured agreement.

"So who were Ḥaāmer and Āakhu? You read hieroglyphics very well." he said.

"Thanks. I don't know who they were...yet. Women weren't held with this much esteem. Hieroglyphics were the religious writing, not the common language. How could these females write it? Some scribe must have written the script for them. This would imply that they had station. Ḥaāmer's name is in a serekh, also an indication of rank or royalty."

"True, I understand what you're saying." He took a deep breath. "Something about that passage bothers me though I can't put my finger on it."

"I know what you mean. It has a familiar ring as if I've read it before."

"You've read it too?" Sanders eyes lit up. "Ani, *Book of Coming Forth by Day*! I researched it extensively as a grad student. I'll have to read my notes from the internet, tonight."

"Yes, I believe you're right. If it is *The Book of the Dead,* then Ani is much more formulaic. Plus he's much later than what all this appears to be. He's Eighteenth Dynasty. Besides this passage seems very personal."

"Nineteenth Dynasty, Ramses II," he corrected her. "But this is way cool. Ani's scroll was supposed to have been copied from early works that may be connected with Āakhu. That would solve our Fourth Dynasty serekh problem."

"To come to that conclusion, we've got a lot to prove."

"Yeah," he said. "We'll have to carbon date everything organic. I could've used your help on my Master's Degree translating hieroglyphics in the British Museum every day. Day in and day out."

"You studied the Budge debacle?"

"Yes...?"

"Damn, him. He bought the Ani papyrus. Bought it!"

"The preservation aspect, right? We don't agree with him now, but that was accepted practice back then."

"Maybe so, but then he cut the scroll into seventeen pieces!"

"Yeah, I agree with you, that sucked, but be easy on Sir Ernest."

Lisa bared her teeth. Sanders laughed at her expression.

Shaking his head, he said, "We don't know what forces were working on him. He may have saved the scroll from becoming kindling. Maybe he needed to get the scroll out of the country quickly to keep it from going on the black-market. It could have disappeared forever. At least, he gave us a start on the afterlife traditions."

ABYDOS, EGYPT, THE FEATURE, JUNE 25TH, 12:22 P.M.

Sanders cleared the table after lunch.

"I've been thinking about our video problem," said Sanders. "I've concluded we can do *some* work with the camera."

"But I thought you said we're risking breaking through the ceiling," said Lisa.

"If we confine the arm to a couple feet from vertical, we should be OK. I did the math. Besides I need to satisfy my curiosity. Don't you?"

Lisa took her seat at the lefthand console.

"Yes, but no accidents. OK?" she said.

"Right. No accidents. We'll track the camera in a cone-shaped path around the vertical, We'll stop at fifteen degree increments to turn the camera through a complete circle."

"That'll be tedious. How can you be sure you won't hit something?"

"Using our initial scans, I've programed the path into the computer controls. In this way, we can miss all the artifacts yet maximize the stereoscopic effect of our video."

"Fantastic!" she said.

"The computers can chew on these frames to produce a three-dimensional rendering of the room. The measurement will be accurate out to three or four feet then less accurate as the distance from the camera increases."

"I understand. How accurate?"

"Out to four feet, the accuracy will be in millimeters."

"Oh, wow!"

They observed the room for the next five hours through the video camera. Their excitement grew as they observed. Holding the camera close to vertical, the method did not explore the corners of the room. The majority of the room was not viewed.

"So how old do you think it is?" he said on one of their spin pauses.

"I've been thinking about that. With the wooden funerary box and stelae, I'd say three to four thousand years old—2700 BCE max," said Lisa. "A thousand years before Ani."

"I came to the same conclusion, but that's pushing early dynastic. That's really exciting. This is the first time anyone's found a collection with this many artifacts from the Second or Third Dynasty."

"Yes, if what we believe is true, but I'm still having problems with a cave burial, women being honored, and which royal family she's from."

"I agree. Cave burials started during what...?"

"Sixth or Seventh...."

"Probably later."

"Which makes no sense. The Second and Sixth dynasties were hundreds of years apart. People during the Second Dynasty were just buried in the desert sand unless you were Djoser or Khufu. Then you got a pyramid. Only pharaohs were formally buried."

"Yeah, and no one was buried in underground tombs. However, to find this much stuff from any dynasty is wonderful," he said.

"You're right, but I'm trying to hold down my enthusiasm until we can prove all of it. Hopefully, some tomb robber didn't just stash all this stuff in here."

"Do you believe that?"

He glanced over at her, smiling into her large blue eyes watching him. He wondered what other tidbits were swirling around inside her head. She looked at him staring at her then turned away.

"No, it's too ordered—placed," she said.

"Agreed."

"The fact that Ḥaāmer's name appeared in a serekh suggests that she's royalty, but Horus usually appears on the serekh and he's missing. Damn this is a pain." she said.

"A painful, interesting puzzle."

"Yes, an interesting puzzle."

"Why is she buried so remotely?" he asked.

"I thought about that when I first arrived, but I saw the panorama of the Nile Valley and it's so beautiful. They could come up through the valley rather than the ravine behind us that's now the road."

"True, but this is still out in the sticks especially back then. Still is. The closest town is Abydos–Abtu. This is away from all the worship centers."

She threw up her hands in defeat. "We need more information. Dating will help."

"Recovering wood will help. Wood splinters from the funerary box and ushabtui would also be a dating source," he said.

"Can't we use your telescoping arm to pick up something to date? I thought I saw a gripper on the end."

"It's not delicate enough to use. You'll just have to be patient."

"OK," she said, giving him a sardonic grin. "We do want samples from a wide number of objects to increase the number of independent data points. I'm looking for a cluster, then we can be confident that the tomb dates from that era."

"The mummy and its wrappings will be the most demonstrative," he said. "But we are only doing preliminary analysis. We must be careful how far we go. We probably won't open the funerary box or even see the mummy this go round."

"Yes, I understand. Other objects might be passed down from generation to generation, but the mummy was wrapped with fresh linen at the time of internment." she said. "We really need to view her."

"Yes, but.... " he shrugged. "I hope the tomb has more rooms than we can see. I think the side looking radar has to be a priority."

"True," she agreed.

"We can start the computer working on the video we've produced."

"Maybe Captain Jagardii's men can help with carrying the radar equipment."

"Right. Unfortunately, it doesn't look very far left, right or deep."

ABYDOS, EGYPT, THE FEATURE, JUNE 26TH, 7:37 A.M.:

The next day the pair arrived with the side-looking radar to begin the underground survey. Lisa lugged one end, Sanders the other.

"Damn! This is heavy," said a struggling Lisa, setting her end of the crate down with a thud.

"Easy on the equipment," said Sanders. "Please ask the captain if we can use some of his men to carry the radar."

"The terrorists haven't used airplanes before," Jagardii said to Lisa.

Lisa smiled as she observed the confusion playing across the two men's faces. She toyed with letting them remain confused, but decided that productive work needed to get done.

"It is radar that looks into the ground," she explained to Jagardii not translating for Sanders. "It will give us a picture of the tomb site and some idea how strong the ceiling is structurally."

Jagardii's face showed that he comprehended.

"Ah, you Americans have all the technology. I'm envious. Yes, the men need something to do to keep them out of mischief. I'll have the lieutenant set up thirty minute shifts."

Lisa explained the arrangement to Sanders.

"Tell Jagardii that we'll make observations in between the thirty minute shifts calling the next shift when we need them."

Within a short time, and with the military's help, the scientists ran the radar across the top of Ḥaāmer's chamber. They observed the thickness and cracks in the stone ceiling.

"The damage is stressing me," said Sanders.

"I don't think the truck caused the original structural problems. The building of the highway may have started the trouble. The crash may have exacerbated the situation."

"Yeah, I suspect they parked their road construction equipment in this natural horseshoe." Sanders swept his hand over the flat area of the site.

"Yes, I believe you may be right. That would also imply that the tomb structure is not out here otherwise it would have caved in from the heavier equipment. Luckily, Ḥaāmer's chamber is over here off to the side. Perhaps a limited amount of equipment was parked over her space," said Lisa.

They drank a large quantity of water and began the next shift. They moved along the cliff face to see what else the site held. A faint, ghostlike fuzz appeared across a corridor from Ḥaāmer's room. They concluded there was a room of nearly the same dimensions as Ḥaāmer's, but they couldn't see any detail. They wondered if this was Āakhu's resting place or an even more important person. Turning the other direction, they traveled to the road, but all substructure departed with the move toward the highway. The day ended with no further discoveries.

ABYDOS, EGYPT, THE FEATURE, EVENING, JUNE 26TH, 6:20 P.M.:

"Anything?" asked Jagardii that evening when the three got together.

"There's a room across the hall," Lisa said. "But that's all we found."

"And that makes the site all the more mysterious," said Sanders once Lisa had translated around. "Why would the Egyptians honor a woman in a small tomb site or is there a complex that we're not seeing?"

"Yes, that's intriguing," said Lisa.

"You need to see more?" said Jagardii.

"Yes, and we intend to continue tomorrow with your assistance. We'll have to scan along the cliff face and the part that goes through the bivouac area," said Sanders.

"Of course we will help you."

Sanders rubbed his chin.

"Think about it, the Egyptians weren't magicians. How did they get into the space? Their entrance can't be through solid, native rock. The radar should see the differences in the rock density. We haven't seen the entrance yet. They buried it well, but it's still here."

"True, but where?" she asked.

"I don't know, but it's somewhere close."

"I'll have the men help, tomorrow," said Jagardii as he left the trailer.

"We'll get a much better picture where the rooms, caves and faults are if we do multiple scans and use the computer to build an enhanced image. We may discover the original entrance to the tomb."

"Yes," said Lisa. "Have you noticed that he's become very helpful? He asked if I'd teach him about the computer."

Sanders' face clouded with skepticism.

"I'm not sure I want the captain working on the computer. Our progress the past two days pleases me, but data security concerns me."

"I'll make sure that he doesn't mess anything up."

Sanders considered this.

"You're a tremendous help, Lisa. You read ancient Egyptian hieroglyphics as if they were modern English. Your Egyptian translation skills made working with the military possible. Things are going great. Are you sure you can process and save the data?"

"I know how to manage data."

"Well, if you are confident the captain will help as well, maybe it's a good thing."

He dropped the subject. "I need to start the radar data reduction," he said. "That'll take forever. If we use the Chicago supercomputer, we'll have to load a huge amount of data across our link. This modern radar with the raw-data feed can produce enhanced results, but it's a pain with the sheer volume of data."

"Maybe I can work on that," she said.

Sanders looked puzzled. "How's that?"

The satellite phone rang and he jumped up to answer it. Reading the caller-id, Sanders put his finger to his lips and punched the phone to speaker.

"This is Dr. Tu'hut."

"Yes, sir. What can I do for you?"

"You sound like you are in a tunnel."

Lisa held her breath.

"Yes, sir, I have you on speaker phone so I can work on a computer problem."

"Something is happening at the site that I do not understand. Why are *you* mounting a military operation there?"

"I know nothing of any military operation."

"I understand you requested a military helicopter be sent to the site. When the general in charge queried his personnel, they said it was for you. You need to return to Cairo immediately so we can discuss these matters."

"Dr. Tu'hut there is a logical explanation for this. I'll be more than happ...."

"Good. I will send a transport tonight and will see you tomorrow morning at ten." The connection broke.

"What the heck was that about?" Sanders said once he was sure the line was disconnected.

Lisa let out a sigh of relief.

"Welcome to the world of Dr. Tu'hut."

"I need to call him back. He doesn't understand what we're doing, but he's wasting a lot of my time."

Lisa shook her head sympathetically. "Diplomacy."

He sighed. "You're right. For diplomacy sake, I need to go to Cairo and see what he wants. Damn! This'll slow progress on the feature."

"I'll be here."

"Yeah. I'll definitely leave you in charge. I want progress on the tomb to continue during my absence. I won't mention you."

"Thank you."

"From what he said, the only helicopter coming is to pick *me* up. We won't be moving the truck."

"Why can't we use your helicopter to move the truck?"

"It won't have the lift capacity. It's only for transporting people. You need to push hard tomorrow to get the radar work done by evening."

"Slave driver."

He laughed.

ABYDOS, EGYPT, THE FEATURE, EVENING, JUNE 26TH, 6:50 P.M.:

"The white minions of sin have been busy today."

"Yes, my brother. We must be careful, but we will teach the unbelievers not to defile our ancestors. They must pay for their sins with their lives. The white minions of Shaitan must be taught a lesson.

"When we kill these, their government will cause the rest to leave the country," said Colonel Fiqar.

"Will the leader favor this move? We have not received his approval."

"We further his cause, if it still *is* his cause."

"His other plans for us concern me."

"I as well. He loses his nerve. I don't like his words. He'll try to make us the dog," said a furious Fiqar.

"You're right, brother. We need to dissolve our commitment with Aboud. We'll gather weapons from these Egyptian military fools and disappear."

"The woman walks into our hands. We can not let this opportunity pass."

The brothers hunkered down waiting for darkness. At dusk, a jeep pulled up to the trailer. They tensed again as the beating sound of a helicopter approached their position.

"We mustn't be seen against the twilight," said Fiqar digging in deeper.

The helicopter didn't approach them, but touched down a quarter mile away on the highway. Slamming the door, a man ran from the trailer. He climbed into a waiting jeep. As the clutch was popped, grinding the gears, the jeep jumped ahead toward the helicopter. The ugly one raised as the jeep sped away. His brother pulled him under cover.

"As you say, brother, we can't be seen."

"He's getting away," said an angry Fiqar.

"We can't be discovered. The whore remains in the camp. She'll be a great prize."

ABYDOS, EGYPT, THE FEATURE, THE ARCHAEOLOGICAL TRAILER, JUNE 27TH, 12:17 A.M.:

Lisa awoke with a start. She stopped breathing, listening intently. She took a deep breath, exhaled slowly, silently, wondering what had awakened her. The air conditioner throbbed monotonously.

Nothing. What time is it?

Rubbing the sleep from her eyes, she looked at the digital clock on the nightstand by her head. The large, fuzzy blue numbers six inches from her face displayed twelve seventeen. The wind kicked up and the trailer shook slightly.

The wind must have disturbed me. That was it.

She rolled over on her side to go back to sleep. A few seconds later, Lisa heard the trailer door lever being turned over as far as the lock permitted with a slight click. She was instantly awake. Her fingers did a toe dance across the top of the nightstand, searching for her glasses. She heard the latch groan, as someone tried to break the lock. The lock held. The latch slowly, gently turned back to its starting position.

Down the side of the trailer, the first window was tried. She swept her hand in a circle determined to locate her glasses. A single grunted word was uttered in a hushed tone. There were at least two of them. Lisa found her glasses and put them on. She swung her legs over the edge of the bed, sitting up.

The trailer was full of valuable things. If they were after the equipment, they would silence her. If they were after her, she didn't want to think about a reoccurrence of Cairo. She was out of bed on her tiptoes. She wished she had the gun she'd left in the States. She was trained, her father insisted, but she'd never pointed a weapon at anyone.

Damn! Nothing to use!

The shadow of a head passed the second window, stopped and tried to pull it open. She knew all the windows were locked. She tried each one before retiring for the night. Eventually, when whoever was breaking in discovered all were locked, they would use additional force. She must get help before then. The third window drape was slightly askew. She saw the two.

Oh, my God! The men from Cairo. How did they find me? What am I going to do?

She doubted whether her screaming through an open window would awaken anyone over at the Egyptian camp, let alone get them here in time to rescue her.

She was in the main room with the computers. She jumped as the third window screen ripped from the frame and the glass broke. A hand reached inside to turn the catch. One of the attackers gripped the window sill, pulling up. His revolver and ugly face appeared in the window.

Chapter 11

jmw-nswt ḥr jtrw ḥsbt 18 ꜣbd 2 prt sw 29 ḫr ḥm n wsỉr

Pharaoh's Boat on the River,
Year 18, Month 2 of Peret, Day 29 under the Majesty of Ạsạr

Dawn was no more than a hopeful smudge on the eastern horizon. Cradled in the embrace of the royal boat, Pharaoh and Īset glided through the mist silent as a god come down to walk upon the river. A finger of cool night air around the window cover pushed Īset closer to Pharaoh, to the warm secure spot he made in the bed. She sighed, caught in a dream, and whispered: "It will be all right."

Ḥaāmer was far away now, gone to the gods. Safe in her underground room, quiet, undisturbed, she too could dream of more pleasant days to come. It could be all right, if the days ahead were peaceful and calm so that Pharaoh and Īset might heal the wounds that Ḥaāmer's short and painful life had left on them. All right if the the governors would suspend their squabbles for a season and the land owners settle their boundary disputes one with another. Maybe the land would grant Pharaoh peace for a season and it would be all right.

Īset awoke to a soft rustle at the door tapestry. A voice called: "Pharaoh?"

Īset rose, wrapped herself in a blanket and stood just inside. "Ṭeḥuti," she whispered. "What is the meaning of this? Pharaoh is tired."

"Apologies, Lady. Pharaoh's commanders are waiting at the Ukher. They need to talk with him the moment we dock."

Īset pushed her head through the curtain. Across the carpet of mist that tumbled over the River, oil pots burned to light the docks. Masts pushed up from anchored boats like fingers pointing to the sand-sprinkled sky. The shadows of men loomed beyond them, men with gleaming armor and sober faces. Īset shivered, the deck cold beneath her bare feet. Her breath made small clouds before her face. She felt the first stirring of fear in her chest.

"So many soldiers so early in the day. I will wake him," she said and disappeared back into the cabin.

wsḫt nt jwsw m wꜣst ḥsbt 18 ꜣbd 2 prt sw 29 ḫr ḥm n wsỉr

The Hall of Balance in Uas,
Year 18, Month 2 of Peret, Day 29 under the Majesty of Ạsạr

"Betnu·ȧḥa, what happened?" Pharaoh asked. He slumped on his gold and ivory throne, his great dark eyes dull with fatigue.

The chief of Pharaoh's armies, stepped forward and dropped to one knee. His weapons clattered. "Men from the northern kingdom have attacked prince Maaạ. provinces Un and Atef-peh may have fallen."

In the silent Hall of Balance, in Betnu·ȧḥa's respectful face and the calm, deliberate detachment of Pharaoh's soldiers, unasked questions shouted for attention: *Why was there no agreement with Maaạ? Why did we not have a force there to prevent this?*

Pharaoh shook his head sadly. "How did this happen?"

"We only have a few reports from the first boats out of the area. They told of a large force raging across the border before dawn three nights ago, slaughtering villagers and destroying temples along the river," Betnu·ȧḥa said.

Pharaoh nodded but said nothing. He closed his eyes a moment, rubbing his chin between thumb and forefinger. He took two deep breaths, rasping like wind over hot sand.

"Maaạ had most of his armies along that border," Betnu·ȧḥa continued. "If the northern force has broken through them, he has little additional protection other than a few palace defenders. If we do not intervene, Maaạ and his four provinces may be lost to the north."

"Maaa rejected our help."

Betnu·ȧḥa nodded. "We have counted on Maaạ's friendship, if not his allegiance, for years. If this northern force is as large and fierce as some say it is, there is no reason for them to stop once they reach our border. We do not now have the men there to halt them if they decide to keep going."

Silence again in the great hall, as beyond the closed doors dawn came from the east, passing Uas on its long journey to the west. Pharaoh stood, dispelling the hesitation. "Then we will go. Gather the men and material that you need in my name and set out as soon as you are prepared."

Betnu·ȧḥa bowed to his Pharaoh and signaled his staff. He was already prepared.

Pharaoh called his chamberlain. "Restock the royal boat. We will sail as soon as it is ready."

Betnu·ȧḥa turned. "I pray, Pharaoh. Do you think that wise? There could be danger."

"Yes," Pharaoh said. "And my people are in the midst of it. I vowed before Ptah to defend them. I must not fail."

Ṭeḥuti witnessed the determination like a fever flushing Pharaoh's tired face. He stepped forward and bowed. "I wish to go with you."

"You shall have a cabin aboard my boat," Pharaoh said.

Ṭeḥuti nodded and hurried from the Hall of Balance, unsure about what he had just done. If the reports of slaughter were true, famine and plague would soon follow.

ḥwt-nṯr nt ptḥ m wȝst ḥsbt 18 ȝbd 2 prt sw 29 ḫr ḥm n wsỉr

The Temple of Ptah is Uas,
Year 18, Month 2 of Peret, Day 29 under the Majesty of Ạsạr

Ḥenḥen found the high priest at a table, focused on a scattering of papyri stretched across its surface.

"It has come to my ears that my brother is planning a trip down river," Set said, looking up. "Can I trust you?"

"You can trust me, as always."

Set rose and came around the edge until the table was no longer a barrier between them. The papyri whispered as he pushed them together into a pile. Set leaned against the table and said: "I have messages for the temples along the river, sensitive messages, so that the priests might be prepared should Pharaoh visit them. I would not have Pharaoh know the content of these messages or even that they exist. Can I trust you?"

Ḥenḥen frowned while his lips curled into a nervous smile. He spread his arms. "Yes, you can trust me. Many times have I served you, never have I failed. It is an honor and a pleasure to do your will."

"Good," Set said. He turned and lifted a papyrus. Beneath it lay a bundle wrapped in new, soft leather the color of harvested wheat. Set pulled the tie and it unraveled. He folded the edges back one by one to reveal a polished bronze blade set into a carved ivory handle. The god of war, Onuris, smiled from the handle's surface, holding up the severed head of his enemy. Around him an inscription flowed that Ḥenḥen could not read.

Set lifted the blade, studied the light from its flawless surface, tested the edge on a fragment of papyrus, shifted his grip to be sure of its balance.

"Come here," Set said.

The blade flashed as it cut through a shaft of sunlight, too quick to disturb the motion of the dust. It stopped beneath Ḥenḥen's ear. He felt the prick of its tip, his rapid pulse beckoning it deeper into his flesh. Leaning close so Ḥenḥen could feel Set's hot, excited breath, the high priest asked softly: "Can I trust you?"

jmw-nswt ḥr jtrw ḥsbt 18 ꜣbd 2 prt sw 29 ḫr ḥm n wsir

Pharaoh's Boat on the River,

Year 18, Month 2 of Peret, Day 29 under the Majesty of Ạsạr

Pharaoh's boat set sail in mid-afternoon and by evening Ṭeḥuti felt alone and distant from Uas and Āakhu. The current, pushing ever on to the great sea, helped their speed. Ṭeḥuti stood alone at the stern, watching landmarks the boat had passed grow small and remote. Other boats hosting Pharaoh's soldiers spread out around them, silent, protective, the men busy on deck pointing and feathering arrows, polishing swords, preparing themselves to spill blood.

Pharaoh leaned forward on his throne at the front of the boat, watching the banks of the Nile slide past. He remained silent and still as a carved wooden god placed there for good fortune and safe passage.

Small boats passed, hastily provisioned and inexpertly guided. Boats loaded with silent, dirty men and women, boys and girls, each laden with bundles that were all they could carry. They told a similar story. Raging men attacking without warning or mercy, killing those who did not flee, destroying that which could not be carried off. The stories reinforced one another: burning villages along the riverbank, bodies floating in the shallows.

Pharaoh said little, other than to offer food and shelter up river. Ṭeḥuti joined him as the boats passed, watched as Pharaoh's face became grim like one of those fleeing the trouble rather than the one who would halt it. Ṭeḥuti hoped they would pass Abtu during the night; Pharaoh became quieter as they approached the place where Ḥaāmer rested.

Pharaoh's cook brought him roasted duck some soldiers had snared along the River, a porridge of vegetables and roots, bread with honeycomb, and beer. It sat, nearly untouched, in front of the brooding Ạsạr.

"You should eat, then you should rest, Pharaoh," Ṭeḥuti said.

Pharaoh turned back from his pensive study of the riverbank, his eyes focused on Ṭeḥuti, returning from whatever far distant object they had been fixed upon. "You sound like Īset."

Pharaoh's tray was heaped full: duck, bread, onions and garlic. He took a sip from his bowl of beer instead.

The fading light of the Aten, in his role as Atmu, the closer of day, cast an orange glow across Pharaoh's face. The sunset was quiet except for the sound of the water breaking against the bow of the boat and the muted commands of the sailors as they steered her.

Near sunset, they anchored at Qebt, capital of the province Herui, one of the original provinces of Pharaoh's kingdom. Men waited at the docks, an honor guard to escort Pharaoh and Ṭeḥuti to the governor's house.

Gemgem, governor of Herui, was a small, intense man. When his body was still, his eyes were in motion, his gaze sweeping rapidly across a scene. Ṭeḥuti could see the intelligence in the man, and the devotion to Pharaoh.

Gemgem wrung his hands together as Pharaoh related the story of the revolt, and his intent to liberate his people from invaders.

Gemgem's face betrayed a moment of worry. "Any news of Khnemes? He was my friend too."

"None," Pharaoh said. "There is still confusion as to what happened."

An uncomfortable silence settled in the room, except for the sound of a wasp building a small mud nest in a high corner. The two men were at a loss for words, each born to power, each so familiar with the other that over the years they had become strangers.

Gemgem introduced his wife Neqa, a tall, willowy beauty who brought them beer. When she sat beside Gemgem, she eschewed her coppery throne for a stool beside her husband. On the low seat she was shorter than her husband. She placed an arm about him.

Neqa nudged Gemgem. Ṭeḥuti found the gesture so comical and touchingly familiar that he smiled and for a moment thought of Āakhu so far away in the Queen's house.

"I don't know," Gemgem said, gathering his courage, his head following his eyes in a side to side motion. "Something isn't right. I've met the governors from the north. They are all tough, fair-minded men. They are not the sort of ruthless killers who attack and slaughter whole villages."

"But that is what happened," Pharaoh said.

"So the refugees say. But something else is going on."

"What?" Pharaoh asked.

"Ask your brother," Gemgem said. "I've heard rumors of midnight visitors to the temples. The priests here seem unnaturally distracted. Has Set mentioned why priests might be quietly traveling north?"

Pharaoh frowned, taking a long, slow drink from a bowl of beer. "I was unaware Set was sending priests northward."

Gemgem shrugged. "I doubt the northern governors would overreact to the mere presence of priests on their southern border. Might they have provoked the North? Even unintentionally?"

"My brother does not meddle in affairs of the realm and would not involve himself with other provinces and kingdoms without seeking my approval. But I will hear from him why he is sending priests northward."

The meeting ended soon thereafter. Ṭeḥuti followed Pharaoh back to the boat. Outside his cabin Pharaoh looked up into the clear night skyand spoke: "I was once told that everyone who crosses the River becomes a flame in the night sky and can look down on those they left behind. Is Ḥaāmer watching over me?"

"I have no doubt but that she is, Pharaoh," Ṭeḥuti said.

"Which one do you think is my daughter?"

"The brightest of all," Ṭeḥuti said, and pointed off to the south, toward Uas. "She also watches over her mother and sister. See how she winks at you?"

Pharaoh followed Ṭeḥuti's direction, watching the stars for a time. Then he wiped his eyes and disappeared into his cabin.

pr ḥmt nwst m wꜣst ḥsbt 18 ꜣbd 2 prt sw 30 ḫr ḥm n wsỉr

The House of Pharaoh's Wife in Uas,
Year 18, Month 2 of Peret, Day 30 under the Majesty of Ạsạr

Kefa·ạb brought a tray of fruit, freshly baked bread, and wine with honey to Īset in the garden.

It was a rare day, cool in the shade, warm in the sun, a breath of breeze setting the leaves in languid motion and sending shivers across the surface of a reflecting pool.

Īset sat at the pool's edge, dangling her feet into the water, soothed by the balance of the warmth, wind, and water.

"You should eat before you go to the Hall of Balance," Kefa·ạb said.

Īset looked up. "You sound as if you disapprove."

"I think men are better at the callous deceit and cruelty that goes into trade and diplomatic negotiations."

Īset smiled. "It doesn't need to be that way."

Kefa·ạb shook her head and sighed. Looking away, she frowned. "Set," she hissed. "He shouldn't be here while Pharaoh is away. Let me call the guard."

"No," Īset said, frowning. "It may be news from Pharaoh. I will summon them if necessary."

Kefa·ạb bowed and plodded away in the other direction before Set could hail and press her into service.

Set followed the path through the garden, never pausing or slowing to look at any of the plants and flowers that grew there. When he saw Īset watching, his face twisted into an ugly smile that was not reassuring.

He pulled a chair around to face her across the narrow width of the pool. She stayed at the pool's edge, her feet and legs stirring the water in a slow kicking motion.

"If your feet hurt, there are servants that can wash and massage them for you," Set said.

She lowered the hem of her dress to her knees. "Sometimes I put my feet in water for the simple pleasure of it."

"I see," Set said, when the pique in his voice told her he did not. "It must be very quiet for you with Pharaoh gone."

"I hadn't noticed. There is always so much to do."

"Are you going to eat this?" Set asked, motioning to the tray of food.

"No," she said.

He picked at the fruit and tore the side from one of the breads and stuffed it into his mouth. Īset looked into the pool at his fractured image, curious as to why his every motion angered her. Maybe it was the water that showed the true Set, how he was twisted and broken behind the handsome, boyish face, inconstant, untrue beneath his tall, muscular body. She focused on the coolness around her ankles and calves, the tickle as the water passed between her toes. She must not let Set anger her. She must stay balanced, peaceful and at peace.

"I was told you plan to open the Hall of Balance today." Set said.

"Yes."

Set's voice was a little too eager. Īset shivered as he spoke: "I would like to sit with you."

"Pharaoh's throne will remain empty while he's away."

"I am high priest of Ptah," Set said.

"You worship Ptah and keep his temple; you do not speak for him," she said.

"And you do?"

Īset looked up and met his gaze, calm, earnest. "I am wife to a god and sister to a priestess who speaks with the gods just as I speak with you now. I sit with Pharaoh, I hear and learn his wisdom. I participate in his judgments. Do I need to remind you of your own disrespect, disruption, and opposition?"

Set drew back, his eyes widening—whether in genuine surprise or a well-practiced bit of priestly acting Īset could not be sure. He looked down and took a sip of the wine. He stumbled when he spoke: "My . . . my apologies. I seek only what is best for Uas. I thought my presence with you in the Hall of Balance might abate the uneasiness people may naturally feel in the absence of a leader."

"Callous deceit and cruelty," Īset said absently.

"What has happened between us?" Set asked.

Īset sighed, and her eyes clouded up. She was not going to find balance today. "You have dishonored my sister. I saw the bruise on her cheek. For that I will not forgive you."

"She was never intended for me. Is it my fault there was never love between us?"

The words brought a sudden fire to Īset that entered her ears and sent a flush the length of her body.

"You never tried. She loved you and you did not care."

"As you did not care for me?" Set retorted, then sighed, leaning back, guessing that he might have spoken harshly and contrary to desire. "Do you remember how you met my brother?"

"I remember."

We walked together along the river, Set and I, laughing and stealing shy kisses, when I saw a beautiful lotus blossom in a quiet river pool. I asked him to bring it to me, but Set, ever conscious of his position and appearance, refused.

His younger brother Ạsạr played nearby, releasing small reed boats into the river, watching the current catch and carry them away. Ạsạr waded into the pool without hesitation, cut the beautiful flower, and presented it to me. To shame Set, I kissed Ạsạr.

I cannot forget the look in Ạsạr's eyes as our lips touched or the fire that burned through me. I knew in that moment it would be Ạsạr—not Set—with whom I would spend my remaining days.

The remembrance faded pleasantly, agonizingly, away. Set was speaking again. She touched the hollow at her throat, felt the quickened pulse and a flush of warmth, and strained to hear his words: "Everything I have ever desired was *given* to my brother. Now he is away; only you and I remain. Once you loved me, Īset. What remains of that love?"

"How dare you," Īset growled. "When Pharaoh hears of this—"

"He will do nothing. The word of a sad and distraught queen against Pharaoh's brother, the high priest of Ptah? Why would I make such a proposition in this public place? Perhaps you mistook a simple concern for your safety. If you speak against me I will make you look confused and ridiculous."

Īset shook with indignation, wishing she had a knife to provide a much more final answer to his solicitation. She kicked her foot, sending a spray of water over the edge of the pool to splash at Set's feet. "We were never intended for one another. Thankfully, the gods knew that and separated us. What you remember is no more than water on the sand. It is gone."

With a whisper of marching feet, four guards appeared beside them, their stance casual but their eyes wary. The leader bowed to Īset and glared at Set. "Kefa·ạb said you called for us. May we show the high priest out?"

"Yes," she said. "Then send a runner to the Hall of Balance to announce my arrival."

Set nodded and rose. "So be it," he said.

The men assumed four points around him and escorted him away. Īset watched his brooding figure grow smaller, felt the tension inside her diminish, as he walked in step with the young men—as if they were an honor guard—out of the garden.

jtrw r ḏkꜥ sbt 18 ꜣbd 3 prt sw 2 ḫr ḥm n wsir

The River at Qua

Year 18, Month 3 of Peret, Day 2 under the Majesty of Ạsạr

Ḥenḥen pulled the boat to shore at Qua. His arms drooped at his sides, spent from the rowing. The current carried the boat down river. Rowing added speed and brought him ever closer to Pharaoh. He limped toward a fisherman mending a net spread across the sand.

"How long ago did Pharaoh's boat pass?"

The fisherman shaded his eyes and studied the exhausted priest. "Just before the midday meal."

Ḥenḥen considered the news. He had closed the distance to less than a quarter-day's journey. But it was not enough. He would not overtake Pharaoh's boat now without Ptah's intervention.

"Where is the local temple? I have business with Ptah's priests."

The fisherman motioned to the path behind him. "That way. All roads here lead to the temple."

Ḥenḥen nodded and left to deliver his message of rebellion from Set.

ḥr ỉtrw mḥꜣw zꜣwt

ḥsbt 18 ꜣbd 3 prt sw 4 ḫr ḥm n wsỉr

On the River Near Saut

Year 18, Month 3 of Peret, Day 4 under the Majesty of Ạsạr

The River filled Ṭeḥuti with a longing he had not felt since childhood. To shiver once more at its cool touch, to be wrapped within it and feel its pull against his arms and legs. To rest, to float, to let it carry him along from Kush to the sea. Instead, Ṭeḥuti gripped the railing so hard his arms trembled so as not to shed his garments and dive in.

It whispered impossible dreams to him. To fish again as when he was a small, quiet orphan boy with the man who loved him enough to call him son and who taught him to respect the water and the life within it. To see, as they had dreamed together, where the river began and where it ended.

Ṭeḥuti held tight to the boat for Āakhu, for Pharaoh, for his students, for Ȧamȧam. He called them childish, selfish thoughts, to yield to the river's call, to flee his obligations, his loves, his responsibilities. Nevertheless, he felt the yearning within and how badly he wanted to answer it.

Since entering the temple school as a student, a few tattered clothes and simple carved toys tied into a bundle on his back, his time on the River was limited to yearly travel to the temples in neighboring provinces. No trip lasted more than a day. He was only a passenger, busy in conversation, teaching, or study. He sometimes heard the shouts of the steersman or paused long enough to watch the men repositioning the sail. He dipped his hand into the cool water and felt it slip through his fingers again. Few were the chances to allow the sound of the river into his ears, the fragrance of it into his nostrils, the sparkle of its leisurely motion into his eyes.

He looked away. Beyond fields of young flax, the land was broken, like the hopes and dreams of men. It soared into steep red bluffs, plummeted into deep, narrow ravines, some softened over generations as they filled with tumbled rocks and sand.

The River remained smooth and constant, rising every year in Semet, falling again in Peret. Like women, the same and never the same.

Āakhu was often in his thoughts. She was sunlight and air to him. As much as he loved her, he did not want to be Pharaoh.

While Ḥaāmer lived that was not a possibility. But Ḥaāmer was dead and it seemed she had taken much more than her possessions and offerings to rest with her in that dark underground room.

The way Pharaoh regarded him, the way Pharaoh suddenly sought his opinion and requested his attendance in discussions with important visitors filled Ṭeḥuti with uneasiness. He had no desire to sit upon a gold and ivory throne, his hands gripping the golden lion's heads on the armrests, deciding men's destinies.

The water mocked him, shattering his image, stretching it into creased, elongated shapes. *I don't want to be Pharaoh. I don't want you, River. I just want Āakhu, my scrolls, and my writing.*

Pharaoh had other distractions. Drifting past their docks on his royal boat, the magnificence of his army strung out before and behind, Pharaoh presented a rare opportunity for every governor, chief, and elder along the route. After the surprised shouts and hasty assembly of offerings, everyone of consequence boarded a boat and paddled out to greet and talk with god.

Each visitor, great or small, was a candle, and Pharaoh a dark, empty room. While together, he was illuminated. After reaching a decision and dispatching couriers with his commands, he sank once more into silence and darkness, solidifying into stone like his images on the temple walls in Uas. Only his eyes remained alive, scanning the river and hills. Tired, sad eyes that knew tragedy waited somewhere ahead.

*   *   *

The first of the refugees from Atef-peh appeared near the village Saut, a day and one half north of Uas. Caught like sand in the wind, they swirled together in small groups, pushed about the hills and valleys. Faded, dusty people trailed along the slopes like teardrops as the land cried and bled out its misery and pain in broken men and women.

No cheer rose from those scattered along the riverbank when Pharaoh's boats came in sight. Dark eyes, wounded faces, mud-soaked and tear-stained, watched in silence. Children clung to the women, but even the children were quiet, too tired and frightened to do more.

Pharaoh called Ṭeḥuti forward to watch with him. The tattered clothes and wounded bodies shamed him. Watching from the safety of Pharaoh's boat made him feel a participant or sympathizer in the attack. He looked down into the water at the reflection of the sky, but Pharaoh reached out in an uncharacteristic, almost fatherly gesture to call him back. "They are my people too. Some day they may be yours."

"I am a man of papyri, learning, and quiet thoughts. I would not know how to care for such a people as this."

Pharaoh gripped his shoulder tighter. "I wanted to grow flax and sail the length of the river trading it. Set wanted to rule. But the gods choose who will be their eyes and ears in this land." Pharaoh swept his arm in a line encompassing the scattered souls. "What do you think when you see this?"

"That I do not wish to be a spectator to their suffering, passing in comfort and safety on a well-stocked boat."

"Neither do I," Pharaoh said. "Let's help them."

The sight of the boats turning slow as giant, wooden hippopotami towards the shore sent a ripple through the bedraggled refugees. Some looked up then returned to the immediate matters of survival, some pointed and whispered. The sight of the ships sent a visible wave through those huddled along the riverbank like a gust through a field of wheat. But the sight of so many soldiers crowded on the decks frightened them—many moved away like a shy, nervous herd, toward the sheltering hills.

"What do you need?" Pharaoh called. "How can we help you?"

The response was a murmur, a hundred voices calling for one thing or another: Food, clothing, and healers.

The shouts grew louder. More people abandoned their tasks or their lethargy and sought the river. The order resulting from general exhaustion dissipated. Hope threatened to turn them once more into a mob.

"Stay where you are!" Pharaoh shouted, his voice rolling across the water like a mighty wave. "We will share what we have. The soldiers will divide it among you. Everyone will receive a share. Do not crowd together."

Pharaoh turned toward the boat master to find him anticipating the request: "Deploy the rest of the skiffs. Open the hold and bring the stores on deck."

Pharaoh strode to the other railing and called to the nearest boat. "General, arm your men and take them ashore. Disperse among the people and establish distribution points. Question them and record their needs. We will send the supplies when you have the means of distributing them."

"Take control of the healing areas," Pharaoh said to Ṭeḥuti.

Ṭeḥuti inspected the stores as the crew brought them up from the hold. He opened jars and boxes, sampling the powders and oils each contained, setting aside those he considered useful and motioning for the remainder to be returned below deck.

He found the powders and oils primitive, suited for treating blisters, insect bites, and sunburn. If the injuries and sickness among the refugees were not too severe, he might have a chance to scour the hills for the necessary leaves, roots, and berries with which to create more adequate potions.

The sound of sandals scraping the deck nearby broke Ṭeḥuti's concentration. He looked up from a pot of spiced ointment to see a soldier.

"I have orders to escort you to shore. There are many who need your attention."

Ṭeḥuti tucked a few final items into a leather sack tied to his belt and followed the soldier to a skiff. Four oarsman pulled together to a wordless, rhythmic song, the little boat knifing through the slow current toward the east bank.

The skiff smelled of sweat and damp wood. Leather squeaked in rhythm to the pull of the oarsmen who covered their hands with cowhide to protect them from blisters. Water slapped against the hull.

Ṭeḥuti heard the growing anticipation of the people on shore. Dust rose among them like incense up to where Aten rode fierce across a cloudless sky.

A cooling breeze ruffled Ṭeḥuti's hair. *They are my people too.* Like Āakhu, like sad, lost Ḥaāmer, like wizened old Ȧamȧam and the many orphans who had truly through the years become his brothers and sisters. A whole stretch of riverbank overflowing with orphans who wanted a friend, wanted a chance to relax and heal and smile once more.

Soldiers dispersed the crowd, urging them to return to their places along the riverside. Ṭeḥuti noted the care that they took, listening, offering hope, assisting those who did not have a place. Accompanying the soldiers were scribes, recording names and needs.

A soldier guided Ṭeḥuti to an open area where a large, heavy linen, suspended from poles, shaded a patch of ground from the burning touch of Aten. A few of the sick and wounded were there, lying on blankets or mats stretched over hot sand. Ṭeḥuti arranged his small collection of healing herbs and powders.

He quickly walked down the ragged row—out of the shade into the burning sun the row stretched—observing and asking questions. He moved them about, sorted them into four groups, from simple cases of overexposure to the Aten to those who would need a miracle from the gods to survive the day.

They exhibited the typical injuries, exposures, and deprivations of people caught in battle, fleeing without preparation or destination. Those who had made it this far were the strong ones, the fortunate ones. Ṭeḥuti knew that the path northward was littered with those older, weaker, less fortunate, dying or dead, food now for animals unless there had been time and strength left to stop and bury them.

That was why they were so quiet, why they did not look up, why their answers were simple yes or no. They had seen too much in too short of time, witnessed in a few days what those born and raised in palaces never saw in a lifetime. They could not cry, could not weep or even curse the gods. They could only suffer and endure and survive.

Two girls ministered to a woman who was clearly dead, wiping the flies from her face, arranging her blankets, refreshing a bowl of water resting by her head. The older was nearly of an age to wed, the other two or three inundations younger.

"What are you doing?"

"She hurt her foot," the eldest said. "See?"

She lifted the blanket. The foot was still there. It had taken an arrow or she had broken it in flight. It was dark and twisted. The bone stuck through the skin, darkened with dried blood. The evil that had gotten in had swollen and darkened the leg to the knee. Mercifully, she had finally died.

"Come with me," Ṭeḥuti said.

"But she *needs* us," the younger whined. Her face melted into tears, that Ṭeḥuti did not think he could bear.

"Others will see to her now," he said, hastily motioning to a soldier. "You have done well. Come. Others need you now."

He reached out a hand to each girl and pulled them along with him. He started with the third group, broken bones and simple wounds. He set the broken bones by wrapping and moving them into place. He told the victim to bite on a stick wrapped in linen to hold in the screams. Afterward, he turned the task of bringing wine and food to a loved one, a volunteer, or one of the girls. The sisters learned quickly, finding and bringing splints and linen, holding the victim down, distracting him or her with childish chatter while Ṭeḥuti worked.

The second group were internal ailments, bad food or bad water or both. Ṭeḥuti lifted two bags from among his potions and showed the sisters how to mix them with wine or beer or water. They mixed the drinks and took the bowls down the line of people who sat up, pale, smelling of vomit and excrement, sometimes moaning, sometimes silent, sometimes clutching bloated abdomens or doubled over with cramps.

Ṭeḥuti called to a soldier. "Fetch a load of sand from the hills to cover the mess. Leaving them among it will only make it worse."

The solder nodded and wiped his dusty brow. "We are busy," he said and then saw the line of sick people and smelled the filth building up around them. "I will, as soon as I can."

The first group were those who had been exposed to the Aten's fiery face too long. Ṭeḥuti opened a pot of sweet oil and showed the girls how to apply it to the red blisters. Then he smeared a pungent grease over the sores to keep the insects away.

"Simple cases of burning can turn deadly when insects laid their eggs in the raw flesh," he told them. "Now you try. I have others I must tend."

They each accepted a pot and turned to the next person when a scream filled the air. A woman near group two doubled over in pain. Ṭeḥuti turned on the sisters. "Why didn't you tell me there was a woman with child here?"

The older shrugged. "There are so many to treat. It did not seem important."

Ṭeḥuti searched. Young men, old men. Two old blind women. Three younger women with feet so bad they could no longer walk. Girls younger than the two sisters. Another two women sleeping or dead. "Have either of you midwifed before?"

The younger sister, eyes large with fear, shook her head.

"I have," the older sister said. "Twice. With my mother."

The woman screamed again.

"Go," Ṭeḥuti said, "Show your sister what to do."

* * *

Ḥenḥen pulled the oars into the boat, leaned over the side, and stuck his head into the water to dispel the strange vision that assaulted him. But when he cleared his eyes and looked again, Pharaoh's boats were still stretched out before him along the east river bank. Ḥenḥen looked to the sky and whispered a prayer of thanks.

He pulled for the anchored boats with one last burst of energy, dreaming of the treasures Set would heap upon him after he killed the false god Ạsạr.

"I have an urgent message for Pharaoh," Ḥenḥen shouted. "Help me aboard."

"Apologies, holy one. Pharaoh is on shore."

Ḥenḥen looked across the remaining strip of water that separated him from his reward. "Take me there."

wḏb jtrw mhꜣw zꜣwt

ḥsbt 18 ꜣbd 3 prt sw 4 ḫr ḥm n wsír

The River Bank Near Saut

Year 18, Month 3 of Peret, Day 4 under the Majesty of Ạsạr

It was late afternoon before Ṭeḥuti saw Pharaoh again. He was on a final tour of the area, checking dressings and splints, when Pharaoh arrived accompanied by one of his guards.

"I have come to speak with witnesses," Pharaoh said.

Ṭeḥuti led Pharaoh to a man whose feet had been badly blistered. Ṭeḥuti had soaked them in oil and powder and bandaged them in linen. The effect was a curious one; he looked like a man whose feet had been mummified.

Ṭeḥuti touched the man on the shoulder and waited for his eyes to open. "Do you know who this is?"

The man's gaze moved from Ṭeḥuti's face to Pharaoh's, and back again. "No, kind priest. Is he a friend of yours?"

"This is Pharaoh Ạsạr. He wishes to speak with you."

The man's eyes narrowed. "He does not look like god."

"He has come in the form of a man. His heart is heavy with news of the attack on Atef-peh. He wants to know what happened."

"I am a trader down from Atfih to exchange grain from the north for tools."

"What happened in Atef-peh?" Pharaoh asked.

"Some say the Northern provinces attacked without provocation. Others say the North was retaliating for a massacre Atef-peh committed against them."

Pharaoh frowned. "They claim Atef-peh attacked first?"

Setchemu looked to Ṭeḥuti, then back to Pharaoh. "I passed burned out villages."

A high, piercing scream startled Ṭeḥuti. He looked to see the woman whose child the sisters had delivered.

She cried so hard her words were unintelligible. The older of the sisters ran to them and handed her child not to Ṭeḥuti, but to Pharaoh. "Heal her," She pleaded.

Pharaoh accepted the child, still bundled in a blanket and looked at the tiny face. His expression paled. Ṭeḥuti saw the motionless limbs, the gray pallor of the baby's skin.

Water, sun, and wind break and wear away rock. Tears, tragedy, and daily disappointments break and wear away the ka, the spirit. Ṭeḥuti could see the wear in Pharaoh's face, the large, liquid brown eyes, the taut cheeks, the grim lips, in how hard he worked to keep the misery from his face. It wasn't a dead, nameless newborn in his arms, it was Ḥaāmer, it was a battered woman in the Hall of Balance, it was a son, a sibling, a parent struggling to safety and falling along the River bank.

"What is her name?" Pharaoh asked.

"She had none," the older sister replied.

"My Ḥaāmer will giver her a name."

Pharaoh handed the dead child to Ṭeḥuti and walked away.

* * *

Ṭeḥuti watched Pharaoh retreat through the throngs of refugees, back to the solitude of his tent. He wanted to follow, even as the dead child settled into his arms and the girl sobbed, far too young for the responsibility of midwifery. People tugged at his arms, called for his attention. He pushed through them and went in search of a burial shroud.

The sisters followed him. "What happened?" he asked.

The older shook her head, wiping tears from her eyes even as more appeared. Her voice sounded young, girlish, and made his wish there had been someone, anyone else he could have sent. "The child was already dead."

Farther along the hillside Pharaoh slipped away into the anonymity of the refugees. Closer, a bedraggled priest approached.

"Holy one," Ṭeḥuti called.

The man jumped. A moment of fear passed across his face and disappeared. "Was that Pharaoh?" he asked, nodding in the direction Ạsạr had taken. "I must speak with him."

"There will be time for that. Come help me."

The priest glared at Ṭeḥuti, but started over.

"Do I know you?" Ṭeḥuti asked.

"I think not," the man shrugged.

"You look like someone I've seen in Uas."

"I've never been there. I'm from Atef-peh."

Ṭeḥuti nodded. "Pharaoh would indeed see you. Men tell different stories about what happened there."

Ṭeḥuti handed the dead child to the priest. "Place this one with the rest of the dead. Find a shroud. Then I will take you to Pharaoh."

The priest walked away when Ṭeḥuti spoke again. "You should wrap your hands in leather when you are at the oars."

He stopped and looked over his shoulder, his face set in a puzzled frown.

"The blisters on the palms of your hands," Ṭeḥuti said, raising and pointing to his own hand. "A long spell at the boat oars will cause them. But if you wrap your hands in leather, they will not appear. You brought a boat from Atef-peh?"

"Yes," he said. He reached with one hand to swat a fly that was buzzing about his face. Flies were already gathering around the dead newborn. "But we took it apart and used it for firewood."

"It would have been more valuable intact."

"I could not argue with the mob."

Ṭeḥuti nodded. "I suppose not."

jmꜣ-nswt mhꜣw zꜣwt

ḥsbt 18 ꜣbd 3 prt sw 4 ḫr ḥm n wsir

Pharaoh's Tent Near Saut

Year 18, Month 3 of Peret, Day 4 under the Majesty of Ạsạr

"He doesn't want to see you," said the soldier.

Ḥenḥen turned away but Ṭeḥuti caught his arm and pulled him back.

"I am Ṭeḥuti and this is a priest from Atef-peh who has information about the attack."

"Pharaoh ordered that all be kept away."

"He would see me," said Ṭeḥuti.

The soldier snorted and poked a finger into Ṭeḥuti's chest. "Look, priest, Pharaoh's last words before sealing the flap of his tent were *I will behead anyone who disturbs me.* I will not lose my head for announcing a priest. Now go away."

Ḥenḥen turned away again. "Come Ṭeḥuti, Pharaoh will still be here tomorrow. A good meal and a night's sleep will improve us all."

Ḥenḥen was relieved to descend the path that led away from Pharaoh's tent. If Pharaoh had given them audience, Ḥenḥen would have had to kill both Pharaoh and Ṭeḥuti. If he could not execute the double killing perfectly, one or the other would raise an alarm and bring the guards down on him. And the perfect killing, with his arms limp, his legs stiff and sore, was nearly impossible. There would be no mercy if he failed. All he could hope for would be to die before the torture progressed too far.

Ḥenḥen looked at the young priest beside him. He had no desire to kill Ṭeḥuti, but he could not have left the priest as a witness. He saw much that he once was in the younger man: before he began stealing small portions of the tribute, a handful of grain, a cup of oil, a bowl of beer; before he came to High Priest Set's attention and was entrusted with a series of *small* tasks, each less honorable than the one preceding it. Now, ten years later, he was plotting to kill Pharaoh. *How have I come from one to the other? And why can't I go back?*

His journey had made him too philosophical. Time alone with the river could do that, with nothing to do but listen to the gods whispering in the sounds of the water.

Ḥenḥen had no more power now than when he first sought it as a young priest. He had been nothing more than a tool of those having power, manipulated to do their will for a promise that was just one more favor away, performing the tasks they could not dirty themselves with.

Soon that would change. A knife waited, hidden beneath his skirt, the leather scabbard rough against his thigh. *Tonight,* it whispered to him. *Tonight, when the soldiers sleep . . .*

wsḫt nt jwsw m wꜣst ḥsbt 18 ꜣbd 3 prt sw 4 ḫr ḥm n wsỉr

The Hall of Balance in Uas,
Year 18, Month 3 of Peret, Day 4 under the Majesty of Ạsạr

Once the doors to the Hall of Balance were opened, after the day's petitioners had assembled in groups and been received by the scribe, Īset spoke: "I am not here to replace Pharaoh. I am here to complete the justice he gives you. It takes both man and woman to create new life. I believe, Pharaoh believes, it takes both man and woman to create a land where people can endure and prosper.

"Those of you who desire to wait for Pharaoh to return from his campaign in the North may do so. Those of you who wish to remain and submit yourselves to my authority, be assured that I will judge in Pharaoh's wisdom and in the wisdom given to me by the gods."

A few left the hall. Others assumed their places. Set sighed and shook his head with slow, weary sadness, his focus on the stone floor, the decorated walls, the petitioners, his fellow priests, anywhere except the throne and Īset.

Perhaps we should seek Pharaoh's opinion, Set said to one petitioner. *Pharaoh may have additional thoughts,* he said to another. While hearing a petition to purchase land, Īset watched with growing irritation as Set frowned and rubbed his chin once more: "Lady, the laws and traditions regarding large land transactions are complex. There are many details to consider. Perhaps we should wait until Pharaoh returns."

By which he meant bribes, taxes, and generous donations to the temple. To his credit, the petitioner, a tall man dressed in a fine linen skirt, his wrists and ankles circled with gold and lapis bracelets, defended her. "High Priest, I think our Lady quite capable of making this decision. Many times she has sat with Pharaoh and joined him in similar considerations."

He might have believed the words he spoke. Or he might have anticipated receiving a more favorable decision from the wife of Pharaoh than from Pharaoh himself. Īset rubbed thumb and forefinger above her eyes in a fruitless effort to diminish the pain growing in her forehead. "Why do you want this land?"

The question caught him unawares. He repeated it, gesturing with his arms, bracelets tinkling and catching the light. "Because the family can no longer farm it."

"And what will happen to them?"

He smiled, uncertain, and lowered his arms. His eyes lost some of their sternness; his posture its stiffness. He flowed back into himself like water draining into a depression. In a softer voice he said: "I assume she will return to her father's house or other close kin until she can marry again."

"Have you asked her?"

"I would not presume to interfere in matters of family, Lady."

Īset leaned back on her throne. Her dark eyes were dusky jewels, showing different aspects with changes in light and the tilt of her head, glowing wise, wistful, concerned, caring. She took a deep, slow breath and bent forward again as she had seen Pharaoh do, her fingers curling over the golden lion's heads set into the arm rests. "He was your partner before he married and gave his wife children. You have always been a part of their lives. To them you *are* family."

He shrugged. "If it is a matter of price, I can offer more. I would not have it said that I did not share the wealth we made together."

"It is not a matter of wealth. Wealth cannot return her husband to her. It cannot buy love or happiness. The land you want is her life. She made a home there, loved a good man, raised her children. You cannot buy that. You can only take it from her."

A murmur passed through the gathered petitioners and attendants. The priests raised a few eyebrows but kept a stoic silence. More people stopped their whispered conversations and turned to listen to their queen.

The petitioner bowed his head. His voice softened further, shy now, uncertain. "I own a large amount of good farm land. Some fields nourish grain better than others, but I have no desire for one place over another. I understand how each seed puts down roots to become one with the land on which it grows. I never thought that people might do the same. Lady, what would you have me do?"

"This is a land transaction. Do you approve the sale or do you want an adjustment?" Set asked.

Īset held up a finger to silence the High Priest. She peered into the shadows between and beyond the painted columns to beckon a woman and three small children out from among the other petitioners.

The woman stopped in the open area before the dais and bowed to Īset. Her children, a boy, a girl, and another boy ranging from four to eight inundations, stayed close to her, the girl leaning against her leg. Their eyes were dark and wide, looking everywhere but always returning to Īset on her throne, her face gazing like the face of Aih from the encircling ivory headrest.

"Rent her land," Īset said, holding out an open hand to him. "Give her her home and her memories and a share of the profit. When her sons are grown, should they wish to be farmers, hire them. Maybe they will be as worthy partners for your sons as their father was to you."

The petitioner looked at the widow and the children. He nodded to Īset. "Your words are wise and just, Lady. I—"

Īset pointed. "Speak to her."

He nodded again and swallowed. He did not speak right away, using the moment to study her round eyes, her high cheeks, her full lips, the way her heavy, dark hair flowed around her face and splashed across her shoulders. He saw her children, how they were small copies of her and her husband, his business partner. Again, he gazed into her eyes and felt a flush of shyness, as if seeing her for the first time. He struggled with the words: "His table is still there in the market house where we sell our grain. The documents he last worked on are scattered open across it. A pair of stained leather shoes that he laced on each time he went to walk the muddy fields sit beside the door, waiting to be needed again. Each time I think of him gone, each time I move to roll up the documents or take away those ugly old shoes, he seems to die again."

The widow bowed her head. Her youngest son fidgeted beside her. She placed a hand on his head and ruffled his hair. When she looked up, there were tears in her eyes. "I've heard him walk through the house singing only to discover it was only the wind, or a bird, or my own spirit wanting so much for it to be so. And in that moment when I knew it was not him, as you said, he died again."

"Lady," he said, turning to Īset, his voice breaking, "we each know how to die. Tell us how to live with death."

Īset remembered, the moments returning like dreams: *A dusty plateau, a man and woman sad, broken. The body of their only child wrapped in a funeral cloth, secured to a rough litter. Neb-t-ḥe-t inspecting a circular depression lined with stones.*

Ȧpnu, a golden figurine one moment, the next a living god, the sun shimmering from his dark fur. His pink tongue protruded from his snout, panting in the heat. His erect ears twitched to catch voices borne on the wind.

Precious stories of the child's short life. Īset's own spirit at last taking a breath and coming alive again. Food shared. Symbols that glowed with fire and turned to stone.

The images flashed through her like sunlight off the water; the words suddenly poured from her: "They sleep now, maybe they dream. The gods watch over them as you might watch over a sick child as she sleeps through the night. We don't know what comes after. Maybe it is we who slumber and stir in the grip of a strange dream and they who are finally awake.

"My sister Neb-t·ḥe-t is a priestess who buries the dead. She also listens to and talks with the gods. She knows more than I do, more than any of us do. Go to her if you wish. She can teach you how to live when death is all around. I only know how she helped me through the lonely, quiet days when I mourned my own daughter.

The Hall of Balance fell silent. Here someone nodded, there someone reached to dry an eye. Couples drew closer to one another, their hands clasped. The widow came to the petitioner and lifted his hand in hers. "If he was like a brother to you, then I am a sister. I want to stay in my home. I want you to see his sons grow into men."

Īset touched the palm of her hand to her heart. "Go in peace."

"Deftly done, Lady," Set said when the two had left, her children trailing in a line behind them like ducklings. "You bring a woman's touch to our laws and our justice. But how did you know of the widow?"

"When the recorder first entered the petition, Pharaoh and I discussed it. I sent a servant and she returned with the widow's story."

Set smiled and turned in a circle to address those present. "We thought it just a land transaction, but you have made it a reconciliation. A pity we will not receive the tax from the land sale, but the harmony you have created must surely be worth more."

Īset frowned and rubbed the skin above her eyes. "Who can put a price on harmony, High Priest? Certainly it is worth more than a few baskets of grain in the temple granaries. The law is flexible, that is why we have Pharaoh to hear and to judge. Some things are not all they appear. Would you not agree?"

Set smiled and nodded, standing secure among his associates.

The recorder called the next petitioner. A man in a fine skirt and jeweled collar came forward and bowed to Īset. "I petition you for a man accused of murder. With your permission, Lady, I will call him."

Īset nodded.

A soldier holding a polished bronze dagger point up before him led the accused into the Hall of Balance. Bruised, dirty, his hair tangled and plastered to the sides of his face, he limped forward slowly. His skirt was stained with reddish brown spots, a threadbare cloak covered his shoulders. Heavy ropes bound his hands together before him; another heavy rope hobbled his feet. His swollen, grayish hands and feet testified to how tight the ropes were and how long they had been in place. Īset frowned, displeased the care provided by his captors was itself little short of a crime.

"What is this?" Īset asked, turning to the scribe sitting cross-legged to the left of her throne.

He fumbled through a pile of papyri stacked beside him, pulling one out and tracing the lines of symbols with his finger. He squinted and read: "A confessed killer requesting Pharaoh's justice."

The circle of petitioners about the dais fell silent. Beyond them, more people had come in out of the heat to watch.

"He has requested that you perform the execution personally," Set explained, a brightness in his eyes and a flourish to his arm gestures as if pleased at the prospect. "Perhaps we should wait—"

"I know what Pharaoh's justice is, High Priest. Before I do anything, I want to question him."

Set frowned. "What more is there to ask? The law does not require—"

Īset's temper flashed. She pointed at her husband's brother and said: "Do not lecture me on the law as if I were a temple novice. I am *wife* to the law."

"You are wife to the law, not the law itself. Being wife to a priest does not make a woman a priest. Wedding a farmer does not make a woman able to raise and harvest crops. I know how highly my brother regards you, but his regard does not make you capable of giving and deciding and executing the laws of this land. I beseech you to wait until Pharaoh returns."

Īset turned to the guard. "If the high priest speaks again without my bidding, remove him. If he resists, beat him and throw him into the street."

Set closed his mouth and stepped back. His face darkened, his jaw clenched, but his expression was more satisfied than contrite or angry.

A murmur passed though the Hall of Balance. Set had succeeded in shifting attention away from the accused and focusing it on him and her. It was no longer an exercise in justice, it was a contest of wills, of ideologies, of the proper roles of men and women.

A square of sunlight crawled across the stones to cast a shaft of radiance across her ivory throne. Īset looked over those gathered: priests, land owners, leaders of one form or another, to see her sister, somber and still, in the shadow of a pillar.

Neb-t·ḥe-t mourned even when not leading a burial procession. Quiet, respectful, a lingering sadness that peeked from her eyes or from the straight line of her lips. Īset wondered what the gods had done with the laughing, happy child who loved to stalk kittens and talk to wooden dolls.

Neb-t·ḥe-t nodded once as if someone were speaking to her. Before Īset could call out to her, she took the end of a fine linen scarf that covered her head and wrapped it over her nose and mouth then turned toward the entrance. Īset gazed once more on the wretched man trembling before her.

"Did you kill a man?" Īset asked.

The prisoner said nothing until his guard prodded him in the shoulder with the hilt of his dagger. "Yes, Lady, I killed him."

"Why?"

A second prodding, harder. The prisoner fell forward a step before regaining his balance. He remained mute.

Īset rose and stepped down from the dais, her fine linen gown flowing around her like mist. Her sandals whispered across the stones. A song bird chattered high overhead in the ceiling rafters.

She cupped the prisoner's chin in one hand and lifted his face. He shivered at her touch. She squeezed his cheeks until he looked at her.

"You have given your life into my hands. Before I take it away, I shall know why."

His was a smooth face with no scars. In other circumstances it might have been a youthful, handsome face, capable of attracting a maiden's interest. "So young. What are you, 15, 16 inundations?"

He nodded.

The same age as Ḥaāmer. "Have you grown so weary of living that you wish for death? Why did you kill him?"

"He forced my sister."

"And you came to her defense?" Īset looked up. "Magistrate. What are the facts?"

The scribe tugged at his chin and batted at a fly circling his head. "We found no sister. The dead man was alone."

"Where is she?" Īset asked. "Can she verify your words?"

"She fled north."

Īset left the prisoner and returned to her throne. "I can pardon you," she said. "I can forgive your action and free you. But I need a reason. What happened?"

"I came home early," he said. He clenched and unclenched his fingers as if something, perhaps the truth, were struggling to get out. "I heard a noise in the back and thought maybe an animal had gotten in. I found them, him, with my sister. She was crying. There was a rock in my hand, I don't know where it came from. I crushed his skull. I told my . . . my sister to run, up river, back home."

Īset hid her face in her hands as he continued on about how close he was with his sister and how pure and chaste she was and how this man had made repeated attempts to find her alone and defile her.

"Enough," she said, standing. "The next lie you tell me, the next lie I *think* you tell me, will be your last."

He nodded.

"She was not your sister."

"No," he said after a deep, painful breath.

"Was she your wife?"

"She—"

"Think carefully before you answer," she cautioned, hearing the lie crawling up his throat, over his tongue, between his teeth.

"No, not my wife."

"Who was she then?"

"A woman I loved and whose love I sought."

"She chose another," Īset said. She sighed, exhaling her sadness. It spread through the hall like a rare, dark perfume, touching each person, finding the spirit, summoning old and familiar sorrows.

"She did not go north," Īset said in a small, quiet voice. "Is she buried in the hills or lost within the River?"

His voice came from a far place, a cold place where he struggled to speak and not to feel or remember too clearly. "The River. It carried her away. North. Toward home."

His words slowed and died away into silence.

"I wanted to save you," Īset said. "I was willing to defy my husband's brother and the entire priesthood of Ptah to spare your life. I would have done this because you defended your sister's honor knowing what it might cost you. But you lied to me."

"I lied to myself," he said in a fleeting moment of honesty.

Īset let the pain and frustration pour out with her words. "How could you do such a thing? And how will I?"

"You have a choice, Lady," said the scribe. "Pharaoh's justice is sword, water, or stake."

"You choose," Īset said.

Surprise rippled through the audience, raised eyebrows, open mouths, small, audible gasps, moving like a wave across a pond or wind across a field of grain. Some called for one thing, others another. Īset understood then why Pharaoh never offered a choice. She raised her hand for silence.

The accused shook his head and sighed. "Dead is dead. They don't wake up."

Pharaoh always used the sword, severing the head in a single stroke as he did to Neshti for killing his wife Hepaba-t. A quick, painless execution. Īset did not have Pharaoh's strength and had never wielded a sword. "Water," she said.

"Water," the scribe echoed and wrote into the record.

The young man groaned and trembled. Īset looked to his guard. "Take him away."

The guard pulled on the rope and the young man stumbled away, head down. He trembled and shook with silent, tearless sobs. Beads of sweat welled up on his face and arms, dripping to the floor instead. He sniffled but could not wipe his nose.

People began to disperse, vaguely uneasy, unsettled, wary. *Our goddess of love and faithfulness has condemned a man to death.* It was always possible, she had the authority, but there was no story, no record of the wife of Pharaoh executing a man. Pharaoh always performed the execution at her request. The men and women in the Hall of Balance looked back with sober faces at the dais, at Īset, unsure of what they had witnessed or what it meant. *Perhaps we should wait for Pharaoh to return* each seemed to say.

"This session is ended," Īset said, listening to the shuffling of feet and uncertain whispers. Above, a bird continued to sing among the rafters. Leather squeaked as the guards moved into a circle about her.

Pharaoh performed executions in a private high-walled enclosure behind the Hall of Balance. There were three stations: a pool the size of a small room with a modified coffin waiting beside it, a thick, weathered block cut from a massive old tree, and a rack built from undecorated saplings with a stained wooden pike suspended upon it.

Īset had visited the enclosure out of curiosity but never to witness an execution. Even in the warmth of the sun the place had a coldness about it. The alignment of the opening funneled the wind, forcing it inside. It moaned as it caught on the pikes and scraped across the block. The gravel crunched beneath sandals like bones breaking. Each mark in the block spoke of a severed head, a death, a font of blood. The pike, darkened from tip to center, testified to the lives lost drip by bloody drip. She struggled to control herself, to keep the tears from her eyes and the screams locked safely within. She looked at her hands, whether it was merely a shiver or shudder or shaking, she refused to surrender to it.

Beside the pool was a bare coffin with eye-sized holes along its sides. The lid was off, the bottom was lined with smooth, flat river stones. The guard positioned the young man beside it while Īset and her guards, Set and two priests, the executioner and three assistants, and the scribe looked on.

After a silent, uncomfortable moment, Set said: "It is customary to ask if the condemned has any final words."

Īset nodded and swallowed the lump that had boiled up into her throat. She pushed away a wisp of hair that had strayed into her eyes. "Do you have anything to say before we give you to the water?"

He shook even as Īset forced herself not to. He sweat now, the drops running down his cheek, one dripping from his chin. "I'm sorry," he said. "I didn't mean to."

He cried finally, there at the end. Tears and sobs. Half-formed sentences poured from him, for his love, for her lover, for himself. Īset felt tears in her eyes but would not wipe them away.

He gasped and struggled when the executioner's assistants took him by shoulders and feet and laid him into the box. They removed the hobble and bound his feet together.

Their actions were quick and methodical and well-rehearsed as they fastened the lid on the box and secured it with ropes and pegs. They did not speak, but when a hand reached out for the end of a rope, a peg, or a hammer, another hand was there holding it. They lifted ropes that cradled the coffin and shuffled as one to position it over the pool. Screams echoed through the holes. The coffin bounced on the ropes as the men struggled to hold it aloft.

They looked to Īset. Behind them, Set nodded, his face impassive. Īset repeated the gesture and they played out the rope, lowering the coffin into the pool and tying the ends to posts. Air bubbles boiled out of the holes and upward like panicky birds. Īset thought she could still hear the youth's screams.

She could no longer suppress the shaking. Tears blurred the image of the coffin beneath the water. She did not care. It rocked from side to side, sending desperate ripples across the surface. Reflections distorted and fractured. Īset felt the same rending within.

She looked up to see Set focused on the youth's final struggles, almost as if he could see through the wood to the desperate, tortured motions within. Lips parted, his tongue crept from tooth to tooth and back.

With a last, small trail of escaping bubbles, it was over. The box came to rest, the ripples died away until the water was once again calm.

Tears continued to spill from her eyes. Pharaoh would not cry, he might even smile, a grim, satisfied smile. He would swing his sword with no more concern than swatting a fly, assured that he had removed evil, applied justice, and restored balance to the land. But she saw a child once held and suckled by a mother. A child that had strayed, killed, and was no more. There was no justice, no balance now, only loss: children lost, balance lost, innocence lost.

The executioner's assistants and the scribe stirred and drifted off, around the block, around the pike and racks that held it, returning to duties elsewhere, melting away like clouds over the hilltops.

"We will raise the coffin at sunset and give him over for burial. You have fulfilled your role. I will remain here," said the executioner.

Īset nodded stiffly, barely able to swallow, and closed her eyes.

A shadow passed across her eyelids, a touch of warm breath tickled her cheek and ear. She opened them again to see Set bending close, a smile curling his lips that only she could see.

"When you struggle, it excites me all the more," he said.

Īset slapped him, her open hand leaving a blush across his cheek. Those close by whirled with surprised expressions. A guard stepped forward, his sword already in hand. "At your word, I will kill him," he said.

Set's eyes flashed with anger, then he smiled. "Do it. See if my brother forgives you."

Īset motioned the soldier to put away his sword "He always forgives me. Will he forgive you?" she asked.

She returned to the privacy of the queen's house before the violent purging took her. All that she had eaten and more came up in painful, clenching heaves until her whole body ached.

Īset wanted to scream, she wanted to run. She wanted to cry until she was blind. She did nothing except tremble, while her thoughts of guilt, confusion, and terror soared away like birds, out of her body and up into the air, across the River, over the sand, rising above the hills and mountains, higher than the sky. Far away from the pool with the lifeless coffin at its bottom, far away from Set and his crude advances.

Her maidservants Steppu and Tchefeṭ-t, silent, eyes wide, ministered to her as best they could. The youngest two, frightened to tears, they sent away. Tchefeṭ-t held a bowl, Steppu held her Lady's hair and rubbed her back while Īset retched. Later they exercised all their healing arts: herbs in fresh water to settle the heaving, fire and blankets to warm away the shakes, oils and salves to lessen the puffiness about her tear-stained eyes and ease her ragged, gasping breaths.

Īset did not speak, she could not, there were no words inside her, only horror and sadness and grief. Each time she closed her eyes she saw the coffin rocking back and forth at the bottom of the pool. She heard Set's voice: *It excites me all the more.*

With the last of the afternoon light streaming through the windows, Īset finally spoke to her maidservants: "Please go away."

Steppu and Tchefeṭ-t gathered their pots and pitchers, silent except for the sounds of lids and stoppers seating. Their faces could not hide their concern or fright. They moved almost reluctantly, compelled to obey but worried for what might come to their Lady in her isolation.

"We will wait close by," Steppu said.

Īset pushed her way out of the confining blankets as the sound of sandals on stone died away outside her door. She rose painfully, as if she had suffered a beating. She slipped the straps of her dress off her shoulders and let it fall in a puddle at her feet.

She dried herself with linen towels and applied only the barest of perfumes. She went through her clothes without knowing what she sought, only those she did not: clothes for celebration or ceremony, clothes that featured or displayed her, clothes finely made, expensive or regal. She dropped the discards in a careless heap. At the bottom of an old box, she found something plain and shapeless, white, without decoration, a wrap to cover her head and conceal her face. It was a dress she never wanted to wear again and had to wear now, a dress for mourning.

At sunset she returned to the pool in the place of execution. The block had grown a long shadow and seemed larger and more ominous as she passed by it, the cuts projecting like jagged teeth across the sand. The pike and rack cast a glyph against the wall that moved and changed with the setting sun. It seemed to say *despair.*

The executioner peered into Īset's concealing shawl. "Are you here for the body?"

Īset shook her head.

He frowned. "Neb-t-ḥe-t?"

She shook a second time. "No."

He drew back and dipped his head. "Lady," he said.

The executioner and his men undid the ropes from their anchoring posts and raised the coffin. Progress was slow, punctuated by their grunts and strained pops from the ropes. The coffin was much heavier soaked with water.

They paused as the coffin cleared the surface, securing the ropes about the posts. Water poured from the holes in the sides and bottom. When the flow diminished to a trickle, they took up the ropes again, raising the coffin higher and setting it down beside the pool.

They worked in silence, removing the pegs, untying the ropes. One man at the head, one at the foot, they lifted the lid.

His ruddy skin was pale, washed out, bloated. He had faded to the color of linen sails, dirtied by a long time on the River. His eyes were open, glazed over, white. His mouth was open: Water tinged with a reddish froth trickled out and down his cheeks and chin.

His skin was shredded and torn away from around his wrists and feet where he had struggled to free himself from the ropes. Threads of muscle lay exposed, strands of gray string tangled with purple veins among patches of slick, white skin. One arm was bent wrong—pulled from the joint or broken.

Īset's insides were rising into her throat again even as she gave in to the shaking.

A hand touched her shoulder. Another went about Īset's waist and drew her back a step from the pool into the shadows of the enclosure. Īset recognized her sister's face.

"I killed him." Īset said, unable to close her eyes or look away.

"You executed Pharaoh's justice, sending him to the gods."

Dead is dead. "He will not wake up."

Īset sobbed, Her knees folded. Neb-t·ḥe-t caught and held her. "They never wake up. Loved ones, innocence, youth—they never wake up again once they've left us."

"I wanted to free him, I wanted him to live," Īset cried. "I was looking for a reason to spare him and all he did was lie to me. Why wouldn't he let me help him?"

"Maybe you should have waited for Pharaoh to return," Neb-t·ḥe-t said.

Īset screamed her rage and grief. "Would that have made me innocent? Being judge but not executioner?"

"You think you are the only one to ever judge and execute another? You think the gods are cruel and unjust to you?" Neb-t·ḥe-t yelled back at her. "Everyone has faced this or worse. Find someone who has not and I will grant you the right to carry on like a sheltered child."

With an intake of breath Īset stopped sobbing. Her eyes widened and narrowed once more. She slapped Neb-t·ḥe-t with unexpected fury.

Neb-t·ḥe-t did not react, other than to center her head after the blow. Her cheek reddened, hiding the last yellow-grey traces of the bruise Set had given her during Ḥaāmer's funeral ceremony.

Īset saw it and began to cry again. "I am so sorry," she said, reaching out, clasping Neb-t·ḥe-t's hands. "I didn't mean to do that."

"Yes, you did," Neb-t·ḥe-t said. "You've always meant it, because I remind you that you were not always the first choice."

"That's not true."

"It is," Neb-t·ḥe-t said. She opened and closed her jaw ad raised a hand to rub her cheek, already dark and swollen. "I wish I could tell you that this is the worst day of your life, but it isn't. I wish there were no more tears, no more death; I wish your life was going to be long and happy and easy—then I could be free of you and go my own way. But none of that is true. People who live extraordinary lives rarely find those lives long or happy or easy.

"Pharaoh was right. The gods hurt us as they make us into their tools. They've hurt you today. So take this as a warning, Īset. There's worse to come. *Much worse.*"

jmꜣ-nswt mḥꜣw zꜣwt
ḥsbt 18 ꜣbd 3 prt sw 4 ḫr ḥm n wsỉr

Pharaoh's Tent Near Saut
Year 18, Month 3 of Peret, Day 4 under the Majesty of Ạsạr

Pharaoh's voice broke the still darkness within the tent: "What are you, shadow?"

Ḥenḥen stopped and slowly turned his head, searching for a sound, a breath, a whisper of fabric, a rasp of feet on sand to reveal how close Pharaoh was.

He took a short, sliding step. An arm closed about his throat, pulling his head back. A hand clenched his wrist and twisted it behind him, igniting a fire in his shoulder. The knife he carried fell silent to the sand. He struggled, lashing out, but the pressure on his neck and shoulder increased. He could not breathe, points of light flared in his vision, the throbbing pain in his shoulder grew more intense and more distant.

His captor pulled him deeper into the tent. He struggled once more for breath, but no air could get past the arm tightened beneath his jaw. He was almost beyond caring. His thoughts were drifting away; he no longer felt his feet dragging across the sand. The hard River pursuit, his muscles exhausted from pulling at the oars, watching, hoping for Pharaoh's boat around each bend of the River—all had come to this.

Then the hold was gone. He fell in a limp heap, a distant, passing thought of trying to break the fall going unheeded by his numb limbs. He landed on a pile of soft pillows. He gasped for breath, reaching up to rub his throat with his good arm.

"If you move from this spot, I will kill you," Pharaoh whispered in his ear.

He began to tremble, except for his twisted arm. He moved it and bit his lip to keep from screaming. He thought it might be broken.

The light from an oil lamp flared in his face, blinding him. He squeezed his eyes shut. The light moved away and he squinted to see a man's outline.

"What did you drop?"

Pharaoh picked up the bronze knife and studied its markings, frowning, turning it over several times in the shadowy light. He brought the lamp to a low table in front of Ḥenḥen and sat down across from him.

"Sit up," Pharaoh commanded. "Why do you carry my brother's knife?"

Ḥenḥen struggled to a sitting position, one arm balancing him on the cushion, the other hanging useless. "I found it."

"Why would you use it to kill me?" Pharaoh's voice was soft. His dark gaze never left Ḥenḥen's face. "Did Set send you or were you to leave this behind to implicate him nd start a cycle of revenge that would destroy us both?"

"I have no answer for you."

Light from the oil pot danced in Pharaoh's eyes but did not give them warmth. "I could show you mercy, though you deserve death. Give me a reason to be merciful."

Ḥenḥen looked at the sand and said nothing.

"I asked you a question and I will have its answer before I send you to the house of the damned."

Ḥenḥen released a slow, painful breath. The flame above the oil pot shivered and spit at its touch. "You are not a god, Ạsạr. Egypt cannot afford to think that you are. We cannot afford to see you every day in the temples, the markets, the fields, and think that god is here to watch over and protect us because it isn't true. Life is still dangerous and uncertain. Evil remains. Good people die. You promise us much but give us only false hope."

As punctuation to his words, soldiers out beyond Pharaoh's tent laughed quietly at some shared joke.

"You would drive a knife into my heart to show I am mortal? Is that your understanding of what it means to be the eyes and ears of the gods?" Pharaoh asked.

Ḥenḥen wished for wine or beer, anything to dull the senses and still his heart. His twisted arm throbbed. The pain made his words sharper than he intended. "I know something of your history. Your father believed the way to conquer Egypt was to unite the civil and religious authority in one man—a man who was god. He chose you to be god and Set to be your high priest.

"But you are not a god and your brother does not worship you. Your daughter died because you had no spell to save her. The gods don't hear you any more than they hear the wind."

Pharaoh rose suddenly and put his fist through the wooden table, breaking it into two pieces. Ḥenḥen lurched forward to catch the lamp before it could overturn. The pain in his injured arm brought tears to his eyes. He looked up at Pharaoh, ready for death, but saw a grimace of pain instead.

"Come," Pharaoh called.

A small circle of soldiers huddled outside around a fire, driving the night chill from their hands and legs as they told stories. They straightened and stopped their whispers when Pharaoh emerged from the tent. The chief of the guards detached himself to approach and bow before Pharaoh, eyeing Ḥenḥen as he sunk to both knees.

"This man found his way into my tent. He came to kill me with this knife."

Ḥenḥen did not have time to frown. Pharaoh swung his arm in a wide, deadly arc, burying the knife to the hilt in Ḥenḥen's ribs. Ḥenḥen gasped at the impact and reached to pull it out, but his knees gave way as he fumbled for it and he toppled forward, twisting to land face up.

Ḥenḥen saw the large, surprised eyes of the guard leaning over him, the whites showing pale and round like two reflections of the Aih. Pharaoh watched, emotionless, as if he had just swatted a fly.

Ḥenḥen stopped breathing. His vision faded.

Pharaoh spoke again. "At dawn, gather the company. Then execute the guards who were watching the north side of my tent this evening."

Ḥenḥen died hearing the sounds of Pharaoh's sandals retreating across the midnight sand.

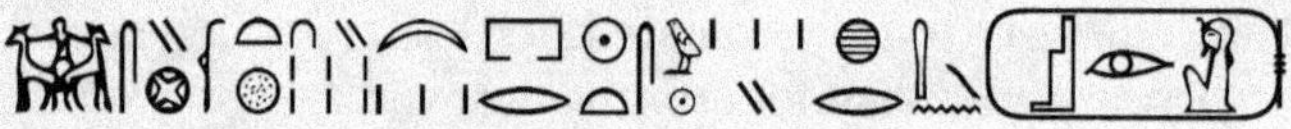

kjs ḥsbt 18 ȝbd 3 prt sw 5 ḫr ḥm n wsỉr

Qes

Year 18, Month 3 of Peret, Day 5 under the Majesty of Ạsạr

The temple and the house of Governor Khnemes still stood stark and white against the azure sky, but the capital of Atef-peh was otherwise in ruins. The streets were littered with death. Buildings were broken down. Foundations and jagged stretches of wall poked up from the sand and rock like bits of broken bone, blackened at intervals by fire. Ṭeḥuti had never witnessed such destruction and for a long time that warm afternoon, as Pharaoh's boat drifted silently closer along the River, could not comprehend what he saw.

Workmen held in place by ropes let down from the roof patched holes in the upper reaches of Khnemes' house. One pointed at Pharaoh's boat and shouted to those below.

Maaạ's boat stood anchored at a makeshift dock erected on the ruins of the one that stood before it. Several small boats waited beyond, close to shore, their sails down, colorful hieroglyphic pennants waving lazily in the light breeze.

Ṭeḥuti expected to hear families wailing for their dead and the wounded crying out for help that would not come. He expected to see those too frightened to stop crying and those too frightened to start. He did not expect what he saw.

"They're working," he said, unaware he was speaking aloud. It was such a normal sight that it almost shouted at him. In the midst of the devastation, people were going about the process of recovery.

"Give them a purpose. Keep them busy so there is no time for despair. Show them others, worse off, to care for. Maaạ did this," Pharaoh said.

Men cleared debris and sorted it into piles of materials that could be used again. Others restored those structures that could be restored. A more solemn group gathered people either in their arms or on hastily constructed litters. If they still moved or called out, they were taken one direction. The dead went another.

Women gathered food and water, preparing it in a large communal area stretching the length of a street. Cook fires smudged the sky. Baskets of wheat and fruit were arranged in groups, plucked birds and butchered animals hung from poles, waiting their place in pots and roasters. Tired, dusty people came by to collect a piece of bread, a bowl of beer, a handful of dates, then wandered off to where they were needed next.

This was the first of Maaa's provinces, Pharaoh had spoken of knowing little of Khnemes, who had come to Uas only twice: once to ensure peace, once to pursue trade.

Ṭeḥuti closed his eyes a moment against the bright sun on the water. Pharaoh stood alone at the bow. A group of buzzards gathered in a tight circle, squawking and picking at something hidden in the rocks. Their wings unfurled as they contested for a chance at whatever dead thing they had found. Ṭeḥuti tried not to think of what it might be.

Pharaoh's boat turned its side to the current as it neared the dock and found an open spot across from Maaạ's boat. The sailors, conscious of the quiet, deserted city, worked in whispers. Only the scraping of the ropes, the creaking of the oars, and the rustle of the sails as they were taken down and tied disturbed the somber mood.

Soldiers on the dock pulled a ramp into place and bowed as Pharaoh and Ṭeḥuti approached. Maaạ waited at its foot, his head down. He looked up when Pharaoh touched his shoulder.

"It saddens me to be the bearer of such tidings," Maaạ said.

"As it saddens me to hear them. What is your news?"

"The revolt has been stopped. But Khnemes and his family are dead."

Pharaoh studied the people gathering around Maaạ, settling on one in particular, a woman with red, tear-stained eyes. She was beautiful even in her sorrow.

"I grieve with you, Tehāra," Pharaoh said.

She nodded, new tears slipping down her cheeks. Pharaoh moved as if to wipe them away, then stopped and let his arm fall back to his side. "Let us return to the house of the Nomarch and decide what must be done."

Pharaoh gave other orders. He set some to establishing a camp. He sent soldiers to join Maaạ's men in the hills, looking for signs of those who had attacked the city. He set a third group to finding any remaining excess stores and carrying them up to the women preparing the food.

The guards arranged themselves around the party and guided them through the streets, around debris, to the house of Nomarch Khnemes. In sunlight the walls gleamed, but as they neared, stains and pits in the clay facing told Ṭeḥuti that bloodshed had occurred right up to the Nomarch's door.

They passed people entering and exiting the main palace gate. It leaned, hanging by a single bronze hinge, the dusty old wood pitted and cut. Guards ushered them through. The courtyard was littered with blankets and linens holding the wounded, a patchwork of pale squares on red earth. Those able to walk tended those who could not.

It was cooler and quiet inside the house. The sounds of soldiers and workmen toiling, of the sick and wounded moaning and crying outside the doors were muted and distant. The walls were bare, unpainted. The linens and tapestries had been torn down to become blankets and bandages.

The guards showed them to the Hall of the Nomarch. Pharaoh sat in Khnemes chair on the dais. Servants appeared in haste with chairs for the others, Tehāra and her retinue, prince Maaạ and Ṭeḥuti. The soldiers took stations at the exits.

Pharaoh surveyed the small group, his gaze coming to rest on Maaạ's tired face. "What happened here?"

Maaạ pulled himself up from his chair. "I came as soon as I heard. I was too late and the force I brought too little. The attackers were gone. My men are following trails leading northward through the hills, but have reported seeing no one."

Maaạ looked up at Pharaoh as if seeking a reason or explanation, his face haggard, shoulders sagging. "These people are not soldiers. They had not taken this land by force. They were farmers and simple merchants. They have been here for generations. This was not a battle, it was a slaughter."

"How were Khnemes and his family killed?"

Maaạ bowed his head, took a deep breath, and answered: "Khnemes herded as many as he could to safety behind his own walls. He took an arrow in the chest and another in the neck just outside the gate."

Pharaoh's voice was little more than a whisper. "And his family?"

"His wife and son were in the Temple of Ptah when it was attacked. They died there."

The stillness of the room was broken by Tehāra's soft sobs, her tears spilling once more for her brother and his family.

"This could have been avoided," Maaạ said. "Instead, Set sent priests here to defend us—priests who fled once the fighting started."

"Priests?" Ạsạr asked.

"After your dimissal, Set sent me priests trained as soldiers. They drank my beer and ate my food then disappeared at the first sign of trouble. They left my people defenseless, grain before the scythe."

"My brother sent priest soldiers to defend you?"

"Yes," Maaạ replied. "But they left before the attack."

"Where did they go?"

"Away, that is all I know. They were thick in the streets and hills one day and gone the next."

Pharaoh frowned and tugged at his chin, his gaze troubled and distant. "I would question the survivors. Someone may have heard something." Rising, he shook his head and muttered, "Priests sent by Set."

"I wish to return to my rooms and mourn my brother and his family," Tehāra said.

"Yes," Pharaoh replied. "I will visit you later."

"That isn't necessary," she said. "Pharaoh must have more important things to do here than comfort an old friend." Tehāra turned and walked away with her hand maidens following.

Ṭeḥuti watched the color rise and then fall from Pharaoh's face. Tehāra meant something to him, Ṭeḥuti could see that. Something more than just an old friend.

* * *

There were the sweet scents of the flowers cultivated for their perfumes, and aromatic, sometimes pungent fragrance of the herbs and spices savored as seasoning for food. But underneath these were rank, unappealing odors of injury, sickness, and death.

Maaạ took them to a makeshift tent tied between two palm trees. Several young men lay on linens spread in its shade. Maaạ settled to his knees beside one who looked no more than fourteen or fifteen inundations old. The youth had a gaping leg wound that had been carelessly bandaged. The leg was swollen and purple-black. Milky fluid leaked from the wound. It smelled of death.

Maaạ touched the young man's shoulder. His eyes fluttered open, bright with the intensity of fever.

Ṭeḥuti knelt on the other side and placed his hand on the young man's forehead. It was like placing his hand on a sunny rock. "He has little time left," Ṭeḥuti said. He saw a woman nearby kneeling over another man. "Quickly, bring me some cool water and linen."

"Will he be able to speak to Pharaoh?"

"Speak?" The young man croaked his lips dry and his tongue swollen.

The man broke into an eerie giggle that ended in sobbing tears. He closed his eyes. His breathing labored on for several moments and stopped.

Maaạ leaned forward. "Tell Pharaoh what you saw and heard."

"He's dead," Ṭeḥuti said.

"Is there another?" Pharaoh asked.

"I will tell you."

The woman left to do as Ṭeḥuti asked. The man she tended struggled to a sitting position and clutched his head. Beneath the bandage that covered his skull a large black bruise darkened one cheek and eye.

"They said we started it. They said we attacked and slaughtered their fishing villages first. Their battle cries were for vengeance and justice—not conquest. I heard the dying cry out to the women and children they had lost."

Maaạ looked up at Pharaoh. "Where were your brother's men?"

The wounded man looked long and hard at Ṭeḥuti. "I will say nothing more with him here."

"I trust Ṭeḥuti with my life."

"The priest must go."

"I will tend to the injured on the other side of the garden," Ṭeḥuti said.

A shadow slithered across the sand, cast by something on top of the enclosing wall. Ṭeḥuti looked up to see a man with a bow in his hand.

Ṭeḥuti turned to shout at Pharaoh. Maaạ also looked toward the wall and lunged to cover Pharaoh as the arrow hissed over Ṭeḥuti's head. It glanced off Maaạ's bronze armor and struck Pharaoh high in the chest near his left shoulder, knocking him to the ground.

The figure brandished his bow triumphantly in the air. "Death to Pharaoh," he shouted. "Life to Egypt!"

He tumbled from the wall to the safety of the ruined city as a hale of arrows pierced the empty air where he had been.

wh ꜣnt m ḳjs

ḥsbt 18 ꜣbd 3 prt sw 5 ḫr ḥm n wsi̓r

The Governor's House in Qes

Year 18, Month 3 of Peret, Day 5 under the Majesty of Ạsạr

"How bad?" Pharaoh croaked through dry lips.

Ṭeḥuti motioned for beer. "Maaạ saved your life. The arrow was aimed for your heart but he changed it enough that it struck your shoulder instead. With the right magics and rest, you will recover."

A guard returned with the beer. Ṭeḥuti accepted and held it out to Pharaoh. "By your command."

Pharaoh nodded. Ṭeḥuti lifted Pharaoh's head and pressed the bowl to his lips. Pharaoh took several swallows before tipping his head away.

A voice at the door tapestry interrupted them. Ṭeḥuti went to pull it aside. Tehāra was there, seeming little more than a child standing before the two hulking, armed guards. She would not look at Pharaoh or Ṭeḥuti, addressing the floor between the two men instead. "I would visit Pharaoh."

Pharaoh answered before Ṭeḥuti could refuse: "Come in."

Ṭeḥuti let Tehāra into the room and lit another pot of oil to push away the gloom. He looked carefully from one to the other, searching for an echo of what once passed between them. Ṭeḥuti stumbled over his words as he searched for a convenient escape. "There are sick and wounded to attend."

"Before you go, Ṭeḥuti, I would sit up."

"The wound is too recent."

"I would sit up," repeated Pharaoh.

Ṭeḥuti sighed. "This will hurt. And if the wound begins to bleed you must lie back again. The arrow can no longer kill you, but failing to allow for Ptah's healing can."

"I understand." Pharaoh said.

Ṭeḥuti helped him into a sitting position at the edge of his bed, resting his feet on the cool stone floor. His arm was bound tightly to his side. He wanted to rub his chin, and struggled a moment before raising the other hand.

Tehāra drifted close and settled silently in a chair beside him.

"I grieve with you for the loss of your brother," Pharaoh said.

She rubbed her hands together, stopping when her fingers touched the gold ring Khnemes had given her as a wedding gift. "How could you do such a terrible thing."

Her voice was cold and raspy like the sound of dried reeds dragged across stone. Pharaoh frowned. "I don't understand."

"Did you think Maaạ wouldn't tell us? He warned us to prepare because you were not sending help. Did you really say you would be as pleased to bargain with his enemies after they killed him?"

"That is not what I said. He was demanding, bargaining, when he was not in position to do so."

Tehāra shook her head. Hair covered her face. "Was it worth it? Your pride and position are intact. You punished Maaạ for daring to bargain with you. My brother and his family are dead as a result."

Her shoulders slumped. She looked up with fresh tears in her eyes. She wore no kohl, no sweet perfumes that whispered of flowers and rare oils. She wore a simple, shapeless black shift for mourning.

"I did not know this would happen. He demanded Āakhu. I was not going to trade her for his loyalty."

The tear tracks were etched on the tight, drawn cheeks. Her lips were a straight, thin line, paling from being so tightly pressed together. "You certainly gamble with other people's lives like a god. You still have your daughter and I have a hundred funerals to attend. You could have reached agreement with Maaạ, sent men to protect us and settle our disputes with the people to the North. But you could not abide another man as bold as yourself. Instead you let your brother send priests to make empty promises and then abandon us."

"Set acted without my knowledge. I will deal with him."

"And every man and woman murdered here will still be dead," Tehāra cried, a bitter hollow sound that struck his ears sharper than the arrow that had pierced his shoulder. "Even should you gain our allegiance, there will be little tribute this year. Much of the land will be given over to graves. And when a basket of our grain or fruit or spice comes to your table, remember what it cost. Remember the dead, broken bodies. This is your fault. These people are dead because of you."

She stumbled to the door sobbing, threw the tapestry aside, and never looked back.

wh3nt m ḳjs

ḥsbt 18 3bd 3 prt sw 9 ḫr ḥm n wsỉr

Ruins of Qes

Year 18, Month 3 of Peret, Day 9 under the Majesty of Ạsạr

The sun rested like a great orange fruit on the western horizon. Pharaoh sat on the broken base of a pillar and watched it. In the distance he heard the soldiers talking, far enough away that he might have privacy but close enough to come to his assistance should danger approach.

The reddening light stained the pale amber stones scattered around him. The lengthening shadows played tricks with his sight. For a moment, he imagined that the land was littered with the eggs of a great stone beast. *What might hatch from such eggs?*

He spoke: "Your birth as a great people will not be an easy one, my Egypt. Women claim that giving birth never is and no woman has ever given birth to one such as you.

"Many good men and women have died to see you born. Would my Ḥaāmer be alive this night if I had devoted more of my life to her and less to your care? Would Khnemes still be if I had not seen the vision of a single Egypt stretching the length of the River?"

Tehāra's anger and accusations, the accusations Maaạ made only with his eyes, the dead and dying he had encountered, the sad, frightened faces, the disappointment: Ạsạr was drowning in remembrance of them. *I have failed and others have paid the cost.* Pharaoh felt tears stinging his eyes that had not come to them since the days of his youth. He tried to look up at the sky, but the strain on his shoulder made him wince. He looked back to see Ra slipping behind the hills to the west.

"Great gods of Egypt," Pharaoh cried. "All I ever wanted was to gather your people together in wealth and happiness. Instead, I bring death and distrust and rebellion. My brother taunts me and seeks to replace me. Tell me what you want me to do."

A breeze from the hills touched his cheeks, taking away the tears that tarried. The sunset was otherwise silent.

A shadow moved among the rocks. He watched as it approached to be sure it was not another trick of the fading light. He thought of calling out to the guards, but did not. *Perhaps this is my answer. Perhaps Ptah has finally sent his assassin with quick death to the Pharaoh who failed.*

It was only a few feet away, a small thing of tattered rags. Pharaoh closed his eyes and waited. He listened to the sound of the sand and gravel as the footsteps neared. He braced for the impact and did not flinch when it came.

But there was no sting of a knife as it slid between his ribs, seeking his heart. He opened his eyes to see a small child, shivering, clinging to him.

Pharaoh's voice, when he found it, was husky with the tension of expected death. "Who are you?"

Two large, round eyes peered at him from the midst of the rags. "I'm frightened," the girl said.

"So am I," said Pharaoh.

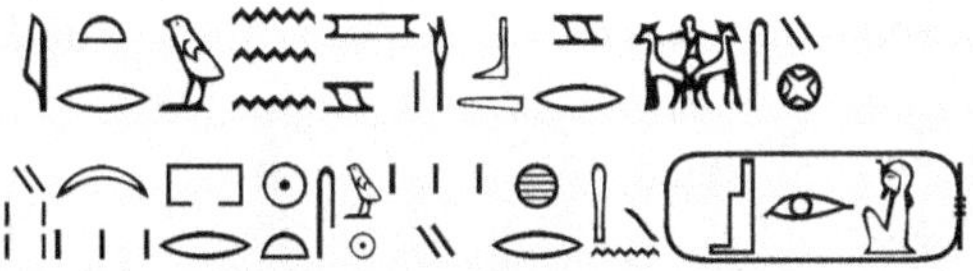

wḏb-jtrw r ḳjs

ḥsbt 18 ꜣbd 3 prt sw 5 ḫr ḥm n wsỉr

The River Bank at Qes

Year 18, Month 3 of Peret, Day 12 under the Majesty of Ạsaṛ

A tent sprawled before the dock that led to Pharaoh's boat. The sides were open, the roof lifting and falling drowsily, as if savoring the first of the morning's breeze.

Maaạ sat in its shade on a unadorned wooden bench, leaning into a small circle of people. The woman who directed the preparation and distribution of food sat across from him, a cat in her lap sniffing at her soup-stained skirt. Beside her, a tired young man who oversaw the clearing of rubble bent as if a heavy weight still pressed on his shoulders, his arms scratched, bruised, and dirty, his skirt encircled with a dark line of sweat and dust. On either side of Maaạ soldiers just returned from the hills, sandals worn, dust coating their bronze weapons, discussed the reports from comrades who still searched for signs of attackers.

Maaạ looked up as Pharaoh and his party approached. "Going?" he called.

"My soldiers are no longer needed. It is time I returned to Uas."

"How is your shoulder?"

Pharaoh shrugged as much as the tight bandages would allow. "Ṭeḥuti tells me I must rest and heal. I never thanked you for deflecting that arrow. You saved my life."

Maaạ made a small nod to dismiss his visitors. They left together, whispering, stealing glances at Maaạ and Pharaoh, drifting back to their places in the ruined city. "I would think your gratitude might transcend mere words, seeing how much devastation you've seen here."

Pharaoh sighed and winced as the effort tugged at his shoulder. All those with him but Ṭeḥuti and his personal guard continued on to the boat, winding around Maaạ's tent to the dock. "How can I reward you? What can I give you that honors you for what you did?"

"I want what I've always wanted."

"Āakhu?"

Maaạ nodded.

"I gave you one daughter."

Maaạ nodded again. "I loved Ḥaāmer. Āakhu is beautiful, but beauty fades. Ḥaāmer heard the voices of the gods. In the days ahead, knowing how they would have me navigate the unfamiliar waters I must travel would have been far more valuable."

"Āakhu is promised to another."

Ṭeḥuti shifted from foot to foot as if the sand burned through his sandals into his feet.

"Promised but not yet given," Maaạ said.

A solitary cloud passed across the fiery disc of the Aten. For a moment the air, the earth, the mood between Pharaoh and Maaạ cooled. The shadow crept over them and away, to the broken, quiet city and the hills beyond. The Aten glared down in blistering warmth once more.

"The provinces I govern are my children. You demand I give them to you while refusing me your own. Why should I acquiesce?" Maaạ asked.

"So this never happens again," Pharaoh said. "If you love these provinces as children, give them that assurance."

"I want a visible sign joining our houses together. In lieu of a son, I want to be your heir."

"I cannot."

Maaạ lifted a bowl of beer to his lips and sipped. Pharaoh stood in the sun with his guards, a few steps from his boat. "Do you dislike and distrust me because I am not like you or because I am? Go back to your boat, back to Uas. You asked me what you could give me for saving your life and I have told you. If you won't honor the choice then we have no further need of one another."

"I could take these provinces, leave my soldiers here and declare them mine," Pharaoh said. "You haven't the force left to oppose me."

"You could. But you could not take our love. It would be difficult to keep so distant a people if they did not love you. Especially after what has happened." Maaạ set down his beer and folded his hands in his lap. " How much are we worth to you? How much is our forgiveness worth?"

Pharaoh frowned and looked over his shoulder toward his boat and the River beyond. The last of the morning mist drifted among the reeds, lingering as gems of dew. Colors swirled on the surface of the River. Flashes of light reflected back at him, giving birth to images, faces, memories. The water whispered to him.

A child trembled in his arms. Two glistening lines of tears flowed down grief-stricken cheeks, the first of the precious water Tehāra would return to the sand. The anger and hurt, and worse, the disappointment in her dark eyes wounded him still. Darkness, a murderous priest with a familiar, decorated bronze knife. The displaced, refugees who had not died in their homes or in flight, drifted across the evening hills like smoke, looking for a place to rest.

He squeezed his eyes closed, but only the sight of the boat and the River left him. The other images continued to move and accuse him. When he opened his eyes once more, he turned to Ṭeḥuti. "Accompany my guards to the boat and wait. I have a matter to discuss with Maaạ and it may take the morning."

Ṭeḥuti, pale as freshly washed linen, jaw tight, nodded and turned stiffly away.

Chapter 12

ABYDOS, EGYPT, THE FEATURE, THE ARCHAEOLOGICAL TRAILER, JUNE 27TH, 12:20 A.M.:

Lisa remembered a geologist's hammer in the desk drawer under the window. She snatched it out, smashing it on the intruder's hand with a sickening, bone-shattering crunch. He screamed, jerking his hand back. His gun fell with a clatter on the desk. His face disappeared. Grabbing the gun, Lisa's eyes never left the window. Backing away to the computer desks, she would shoot the next face that appeared.

The other man pulled up into the window. She fired the gun at him, jerking with terror. He dropped.

Missed! Damn!

Her ears rang. She shifted to a new position, knowing they would come in shooting. A minute later, shouts came from the direction of the Egyptian military camp, followed by lights playing over the windows. Lisa must have gotten the sentries attention. Someone pounded on the trailer door, the accompanying voice sounded like Captain Jagardii's. Pulling the drape aside she saw the shirtless captain.

Lisa dropped the drape while shoving the gun into the open drawer and slamming it closed. Thumbing the lock, she turned the knob. Jagardii crashed into the room.

"We heard a scream. Why did you fire a gun?"

"Two men were breaking in."

"My men?"

Lisa shook her head negatively.

Captain Jagardii shouted orders to his men, directing them to search in different directions. Lisa began to shake. He bent forward getting eye contact to steady her.

"We will talk again once I catch them."

ABYDOS, EGYPT, THE FEATURE, THE ARCHAEOLOGICAL TRAILER, JUNE 27TH, 12:57 A.M.:

Captain Jagardii returned to the trailer.

"They escaped. Do you know who they are?"

Lisa drew a deep breath.

"Yes, They're from Cairo. I saw them bomb a car a week ago. Here," she pulled out her cell, playing the video for him.

"The Minister of State for Antiquities! Why didn't you tell me, the police?"

"I am afraid of the authorities. I don't know who to believe."

His eyes narrowed, considering her statement. A moment later he nodded understanding.

"You may be right about not trusting anyone. You must have a guard around your trailer. How did they follow you here?"

"I don't know. No one in Egypt knows I'm here," Lisa said. "Until now."

"This is amazing! E-mail those pictures to me. A gun was fired outward not into the trailer. He pointed to the bullet hole. Foreigners are not allowed weapons like they are in the United States," he said.

Foreigners aren't allowed to have guns in the States either.

"I have a gun is in the States, but I did not bring it. It was the terrorist's. They must have taken it." she said.

Lisa needed to protect herself. He looked at her hard for a long moment.

"I see. We'll talk again."

He jotted his e-mail address for her. Captain Jagardii went out to determine whether his men had captured the terrorists. Lisa slumped down in a console chair. She doubted whether she would get any more sleep.

ABYDOS, EGYPT, THE FEATURE, THE ARCHAEOLOGICAL TRAILER, JUNE 27TH, 8:15 A.M.:

Jagardii left about 1:30, having gone over the whole story again. As she predicted, she had not slept after that. She felt wasted.

How did they find me? Did they trace me through the hotel? They couldn't have followed me to the site unless they saw me at the hotel and followed me to the air cargo terminal. Then again, we could have a spy here who is informing the terrorists. I'll suggest that to Jagardii.

Now that they've found me, they'll never stop trying to kill me. If I go to the authorities, they'll deport me, or worse, detain me indefinitely. My embassy will force me to go back to the States. None of this allows me to do archaeology.

"Damn!"

I need to find out what they know at the hotel. When I have the staff send my personal belongings from the hotel baggage room to my university office closet, I can ask the hotel staff about any inquires for me.

"Bell station, please," she requested after the call went through. "This is Lisa Hampton."

"Oh, yes, mademoiselle. Please hold while I put you through to the hotel manager."

"Wait!" she said as the phone went to Middle Eastern music.

Lisa waited several minutes. Just as she decided to hang up, the manager came on the line.

"Ah, Dr. Hampton. Would you please come to the hotel immediately?"

"I'm sorry that's not possible. I'm not in Cairo. What is it?"

"I hesitate to tell you, but police would like to speak with you. You are such a long standing, honored guest, mademoiselle.... Ah,...they do not wish me to tell you this shocking thing, but a maid was murdered in your room four days ago. Her throat was cut."

"Horrible!"

"I told them you could not have done it. You checked-out at 4:30. The unfortunate girl did not come to work until 6:00. You could not be involved. I told them, but they persist. I would call police to tell them your telephone number, but it is blocked. Please tell me how police can call you?"

A stunned Lisa stared at the phone cradle on the wall. Unconscious of her actions, she placed the receiver into it. Staring at the disconnected instrument, her mind swirling incoherently, her stomach refluxed, threatening to heave its empty contents. Bile soured her mouth. Rising, she stumbled down the hall to the bathroom. After several dry heaves, she placed her throbbing temple on the toilet seat.

My God, I caused that poor girl's death. I didn't even know her, but she was murdered because of me.

She rocked side to side in agony, her head hitting the wall. The toilet paper holder stabbed into her shoulder. Her hand fell on it. Tearing a wad from the spool, she wiped her mouth. Pushing herself from the floor, she crashed against the door frame and staggered into the bedroom. Crawling fully dressed into bed and dragging the covers over her head, she pulled her knees into a fetal position. She began to weep.

ABYDOS, EGYPT, THE FEATURE, THE ARCHAEOLOGICAL TRAILER, JUNE 27TH, 9:30 A.M.:

Lisa awoke from a tormented nightmare. She rolled onto her back. Her dried tears stuck to her eyelids scratching them. Returning to the bathroom, she swirled water in her mouth and splashed water on her face. Toweling her face dry, she put on her glasses.

She no longer wanted to be in Egypt. She wanted to leave this awful place. Having done nothing, death spun everywhere around her. She would take her pack and go directly to the airport. The terrorists or the police would be there and she would either be killed or arrested. If she avoided the terrorists, she did not want the hospitality of the police. The city of Cairo was out.

I won't be calling the police. What should I do?

Lisa had wanted to believe that she was as safe here as anywhere, but she no longer believed that. The periphery of the camp was being patrolled with greater care now that she had been attacked. Anwar promised her. Two soldiers guarded her trailer. More soldiers were posted up and down the highway. These modifications were in addition to the soldiers already posted on the cliff tops on both sides of the road.

She did not want to work, but her churning thoughts were causing her stomach problems. She had to turn her thoughts. Dragging herself back to the main room, she flopped at a computer keyboard, staring several minutes at the immense, blank monitor.

She pressed the start button for the system, watching the screen light. Hundreds of file icons appeared.

Sanders' has been hard at it.

Trying to open a file, she found it password protected.

Strange. We haven't been protecting our work.

After several attempts, she found a file, containing archaeological notes.

I wonder what he's writing, protecting.

Lisa created a new file, naming it by their archaeological standard. On a whim, she added a password. If she wasn't staying, she needed to get her ideas recorded. Pushing her problems as far back into her mind as she could, she pounded out her scientific thoughts, as fast as they streamed into her mind. She documented her observations, stated theories and suggested lines of research.

At ten-thirty, the foul taste in her mouth drove her to sip water. Her gut ached, but she couldn't eat. She returned to her work. She saw the radar program icon at the bottom of the screen. She selected it.

Sanders's radar program is pretty sophisticated. I'll read the notes and figure it out.

Leaning back in her computer chair, she displayed the program notes on the screen.

CAIRO, EGYPT, MILITARY HEADQUARTERS, GENERAL FADI'S OFFICE, JUNE 27TH, 10:00 A.M.:

"We finally meet, Your Excellency," General Fadi said as he searched his guest's face. The Kuwaiti ambassador lifted his chin from his chest. Fadi continued. "I'm most sorry...."

The ambassador raised his hand motioning for Fadi to stop.

"I've heard this too often. I'm resolved to eliminating the evil ones who murdered my wife."

Fadi nodded, waited. Fadi's eyes continued to scrutinize the ambassador. His wrinkled shirt collar looked as if he'd slept in it, but Fadi knew better. The other man had not slept.

"My intelligence service forwarded you our information?" asked the Kuwaiti.

"Yes, Your Excellency. I've distributed it to our intelligence officers. Thank you for your help."

"I want the bastards!"

The ambassador's emotional outburst surprised Fadi. Diplomats were stoic, the man's loss must be preying on him.

"They're mercenaries," the ambassador continued. "We've already encountered them in my country. Unfortunately, all we succeeded in doing was driving them to yours. It would have been better if we had not."

"You've dealt with them, Your Excellency?"

"Yes, the man who murdered my wife has an Arab crescent moon and star tattooed on his wrist. A pair of yellow and purple snake-eyes are below the symbol. He was interrogated in Kuwait, but he had no information so we released him. I wish now for other results."

"So they're not religious zealots as they proclaim?"

"Their chief desire is money. Their controller, the person with other motivations, is who you must find."

Fadi nodded. He did not like being told his job, but recognized a good point.

"We'll find that Shaitan," said Fadi. "We'll allow your intelligence service to interrogate the terrorists once we have them, Your Excellency."

"Very well then. Keep me informed," said the Kuwaiti as he heaved his bulk from the sofa.

"Yes, Your Excellency."

Dealing with the Kuwaitis might prove difficult and certainly against protocol, but Fadi needed a break.

CAIRO, EGYPT, MILITARY AIRBASE, JUNE 27TH, 10:30 A.M.:

Bill had no clue what Dr. Tu'hut wanted to discuss. A military operation made no sense. If Dr. Hampton topic came up, he decided to temporize with the Secretary General. He appreciated her help despite Dr. Tu'hut's nasty comments, as long as she stayed safe.

Bill recognized that Lisa is a superb scientist. She is inquisitive, careful and methodical. She wanted to preserve the find for study by any future investigators. She was in direct disagreement with Dr. Tu'hut's desire to move the artifacts to the Cairo museum for his study which very well might be the source of their conflict. She didn't seem to have any desire for self-aggrandizement or profit. Bill felt she was a significant asset.

The only negative seems to be Dr. Tu'hut's feeling that she is a difficult woman. I know she can be that, but it's nice having her on site.

When Bill arrived at the Cairo military base, Dr. Tu'hut met him in a new limousine to drive them to the Ministry of State for Antiquities where he had moved his offices since the death of their previous owner. Tu'hut had taken over the minister's responsibilities after his boss's death in a recent car bombing. Shifting uncomfortably, Bill realized he was sitting in a similar vehicle that could end in the same way. He wondered at Tu'hut's quick move to take over his superior's position. Perhaps Tu'hut was a social climber.

"How are your explorations going Dr. Sanders?" asked Tu'hut. Recognizing the trip to the ministry would be spent in non-substansive pleasantries, Bill settled back in the plush seat, attempting to release his tenseness.

Upon arrival at his office, Dr. Tu'hut ordered his aide to prepare tea for them which Bill accepted understanding the importance of Middle Eastern manners. Taking the scalding cup from his employer, Bill sipped on its edge. Tu'hut smiled at Bill, offering him sugar as he added half the bowl into his own cup. After a few sips, Tu'hut began.

"You requested a helicopter? I was unaware that archaeology was carried on using military equipment, Doctor."

"The military truck that discovered the site must be removed to continue my exploration. My internal survey shows a significant weakness in the ceiling structure."

"Can the ceiling fail?" asked a concerned Tu'hut.

"Yes. I'm amazed that the truck didn't crash through the roof into the chamber below. I need a piece of equipment that will lift the truck, but at the same time will not put additional pressure on the ceiling. The military adviser, Captain Jagardii, suggested that we use a helicopter."

"I see. So it was military's idea that this method be used?"

"Yes, sir. I thought it quite enterprising on his part."

"I am sure you did. Did he indicate that he had any other use for the helicopter?"

"No, I'm unaware of further use for the equipment once the truck is moved."

Tu'hut summoned his aide and spoke in Egyptian to him.

"There is the additional matter—the American woman," said Tu'hut after the man had left the room.

"Woman?"

"Dr. Hampton. You met her in my office. She has disappeared. I assume she has left the country as I requested," Tu'hut responded.

"How unfortunate. I certainly could use her skills as an archaeologist."

"The feature is no place for *that* woman," said Tu'hut.

"From what I've seen of the feature, there're no security concerns there," said Bill ignoring Dr. Tu'hut's obvious ill feelings for Lisa.

"The security of the site is General Fadi's responsibility and solely his responsibility. He will make all decisions about security. I am troubled by her for other reasons."

"She could be a tremendous asset to my exploration."

"I am not sure Dr. Sanders. There are other questions being asked concerning her that I am not able to say, but I have worked extensively with her. She is a good scientist with understanding of all of the archeological techniques, but she consistently shows that she does not work well with others. Her graduate students complain about her directives. She does not follow the planned activities. Now with these additional problems, she is completely unacceptable."

I've seen some of these weaknesses, but I do appreciate her thinking outside the box. Now what has she done?

Bill nodded at Dr. Tu'hut, as concern about Lisa began to rise.

"I had tried to restrain her, but she does what she wants to do. You saw how she called me a chauvinist pig."

Ahh, another one of Tu'hut's paranoias with Lisa.

Ali entered and spoke to the Secretary General.

"Enough about these unpleasantries. I have received word from the general. He informs me that he will send a helicopter for the purpose of lifting the truck. Once that is complete, it will return to Cairo. He will transport you to the site at five o'clock this afternoon."

Five, Damn! What a waste of time! I must accomplish something else.

CAIRO, EGYPT, EL'ARAFA (THE CEMETERY CITY), JUNE 27TH, 11:30 A.M.:

Bill wound his way through the narrow 'streets' of el'Arafa, Cairo's cemetery city. Rapidly increasing rents forced some of the indigent population to live inside the city cemetery in the burial mausoleums. People staked out their claim having semi-permanent locations, 'neighborhoods.' During the 1960's, President Nassar sanctioned this *temporary* occupation. President Mubarak, during his tenure, had made changes so the occupancy continued. A tomb guard watched over the dead. A headman controlled the areas occupied by the living inhabitants. With one such man, Bill had made an arrangement.

Bill and the headman moved into the man's 'home.' The resident took a seat in his tattered recliner, his prized possession, his throne and his favorite place when entertaining guests. As usual, Bill sat on the movable slab that covered the area for receiving the dead. Originally, the seat, and for that matter the place, had given him the creeps, but with familiarity it had become a natural resting place for him to talk with the headman. Often the pair shared a brewed beverage, rotgut beer, not being an orthodox Muslim, the headman provided the refreshment. Today; however, Bill had other, serious business on his mind.

"Have you seen Khidr?" he asked.

"I have not heard from him," said the headman. "I am concerned for him. Several people from 'here' have disappeared."

"How long has he been gone?"

"I do not know. He comes and goes, but I have not seen him in the last week."

"Damn! I'm concerned. Here's the usual money to cover your expenses. Keep an eye out for him."

"I will, but as you know, bad things are happening in Cairo. I will watch."

"I should be back in town in a few days. I'll check with you."

CAIRO, EGYPT, MILITARY HEADQUARTERS, GENERAL FADI'S OFFICE, JUNE 27TH, 10:48 A.M.:

General Fadi and Minister Aboud met at Minister Aboud's request. The general knew the minister had spies. Aboud knew that Tu'hut had interviewed the American? Tu'hut communicated the results of the interview and the reason for his needing a heliocopter.

"Does he know where Dr. Hampton's disappeared?" asked Aboud.

"You mean the American woman? Apparently not, minister. He said it's unfortunate that she can't help him with his explorations."

"I see. Are you satisfied that activities at the site aren't involved with the terrorists?"

"I'm not satisfied with anything that's occurring in the south. I believe that Dr. Sanders appears to be doing archaeology. Beyond that I'm not sure of anything."

"You need to watch your group there."

"I'm aware of my duty."

ABYDOS, EGYPT, THE FEATURE, THE ARCHAEOLOGICAL TRAILER, JUNE 27TH, 2:00 P.M.:

The captain knocked on the door. He handed Lisa a cup of coffee that she placed on the console without drinking.

"You look unhappy." His eyebrows knit together.

"A problem where I stayed in Cairo. I will tell you later," she said.

"I do need to know if it affects security here. What are you working on?" he asked with a speculative look at her.

"I started the geological substructure. The radar program is working."

"How long will it take?" he asked.

"The program estimates eighty-five hours."

"You people don't do anything very fast," said Captain Jagardii.

"That is true," said Lisa, "but look how long it took yours to bury all the stuff we are going to dig up."

They both chuckled. Lisa felt that the captain and she were making progress toward a better relationship.

"Let me try another technique."

She selected another, less comprehensive analysis, The program estimated fifteen hours. Lisa knew the results would not be as good as her original choice. She looked at her watch.

"About seven tomorrow morning," she said starting the new analysis.

"I noticed that you've been recording the inside of the room. How are you going to use that?"

"The programs will build a model from the pictures we take."

"You mentioned that before. Will it make the pictures better?" Captain Jagardii struggled with the Arabic to ask the question. "Can it take a picture and make a better picture?"

"I think what you are asking is called photo enhancement. Yes, that is one of the stages of building the virtual reality."

"What's that?"

"The program analyzes all the data and creates a three-dimensional image. With special glasses, the person viewing the room can walk around each object and see it from all sides as if they were walking around inside the room."

"Can your program use data from a DVD?"

"Yes, the machine has that input too. Why? We are using direct feeds."

Anwar studied her for a moment.

"Does your boss mind your using his equipment?"

"We have discussed my using them. He is satisfied that I know what I am doing."

"I'd be happy to do analysis for you in exchange for allowing me to evaluate the terrorist recordings that I've received on DVDs. I wish to pursue them through technical methods even if I can't do it physically. Would you show me how to use the program?"

"If you have disks of the terrorist activities, perhaps you could assist in capturing them. That would help me. For the time being, we probably should not tell Dr. Sanders."

Anwar looked at her in disbelief. She was smiling at him. For certain, he wouldn't be telling Sanders anything. Then he understood she was being humorous so they both laughed.

For the next two hours, Lisa tried her hand at the program, demonstrating its use to Anwar. Together they learned how to control its capabilities. The captain tried his hand at loading one of her recording and doing the initial work on the pictures. They were both amazed at how fast he caught on and the quality of pictures he was able to produce from inside the feature.

During a water break, Lisa told Anwar about the death of the maid.

"I agree the terrorists are after you. The airport will be unsafe for you. You must be careful in all ways. I will protect you," he said.

"Could they not just shoot a rocket into the trailer like they shot at you?"

"It was a grenade. I have sentinels on the cliff tops and all around."

"Thank you. That is why I am staying here."

THE ABYDOS FEATURE, EGYPT, JUNE 27TH, 3:00 P.M.:

With Sanders in Cairo and the computer grinding on her problem, Lisa went looking for work. She found the lieutenant and asked him for a tour of the military area. The tour turned out to be more than she expected.

"Ma'am, we discovered a cave while looking for the terrorists who attacked you. Actually, we found three. Two are nothing. You can stand up in them, but that is all."

"Really? I want to see."

"Apparently, the ancient slides created natural openings back into the rock. In the third place, the soldiers found cool air coming up between the rocks. They are using the space as a cool place."

"Damn! You should have told me."

"We just discovered it, ma'am."

Inside the cave, following the current, she low-crawled into the cramped space that none of the soldiers were willing to explore. Lisa found a hole in the floor where the air came from between the rocks.

Wiggling out again, she said, "Lieutenant, I need the men to help me lift these stones. This may be an opening into the tomb complex below."

A twenty minute fire brigade, led by Lisa's pointing, cleared the area around the opening. A halogen light pointed into the opening showed a sheer drop of ten feet, a wall and the floor, but nothing in the room.

Lisa went to the trailer for recording equipment. Using ropes and squeezing through the tight opening, she was able to go into the space below.

She found the tomb seal.

The discovery ended the occupation of the cave by the military. Centered on a giant, flat rock slab was a carved serekh: *Ptah*. Included were hieroglyphic enchantments forbidding entrance into the tomb, but the serekh contained no Horus falcon. From the size of the opening above, Lisa was sure it would be difficult to explore the area. She was concerned how Bill and she were going to get into the tomb.

How did the Egyptians get in?

"Are you all right, ma'am? None of us can get through the opening."

"I'm OK."

She found a shard of a bowl or a pot. Hieroglyphics on its edge stated: *Food by Ptah, for pleasure....*

Lisa turned to see what else the space contained. Carved into the wall facing the entrance were three lifesized figures. She recorded them. To the right, the floor sloped up to a pile of boulders.

This must have been the original opening to the tomb.

"You better come out, ma'am. We're worried about stability."

"OK, haul away."

As they hoisted her from the room, she looked around the space, deciding to explore the room once they were confident that it wouldn't cave-in. She was unable to see anything but black to the left.

ABYDOS, EGYPT, THE FEATURE, THE ARCHAEOLOGICAL TRAILER, JUNE 27TH, 7:30 P.M.:

With her lack of sleep, Lisa's headache would no longer go away. Her pill consumption was causing her stomach problems.

While reading her e-mail, one from Robert popped up. She wondered what he was doing with all the site water. She'd been there only the week before, but it seemed like ages. He wrote:

> Lisa: How are you? I'm fine, but things around here have taken a strange twist. I extracted the pot you were digging. Your find is huge.
>
> It has glyph text depicting the battle between Set and Horus. The Horus' hawk head looked strange, like it was painted later, So I had it analyzed. Using laser and x-ray scanning, I see 2 layers. Have computer working on it.

I'm impressed. Robert has always been my best student. Knowing Robert's computer skills, he probably had his girlfriend do the computer analysis. I should talk.

> I'm driving the other grads like slaves. We're excavating a channel to the Nile. right thru the farmer's field. Remember the plat map. Channel's ancient. Looking for material to date. I think this site is really important. Looks like a cult center. Tu'hut's driving me nuts. won't agree to anything.
>
> Speaking of him, he's going crazy looking for you. Hope you're OK. Write me soon and update. Robert.

Sounds like he's really busy, doing good things with my—his project. So I need to write him, but getting some sleep would help. A clear mind can handle a lot more.

She stood and stretched. She marched down the hall to bed.

ABYDOS, EGYPT, THE FEATURE, JUNE 28TH, 10:15 A.M.:

The still, clear air broke with the beating sound of the approaching helicopter. The entire camp paused. A few looked toward the sky to locate the mechanical beast. Others readied their weapons in case of attack. Lisa paused looking toward the sound as she studied the printout that had just come from the computer.

Holding in her hand an amazing facsimile of the site sub-structure, Lisa had no doubt that the underground looked like what the machine had printed. It displayed too many known details not to be an accurate depiction of Ḥaāmer's room. The semi-circular ring of the cliffs surrounding the bowl were shown and the tomb entrance below the cave. The program was a wonder, even giving her three dimensional profiles and perspective views.

Across a 'corridor' was another rectangular room carved purposefully by human hands from the native rock: not just a prayer room or food storage area, but a full-sized, object strewn room. White space represented voids in the rock. Gray furry areas indicated objects in the space.

Maybe, Ḥaāmer's husband / consort is across the hall. The important guy.

The perspective views gave a wonderful picture that with some computer tinkering, Lisa was able to reconstruct into a pseudo-original entrance. Using computer rendering, she removed the outer landslide debris covering the tomb seal and righted the fallen columns. She drew how she believed the grand archway must have looked. A huge lentil, now canted at a strange angle, had once garnished a massive portal with carved side columns and three life-sized statues of the Egyptian gods to the right.

This tomb has to be for an important person.

An imposing approach to an elaborate tomb, surrounded a vestibule guarding the passage leading downward to the tomb seal, much more than expected for a common woman. When she had been underground, she had not imagined this magnificence. The cave-in had hidden most of these details, giving the space a twisted obscene appearance.

Progressing along the internal passage to its low point, she saw that the corridor began to slope upward toward the surface. Lisa now had a new direction to explore. She needed Sanders and Jagardii to run the radar at that end to investigate how close it comes to the surface. They might be able to dig through into the tomb. Although she didn't see any rooms, she hoped that others might branch from the corridor closer to the upper end.

Fearing the arrival of Dr. Tu'hut and never being sure of who might be arriving, Lisa headed for the trailer. The helicopter, a strange, large preying mantis-like machine, landed on the road fifty meters from the trailer. Although only a dozen vehicles passed in the last five days, soldiers ran in each direction to warn off traffic. Kicking off her shoes, Lisa knelt on the living room sofa peering out of the trailer front window curtains. She cranked the louvers open to hear. Sanders climbed from of the helicopter, ducking low under the rotors. He scanned the area, looking for something or someone.

Four robed men, shuffled after Sanders. They were followed by a stiff, polished army officer in a splendid uniform. He was angular, tall and thin. Captain Jagardii came to attention in front of the officer and saluted. A short exchange took place between them. Jagardii saluted again then trotted to the helicopter, receiving something from the pilot. Soldiers attached cables to the truck and helicopter. The captain climbed the rock face while speaking to the pilot with the device he had obtained.

Sanders flapped his arms to get the captain's attention; but Jagardii, concentrating on maneuvering the helicopter, did not hear him. As the cables raised and became taut, he directed the position of the helicopter to lift the truck. The front of the truck lifted first as it rotated onto its back wheels. Slowly the rear wheels slid forward. The truck raised a foot above the ground. Suddenly, the ring connected to the helicopter hook shifted. The screech of tortured metal dragging across the rock surface tore the air. The rear of the truck swung forward striking the camera mount bending it at a hideous angle.

As the truck's weight shifted forward, Lisa watched in horror as the helicopter lost altitude, twisting around its lifting hook. Lisa did not know how the pilot kept the helicopter aloft. The suspended truck swung toward the highway, crashing into the ground away from the hole. Everyone ran toward the truck as the helicopter slipped sideways, continuing to drag the cable and the truck away from the cliff face.

"Back. Get everyone back," shouted Sanders. "The ground is unstable here."

Sanders went to the camera mount. Lisa saw that the truck had sheared through the computer connections. Loose wires dangled from the bent telescopic arm and smashed controls. The trailer data cable lay shredded, useless, five feet away.

A livid Sanders charged Captain Jagardii as he arrived from the top of the rock slide. Unintelligible words were exchanged between the pair. Lisa heard the captain say it was safe to winch the truck completely away. The lieutenant translated for Sanders. This didn't satisfy Sanders who continued to scream at Captain Jagardii. Lisa watched as seconds stretched, the lieutenant stood between Jagardii and Sanders, keeping the two men apart.

Soldiers detached the cable and ring from the twisted helicopter hook. A military truck drove into the area. Soldiers unreeled a winch cable from the front spool connecting it to the damaged truck. The pointed axle gouged deep furrows into the exploration site floor. The screaming of raw metal on stone reverberating off the cliff walls sent chills through Lisa. In a short time, the damaged truck was dragged to the center of the area well away from Ḥaāmer's room.

Once the truck was moved, Captain Jagardii trotted after the other military officer who climbed aboard the helicopter. The lieutenant standing away from chopper signaled the pilot to take-off. Fists balled in anger, Sanders watched as the helicopter disappeared into the distance.

"Bastard!" spat Sanders as he entered the trailer.

"Oh, Bill, I'm so sorry."

"You'd think the idiot would've cleared the area first."

"Do you have spare parts to fix it?"

"No!"

"Who...?"

Ignoring her, he picked up a tool box, heading out of the trailer toward the ceiling opening.

"Before we work with the camera, we need to clear the area of debris," Lisa trailed after Sanders.

"I know that!" snapped Sanders.

CAIRO, EGYPT, MILITARY HEADQUARTERS, GENERAL FADI'S OFFICE, JUNE 28TH, 2:42 P.M.:

An apprehensive Captain Jagardii sat outside General Fadi's office, wondering why Colonel Mohieddin had arrived at the archaeological site with the helicopter. The colonel said Fadi wanted to see him immediately. He provided no explanation. Anwar and the colonel had never been on the best of terms, but the colonel was particularly aloof.

He sat rigidly at attention trying not to fidget. He reviewed in his mind everything that had happened since the last time he had spoken with the general. Colonel Mohieddin appeared at the door.

"He'll see you."

"What the hell are you doing?" said Fadi with no preamble.

"Pardon me, sir. I don't understand."

"Dammit, you requisitioned a piece of equipment you are not allowed to have at a time we are under great pressure."

"The American scientist needed Omar's truck moved."

"In the process, Colonel Mohieddin tells me you almost lost the helicopter."

"We had a mishap that caused no damage to the chopper, sir."

General Fadi grunted.

"You had no further use for the equipment?"

"No, sir."

General Fadi settled back in his chair—relaxed. "At ease, Anwar."

"Sir?"

"Anwar, come sit. Tell me what really is happening."

Anwar told the general everything occurring at the Abydos site with the exception of his interaction with the Kuwaitis, his computer work and Lisa. This did not leave much. Their discussion did not encompass much that the general had not already received through Anwar's reports. He did enlighten Fadi about Sanders's anger with him.

"We are interacting only when necessary," said Anwar.

"That is sufficient," said the general. "Keep the asshole safe if not happy. The Minister of the Interior would like to speak with you. I've released you to him. A driver will take you to his location. Anwar be careful with him. As you know, he is a slippery eel. Return here when he is done speaking with you. I will give you your orders."

"Yes, sir."

CAIRO, EGYPT, MINISTRY OF THE INTERIOR, MINISTER ABOUD'S OFFICE, JUNE 28TH, 3:30 P.M.:

The knowledge Lisa was a witness to the Antiquities Minister's murder plagued Saladin. The brothers told him she was working at the feature. With some pleasure, he saw that a mere woman had wreaked havoc on Colonel Fiqar. Saladin doubted whether he'd regain full use of his hand. The ugly one deserved what he'd received for disobeying orders; however, Saladin would enjoy watching when he finally released her to them.

"Good afternoon, captain. How are your efforts in the south?"

"Sir?" The captain looked puzzled. "I'm simply guarding the American scientist as he explores."

Saladin wanted to have him to admit that the woman was at the Abydos site then he could get her back to Cairo. He would arrange for her capture and elimination. The murder of the Antiquities Minister led through her to him. Once he'd handled her, he'd rid himself of the brothers.

This torture is unbearable. She will put a sword to my neck.

"Do you know where the American woman is?"

"Of what woman are you asking?"

"An archaeologist from America."

"We have a man at the site from America."

"So you know nothing about the woman?"

The captain did not respond. He continued to look puzzled.

"Never mind."

Saladin couldn't risk the captain suspecting his knowledge.

"Thank you, captain. You may return to your superior."

Anwar stood, saluted and left without further comment.

Saladin called Fadi.

"He's too incompetent to command the terrorists, but he may be one of them. I suggest you recall him."

CAIRO, EGYPT, MILITARY HEADQUARTERS, GENERAL FADI'S OFFICE, JUNE 28TH, 3:56 P.M.:

Fadi sat at his desk drumming his fingers. The Minister of State for Antiquities had been car bombed. The Kuwaiti Ambassador's wife had been murdered. Now the news that rocked Cairo was the death of the Prime Minister the previous evening. The filthy bastards, wearing ski masks, shot the minister in the head on streaming video. It was all over Egypt. The minister's body had been recovered from the Nile this morning, mauled by alligators. The terrorists celebrated his death, firing automatic weapons into air, as if it were a holy victory over the evil government. The people were chanting in the streets. The terrorists said that Egypt should stop assisting the Israelis and Americans. They'd said the president should be removed for his perfidy—by force if necessary.

Looking down at the telephone ringing on his desk, Fadi saw it was the field marshal. He contemplated not answering, but his receptionist buzzed him.

"I'm sure you've seen the news, Fadi," said Aaliyah. "What do we know?"

"We are just beginning our investigation, sir."

"You'd better have answers. The president is calling all of his ministers home from their overseas assignments. I will be updating him personally until the cabinet assembles. He will begin holding daily cabinet meetings in two weeks. You are very lucky for this delay. As the lead army investigator, he expects you to provide the cabinet with your solution."

"Yes, sir."

The phone connection broke. The general slumped back in his chair—an impotent failure to his country. He had nothing to offer. His only ally was Minister Aboud who was calling for Anwar's recall to Cairo. Jagardii is very smart. He probably double-talked the minister.

Good. Jagardii's recall is not going to happen. How will I explain that to the minister? Allah, I'm not in control. Evil of Shaitan! What am I going to say to my president?

* * *

"He asked me questions about the archeological site. I didn't believe he needed information so I acted dumb."

"I appreciate your not telling him anything, Anwar. You need to be back to the site before dark," said Fadi. "No more of your damnable unauthorized equipment requisitions. Keep tight control over the site and there will be no incidents."

"I understand, sir."

"Dismissed."

Anwar saluted and spun on his heel. If he hurried, he might be able to see Nefri on the way to the airbase.

CAIRO, EGYPT, NEFRI MULHAN'S HOUSE, JUNE 28TH, 5:03 P.M.:

"It is so nice of you to come see me," Nefri said smiling warmly like her old self.

"Is there anything I can do for you?"

"I'm doing fine. The boys look after me like they always have when you men are in the field. How is the Company? I haven't seen anything about you on the news."

"I'm still babysitting the American scientist."

"From your voice, you don't seem pleased with the assignment. Has the American been troublesome?"

"No, he gets all excited about his toys and what they can do, but he doesn't progress very quickly."

A merry twinkle appeared in her eye.

"I've seen you hold a bit of clay in your hand and stare off into space for hours."

Anwar sighed, raising his hands in resignation.

"True, but I want to be searching for our country's enemies, not sitting on my ass looking after a foreigner, an American."

Nefri's expression became sad, the twinkle gone. She nodded. "I know you. Always looking for a fight. I hope you are keeping safe."

"Safe! There's nothing to be safe from."

"You need to be careful. Trouble always seems to happen where you are. Omar happened there," Nefri's breaths came as gasps, tears forming in her eyes. She looked into his face.

Damn! I hate the terrorists.

Something upset her for the tears disappeared and the sadness returned. She turned away from him.

She finally said. "Why are you having me make the awful disks of the things these men do?" she indicated a bag containing disks that she had burned from the internet.

"The American computers build pictures from the DVDs. I am creating a dossier for each of the terrorists. I will know them all by sight."

"The American brought computers to film our past? He's doing a good thing. He's allowing you to use his machines to find the terrorists?"

"He's not aware of what I'm doing."

"Oh, Anwar, why are you pursuing this evil so strongly?"

"I *will* avenge Omar."

Nefri gasped, her hand going to her mouth. Her eyes opened wide as she looked in horror at him.

"Omar does not want to be avenged. Your hatred is not helping him. You're doing this for yourself. It is wrong."

She picked up the bag, pressing it into his arms.

"Here, here are *your* disks. You must leave now. This revenge is no good."

"Omar must be avenged!"

"I can't bear to have another person killed. I won't collect anymore disks."

She broke into great heaving sobs.

He left her house, walking stoically to his car. Once again Nefri ended sadder than when he arrived.

I do not know what to do for her.

"Captain Jagardii."

His head down, not paying attention to his surroundings, Anwar was startled by a person approaching him. Anwar was angry with himself for not being more careful. Not recognizing the man, he tensed ready to fight.

How did he know my name?

"I'm from the Kuwaiti Embassy. My principal would like to speak with you. Would you accompany me to his car?"

A black, diplomatic limousine stood angled before Anwar's car, blocking it. Kuwaiti flags flapped on short staffs on each end of the front bumper.

ABYDOS, EGYPT, THE FEATURE, JUNE 28TH, 7:37 P.M.:

Satisfied they would cause no further surface damage to the tomb, Sanders and Lisa examined the camera. An angry Sanders realized that he could not reattach the camera to the mounting. The truck had sheared the small bolts connecting it to the steel assembly.

"This is hopeless," he told Lisa. "I'll have to drill out each bolt and re-tap the holes. What a pain. I should start working on this mess."

"It's getting dark."

"I can set up lights. It'll get me ahead."

"You'll be more productive in the morning."

A helicopter landed on the road across from the site. Jagardii jumped out and the aircraft took off. Sanders stopped following the captain with his eyes. Lisa touched his arm.

"So who was the army stiff who came with you earlier today on the helicopter?" Lisa asked as they turned, walking to the trailer.

"A Colonel Mohieddin. He's General Fadi's aide. General Fadi is that bastard's boss. He was here to take the captain and the helicopter back. The general was pissed Jagardii requisitioned the chopper. Why don't you bring me up to date on your work during my absence," he said as they entered the trailer.

Lisa hurried into her exploration, skipping the attack on the camp. She told him about working with the program to produce the radar study. She indicated the parameters she had used.

"Thank you. You've helped immensely in this exploration. I'll up-link to Chicago the raw data and program over the next several nights. So you have a decent picture from the shorter run?"

"Yes, here's the schematic."

He nodded, drawing the paper close to his face squinting at it.

"Please hand me the ruler on the desk."

She turned, wondering what he was doing. No scale was indicated on the diagrams though she knew their relative sizes were correct. He measured the two rooms from the multiple views.

"They are identical in size," he informed her.

"I told you the two rooms were similar."

"No, I assume the pictures are to the same scale."

"Yes."

"So, they are identical. They've been purposefully carved the same size."

He drew his cell phone from his belt and started punching numbers as he remeasured the dimensions. He turned his phone around and showed her his calculations.

"Did you notice the ratio? Three by four by five. The Egyptians are into perfection—their godly numbers."

"Wow! I missed that."

He nodded.

She continued, "Talking with the lieutenant, I discovered the military was guarding a small cave that proved to be the entrance to the tomb complex. I manipulated the picture of the collapse. From my reconstruction, you can see the entrance was once a grand portal."

"You found it! You've done a wonderful rendering. The picture you created is beautiful. Excellent!"

"Not so fast. There's more. One of the soldiers discovered cool air puffing from a hole in the floor at the back of a cave. I dropped into the area below and photographed underneath."

"You went underground? You're always taking dangerous chances."

"No, big deal. That's how I photographed the carvings of the three gods and the tomb seal you see in the rendering."

"So we'll be able to enter the tomb with a little excavation around the front door?"

"I don't think so. It is pretty hard to get to. It's collapsed solid blocks."

"Then how did the ancients get in?"

"I don't know. I've been thinking about it ever since I went below. Ḥaāmer had to be important since she is buried in a carved tomb. Maybe an accidental cave-in buried the entrance."

"If she were important, wouldn't they dig her out?"

She shook her head negatively.

"It's a pretty bad heap. Might have been impossible."

"So I assume you're telling me it'll be equally hard for us?"

"I'm working on another possibility."

"Good, I hope you can come up with an easier way," he said.

"Perhaps tomb robbers caused the problem. They sealed the entrance by accident," she speculated.

"Maybe the builders did it. That's why this tomb was never chronicled."

"That would have caused a real who-ha," she said.

"Some heads would have rolled unless they were through burying people there," Bill agreed.

"That would imply more rooms and more people. I don't see that."

"Yeah. So let's continue with your discoveries."

She played the recording of the cave entrance showing him the short version. The size and clarity of the relief carvings astounded him.

"Someday we'll have to explore this entrance even if it is hard to get to." He looked at his watch. "I think we'd better knock off for the night. I assume you're sleeping in the bedroom."

"Yes, I would appreciate that."

He sighed and shook his head understandably.

"I'm going to move back in here again to the couch. I hate sleeping in the back of the truck like the other night."

"Yeah." she said with a sober face.

"But you'll keep the door locked anyway, right?"

She stood and moved behind him. She began to rub his shoulders. His shoulders sagged.

"Please stop. I can't handle that right now."

Surprised she responded, "You do look exhausted."

"Yes, I'm exhausted. Today's been full of crap. I notice you're locking down your archaeological files," he said.

"Why are you protecting files as well?" she fired back.

Her remark startled him.

"Those are private files."

"So why are you keeping secrets?"

"Let's change the subject. In the future, please don't lock your archeological notes."

Sanders stretched his neck. He stood, going to the small kitchen sink to run water over his head. As he turned to face her, he saw the damaged trailer window.

"The trailer window is broken. Someone tried to break in here last night didn't they?"

Lisa spread her fingers to indicate no big deal.

"That's a bullet hole," he bent forward and peered into the hole. "There's a bullet in there, Lisa. A gun fired in here isn't a 'small' deal. Did some idiot soldier try getting to you?" he asked.

When she didn't respond, his thoughtful expression changed to one of understanding.

"This is the terrorists. Tomorrow, I want you packed. I'll have the army transport you to Cairo."

A huge silence hung between them. Tears formed in Lisa's eyes.

"But,...but they'll kill me."

"What!" Bill's mouth gaped open.

"If you send me back to Cairo, they will kill me."

"Who?"

"The terrorists."

"Wait a minute," he shook his head. "I'm confused. You say the terrorists are trying to kill you here and in Cairo too?"

"I contacted my hotel in Cairo to move my personal belongings. They told me a maid had been murdered in my room. The police know I'm not involved."

"Shit! I don't believe this. You're involved? It was your room, and now here?"

Lisa's shoulders sagged. "The hotel manager said two men asked where I'd gone. The police are looking for them. The police are looking for me too, but the hotel doesn't know where I am."

"So as usual, you're crosswise with the authorities. Why are the terrorists after you, Lisa?"

She heaved a great sigh.

"I wanted to be here to explore, but the bad guys were trying to get me too. I saw them murder the Minister of State for Antiquities so I fled Cairo to escape them."

"The car bombing? Tu'hut's boss! You saw the murder?"

"Yes, the debris fell around me. I was watching them and they tried to catch me. They tackled me on the MSA steps, but the ministry guard saved me. They're the guys the police are after."

His mouth opened in shock. "Was that when we met in Tu'hut's office?"

"Yes, I was running on so much adrenalin that I didn't know what I was doing."

He shook his head. "Good Lord, you're a crazy lady. They followed you here?"

"I don't think so. I sneaked here in to the back of your truck. I didn't tell anyone that I was coming."

"But they know you're here now. You have to go back."

"They'll find me there and kill me."

"So go back to the States."

Tears formed in Lisa's eyes, spilling over and running down her cheeks.

"Come with me," Sanders said throwing open the trailer door. He tromped across the feature to the Army area, Lisa trailing after him. The sentry challenged them.

"Captain Jagardii," was all Sanders said.

The lieutenant came with Jagardii. Lisa looked at the ground.

"What is it?" Jagardii demanded through the lieutenant.

"I want Dr. Hampton on the next supply truck going to Cairo."

Chapter 13

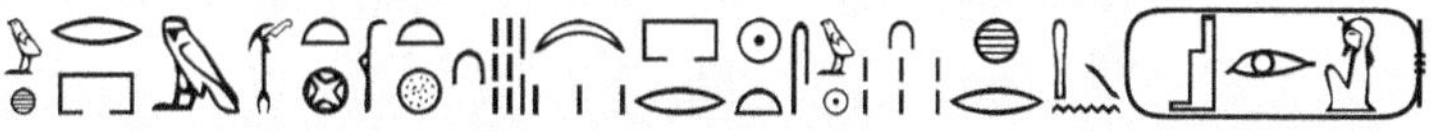

wḫrpr m wꜣst ḥsbt 18 ꜣbd 3 prt sw 16 ḫr ḥm n wsỉr

The Docks in Uas

Year 18, Month 3 of Peret, Day 16 under the Majesty of Ạsạr

The gods awakened Neb-t·ḥe-t deep in the night with a single word: *daybreak*.

She rose and dressed by candlelight, a long linen dress and a warm cloak, then pressed her feet into soft sandals. She passed from her rooms into the temple. Scattered oil pots cast large, flickering shadows across the walls and columns. A lone novice polished a patch of floor—punishment ordered by one priest or another.

The streets of Uas were empty. Moonlight brightened her cloak so she drifted like a patch of mist between the buildings. At Pharaoh's pier, she came to a small, mud brick hut. An old man sat on a stool near the door in a circle of oil light, twisting reeds and bits of grass together into the shape of a doll. He did not look up.

She stopped at the end of the pier. An oil pot atop a post sputtered nearby, the watch fire dying. The old man limped out from his hut to fill it from an urn slung across his shoulder. He poured some in and paused to look up at the night sky. Then he added a little more. He left without a word and returned with a ragged piece of flat, coarse bread and a small, clay bowl of beer. He held them out in silence until she accepted them. She thanked him, and with a shrug he left her.

The stars drifted West, carried along on their own dark river. To the East, the sky revealed the first traces of purple and pale blue as the new day approached. Neb-t·ḥe-t sipped the pungent beer and chewed a mouthful of bread, watching and listening.

The River had its own sound, its own voice that changed with the seasons. It chattered, laughing, joyous, and bountiful during the inundation, spilling across the land, spreading gifts of soil and water to ensure another crop. During the growing season the River exhaled and quieted and drew back into itself, weary, pensive, the water clearing, the sounds more introspective as the River healed and slowed to watch the life it nourished rise from the fields.

With harvest over, with the cooler, shorter days, it now slept, burrowed deep within its muddy course, its voice little more than a whisper, words and sighs muttered in a dream, the ebb and flow languid like breaths taken in the still night.

Mist spilled over the edge of the dock and covered Neb-t·ḥe-t's feet. Few things in Egypt were cool to the touch during the day. The fiery Aten, the blistering sand, and the feverish, shallow waters saw to that. But when the Aten was gone from the sky, when the sands had lost the warmth of his smile and the waters had a chance to rest and sigh and breathe, the nights could reach deep into you and send a cold shiver along your spine.

Neb-t·ḥe-t felt that shiver building and smiled, a secret nighttime smile only the gods could see. "Thank you," she whispered. She shook off her sandals, standing on the wet stones, wiggling her toes.

Yesterday the wind had turned cool from the North. The days were shorter with the Aten drifting across the sky far to the South, his brightness dimmed as if in contemplation or shyness or fatigue. The River was near its lowest point, the current sluggish. The mists lasted further into the morning, making navigation less certain for large boats.

I will not cry, she prayed. *Let me be strong.*

Neb-t·ḥe-t had not cried the first time she found Set with a temple dancer. Nor did she cry the second time. Nor the third.

She did cry the day her father came to her and announced that the line of succession had changed and she would wed the older brother Set instead of the younger brother Ạsạr.

But she couldn't remember if she felt worse for herself or for the young prince who was happy to be the second son, who would gladly give up ruling Egypt to sail every water known or rumored, to see every port from the deck of his own boat. Did she regret that he would not take her with him, away from the responsibility and politics? Or did she regret that Ạsạr would never sail the River and visit the fabled lands and waters beyond, that he would instead sit on a gold and ivory throne, bound in chains of power and obligation? Instead of the sound of water, he would listen to greedy, power-hungry men day after day for the rest of his life, offering sincere advice as to how he might better rule to the advantage of everyone in general and themselves in particular.

Dawn was imminent and a moment later the Aten crested the horizon to begin another day's journey. Neb-t·ḥe-t turned away toward the West and felt the warmth on her cloak and against her neck and shoulders. The watch fire sent up a last puff of flame and smoke and went out. The mist fluttered about her feet, gentle, like delicate fingers massaging the aches away before tumbling off the edge of the pier and back to the waiting River.

She looked up. In the distance, Pharaoh's boat slipped through the water, the first of four boats to peek around a bend in the River. The Aten painted their sails in gold and orange.

The cool, uncertain breath of wind pushed the center of those sails. The hypnotic cadence of the rowers, pulling easily on their oars, provided most of the motion up River. Soon she heard their rhythmic song as the oars went up, forward, down, and back. The morning, the sleepy, waking town, took it as their own beat, emerging from houses, the Aten lifting in his own serene motion on invisible oars. Pharaoh's boat finally drew even with and past the pier. Ten lengths beyond the boat master halted the rowers and turned the boat broadside to the current. The River carried the boat to its berth, the rowers reaching out with poles to bring it to rest.

Fishermen, with Pharaoh's boat no longer a distraction, pushed their boats into the River. Lazy columns of smoke curled up from the city like tiny whirlwinds.

Vendors began their individual calls, competing for attention through the city streets: warm bread, fresh fruit, smoked fish, newly fermented beer.

No longer needed for rowing, the strong, dark men threw coiled ropes from the boat to the pier and leaped the short gap from the boat to secure them and winch the boat closer. The master nodded and more men lifted a ramp and fitted it in place. A brief command from the captain and the guards formed into two equal columns, faces serious, eyes alert, weapons gleaming like bits of flame in their hands. Another word and they marched forward in unison.

The ramp flexed beneath Pharaoh's feet, the boat rose and fell and sighed as he descended.

"Whatever you want, Neb-t·ḥe-t, will have to wait."

"Where are you going?" She asked.

"To see my brother," Pharaoh said as he passed her.

"He's gone," Neb-t·ḥe-t said. "A temple runner arrived midday yesterday with news of the North. When Set heard that you were coming for him," she looked at Pharaoh's bandaged shoulder, "he left."

"Where? Do you know?"

"No," Neb-t·ḥe-t said, looking down into the water and seeing a fish rise to the surface, leave a bubble, and dart back into the dark, silty, depth.

"Who is in charge at the Temple?"

"Temu handled the day-to-day activities when Set was here. I believe he still does."

"Would he know where Set went?"

"He is Set's friend. He would not tell you."

"I could put him to torture."

Neb-t·ḥe-t sighed. "Set knows that. He didn't tell Temu or anyone else where he was going. He might not have known himself. He was in a hurry to be well away before you arrived."

Pharaoh hesitated. "He must be stopped. He has gone too far this time."

"He will be stopped. But not by you."

"What are you saying, Neb-t·ḥe-t? Speak plainly."

The tears came, Neb-t·ḥe-t felt them, unable to stop them any more than she might stop the River. She let them trail down her cheeks as she spoke. "I know how this ends."

"Will I find him?"

"He will find you."

Some of the fire went out of Ạsạr, his eyes lost their frown, his cheeks and jaws relaxed. He reached out and wiped a tear from Neb-t·ḥe-t's cheek and let his hand rest on her shoulder. "The last woman who cried before me also cursed me. Is this your curse?" Pharaoh asked.

"No, Ạsạr. I find no fault in you. No curse I could name would match those you already carry," she said.

"Why are you telling me this?"

"Because you won't believe me any more than you will believe that giving Āakhu to Maaạ has saved her life. Go to Īset. Each of you needs forgiveness to endure the days ahead. Forget Set. The two of you shall have your reckoning soon enough."

She could see it in his eyes, just for a moment. All the things he wanted to say and those that he didn't. Why things had never been the same between them after his father changed the line of succession. Why, after being destined to marry, nearly lovers, she was suddenly no more than his wife's little sister. Why he never offered her a sweet, empty word of parting. Never a goodbye. She watched for signs of regret or sadness and saw many. But she could not tell if any of them were for her.

Through with her again, uncomfortable with her nearness and the knowledge of the things she could see, Pharaoh turned and signaled his men. They marched, silent, confident, unaware of the bad days to come, unaware how short life could be, how unexpectedly it could end and yet how long the days seemed when your dreams were cold ashes and dead embers and you had only duty and obligation to look forward to.

"He will not let this go," Neb-t·ḥe-t said.

The boatmen went about their duties, securing and inspecting, ignoring Neb-t·ḥe-t. The boat master called a greeting to her and motioned her aboard. She shook her head and tried to smile back at him, but tears and smiles rarely complement each other.

Sounds whispered from the water, the air, from a bird circling far overhead. Neb-t·ḥe-t turned the other direction to see Pharaoh and his party trooping up the narrow street to the House of Balance, growing smaller, less distinct now that she knew their destinies.

She wiped her cheeks and spoke to those only she could see. "I do not like being your voice when words are not enough."

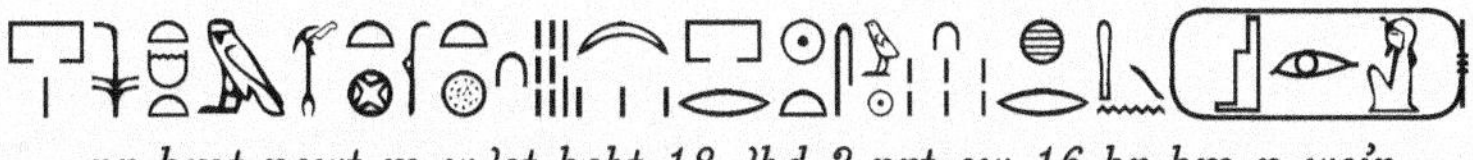

pr ḥmt nswt m wꜣst ḥsbt 18 ꜣbd 3 prt sw 16 ḫr ḥm n wsỉr

The House of Pharaoh's Wife in Uas

Year 18, Month 3 of Peret, Day 16 under the Majesty of Ạsạr

The cat led Pharaoh to Īset.

Once Ḥaāmer's, Baka stayed behind, disappearing for days at a time, eventually finding his way past the doors and walls and armed guards to curl up during the night at the foot of Pharaoh's bed.

He lay stretched on the stone, morning sunlight warming the soft sand-colored fur along his belly. Pharaoh encountered him after passing through an arch and beside a garden.

Blocking his path, the green eyes opened and watched Pharaoh's approach. The tilted head seemed to say *Where have you been?*

Baka licked a paw, rolled over and onto his feet, stalking quietly, Pharaoh behind, into the Queen's house. The sound of Pharaoh's footsteps sounded like whispered accusations hurled at him from the walls.

It was dark and quiet. Several torches had been allowed to go out. Baka stopped and gave a single meow when Pharaoh fell behind looking into the shadows.

There was sound, the further they went down the hall, past doorways opening on gardens and pools. At first Pharaoh thought it was the sound of water, but it became clear with each step that it was someone crying.

He turned a corner. A maidservant, lit by dappled light through an archway, washed the floor. She stood at the sound of approaching footsteps and seeing Pharaoh, went to her knees again, bowing so that her forehead touched the floor.

"Get up," Pharaoh commanded.

She rocked back onto her feet and stood, head down. After a moment, she self-consciously leaned and dropped the rag into a pot of water.

"Why are you crying?" Pharaoh asked.

"I am worried for the Queen. She doesn't leave her room. She doesn't eat. She will not let us enter."

Pharaoh left her. Baka had gotten ahead again and stopped to wait for him. He proceeded more slowly, uncertain. Īset was not prone to bouts of solitude and sadness, though nothing was as it had been before Ḥaāmer was taken to Amennt. He had gone a few slow steps when he heard the creak of knees bending and the rasp of a rag scrubbed across stone behind him.

The common room was empty and dark when he reached it. Enough light filtered through the high windows that he was able to make his way around the couches and tables to the door that led to Īset's private chambers. He was unaccustomed to announcing himself or asking her permission, but he did both as he reached her door. "It is Ạsạr, may I enter?"

A shiver passed through him at the thought that she might be gone, the room empty. Then a sound, a muffled word he could not make out, which he took as acknowledgement. He exhaled a breath he had not realized he was holding and pushed through the tapestry.

Baka sniffed the air and preceded him, a spot of darkness in the shadowy room, flowing across the floor and up into Īset's lap. She sat in a chair, alone, her face and hands like stains against the lighter shades of her dress. It was too dim at first to make out her eyes, her cheeks, her lips.

"Īset?" He whispered, suddenly afraid the the room might indeed be empty.

A hand trailed along Baka's spine. "I killed a man," she said, her voice a dry, brittle sound.

There was a chair across from her, polished, reflecting what little light passed through the darkness, glowing soft, sandy gray. Poised on four legs, it was like an attentive beast, regal, silent, facing her. Pharaoh sat. "You did so in anger?"

"Not anger, Pharaoh's justice. He beat a man and woman to death and lied to me before everyone in the Hall of Balance."

"You could have waited for me. I would have spared you this."

Īset tilted her head back, allowing the hair weighed with beads to fall away from her cheeks. "Set said the same in that tone that makes you look and feel like an idiot for taking his advice. He cornered me. I felt I had no choice but to carry out the execution."

She raised her head again, her eyes two bruises before the curtain of her hair slipped forward and shadowed them again. "I never knew it would haunt me so."

"It isn't easy—it should never be easy—to take a life," Pharaoh said.

"It wasn't heroic or glorious," Īset said. "He wasn't facing foes on the field of battle, doing brave and noble deeds. I tied him up and shut him in a coffin. Then I drowned him at the bottom of a pool. Where is the justice in that?"

"Where is the justice for those he killed? Justice would have been served only if none of those deaths had happened. But they did and the only response you or I or anyone in authority can make is to seek compensation or punishment or revenge and call it justice."

"My chu tells me you speak true, but my ka sees only a tied up body whose life I drove away."

If there were words that could take away her pain, Pharaoh would have spoken them. But there was only emptiness and quiet. Baka shifted on Īset's lap, pushing his head beneath her hand and purring.

Īset turned her face to the walls, the ceiling, the floor. She watched each attentively, as if something came to life each place her gaze found and spoke to her. Finally her gaze found him. "What did you do to your shoulder?"

"It is nothing," Pharaoh said. He shrugged, but only the good shoulder moved.

"Why is it wrapped so tightly if it is nothing?"

"I was struck by an arrow. Just grazed."

Īset's face grew paler, her eyes larger and rounder. She gripped the arms of her chair with a talon-like ferocity. "Someone tried to kill you?"

There is no hope except in the truth. Surprise her, hold nothing back, nothing that she can grasp and worry over until both of us are angry and alone. "Twice, a priest in my tent with a knife and a man with bow and arrow atop a wall in Qes. The priest died for his failure, the other escaped."

"Have you arrested Set?"

Pharaoh shivered in the warm semi-darkness at the coldness in her voice. Her brows had settled heavy over her eyes, forcing them smaller again, little more than slits above her cheeks. "Set has left Uas."

"Will you go after him or will you leave leave him free to try again?"

"I am not convinced that he is behind this."

"Who does he need to convince? Is there anyone in Egypt who would turn against you if you went after him and put him in prison? Is there anyone who does not know that he hates you and wants to replace you?"

"He is my only brother."

"Yes," Īset said, her voice bitter as bad water. "It always comes back to that. So I must pray to the gods that in the end he feels the same."

Baka jumped from Īset's lap and crept off to prowl a dark corner. Outside, the birds were silent, the wind still. People that passed beyond the walls of the Queen's house passed without laughing or speaking.

One thing still burned in the back of Pharaoh's throat like a live ember and pressed on his heart like a heavy stone. "There is something more. We must plan a wedding," he said, letting it go.

Īset looked up, the pain and sadness a little less prominent in her eyes, the lines of her cheeks, her lips. "Āakhu and Ṭeḥuti?"

Pharaoh sighed and looked away, shaking his head. "Not Ṭeḥuti. Āakhu and Maaạ. Our daughter will be the governor's wife."

All that had been gained was lost. The light died in her eyes, her face lost its animation as if a veil had been drawn across it. "Have you told her?"

"I leave that to you."

"She is planning to wed Ṭeḥuti. How could you do this to her?"

Her chair was a step from his, a single square of stone set into the floor measured the distance from his knee to hers. But the distance seemed wide, and growing wider. He studied her blank face, her eyes hollowed into her face even without kohl to define them. Her dark hair, unwashed, cloudy rather than shiny now, hung in beaded strings about her ears and neck. She shrank into her chair, grew smaller, her shoulders slumped. She was like Uas seen from the deck of his boat, diminishing as the current carried his boat away. Tiny people, tiny lives, dwindling in the distance, gone, except for the first pangs of missing them.

"Come here," Pharaoh said, opening his arms to her.

She rose stiffly, as if his voice were a royal decree rather than the plaintive call of one broken heart to another. She settled on his lap and he surrounded her with his arms as if at any moment she might turn to wind and be whirled away. Their heads found each other's shoulder.

"I am so sorry," he cried. "If I could take these days away, smooth away all trace of them from the sand, if I could bring our sweet Ḥaāmer back, I would. But I can't. The gods have given me only enough power to dream of what might be and grow bitter that I cannot bring it to pass. Maaạ saved my life, deflecting that arrow from my heart. He wants Āakhu. I offered him a gift and when he named it, I could not refuse."

"She will not understand. Her heart has been set on Ṭeḥuti since they were children. Could you not have given Maaạ something else?"

"I would have given him more boats and armies than he could dream of. He only wanted Āakhu. Neb-t·ḥe-t told me that I have saved her life by giving her to him. She sees something terrible coming. To us, our family, to Uas."

"She said as much to me—after the judgment. There is worse to come. Each day now I hope that this is it. That this is the worse to come. And each night I go to sleep knowing it is not."

"Will you tell Āakhu?"

"Yes," she whispered. "And now I know how tomorrow will be worse than today."

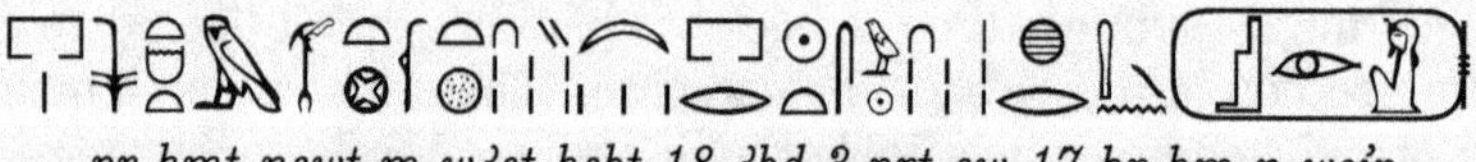

pr ḥmt nswt m wꜣst ḥsbt 18 ꜣbd 3 prt sw 17 ḫr ḥm n wsir

The House of Pharaoh's Wife in Uas

Year 18, Month 3 of Peret, Day 17 under the Majesty of Ạsạr

"Āakhu, where are you going?"

Having asked, Īset felt with an aching inside that she knew the answer. The fresh kohl around Āakhu's eyes, and the exotic scent that drifted about her were as plain as if Āakhu had written hieroglyphics across her forehead.

"I was off to the temple to pray and visit Ṭeḥuti. He's been back almost a day. It surprises me that he has not yet asked to visit me."

The moment arrived despite Īset wishing that it somehow never would. She could delay no longer. "Come and sit with me. There is something I must tell you."

Āakhu frowned, her delicate eyebrows drawing together. "Are you well?"

Īset lowered her head, the beads woven into her hair falling forward across her shoulders to obscure her face. "No," she said.

Īset turned towards the common room. She could hear the whisper of Āakhu's sandals behind her. She took to her couch on the dais. Āakhu stood next to her. "What's wrong?"

"Come sit with me, daughter. Let me hold you. It has been a long time since I have held you."

"It has been a long time since I was small enough to hold," Āakhu said.

"I remember your scraped knees, and bug bites, and cat scratches . . ."

"What are you trying to tell me?"

Īset's heart sank slowly, like one of the poorly constructed reed boats being gradually swallowed by the River. The ache inside grew to encompass her.

How would Īset kill her daughter's happiness, her dreams, her future? Would she do it with one sharp thrust as Ạsạr's military men would suggest? Īset weighed the idea of a violent, swift assault, thrusting her words at her daughter in a sudden, cold torrent as a soldier would thrust a knife. She could bluntly announce that Āakhu would now marry Governor Maaạ instead of Ṭeḥuti.

But should she do it slowly instead? Should she try to explain, should she try to soften the blow, lead up to it, while she watched the life slowly drain from Āakhu's face? She thought of that, too.

When her daughter's happiness lay dead, when the warmth of love had been wiped away and replaced with the coldness of duty, would it matter? Would it matter whether hope disappeared in one swift stroke or in a flood of pale words about destiny and duty?

Īset could not answer those questions in the moments between heartbeats. They were questions left to the thinkers among the priests. It was so much easier when looking into the eyes of a stranger to know what to do, but so hard when looking into the trusting, innocent eyes of your own child.

Īset would see those eyes in this final moment forever in her dreams. She would remember them and a river full of tears would never wash the image away. Īset could only sail ahead, and hope that Āakhu would forgive her.

"You're frightening me," Āakhu said.

"Your father was hurt when he was in Qes to stop the attack. There are those who would see Pharaoh fail. They still have the memories of the small bands that once roamed this land and led simple lives. They are unprepared for the future and seek to keep it from coming. They are neither strong enough or numerous enough to do it with their voices. They think they can keep their simple ways by killing Pharaoh. They have sent assassins."

Āakhu drew back. "Is he—?"

"He was wounded. It will heal. Maaạ saved his life."

"If Maaạ saved Pharaoh and Pharaoh will be well, why are you sad?"

"Pharaoh offered Maaạ a reward for his bravery and allegiance."

Īset could not control herself. Tears came to her eyes; her breath came in short gasps. The words stuck in her throat.

"Has he asked for too much?"

Īset reached for her daughter and clung to her. "Yes," she whispered. "He asked for you."

Āakhu stiffened and tried to pull away. Īset held her tightly.

"I am betrothed to Ṭeḥuti!"

"That betrothal is dissolved. You must now go to Maaạ. Pharaoh has granted it."

"No!" cried Āakhu.

Īset rocked her daughter. "I know it will hurt."

Āakhu shook her head and shouted. "This is wrong! Ṭeḥuti and I were ordained by Ptah and by father to be together. I will not do this, I will die first!"

Āakhu stumbled from the dais and ran toward the entrance that led to the courtyard and the gate beyond.

"Come back!" Īset pleaded, but she was already talking to an empty room.

"Āakhu!" Īset called once more. Her voice sounded desperate and pleading even to her own ears.

The curtain at the door was still. The sound of Āakhu's sobbing diminished in the distance until it was nothing. Īset buried her head in a pillow and wept, convinced she had somehow failed both her daughter and herself.

ḥwt-nṯr nt ptḥ m wȝst

ḥsbt 18 ȝbd 3 prt sw 17 ḫr ḥm n wsỉr

The Temple of Ptah is Uas

Year 18, Month 3 of Peret, Day 17 under the Majesty of Ạsạr

"Run away with me," Āakhu said from the doorway. She had barely pushed the tapestry aside.

Ṭeḥuti looked up to see her eyes, large and frightened, tear-stained and frantic. He could see her shaking, and yet the sight of her was like a dream come true.

Āakhu slipped into the room and let the tapestry fall behind her. She was alone. No guards. No servants.

"Father has given me to Maaạ," she said, her voice breaking at the end.

"I know."

"You . . . knew?" she asked, her eyes too wide for the soft light, her delicate eyebrows raised.

"Pharaoh has forbidden me to see you. I have spent every moment since my return planning how I would get you away from Uas. I've enlisted one of your guards. I was coming for you tonight."

Āakhu shook her head. "We must flee. I want to live my life with you—not Maaạ. I don't even know him."

"Be sure of this," Ṭeḥuti said. "Love motivated by fear can be lost when the fear is gone. You will not be a daughter of Pharaoh. Life will be hard.

You saw Ȧamȧam and the children. We will be little better off until I can establish myself fishing or handling legal agreements in a distant village."

"I don't care!" she shouted. "I will not be given to another as part of an agreement. I love you, that is all that matters."

"You are trembling," Ṭeḥuti said, rising from his bench. He went to her and surrounded her with his arms. "I love you, my soul and my heart. Let me gather a few things. The sooner we are away the better our chances."

He smelled the sweet scent of her hair, felt the warmth of her breath against his chest. He had a moment of hope but also saw all that might lie between them and happiness. Could she cook her own meals? Wash her own clothes? Could she give up what she was and become one of those who served rather than ruled?

What was it that Ȧamȧam had said about her? Was Āakhu's destiny so different, so far away, that love could not overcome it?

Ṭeḥuti went to the shelves and found his medicine bag. He dusted it off and filled it with sealed jars and small boxes of dried herbs. He gathered his amulets, images of his personal gods, and put them inside as well.

A second pair of sandals for each of them, a few fruits from a bowl on his work table, were all the bag would also hold. He found two traveling cloaks in a box, one for himself, and one smaller but still too large for Āakhu.

"Put this on," he said. "The less you look like the daughter of Pharaoh, the less likely we will be caught."

"You think father will be looking for me so quickly?"

"As soon as he knows you're gone," he said, wrapping himself in the long, linen robe, its hem stained with traces of the red clay found along the many paths between the River and the sandy hills.

He went to another shelf and dug through a stack of rolled scrolls. He chose three of the four he pulled out and stuck them into pockets inside his robe.

"Let's go," he said, taking her arm and pausing only long enough to extinguish the oil pot on his table.

"Which way?" Āakhu asked.

"To Ȧamȧam. She will have more food and clothing. She will let us use the boat."

They fled the temple wearing wraps that covered their nose and mouth and protected them from the blowing sand. There were no brown or red stains on the blue sky that would presage a sand storm, and that drew some curious attention, though not nearly as much as parading the newly-betrothed daughter of Pharaoh out of the city.

Their passage was neither as quiet or quick as Ṭeḥuti hoped, and he had to recognize and control his growing frustration and trust that the gods would see them away in order not to make even more of a spectacle.

A man, recognizing their priestly robes, stopped them in the street and asked for a blessing for his wife and their first child. Ṭeḥuti sighed and whispered a prayer of deliverance. Then he and Āakhu followed the man to his house. Āakhu said nothing as she knelt with Ṭeḥuti in the small, windowless mud brick room, a single smokey candle casting wan shadows on the bare walls. The young mother smiled as she suckled her child.

Ṭeḥuti offered a brief blessing, sprinkled water from the River on the child, and passed the mother a copper ankh from his bag, folding it into her hand. Her eyes and her smile widened as she held it up and saw the metal glow in the light. Āakhu patted her shoulder, stroked her child's small head, and wished her well. Then they were out of the house, commending the small fee the husband offered back to his child's care.

They made it to the end of the street and turned up another toward the hills. Ṭeḥuti watched for signs of Pharaoh's guards and saw none. Nor did he see people staring and pointing. No one seemed to be looking for a man and woman traveling nervously and in a hurry out of Uas.

A woman hailed them in the street, praised Ptah that he had sent them, and asked them to come see her sick husband. Ṭeḥuti looked at Āakhu. "I will see to this if you want to continue. I can catch up."

"I go where you go," she said, taking his arm.

They followed the woman into her house, mud brick and reed, small but clean and airy, aligned so that the breezes between the River and the hills might pass through open doors and small windows to freshen the length of its interior. She took them to a darkened room large enough only for a bed and a clothing box.

"It is nothing," the husband said as they lit a candle. "My Ārit worries. You need not have come."

"Hush," she said.

Ṭeḥuti knelt by the bed. He touched the man's head, his neck, his chest and stomach. He checked nose, mouth, and ears for signs of evil spirits or poisonous bites and found none. Āakhu stood quietly behind him.

"What is it?" Ārit asked.

"I have something that will make you well," Ṭeḥuti said as he stood. He took a small box from his pack, lifted the lid, and inhaled. He made a face and sneezed. "You will not like it but it will help."

He turned to Ārit. "Crush a pinch of these herbs between your fingers each morning and put them in a bowl of water. See that he drinks all of it. As he drinks, speak this prayer:

"You are Amun, god of the silent,
who comes at the cry of the poor.
I call upon you when I am ill,
You come that you might rescue me.
Give your breath to one who is weak,
Bring forth one who is shut in."

He found an amulet of Amun and placed it beneath the man's headrest. "Leave this here until he is well. Then take an offering to Amun in the temple. He will be well in three or four days."

Ārit smiled, put her hands together, and fell to her knees. "Thank you."

"We must go," Ṭeḥuti said to Āakhu. "We have delayed too long."

"You shall not leave without my thanks," Ārit said.

She led them to her kitchen and put two small, salted fish and a handful of dates into Ṭeḥuti's bag.

"You wrap your faces. Is there a storm coming?" Ārit asked.

"Yes," Ṭeḥuti said. "But not the sands. We travel in secret and do not wish to be seen."

Ārit frowned. Ṭeḥuti and Āakhu left her house and continued up the street.

"Was that a wise thing to say to her? She will tell everyone."

"I know," Ṭeḥuti said. "We are past wise now. We must get away."

They sought quiet streets, passing the houses like two shadows. They prayed that they might not be seen or long remembered. They asked that Pharaoh's guards might not chance this way.

The houses were simpler, poorer, patchworks of mud, wood scavenged from the River, stones rolled down from the hills. The people were plainer, thinner, dressed in worn, ill-fitting, yellowed clothing, having few concerns beyond living another day. Children played as they worked, singing simple songs as they fed animals, tended cook fires, ground grain or washed and cut vegetables. They had no time for more than a smile and a quick greeting as Ṭeḥuti and Āakhu stole past.

With a sigh of relief they reached the hills beyond Uas. Āakhu did not tire or falter, she did not ask Ṭeḥuti to slow or stop for rest. She cast an occasional glance back at the city, searching for anything that might be following. Fear and love and hope all sustained her.

Half the distance to Ȧamȧam's behind them, the Aten past midday, descending, Ṭeḥuti called a halt atop a hill that gave them clear view of the lands about them.

He removed his cloak and spread it out for them. "Salted fish and dates," he said, removing part of Ārit's gift from his bag.

Āakhu nodded and lowered herself to the ground with a sigh. She removed her sandals and rubbed her feet.

Her eyes had lost their redness, her face that sense of panic he had seen in his room back at the temple. The fear was draining away now that they had made it this far without incident.

"Will you miss the life of stone palaces and temples?" Ṭeḥuti asked.

"There has never been a palace or temple as grand as this," she said, turning to take in the view.

The River switched back on itself like a lazy, contented serpent in the valley below, basking in the embrace of the dormant fields still stained with dark patches of soil left by the inundation. Hills stretched away to the east, the valleys, dunes, and wadis pointing with hieroglyphic precision from the River valley to the eastern desert. A land of golden sand, orange and red stone, stark, barren, wildly beautiful in its own way. The winds sang among the hills and down the valleys, the gods whispered and spoke timeless wisdom to anyone who would listen.

"I hope you can grow to love it as I do," Ṭeḥuti said.

"I love you," she said. "That is a start. Today, it is easy to love this new, strange life we are fleeing towards. Tomorrow, it may be hard. But while I have your hand to hold, your lips to kiss away my tears, your voice and your strong arms as comfort, I will have enough."

He would have liked to stay there with Āakhu on the top of that hill. He would have liked the Aten to halt so the day might last forever. He would have liked to lay with her on that weary old cloak and taken and given her his love. But the Aten continued his descent, there was still a fair distance to Ȧamȧam's, and they were not yet far enough away that he could relax and pronounce them safe.

Ṭeḥuti smiled at her, and tried not to let his disappointment show through. He hoped there would be other timeless, perfect days, when her smile was once again as bright as the Aten, her eyes as cool and deep and inviting as fresh water, her lips, her mouth sweet and tantalizing as succulent fruit, her body as perfect and inviting as it was this moment.

"We should be going," Ṭeḥuti said.

She watched him a moment. Perhaps her thoughts had run similar to his. Then she smiled and there might have just been a trace, an instant of that same sadness and disappointment. But the moment was already lost and that knowledge was there as well. "Yes," she agreed.

They continued on to Ȧamȧam's hand in hand, talking very little. Āakhu sang in a soft clear voice, a praise to Ra, a praise to Ptah. Then she sang a song of the boat men, one he was surprised she knew, though the words she sang were more appropriate to Pharaoh's daughter than the coarser expressions the boat men used. Ṭeḥuti joined her when he knew the words, adding a deeper melody to her songs. He had a fair voice though he seldom sang. But there came moments when he hit a precise note, harmonizing perfectly with her, that they would look at one another and smile. Then Āakhu sang him a love song:

I shall never be far from you
while your hand is in mine,
And I shall stroll with you
in every favorite place.

Threading her arm through his and around his waist, she walked close to him. It would be so easy, under a clear sky on a warm day, the breeze from the River whispering encouragement and pushing them together toward tomorrow, so easy with Āakhu's hand in his, her sweet love poems filling his head with dreams, to forget that he did not know where their next meal would come from, or where they would sleep tonight, or what they would do tomorrow or the day after that, or whether they would ever be free of Uas or the obligations that bound them there.

Ṭeḥuti did not voice his thoughts. They did not linger and trouble him, not with the sound of Āakhu's laugh and her breathing, the sound of her sandals keeping time across the hot sand with his. They did not speak except of trivial things, a stone that looked like a bird, a cloud that looked like a cat, a whistle of wind down a ravine that sounded like an old song.

Their pace slowed from an escape to a lover's stroll as Uas fell further behind them. In mid-afternoon, they reached the edge of the bowl in which Ȧamȧam's house sat. They stopped, still arm-in-arm.

"Where are the children?" Āakhu asked.

"Something's wrong," Ṭeḥuti replied.

Untended fields circled the house, empty of the children who normally tended them. Rough tools lay scattered about, hastily dropped. A water pot rested on its side along the path down to the River next to a splash of dried mud. A spotted brown goat nudged it, pushing his tongue inside for a few last drops. Other animals crouched or lay listless in small patches of shade.

Ṭeḥuti guided Āakhu away from the edge, out of sight of the house. "There's a path down to the River," he said. "Let's see if the boat is here."

The path, little more than an animal trail, curled around the basin through a head-high ravine, Its mouth opened onto a narrow plain of short grass and young palms whose seeds had been deposited in some past inundation. At the River bank, Ȧamȧam's boat was tied in is usual spot. Beside it, a newer, bigger boat, rocked gently on the River's current.

"Father's guard," Āakhu said.

Ṭeḥuti scanned the hills leading up from the River for any sign of them. "How could they have followed us here?"

"I told mother and Pharaoh about this place. The servant who returned the boat must have led them. What will we do?"

Ṭeḥuti motioned her silent. He took her hand and listened, but the only sounds were birds and wind and water. There were no sounds of the guards. "They must be holding Ȧamȧam and the children inside, waiting for us. Did your servants repair Ȧamȧam's boat before returning it?"

"A new mast," Āakhu said.

"Then we will take Ȧamȧam's boat and set the other adrift."

"Why not take theirs?"

"Too big, too recognizable. Come."

Ṭeḥuti led her across the stretch of sand and grass to the boats, glancing at the rise for any sign of a lookout, praying Pharaoh's guard did not think it necessary to leave someone to watch their boat.

He put his hands of her hips. "Jump," he said and boosted her into the boat. He untied the solder's boat and tied it to Ȧamȧam's, then pushed both away from the bank.

With a last look at the hills leading to Ȧamȧam's house, he pulled himself aboard and settled at the oars.

The rowing was hard, towing the larger boat. Rather than struggling south against the current, he risked being carried with it toward Uas while he pulled the guard's boat to mid-River. The current was strongest there, he could release the boat with a better chance Pharaoh's guard would not recover it in time to pursue.

Āakhu sat before him, still now that she had nothing to do, nowhere to go, alternately offering quiet words of encouragement and watching the River bank.

A shout carried across the water to them. Āakhu stiffened and pointed. "Pharaoh's guard," she said. "Four of them."

The men ran down the hill and stopped at the water, cursing themselves as much as Ṭeḥuti. One quickly stripped off his weapons and sandals and dove into the River.

"Time to go," Ṭeḥuti said.

He lifted the oars. The two boats were nearly halfway to the River's center, not as far as he wanted, but far enough to delay them. He untied the soldier's boat and tossed the rope aboard.

He removed the ties and loosed the old, stiff sail on Ȧamȧam's boat. It squeaked in protest as the afternoon breeze filled it. He swung it into position. The boat slowed and finally stopped drifting with the current, beginning a painfully slow, almost imperceptible crawl against it. Ṭeḥuti tied the rope for the sail loosely to the boat and motioned to Āakhu. "Watch this. Pull on the rope to keep it filled with the wind."

She nodded and moved over to sit beside the rope. Ṭeḥuti dipped the oars again and pulled, increasing their speed against the current.

Several fishing boats glided along the River, as well as two trading boats moving in tandem. Ṭeḥuti would have liked to hide among them. But as the afternoon lengthened toward evening, the boats all headed with the current toward Uas, the wrong direction.

Āakhu frowned. Ṭeḥuti looked back. The soldier was a good swimmer. He had already covered half the distance to his drifting boat.

"Fetch me those leather straps," Ṭeḥuti said. "My hands are getting raw."

Āakhu gathered and held them out to him. He put his fingers through the crude holes. Wrapping the leather comfortably between his palms and the oars, he resumed rowing.

The water sizzled as it broke against the bow and slipped along the sides, but their progress was slow. Ṭeḥuti steered them gradually toward the western bank, seeking that magical combination of slower current and favorable wind that would take them south out of the reach of Pharaoh's guard.

"Will we escape them?" Āakhu asked.

Ṭeḥuti glanced at her, small now, almost child-like, still holding the sail rope. Her eyes had grown large, her face pale, the first doubts and fears, perhaps regrets as well, stealing over her in the fading afternoon.

"If we can reach Tod by dark. It's easy to follow us on the River, but nearly impossible in a city. I think we will be safe there."

But he looked back and saw the soldier paddling the boat, halfway back to pick up his comrades. Ṭeḥuti knew it would come down to how skilled Pharaoh's soldiers were as boat men and whose boat proved to be the fastest.

"Where will we sleep? What will we eat?" Āakhu asked, discovering the same questions he had asked himself earlier.

"Ptah will provide," he said.

"Ptah isn't here."

"Then I will provide," he said. "I have items for exchange. I have my magics. Healing someone's sickness should be worth a meal or two, perhaps even a quiet place to stay for the night."

"I don't know . . . " she said.

Her enthusiasm had not survived the day. He hoped her love would survive much longer. "You came with me, now you must trust me. I will see that you have food and shelter. Smile for me and tighten that sail."

She looked down, smiling shyly, then turned to watch the River, the waves, the other boats, before turning back to Ṭeḥuti. "Will we one day laugh about this and tell our children about our escape from Uas? Will they ever believe that I am Pharaoh's daughter."

"Whether or not they believe," Ṭeḥuti said in time with his pulling on the oars, "it will make for an entertaining story."

Āakhu sang in time with Ṭeḥuti's rowing:

We embark on a ship of cedar wood,
I hold the sail and my love the oars,
We seek our fair mansion,
one we will build ourselves.

Our mouths will fill with wine and beer,
With bread and meat and cakes,
Oxen slain and wine jars opened,
And pleasant singing awaits us.

Praise to thee, oh River,
Who comes from the south to nourish the sand,
Carry us to safety,
Carry us home.

He smiled and rested as she finished. Āakhu let go the sail rope, leaned forward, hand on his knee, and kissed him. It seemed too brief, the time that their lips touched, but long enough that he no longer felt quite so urgently the fatigue in his shoulders and arms.

The soldier had reached shore and his comrades scrambled quickly aboard. They had pushed away from the bank. When Ṭeḥuti resumed rowing, Āakhu was holding the sail rope again, watching the soldiers.

"A pursuit on the River, against the current, can last all day as the distance between pursuer and pursued diminishes with the whims of wind and current," Ṭeḥuti said. "Though we can still see the soldiers behind us, they are nearly a quarter day away on the River. We will be lost in Tod before they can reach us. And by the time they rally forces in the city, with a little favor from the gods, we will be further away."

"It would be faster on land."

"It would, if the land were even, if there were trails and paths close to the bank. They could move faster on land than we could on the River and would eventually get ahead of us. Some River pursuits end that way. But while they tried to get ahead of us on the east bank we would go west, the other side, and we would lose them that way. Until they can enlist others, they must follow us, on the River while we are on the River, on land while we are on land."

"They cannot go for help," Āakhu said.

"No," Ṭeḥuti said with a smile. "You have taken your first step as a military strategist. The guard cannot stop or go back for help or they will certainly lose us."

"So we wait."

"And row, and keep the sail positioned to catch all the wind the gods send us, and pray," Ṭeḥuti said.

The mast creaked, the sail squeaked and shivered as it filled and emptied with a fickle breeze, diminishing in strength with the passing of the day. The coarse linen caught as much of the Aten's yellow-orange light as it did wind. The water settled into a monotonous, soothing tone, slapping and bubbling against and along the boat's sides. Ahead, the cook smoke and dust from Tod were a smudge above the hills. Sails clustered about the piers there as fisherman came home early.

Ṭeḥuti's thoughts drifted away, lost to the rhythm of rowing, *pull, lift, push, drop,* in constant, seemingly eternal succession. He failed to notice the darkening to the west behind the boat's sail.

"They are getting closer," Āakhu said.

"There are four of them and they haven't been rowing as long. But they haven't let out their sail."

"Why are they pointing and shouting? What are they saying?"

Ṭeḥuti turned. For the moment, two of the soldiers had let go their oars, standing, pointing, shouting something he could not quite hear. In the other direction, the reason for their concern was evident. The Aten, though still well above the horizon, was growing red and dim as streaks of something like smoke passed over it.

"Sand storm. Let's get the sail down," Ṭeḥuti said, even as the last of the breeze died and the sail slackened.

Ṭeḥuti reached and loosed the rope that held the sail, letting it all the way out so the linen fell to the deck. "Sit by the mast," he said. "The boat won't rock as much and you can get beneath the sail for protection."

"We need to get to shore."

"Too late for that, we'll have to stay low and keep covered until it passes," Ṭeḥuti replied.

The first gust hit them, sending a shiver through the boat as if it had run aground or hit something in the water. The boat rocked. Āakhu struggled for balance as she stumbled for the mast. A second gust hit, sand this time stinging their faces, arms, and legs like countless insect bites. The boat rolled. Ṭeḥuti and Āakhu both reached for the mast. The wind and sand caught a corner of the sail, throwing the linen up into their faces. The boat tipped again and went over, spilling them into the River.

The boat turned over completely, the bottom, like the hump of a turtle's shell, all that remained above the waves. Ṭeḥuti came up first, grasping for the boat's side, and shouted Āakhu's name. He tried to follow the contour of the boat, shouting her name again and again. The day had suddenly become a reddish-brown twilight, even head-high above the River it was hard to see through the sand and water the wind had raised.

He went around the bow. There was the weak cry and the sound of choking. He wiped at his sand-crusted eyes and saw a hand, a face, fighting to stay above the water. Ṭeḥuti pushed away from the boat, caught her, and pulled her back. She was still gasping and crying, but there was no struggle left in her. He got both of her hands onto the boat and guided her back to the other side, out of the wind.

He got her arms spread and boosted her up onto the side of the boat still shielded from the wind. He spread across her, protecting her, keeping her warm, boosting her higher even as the boat slowly sank beneath them.

The wind screamed across the boat's spine, mud rained down on them. Ṭeḥuti used handfuls of water to wash it from his eyes

Āakhu choked for awhile, expelling mouthfuls of water that had gotten inside her, then she sobbed. It was a sound that wounded him more than the wind and the water, the overturned boat, their failed escape. At one point Ṭeḥuti heard her whisper "What do we do now?"

"Hold on and pray for a miracle," Ṭeḥuti said with a shiver.

The boat settled lower. Ṭeḥuti tried to peek around the bow and see how close they were to the River bank, but in the mud and wind he could see no more than three or four paces distant. He could not see the bank and did not know how far away it might be. With the River whipped into a muddy froth by the sand storm, it was doubtful they could swim much further than he distance he could see.

Āakhu wailed as the boat sank beneath the waves. The wind and mud attacked them again. Instinct got them facing away, but the mud was like knives stabbing into the backs of their heads. Āakhu's hair blew across the water, obscuring her face.

They kicked to keep their heads above water, but the waves were building, washing over them. They were both sputtering in the troughs to expel the water each wave drove into them. But they were tiring, the escape from Uas, their walk to Ȧamȧam's, the River chase, had taken its toll. Āakhu slipped further into the water. Ṭeḥuti held her up, but knew his strength was nearly at an end.

Ṭeḥuti's head went under and did not come up. Something pried his arms away from Āakhu and pulled her away. He struggled and clawed back to the surface, groping blindly for her. One of Pharaoh's guard pulled her into their boat and passed her to two of his comrades. As Ṭeḥuti reached desperately for the boat, the soldier looked down at him and growled, "I should leave you to drown for your stupidity."

For just a moment, Ṭeḥuti thought and wished he would. Āakhu was safe in their boat. She had her family, her life, her future. Ṭeḥuti had nothing now, he had lost her and failed.

The soldier cursed and shook his head, then reached to pull Ṭeḥuti aboard.

* * *

The storm died with the day. The wind diminished from a wail to a whisper and soon the soldiers emerged from the sheltering linen to clear the boat of mud and sand. The Aih emerged first from the darkness, a welcome sight even to Ṭeḥuti, followed by a sprinkling of the brighter stars.

The guard escorted Āakhu to a shelter at the back of the boat and were generous in giving her their food and water. They ignored Ṭeḥuti.

"I'm sorry," Ṭeḥuti said, as if an explanation might somehow absolve him. "We wanted to be together."

After a few cold glares, the guard resumed clearing the boat, folding and stowing the sail and the linens that covered them during the storm, finally turning the boat toward Uas.

They tied Ṭeḥuti, sitting, to the mast. Their anger dissipated in hard work, they treated him with grudging respect, ordering him to sit and put his arms out behind him, leaving the ropes loose about his wrists. Ṭeḥuti could flex his fingers for all the good it did him.

Āakhu sat in the Aih's shadow beneath the shelter at the back of the boat, by turns silent or softly weeping. The guards were quiet as they guided the boat back into the sluggish current and let the River carry it toward Uas. Huddling together near the bow, they glanced back at Ṭeḥuti and Āakhu, relieved they had saved her, but uncomfortable that everything they had done since only made her cry.

wsḫt nt jwsw m wꜣst ḥsbt 18 ꜣbd 3 prt sw 17 ḫr ḥm n wsỉr

The Hall of Balance in Uas

Year 18, Month 3 of Peret, Day 17 under the Majesty of Ạsạr

It was night and the hall was dark except for the scattered torches that burned at the front where Pharaoh sat. Few people were here this late. Pharaoh and Īset, a sleepy looking scribe, Pharaoh's guard, four maidservants, Ṭeḥuti and Āakhu.

"Do you understand the cost of your actions?" Pharaoh asked. "You could have both died when the boat capsized."

"It was my doing," Āakhu cried.

"You will be silent," Pharaoh said, pointing at her, "until I grant you permission to speak."

Īset reached and caught his arm, tugging it gently back to the armrest, away from the tear-filled eyes and trembling lips of their daughter.

"I only know what it would have cost had I not tried," Ṭeḥuti replied.

He wanted to wrap an arm about Āakhu and pull her close, for support as much as comfort, but the bonds on his wrists prevented him.

Pharaoh grumbled. "The fate of four provinces, all those people and their safety, depend on this marriage. I thought you were wise enough to recognize and honor that. Instead you jeopardize all the gods have set in motion."

"You need not have given Āakhu to him. You should not have broken the promise you made to your daughter. Maaạ would have joined you anyway, he had no where else to go."

"It is the will of the gods that Maaạ be part of the house of Pharaoh."

"Then why did you not declare it so?"

Pharaoh nodded. The chief of his guard struck Ṭeḥuti in the mouth. Ṭeḥuti went to one knee, looked up at Pharaoh, and ran his tongue across his bleeding lip.

"Was that necessary?" Īset asked. "They are in love, they were promised to one another. How can you be surprised at what happened?"

"You think I know nothing of the pleasures and disappointments of love?" Pharaoh asked without looking at his chief wife.

Īset blushed. Her lips, compressed into a thin, angry line, trembled as she spoke: "Not love. But what has become of your mercy?"

Pharaoh turned his head to glare at her. "If you question me again I will have you escorted home."

Īset folded her hands in her lap and said nothing.

Pharaoh rubbed his chin. His shoulder was no longer wrapped but he did not use it. His eyes were tired, sunken, haunted. His cheeks were gaunt. His hand trembled ever so slightly when he lifted it. "Enough of this. She is Maaạ's now. You have betrayed me. You will be held until the cargo boats return from down the River and placed aboard one when it departs. You are never to return to Uas. If you disobey me a second time I will put you to the sword."

Ṭeḥuti bowed his head. Āakhu gasped.

"And you, my own daughter," Pharaoh said. "I thought you better than this. Maaạ wants you. He has offered to join me. You may well be the wife of the next Pharaoh and sit where your mother sits now. It is important to everyone that this marriage occur, that our two lands join together in unity and strength."

"You broke your promise."

"You should know by now how rarely any of us gets what we want or think we deserve. The gods have their purposes for each of us. Their purposes are rarely our own. Maaạ is a good man. You should consider yourself blessed."

Āakhu did not answer. Instead, she removed her sandals, stepping backward out of them, first left, then right.

"These were given by a father who honors his word to his daughter. They are no longer mine and I can no longer walk in them," she said.

She shrugged out of her gold and jeweled bracelets. They clanged and bounced as they tumbled to the floor, some of the jewels coming loose, scattering, the hoops rolling in circles about her sandals.

Āakhu watched them a moment and looked up. The sound of her jewelry coming to rest was the only sound in the Hall of Balance. Everyone was spellbound, watching in disbelief as Pharaoh's family splintered and came apart.

"These gifts were given to a daughter by a father who would not sell his children for land in the North. I no longer have that father so these can no longer belong to me."

Āakhu stood alone, still wearing the too-large traveling robe Ṭeḥuti had given her. Tears ran down her face but she held her head high, her shoulders and back straight as she had been taught. She focused her gaze on Pharaoh, wounded and defiant at the same time. Then she turned away.

Pharaoh looked at Īset. "Call her maid servants to take her to the Queen's house. See that she does not leave until her wedding."

It was over just that quickly, having taken less time to pronounce judgment than to open the hall, light the torches, and see the two captives inside.

The guards came forward and took Ṭeḥuti. He was still too numb to realize what had happened. Banished?

He wanted to say that there had been a mistake. Banished? Love was not supposed to be banished or sent away. But how could he tell Pharaoh that Maaạ was the mistake? That Pharaoh's giving Maaạ another daughter was a mistake?

"Wait. No," Ṭeḥuti said. But no one was listening. Pharaoh's guards tugged at his arms to lead him away. Pharaoh had already stalked off into the darkness, followed by a silent, angry Īset.

Ṭeḥuti searched for a last glimpse of Āakhu but her maid servants had surrounded and herded her away. They would not look at him.

"I will find you," Ṭeḥuti tried to say. But his voice was thin and broken, and only the first two words came out before the guard slapped him into stunned silence.

* * *

Pharaoh and Īset reached the gate to the her house. She turned to go in, her movements stiff, refusing to say a word to him.

"I'm sorry," he called after her. She did not slow her steps or answer.

"Everything I do goes wrong now. I did not want to anger you or Āakhu or even Ṭeḥuti. Neb-t-ḥe-t said I have saved her life by sending her to Maaạ."

Īset was lost in the shadows. Only the sound of her footsteps persisted.

Too softly for her to hear, he said: "I think the gods will come for me soon. They must be weary of the Pharaoh who fails. Will you forgive me before I am gone?"

* * *

It is always night in the prison behind the Hall of Balance, dark and cold. A torch burned in the corridor beyond the tiny window like a single far-off star. A guard came and exchanged it for another each time it burned low. Ṭeḥuti could not stand upright, but got to his feet, stooped, each time he heard that guard approach, hoping Pharaoh had reconsidered, that the anger had left him and compassion and mercy had convinced him to set Ṭeḥuti free. Each time, the guard lifted the dying torch from its holder, twisted the new one firmly into place, and left, the sound of his feet dying away in the distance.

Ṭeḥuti thought he saw shadows move. He heard sounds, squeaks and scrapes, the crack of an insect crushed by small unseen jaws. He slid to the other side of his prison away from them. He nodded and dozed, haunted by half-remembered dreams of a terrible chase, and woke with a start.

A shadow lingered in the dark corridor just beyond the feeble light, a woman veiled in linen.

"I wish you had succeeded," she said, her voice soft with regret.

"So do I, Lady," he croaked, his voice suddenly a foreign, uncertain thing.

She stepped forward, the light shifting to make the veil transparent. It was Neb-t·ḥe-t.

"You have played at love since you were both children and treated love as if it were something already bought and paid for. Now you know better. Do you love Āakhu?"

"More than my life."

"Take care what you say when the gods can hear. You may yet be together, but not until you have tasted the poison that is love as well the sweetness. Clay is burned to make brick. You and Āakhu must be tested with fire and reshaped into something different if your love is to endure. I will pray that you live and find your way back to her. Someone should have a happy ending."

Then she was gone, a cloud of linen mist drifting into the darkness, leaving him alone and broken.

Chapter 14

ABYDOS, EGYPT, THE FEATURE, JUNE 28TH, 8:25 P.M.:

"Why do you want her to go?" asked Captain Jagardii.

"She's a witness to the Minister of State for Antiquities's murder."

"Yes, I know. I'm protecting her. She's staying here,"

"I'll contact Dr. Tu'hut and through him your General Fadi."

"Do not threaten me. You'll do nothing. Things around here will become most unpleasant."

"Now you're threatening me! You'll be replaced."

"I doubt that."

Sanders took a step toward the Captain, poking him in the chest. Jagardii stiffened, wiping Sanders' hand away and bringing his fists up. The lieutenant stepped between them.

"Unbelievable! How did I get in the middle of this?" asked Sanders. He turned to a dejected Lisa looking at him.

"I'm sorry," she said. "I didn't mean for you to be put is this position."

"Good night, Dr. Sanders," said Captain Jagardii as he and the lieutenant turned back to their area.

Lisa and Sanders faced each other in the center of the archaeological site.

"So I guess you're in charge now?"

"I don't want that. That was never my purpose. You're the Project Manager."

"If that's the case and since I'm hamstrung by the Egyptian Army, I want a military guard around you at all times."

"I already have that."

"No, I mean when you walk anywhere in the area. After what happened tonight, I don't know what I'm going to do about your being here—no promises."

"I just want to work."

"So what am I supposed to do?"

"Fix your damn camera."

"You're too pragmatic! And by the way, the next time you want to get the army's attention, blow the horn on the top of the trailer rather than shooting a hole in my wall."

I was shooting at the terrorist not your wall.

"How do I do that?" she asked.

He showed her.

ABYDOS, EGYPT, THE FEATURE, JUNE 29TH, 6:15 A.M.:

With difficulty, Bill removed the head of the telescopic arm. He disconnected the remaining computer wires so he could extract the camera from the hole.

"What a mess. I'll have to splice the wires into the camera to see if it's even functional. I must remove everything from the opening and start all over again," he groused to Lisa. "Maybe I'll be able to rebuild parts of it. Until I get it recalibrated, it'll be useless for accurate measurements. Damn! This is a major setback."

Bill had the lieutenant draft two soldiers. With their assistance, he lifted the entire assembly from the hole.

"Why don't I explore along the cliff face down the road?" Lisa suggested, not wanting to be around as he vented.

"You're going out of camp?"

"I'm going to explore the other possibility for getting into the tomb that I mentioned last night. I'll take soldiers with me."

A firm lipped Sanders gave her a curt nod. Lisa left with the lieutenant and armed guards.

Bill had the camera functional four hours later. Next, he cursed over the telescopic arm. The drive mechanism was beyond repair. Luckily the University understood that sand wears out nylon motor gears at digs such as his so he came with a spare.

The telescopic arm was another story. Unable to repair or retract the camera support into the bent first section, he would have to replace it. With it extended, he would have to be careful not to hit anything.

Damn! It's worthless for measurements. The calibration is shot.

He calculated the distance to all the known objects close to the opening to see if he had clearance once he reinstalled the camera with the arm in its shortest configuration.

I miss everything that's my first bit of luck.

He'd have to twist around the high items, but he could program the computer to avoid these artifacts. He went to the tomb roof opening and began the process of reinstalling the camera and arm. His stomach growled.

Crap! I've missed lunch again.

* * *

Lisa slung her pack over her shoulder and gathered her guards. Their nervous tension showed as they scanned the heights and the sides along their path. Their heads and eyes were in constant motion. Their nervousness transferred to Lisa who eyed the cliffs as well. After a time, she decided to trust the soldiers because her worry was accomplishing nothing.

She was happy to be away from Sanders. Since their encounter, he was giving her a lot of leeway, but she had to become indispensable. She must find easier access to the tomb complex.

"Stop!"

Lisa jumped. Looking down, she had nearly stepped off the edge of the path into a ravine, a vertical drop of fifteen feet.

"Thank you, lieutenant. I could've been injured."

He nodded.

I'd better wake-up. Get my mind on what I'm doing.

Stepping back from the edge, she pulled her map from her hip pocket and found her place next to the ravine. They'd traveled a hundred meters down the modern highway then turned left into the cliffs on this trail. Assuming they'd gone far enough along it, they should be able to circle back to where she calculated the subterranean corridor extended. She agonized over how she was going to 'blast' into the tomb.

"We'll go that way, lieutenant."

They trudged off again skirting the edge of the ravine and backtracking around the cliff face along a narrow side path. She turned a corner to find her path blocked by a shoulder-high rockslide flowing over the path and down into the ravine. A shallow depression curved back into the cliff wall—a dead end.

Damn!

Lisa rocked back on her heel, pulling the paper once again to review how far she was from the intersection point. If she had to crawl over the rock slide, further exploration by this route was going to be a pain. She was close. She glanced from the paper to the wall, looking at the base of the heap. Her heart skipped a beat.

Wait a second! That stone looks dressed. Its weathered, but those look like tool marks.

Lisa went down on her knees, motioning for the others to stay back. As she brushed the debris from the top and sides of the rectangular piece, she discovered a footing stone. Finding another flat surface to the side of the first that disappeared into the rock slide, she continued to expand the area. Cleaning upward, she found a stone stacked on the first. As she continued to expose more, she found additional slabs.

This rockslide was 'built.'

The ancients had hidden the structure by piling stone, gravel and sand, a fake rockslide, over the path and down into the ravine. Over the millennia, the infrequent rainfall had washed the disguise away. Lisa could see the gradation of stone and sand from the top to the bottom. The ancients were pretty ingenious. She photographed everything.

"Lieutenant, this rock slide is artificial."

He stared at the rock wall for a moment.

"Yes, ma'am," his voice hushed full of awe.

If the ancient Egyptians pulled it off, after the first hundred years, the tomb may have remained undisturbed lost and forgotten through the ages. This tomb could be a find as significant as Tut.

"Lieutenant, would you please have the men remove those stones from the top of the slide. Start here."

Using their bare hands, heavy labor and two hours work, the soldiers opened a small hole large enough for Lisa to peer inside. They stacked the stones by the side of the path.

"These stones are placed," remarked the lieutenant crouching beside Lisa looking through the opening.

"Yes, From the inside, it's obvious that the rockslide is a stone wall," she said.

Lisa documented everything. After brushing the loose material away from the opening, she was ready to proceed. The soldiers widened the opening under Lisa's supervision until she could fit through.

Inside the opening, a meter back, Lisa observed a flat surface—*perhaps another tomb seal.* From the backpack she had brought with her, she pulled pitons and a rope harness. Using her geologist hammer, she hammered the pitons above the opening in cracks in the native rock. Slithering through the small hole, she rappelled down the flat slab face avoiding any projections. The lieutenant wedged in behind her, bracing between the tomb seal and the rockslide wall.

"Stop! What are you doing?" asked Lisa.

"I am here to protect you."

"From people who have been dead several thousand years? Don't move."

Twisting on her ropes to turn upside down, she visually inspected then photographed a protuberance on the flat surface. Taking a soft brush from her pack while hanging inverted, she brushed a small dust mound—an accumulation over the millennia. Her hands shook as she exposed the serekh of Ptah chiseled into the tomb seal with the carved hieroglyphics forbidding entry like the first entrance. Her trembling hands dropped the brush.

Damn! I will retrieve it later.

"Ptah's seal and a stacked facade! This entrance was deliberately cut."

Lisa's breathing became unsteady. The significance of a second, pristine tomb entrance overwhelmed her. Placing her hand to her forehead, she uprighted herself, leaning back against the inside surface of the rockslide, her feet planted on the flat slab.

"Ma'am, are you all right?"

"Not this second." She took a long swallow of water from her water bottle. The lieutenant eyed her nervously.

"Are there spirits?" he asked nervously, irrationally. Lisa could not believe that a military officer would believe such nonsense.

"No, I'm just surprised, facing a several thousand year old, untouched tomb."

The lieutenant contemplated that thought.

"You said no one has been here for several thousand years, but you walked right to this place as if you knew where it would be," he said.

"I did know where," she said as she showed him the map.

"You, Americans, are amazing with your computers."

Lisa nodded. She completed cleaning and photographing the area. There could be no carved gods in this tiny space. With its ornate structure, the other end had to be the main entrance, but this one was easier to get to. It made no sense. If the first entrance had caved in, perhaps they turned to this end. If that were so, she was truly impressed with the architect who burrowed in from the outside to meet the original tunnel. She had great respect for the ancient Egyptian's surveying techniques. This entire tomb complex became more mysterious and amazing by the moment.

"Let's go back and tell Dr. Sanders about our discovery. Please leave the guards posted at the top. No one's allowed in here."

* * *

Lisa saw Sanders hunched over the tripod mounted in the ceiling opening. He'd made significant progress to be working in the hole again. He looked up and waved at her.

"The camcorder is working again and I've the telescoping arm jury-rigged."

"Great! How soon will we be seeing pictures again?"

"Right after lunch."

"Lunch!" Lisa snorted. "It's half past four."

"That's why my stomach's been growling."

They fell into step, walking back to the trailer.

"You're all covered in dust and rock fragments," he scanned her. "Where are your guards?"

"We found a second entrance," she said. "I left them to guard it. The lieutenant protected me coming back."

"I wish you would follow procedure. A second entrance?"

"Yup. We walked right up to a fake landslide which I dug into. Hence the chad. The serekh of Ptah is centered on a second tomb seal."

"You found a second tomb seal. Wow. Is the seal damaged?"

"Nope. Unless there's another tunnel somewhere, we have a pristine find."

"Oh my gosh!"

ABYDOS, EGYPT, THE FEATURE, JUNE 29TH, 4:20 P.M.:

After 'lunch'—a light supper Lisa prepared in the microwave, they wired the camera into the computer. Turning the camera over, they discovered that a chunk of the ceiling to the side of the opening had fallen crushing the artifacts below.

"Damn," said Bill.

"We lost some artifacts," Lisa nodded, having become fatalistic with the truck move. "It's unfortunate. We could have lost much more if the truck had fallen through. "

"Yeah, unfortunate" he said simply. "While I was rebuilding the camera installation, I was able to spread the bracket weight away from the hole. We should be able to extend the arm to all areas of Ḥaāmer's room. I can't retract the first section. I've programmed the camera controls to avoid all the high artifacts."

"Cool."

"However, there is no calibration."

"I've been thinking about that. I have a friend who works for the USGS, the Geological Survey. We could use photogrammetry to complete high accuracy measurement."

His head jerked back. "That's right. We could. Is there any scientific method you don't know about?"

"It's lucky you got preliminary measurements to use as calibration."

He just stared at her.

"And you surveyed the bracket in the first day so we can calibrate," she finished her thought. "What...?"

* * *

At dusk, Anwar walked from the camp. He went a hundred meters down and across the modern road to the right into an area strewn with shoulder high boulders and small, winding trails.

The Kuwaitis present a new angle. Am I betraying my country? I'm sure Fadi would not approve. This could be treason, but they said they'd bring new disks as they were shown on the internet.

The Kuwaiti diplomat and Anwar agreed there'd be more incidents until the terrorist leader was caught and the vermin eradicated. Anwar saw the Kuwaiti ambassador had the same objectives as he. For now, they'd provide him important information in return for.... Anwar was ignoring those concerns.

Who are these terrorist bastards?

He had lots of DVDs, but absolutely no answers. With the dossiers he was building, he'd pursue them even if he was sitting on his ass.

ABYDOS, EGYPT, THE FEATURE, THE ARCHAEOLOGICAL TRAILER, JUNE 30TH, 5:45 P.M.:

Exhausted, shoulders aching from swinging a hammer and desperately needing a shower, Lisa entered the trailer to smell a wonderful dinner cooking. She decided to add 'famished' to her list of ills. The oven exuded odors more sumptuous than the microwave dinners she'd prepared the night before. Bill smiled at her.

"Hi, how was your day?"

"I made progress, but I'm pooped. So when did you have time to fuss around the kitchen. Hmm, it smells like pot roast. Where did you get the pot roast?" she asked.

Even with her exhaustion, Lisa noticed that he was going out of his way to be kind to her—a first since their disagreement over her staying.

"Let me see what's going on here," she said.

Opening the stove door, she lifted the cover of a dutch oven with a pot holder. The steam puffed in her face, fogging her glasses and bringing the rich aroma of cooking meat and vegetables to her palate. She saw bubbling potatoes and carrots churning in the boiling juices.

"You went to a lot of trouble."

"Thanks, but it's really no trouble. The oven does all the work. Where I got the roast is a state secret."

"I'm looking forward to tearing into it just as soon as I knock off some of this dust. Is ten minutes OK?"

"Sure."

She went off to contemplate his motives. With the discovery of more protected files and his spending more unexplained time in Cairo, she was having increased trust issues.

I hate being in the dark about what he's doing, she thought while luxuriating in the hot shower pummeling her bare skin, running through her sun bleached hair in rivulets down her back. Stepping from the shower, she toweled her body then blew-dried and primped her hair, tying it up in a knot.

When she returned in a fresh jumpsuit, her body felt physically refreshed, but starved. She suspected that she looked a good deal better as well. She caught Bill looking at parts of her other than her eyes. Sliding onto bench behind the table, she tore into her food, noting that he smiled at her.

"As tired as you look and as ravenous as you're eating, you must have had a day filled with hard, physical labor."

She nodded, laughing without mirth.

"I chipped at the top right section of the seal and peeked inside. The cupboard is bare. All I see is black even with a halogen lamp. I started expanding the entrance around the edge of the seal. I have a small opening, having beaten the rock senseless. That leaves only a day or two before I can go in. So what did you do today besides cook a great meal?"

I need to continue with a gentle attitude and genuine gratitude. He makes me happy.

"I went for my daily run. After I cleaned up, you were gone so I used the shower."

She cocked an eye at him as he grinned at her.

"Too many details?" he asked.

"I saw your shaving equipment."

"So I invaded *your* space, right? I put in the roast then started recording the rest of the tomb. I extended the arm out to each of the corners so we can get a maximum view of the space. I hope your idea of using a computer program to correct all of our measurements works."

"Can you see the door seal?" she asked.

"Yeah, but artifacts are piled everywhere and especially near the door. In some cases to the ceiling."

"Tut was stacked to the ceiling."

"This is the same. I haven't found a place we can go through without running into something. If you've any energy left, I'll show you a fast scan of the room."

She nodded.

"There's not as much gold as with Tut, but from an archeological sense we've found a treasure. The funerary box does appear to be covered with gold. With paint and inlays, I can't tell the extent of it. I'm going to spend time tomorrow recording from the door to the box. I figure that when you're inside, you can temporarily move the items near the door into the hall, and x-ray the mummy. After we're finished, everything goes back where it was when we arrived."

"I thought we're only doing an initial survey. You want to view the mummy?"

"Yes, I've decided that's the only way we'll get an accurate dating. The mummy is the most indicative."

She nodded.

"I'm glad to hear that you're a preservationist," she said.

His comments indicate that I'll be doing the work. Maybe he's resolved to my staying. I can hope.

"Right. But from everything I've seen, you're the real preservationist. I'm just a tag along. I've been reading your papers online. Sometime you'll have to tell me all about Crain."

Reading my papers?

"Yeah, he's a character," she said.

"I've loaded your photogrammetric program into our computer. I studied the manual so I can run it. We'll have to load our calibration data manually. That'll take some time. I'm not impressed with the estimated run times.

"Additionally, I received a revised map from the super-computer. It doesn't give us much more detail about the site, but it does show rooms full of objects. I don't see a second door," he said.

He slid a paper across the table to her.

She glanced at it having to agree that it didn't indicate anything startling. Still no additional rooms. The image was sharper. It did show the structure of the first tomb seal. Getting in from there would be a pain.

"We need to bring the radar inside the hall once you're there. We need to expand this complex. Otherwise, none of this makes sense, " he concluded.

She nodded as she studied the diagram and chewed a piece of meat.

"I've been thinking about the occupants of the tomb," she said between mouthfuls. "We need to know how old the contents are. The mummy is the best source. If we're ever going to get a perspective on the timeline, we'll have to know where to place this feature."

"I agree."

"One can see the tomb must come from the Old Kingdom. The contents don't have the development of the Middle or New Kingdoms. Besides, the formality of the Book of the Dead is missing." she said. "There're snippets of it here, but not enough to satisfy my understanding of the Egyptian religion,"

"Right, I studied my notes again and these bits from the Book of the Dead really don't make sense. We could place the tomb in the Sixth or Seventh Dynasty, but that compresses our timeline. We know, with Ani, the Book of the Dead was quite formal. Ani copied from earlier works, say in the Second Dynasty. We may be looking at some of these very ancient works."

"Great concept, boss, but this Book of the Dead is informal. We've one sister writing to the other in hieroglyphs no less. Perhaps she was paraphrasing a text. If that's so, I'm impressed that she had a working knowledge of the Book."

"Right, how was she so educated? Maybe a scribe did it for her. That would explain the hieroglyphs. Please, continue your summaries. They help."

"I'd like some solutions. By the way, you're a great cook. I vote you perpetual kitchen duty," she laughed feeling revived by the food.

He smiled at her shaking his head negatively. "You've reached my limit with this one."

"Well, I appreciate your doing it," she reached across the table and squeezed his arm. "So where'd you learn to cook pot roast?"

"Chef's secret." Then after a pause, he said, "Mom."

"Really? Your mom taught you right. My mother was never much of a cook. She'd rather be exploring the Cairo Museum. We did for years."

"So that's where you inherited your interest."

She nodded. "My mother, under different circumstances, might have been the archeologist. She instilled a great ancient Egyptian curiosity in me."

"So how did you learn the modern Egyptian language and hieroglyphics?"

"I learned Egyptian Arabic while my father worked for an oil company here. I learned hieroglyphics at the University when I was getting my Ph.D."

"You've an extraordinary knack for languages. I studied the ancient Egyptian writing intensely. I can read it straight away, but I've nowhere near your ability."

"Thank you. So what brought you into archaeology?"

"I grew up on a Midwest farm and when I had spare time, which there was very little of, I'd explore for Indian arrowheads in the fields. A college professor got me on a dig and I was hooked."

"I see where you got your strong work ethic," she said, suppressing a yawn.

He looked into her sleepy eyes.

"I'm boring you."

"No, it's not that. I'm just physically tired. So what's on for tomorrow, boss?"

He looked at her steadily for several seconds. He was considering something and this made Lisa nervous. Perhaps he's going to move me out.

"Do you want to continue going through the seal?" he asked without giving any enlightenment into his thoughts.

"Sure."

"I think I'd like to have a more intensive analysis of the hieroglyphic grammar to see if it's a known style. You're tired tonight. Why don't you let me treat?" he asked smiling as he stood to clear the plates. "I'll play the fast scan for you."

Alarm bells were definitely going off in her head, but she was too tired to expend any energy trying to think what it meant.

"OK, if you say so, but since you treated, I should cleanup," she responded, fishing. She noted that he was staring at her in a speculative way.

"Don't worry about it."

She stood and moved to the command chair.

I'm definitely worried about what he's up to. I need to figure it out, but I'm too tired to think.

He started the video recording for her. She wanted to say something, ask something, but she didn't know what.

*   *   *

When he completed the dishes, he went to join her and found her asleep in the chair. He paused, looking at her. He wanted to tell her that she had a job as long as she wanted it, but that wasn't true.

I'm taking a terrible chance allowing her to be here. The terrorists know she's here. Tu'hut could fire my ass too. I love when she calls me 'boss'. She is so cute.

He glanced back at Lisa as he turned the equipment off. She was sound asleep, leaning on her hand, her glasses askew. At the risk of waking her, he removed her glasses, placing them on the console. He looked her full in the face.

Wow! She's quite pretty—beautiful actually. She should wear contacts. She works hard at disguising her great looks behind those thick lenses. I wonder why.

He left her sitting in the console chair. Tossing his sheets and pillow on the pullout sofa, he turned off the lights. Stripping off his shirt and shorts he pulled the sheets over himself turning away from Lisa sitting in the chair.

Good night....

* * *

Lisa awoke with a jolt. Disoriented, she scanned her surroundings. She couldn't see anything. Her glasses were on the console. Putting them on, she found that Bill had cleaned up. He was on the pullout sofa with his back to her. His breathing was soft and regular.

He must have put my glasses there. Why did he do that?

Standing, she wobbled to the trailer door, checking it and each window, finding them all locked. Her fatigue didn't allow her to focus coherently, but vaguely on an instinctual level, she wondered about his motives. She looked over her shoulder at him lying on the sofa.

I wish my life was as stress free as his. He's up before me every day running—I need to do that too.

She went to the trailer bedroom locking the door behind her.

Bill Sanders is a complete mystery. I don't believe I'll ever understand him. He's always in my space. He chews me out then he's kind. If he's trying to protect me, I don't need a nursemaid. Damn!

Her bedside clock showed nine. She looked out the windows, as she checked their locks. *Dusk.* She went to bed.

ABYDOS, EGYPT, THE FEATURE, JUNE 30TH, 8:07 P.M.:

The helicopter landed at the Abydos site just before darkness. They were hurrying for the helicopter would not attempt to land after dark. The lieutenant, walking the site, saw his captain leap from the chopper.

"Are the Americans finished for the day?" asked Captain Jagardii.

"Yes, sir."

Captain Jagardii turned, going out to the road, walking toward the second tomb entrance.

* * *

"I'm here, captain."

Jagardii couldn't see the Kuwaiti intelligence officer among the rocks, but he recognized his voice. The two had arranged this meeting earlier in the day.

"Here are the recordings we agreed to."

"I've nothing in return."

"Nothing is expected for now. Keep working, captain."

ABYDOS, EGYPT, THE FEATURE, THE TOMB, JULY 1ST, 7:15 A.M.:

Hanging from a trapeze, she released the brake, lowering herself into the opening on the inside of the tomb seal. She had vacuumed the opening, but she still avoided touching the sides as much a possible.

"Stay back," she yelled, as they scrambled forward to peer into the opening scattering small pebbles after her. When the shower stopped, she looked up at their faces, using her hat to shield her head from further debris. They had stopped short, fear evident in their eyes. Given what she'd heard from the lieutenant, she could picture the imagined curses and taboos racing through their minds. Her objective was to keep them from plodding through the area above, causing more rocks to fall on her and the floor below. Her attention shifted to her exploration. Shining her powerful light on the floor, she saw no footprints in the dust.

I can only imagine what Carter must have felt, being the first person to view Tut's tomb after it had been lost for millennia.

She began recording outward into the tomb. As her vision adjusted to the darkness, she saw life-sized wall-carvings on either side of the tomb seal. She hadn't seen them with the tiny light during her initial peek inside. Gliding downward, she put her hand and footprints into the dust on the floor. Her heart raced as she imprinted the space. She bent forward and brushed the floor dust aside. To her surprise, it was polished smooth and shiny like the surface of a tombstone. She began recording.

"I'm amazed by the care and preparation of this tomb. It is significantly better than any I've ever seen. The architect was excessive in his detail. For what purpose? Who was the builder? Who is this tomb for?"

She lifted the camcorder and recorded the wall.

"Ptah and Ra stand on each side of Osiris seated on a throne as if they are looking upon a favored son. Once again their names are carved as serekhs next to their images. I've never seen this juxtaposition of Ptah, Ra and Osiris. Isis stands beside the seated Osiris, her hand on his shoulder—a loving wife. Standing beside Osiris and Isis are two young women. Females being honored with the gods? Unbelievable! This tomb honors two women. Their serekhs read: Ḥaāmer and Āakhu. The young women are slightly smaller than Isis. Isis is slightly smaller than Osiris. Typical of Egyptian statuary, scale indicates importance. Someone really liked these women. Bill will appreciate this."

She walked the corridor abandoned for so many millennia.

"Doctor, is it safe?"

Lisa, concentrating hard on what she was saying, jumped. She suppressed her urge to tongue-lash the lieutenant.

"Dammit! How'd you get in here?"

"Apologies, Doctor. I came down the ropes hand-over-hand. I did not touch the walls."

Impressive. Obviously in good shape.

"Your boss said someone must be with you at all times. You are underground. It is dangerous."

"Follow behind me. Don't touch anything and walk in my footprints."

"Yes, Ma'am."

The lieutenant squeezed next to her.

"The figures on the wall are different from the ones on the other end. The men looked the same. Are they gods?"

"Yes, you're observant. How did you see the figures at the other seal?"

"Captain Jagardii showed me your recordings, Ma'am."

"I see. I'll continue to record my notes now, lieutenant. Please be quiet."

"Yes, Ma'am."

Lisa traversed the distance between the two tomb seals, the lieutenant in lock step with her. She recorded the two sealed room doors to the left and right. The door to the left, Ḥaāmer's, was bricked. The door on the right was tied with cord and wood panels.

"Why are the room seals different?" she asked her recording.

Leaning against each door was a hawk-shaped ushabtui. Hieroglyphics, carved into them, were too distant to read. The two Horus figures comprised all of the loose objects in the hallway. They would wait for later analysis for she didn't wish to deviate from the center path until she had made full recordings. She assumed a small, empty area carved next to Ḥaāmer's room was for mourners. The hall was plain, featureless and timeless.

"Lieutenant, we'll leave the tomb and get some liquid. I'm dehydrated." They lock-stepped back to the opening. "I don't want anyone in here without Dr. Sanders' or my permission. Do you understand? I mean the Secretary General and President of Egypt included. Dr. Sanders or I will designate who may enter. This place is a sacred place. This place is a national treasure."

"That would put me in an awkward position if the president came to the site. I'll instruct the guards."

He climbed the ropes hand over hand in a rapid and easy form.

"Haul-away," she shouted to the soldiers above, rising on her trapeze.

ABYDOS, EGYPT, THE ARCHAEOLOGICAL TRAILER, JULY 1ST, 10:22 A.M.:

Neither Bill nor Captain Jagardii had spoken to the other since the disaster with the camera. Bill felt the Egyptian was acting sullen, but not comprehending the language hampered him. The Captain sitting at the console working on a video turned as Bill entered the trailer. He looked strange, like something out of science fiction, wearing the large 3D glasses necessary for developing the virtual reality images. As Bill approached, the picture seemed to change, but he was not completely sure so he looked over the captain's shoulder at his work—a section of Ḥaāmer's room.

"Go back. What were you working on?"

Jagardii said something unintelligible to him.

"Oh, shit!" said Bill, grabbing a coke from the fridge. He left the trailer.

* * *

Anwar switched back to the disk he had been processing when Bill entered the trailer. He had learned he could switch between tasks, keeping the American believing, he was working on his archaeological data. The woman was his ally, as he worked on the dossiers for each of the terrorists. She wanted the terrorists captured. As he originally believed, the computer could reduce each lurid event into its individual actors and actions. He learned to process these sequences frame by frame, compiling them into sequential pictures then back into movies. He also learned how to save an actor as an object, moving him from one disk to the next. For all but one terrorist, he created complete three-dimensional images. He could actually spin each of them before his eyes like puppets on strings.

Amazing this American technology.

He found the terrorists were few in number. He counted twenty-five different people in all. The one person he hadn't isolated, he recognized from his legs and feet, but he'd never gotten a picture of his face. From the way the others deferred to him, Anwar could tell he was the leader, orchestrating all of the terrorists' activities. He wanted to see this person. He closed his analysis until he had more data, having exhausted all of the video disks he had received from Nefri and the Kuwaitis. He switched to the archaeological videos.

Look at all of those beautiful objects. Amazing!

A rich sense of the past rushed through him—expanded, thrilled him. He wished the scientists from the Cairo museum could work on the project rather than allowing the Americans to take credit for the find, but they wouldn't have all of this equipment. Anwar realized that the Israeli military victories of the past were linked in a subtle way to similar but deadlier technology supplied by the Americans. What amazed him was that he did the work at all, but there were several driving forces that kept him going.

His efforts with the computer program allowed him to pursue the terrorist problem with a great deal of skill that he otherwise would not have had. Omar would be proud of his grasping the moment. He discovered that the primary reason he continued was his love for the past. He had not seen this earlier, but with the tedious hours, he now understood it.

Anwar pointed the mouse at an object; the computer identified its outline, colored it and cataloged it. Anwar would make adjustments if necessary. He switched to a different view of the room to find the same object from a different angle. As the number of cataloged objects increased, the computer did a better job finding the objects in the alternative views. Originally, he did all the work. Now the computer was readily finding the objects. Once the computer identified the object in all of the other views, it would build a three-dimensional picture of it. Anwar extracted the object from the background of other items in the room, viewing it separately. He had not figured out how to take the lid off anything to view the inside, but he was thinking about that. He found the work boring, but generally the sense of exploration held his interest.

Amazing. Look at all of these beautiful things that his forebears had created.

Even more interesting, the interpreter told him that he overheard the American woman say that they were working in new territory. The pieces did not fit together correctly. Anwar would ask her subtly to explain it to him. He liked the suspicion of a mystery with his site.

One mystery that he was trying to understand was a hint of color on the wall. It would appear and just as suddenly disappear. It didn't seem to be a shadow of anything in the room. He wondered if it was some apparition in the computer software.

Chapter 15

wsḫt nt jwsw m wꜣst ḥsbt 18 ꜣbd 3 prt sw 20 ḫr ḥm n wsỉr

The Hall of Balance in Uas

Year 18, Month 3 of Peret, Day 20 under the Majesty of Ạsạr

Temu knelt before Pharaoh, his forehead touching the floor, and rose again. Looking at Pharaoh's guards, uncomfortably close on both the left and right, he asked: "Have I displeased you?"

"I will ask the questions," Pharaoh growled. "Where is my brother?"

Temu spread his hands apart. "I know not, Pharaoh. He thought you were returning to kill him. He's gone."

"Why would he think such a thing?"

Temu looked up at Pharaoh's shoulder. The wrapping was off. Though the swelling was down the skin about the wound was bruised red and purple. A scab covered the hole where the arrow had penetrated. Oil covered the scab and a thicker, sour-smelling salve covered the surrounding skin.

"A temple runner arrived yesterday morning with news of what happened. Set saw no other option than to flee from Uas."

Pharaoh frowned, the words sad and poisonous inside him. He found no relief in letting them out. "Why is he trying to kill me?"

Temu drew back a step, his eyes wide. One of Pharaoh's guard reached for a dagger when Temu first moved, but checked his motion and returned to quiet attention. "Oh, Pharoah," Temu said, "he doesn't want to kill you. It plainly grieves him that you would even think so."

The delivery was that of a man comfortable speaking to crowds, who had learned how to draw attention, guide thoughts, stir emotions. The surprise, the widened, respectful eyes, the humble, yet powerful voice capable of filling a temple, with just a subtle hint of hurt, it was too spontaneous and natural not to be a well-practiced act. But Pharaoh saw hundreds of similarly fine performances each day in the Hall of Balance.

"Then who? Did your temple runner know that?"

"No," Temu said. "I can only speculate."

Pharaoh waited a moment. *Here it is. Draw attention, guide thoughts. Stir emotions.* "Speak freely."

Temu brought his hands together and looked down at them, the stance of one praying for wisdom or preparing to impart it. He took a breath and looked up at Pharaoh.

"The people of the North have reason to kill you. You are all that prevents them from spreading their kingdom southward. They must know you and Governor Maaạ are working out an alliance. What better way to draw you away from Uas where they can kill you than to attack a region you must defend? Especially before you and Maaạ reach an agreement."

"Why did Set send soldiers to Maaạ?"

Temu frowned at Pharaoh. "I know nothing of any soldiers."

Pharaoh clenched his hands into fists. "Maaạ told me that Set sent him priests trained for fighting to discourage any attack from the North. Did he or didn't he?"

"Is that what Maaạ said?"

A sharp gesture of Pharaoh's hand brought the captain a step forward. His sword cleared its scabbard with a deadly whisper.

"That isn't necessary," Temu said and retreated a step, his eyes focused on the polished bronze blade. "I don't know anything about these priest-soldiers. Set certainly didn't send them. I doubt they even exist. I was present when Set offered Maaạ six men to aid him in negotiations with his Northern rivals. Maaạ refused them."

"All of Qes witnessed them. The city was filled with priests until the attack. Then they disappeared."

Pharaoh watched Temu's face, his shoulders, his hands for any trace of a lie and saw nothing. Temu looked down and rubbed his chin. The golden bracelets and amulets he wore jingled a soft accompaniment to the motion.

"The good people of Qes saw men dressed as priests who claimed to be soldiers," Temu said, slowly, as if thinking through a problem. His eyebrows lifted and the puzzlement faded away. "I think I know what happened. Maaạ was angry after you denied him your daughter. What better way to change your mind than to cause trouble between you and your brother? Maaạ probably dressed up these men just so he could claim Set went behind your back."

Pharaoh shook his head, allowing the anger to fall away. Beneath that anger loomed a weary sadness. "Many innocent people died. Maaạ's confusion and remorse over the attack were genuine."

"Certainly a miscalculation."

"On someone's part," Pharaoh agreed.

Pharaoh reached and rubbed the skin around his wounded shoulder, soothing away some of the itch that had developed there. It was with growing irritation he could not do the same to the thoughts crawling inside him.

Pharaoh adopted his own persona, his most regal, most godly, most deadly pose, expression, and voice: "I will find Set. He will answer these same questions to my satisfaction and I will decide his fate. Those who have stood with him, those who have hidden him, spied for him, assisted him, will share that fate. Who do you serve?"

Temu did not hesitate. “I serve Ptah and Pharaoh.”

After Pharaoh dismissed him, after his personal guard escorted Temu from the Hall of Balance, Pharaoh motioned to his captain. “Find someone to watch him. See where he goes and who he speaks to.”

ḥwt-nṯr nt ptḥ m wȝst ḥsbt 18 ȝbd 3 prt sw 20 ḫr ḥm n wsỉr

The Temple of Ptah in Uas
Year 18, Month 3 of Peret, Day 20 under the Majesty of Ạsạr

Ṭeḥuti awoke immediately. Footsteps, but different from those of the two torch lighters. More than one man. He scrambled back into a corner and heard a squeak from something he displaced.

The wood bars lifted from the door with a dry rasp of wood against wood and the door pulled away. Light from smokey torches spilled in, blinding him. He threw an arm over his eyes.

Four shapes stood outside about the door. As his vision cleared and he could lower the protective arm, he saw Pharaoh’s guard.

“Ṭeḥuti, it is time to go. We are to take you to the docks and put you on a boat. Pharaoh said you are not to return. Do you understand?”

“Yes,” Ṭeḥuti said, stumbling to his feet.

Two of the guard caught him by the arms and held him up until his legs regained their strength. They pushed his bag and cloak into his shaky, flea-bitten arms and turned their heads away. “We should clean him up. No one will take him smelling like this.”

One guard went to Ṭeḥuti’s rooms at the Temple of Ptah for fresh clothes. The other three led him to a bath.

The Aten rose over the eastern hills. Ṭeḥuti stole glimpses of it as if it might be the last time he would see it. He felt numb. The thought of leaving Uas, the thought of Āakhu being married to another, seemed as empty and hollow as old, dry bones. The pain he felt in the dark of his prison had stayed there. He would not see or say goodbye to friends or students, or prepare for a proper journey, or even put away the linen and papyrus documents still on the table in his room. These thoughts came to him, one after the other and he felt nothing; he didn’t want to feel anything. He wanted to stay in this waking sleep until he could get on a boat and get away. Then he could wake. Then he could plan and let his love lead him back to Āakhu.

The Ukher was a loud, boisterous, busy place. There were shouts, raucous boasts and stories taking wing back and forth among the different crew members. The men went at their jobs unloading and reloading with an almost impatient energy. Ṭeḥuti remembered the feeling. The river was their home, the shore—with the inevitable exchange of one cargo for another—was merely work. A true boat man was always ready, after a quick evening's revelry, to sail at dawn.

Pharaoh's guard slowed as they approached, uncertain how to proceed. Boat men and those assigned to lift and move cargo made way with scarcely a glance.

"Let me go on alone," Ṭeḥuti said to the captain.

"Our orders are to put you on a boat and see that it leaves Uas."

"It will be easier for me to gain passage if I am not paraded along the docks like one despised and dangerous to Pharaoh."

"Pharaoh gave us marked stones to exchange at the temple granary. You need not bargain for passage."

"I want to sign on as crew. I am no longer a priest and will need something to do."

The captain frowned.

"You know me. My word is good. Leave a man to see that I join a boat and leave today."

The captain looked at Ṭeḥuti and then at each of the other three guards. "Agreed," he said at last. "I will stay."

The others saluted their captain and turned together, marching proudly back to the House of Pharaoh, the morning sun gleaming off their bronze weapons and their dark, muscled limbs.

Watching them, the captain said: "Will you try to escape back into the city?"

"No," Ṭeḥuti replied. "I will leave Uas. There will be other days. Āakhu must also leave Uas soon."

The captain nodded his head. "Be some other man's problem. If I see you again, we must be enemies."

Ṭeḥuti bowed to the captain and lifted his face to survey the boats at anchor along the docks, choosing one taking on goods for trade with the Lower Kingdoms. There were a number of such vessels; trade with the towns near the great sea had grown as the provinces became more organized.

The Lower Kingdoms, in particular the delta that spread its fingers into the great sea, were fertile areas for growing food and raising animals. It was also a stopping point for caravans passing west and north and east. Ạsạr traded his kingdom's knowledge of the stone and metal that flowed north from Nubia for the grain and animals from the delta and treasures from distant lands.

Even when the provinces warred among themselves, trade flourished and the boats passed along the river unhindered. In any province foolish enough to interfere with the boats, the boats would no longer stop. Without the boats, cities weakened as needed supplies grew scarce, and the province soon fell prey to less foolish neighbors.

Ṭeḥuti approached the first boat. Sweating men struggled with ropes and logs, hauling a block of stone up the ramp and onto the deck.

"I would like to hire on as a worker," said Ṭeḥuti.

The master squinted, looking Ṭeḥuti over from head to foot. "I need no more crew. I have taken on three this morning. Seems like every young man fancies working on the river today."

Ṭeḥuti nodded. "Ptah's blessing on you. May Merhyt guide your journey."

"And to you," the master called. He raised his arm and pointed. "Try that boat, the Sakhr-Mut, I think the master is looking for a man."

The Sakhr-Mut was an old boat, the different shades of wood, rope, and linen spoke of the different ages of each of its repairs. At one time it must have been a fishing boat, but those days had passed. The hull had been lengthened and widened to give it more stability. Extra support had been added to the deck and deck house. Two workers carried earthen pots full of beer up the ramp and arranged them in rows on deck. A man Ṭeḥuti took to be the Sakhr-Mut's master argued with another man overdressed in the rich jewelry of a merchant.

The merchant waved his arms about in exaggerated gestures. "It is the finest beer in all of Egypt! It is the personal favorite of Pharaoh."

The boat master smiled. "At your cost, only Pharaoh could afford to drink it."

The merchant took a step backward and put a hand on his heart. "Why don't you just slide your dagger between my ribs and steal my beer. It would be a kinder thing than to endure your attempted robbery and the pain of these insults."

"The people in the lower lands know not of Pharaoh's drinking habits—nor do they care. You are not the only one who makes beer or sends it there. Only the taste and the obvious care you take with your grains allow me to continue selling it at all," the master said.

"I do not believe you."

The two acted their parts with a well-practiced grace. The boat master did not chafe at the merchant's theatrics. His face remained placid, his voice calm as he spoke. "I have carried beer north for you these last three inundations. I have never cheated you, and never failed to return you a comfortable profit. I must maintain my boat, feed my family and pay my crew. Each costs me more each day, yet I have agreed to carry your beer at the same price as my last trip."

"I too have increasing costs," said the merchant.

"I have no doubt."

"I cannot sell my beer at last season's price."

"And I cannot afford to carry it at a higher cost."

"Then there is no deal."

The boat master watched the merchant for a moment and nodded. He turned and shouted to the two men carrying the pots onto the ship. "Put those back on the cart. And unload the rest."

The two crewmen exchanged a look, but said nothing. Each hefted a pot that he had just set down and turned back to the merchant's cart.

The merchant's face flushed dark in the bright sun, but he said nothing.

"Ptah be with you," Ṭeḥuti said, stopping before the two men. "I have a question."

Both men looked at him. The boat master studied him with the same calm expression he used with the merchant. "Who are you?"

"I go by the name Ṭeḥuti," he replied and turned to the merchant. "How much do you wish to increase the price of your beer?"

"A pittance. Two pots trade for five small bronze rings. I would ask a sixth."

Ṭeḥuti nodded. "Boat master, could you carry twelve such pots if the thirteenth were given to your crew for their enjoyment on the journey?"

"I could never—" the boat master frowned.

"You might increase your profit. Having worked and fished along the river, I know how much of the cost of a journey is due to the cost of my beer. If beer were offered by the boat master, I would accept that as wage. Would your men not agree, master?"

"They would."

"But—" the merchant now protested.

"And boat men like to talk," Ṭeḥuti continued. "If your beer is as good as you claim, every port between here and the great sea will know about it as soon as the men leave the boat. I suspect this cargo will be sold before it gets halfway to its destination. Are you prepared to make more?"

"I have grain shipments arriving any day now."

"I think you will need them. And I think it generous of the boat master to require only one pot in thirteen for the service he and his crew will be doing as they spread the fame of this rare commodity."

"Well," the merchant hesitated, "I suppose it would be fair."

"Master?"

Nothing in the boat master's calm expression revealed what he thought. After a moment he turned toward his crew. "Stop taking those off the boat. Load them back up."

The two workmen looked at each other. "Ptah have mercy," swore one to the other. They reversed directions with their burdens and trudged back up the ramp to the deck.

The merchant thanked the boat master and hurried off to his cart, a broad grin and two rows of great yellow teeth creasing his dark face. The boat master turned back to Ṭeḥuti.

"Do you have business here?"

"I am looking to join a boat."

The master nodded toward the ramp. "See Ānukhet, my steerswoman. She will show you where to put your belongings. I provide your food, and," a sly smile touched the corner of the master's lips for the first time, "your beer."

wḫrpr m wꜣst ḥsbt 18 ꜣbd 3 prt sw 20 ḫr ḥm n wsỉr

The Docks in Uas

Year 18, Month 3 of Peret, Day 20 under the Majesty of Ạsạr

Ānukhet rubbed oil into the steering oar using a gentle back and forth motion, listening to bits of conversation drifting up from the Ukher. The oil cleaned and protected the precious wood, extending its life, keeping it from warping. It also prevented the wood from soaking up water and becoming too heavy for her to steer effectively.

She had used this same steering oar since taking work aboard the Sakhr-Mut almost six inundations ago. This oar had become her friend and partner. One always looked after one's partner—especially on the river.

The sound of footsteps approaching along the deck stopped nearby. Ānukhet continued her meticulous rubbing.

"Where should I stow my belongings?"

Ānukhet looked up, shading her eyes and squinting into the bright sunlight that loomed over her visitor's shoulder. He had the smooth round face of a young man, but his solemn eyes and demeanor were not those of a young man at all.

"Why didn't you just present your scarab and claim free passage like the other priests?"

A frown crossed his face. "I am no longer a priest."

"You wear a priest's sandals," she said. Leaning forward for a better look she continued, "They're temple issue and judging by the quality, given only to a priest of considerable stature."

She looked up again to see unsmiling lips and distant, veiled eyes that drew a sober shadow about him. *A man with a story to tell.*

"Are you always so remarkably observant?" He asked.

Ānukhet shrugged. "It's a requirement for one who steers a boat. You still haven't answered my question: why is an important priest who is no longer a priest signing on as crew?"

"I fished when I was young. I'll be traveling on the River for many days and thought it would ease the tedium if I discovered what remained of my skills."

Ānukhet nodded. *Half the truth is better than no truth at all.* "There is a chest in the hold next to the boat master's quarters. Wrap up your belongings, put your mark on them and place them inside. When you're finished, the forward deck could use a scrubbing and some oil. We caught a storm near the Great Sea on our last trip. I haven't been able to get the salt out of the wood."

"As you wish," he said.

"What's your name?"

"Ṭeḥuti."

"I'm Ānukhet. Welcome aboard the Sakhr-Mut."

He walked away carrying a small sack that already had his name on it: the Ibis on a standard, a loaf of bread, two diagonal strokes, and the falcon on a standard.

A curious puzzle, she mused, dipping the linen rag into the oil pot and returning to her polishing. *And curious puzzles always make for the most interesting trips.*

wḫrpr m wȝst ḥsbt 18 ȝbd 4 prt sw 1 ḫr ḥm n wsỉr

The Docks in Uas

Year 18, Month 4 of Peret, Day 1 under the Majesty of Ạsạr

The boats from Meḥ arrived during the third hour of the day, their triangular sails filled with a fresh morning breeze and bright, coppery sunlight. Īset watched their stately arrival with equal parts of awe and sadness. *Maaạ is coming to take my daughter away.*

She attended Pharaoh at the docks, he having been forewarned that Maaạ would make his arrival this morning. She and Pharaoh were foremost of the welcoming party. Other dignitaries and guests and those curious citizens not otherwise engaged in work, fanned out behind them in quiet anticipation. But Āakhu remained hidden in the Queen's House, preparing for her wedding and her departure.

Īset no longer knew how her daughter felt. Their conversations in the days since Pharaoh's angry proclamation had consisted of no more words than were required to make a polite request, ask a short question, or give an even shorter reply. Their few brief encounters were characterized by blank faces, dead words, and veiled hearts.

Īset tried many times to tell Āakhu that she was sorry. In her last attempt, early this morning, Āakhu had waved her away and disappeared through a doorway to leave Īset alone, the words half-spoken.

If she would shout at me, if she would pound her fists against the wall or throw a few pots and break them, if she would just let some of the poison out of her ba so I could know she would be well again—

"Maaạ is a good man," Pharaoh said.

Īset glanced up into his deep brown eyes, wondering if his words were spoken more to reassure her or himself. "He is not Tehuti."

"He's not." He agreed. "But he has some of the same qualities. Perhaps Āakhu will one day come to love Maaạ as much as she has loved Ṭeḥuti."

Īset looked back at Maaạ's boat, the sails coming down as it turned and drew near the dock. "I would not presume to know the ways of any heart but my own."

"And what does your heart tell you?"

"I may never see her again."

"You will. And you will see the birth of each of your grandchildren."

"Ptah has told you that?"

Pharaoh said nothing.

The workers tied Maaạ's boat fast to the dock. The gangway was pushed out and down. From the single cabin mid-boat, Maaạ appeared. He wore a knee-length skirt of finest white linen, bare-chested above except for the pelt of a lion that hung over one shoulder. His head was covered in a folded kerchief.

He grasped a beautifully wrought shepherd's crook, banded in gold and lapis lazuli from its curved tip to its base. It sparkled in the sunlight, casting golden flashes across Maaạ's dark skin and the deck about him. The light that cascaded along its length made it seem almost alive.

Maaạ stood motionless for a moment: tall, young, vibrant, solid as a statue. Using the crook as a staff, he came forward and down the gangway. Four of his personal guards closed rank and followed in step behind him, each wearing an impressive bronze knife at his side.

Maaạ stopped before Pharaoh. He and each member of his guard went to one knee and bowed their heads. "Pharaoh Ạsạr and Lady Īset," Maaạ said, "it is an honor for me to come to you here in Uas, and a privilege to accept your daughter Āakhu as my wife."

"Well-spoken, Maaạ. Rise and let us stand together."

Maaạ rose. Ạsạr put a hand on his shoulder. To the people of Uas he said: "Maaạ has joined us from Meḥ. Let us welcome him."

Blessings went up from the crowd and they gathered closer about the royal pair. Maaạ handed the beautiful crook to one of his guards and nodded. The man wrapped it in animal skin, and he and the rest of the retinue returned it to Maaạ's boat.

Pharaoh and Īset introduced Maaạ to the leading men and women of the city. Pharaoh, as was his custom, spoke a man's name to Maaạ and followed it with a personal reference or story.

It helps them remember, Ạsạr once told her. *It is hard enough to remember a single new name and face, let alone the fifty you might meet at a royal event. But it is easy to remember the man who grows the best onions in all of Egypt, or owns the fattest goats, or has the most children—even if they are only boasts.*

Maaạ greeted each with a boyish smile and a few humble, self-deprecating words. After meeting a master brewer, Maaạ caused a burst of laughter among those within hearing when he replied: "the darkest beer, you say. Then you must give me your secret. I have done some brewing of my own, but all my beers can pass through a man without changing color!"

That remark eased the deference that rank and parentage otherwise imposed on these men. They were no longer Pharaoh, prince, priest and dignitary. For a moment they were comrades, familiar friends swapping bawdy stories as a distraction from the afternoon heat, while their wives stood by and marveled at the sudden descent of their men back into childhood.

At length, Pharaoh interrupted: "Let us go up to the Hall of Balance where I am told a feast waits. All are invited."

Maaạ stood beside Pharaoh and addressed the people: "This day my ka, my spirit, overflows with bounty like the Nile in the day of inundation and my ba, my soul, soars like the falcon circling ever higher into the sky. I cannot contain them. I have arrived with gifts from the people of Meḥ to the people of Uas. May I distribute them along the way to your feast?"

Maaạ pointed. Pharaoh and the gathered citizens looked towards the docks. Carts had been rolled down from the boats of Maaạ and were being loaded. Some were piled high with loaves of bread, others with fruit: pomegranates, dried dates and grapes. Still others were stacked with smoked, dried fish wrapped in palm leaves.

Pharaoh smiled. "So be it."

Another cheer went up for Prince Maaạ.

What began as a parade from the docks to the House of Pharaoh became a true festival—one to rival the five days of celebration that began with the end of one year and ended with the beginning of the next. No one there went hungry or thirsty. Small carved scarabs appeared everywhere inscribed with the message: *Peace and prosperity from Maaạ and the people of Meḥ.*

For Īset, it was a time of reflection. She wanted to hate Maaạ for taking her daughter so far from home. She wanted to hate him for dissolving the love between Āakhu and Ṭeḥuti—a love in which Īset found no flaw. But she could find nothing in Maaạ to hate.

Ṭeḥuti was a quiet man who loved his books and his writing. He had a natural curiosity and a need to know the answer to every question. His patience, his wry humor and his gentle manner were those of a natural teacher. He never forgot a face, and always had an encouraging word.

Maaạ, as Īset observed, loved to be in a crowd of people. He came alive there and brandished his words and gestures with enormous skill. With his singular smile, a wink, or a sly remark he made the people of Uas feel as if they had been his friends for all their lives. In Maaạ's presence, even Pharaoh had regained some of the youthful energy and enthusiasm that had been absent during the days of Ḥaāmer's sickness, death, and burial.

Ṭeḥuti was the one to whom you could come for answers and advice. He was the one to whom you could confess your secrets and know they would remain secrets. Maaạ was the man with whom you would share your last bowl of beer.

You could go to Ṭeḥuti for the wisdom and skill to keep a people out of battle. You would go to Maaạ to rally the troops and lead them into it.

Two such different men, as different as—and here Īset caught her breath—as different as Ạsạr and Set. Īset tried to hate Maaạ but could only admire him, drawn by his charm with the rest of Uas.

If the past could be washed away, if the Aten could return the days from west to east, if Īset could meet Maaạ and Ṭeḥuti again and for the first time, who would she say would be the best husband for her daughter: Ṭeḥuti, the man of great wisdom or Maaạ, the gregarious man of the people?

Therein lay the tragedy. Perhaps, in his inexorable perfecting of the people of Egypt, Ptah really did have a plan. It might be that from his height he truly sees further than any human lifetime.

He had chosen Maaạ for Āakhu. Would Īset's only remaining child ever accept that?

wsḫt nt jwsw m wꜣst ḥsbt 18 ꜣbd 4 prt sw 2 ḫr ḥm n wsỉr

The Hall of Balance in Uas

Year 18, Month 4 of Peret, Day 2 under the Majesty of Ạsạr

"I am not ready for this," Īset said to Ạsạr.

"Nor am I, but Ptah will not wait for a readiness that will never be," Pharaoh replied. He took her hand and massaged it gently with his own.

Pharaoh nodded and the attendants opened the doors to the Hall of Balance. The crowd that stretched beyond the hall stirred and began to file in.

The day was already bright and warm. A soft, dry breeze brought the sound of music to Īset's ears.

The priests, diplomats, and merchants of Uas were dressed in their finest skirts and dresses, as evident in the highest quality linen, perfect fit, and jeweled beads or dyed scroll work around hems and sleeves. They were painted, perfumed, and covered with jewels—the men as well as the women.

Maaạ and his retinue led the crowd into the hall. Their murmurs of anticipation were punctuated with soft sounds of pleasant laughter. Maaạ stopped before Pharaoh, the beautiful blue and gold crook held in his right hand. Īset heard the sharp tap as he set the gold point against the stone floor.

The people of Uas and Meḥ filled in the area behind and about Maaạ and spilled out the open entrance and down the street. Īset noticed that more than a few looked sleepy and a bit pale. The parties in honor of Prince Maaạ had lasted far into the night.

Pharaoh raised his hand and the crowd quieted.

He spoke: "Ptah commanded and Nut, the spirit of the sky, came down to mate with her lover Geb, the spirit of the earth. The Land was born.

"Ptah spoke and from Hapi's womb came the river with its cycles of inundation and retreat. From the rich black soil of the inundation, Ptah formed man and woman and breathed a bit of himself into them. We were born.

"Ptah is eternal and unchanging. The cycles that he has established for us are wise and just. Today we reaffirm those cycles as we gather to celebrate the giving of my daughter Āakhu to Maaạ of Meḥ."

* * *

Āakhu felt a strange distance between herself and the events unfolding about her. It was if she were viewing her life in the shimmering waves of heat that rose from distant hills.

She watched from an alcove in the Hall of Balance as her father spoke. She knew that her pain was not gone. But it was suspended for a time.

She wore a gauzy, revealing, flattering dress for her wedding day. Every exposed inch of her had been oiled or painted. Her handmaids proclaimed her a vision, a goddess, the most beautiful woman in all the Land.

Āakhu could only gaze absently at the face of a stranger in her polished bronze mirror. *She isn't me. I will watch this woman become Maaạ's wife, but she isn't me. Ṭeḥuti will come; he will proclaim his undying love and we will run away together on the River.*

The days that Āakhu and her handmaids had spent packing her belongings had all long since settled in the west. *Ṭeḥuti had not come.* The unnecessary hours of wedding preparations undertaken by her mother and father now passed into fruition. *Ṭeḥuti had still not come.* This faraway woman stood waiting, watching Āakhu's father speak, Maaạ standing tall and straight before him. *Ṭeḥuti* must *come.*

The handmaids prodded her and whispered. "Pharaoh has spoken your name. You must go and join Maaạ now."

From the safety of her faraway place she looked down at the numb, traitorous feet that carried her forward. Maaạ's bride entered the Hall of Balance and joined him before Pharaoh and Īset.

Maaạ's hand was soft and warm as it clasped hers. *How can I feel this from so far away?* Āakhu thought.

She glanced to see Maaạ drop to one knee, one hand still holding hers, the other holding a stunning gold-striped crook. He looked up at her, his eyes wide, deep, and richly brown.

"If Aten stopped shining this moment, I would never notice," he said to her. "You are my light."

His was a handsome face: young, quick to smile, expectant, anticipating each moment with assurance. His gaze, as it searched her face, was filled with love.

"Come be the light of my life for the rest of my days," Maaạ said.

Āakhu trembled. She wanted to run, she wanted to find Ṭeḥuti, she wanted to be swept into his arms and carried away, but there was no way past the people who surrounded her, watching her. She heard unexpected words crossing her lips:

I will rise before you in the morning.
I will bring you cool water from the well.
Your house will have happiness;
It will have laughter,
And many children;

Your house will have friends,
And a wife who loves you.
I will welcome you into my arms in the evening.
I will give my love to you through the night.

Pharaoh and Īset rose together. "Prince Maaạ," said Pharaoh, "today, Āakhu passes from my house to yours. Treat her well and she will bring you honor and glory. She will be the completion of your life; she will give you love and friendship. Through the sons and daughters she bears come your hope for the future and peace for the present."

Īset wiped tears from her eyes. "My shining flower, this is the happiest and saddest day of my life. You are mine no longer. Today you pass from the house you have known all your life to the house that will be yours for all the days to come. Go with him; give him your hands and your heart and you will never lack for love and honor. Be the one to whom his thoughts always compel him to return. Give to him your ka, your spirit, so that no matter where his journey takes him, he knows that where you are is home."

Maaạ's bride nodded and felt hot, salty tears forming behind her eyes. *Where is Ṭeḥuti?*

Maaạ stood beside her again. Pharaoh and Īset resumed their thrones. Pharaoh's face was regal, composed, but emotions played across the face of Īset in a progression of slow changes—like all the seasons of the river. Āakhu, in her distant place, remembered her mother's words: *It is the cycle of the river, the cycle of our bodies, and the cycle of our lives: renewal, flowering, harvest. We are raised in a family, taken from it and given to a husband. We raise new daughters from our flesh. They are taken from us and given to new husbands where they bear and raise daughters of their own.*

Renewal, flowering, harvest.

Maaạ let go of her hand and approached the dais. He knelt and placed the golden crook at Pharaoh's feet.

"I am husband this day of the second-most beautiful flower in all the Land, shadowed only by the one who is her mother."

A muttering stirred in the crowd, which dissolved into a sigh. Īset placed a hand over her heart and inclined her head ever so slightly to Maaạ.

"I am now of the house of Pharaoh. As Governor, and the acknowledged ruler of four provinces, I pass the care of these provinces to you. This crook, symbol of the shepherd who faithfully keeps his flock, was given to me. I give it to you. Wield it over me and my people as Ptah directs."

Pharaoh reached down and lifted the crook. He stood with it in his hand. Īset joined him. Maaạ returned to take his bride's hand.

Ṭeḥuti?

A deafening cheer went up in the Hall of Balance, with chants, prayers and wishes for health, happiness, and many children. After a moment, Pharaoh raised his hand to quiet them.

"The sun smiles, the River calls, and a gentle current whispers and points the way. Safe journey to you, Maaạ. Take your wife to see her new home," Pharaoh said.

Īset added: "You have spoken true, Prince Maaạ. You are of the house of Pharaoh and this house is yours as well. Let the floors of this house not gather dust because your feet have been too long absent. Let its walls not forget the sound of your laughter or the sight of your smile. We would see you, and our grandchildren, often in the years ahead.

"Go in peace. Go in health. Go in love."

The crowd echoed the blessing. Maaạ and his bride turned to acknowledge them as they gathered around.

Ṭeḥuti, where are you?

A parade and celebration erupted again along the streets of Uas as Maaạ and his bride made their way back to the Ukher and the boats that would return them to Meḥ.

A thousand hands touched the bride's arm and offered blessings. A thousand faces appeared before her with words of encouragement and hope. A thousand tongues wished her as much happiness as it was possible to find in a world where so many people died before ever having a chance to live.

Strangers pushed gifts of amulets, jewelry, and charms into her numb hands. From faraway in her shock and sadness, she did her very best to smile and cherish each gift for a moment, instructing the maid servant who came forward to carry it for her that it be given a place of honor among all other such treasures.

She scanned the crowd for Ṭeḥuti. Her spirit rose each time she saw the shape of a half-turned face or the robe of a priest. Her heart leapt each time she heard the sound of a similar voice or shy laugh. But each time her spirit fell again, a little lower than before.

Ṭeḥuti is not here.

They reached the Ukher. Maaạ led her to a private cabin aboard her own boat. Her maidservants carefully stored her new treasures and prepared her room before retiring to their own much more humble places at the back of the boat.

She stood alone in her cabin, hearing the distant sounds of the celebration still echoing about the docks and the city streets beyond. The room rocked ever so gently with the River's current washing past.

The distance vanished as if it had never existed. The numbness loosened its grip on her ba and ka, her soul and spirit. With a slow, painful awareness Āakhu knew that it was she who stood alone in this room aboard the boat that Maaạ had given his bride, surrounded by the chests and boxes of clothing, jewelry, and cosmetics that had been carried from her rooms in the Queen's House.

She, Āakhu, wore the beautiful wedding dress. She had become the wife of Prince Maaạ, today—not some other woman as she had earlier watched.

Ṭeḥuti, why didn't you come back for me?

Āakhu sat down on the bed, drew her knees to her chest, and wept.

kbt ẖnw m spt ḥrw ḥsbt 18 ꜣbd 4 prt sw 3 ḫr ḥm n wsỉr

Qebt, Capital of Province Herui

Year 18, Month 4 of Peret, Day 3 under the Majesty of Ạsạr

A messenger from Maaạ's boat arrived at dawn. *Prepare yourself. We will be visiting Governor of Herui at mid-morning.*

Āakhu spent the time in preparation with her maidservants: washing, dressing, applying cosmetics. The maidservants went about their work in silence. They saw her puffy, tear-stained eyes and thought she was missing her home.

With the fields about Qebt, the capital of Herui, in view a second messenger arrived from Maaạ to escort her to her husband's boat.

Husband. The word could still raise an ache out of her numb heart.

Āakhu sat on a bench at the center of the small boat. She held her head high, kept her back straight—proud and regal as a lifetime of training had taught her.

Maaạ was waiting as her boat drew alongside. Another man stood nearby.

"Tell the governor we would be happy to share his table," Maaạ said. "I also want to speak with him privately before we depart."

The man bowed. "I will convey your request."

Maaạ's face sobered as he watched the man walk away. He turned and seeing Āakhu, smiled with innocent delight, a look of reverence in his eyes.

He reached to help her aboard. She looked up quietly for a moment before taking his hand.

He pulled her to his side with hardly an effort, his arm coming to rest around her waist. He drew her close and half-whispered: "You are radiant today. The sight of you makes my ba soar."

She smiled briefly but said nothing.

"Did you sleep well? Was the meal my servants prepared this morning to your liking? Is there anything I can do to make this journey pleasant for you?"

"Everything is fine," Āakhu said.

Maaạ nodded. "We are seeing the Governor Gemgem and his wife Neqa today. I believe they are friends of your father. They will be happy to see you."

The boat slowed and approached the dock, the men pushing with oars and long sticks, others tossing ropes of hemp and bound reeds from the dock to secure it. When the gangway was in place, Maaạ took Āakhu's hand and led her ashore.

"Welcome to Qebt," said Gemgem. "We are honored."

Maaạ and Āakhu bowed. "It is a joy for me to be here and introduce you to my chief wife Āakhu, daughter of Pharaoh Ạsạr and Īset."

Gemgem was a head shorter than Āakhu, but with an impressive physique and a wide, friendly face.

"I welcome the daughter of Ạsạr and Īset to my province," Gemgem said.

"You have your father's eyes," said Neqa.

She was tall and slender, taller even than Āakhu. Neqa had a pleasing, oval face with high cheeks and large, intriguing eyes of her own. Her skin, in the morning sun, was a beautiful shade of burnished ivory. Her arm was affectionately draped across her husband's shoulders.

"But your enchanting beauty—Ạsạr forgive me—must have come from your mother," Gemgem said and boomed with laughter.

Āakhu could not resist the amusement that poured from Gemgem. The suffering that had gripped her so tightly these many days relaxed its hold. In this funny little man's presence Āakhu felt a blush rise to her cheeks.

"I don't know what to say," Āakhu replied demurely.

"Say you'll share a meal with us," Gemgem said.

"We would be honored. I have word from Uas," said Maaạ.

"Excellent! Ptah blesses us with your presence." Gemgem cried.

"And while you talk, perhaps I could show Āakhu my gardens," Neqa said. " With all the time she has spent on the River, she might enjoy the quiet, fragrant surroundings for a spell."

"Not to mention the chance to spend time on ground that is not rocking constantly to and fro," Gemgem winked.

Āakhu blushed and nodded. "I would like that."

"Come, then," Neqa gestured, "let me show you the way."

Neqa and Āakhu left the dock and walked through the streets of Qebt towards the Governor's house.

"Do you not sit with your husband and take part in discussions with visitors?" Āakhu asked.

"I do, when I have a concern or an interest."

"Or when not tasked with keeping me occupied?" Āakhu asked.

Neqa smiled but said nothing. She exchanged greetings with several passers-by, introducing Āakhu to denizens of Qebt as they strolled to the Governor's house.

Qebt was smaller than Uas. It was also quieter, the streets not as cluttered with merchants and peddlers. Qebt was closer to its agricultural origins and its history as a river port than Uas. The creation of the province Herui and the selection of Qebt as the city of the Governor were distinctions awarded a mere two generations earlier.

When they were alone again, Neqa resumed their conversation with a sigh: "Why have you been crying?"

Āakhu stumbled, caught herself, and looked up to meet Neqa's glance. "Do you think Maaạ knows?"

"From his obvious delight in your company, no, I don't think so. But he will, given time."

Āakhu nodded.

"I would like to help if I can. You haven't been married long enough to be so sad—even if the marriage is a bad one."

"I don't think you can help me," Āakhu said, the sadness descending on her once more.

"If you refuse me the opportunity, then we shall never know."

Āakhu paused on the doorstep of the Governor's house, puzzled by her hostess and the casual friendliness with which she treated her visitor. *You speak as if we had shared our secrets since childhood when in truth, we have only just met.*

Neqa seemed to know that her suitability and discretion as a confidante were being evaluated. She smiled and gestured at the open doorway. "Through here."

The Governor's house, lit by pots and torches, was shadowed and cool. A corridor through its center funneled the breeze that came down the River and provided a fresh movement of air throughout. The two women drifted along on that breeze. Servants working within paused to bow to their mistress and her guest as they passed.

The door at the far end of the house opened onto a porch of bright, invigorating green. Before them stretched a pool decorated with lotus flowers, their blue blossoms fragrant in the lazy morning heat. Arranged about the pool were palms, ferns, grasses, and flowers. Rows of onions and garlic stretched along one wall, fruit trees and grape vines hid the other. Above and about them, birds sang. The garden loomed like an oasis, a pleasure of sight, sound, touch, and taste.

Even in Uas, Āakhu had not seen its equal. "This is truly remarkable," she said.

"Yes," Neqa agreed. "I wish I could take credit for it, but although I started it, my time working here has diminished as Gemgem's position has grown in Qebt. I manage the house while gardeners do the work here. But I still find the time to enjoy it."

Āakhu could only nod as her gaze swept across the scene, drinking as much of the unusual beauty into her parched ka as she could. It did not seem a place that could be connected to the house, the city, or the River. This was a place where the Aten never rose or set, but smiled down forever from overhead. This was where the gods came to rest, and play, and think great, godly things—ultimately reminding themselves why they created the world and fought so jealously among themselves to control it.

Indeed, the gods watched over the garden. Placed with honor in small groves, Āakhu saw images of Ptah, Nut, Neb, and Hapi—the spirits of the earth. Their steady eyes and placid faces watched serenely over the plants and animals that lived here.

"Come, sit beside me," Neqa said, motioning to Āakhu.

Neqa led her to a short dais at the edge of the pool. The women settled side by side. Neqa turned and reached to trail her long, slender fingers through the water, sending several small fish scattering for the cover of the lotus pads.

"Where were we?" Neqa mused almost playfully. "Ah, yes, you were in the process of deciding whether to confide in me the reason for your tears. Did you reach that decision?"

Āakhu looked down at the green sparkles that the ripples from Neqa's fingers set in motion.

"I love someone else," Āakhu said finally.

"I see," Neqa replied softly.

Āakhu sighed heavily, lowered her own hand into the inviting water, and stirred it slowly. "My marriage to Maaạ was arranged. Although I had seen him before when he came to court my sister Ḥaāmer, I met him for the first time at the ceremony. Before Maaạ I was betrothed to another."

The quiet, vibrant beauty of the garden, its peace, and the watching eyes of the gods released the pressure within Āakhu. The words tumbled out of her: about Ṭeḥuti, about the cold, quiet days in her mother's house and her father's distance, about her last visit with Ṭeḥuti and their failed escape.

Āakhu began to cry again. Neqa lifted her hand from the pool, dried it on her skirt, and pulled the hair back away from Āakhu's face. "Don't cry, Āakhu. Your eyes are red and puffy enough as is."

Neqa poured wine into two bowls and raised one to her lips. "Maaạ is a good man. He has watched over our northern provinces in peace, justice, and prosperity. His other wives, Merakesh and Marmut, truly love him and he loves and honors them in return."

Āakhu sighed. Neqa sat the bowl down by the pool. "Do not throw away what Maaạ offers you. You have a duty now, a commitment; that is more important. Ask yourself, if this love with Ṭeḥuti was destined, why did the gods give you to Maaạ? There is so much at stake, your happiness, your safety and the safety of your children, your father's dream. We are four provinces here caught between two great kingdoms, we need the safety your presence brings us."

Silent tears trailed down Āakhu's cheeks. Neqa hugged her. "I know it hurts, truly I do. I was not born loving Gemgem, but after being his wife these five inundations, I do not think I could love another. Give Maaạ a chance to earn your love and devotion, for all our sakes."

* * *

"What is the news from Uas?" Gemgem asked.

The two men were alone in Gemgem's private rooms, sharing a jug of cool wine and bread with honey.

Maaạ frowned. "Good and bad, I'm afraid. Ạsạr recognizes the danger his brother represents, but refuses to hunt for him."

Gemgem lowered the bowl of wine and peered soberly at Maaạ. "Does he know how dangerous a game he plays with Set? Does he realize that he gambles not only his own life, but the safety and the future of all the provinces that swear allegiance to him?"

The light sparkled in Maaạ's eyes as he shook his head. "I don't know. I certainly tried to press the point with him, but he kept talking about this destiny he believes Ptah has set before him. He considers the future infallible. He is convinced the bonds between him and Set are strong and ultimately, whatever Set's ambition, he will not be able to kill his own brother to obtain it."

"You have met Set. Is Pharaoh correct?"

"Set tried to kill Pharaoh twice already, two assassination attempts while he traveled north along the River. But he sent others to do his work and they failed. I think he has learned from his mistakes and will launch his own attack soon."

Gemgem placed his empty bowl on the table and refilled it. He held the jar out to Maaạ who took it and poured more of the red liquid into his own bowl.

"Set as Pharaoh—A bad thought," Gemgem said as he leaned back in his chair.

"I agree. Set can rule—ruthlessly—but he cannot govern. He has no concept of diplomacy, consensus, or negotiation. Set as Pharaoh would be a disaster to the unity Pharaoh has so carefully crafted among the provinces."

Gemgem shook his head. "It is almost as if—and Ptah forgive me for saying this aloud—they were each half a man. Ạsạr has the intellect and the passion; Set has the ambition and the compulsion."

"Sadly, I agree. If the two were but one man, he would already rule from the sea to the cataract. I do not see how these two incomplete men could be some great tool of Ptah's."

Gemgem watched his old friend, troubled by the grim look on the youthful face. "What will we do?"

"If Set acts we must join together to depose him. If we do it quickly, we might avoid a costly and potentially ruinous war."

"And if we fail?"

"Gemgem, if Set becomes Pharaoh we are all dead men. He would not allow a Governor to live that might offer a challenge to him. If I am to die anyway, I would do so trying to save what Ạsạr has created."

"As would I, my friend," Gemgem agreed.

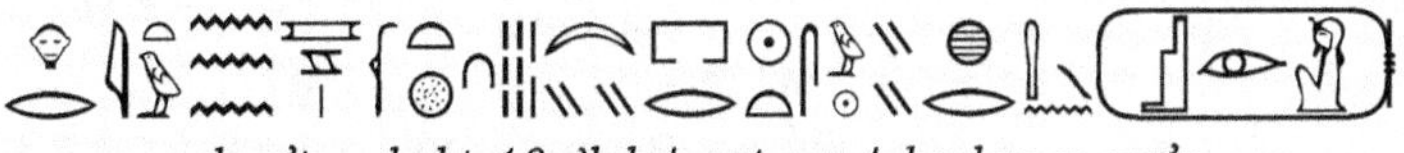

ḥr ỉtrw ḥsbt 18 ꜣbd 4 prt sw 4 ḫr ḥm n wsỉr

On the River

Year 18, Month 4 of Peret, Day 4 under the Majesty of Ạsạr

"Who is she?" asked Ānukhet.

She sat at the steering oar, watching the banks of the River pass by, her eyes scanning the other boats drifting north with the current.

Ṭeḥuti looked up from oiling the deck. He was alone with her at the back of the boat. The other more experienced hands knew to stay forward if they did not wish to have their lives examined by the steerswoman. Ṭeḥuti, as the most junior member, had neither the option nor the inclination to avoid duty at the stern.

"Who is who?"

"This woman for whom you secretly mourn?"

Ṭeḥuti said nothing for a moment. His gaze was level and steady, nothing in his eyes gave any indication of whether he would answer. Finally, without looking away, he raised his arm and pointed to one of Prince Maaạ's boats.

"Maaạ's new wife," Ānukhet said.

Ṭeḥuti resumed oiling the deck.

"So you are *that* Ṭeḥuti. The one responsible for much of the innovation in Pharaoh's kingdom. The one once betrothed to his youngest daughter."

Ṭeḥuti continued his back and forth rhythm as he worked the oil into the wood with measured, constant strokes. He paused only to dip the rag into the oil pot.

Ānukhet sighted forward using a small straight stick that rose from the bow of the boat and made a slight movement on her oar to adjust the course. "Why are you scrubbing the deck when you should be with her?"

ẖmnw ẖnw m spt wn ḥsbt 18 ȝbd 4 prt sw 7 ẖr ḥm n wsỉr

Chemennu, Capital of Province Un

Year 18, Month 4 of Peret, Day 7 under the Majesty of Ạsạr

The last stop on the journey to Meḥ was in Chemennu, where the Governor Teni ruled.

Āakhu had fallen into the pattern of this life on the River: the messengers from Maaa, the hours of preparation, and the brief trip to his boat so she could be seen at his side when he docked and visited with the Governor. At each of these stops Āakhu was led away to exchange vague pleasantries with a woman whom she knew only from a brief coaching from Maaạ or the oblique references once made by her parents.

The repetition allowed Āakhu to slip back into the numbness of existence: to smile at an appropriate moment without awareness of why the gesture was appropriate. She could be demure, she could be chatty, she could be the living equivalent of a fine bronze mirror, reflecting to each person she encountered the image that he or she most expected and wanted to see, while the true image of what had once been Āakhu sank from view—quietly and without a struggle.

The words of Neqa brought her back to herself from time to time as she reflected on what transpired one golden afternoon in that beautiful garden. *For all our sakes.*

Today she was with Tehāra, Governor Teni's wife, a woman of unusual beauty about the same age as her mother. Āakhu walked with Tehāra, while keeping her thoughts and emotions safely distant, when Tehāra looked at her and said: "We have something in common, Āakhu. Neither of us married our first love."

Āakhu stopped, not knowing whether to smile, frown, giggle, tell a story, or yield to any of the other unthinking responses used as cover the last few days. She felt as if she had suddenly awakened in some strange and unfamiliar place far from where she had fallen asleep.

"How did you know?"

Tehāra gestured and Āakhu resumed walking.

"Ṭeḥuti was here with your father when he came North seeking rebels. He cared for your father's shoulder wound. We had the chance those few days to talk about many things—including you."

Āakhu needed to retreat back into numbness before the tears started once more. But Tehāra and her strange, sincere talk drew Āakhu to stay.

Tehāra took Āakhu's hand, gently squeezed it, and said: "My first love was one that could not possibly flower. We were little more than children feeling the first stirrings of adult emotions. It was painful, innocent, and doomed. You will suffer as well until you find someone better, someone who will make you forget. Maaạ is that someone.

Tehāra looked into Āakhu's eyes. "I know you still have sadness ahead of you. But our days on the River are few. Don't waste them twice."

"Twice?"

Tehāra looked at Āakhu. It was all there, written in the fine lines of her face and dark concern peering out from her eyes. *Is this what I would see,* Āakhu thought, *if I were not hiding behind the reflections that each one expects to see? Is Tehāra my true face?*

Tehāra gave Āakhu the answer, but not in time to prevent much of what came later: "Once, in wasting the day in regret; twice, in denying Maaạ and yourself a love you both deserve."

They continued several paces while the words seeped deeper into Āakhu. Tehāra's words were so much like Neqa's. Could they both be wrong? Could she pretend? Just close her eyes and imagine it was Ṭeḥuti instead of Maaạ with her? Should she?

"I see the hesitation in you," Tehāra said, taking Āakhu's hand. "If you feel hurried, there are always the days of purification. If you cannot love him, you might at least find the time to accept him."

* * *

Maaạ and Teni sat on a rooftop terrace overlooking Chemennu. A breeze coming down the river valley tugged at the awning that shaded them and lessened the afternoon heat.

"What was Pharaoh's response to your warning?"

Maaạ looked down into his bowl of beer. "He refuses to take any action against his brother."

"And when Set kills him and takes the throne?"

"We must move quickly to depose him."

"We?" questioned Teni.

"Gemgem has joined me."

Teni closed his eyes for a moment. "Ptah have mercy" he whispered.

When Teni opened his eyes again, Maaạ was watching him. "I'm with you too," Teni added wearily.

ḥr ỉtrw mḥꜣw mḥ

ḥsbt 18 ꜣbd 4 prt sw 8 ḫr ḥm n wsỉr

On the River Near Meḥ

Year 18, Month 4 of Peret, Day 8 under the Majesty of Ạsạr

The boats of Maaạ turned toward the riverbank where another large city loomed. Āakhu, puzzled, hailed one of the crew.

"Why are we stopping? I received no messenger from Maaạ."

The youth smiled to cover his embarrassment. "Lady, we are home. This is Meḥ."

pr-tꜣty m mḥ ḥsbt 18 ꜣbd 4 prt sw 9 ḫr ḥm n wsỉr

House of the Governor in Meḥ

Year 18, Month 4 of Peret, Day 9 under the Majesty of Ạsạr

Maaạ stopped in the shadow of the doorway, watching his bride weep. He had never witnessed such a scene before—not with either of his other two wives, nor with any of the maidens he had loved for a time. When he first came upon her he was puzzled, but as he watched and listened to this very private pouring out of her ka, he found the glistening of tears and the sound of her lament unexpectedly moving.

He stepped back in retreat, wishing to leave her alone with her grief so he could return later when she had released it, but his effort betrayed him.

Āakhu stumbled from the bed, smearing the kohl as she tried to wipe the tears away. "My husband! I did not hear you approaching. Please forgive this poor wife for not preparing you a better greeting."

My husband, not my love.

She went to her knees in a bow much like one would give a Pharaoh. She touched her head to the floor.

"Please get up," he said solemnly. "I'm not your master."

She rose nervously and faced him, trembling as if she had come out of warm water into cool air. Her lips quivered; her eyes filled with tears once more. She flinched as he took a step in her direction.

"Who is he?" he asked.

She tried to smile and shake her head but succeeded only in spilling the tears from her eyes down her cheeks. "It is only sadness for home. This is my first time away in many years."

"I have seen the homesick tears of a young woman far from the comfort and familiarity of home and family. Your tears come from a deeper place, a more fragile place. You shed the tears of one that has lost all whom she loves. I know you were intended for another. Who is this young man for whom your ka cries out?"

The moment stretched out. "Forgive me. You will no doubt learn that in all but years I am still a foolish child."

"I have found love to be neither foolish nor childish. Go on," Maaạ coaxed.

"His name is Ṭeḥuti. He is a priest of Ptah at the temple in Uas."

Maaạ nodded, a thing that had puzzled him suddenly became known. "I met a young man by the same name. He was in the company of Pharaoh when he came North to quell the rebellion in Kes. That Ṭeḥuti was also a priest—an extraordinary priest who brought knowledge and healing instead of empty gestures and tired prayers."

"That was him," Āakhu whispered.

"I saw the sadness in his eyes after Pharaoh considered my request for you. I thought at the time that it was due to the suffering he had witnessed. Now I know better."

An oil pot sputtered for a moment, flaring, and settling back into a soft orange light. A bird called from nearby. A breeze drifted through the room, soft as a sigh, quiet as the crumbling of innocence.

"Āakhu, I did not know this," Maaạ said. He had no wish to hurt her more and did not add: *But it would have made no difference.*

"And now that you know?"

"It is imperative that I be aligned with the house of Pharaoh. He needs a successor."

"My father still hopes for a son. Before we ran, he considered Ṭeḥuti a possible successor."

"A noble gesture," Maaạ said, "seeing Ṭeḥuti's wisdom and learning are responsible for many of the advancements in the provinces. These improvements *granted by Pharaoh* have greatly broadened Ạsạr's influence.

"But Ṭeḥuti is no Pharaoh. He could not endure anything that long took him from his explorations. His heart is too tender. He cannot make the tough decisions that are required of a Pharaoh."

"How could you know that?" Āakhu questioned defensively.

"I watched him stand mutely at the rail of the boat as Pharaoh gave you to me. He made no defense whatsoever of his love for you. He spoke not a word to save your betrothal."

Āakhu began to cry again.

"Please don't. I love you. My heart was yours the moment I first saw you. Please accept it. Give me the chance to win your heart as well."

For the first time since the ceremony in the Hall of Balance, he held her. He wiped the tears from her cheeks and folded her in his arms.

Āakhu stood like a statue, her arms stiff at her sides. "Why must you be Pharaoh?"

Maaạ let her go. "Āakhu, it is the first night we have had alone together as husband and wife. Must we fill it with political discussions?"

"Why?" she reiterated.

"Because there may soon be war."

Āakhu looked at him in disbelief.

"You've lived your whole life in Pharaoh's house. Isn't it clear? Set wants what his brother has. He has spent the last several years moving his followers into position to take the throne of Egypt. If Pharaoh does not kill his brother, and it appears he cannot, Set will kill him and take his throne. Those within Set's circle are becoming restless. They will not wait much longer.

"I cannot let that happen. I am a man of Pharaoh's heart. I understand his vision of Egypt and the importance of men like Tehuti to our future. I have the skill to carry Pharaoh's vision forward. When Set replaces his brother, I must attack and depose him. Having you at my side strengthens my legitimate claim to the throne."

"This cannot be."

"Only Ptah can save your father now," Maaạ said.

Āakhu wrapped her arms about herself and sat on the side of the bed, rocking slowly forward and back. Maaạ came and stood beside her. She stopped moving when he placed a hand on her head.

"I am sorry, Āakhu. I meant this night to be one of great joy for us."

Aakku did not look up. "You deserve better than a wife who does not love you."

Maaạ sighed, and took a moment to compose his thoughts. "That will change. Come, he said, offering his hand."

"I request my days of purification," she said, unable to look at him.

Maaạ said nothing for a time. His offered hand fell back to his side. "You are the daughter of Pharaoh and Īset, raised in the royal house. I do not need proof you are a virgin."

"I request my days of purification," she repeated. This time she raised her head to gaze into his eyes.

"The full forty days?"

"Yes."

Maaạ's face was a mask, concealing all that he might think of his new wife and her request. He studied her face, beautiful even while suffused with sadness, eyes sparkling with tears, ebony hair shimmering in the torchlight. When his gaze became uncomfortable, she looked down again at a spot on the stone midway between them. He sighed. "As you wish."

If relieved, she did not show it.

"There are conditions," he said. "Should I go on?"

Āakhu nodded.

"I will not shame Pharaoh and Īset by announcing this; it will be done quietly. You are my chief wife and will appear with me—affectionately—in public. You will accompany me on trips and be seen as my chief wife. Each night, the maid servants I give you will see that you sleep alone. Do you understand my conditions?"

"Yes," Āakhu said flatly.

Maaạ paused for a breath. His face softened, his shoulders relaxed.

"Should you choose to accept me as your rightful husband, you may do so without recrimination. I will wait for you, Āakhu, as long as it takes for your heart to turn to me. I love you."

Āakhu nodded again but said nothing.

Maaạ offered a final thought: "If Ptah desires that I should precede you across the River, you will be free of me. I know not whether that knowledge will be a hope or a curse to you in the days that lie ahead."

Āakhu, her head still bowed, said contritely: "I do not wish you ill, Maaạ, nor do I despise your love. I gave my heart to Ṭeḥuti and know not how to get it back."

"Then I hope you find a way. What is your wish, my love?"

"I will return to the women's house now and start the days of my purification."

"Then go," he said sadly, turning his face from her.

Chapter 16

pr ḥmt nswt m wꜣst ḥsbt 18 ꜣbd 4 prt sw 11 ḫr ḥm n wsỉr

The House of Pharaoh's Wife in Uas
Year 18, Month 4 of Peret, Day 11 under the Majesty of Ạsạr

Īset dreamed alone in the room that had once belonged to Ḥaāmer.

The sunlight through the high window was occasionally dappled by a stray cloud or passing bird. In the rippling shadows Īset recalled the subtle, precious moments of Ḥaāmer's life.

The breezes that whispered about the stones and bricks of the Queen's house on the otherwise still day were to Īset the sighs of Ḥaāmer and Āakhu as they slumbered together with her during the warm summer afternoons.

The room was empty of anything except memories now. Īset's gaze swept across the bare floors and walls: *her bed was there; the table with her jewelry and cosmetics was against that wall. Behind me rested the trunks that held her clothing. She always kept her sandals nearby in neat pairs, toes pointed to the wall.*

The artifacts of Ḥaāmer's life had been buried with her that she would have them for her next life. It was a duty, but also an unutterable cruelty to those left behind: as if removing all evidence that the sick young woman once lived and loved and cried and died was atonement for something born flawed from the mind of god.

What remained of Ḥaāmer existed now only in the fragile, precious, memories of those who loved her, a few people at best. *And what of those poor who are never known beyond the bounds of their own families? What of the children who die so young?*

Īset did not realize that the tears had returned until the thirsty air tickled and wiped them from her cheeks. What a mystery: *that life can be so beautiful and painful at the same time.*

Īset grew aware of footsteps echoing through the doorway from down the hall behind her. They approached, hesitated at the door, then entered and stopped beside her. The silence returned.

A quick glance revealed the familiar sandaled feet and strong, muscular legs of Ạsạr. He lowered himself to sit beside her on the stone floor as they had not done since they were children. Putting an arm about her, he drew her close.

"I remember how she would be waiting at the door to the Queen's house each afternoon as I returned from the Hall of Balance," he said.

Īset leaned close to him. "She and I and newborn Āakhu would nap together through the heat of the day. But she always seemed to know when you were coming home."

"I held out my hands and clapped once," Pharaoh continued, "she ran and jumped into my arms. I whirled her about like a sling—sometimes by the arms, sometimes by the feet—and tossed her over my shoulder like a sheaf of grain. I carried her that way to the common room, laughing and tickling her feet."

"I remember waking to sounds of the two of you," Īset mused. "I also remember how she loved to go with you to see the new irrigation projects and how you would both return covered in the black dirt looking more Nubian that Egyptian."

"She never showed much interest in the details of the project, but she did the most wonderful impersonation of me," Ạsạr laughed. "She would have the priests in fits of laughter—at least when they thought my attention was elsewhere."

"You should have punished her for making a public mockery of your reign."

Pharaoh shook his head, his eyes still half-focused on distant days. "I could never punish Ḥaāmer."

"No, you never could," Īset agreed. "She was always your little girl."

Ạsạr nodded but said nothing as birds and clouds continued to drift across the face of the Aten, sending shadows and memories spilling across the walls of the lonely room. The breeze from the River, slipping around edges and across rough surfaces, whispered words and phrases in voices not heard since younger days.

"Is this what it is to grow old," Īset reflected at last, "to sit in an empty room, remembering my youth and the days raising my two daughters and thinking that I am happy?"

"This is only a moment's rest in the journey of life, a chance to catch one's breath and reflect on where one has been before resuming the path to where one is going."

"Then I feel as if I could rest for a long time. I find much of my happiness in past days, dreaming of my daughters and my husband—days when we could feed each other grapes, and swim, and share love as the breeze dried our naked bodies—all without half the priests in Uas questioning our wisdom or sincerity or technique."

Ạsạr's hand reached for hers. "It has been a long time since we have had our freedom. A Pharaoh and his wife have many duties and responsibilities—maybe too many."

"And while we were so busy with the people of Egypt, our daughters slipped away from us."

"I'm sorry," he said quietly.

Īset squeezed his hand. "It's not your fault. We both grew up watching from a distance as our parents lived these same lives, their time and affection taken from us by the people they governed. We knew what the cost would be."

"Perhaps we can get away from Uas, toward the end of Peret or the beginning of Shemu—before the land is busy with harvest. The River will be slow and calm; we could follow the current to Meḥ to see Maaạ and Āakhu."

"If wishes were raindrops, there would be no more deserts in Egypt," Īset replied. "I appreciate the thought, but I fear there will always be a crisis, or event, or need to keep us here even during a quiet season."

"I am Pharaoh. I should be able to travel as I choose."

Īset smiled, but it did not mask the growing emptiness inside. She leaned against Pharaoh, reaching around him, her head on his shoulder: "I love you so much. But even my arms cannot hold you tightly enough to prevent the people of Egypt from taking a little more of you from me each day."

Ạsạr returned her embrace. Nestling his nose into her fragrant, dark hair he whispered: "Our best days are yet to come, Īset. Let me show you that it is so."

Īset nodded, wondering what might yet come that would replace the memories of her two precious daughters and her young, eager husband as the best moments of her life.

"There is something else I came here to tell you," he said after a quiet time. "I have created a proclamation and given it to the priests. It is to be carved into the wall of the Temple of Ptah: *The daughters of Pharaoh shall no more be the currency of politics and shall not be wed to husbands beyond our borders.*"

"I was wrong," he concluded with ungodly humility.

"It will not help Āakhu."

"No," Pharaoh admitted, "but she will be the last."

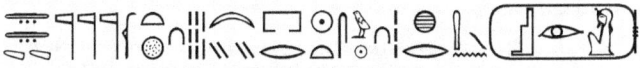

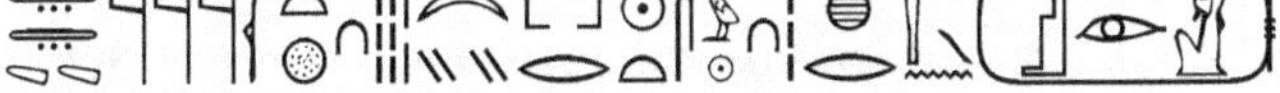

tꜣw nṯrw ḥsbt 18 ꜣbd 4 prt sw 13 ḫr ḥm n wsỉr

The Eastern Desert

Year 18, Month 4 of Peret, Day 13 under the Majesty of Ạsạr

The four men met in the hills bordering the eastern desert, a place all of them knew but where none of them lived. They had arrived as night faded, traveling through the night. Sand and heat were already stirring, obscuring what had been a beautiful view of the Aten launching into the sky over the stark, patterned vista of sand.

"Were you followed?" Set asked, hidden in the comfort of a protective, nondescript linen robe. The air was still cool in the valley shadows about their small camp.

"He assigned a man to follow me. A pair of dancers occupied him before I left."

Set smiled. "Yes, I miss them during these cool nights. So what is this problem the messenger spoke of?"

Shepses held up one of Maaạ's sandstone scarabs. "These accursed things are everywhere."

Set took the scarab and turned it over in his hands, frowning as he read the inscription. "I don't see the danger. They contain a greeting from Maaạ. There are no magic spells written on them."

Shti-ahk stirred and shook his head. "But magic has occurred. In the streets I hear the name of Maaạ mentioned more than that of Pharaoh. And since the food giveaways at his wedding Maaạ has been more popular than Ptah! You have not seen it, but Maaạ has most certainly cast a spell over the people of Uas."

"Maaạ is safely back in Meḥ now. The stir he created will fade. We need only be patient."

"We have been far too patient already," Shti-ahk growled.

"People are referring to Maaạ as Pharaoh's logical son and whispering his name as the natural successor to the throne of Egypt," Shepses continued. "A dangerous idea like that, once voiced, can spread quickly and assume a spirit of its own—a spirit we would find very difficult to put down."

Temu, listening to this point with quiet interest, leaned forward and spoke: "Though you are Pharaoh's brother, you are not nearly so well-loved among the populace. Maaạ, though newly arrived, and despite scattered whispers that his marriage took Āakhu out of Ṭeḥuti's arms, is seen as smiling and friendly and generous. He has a remarkable political presence and the ability to befriend almost anyone."

"What do you want me to do?"

"We want you to kill Maaạ," Shepses said.

"Maaạ lives on the northern frontier of Egypt—far from life here in Uas. He is not a threat to me."

"He is popular, and his popularity is growing," Temu resumed. "We have few men in Meḥ and are not well-informed as to his plans and activities. But if it were to come down to a contest between the two of you for the allegiance of most Egyptians, Maaạ would win. He's winning already. You cannot afford for it to continue."

Set hesitated and pulled at his chin. "But he would be of such value if I could turn him to my purpose."

Shti-ahk asked rhetorically: "Why should he serve you when he could just as easily be your master?"

"Watch your tongue," Set warned.

"Set," Temu spoke into the dangerous silence, "you have gathered us into your confidence over the years as the men you trust to put you on the throne of Egypt. We have served you faithfully and advised you without error. Why is it that you no longer listen to us?"

Set looked at Temu, studied the weathered face, bronzed arms sticking from the sleeves of his robes like old weathered sticks. They were old men now, too many years had passed in hoping and planning. Ạsạr was still Pharaoh and Set was still waiting. "I am listening, I have always listened. While you have remained in Uas frightening yourselves with thoughts of Maaạ's fleeting popularity, I have travelled and listened to others as well."

"And what do these others tell you?" Temu asked.

Set smiled, a treacherous, murderous smile that seemed to chase all the gathering warmth from the day. "They tell me it's time to throw my brother a feast."

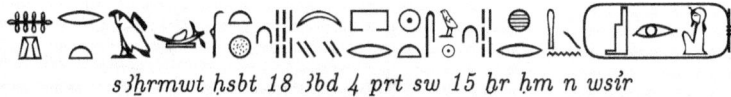

sꜣḫrmwt ḥsbt 18 ꜣbd 4 prt sw 15 ḫr ḥm n wsi͗r

The Boat Sakhr-Mut

Year 18, Month 4 of Peret, Day 15 under the Majesty of Ạsạr

After twenty-five days aboard the Sakhr-Mut, Ṭeḥuti looked less like a soft temple priest and more like a seasoned crewman. His skin had darkened, his hands grown rough and blistered, and he was already showing signs of regaining the lanky leanness of his youth. His river legs had returned, as had his feel for the boat. He no longer asked for assignments, he knew when something needed attention and attended to it.

The days were filled with activity: scrubbing, mending, plugging leaks, and bailing. At night, while the crew settled into welcomed rest, Ṭeḥuti succumbed to his natural curiosity and the habits of his priestly life.

Once the Aten settled into the earth and the stars and Aih appeared, Ṭeḥuti fetched the few simple instruments he had managed to borrow from former students at temples along the River. With his writing stick and whatever scraps of material he could find, he retreated to a quiet, secluded part of the boat and recorded events that took place in the night sky.

The others left him alone. He was still a priest to them and priests were known for doing inscrutable, worshipful things. Occasionally, during the day, a fellow would mention seeing him and ask with friendly curiosity what he saw up there. He would try to explain, but to one not drawn to the night sky, such explanations seemed distant and mystical.

Aih was but a sliver—nearly veiled, or consumed—and would rise shortly before Aten. In its absence the stars and the wanderers were easily visible. He looked and began to see the familiar patterns. With his writing stick and a candle he recorded ascending and descending stars, the location of two of the wanderers within the patterns. On the hunch that it might prove valuable, he also recorded the approximate location of the boat from which his observations were made.

Staring upward, he almost missed the soft sound of bare feet approaching from behind. The sound ceased two paces behind him.

"One time," Anukhet began without preamble, "a woman brought her daughter down to the boat where I worked. She begged me to take the child and make her my apprentice. I refused, for I could see by the child's fright that she had no desire for the water.

"But the mother would not desist. She pleaded and cried, even as her daughter trembled in her arms. But I could not honor her request. It was not for her daughter's future that she truly entreated me, but for her own past. And the Aten had long since carried those days away.

"She had accumulated too many responsibilities and burdens to ever leave them—or her child—behind. But somewhere within her the desire still burned. It was too late for her, but she thought her daughter might still escape the life that she so secretly regretted."

Ṭeḥuti sat his instruments down and turned to study Anukhet's thoughtful face in the candlelight. "Only through her daughter could she achieve her desire and hope that her own disappointment would not be repeated."

Anukhet nodded. "But her daughter did not have that call to travel the River and never would."

"That is a sad story."

"It is an *evil* one," Anukhet corrected. "I can think of nothing more evil that to be born with a desire, a true passion, and no hope of fulfilling it."

"Except maybe to be given a hope when there is in truth none," Ṭeḥuti added.

"Perhaps," Anukhet nodded thoughtfully and continued: "The woman's pleading gnawed at me over the succeeding days. When my boat returned, I determined to find her and offer her an afternoon sailing the Nile on a borrowed fishing boat."

"Did she go?"

"She died of the fever three days before my arrival."

The frogs, the alligators and hippopotami, the birds and fish, all seemed unnaturally quiet as if weighing Anukhet's story. Even the water seemed to have stopped slapping the sides of the boat. Or maybe Ṭeḥuti just failed to hear them over the voices of his own ba.

"You are still alive and so is Pharaoh's daughter."

"She is Maaạ's *wife,*" Ṭeḥuti reminded her.

"She did her duty, just like the woman who raised a family instead of sailing the River. But the yearning never diminished. You owe it to yourself and to Āakhu to know her ka and see if there might yet be a way for you two."

"Soon, I think. We will stop in Meḥ and I will see her. If there is a way, we will find it. But there is much more at stake than our love."

"I have never heard of a thing more important than love," Anukhet replied, "only of things that were for a moment more convenient."

Anukhet's face was calm, no trace of frown or disappointment. But her eyes were alive with emotions that danced with the flickering candlelight until she shook her head and turned away. As her shadow retreated into the darkness, Ṭeḥuti heard her say: "Then I will also have the wasted love of a priest and princess with which to sober the ba and sour the beer of distant evenings."

wsḫt nt jwsw m wꜣst ḥsbt 18 ꜣbd 4 prt sw 16 ḫr ḥm n wsi̓r

The Hall of Balance in Uas

Year 18, Month 4 of Peret, Day 16 under the Majesty of Ạsạr

"Why are you here?" Pharaoh asked after he had settled on his gold and ivory throne.

"As you commanded, I have discovered and captured the men who plotted to take your life," Temu said.

Pharaoh looked beyond the priest to the back of the Hall of Balance. "Where are they?"

"This is an auspicious occasion," Temu said, waving the question away with a hand motion. "You survived the assassination. I have inquired, investigated, and found the men who have plotted against you. I was reading through the records the other day and realized you are completing the eighteenth year of your reign. We at the Temple of Ptah are planning a feast to honor you and celebrate your wisdom and justice. As the highlight of the evening, we will bring out the men that you may question and execute them."

"I would prefer to have them here in the Hall of Balance where I can question them before the people."

"They are evil men for plotting against you. A public forum is not the place to give voice to their poison. A celebration of your power and wisdom—that is the place to show them the evil of what they tried to do. If you wish to take them to the Hall of Balance afterward, by all means do so."

Pharaoh considered this a moment. His shoulder was wrapped in a bright, fresh bandage. He was told daily that it was healing well, but it hurt as much from keeping it still as it did when he tried to move it. "What about this feast?"

Temu bowed his head a moment. When he raised it again, his face was solemn. His voice, devoid of its usual confidence, was soft, his words slow and considered: "We have never led the people of Uas in honoring you before as Pharaoh. We might have lost you. We want to show you the love and respect we have for you. We want to celebrate you in a manner that has not been seen since the day you assumed the throne. It will be an evening forever remembered among our people as a night you were celebrated as you are due."

The solemnity had given way to enthusiasm and fire, the light glowing in Temu's eyes, his hands in wide arcing motions encompassing the dreams he had for the evening. It was another brilliant performance by Temu but Pharaoh found himself hoping that it might be true. But there was one question that crowded out all others, one that haunted him, ate at him, confused his sleep and poisoned his meals. "Was my brother among those you discovered?"

Temu drew back, eyes large, face pale, in a gesture Pharaoh assumed was genuine horror. "Pharaoh, no! Set has always been loyal to you even when he disagreed. We at the temple pray for the day when you might forgive one another."

"So do I," Pharaoh said.

Temu bowed and looked up, his face uncertain, hesitant, struggling to get from his last words to the next. "There is one other thing. The Lady Īset."

Pharaoh smiled for the first time, seduced by Temu's discomfort and his attempts to cover it with a soft voice and raised eyebrows. "I should come alone?"

Temu's face changed yet again to one humble, contrite, but mischievous as well. "I have engaged entertainments that may not interest Lady Īset."

"So I thought," Pharaoh said, leaning back. "I would prefer to question these men here."

"You can still do that. But come to the feast. Celebrate. Let us honor and praise you. Let us entertain you for an evening in a manner to which you seldom see. If, after that, you still wish to defer questioning and hold it here instead, do so, with our blessing."

In the distance, beyond the Hall of Balance he could hear the strains of music and singing celebrating the birth of a child. As it faded away it was replaced by much more subdued music and the unsettling, trilling calls of women in lamentation. *Music from the ends of life. One is born, one dies. One is Pharaoh, one is not. One dies, one continues. One leaves the throne, one takes it.* These thoughts, rising and falling to the pattern of the music, followed one another like the members of a caravan—each in line and in step with the one it followed. He returned after a time, settled, resolved, to the sound of torches flaring about him and Temu's gaze, passionless and unyielding, pressing up on him from below.

"I will come," Pharaoh said.

pr-tꜣty m mḥ ḥsbt 18 ꜣbd 4 prt sw 16 ḫr ḥm n wsỉr

House of the Governor in Meh
Year 18, Month 4 of Peret, Day 16 under the Majesty of Ạsạr

"But what do we do here?" Āakhu asked, her frustration apparent in the sound of her voice.

Maaạ's other two wives looked at her with puzzlement.

"We raise the children here," replied Merakesh, the oldest of the two. She was a quiet, pretty Nubian about Āakhu's age. "We oversee the affairs of the house, we—"

"We prepare ourselves through the day to be summoned to Maaạ's bed," Marmut, the other, younger woman winked. She was already displaying the first visible swelling of pregnancy, and would likely not be summoned to Maaạ's bed many more times before the birth.

Āakhu shook her head again. "Surely there must be more. Don't you ever accompany Maaạ to the judgment hall? Don't you dispute with the priests in matters of law and justice? Don't you study the languages and customs of other cultures? Don't you write poetry?"

Merakesh looked at her sadly and with dawning understanding. "Āakhu, very few women—even privileged ones—have the opportunity to do those things."

"But in Uas—"

"In Uas lives Īset, the most extraordinary woman ever to walk the black lands. To you she is mother, to the rest of us she is one touched by the gods, a woman of unearthly gifts. There are none like her, and though her influence grows, there are few other women capable of following the trail she has blazed."

Marmut rubbed her belly and brightened. "We can order scrolls from the temple library to read. We can get sticks and linen for writing. As for arguing points of law and religion, that would be up to Maaạ. As enlightened as he has been by your father, he has shown no interest in having his wives join him in the judgment hall. But neither of us has ever made the request."

Merakesh shrugged. "I will tell you what I remember of my life in Nubia, and the few words of my native language that I still remember. And there are other servants here in the house who could tell you of their native lands."

Āakhu held her arms out in appeal: "Hearing your stories might do for a time, but if I don't *do* something I shall go mad!"

"I know, Āakhu," said Merakesh, "First you are angry and sullen, but that fades through the dark days to a sad and distant reserve one might almost mistake for shyness. Then your ba and chu withdraw, leaving behind an empty shell. In the end, the light in your eyes goes out; the fire that your mother kindled within you burns to embers that cool and die here so far from where she might continue to tend you. Yes, I have already seen what happens when you are kept from the thing that you love. Your bargain with Maaạ is no secret, nor is your lamenting for your lost priest."

"That is why I need a task: to keep me from that which I have no desire to dwell upon."

"You don't need a task, you need a cause: something to consume you so you have no time for your past and its disappointments. If you insist on not bearing our husband sons, at least do something to make him proud of you. Perhaps some involvement in the disappointments of others might put your own in perspective."

Āakhu was suddenly ashamed, and felt the heat rising to her face. Since her arrival, she had mostly dismissed Merakesh and Marmut as incapable of understanding her or being her friends. To be given wisdom by one she had taken so lightly was humbling.

"My chu hears you," Āakhu said much more kindly. "I am sorry for my behavior of late."

"You have been through a lot," said Marmut.

"Perhaps I do need a cause, but where do I look? How do I know when I have found one that is sufficient to my need?"

"By not looking with the notion of fulfilling yourself," Merakesh agreed. "Look to make our husband proud. Look to make your priest, should he hear of it, smile for a moment, with the knowledge that his time with you might have changed you both into something better."

Āakhu reflected for a moment on her life and the days she had spent with Ṭeḥuti. How had she grown?

She remembered Ḥaāmer, and how her death had hurt so much, almost as much as losing Ṭeḥuti. She had mourned in Ḥaāmer's absence, thinking she might mourn for the rest of her life. She had written beautiful, tragic poetry to accompany her sister to Amennt but had not lost her sorrow.

Then Ṭeḥuti had taken her out of the city. She remembered a warm, sunny day, and grapes, and women washing. But more than that, she remembered children: children in the streets of Uas pretending to be her father and mother, children running to meet her and Ṭeḥuti, children who had so little and gave so much and for a moment she was ashamed all over again at her own selfishness.

Āakhu remembered Ȧamȧam and one precious, quiet little girl in particular. "I know the reason I have been brought here and what I must do."

"Then let us begin," said Merakesh.

sꜣẖrmwt ḥsbt 18 ꜣbd 4 prt sw 16 ḫr ḥm n wsỉr

The Boat Sakhr-Mut

Year 18, Month 4 of Peret, Day 16 under the Majesty of Ạsạr

"If you take a dip in the River, it might relax you enough that you will stop wrestling with sleep," Anukhet called out softly in the darkness.

Ṭeḥuti ceased his restless turning and rolled onto his elbows. In the starlight he could see the outline of the sheets under which she slept.

"Who are you Anukhet? What is your story? Are you a spirit sent from the gods to trouble me?"

Ṭeḥuti heard Anukhet muffle a giggle.

"Seriously," he added. "Your words of last evening have driven away my sleep."

Her laughter died away, lost to the sounds of the River sighing restlessly about them.

"I am just a woman who steers a boat, Ṭeḥuti. My words are lost on the breeze. You are awake because their truth touched your own troubled ka before they drifted away."

"Where did your words come from?"

"I meet people and hear stories. I find patterns in those stories and the people who tell them. When I saw you mourning your princess the other day I was reminded of a woman who mourned in secret her own lost opportunities."

"What do you mourn, Anukhet? What do you love? What words stir your ba and keep you awake nights?"

"I have none."

"I cannot believe that you have no story of your own. I will not sleep until I hear it."

Ṭeḥuti heard the sound of her sigh.

"Come closer then, and whisper," Anukhet said, "for there is no need to keep the whole crew awake."

Ṭeḥuti pulled the pile of folded rags he used as a pillow closer to where Anukhet rested. In the darkness he made out her face as a round paleness above the dark wood of the deck, floating among the cloudy billows of the sails she used as shelter against the cool Peret evenings.

"I took my first journey at the age of four," Anukhet said. "I wandered away from my mother in the marketplace and found my way aboard a boat. I fell asleep and wasn't discovered until they were nearly to Abtu. The crew hailed a boat going the other direction, transferred me, and took an oath from the boat master to return me safely home."

"My mother once told me that from the moment I could roll onto my belly and crawl, I always went directly toward the River. My father told me I could swim before I could walk. 'River' was the first word I ever spoke."

"They must be very proud of you."

Anukhet nodded: "I think they were, in the end, before they died. They indulged me in the beginning because they thought it was something I would grow out of—like diapers and dolls.

"Later, it seemed almost as if they blamed themselves for my behavior, and redoubled their efforts to educate me in the joys of husband, home and children. Every moment of my layovers was spent learning to manage a house and a one-sided discussion of the advantages of bearing strong sons as my sisters were doing.

"But my sisters knew me and accepted me for what I was. They understood that I would be no happier raising a family than they would be steering a boat. I think it was they who finally convinced my parents. I certainly wasn't around enough to make the argument."

"You have never felt the desire to look into the eyes of a child—your child—and see the spirit developing within, knowing that spirit came from you?" asked Ṭeḥuti.

"I see that spirit every time I gaze into the River, Ṭeḥuti. I see it when Aten appears in the east and when he sets in the west. I see it in the ivory face of Aih."

Ṭeḥuti was silent.

"I am sorry I have not had a life as tragic as your own. We do not all seek the River out of loss or despair. If it makes you feel any better, you have touched me."

"What is that supposed to mean?"

Anukhet shifted under her sails, exposing her face further to the starlight. Ṭeḥuti thought he could make out the shadows that were her eyes, and her lips stretched into a smile.

"Women are drawn to stories of love—especially those that involve lovers battling the obstacles that keep them apart. There is something in the shedding of tears for another's struggle that strengthens us to meet our own. Yours is growing into one of the sweeter and more tragic that I have heard. You have my sympathy."

Silence returned, while the waves brushed the sides of the boat and the stars turned ever so slowly overhead. Ānukhet made Ṭeḥuti feel wiser and dumber, happier and sadder, than he had felt since that terrible afternoon on the dock at Qes. He wanted to die and live at the same time.

Ḥes Ȧturres, Song of Egypt: desert and the River, gods and mortals, men and women—all locked in eternal enigmatic struggle.

"Thank you, Anukhet," Ṭeḥuti whispered at last.

He crawled away in the darkness to his mat and went to sleep at last.

Chapter 17

ABYDOS, EGYPT, THE FEATURE, THE TOMB, JULY 2ND, 8:25 A.M.:

Beginning work in the tomb hall, Lisa and Sanders read the hieroglyphics on the two hawk ushabtui that Lisa had seen in her initial exploration.

Speak to your lady of Horus,
her brother,
Who yearns for her laughter as a bird yearns for the sky.

The ushabtui referred to the hawk god, Horus. With no additional information, the feature held another mystery.

Hadn't Robert indicated he was exploring objects associated with Horus? He sent JPEGS showing the pot I was excavating. I need to review his documents this evening.

"How are we going to get into Ḥaāmer's room?" asked Lisa. "It'll be destructive."

"The only place wall painting won't be is the inside of the brick doorway. I want to study their masonry techniques so busting the door apart is going to take time," responded Sanders.

"OK," agreed Lisa.

"The computer model shows the bricks are thin so we will be able to go in at the bottom," said Sanders. "I can drill here at floor level and open a hole our size."

"That'll get us in, but to bring in the x-ray equipment in, we'll have to expand the hole. I don't want to destroy any of the wall."

"We'll be able to slide the x-ray machine in sideway, but the CT equipment is another matter. We need to remove the artifacts at the door so we can get our equipment into the room. Later, we can open more of the bricks down here without destroying anything."

ABYDOS, EGYPT, THE FEATURE, THE TOMB, JULY 5TH, 9:08 A.M.:

It took three days with a rock saw to create an opening large enough for Lisa to get into Ḥaāmer's room. For the time being, Sanders would not fit. She lay on her belly, photographing through the opening before reaching through to hand objects back to Sanders. Once she had cleared a sufficient area for her to get inside, Lisa wiggled in on her belly with chad scraping inside her waistband. To get out, she lay on her back with her arms extended over her head for Sanders to pull her out.

"We need to bring your vacuum to remove the loose stuff. Let's enlarge the opening soon. I'm not liking the indignity," she grumbled.

"Oh, I don't know," he responded. "I'm rather enjoying it."

She screwed her mouth, making an ugly face, but laughed at his remarks.

Lisa sat inside the opening, photographing location, examining, and recording comments about every object she picked it up with her gloved hands. She handed them out to Sanders who created a holding area, placing them on a large linen sheet. As Sanders predicted, every square foot of the floor was covered with Ḥaāmer's possessions.

She provided several organic chips from the floor to Sanders for carbon dating. He carried them to Cairo on his next junket. Slivers from a smashed wooden chair, and what appeared to be a shriveled piece of desiccated fruit were some of the 'representative' artifacts sent to Tu'hut. She agonized whether she should attempt to reconstruct the chair shattered into splinters from a fallen ceiling chunk, but Sanders shook his head, saying the chair was beyond repair.

He could have dated these items with his equipment, but for authenticity, he wanted an independent, documented dating for the tomb. Plus he didn't want to spend his time doing lab work. The Cairo Museum technicians were the logical choice.

Lisa's goal was the wooden funerary box resting in the center of the room. Stelae surrounding it proclaimed Ḥaāmer would triumph in the hereafter. Lisa had read enough hieroglyphs in the room to pique her curiosity about the cause of Ḥaāmer's death. She wanted to x-ray and date the mummy to see if she might find a clue.

Ḥaāmer's name always appeared in a serekh, indicating she must be royalty; even if the Horus falcon was missing. The sheer quantity of artifacts indicated Ḥaāmer's importance. A common person would have only a few items.

Lisa worked diligently, but carefully cataloging and moving the numerous items blocking her path to the funerary box. *Archaeologists must have enormous patience,* she told herself repeatedly, as if only half believing the mantra herself.

She passed the items through the opening to Sanders, requiring her to get up and down repeatedly, exhaustedly. Her eyes fell to a stelae centered by the casket that stood tilted forward and downward. She had another two meters of area to clear before she would be able to read it.

"Lisa!" shouted Sanders.

Lisa jumped. She turned to see him bent down peering through the opening.

"I'm sorry I startled you," he said. "I have to go to Cairo again to see Dr. Tu'hut. I feel as if I'm a shuttle diplomat. In the meantime, it will slow our progress."

"Diplomacy can be a very powerful archaeological tool," she informed him, remembering her recent return from purgatory. Besides she liked to pinch him. His look and growl did not stop her from continuing her impishness. "So who're you really seeing in Cairo?"

"He swears it's to talk about the project."

"No, I mean, what girl are you seeing on the side?" her eyebrow arched. Sanders finally caught her drift and smiled back at her.

"You'll just have to come to Cairo with me and find out."

"You're not getting rid of me that easily."

"I hope we get the carbon dating," he commented seriously. "I want to see how old the place is. Hopefully, I'll be back by nightfall."

Lisa nodded. "I've plenty to do to keep me busy and out of trouble in the mean time."

"Yeah, right. Just be sure you do...keep out of trouble."

Sanders retreated back down the corridor to climb out of the tomb. Their pleasant interactions lifted Lisa's spirits.

I need to be gentle on him. Perhaps I can win him back.

ABYDOS, EGYPT, THE ARCHAEOLOGICAL TRAILER, JULY 5TH, 2:41 P.M.:

Anwar sat at the computer console building his terrorist's dossiers and cataloging Ḥaāmer's possessions. His back and neck ached from his continued hunched posture, but his progressing efforts pleased him. However, he currently was fighting the powerful spotlights in the chamber supporting the archeologist's work.

That blasted light!

Anwar looked at an object; but the backlighting was blinding him. The light was at a high oblique angle.

How am I supposed to work with this problem?

He turned his eyes away from the object to save them and he glanced at the wall. A picture jumped at him—a picture of a young, ancient Egyptian woman.

CAIRO, EGYPT, THE MILITARY BASE, JULY 6TH, 10:42 A.M.:

A smiling Dr. Tu'hut met Bill at the Army base.

"How does your investigation go?"

"I'm making progress."

"Good. I'm making my decision about who will open the tomb and make the full exploration. So when will artifacts begin to arrive in Cairo?"

The movement of artifacts was a quandary for Bill because he didn't know how to respond. He felt Dr. Tu'hut's remark about exploration leadership was an attempt to blackmail him into transferring artifacts. He wanted to place them back in their natural habitat resealing the feature just as Lisa and he had discussed, but he didn't know how to keep them safe from looting. He felt, on the other hand, Dr. Tu'hut wouldn't accept his decision to hold the artifacts. Ultimately, that responsibility would fall on the Egyptians to protect the feature.

"I'm being very careful in this exploration as you can appreciate," he temporized. "I've brought videos of the chamber that will excite your curiosity I'm sure."

"I want to review them with you. Your carbon dating is complete. We will go to the museum laboratory first for the results then we will go to lunch and plan your further exploration."

I don't need to be micro-managed from Cairo.

He did owe the Secretary General a report, but he felt he could manage quite well in the field. He smiled at Dr. Tu'hut in response, wondering just how much the good doctor was taken in by his *politicking.* At the Cairo Museum, Bill followed Dr. Tu'hut to a back area where daily archaeological work occurred. Dr. Tu'hut greeted a technician in Egyptian then continued in English for Bill's benefit.

"They have completed all four samples that you brought the last time. The sample size was excellent, Doctor. We were able to give an equal amount to each technician. You know the process is destructive. I wanted independent readings made by two different people so the results could be correlated and verified."

"Yes," agreed Bill.

"The technicians tell me that they agree within one percent which is phenomenally close for this type of work. I would have been pleased with fifteen percent. I was specific that they should work independently, our standard policy. I wanted them to draw their own, separate conclusions. The variance among all of the samples correlates very well. All of the ages of the samples are within five percent. Did you pick samples from various objects?"

"That's standard procedure when an abundance of material is available. The videos will show you that there's an abundance of material. So what's the age?"

Dr. Tu'hut smiled at Bill. He had been holding back on purpose to raise Bill's anticipation.

"Five thousand three hundred ten years plus or minus sixteen years. More than 3250 BCE. You do realize the significance of this dating?"

Bill let Dr. Tu'hut's statement soak in for a moment, then realized Dr. Tu'hut wasn't just building his anticipation.

That's more than a thousand years before the date Lisa and I are theorizing!

"That precedes the first dynasty!" said Bill.

Dr. Tu'hut nodded his head vigorously. His beaming smile wasn't just one of pleasantry.

"That is correct, Doctor, and from what you have been telling me and what I remember seeing, there are significant numbers of artifacts."

"This is not possible. This makes no sense. Are your technicians sure of their estimate?"

Dr. Tu'hut gave his field director a concerned look.

"This is why I had the two men check each other. This is why I had you fly to Cairo. This is a significant find, Dr. Sanders. This feature precedes the first dynasty by only two hundred years." Dr. Tu'hut raised his hands and shoulders in amazement. "This time is unexplored. We have no information. Until now we knew only one sentence. Now, we will write volumes. We have a great discovery. This is fantastic, Doctor!"

Dr. Tu'hut pounded Bill on the shoulder who stared dumbly at him.

"But this doesn't make sense. I have trouble believing that it happened as early as the sixth dynasty. Events and items are occurring too soon."

He had the Secretary General all but hopping from one foot to the other in front of him. He wanted to make the man stop shouting at him so he could sit and think.

"There must be some mistake. Certain things couldn't have occurred until much later—the Book of the Dead and Osiris."

"I am certain the dates are correct, Doctor. Of what artifacts do you speak?"

"I didn't bring the disk of the most important one, but I'll show you what I have already."

Dr. Tu'hut looked at his watch.

"Immediately after lunch."

Fidgeting, Bill knew that he was stuck going to lunch with the Secretary General. He also knew that this could be a drawn out affair with Egyptians eating much slower than Americans—more of a social affair than a refueling. He didn't wish to offend his employer, but Dr. Tu'hut had no idea the bomb he'd set off inside him with the dating.

He needed to think then talk with Lisa. There had to be some mistake. Many of the artifacts they'd seen didn't come about until the middle of the Old Kingdom—two hundred years later maybe closer to three. Two hundred years was a significant time span. Elements within Egypt just didn't occur out of sequence. Event three never occurred before event one. The things they were discovering just didn't make sense given this timeline. Burying people in caves hadn't been invented yet. The Book of the Dead and Osiris were not invented, or at least not common.

The parts of the puzzle weren't fitting together, but wasn't that what Lisa kept telling him from their initial viewing? Bill accepted the report from the technician hoping Lisa would be able to decipher the information to shed light on the discrepancies.

"Many points of view on this find are contradictory," Bill said.

Dr. Tu'hut became curious. "In what way?"

Bill didn't like leaving Lisa out of the discussion because he felt he was taking credit for her work, but he had her interests to protect. He began to describe the feature as he understood it.

"There're so many contradictions it's hard to know where to start. Why are two young women honored with statues of the gods? A personal note from Āakhu to Ḥaāmer paraphrasing the Book of the Dead. The timeline is too compressed."

Dr. Tu'hut became increasingly excited as Bill continued to describe the contradictions for the next several minutes.

"I have to come south and visit the site as soon as possible. Unfortunately, with the death of the Antiquities Minister, his duties as well as mine fall on me. I have to catch up. I want to see these things you describe, but they will have to wait. You are making me more and more curious. I now want to see the video you have brought with you."

Bill could see the inner turmoil working on the Secretary General. Dr. Tu'hut broke into a smile.

"We will have to...what do you Americans call it? We will have to get food fast. Perhaps a hamburger...I am joking."

Bill smiled. They were making progress. As it was, it took over an hour to complete their lunch even as Dr. Tu'hut grumbled.

"You Americans eat too quickly. It will give you bad digestion. Let us see your recording."

Bill played the video through once without commentary then again stopping when he had a comment or whenever Dr. Tu'hut had a question. Bill could tell the work excited the Secretary General from his movement and the questions being raised.

"I need you back on site tonight unless you are having problems with the terrorists?"

Bill shook his head negatively. "I'm not."

"That is well, but their activities here in Cairo are increasing. The skirmishes between the muslim radicals and government troops are increasing. The terrorist acts are causing this. You will have to be careful at the site. Call me daily with reports on your progress."

ABYDOS, EGYPT, THE ARCHAEOLOGICAL TRAILER, JULY 6TH, 5:12 P.M.:

Lisa decided she wanted a third mind working on the problems they were encountering. She hadn't spoken with Randall Crain since she left Cairo so she thought this was an opportune time.

The last time she spoke with Randall, she'd called him in the middle of the night. She glanced at her watch, mentally making the seven hour conversion.

It'll be midmorning there. He shouldn't mind my calling.

She called Providence. Randall picked up on the third ring.

"Hey gal, how are you doing?"

"I went south to the feature and am working on the team."

"So you're out of Cairo. Good. Tell me about that adventure."

Lisa gave him a thumbnail sketch of what had happened since she left Cairo even telling him about the trailer incident.

"Good lord, Lisa. They were going to kidnap or worse shoot you. I'm worried about you, girl. I don't want you getting hurt."

"I can take care of myself."

"That sounds tough, but the people you're dealing with are pretty nasty. I'm following the deaths on the news. The Egyptians have lost a couple ministers and a bunch of citizens. I'm not excited about your being involved."

"Now you're beginning to sound like my project manager."

"He sounds like a sensible guy."

"You would stick up for him," Lisa groaned.

"There's nothing as important as you. Keep that in mind."

"Thanks, Randall. I called you about something else. This feature is turning up one anomaly after another. Nothing really makes sense."

"Tell me about it."

She told him the facts that she felt were relevant.

"Lisa, that's a real mystery—you're right, nothing adds up. It's wonderful you've so much material to work with though. Amazing, actually. But in your report, you'll have to explain all of it. What's the age?"

"Don't know. I'm hoping that Bill can tell me this evening."

"Bill?"

"Bill Sanders, the project manager in charge. He's in Cairo now."

"Oh, *Bill....*"

"It's not like that."

"Right. When you were in Cairo, I told you I knew Dr. Sanders by reputation. He's a good man, Lisa. In the mean time, I'll think about what you've told me. If I come up with a theory, I'll e-mail you and you do the same. For now keep out of trouble, safe."

"OK, OK."

"Say hello to *Bill* for me," he chuckled, hanging up before she could respond.

EGYPT, THE TERRORIST VILLAGE, JULY 6TH, 5:15 P.M.:

The terrorists walked the streets of the deserted village, dragging the bodies into piles. The television cameras swept over the disgusting wreckage of human life pausing on a news reporter now well known on Egyptian streaming Internet. He reported the latest death count. A tremor of disgust rose in his voice as did the bile in his throat. He suppressed a gag as he always did after watching the scene he'd witnessed several times before. The cameras were already turned off as he retched. Saladin looked at the reporter with no sympathy, turned and walked back to the helicopter, seeking relief from the heat. When the reporter finished, he joined the minister in the aircraft.

"You are lucky I put up with you," said Saladin. The reporter hung his head realizing that in a short time he'd be a victim just as these poor wretches in the street. He knew too much.

ABYDOS, EGYPT, ḤAĀMER'S ROOM, JULY 7TH, 8:37 A.M.:

Lisa looked forward to her labors today. She had cleared the remainder of the artifacts between the door and the funerary box. The ancient Egyptians placed the box on a pedestal of native rock left in the center of the excavated room. Figures carved into the pedestal with their arms upraised appeared to hold the box in their hands, providing a beautiful image. She had reviewed her archaeological records while eating dinner. She read Robert's notes and pictures to see whether they correlated with her explorations. They didn't appear to, though she could tell that Robert was doing some wonderful work.

Archeologists never have enough hours in the day. We review our findings at night while the troops sleep.

She suppressed a yawn.

Last evening, she moved the ushabtui figures that encircled the pedestal. She found a small bowl at the base of the funerary box. At the time of the interment, it probably contained water from the Nile to be poured over the casket. Its simplicity and perfect symmetry impressed her. She viewed it on the video and wanted to examine it today.

She planned to x-ray Ḥaāmer, if she could remove the lid of the funerary box without damaging it. Diggers would lower the x-ray machine into the tunnel.

Bill didn't return. I wonder about his numerous trips. We haven't discussed his files either. They've disappeared, but what's going on? He promised to return with the carbon dating. I hope he's back today.

Worse, she had a nagging concern about the captain. He spent inordinate time on the computer, analyzing her data, but completed very little. Nurse-maiding him did not appeal to her with no extra time. When she went looking for him the previous night to discuss his progress, he was not in camp.

Where the heck is he? The lieutenant has no idea.

On her way to the tomb, Lisa met Anwar. He looked the worse for wear. He must have been up a considerable portion of the night.

"How is the data reduction going?"

"I should finish today," he shrugged. Lisa wondered at his ambivalence.

"If you're spending too much time on your other project, you need to complete the archaeology."

"No, problem. It just takes time," he said irritably.

He's tired. I won't push on him now, but I'd better get him finished or Sanders will be on my back.

Anwar headed to the archeological trailer. She met the lieutenant on her way to the diggers' tents.

"How are your explorations going?" he asked speaking to her in English. He always spoke to her in English for he wanted to perfect and maintain his language skills.

"Fine. I'm going to x-ray the mummy." she explained, as a way of checking her own thoughts. "I need the diggers to carry the x-ray equipment to the tomb entrance."

She instructed the diggers then went to the second tomb entrance. The lieutenant accompanied her from the camp to the tomb entrance with the usual two soldiers accompanying them. "Has anyone been here since I closed yesterday?"

He consulted a sheaf of papers he was carrying.

"No one, ma'am. We follow your procedures exactly. We pass all that happens during each guard duty to the next group. You closed the entrance at seven last evening when you left. No one except each guard team has been here until you came. No one is allowed inside."

"Thank you, lieutenant."

She watched the diggers drag the equipment through the opening—lowering it on a platform suspended from her trapeze. After they hefted it down the corridor to Ḥaāmer's door, she uncrated the x-ray, setting it up ready for use.

"Go back to the trailer and bring back the stack of concrete blocks and timbers. Thank you."

She examined the wooden casket to determine how she should open it. It had been painted then sealed with beeswax. Although she was confident that the funerary box had remained sealed, the majority of the seam still being filled in, she could see several places around the lid where the wax had popped out. She hated 'breaking-in.' Until she completed recording the untouched seam, she hesitated starting the process of opening the box. She circled the box twice with the camcorder, walking slowly, recording her translation of the hieroglyphs and her additional comments. Using a high-definition digital camera, she made the trip around twice more taking overlapping still photographs. She collected the small bits of loose beeswax hoping it could be dated. The gaps indicated the spots where she should start.

She applied a very thin knife to the seam. The beeswax was so dry with age that it popped out. Frustrated, she thought about what she could do better, resolving that heating a knife in an acetylene flame before trying to cut the wax would be the best option. Since this method was destructive to the paint and seal, she decided to wait for Dr. Sanders to see if he had a better plan.

Lisa shimmied out into the cooridor to rest her back. She remembered the small bowl she wanted to examine. She went to the area containing the labeled artifacts. Each area equated to a different place within Ḥaāmer's room. She knew specifically where the interment bowl should be and knew instantly that it was missing.

She spent the next thirty minutes searching all the other areas to be sure the bowl hadn't inadvertently been placed in the wrong spot. The bowl wasn't among the artifacts. Using the camcorder, she recorded all of the artifacts in the corridor. Later today, probably the evening, she would use the captain's processed work to determine if any other artifacts were missing She hoped she was simply overlooking the bowl among everything else. She had the sinking feeling the bowl was stolen. Having dealt with artifact theft before, she was outraged.

Either the guards lied or a digger carried the bowl out of the tomb. Only these people were allowed near or inside the second entrance. She would have the diggers' personal belongings searched by Captain Jagardii, but the soldiers guarding the door presented another problem. She would obtain the list of the names of those on duty through the night. She would recommend to Captain Jagardii that the pairs of guards be shuffled so friends would be separated.

Damn!

"Lieutenant! I want everyone out and back to camp. Please post a fresh set of guards at the entrance. Ones who didn't serve here yesterday."

"Ma'am?"

"I want everyone who served yesterday to be assembled in the camp parade area."

"Yes, Ma'am."

Thirty minutes later found everyone who had been on duty the previous day, standing in a small circle in the center of the camp—the four diggers and the army guards. Captain Jagardii came from the trailer to investigate the disturbance. Lisa drew the captain and lieutenant aside for a hushed conference.

"Captain, an artifact is missing. I want to know if anyone else was in the tomb? The people assembled in the center of the camp are the only ones who were by or inside the feature yesterday."

"Allah preserve the man who steals objects from the past. Lieutenant, you and I will personally conduct the search of these men's belongings."

Taking the two soldiers inside the trailer, Lisa showed them the video display of the missing bowl. After an intensive search, the missing artifact was not found.

"In the future, I will have the men searched when they leave the tomb," said Captain Jagardii. "I will debrief everyone to determine whether anyone entered or left the site."

Lisa nodded.

"The guards who were paired together yesterday will not be together again. The soldiers guarding the entrance will be mixed and rotated daily to stop a conspiracy being formed."

"Thank you, captain. I'd like a full inspection of the camp. I want to find the missing artifact. I'll review the disks to determine if anything else was stolen. I'm closing the tomb until Dr. Sanders returns."

Captain Jagardii wore a frozen mask of rage. He nodded.

"It will be done," Captain Jagardii said flatly. "I will kill whoever did this."

Lisa agreed the thief needed to be stopped.

ABYDOS, EGYPT, THE FEATURE, JULY 7TH, 3:43 P.M.:

As the military helicopter neared the feature, Bill's excitement mounted. The previous day with Dr. Tu'hut ended too late to make the trip back. This morning, he went to the Cairo museum to review the notes with the two technicians who did the carbon dating. They proved to him beyond any doubt the dates were as accurate as could be produced using the dating technique. What was Lisa going to think when he returned with the news? Their exploration placed the feature in the center of the Old Kingdom. Now he knew this tomb preceded the First Dynasty—before the Old Kingdom era began. He updated himself on the period before he made the trek back. The information was minimal.

Amazing.

The remainder of the day, he searched with the headman through the cemetery city to see if they could find Khidr or hear news of him. They checked his local haunts, but found no sign of him. They talked with his friends, but discovered nothing further. Bill's dark concerns were increasing.

The helicopter landed just above the feature and almost immediately lifted off for the return to Cairo. Bill trudged down the highway. The camp seemed quiet enough, just as he had left it. He felt relieved and slightly piqued that he'd worried.

He knocked on the trailer door, wondering whether Lisa was there or inside the tomb. The curtains drew aside and she flung open the door.

"Hi, how are you?" he asked.

"I'm pleased to see you. I was worried when you didn't return yesterday."

"I'm sorry I upset you. It was too late to fly."

She nodded, concern painting her face.

"Thanks, but I have bad news for you," she said.

His spirits fell. Lisa definitely looked serious. She also looked exhausted.

"Was there another attack?"

"No, no. Nothing like that. An artifact was stolen."

"Stolen! How did it happen? We're being so careful. What's missing?"

"We don't know how it happened, but this morning, I went to Ḥaāmer's room looking for a small bowl I'd seen, but I couldn't find it. I recorded all of our holding areas then asked the computer to locate the bowl among everything."

"That's a good idea."

"Yeah, but it wasn't there. When I discovered the object was stolen, I shut down the feature. Captain Jagardii posted new guards. He searched the diggers and the soldiers guarding the feature yesterday. Nothing! Captain Jagardii is livid. I think he'd personally rip apart any thief. I compared the recordings against each other to determine if anything else was missing. The bowl was the only one. It's small enough to conceal in a robe or a military pack."

"Shit!"

"I had Captain Jagardii change procedures with the guards. You know we've been strip searching everyone back in camp, but I changed to having a tent outside the second entrance with the two officers managing it. It's not a great plan, but that's all I've come up with."

"It will be rough on everyone. It's manpower intensive It'll delay entering and exiting the tomb, but I think its appropriate."

"So if we're done with that crap. How did your trip to Cairo go?" she asked.

He paused, smiled, nodding at her.

"Actually, wonderfully. I have the carbon dating results. I spent today in the Cairo museum boning up on the period so I'd have half a chance of keeping up with you."

She smiled at him for the first time since his arrival.

"Thanks, don't keep me in suspense how old is the feature?"

"Fifty-three hundred ten years plus or minus sixteen years."

Lisa thought for a second, her eyes opening wide with realization.

"That's greater than 3250 BCE. That's impossible. You're pulling my leg," she said.

"I know it's impossible and no, I'm not pulling your leg. I didn't believe it myself. So I checked all of the results with the technicians. I followed their notes and procedures to be sure they were accurate. The dating is correct."

"The First Dynasty began between 2700 and 2900 BCE," she said.

"Yes, I know. The tomb is pre-Dynastic."

"I don't believe we picked up objects handed down from previous generations. The samples looked reasonable for dating. The dried fruit was the most representative."

"If we'd by coincidence picked only older objects, the objects would not correlate among themselves. Some objects would be significantly older than others. All of the objects are peers. Normally in an investigation, I wouldn't open the funerary box, but we need to date the mummy and her wrappings."

"Bill, it's not possible. Osiris and Isis weren't invented yet. Ptah was around. Ra was on stage, but Osiris came much later. We're talking apples and oranges here."

"Yes, I know, I know," he said. "The legend of Osiris settled down during the second dynasty—three to four hundred years later. Yet, we've direct mention of Osiris and Isis in a final form. The religious dogma began settling at this time. Abydos is the shrine of Osiris. They may be a little earlier than the rest of Egypt."

"We have to solve this mystery."

"The Egyptians didn't plant this tomb as a mystery. I agree we must make sense of it," he said.

Lisa stared at him. She stopped looking over the top of her glasses, pushing them up her nose. He wondered what she was thinking. Maybe a big fall was lurking, but he couldn't see it. He knew they'd followed archaeological procedure.

"I'll contemplate that one, boss. In the mean time, what'll we do with our modern problem?"

"Continue our exploration. I want your new security procedures implemented. I want to check the artifacts daily for theft. So what did you cook for dinner?"

He laughed at her shocked face. "I'm just joking. Maybe I'll invite you out to the restaurant down the road."

"Maybe I'm going to start throwing things at you."

ABYDOS, EGYPT, THE ARCHAEOLOGICAL TRAILER, JULY 8TH, 6:23 A.M.:

At dawn, the two archaeologists continued their work. They crunched the data to determine whether anything was stolen during the night. The computer reported nothing new missing.

"Anwar's efforts allow us to check the objects," Lisa told Bill. "He did all of the categorization."

"I want to speak with you about the captain," he said steadily. "I know you are high on his work, but I'm concerned"

"He disappears at night. No one knows where he goes," she admitted.

"He could doctor the videos so objects appear to be there. Their value makes the effort worthwhile."

"That would take a lot of technical savvy. You have it, but who else does. Damn. I hate loosing him as a resource," moaned Lisa. "If he's legit."

"Thanks, for the compliment. He could be trained in Military Intelligence. I think he's a risk. Haven't you told me he uses enormous amounts of computer time?"

"Yes, but we're so short-handed. How are we going to get the work done?"

"We have an artifact missing. If he's doctoring the results, I don't want anything else gone."

"OK, OK, I'll have him stop."

"Thanks, Lisa."

* * *

The archeologists spent the morning enlarging the hole so Sanders could go inside too.

"You remember it took Carter over a year to open Tut's sarcophagus," said Sanders once they both were inside.

"Yeah, and it weighed one and a half tons with three embedded coffins, one of solid gold buried in resin. I don't think we're dealing with the same thing. It's not big enough."

The archaeologists began their work on Ḥaāmer's funerary box. Lisa explained her thoughts from the previous day. To facilitate their work, they built a free standing platform from concrete blocks set around the box on tarps to protect the floor. From this platform, they assembled a series of pulleys for lifting the lid and the mummy. They set up halogen lamps to illuminate their workspace.

"One of us should apply pressure on a corner of the lid while the other holds steady pressure along the major seam," she suggested. "If anything cracks, we'll have to stop. We must heat a knife to melt the beeswax, otherwise it just pops out damaging more then I want. I did a test yesterday. The lid is dryer than tinder. I hate using a torch in here."

They worked on the fragile lid for several more hours stopping periodically for water, until they were finally able to cut the beeswax all the way around. The lid was a half inch thick. Once the seam opened, they attached multiple silicon gel coated plastic clips to the lid, lifting it straight up eight feet with the pulleys to move it out of the way. They placed a board underneath and lowered the lid onto it.

The casket was not nested, but contained the mummy in the only box. A linen shroud covered the wrapped mummy. They spayed the linen with a modern resin designed to solidify the cloth, but not change it chemically. Beneath the shroud were flowers, amulets, and the residue of ancient unctions. They attached their plastic clips to the mummy, resting on her sand bed. Using the pulley system, they lifted Ḥaāmer above the funerary box. They placed her on a sheet, allowing them to move her without exerting additional pressure on her or the wrappings. They had no intention of unwrapping her. They positioned the x-ray equipment to expose sequential skeletal segments without further movement of the mummy. Leaving Ḥaāmer's room, they viewed a black and white florescent picture on their computer screen in the hallway.

"She appears to be sixteen or seventeen from her teeth. Look at the third molar. Her skull appears intact and undamaged"

"I concur," said Lisa. "She was an adult in their society. We'll have to determine whether she was married."

"Right."

They turned off the equipment, crawling back into Ḥaāmer's room. They repositioned the x-ray on Ḥaāmer's neck and shoulders.

"She appears to have died of acute tuberculosis. Look at the reductions of the calcium in the spinal column," Lisa said, pointing at the computer terminal.

"Yeah," said Bill peering at the thin white lines at the ends of the spinal vertebra. "We now know the ancient disease referred to by the hieroglyphs, but tissue samples will confirm our suspicions. We can insert a hypodermic needle into a muscle group through the wrappings to obtain a tissue sample. We'll need Dr. Tu'hut's permission."

Lisa made a face. Bill smiled at her.

"I'd like to rehydrate a tissue sample, carbon date it and obtain a DNA analysis for historical purposes. If we obtain additional remains, we'll be able to determine whether she is a member of the family group."

Lisa nodded. "This answers several of my questions about the young woman. I can access the room across the hall. I hope to find her consort."

"Let's finish x-raying her now. Tomorrow, I will bring my CT machine to scan her. I'd like to produce a 3D picture of her. We can use the clay molding software to build a lifelike appearance."

"You're the boss," grinned Lisa.

ABYDOS, EGYPT, THE FEATURE, DUSK, JULY 9, 6:53 P.M.:

Lisa's shoulders ached from her afternoon exertions. This was becoming a chronic occurrence each evening. She swallowed two pills to ease the tension and pain. She needed to be mindful of her stress. She would dismiss the aches in her back, shoulders and arms caused by the physical exertions, but she had to watch for the aches growing in her jaws, teeth and back of her neck. She knew the warnings of stress related pain. She popped the tab on a diet soft drink, guzzling the welcome cold down her throat. She craved her bed, but she craved relaxation more.

She stepped from the trailer door and looked up to the heights above her.

How beautiful. I need to look at the stars and desert again.

She locked the trailer and headed across the feature. She made the slow, tedious climb to the summit, concentrating on her footing, not wanting her weariness to cause a careless slip. She warned the sentinel of her approach as she came to the top. Barely discernable in the fading light, she knew he would be on hyper-alert with the noise she produced during her climb.

"You should not be here," he told her.

Agreeing, she set off across the top of the cliffs looking for the spot to sit. The captain was well hidden and Lisa wouldn't have seen him if she hadn't expected him to be there. As with the sentinel, she warned him of her approach. He grunted, but didn't chastise her for climbing the cliffs. Perhaps he understood her need to be here.

"Come to observe the sunset again?" he asked.

"And the desert. I've come to relax, to look into the past, to see what this tomb is telling me. I've come to forget my troubles and to allow the physical aches of my body to ease out of me."

He snorted.

"You come seeking much."

"No, not much, just a few simple pleasures."

His head tilted toward her continuing to contemplate her. She slid down to the ground beside the rock, her back leaning against it. Closing her eyes, feeling the heat soak threw her, she took a deep breath letting it out slowly.

"The last time I asked you about your appreciation for your heritage. From the work you do for me, it is apparent you have a great love for it."

She sensed his nod without seeing it.

"Yes, I study the ancients, but it's obvious you understand far more than me about that time in our history."

"With this tomb, I understand very damned little."

"What do you mean?" he asked.

"The artifact evidence does not support the carbon dating. This tomb is pre-Dynastic."

"That old. Amazing. I'm sure you'll understand it. You are an expert."

"Thank you. I have made it my life's work just as you have made protecting Egypt your life's work."

He snorted again. "I've been poor at that. I haven't caught these damnable terrorists. How did you begin studying our heritage?"

Amazing. He's asking the questions again.

"I told you before, I grew up here. I gained a great appreciation and respect for what is yours."

He did not respond immediately.

"It's not mine. It's not even Egypt's. If anything, it belongs to all mankind. Egypt is a great treasure for all man. The great art and stories have meaning for everyone. Every time I look at the objects from the tomb, I see their beauty. Every time I hear your translations of what they said, I hear them speaking. These people lived, loved and died. What right do we have to disturb their death. Still I can't escape from my curiosity, my fascination."

I've only suspected the depth of his love for his heritage. I need to keep him speaking.

Murmuring her agreement, she waited for him to continue.

"Our ancient myths tell of what they would do for love."

Like Ḥaāmer and Āakhu.

She searched her mind for the specific story to which he referred. He got to his feet.

"Doctor, it's time to go," he said taking her by the hand, another thing she didn't expect.

"My name is Lisa."

"Then you must call me Anwar."

He led her down the cliff face. Lisa wondered at what she had just heard.

* * *

"Did you stop him from working with the computer? Did you speak with him about his computer usage?"

"No, Bill, I didn't, but I will. I haven't found the right moment, OK? I will."

His eyebrows rose. Bracing for the barrage, she waited for his chewing out. He shook his head negatively as he went out the trailer door. In the past, he would have told her off.

"I trust you," he threw over his shoulder. This time Lisa's eyebrows lifted.

ABYDOS, EGYPT, THE ARCHAEOLOGICAL TRAILER, JULY 10th, 12;00 P.M.:

Lisa entered the trailer, finding Anwar sitting at the computer. Perhaps this was good a time for their discussion.

"Anwar, we need to talk," Lisa sighed.

"You look unhappy."

"I am. I want to talk with you about your use of the computer."

Anwar regarded her evenly. "Yes?"

"You are using large amounts of computer time without progress on the archaeology. Would you please explain?"

"I've prepared a gift for you—my contribution. I've completed the work that you requested, but I made an additional discovery."

"Your categorization is excellent. What is your discovery?"

Anwar turned to the computer and brought up the photo enhancement program. Calling up a project file, Lisa saw the flat, polished unremarkable wall of Ḥaāmer's room.

"When the light was set right, I saw strange shapes," he showed her the purple smudge. "Then with the light set at a blinding angle, I saw this."

Anwar showed her the woman. The oblique angle distorted her.

"Wow! The original paint has faded, but their tones remain. Through color interference you've developed a picture."

"It occurred to me I could turn the image as if I were facing it and improve the colors. I eventually developed this picture."

Lisa knew he would have used an enormous amount of computer and personal time to create the image. On the screen, Lisa saw the freeze of the wall. The person was the sad faced woman in the hall, standing with the gods—hieroglyphic streams ran everywhere. It would take hours to read all of it.

"Amazing! Please, keep working on all of the walls. If you need me to place the lights in the room, I will help you. We need to do a three dimensional, high definition scan of the wall to develop the texture and color. Maybe we can do the initial work in the computer."

*   *   *

"Bill, we need to talk about Anwar."

Chapter 18

mḥ ḥsbt 18 ꜣbd 4 prt sw 25 ḫr ḥm n wsỉr

Meḥ

Year 18, Month 4 of Peret, Day 25 under the Majesty of Ạsạr

Ṭeḥuti came to the temple at dawn to pray for strength, for success, and for love. He prayed that Neb-t·ḥe-t had been mistaken and that the road which brought him back to Āakhu would not be long or dangerous and that the happy ending he envisioned with Āakhu would not be at great cost to either of them. He had just concluded those prayers and left the temple for the governor's house and an audience with the new chief wife when a nervous young man, gasping for breath in the mid-morning heat, blocked his way.

"Are you Ṭeḥuti?"

"I am."

"There's a cart overturned in the hills," the youth said. "Children are hurt."

"Which way?" Ṭeḥuti asked.

"Follow me," the young man said, turning away.

Ṭeḥuti followed at a jogging pace from the temple along streets the merchants used to bring their wares to the market. Their route left the city, ascending into the hills bordering the eastern desert. Dust clouded the air from scuffing feet and the occasional cart still heading into Meh. The sun, one-quarter of the way above the eastern horizon, blazed bright and hot.

The young man increased the pace and Ṭeḥuti, on his left, matched him stride for stride. The path followed the contours of the land. There was no other traffic, allowing the two runners to increase their speed.

Ṭeḥuti was pleased that he did not tire as quickly as he once might have. His legs were strengthened by his days on the boat and the hard work that had occupied him from Aten's taking flight in the east until his landing once more in the west. He thought briefly of Aamaam and her orphans, Uha-tet, Netch, Sabi and the others. He thought of them scattered, broken, about the wreckage of a cart. Any fatigue he might have felt vanished again.

His guide turned off the main cart path onto a series of smaller, less-traveled paths used by the herders.

"Is it much farther?" Ṭeḥuti called.

"No," the young man huffed over his shoulder.

The incline increased as the path climbed to rejoin the road that had turned back along the face of the rise into the eastern desert. Ṭeḥuti felt the strain in his legs as they flexed and pushed him forward. The air seemed to both burn and parch Ṭeḥuti from the inside out as he inhaled greater breaths of it.

The path wandered among the reddish-brown rocks and sand, opening onto a small ledge just below the main road. The young man stopped and Ṭeḥuti stopped with him.

A group of priests were gathered, young priests, unfamiliar to Ṭeḥuti from his days in Uas. They watched the two men in silence. There was no overturned cart, nor were there any children—injured or otherwise. Ṭeḥuti focused on quieting his breathing as he studied the men. His companion, younger and fitter, slithered over to join their group.

"There is no accident," Ṭeḥuti stated.

"No," said the leader, a young, hard-faced man with a scar along the line of his jaw.

The young man came forward and placed a hand on Ṭeḥuti's shoulder. The look in his eyes indicated no particular malice as he made a fist of his other hand and drove it hard into Ṭeḥuti just below his ribs. Ṭeḥuti doubled over and fell to the ground on hands and knees, trying to gasp once more for air and to vomit at the same time. A couple of agonizing breaths later, before he could regain his wind, a vicious kick to his ribs flipped him over on his back.

Pain tightened lungs and ribs. His vision darkened and for a moment the blinding sun was gone. Ṭeḥuti continued struggling for air, instinctively drawing his arms and legs close for protection. He was not aware that his vision and the eye watering sunlight had returned until a shadow enveloped his head.

"Why?" Ṭeḥuti cried out. "Are you from Maaạ or from Set?"

"Maaạ and Pharaoh and Set all want you dead. One for what you were, one for what you are, one for what you could be. How could you have made so many powerful enemies so quickly and not feared one of them would kill you?"

Other shadows passed over Ṭeḥuti as the priests joined their leader and gathered about him. Ṭeḥuti looked up to see them standing over him, grimacing almost as if they were also in pain.

"The word has come that you are cursed. We are to beat you and leave you here to Ptah's judgment."

"You are mistaken," Ṭeḥuti wheezed.

"There is no mistake. You are Ṭeḥuti, the priest from Uas."

"It isn't true," Ṭeḥuti replied. He struggled to roll over and push to his hands and knees once more. "If you would let me—"

Another kick sent him back to the ground. Dust filled his eyes, nose and mouth.

The priests closed the circle around him. Blows suddenly rained down on him from all sides. The first several hurt enough that he cried out, but after that the sensation faded, as did the taste of blood in his mouth and the smell of dust in his nostrils. His vision faded again, taking with it the image of eyes bright and feverish with hatred above the crooked, almost salivating smiles of young men who looked hardly human at all.

In his own private night, his thoughts wandered. *Is this death?*

After an unfathomable time his sight brightened again. He felt warmth and peace. He saw the green of the River valley stretched out before him. *Is it possible? Can it be that a lowly priest like me could be given such an honor?*

A voice called to him. He turned to see Āakhu approaching through a field of new flax—Āakhu smiling, Āakhu in a sheer summer shift, her breasts lifting and falling, teasing him from beneath the revealing fabric. She drifted sensuously toward him through the shin-high flax, like Aih drifting across the summer evening sky.

"How can this be?" he called. "Āakhu, how can you be with me here in Amennt when you are with Maaạ in Meḥ?"

Āakhu reached and pressed against him. He closed his arms about her, savoring her closeness. He drew his fingers slowly up and down her back, excited by the supple softness of her oiled skin. Her breath was warm on his neck as she stood on her toes to whisper in his ear: "Maaạ and Meḥ were of another place. I am yours forever now. We have waited long for this day. Come my love, let us take our pleasure here in the field while the day is young."

Ṭeḥuti's final fading thought, as the priests of Ptah continued to kick and punch the life from his broken body, was a simple one: *If I had all the gold in all the world . . .*

ḳꜣꜣw mhꜣw mḥ

ḥsbt 18 ꜣbd 4 prt sw 26 ḫr ḥm n wsỉr

Hills Near Meḥ

Year 18, Month 4 of Peret, Day 26 under the Majesty of Ạsạr

"That's enough," Atchaut ordered the others. "Let Ptah judge now whether he lives or dies."

The last of the priests still kicking at Ṭeḥuti's still form stopped. The fight lust was gone from their faces—as if this had ever been a fight. The sound of their spent, heavy breathing, a consequence of their excitement and the beating they had inflicted on Ṭeḥuti, was the only sound heard on the ledge.

Atchaut did not know if Ṭeḥuti was dead. He could not tell if blood was still bubbling from Ṭeḥuti's nostrils or half-open mouth. He did not care to check. He had done as Set's messenger ordered and would soon be sending the acknowledgement back to Uas.

"Throw him over the side," he motioned to the two priests nearest him. His hands were shaking; he clasped them quickly behind his back.

The two men laid hold of Ṭeḥuti, one lifting him under each shoulder. They dragged him to the edge, his hands and feet cutting shallow, straight, pink-stained trails in the sand, and slung him over. The sound of Ṭeḥuti tumbling and sliding over the rocks and sand masked for a moment the scuffling sounds of the restless priests.

"You may find what we did here distasteful, but it was necessary. Not all of our work is prayer and collecting grain and gold for the temple. There is evil in Egypt as well as good. We must physically oppose that evil. You have done well, but Ptah and the high priest forbid you to ever talk about it—on the pain of suffering a similar fate. Split up and return to the temple either singly or in twos. Use different routes." Atchaut said.

He turned away and purposely strode off to hide the shaking that had spread to his legs. He clenched his teeth together to keep the rising bile down. He was in desperate need of a large bowl of the strongest beer he could find.

sꜣḫrmwt r wḫrpr m mḥ

ḥsbt 18 ꜣbd 4 prt sw 26 ḫr ḥm n wsỉr

The Boat Sakhr-Mut at the Dock in Meḥ

Year 18, Month 4 of Peret, Day 26 under the Majesty of Ạsạr

Ānukhet pushed her way from beneath the old linen sails she used for bedding. A glance to the east showed the Aten already clear of the ridge that marked the rise into the eastern desert.

We're late, she thought, yawning once and reaching towards the sky to stretch her legs and arms. *We should already be underway.*

Others had stirred or were stirring. She tasted the pungent, smoky scents of breakfast brought to her by the first kiss of the morning air.

The motion of a man shifting from foot to foot at the bottom of the ramp attracted her attention. It was the boat master, his back to her, looking toward Meḥ. She glanced briefly at the untouched blankets, neatly folded, where Ṭeḥuti often spent his nights and knew he had not returned to the Sakhr-Mut.

Ānukhet wrapped herself in a shawl and padded silently down the ramp to join the boat master.

"The River is running. We should leave now," she said.

The boat master studied the streets leading up into the city. "Just a little longer."

Ānukhet placed a hand gently on his forearm. "I will miss him too, master. But he is either with her now or he has fled. We must go."

The boat master turned his head to regard her. "What passed between you two?"

"Not what you think," she replied.

The boat master continued to study her face, waiting for more.

"It's a long story," Ānukhet sighed, "one better left to a cold night, a warm fire, and a deep bowl of beer. Come, the boat is ready, the men are eager, and our buyers are waiting. It will do you no good to wait here for one who can never be your son."

Ānukhet saw the wound her words inflicted in the tightening about his eyes and lips. "There are no secrets to be kept from you."

"I'm sorry," she said softly. "I didn't mean that as a barb. Ṭeḥuti can handle a boat, but is not a boatman. He is something far different. And for all the affection each of us has developed for him, his heart calls him elsewhere. There was never any hope he would stay. In that way he has been like a son: ours to have for a time, but never ours to keep."

The boat master cast a final look at the awakening streets that led into the heart of Meḥ. "You are right. Let's be off."

Ānukhet remembered Ṭeḥuti's belongings in the box by the boat masters' room. "There is something I must do for him before we leave."

The boat master nodded his assent and turning away added: "I hope he finds his happiness."

Ānukhet nodded. "He may yet. But he has a tender heart. I think he will pay dearly for it first."

ḳꜣꜣw mhꜣw mḥ

ḥsbt 18 ꜣbd 4 prt sw 26 ḫr ḥm n wsỉr

Hills Near Meḥ

Year 18, Month 4 of Peret, Day 26 under the Majesty of Ạsạr

Herti scrambled over the rocks back onto the caravan trail, running a few steps before slowing to walk beside his father's dromedary.

"There is a man down in the rocks," he said. "He's hurt."

Khashta, his father, the caravan master frowned. "Where?"

"Down there," Herti pointed. "He needs our help."

Khashta raised a hand and looked back at those behind him. "Merptah, you lead for awhile. Herti found a body off the side of the road. We'll catch up."

His chief nodded and took the lead as Khashta followed his son off to the side.

"Lead the way." Khashta motioned to Herti.

Herti scrambled back down the rocks, Khashta moving slower, picking a route with better footing for his dromedary and himself. Herti was already crouched next to the man when Khashta rounded a finger of rock and sand that had broken loose and slid from higher up.

"He still breathes," Herti declared before pointing uphill. "He must have fallen. There are fresh marks down the face of the hill where he tumbled."

The man was lying on his back in a shallow depression between two weathered fingers of gravel. His pose was natural enough that he might only be sleeping—except for the blood and bruising. His arms were close to his side and straight seeming to indicate no serious breaks. His legs were also straight, his feet only a forearm's length apart.

Khashta looked at the dried blood about the man's nose and mouth, the scrapes on his arms and legs, and the welts and bruises that covered every other visible part of him. Khashta instinctively checked that his knife was ready at his side and quickly scanned the hilltops about him.

"There are too many bruises for just a fall. He was beaten and probably robbed. Did you see or hear anyone else?"

Herti looked cautiously about as he shook his head. "No."

"Keep your eyes on the hills and stay close," Khashta ordered.

He turned to his packs. He found his water skin, and a second skin with a strong beer. He also found a few linen rags that he could use to get the dirt and the blood off the man.

"Has he said anything?" He called to his son.

"He has not stirred, even when I tried to wake him."

"He looks to be halfway to Amennt. There may be nothing that we can do for him."

Khashta brought a bowl, the water skin, and some rags. He poured water in the bowl and wet a rag. He gave the remaining rags to Herti. "Clean his face and arms and legs. Be gentle, we don't need to hurt him any more."

Khashta applied the rag to the man's cracked lips, squeezing gently to allow the water to drip into the man's mouth. The man moaned softly and swallowed but did not open his eyes.

He went back to the dromedary as Herti carefully washed the man's head and neck. Khashta fetched another bowl and the beer. He put more water in the bowl and used the rag to give it to the man squeeze by squeeze.

When the bowl was empty of water, he poured some of the beer in it, the malty, sour, alcoholic scent wafting up to tickle his nose. It would not be a kindness for the man to wake without something to dull the pain.

He emptied the last of the bowl of beer into the man's mouth as Herti finished washing the man's feet. Wiping his brow his son looked up at him: "He is wearing very nice sandals. And his skirt is very good material."

Khashta smiled. Not yet nine inundations and already seeing the world as a trader. "The garments are those of a priest."

"But he isn't a priest?" Herti asked.

"Priests don't usually have calloused hands." Khashta indicated.

"Who would beat and rob a priest?"

Too many would these days, Khashta thought. He shrugged and felt carefully the length of each of the man's arms and legs. There were hard, purplish lumps, indicating cracked bones, but nothing bad enough that Khashta suspected any serious breaks.

The man's nose was broken, his face was swollen. It was possible that his jaw was out of place, but Khashta would not be able to tell until the swelling went down.

He checked the man's chest and abdomen. This elicited a couple of soft moans as he felt the ribs. *Yes, definitely some cracks there. The abdomen was bruised but not swollen. Whoever beat him did most of the work on his ribs—a natural protection. His attackers were either not trying or did not know how to beat him to death.*

"What are you doing?" Herti asked.

"I'm feeling for broken bones as well as hidden wounds serious enough to kill him. But it appears there is nothing destined to kill him today. Ptah has smiled on him: he may not live, but if we care for him he has a chance."

"We are taking him with us?"

"It's all we can do for now. It would cost us too much time to return to Meh and put him with someone who might care for him. We can wrap him in linens and put him on my dromedary."

"I can run and fetch Merptah," Herti offered.

"No, I don't want you running through these hills alone when there might still be robbers about. We will do this together."

Khashta fetched a linen roll from the dromedary and he and Herti carefully wrapped the unconscious man in it. This action immobilized him and protected him from the burning smile of the Aten. Khashta fed him more of the strong, bitter beer before Herti tied a cloth loosely over his face.

Khashta led the dromedary closer and persuaded it to kneel. He and Merti worked together to gently lift the stranger and secure him face down lengthwise along the dromedary's back.

Khashta looked up to see that the Aten had moved nearly a third of the way across the sky in the time he and Herti had spent finding, treating and bundling the stranger. He shook his head. "It will be nightfall before we can rejoin the caravan. We best be on our way."

"Will we be safe?" Herti asked, scanning the hills again.

"Once we reach the main road. You should ride, I'll lead."

Herti scrambled up onto the dromedary. The beast barked once. Khashta took the reins and pulled the beast to its feet and guided it around the shifting sand and loose rocks toward the caravan road.

"I don't think it a good idea for you to wander these hills alone anymore. I wouldn't want anything to happen to you. Stay in sight of the caravan from now on."

Herti looked at the still, white linen form. "Yes, father."

pr-tꜣty m mḥ ḥsbt 18 ꜣbd 4 prt sw 26 ḫr ḥm n wsỉr

House of the Governor in Meḥ

Year 18, Month 4 of Peret, Day 26 under the Majesty of Ạsạr

Āakhu looked happier than the last time Ānukhet had seen her. Then she was the tragic bride being led to her boat, destined for a life far beyond Uas, torn from her betrothal and given to a man whom she barely knew. But today, as she sat on her dais in the common room of the women's house, her eyes were clear and calm, without the redness that spoke of tears. Her face was serene; her lips were relaxed and straight with no hint of sadness. *Someone has lifted her spirits. Perhaps Ṭeḥuti has been here after all.*

"You requested an audience," Āakhu said.

"I did, Lady. I am called Ānukhet. I steer the trading boat Sakhr-Mut."

"Welcome. I am Āakhu, chief wife of Governor Maaạ. With me are his other wives, Merakesh and Mermut," she said indicating first a striking Nubian, then a younger woman already swelling with child.

"Blessings, Lady. I come seeking a young priest named Ṭeḥuti. I believe you know him."

Ānukhet watched the color drain from Āakhu's face as she spoke. *So he hasn't been here.* Merakesh and Mermut exchanged a puzzled look.

Āakhu recovered during the ensuing silence, but her hand trembled as she held it out. "I do know him. Why would you seek him here?"

"He told me somewhat of your friendship. When he left the Sakhr-Mut yesterday, I thought it might be to visit you."

"Ṭeḥuti was a passenger aboard the Sakhr-Mut?"

"No Lady, he hired on as one of the crew."

She didn't know, Ānukhet realized, watching the frown return to Āakhu's face, and the lost, searching look in her eyes. She had learned more from Āakhu about this strange relationship between the priest and princess than she had from him.

"When did this happen?" Āakhu asked softly.

Ānukhet debated how much she should reveal. She enjoyed telling these stories of love struggling against impossible odds up and down the River on those dark, late nights when she could attract a good audience, but she did not like to be a part in the tale's creation.

"He joined us in Uas a week before your wedding."

Āakhu said nothing for a moment. She straightened her back, the beads in her headdress whispering. A cat the color of sand appeared from behind Āakhu. Its bright amber eyes briefly regarded and dismissed Ānukhet as it rubbed against Āakhu's legs. The chief wife slipped a foot from her sandal and trailed it the length of the cat's back, at which time it stretched and purred.

"You are much like the River you travel," Āakhu said, looking up from her pet, "One can draw the water bowl by bowl without ever coming close to the end of it. I would hear all of your time with Ṭeḥuti without the need to pull it from you."

"As you wish, Lady," Ānukhet bowed, realizing the folly of keeping secrets from one to whom secrets were a way of life. "We were one of the trading boats that followed you to Meḥ. He watched you each day, which is how I came to know of his relationship with you.

"We stayed here a day before taking goods to Qes. We returned to Meḥ two days ago. We're leaving today for the great sea.

"Ṭeḥuti left the boat at mid-morning yesterday and did not return. I thought he might have come here or that you might know where he is. Before we departed, I wanted to leave his belongings where he might find them."

Āakhu looked at the bundle resting on the stone floor at Ānukhet's feet. "Let me see," Āakhu pointed.

Ānukhet hefted the pack and carried it to the dais. There she opened and spread the items at the feet of Maaạ's chief wife.

Āakhu leaned forward to inspect Ṭeḥuti's instruments. She lifted but did not unroll his journal, placing it tenderly back with the other pieces. Her face was the calm, inscrutable face of royalty as she inspected each item. Ānukhet could see in the downward turn of her lips and the tightening and wateriness of her eyes that she had been affected.

Ānukhet said softly to Āakhu: "He still cares a great deal for you, though he works hard to hide it."

"That is not possible," Merakesh spoke. "Āakhu is chief wife."

Ānukhet allowed a whimsical smile to tighten her cheeks and curl the corners of her lips. "I have never known the facts of a situation to be of much concern to one in love."

Āakhu leaned forward farther, her brows pressed together in a frown. "Ṭeḥuti is in Meh?"

"I don't know for sure," Ānukhet cautioned. "He was, and I thought he might visit you. He is such a steady, dependable boatman that I fully expected him to return to the Sakhr-Mut at sundown last night. I guess I should hope now that he is in the embrace of a lusty woman or a nasty hangover and will surface again in a day or so."

Seeing the horror creep into Āakhu's expression she added: "But he has shown no inclination for either women or drink in the short time I have known him."

"Lady, you should not accept these things," Mermut said. "It would not be good to see them in your rooms. It would not be good to see him again."

Merakesh agreed. "Ānukhet, please take these things away."

Ānukhet acknowledged the Nubian with a nod, but focused on Āakhu. "Lady?"

Āakhu returned the writing stick she held and rose to her most regal pose. Her face was distant and unemotional as she said: "Yes, take these things away. I cannot have them. He has not been here and will not come here."

Ānukhet bowed in acceptance. "As you wish, Lady. Might there be another who would take them?"

"If you return to Uas, take them to the temple. He has—or had—rooms there," replied Āakhu. Her eyes looked away toward the doors of the common room for a moment, lost in thought, before she continued: "There is also a woman named Ȧamȧam who lives along the River south of Uas. She raised him after his parents died."

"How shall I recognize Aamaam?" Ānukhet questioned, intrigued by the idea of another who might know of Ṭeḥuti and Āakhu.

"Look for the children."

ḥrty ḥsbt 18 ꜣbd 4 prt sw 28 ḫr ḥm n wsỉr

A Caravan March

Year 18, Month 4 of Peret, Day 28 under the Majesty of Ạsạr

"I don't think he'll survive the desert," Merptah said, popping a dried date into his mouth.

Khashta glanced at the injured stranger. "Probably not."

Herti napped next to the man during the hot afternoon so he might awaken if the stranger stirred. Khashta was pleased and surprised that his son had taken responsibility for the man's care: washing and tending to wounds, giving him water and bits of food, talking to him on those occasions when the man's eyes flickered open for awhile.

"What will you do with him?"

"I thought I might leave him with Sefher at the oasis," Khashta replied.

"She doesn't need another mouth to feed."

"She will do this for me."

Merptah grinned. "She would do *anything* for you. When are you going to take her as your wife?"

"When I finally tire of seeing your face every morning," Khashta replied, and continued in spite of his friend's laughter: "Living at the oasis with her would be a relaxed and peaceful life." *Except it would kill me to watch the caravans come and go without me.*

Overhead the stitched-together linen strips of the shelter rippled in the shifting desert breeze. The sticks that supported it creaked and swayed. The Aten settled lower in the west, staining the linen more orange now than gold. Soon it would be cool enough to pack up and resume their journey.

Aih trailed the Aten across the sky since its recent rebirth. She grew larger and brighter each night and guided their journey almost a quarter of the night now before she followed the example of her lover the Aten and descended with him into the land. Khashta figured they would reach the oasis before Aih's setting forced them to journey by starlight.

Khashta glanced at Merptah to see him putting the remainder of his dates back into a goatskin pouch. Merptah and Khashta had worked together for many years, trusting their lives to one another, learning each other's skills, habits, and failings. They had developed their own form of communication.

"I'll tell the men to pack the dromedaries," Merptah said, correctly interpreting his friend's glance. "We'll be ready to move when the Aten is down."

pr-zfhr mhꜣw šdšr

ḥsbt 18 ꜣbd 4 prt sw 28 ḫr ḥm n wsỉr

Sefher's House Near Shedesher

Year 18, Month 4 of Peret, Day 28 under the Majesty of Ạsạr

Sefher looked up from her weaving. "Khashta! I didn't hear you come in."

She made some final adjustments to the loom, touched some balm to her lips, and pushed her hair girlishly behind her ears. She stood as Khashta approached.

"You're working late," he said and took her in his arms and kissed her. Her lips were warm and inviting and tasted of fruit. She had been experimenting again.

"You taste of strawberries," he said as he let her go. "What enchantment is this that you cast on me?"

Her eyes were shining. "Do you like it? I've made several jars and thought you might take some when you return to the River. A poor widow can always use a few extra things in trade."

"I will. It should fetch considerable trade in Meh among the women—and their lovers."

Sefher smiled and kissed Khashta again.

"I have a gift for you as well," he said.

Khashta called through the doorway to Herti, who entered carrying a basket. Sefher accepted it from him and set it down. She pulled the lid away and reached inside. "Dates, fruit, new sandals for Inuaabb, a new dress," she said, holding it up and inspecting it.

"Rather revealing for a woman of my years," she noted, lowering it enough that she could peer at Khashta.

"You weave so much cloth, but never keep any of it for yourself. You make clothes for your daughter, but not for yourself. If you are to have a nice dress, it seems that I must bring it to you. Can you blame me for choosing something that reveals those charms that I so often dream of?"

She can still blush like a maiden, Khashta thought as she carefully folded the dress and placed it back in the basket.

"Herti," she said. "Inuaabb wanted to wait up for you, but her eyes just would not stay open. She made me promise as I tucked her in that I would wake her the moment that you arrived. She is in her room. Why don't you go see her?"

Herti grinned and disappeared through the doorway into the next room.

"How long are you here?" Sefher asked, reaching into the basket.

She put her gifts away, storing them in jars and boxes, stretching to reach the shelves above, bending to peer into pots in ordered rows on shelves below.

"Only for the day. We leave for the Red Sea coast tomorrow evening."

Khashta liked to watch her move, liked to see her calves tighten as she went to her toes to reach a high place, liked to see her skirt pulled tight across her hips as she bent to peer into a dark corner. Sefher had been a dancer and singer in her youth, but refused now to speak of those times. The habits of her training still showed in her grace, the fluid movements of her arms and legs, and the economy of her motions. Watching her put away a basket of groceries was its own strange, enchanting dance.

She caught him watching her and chided him: "You embarrass me when you stare like that."

"I cannot help it. I have never seen a woman move the way you do."

"Every dancer moves the way I do."

"But they do it because they have been hired and are being paid, or they do it to seduce a partner for an evening's love play. But it is a natural part of you; you do it unconsciously and regardless of whether one watches or not."

Sefher paused, a pomegranate halfway out of the basket, and looked at Khashta. She smiled. "It is a pleasure to hear words like that from time to time."

Then she was on her toes placing the pomegranate on a shelf with several others.

"Have you eaten?" she called. "You look as if you've lost weight."

"It's just the desert this time of year," Khashta said. "I think it draws the moisture from me so that I look thinner—sort of wrinkly, like a dried date.

I've actually been nibbling on bread and smoked fish since the Aten entered the earth."

"What of Herti?"

Khashta went to the door of Inuaabb's room and peered in. Inuaabb was asleep in her bed, her arm curled about a small straw doll that Herti had brought for her. Herti was curled up on a mat in the corner, almost hidden in the shadows cast by the small oil pot, his eyes closed, his soft breathing barely audible.

Khashta ducked quietly out again and shook his head for Sefher. "Both fast asleep."

"I suppose you are also ready for bed," Sefher said, standing beside the basket again. She took the delicate dress in each hand and held it against herself, smiling to him as she turned smoothly from side to side.

"Actually, there is one other thing," he said. "I need a favor."

"You have been kind to me over the years, Khashta—even when it was not good business. You have only to ask."

Khashta nodded. "We came upon a young man as we ascended the hills beyond Meh. He had been badly beaten and would have died if left behind. We brought him with us, but the journey to Quser may be too much for him. I would like to leave him here until he is well enough to accompany me."

Sefher said nothing for a moment. She watched him thoughtfully. Khashta found even the blinking of her eyes an enchantment.

"You are not secretly bringing me a husband or a lover, or even a son, are you? This is not a match, this is just a guest?"

"Just a guest, Sefher. I am too selfish to ever bring you one that might make you forget me. If you would accept a caravan man or I could ever stay in one place, I would be your husband and your lover."

Sefher lowered her eyes as her dark cheeks grew ever ruddier. "And you know that I would welcome you."

One of the children stirred and sighed in the other room. Outside, the stillness of the night was broken by the plaintive call of one night bird to another. Khashta and Sefher stood only a few short paces apart, their faces hidden and revealed, shadowed and brightened by the flickers of lamplight that passed through the room like clouds.

If I could keep my gaze focused only on her face, if I could hold her soft hands forever in mine, would I find peace even as the caravan went on without me? Spending the quiet days with her and Inuaabb and Herti, would I be able to look at distant hills without being drawn to them. Is this the night to begin that discovery?

Love was so close and so far away. Each needed something the other could not yet give. There are seeds that lie dormant for years in the dry sand, awaiting only the miracle of rain to awaken and bring blooms to the desert. There are human beings that live their own dormant lives, awaiting the day that a kindness, commitment, or tender word might awaken their own sleeping love.

"Where is my new guest?" Sefher asked.

"He is with the caravan tonight. We can see to him in the morning."

Sefher nodded. "Would you like a back rub before we sleep?"

Khashta took a step toward her. "I would offer you the same."

"I would like that."

They met in the center of the room. Khashta held her and kissed her, a taste of strawberries still lingering on her lips. He could almost feel the love trembling and stirring within her as it was in himself, distant and unfamiliar as the call of a solitary night bird.

Chapter 19

ABYDOS, EGYPT, ḤAĀMER'S ROOM, JULY 11, 9:40 A.M.:

"I've done a complete scan of the mummy," said Sanders.

"Any other trauma, other than her disease?"

"Nope. I also determined she never had children."

"Her young, painful death upsets me," said Lisa. "TB's a bad way to go. Normally, I don't attach to a mummy with this much sympathy, but I am strongly connected having read Āakhu's poem and studying Ḥaāmer as a mysterious royal woman."

"Yes, very sad. I've made a full body scan of Ḥaāmer. I'll start the clay modeling software."

"Good."

Following a simple lunch, soft drinks, a knife stabbed into a jar of peanut butter and stacked slices of bread, the archaeologists began their separate tasks. Bill placed the robotic rover into Ḥaāmer's room. He electronically connected it to the data collection relay computer he had set in the corridor. The wide-tired robot, weighing only seven ounces, transmitting a wireless, high density data signal, climbed over the strewn artifacts without causing them damage. Checking the telemetry, he drove the machine through the eyes of the rover around the chamber like a kid with a video game.

Indeed, he admitted to himself, *this is too much fun.*

"You'd better be careful with your toy," warned Lisa.

"Yes, ma'am," he grinned as he reduced the speed by a notch.

Using their overhead scans, he had found a semi-open path through the room. He drove between chairs and a bed. From his previous experience at the Cairo museum from other treasure troves, he knew the chests probably contained clothes. Urns contained grains to plant or eat and wine to drink.

We could date the grain.

As he came to the end of the first pass, he stopped.

No wires. Nothing drags. This is going well. We'll have a ground level scan to enhance our calibrations.

Bill turned from his control screen to gaze at Lisa over his shoulder. Working to remove the cord seals from the second room opening, Lisa's brow furled in concentration. She lifted the clay blobs encasing the rope ends supporting the wooden door edges. He watched with rapt admiration of her delicate hands, separating with slow, precise movements the rope layers.

She's an incredible woman. I'm amazed with her ability to hold her hands so steady at eye level without a tremor. She could be a surgeon.

Lisa paused, stepping back from the door to rotate her shoulders and arms to reduce the tension building in them. He ducked his head when she turned a quizzical eye on him, staring at her. He made several passes across Ḥaāmer's chamber before he looked at her again.

"We're through," she shouted as she sagged with her stress release.

"Good job, preserving the door and fasteners."

She nodded.

She supported the door with the soft silicon clasps joining the fragile structure to a thick, soft plastic pad. Sanders moved across the hall to help her lift the mounted, wooden door panel. They laid it aside for later microscopic scanning and examination.

"Thanks," she smiled at him.

"Sure. The door is as delicate as a dried flower," he said, returning her smile. "Probably more delicate."

She agreed.

Lisa picked up a tripod, extending the legs to set up a video camera next to the doorway. Bill rested, watching her movements, having a hard time containing his curiosity. The camera resolved objects in the second room. Once again, he observed stelae, stone ushabtui and wood litter on the floor. Lisa turned the camera to each side. Bill concluded that they could work safely in the room, but waited for her to inform him.

"I guess you'll have plenty to do then," he said dryly.

"True. One strange thing. I don't see a funerary box."

"So where's Āakhu?"

"Or better yet Ḥaāmer's spouse; but no, there's no funerary box," she said.

"Strange stuff keeps piling up. If it's a storage room for more of Ḥaāmer's posessions, then we have a real problem with a highly-honored pre-dynastic woman. Do you see any other doors?"

"Not yet."

Bill returned to his work, puzzled by this latest problem. He continued with his floor surveys. Within the hour, he finished the floor in one direction. Then he set the robot to scan the floor obliquely when Lisa's whoop startled him. Bill turned to look at her screen, observing a small stone ushabtui centered in her monitor.

No, it's a small statue of Osiris.

With no reference point on the screen, the size of the statue was indeterminate.

"What do you think of that?" she asked rhetorically.

"A pharaoh?"

"Osiris, but what's wrong with him?"

Bill's brow wrinkled as he contemplated the Egyptian God of the Dead, trying to understand what she saw that he didn't. He had seen many statues of Osiris and they looked like this one carved from stone. Formally dressed wearing the crown of the Southern Egyptian kingdom, Osiris stood with his arms folded across his chest, a flail in one hand, a crook in the other. Bill frowned as Lisa smiled at him for having missed the significance, but her expression changed as her eyes defocused, her mind looking back across time.

"Osiris is not wrapped as a mummy as he normally appears," he said. "Are you sure it's not just a pharaoh?"

"No, he looks like the guy out front labeled as Osiris. You're right, he's not dressed like the keeper of the underworld. He's fully formed, but without his swaddling."

"And only the southern crown," said Bill.

"Right, he's missing the double crown. Good observation. As with everything else, he appears strange, out of place. We're out of sync with time. Characters, important characters, appear on stage too soon and off timeline as if they are from a different civilization. Not Egypt. We need to get another, carbon dating and put this mystery to rest."

"We'll have to explain why the previous artifacts were archaic," he said.

"We know where we found them so we can analyze them again. The dried fruit should've been indicative. We'll have to figure why they're different," she said.

"I'll take the robot video for Tu'hut. Let's gather wood chips for the next dating. I need a sample of the mummy and her wrapping."

Lisa nodded, but he could tell that she was not happy with the situation. They continued with their separate tasks. After posting the guards, the tired pair strolled back to the trailer with their guards in tow. The lieutenant met them.

"A communique came in this afternoon for you, Doctor," the lieutenant told Bill as he nodded a greeting to them. "I believe you are to contact the Secretary General of the Ministry of State for Antiquities in Cairo."

Bill looked at his watch. Deciding Dr. Tu'hut might still be in his office, he jogged ahead to the trailer. Reaching the Secretary General at his desk did not surprise him.

"How does your work progress, Doctor?"

"I'm making good progress."

"Good. I will send a helicopter for you. It should arrive tomorrow morning."

"Oh. Any thing you're concerned about?"

"No, your work is excellent. Do you need more carbon dating?"

Bill sighed with mental relief.

"I've gathered samples. These include the mummy and her wrappings. I entered the second room today. I've samples for carbon dating to be done and a video to show you in the morning. I've also made a complete survey of the original room. I expect to finish the mapping of this room on the computer tonight."

"You are a remarkable man, Doctor. It is as if you are two people."

Bill needed to guard his statements. He decided to treat the comment as a compliment.

"Thank you, Dr. Tu'hut."

"I hope you are taking good care of the artifacts."

This comment irritated Bill.

"Of course. I use extreme care. I am documenting everything."

"Of course. I have complete faith in you or I would not have selected you. I am disappointed that once again I am unable to come to the site. The Antiquities Minister's death, keeps me doing double the work. I wish to see your exploration. Perhaps soon. As we discussed, I want to move the artifacts to the museum. One day I will just have to 'pop' in on you so I can understand the situation."

"Yes, sir."

Tu'hut hung up the phone.

"How soon do you expect to return?"

Bill whirled to see Lisa standing in the door.

"I hope to return tomorrow evening. Be careful while I'm gone."

Lisa grunted, getting a drink from the refrigerator. She went outside to sit in one of the canvas chairs.

ABYDOS, EGYPT, NEAR THE FEATURE, JULY 11TH, 8:45 P.M.:

The digger cowered with the barrel of the automatic weapon stuck in his right ear. Snake expected this or he would have messed himself. He didn't know if Colonel Dhul Fiqar would decide to pull the trigger. He knew the ugly one was insane. He hoped his position in the camp and the possibility of looting stayed the colonel's finger. The weapon lowered and the digger relaxed internally. He was careful, keeping his eyes down showing the proper deference. This one made his life unpleasant. He must tell this monster the problems with leaving the camp without incurring his wrath.

"You're late."

"Apologies honored one. The Americans started new security procedures that delay departure. They would suspect me if I tried to avoid their procedures."

"Americans!" spat the ugly one who continued into a tirade of epithets. Snake knelt, looking at the ground, listening to the colonel's ranting. With a gasp of air, Fiqar stopped.

"What have you brought me today?" he snapped.

"Nothing. I was searched."

The ugly one swung his fist, dropping the digger with a single blow to the head.

"Imbecile! I know you are stealing from me?"

"No, colonel. We are watched," he cowering again as the weapon pointed at him. Fiqar hesitated. He looked with disgust at the man on the ground.

"Bring something next time. Do these weak Americans outwit you, stupid one? Disrupt their work. We need funds for the cause."

Snake understood the enormous profit from black market artifact theft was the primary reason.

"We remove the infidel idols and they pay for the holy cause. Bring more objects to me. Do you understand?"

He kicked the helpless man on the ground. Snake rolled over in the dust, crouching, out of reach. He knew a failure would bring his end, but satisfying the ugly one would be difficult to do. This was not the great jihad he envisioned when he joined the cause.

Colonel Fiqar stalked away. Snake shuffled back to camp, entering the only way he knew he could go undetected. He didn't know how to obtain another artifact.

ABYDOS, EGYPT, THE CLIFFS ABOVE THE FEATURE, JULY 11TH, 8:45 P.M.:

Taking care as he ascended the cliff face, the climb didn't seem as difficult as the first time. Wanting to talk with Lisa, Bill had seen her climbing a few minutes earlier. He followed her.

Wasn't I just here? he thought. *Didn't that encounter end badly? I have to find a way to talk with her. We need to start building trust. Besides, I'd like to extend our relationship.*

He looked up. The cliff tops loomed well above him, seeming to be a long ways away, echoing his feelings about their relationship.

How am I going to tell her my feelings? She seems so aloof not interested in anything—in me—only her exploration. She is a solid professional, not the beautiful woman that I see.

He gripped an outcrop, using it as a handhold.

Wasn't this where I lost skin before? Damn!

He paused, drawing a deep breath, gathering his thoughts.

It's that aspect about her, being a woman, that I want to explore with her. She is beautiful, sexy and intelligent, all of which she avoids. Why? For Pete's sake, she always wears a man's shirt. The shorts aren't bad though.

He shoved those thoughts aside, continuing his ascent.

"How do I bring up any one of those topics?" he mumbled under his breath. "So what are my feelings? They're rather amorphous."

His head broke the top of the track.

"I'm not sure it's really love, but I would like to explore a deeper relationship."

He nodded at the guard and traversed the cliff-top path.

"I'd like to develop a more personal relationship with her."

Lisa sat in the same spot as before, staring off to the east. She acknowledged him.

"Hi, what were you saying?" she asked.

"Nothing. Just thinking out loud."

Her demeanor didn't seem as put out as the last time. He eased in beside her, closing his eyes, soaking of the warmth from the rock against his back, swinging his legs to and fro over the edge, contemplating what he was going to say. His hip pressed hard against hers. She reached over, pressing down on his knee with her hand. He looked at her. She smiled at him. He relaxed again, closing his eyes, continuing to absorb the warmth against his back. . Absently not thinking, she twisted the hair on the inside of his leg just above his knee.

"Is Tu'hut asking about me?" she queried.

She's worried about her situation. Her fingers are not helping me.

"Hey, I'm meditating," he groused, opening an eye to look at her. When her lips pursed in mocking disgust, he continued. "No. When am I going to start sending him artifacts? He needs to come here and on and on."

Smiling at him, her shoulders relaxed, her body showing less tension.

"You seem vexed. Dealing with him is why you make the big bucks."

"Yeah, right. A college professor... big bucks," his voice laced with sarcasm.

"I understand your situation, professor."

"I've thought a lot about your being here," he changed the subject.

"Yes," she interrupted retracting her hand to cross her arms across her torso. "I want to thank you for treating me so professionally. We've kept our interactions on a strictly business level and I am glad for that."

Bill felt crushed. This conversation was going in the wrong direction. She seemed to detect his upset and her eyebrows went up in a questioning expression.

"Did I say something wrong?" she asked.

"No, I...."

"Well I...," she started to interrupt. He reached forward, touching her lips with his fingertips. She pulled back surprised by his contact.

"I'm not upset with you, Lisa, but please listen to me. Certainly you're a talented archaeologist. You are capable of running this project on your own. I rely on you daily."

He paused.

"But, you were about to say, but...," she interjected unable to contain herself, scanning his face intensely.

"No buts...," he responded holding back any aggravation with her lack of trust in him. "I'm resolved to your being here. I wanted to say thank you."

And a whole lot more.

Her face twisted into a perplexed expression. She really didn't understand his motives. He sighed. He supposed he had to show her his trust.

"Look, Lisa, I want you to stay here and help me. I'm willing to take the heat if we're discovered. I'm not concerned about my professional reputation or worse getting us both kicked out of Egypt."

After a long pause, she said. "Ah..., thank you," He thought her response was a little weak. "Bill,... thank you. That puts my mind at ease, but I sense there's something else."

That wasn't quite the pathway he was looking for. She didn't sound at ease. But what response was he expecting? He gave her a nod and a crooked smile. She continued to study his face as if she were trying to read his mind. She reached across, taking his hand, squeezing it.

"Thanks," she repeated. He nodded. Her expression turned speculative as she continued to study him.

"There *is* something else. What?"

"We'd better get down before it gets dark," he said, not knowing how to continue from here. *Damn!*

Nodding, she took a deep breath. She turned once again toward the disappearing, purple desert sand. He followed her gaze to the silver thread of the Nile, fading with the twilight.

"OK," she said rising, pressing on his knee to leverage herself standing.

She offered him a hand to assist him. Turning to face him as they stood, she studied him in an introspective way.

The gravel shifted under her feet. He reached forward to steady her, his arms encircling her waist, but this time instead of storming off, she pitched forward into him, her chest pressing hard against his. Surprised, he held her locked in the embrace to steady her, feeling her body warmth against him.

On a sudden impulse, he bent forward giving her a light kiss on the lips. He watched her eyes grow wide. Embarrassed, feeling he had made a mistake, he pulled back. She looped her arm around his waist, lifting her chin, her other hand reaching for the back of his neck, drawing him tighter, pressed her lips hard to his. When they broke apart, both gasping for breath, they stood looking at each other.

"Oh," he managed.

"Yes," she responded with a long sigh.

He smiled at her.

"We'd better go," he said.

They went down carefully with Bill in the lead. She allowed him to grip her hand when the path was treacherous. When they reached the bottom, they crossed the area between the cliff face and the trailer, walking close to each other.

"A digger," Lisa said nodding in the direction of a robed figure. He entered the camp along the cliff face, coming from the direction of the second tomb entrance.

Anwar stood at the entrance to the laborer's tent area. He spoke to the man.

"He's signed that he went for prayers," said Bill.

"Strange, there are many Muslims in the camp. They don't leave for prayers," she said as the digger gave Anwar a deep bow then turned to enter the tent area.

"We'd better check if he went to the tomb," said Bill. They took an escort with them around to the second entrance.

* * *

Lisa and Bill returned to camp, having determined the digger hadn't gone to the tomb. They sat in the canvas chairs outside the trailer, finishing their discussion about the digger's reason for leaving the camp.

"He must have gone for prayers," repeated Bill.

"His leaving makes me uneasy."

"We'll ask Jagardii tomorrow about the digger," said Bill.

Lisa untied her boots, pulling the laces from their hooks, dropping them into the dust beside her chair. She pulled off her heavy socks, wiggling her anaemic, white toes that were in dramatic contrast with rest of her skin. She rocked back onto her hip, putting her bare feet into the seat with her. Looking at Bill, she saw him, gazing at her legs. Ignoring him, she leaned back, looking up to the heavens, absorbing them, not speaking for several minutes. Her mood changed. She relaxed, feeling a calm begin to flow through her. She.enjoyed the cool evening breeze, letting random thoughts slide around inside her head. Bill reached over to hold her hand. She thought about the mysterious, maybe magical moment on the cliff top.

What is going on?

Doubt crept in again.

"I'm tired of all the problems," she told Bill, avoiding her non-professional thoughts about him.

"How so?"

"The theft, Tu'hut, the terrorists and a feature that doesn't make sense."

"I'm glad you didn't mention me in there," he said smiling as he faced her.

She gave him one of her weak, wrinkled smiles.

"If you insist, I can add you. I don't need a nursemaid."

"I understand you are a strong, intelligent and independent woman. I just want you to be safe," he said. He released her hand. His fingertips traced along her bare thigh from her shorts to her knee, squeezing it.

"I've discovered that," she said putting her hand on top of his, holding it in place, feelings stirring inside her.

"I've learned to live with your strong will," he said.

She paused, thinking, finally saying. "I know you have. I appreciate that. I'm not always easy to work with."

"Your insights have made it a pleasure," he smiled.

"Hmm," she thanked him with a smile.

They returned to silence, setting her thoughts wondering again. When the cooling air caused her to shiver, he said.

"You ready for dinner?"

"I had something else in mind," she said giving him a look.

"Oh," he said as he stood looping his arm around her waist. Holding her, he kissed her.

* * *

Later, they prepared dinner together jostling each other playfully. They ate a feast of chicken potpies, canned sugared fruit and because it was a special occasion, a wine Bill had tucked away. At the end of the meal, Bill shoved his empty plate to the center of the table, rubbing his stomach.

"This has been a great evening," he said.

"Yes, I agree."

"So much for a strictly professional relationship."

She smiled.

"Let's tackle one of those problems you mentioned earlier," said Bill.

Her face transformed into a concerned look. He continued.

"How about 'a feature that doesn't make sense.'"

"Oh, OK," she said with apparent relief. Lisa reassembled her thoughts, "The characters appear on stage much too early. This tomb is so out of...time...sequ...."

* * *

Bill smiled as he watched Lisa's eyes turn introspective. She stopped speaking mid-sentence, not even appearing to remember his presence. His grin broadened as she stood beginning to pace back and forth in the short space between the dining area and the kitchen, her steps becoming shorter, faster as her thoughts progressed. Something elusive had launched in her mind. He enjoyed watching her movements. Her eyes ticked back and forth as if she were checking each item. She jerked to a stop, gripping the edge of the kitchen counter to steady herself. She swayed.

"Oh, my God," she whispered. She slumped into her chair again. "Oh, oh!"

Looking wildly at him shaking her head negatively as if not believing herself, she put her hand to her mouth her eyes opening wide, shocked by her own idea. He waited for her to speak, but finally prompted her.

"I understand it," she responded in a whisper awed by her discovery. She nodded. "I completely understand it."

"Don't keep me in suspense."

"Oh, Bill, it's impossible. Anwar planted the seed."

Her short, rapid breathing showed her excitement. Bill leaned back in his seat readying himself for her revelation. He trusted it would be remarkable. When she explained it to him, it was indeed remarkable.

"Lisa, I believe you, but I'm aghast. It makes complete sense, but you'll have a huge mountain to climb to prove it to the rest of the archaeological community, if you expect them to accept it."

"We've gone over the details so many times I see all of the points, but our theory will be a tough sell," she said.

"Your theory," he corrected. "We've no direct evidence. We need to find the rooms of the remaining occupants. The corridor walls are solid stone. Radar in the hall proved that, but you said the second room had no funerary box."

"What if the cave-in sealed the tomb and there are no other occupants?"

"That would be a bummer."

"Hopefully, Āakhu's room is the entry to a complex? I think the first tomb seal may have some bearing as well. Maybe there's a corridor off to the side we don't see. It's deep enough that the radar scans wouldn't show it."

"A second series of carbon dates will time lock this tomb. I'll drop the samples while I'm in Cairo."

"I think I'll e-mail Professor Crain in Providence with our theory."

"Right, I remember you're from Brown. Is telling him wise?"

"He's trustworthy and he may have some insights. Why are you going to Cairo again?"

"It's a private matter."

"I've been meaning to talk to you about your *private matter*. You need to trust me. I don't want to pry, but it worries me when I'm here all alone."

She lifted her hand to halt his comment.

"No more opinions about my staying. You need me for technical support and artifact protection."

"Yes, I do. I wasn't going to say that. I've been supporting an Egyptian teenager. I have been taping our sessions. That's the protected files you saw."

"Oh," she said.

"Khidr's from lower society. He lives in the City Cemetery, but has gone missing. I've been searching for him."

He went to the console and brought up a video file. He played it for Lisa.

"Oh, my gosh," said a horrified Lisa. She fumbled in her shirt pocket for her phone, manipulating it to bring up a picture to show Sanders.

"Where did you get a picture of him?"

"When I saw the terrorists bomb the minister, they were hustling this boy into the back of their truck."

"You're saying the terrorists have taken him?"

"Maybe. I thought it was strange that the army was picking up random people. That's why I took the picture. The two who bombed the limousine were in this army truck. A soldier was putting this boy in the back."

"So the terrorists have him. They've either killed him or worse he's joined them."

"I don't know, Bill," Lisa reached across the table to touch his arm. "I'll try to help you in any way I can."

ABYDOS, EGYPT, THE FEATURE, JULY 12TH, 8:00 A.M.:

Bill's helicopter arrived to take him to Cairo. Lisa came to him carrying the samples they'd collected for carbon dating.

"I wish I wasn't going. Your theory has dropped a bomb on me. You are incredible."

"Find the boy."

"Don't do anything rash today," he said.

"I'll verify the artifacts with the computer. I'm going to document my thoughts into the machine."

"Good idea. You do the initial work. We'll start together when I get back."

"You won't discuss our theory with Tu'hut, will you?" she asked.

He shook his head. She stepped to him, kissing him hard on the mouth. "Please, hurry home, Bill."

He smiled at her, "Right. You're brilliant and beautiful."

ABYDOS, EGYPT, THE ARCHAEOLOGICAL TRAILER, JULY 12TH, 9:00 A.M.:

"We're missing another artifact!" Lisa screamed angrily, as she scanned the inventory list. A small well-formed statue of Ȧpnu was missing. When she first examined it, she placed it on a linen sheet. The gold cat-god had warmed her heart with its lifelike characteristics: its paws outstretched, black obsidian eyes glowing at her and striated marks on its sides representing fur.

"How could this happen?"

I've a prime suspect. I know who was out and about last evening. I'll talk with Anwar to get an immediate search before the artifact gets away.

Thirty minutes later Anwar pulled everyone into the camp assembly area. She'd told Anwar her suspicions. With all accounted for, Lisa noted her suspected digger had his head down not meeting anyone's eyes. Anwar began a systematic search of the bivouac starting with the diggers' tent and their personal belongings. Lisa's prompt action bore fruit. After a brief search, they found Ȧpnu buried in the sand in the center of the laborers' tent. Lisa was ecstatic with the recovery.

"We've found the filthy bastard who pillages our heritage," shouted a livid Anwar.

"Wait, Anwar. We don't really know who stole the relic. We found the object in the center area of the tent. It could have been any one of the diggers or for that matter someone being very clever."

"Oh, I think I know who did this. The man who came back last night. I believe I'll be able to get a quick confession."

Anwar slapped back the door canvas, shocking Lisa with his vehemence. She stared after him. She heard shouts and the various sounds of a scuffle.

Once the noise of the struggle subsided, the group outside began to move away from the assembly area.

Perhaps they'd resolved their problem; however, there were others who might be stealing. Anwar seems pretty quick to jump on the one suspect we have. Is he covering something up? I don't know where Anwar goes at night.

Lisa was determined to have Anwar get as much information as he could from the digger, if he was indeed the culprit. Walking from the tent, she saw the lieutenant in the center of the area talking with two of his men. When the lieutenant saw Lisa heading toward him, he broke away from the group.

"Lieutenant, where is Anwar?"

The lieutenant's eyes widened. He shifted, looking nervously at Lisa.

"He said that you two caught the thief."

"Yes, we have a suspect."

"I've never seen the captain so angry."

Lisa frowned. "The digger, if he is the thief, will be prosecuted under Egyptian law for grave robbing. But he's now only under suspicion. I'd like to find out whether there're others here who're working with him."

"You'll have to catch him because he dragged the man out of the camp." The lieutenant pointed toward the second entrance. "I would not interfere with the captain's interrogation, ma'am."

"We need to find out if there are others," said Lisa as she walked in the direction the lieutenant indicated.

"Ma'am, you need an escort."

Ignoring him, Lisa trotted after the captain. She rounded the cliff face that led to the second tomb entrance. The road sloped down below the camp, winding into the rocky plain. Instead of going in that direction, she saw the pair across the road entering the rocks along a side path. Anwar dragged the man. Looking both directions, she crossed the highway, heading along the same path.

She slowed, walking at a fast pace to overtake them. When she cut between a pair of sentinel stones, she saw Anwar and the digger just ahead stopped at a widening in the trail. She could not hear them, but she could see Anwar shaking the other man as if he were a limp, rag doll. Anwar lashed out with his fist across the digger's face. The man fell to his knees backing away from the army captain.

The digger suddenly jerked, collapsing to the ground. Anwar followed him down, a rifle report echoing from the cliffs above and behind Lisa. Lisa, not knowing what to do, went to the ground like Anwar.

Anwar, his service pistol out, fired into the cliffs. Lisa moved around the boulder to put it between her and the direction Anwar was firing. No additional shots came from the rocks above. Time shifted into slow-motion, with Lisa clinging to the rock. The sounds of people running came from behind her and Lisa twisted to see. Soldiers crossed through the various paths in a crouching run. Still no shots were fired.

"Up there," shouted Anwar pointing in the direction that he'd fired. "Quickly."

He turned over the digger to examine him. Anwar signaled a soldier approaching his position not to rush. The digger was dead. The troups, who had been climbing the cliffs, reached the place indicated by Anwar. They signaled that no one was there.

A group of soldiers formed around Lisa. She was frogmarched back to camp with a pair carrying the digger. She heard Anwar say that he and the remaining soldiers would scour the area for the sniper.

ABYDOS, EGYPT, THE ARCHAEOLOGICAL TRAILER, JULY 12TH, 10:18 A.M.:

Lisa called Bill's cell phone.

"Bill, you have to come back now! A digger is dead!" she gasped, out of breath.

"Lisa! Calm down. I'm having a hard time understanding you. You need to slow down. Are you locked in the trailer?"

"Yes."

"Now start again and tell me what has happened. You said that a digger is dead?"

With several false starts, Lisa explained what happened in the camp after Bill left. She explained her searching for the missing artifact. She explained how she had followed Anwar into the rocky cliffs and saw the digger's death.

"Going after Anwar was a foolish thing to do, Lisa."

"I had no idea that a terrorist was there."

"You need to be out of there," he said.

Lisa didn't respond. At the moment, terrified, she had to agree with him.

"Stay in the trailer. I'll drop the material with Dr. Tu'hut and come back immediately."

"Please hurry."

CAIRO, EGYPT, THE CAIRO MUSEUM, JULY 12TH, 11:09 A.M.:

An hour later, Dr. Tu'hut asked one of the lab assistants where Dr. Sanders had gone.

"He has a problem at the site?" he told the Secretary General.

"Hmm, thank you. Please proceed with the dating quickly."

Dr. Tu'hut mused over Dr. Sanders' strange behavior.

I can't continue to clear matters at my desk.

ABYDOS, EGYPT, THE ARCHAEOLOGICAL TRAILER, JUL 12TH, 12:32 P.M.:

"Lisa!" shouted Bill, pounding on the trailer door.

Lisa pulled back the drape. The lock released. Stepping into the trailer, he found her in an agitated state. A gun lying on the counter next to the door surprised him. Lisa slammed the door behind him, re-locking it. She rushed into his arms clinging to him, trembling. He could feel her heart thumping against his chest,

"A sniper murdered the digger. He fired from the cliffs above," she told him, terror etching her face.

Bill nodded, not challenging her.

"What are we going to do?" She asked him, desperate for an answer.

"Getting you out of here is high on my list. Why did Anwar take the digger out of camp?"

"He was interrogating him," she said.

"Did Anwar or anyone else come here?"

"No, I haven't seen anyone. I've stayed away from the windows."

"Good. Where did you get that?" he pointed at the desk.

"From the previous attack."

He shook his head.

"With you here, I feel much safer," she said, her composure having returned. "We need to find Anwar."

"The terrorists are out there. They may shoot us."

Chapter 20

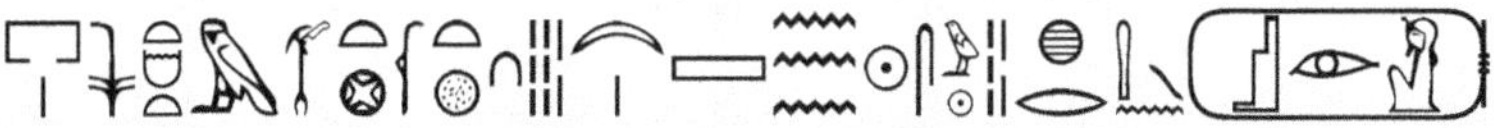

pr ḥmt nswt m wꜣst ḥsbt 18 ꜣbd 1 šm sw 5 ḫr ḥm n wsỉr

The House of Pharaoh's Wife in Uas
Year 18, Month 1 of Shemu, Day 5 under the Majesty of Ạsạr

Īset walked from her bath to the Queen's House as the Aten lifted above the eastern hills. His touch was soft and warm on her bare back, his smile brightened the new day. She twisted water from her hair with one hand, and combed it through the fingers of the other. She moved slowly; a sigh of a breeze drifted about her, caressing her, complementing the golden sunlight.

Kefa·ạb waited in her chamber with a shift and sandals. Īset threaded her hands through the shoulder straps high over her head and let the hem fall to her ankles. She glanced at the sandals and sighed.

"Must I?"

A smile creased the weathered old face as Kefa·ạb held them closer. "How many times have I told you, my lady, that you cannot go to the Hall of Justice in bare feet?"

Īset slipped her feet into them, a smile tugging at the flesh of her own cheeks and lips.

Tchefeṭ-t and Ạaātchṭạ-t waited with discs of cosmetics for the wife of Pharaoh. Oils, pressed from plants and herbs for her skin; creams from pulped fruits and flowers for her face, hands, and feet; perfumes from rare herbs and spices; stains from flowers, berries, and fruit, for her lips and cheeks; and kohl for her eyes.

"Sit, Lady," Kefa·ạb said, motioning to a chair.

Steppu fixed Īset's hair and colored her face; Tchefeṭ-t applied oils and creams to Īset's arms and hands; Ạaātchṭạ-t to her legs and feet. The youngest, Ramatet, only seven inundations, watched and learned, hovering about the other three, occasionally taking an order to assist.

"Tell me of your classes," Īset asked. "What have you learned?"

Tchefeṭ-t, her unusual green eyes bright, cool, and clear in the morning light, looked up from staining a nail of Īset's hand. "I have learned how special and rare we are. There are few women in the classes you have chosen for us. None of those other women are servants."

"I would like to change that," Īset said.

"You will. In small ways, you have already," Steppu replied, taking up the narrative. "In those first few days we were ridiculed. The young men thought perhaps we were lost and offered to escort us back to the kitchens and the laundries. Each morning we would find smooth stones for beating washed linen, or small bags of grain for making bread, placed with our tablets and sticks. We smiled innocently—as you instructed us—and thanked the young men for their gifts, then went about our tasks. We studied hard, answered the same questions, bore the same examinations, and did as well as they. But we did so *quietly.*

Tchefeṭ-t resumed: "I remember your wisdom:

Change a man not by strength,
for strength is his advantage.
Change a man not by wounding his pride,
for wounded pride is slow to forget and to forgive.
Change a man not by being a man,
for he will never see you as such.
Change a man slowly,
as water changes rock."

"I said that?" Īset asked.

"Yes," Tchefeṭ-t replied.

"The others no longer see us as servants or pleasant diversions," Steppu said, her soothing voice like honey on bread. "We are friends and comrades."

"But we're prettier," Tchefeṭ-t added.

"And we smell better," laughed little Ramatet, rubbing her own face and arms with one of the aromatic creams.

"That is how it should be," Īset agreed. "Pharaoh has a dream that Egypt will some day be one people, from the Great Sea to Kush and beyond. I think that might be. But for Egypt to be strong and to persist will take the thoughts and spirits and hands of *all* the people—the women as well as the men. I work a little each day to show Pharaoh that truth as well.

"We bear children, we care for them. We do many tasks that accomplish no purpose other than to support the men and free their lives for the physical work. We are more than our tasks, we can *be* more. We are ka and ba, and chu and cha; we have hearts that beat, eyes that see, and hands that hold."

"I do not think the men believe that," Tchefeṭ-t said.

"Somewhere in their ka they do, they have only forgotten."

"We will help them remember," said Ạaātchṭạ-t.

"If they are to reach this great goal for which they continually grow and change and build, they will need us at their sides: not as domestic servants, but as equals."

Steppu frowned. "How do we make an *equal* watch children?"

"Or cook?" asked Tchefeṭ-t.

"Or wash clothes?" added Ạaātchṭạ-t.

Īset pointed to each questioning face in turn as she spoke, emphasizing her words: "In *love.* In *patience.* In *hope*—remembering that their days are long but their years are short."

"And because we smell better," Ramatet said.

Laughter echoed through the room, laughter that subsided and left wistful smiles in its wake. Steppu paused in tracing lines of kohl about Īset's eyes and appraised her work. "How fare your evenings, Lady?"

Īset tried to smile again, but it flickered and died. "I spend my evenings here in the Queen's House, sipping a fine wine brought from a land I will never see, Baka purring in my lap. Sometimes I go to the roof, communing with the evening breeze, listening to the song birds, watching the small lights trace pictures across the night sky."

"He has not sent for you?" Steppu asked, surprised.

"No," Īset said softly. "He has not sent for me."

She lowered her head unconsciously, only to have it lifted again in Steppu's soft fingers. "Why? Have you offended him?"

Steppu realized that she had reached out and touched the wife of Pharaoh without permission. There was a moment of clumsy silence before Steppu pulled her hand away. But Īset reached and took it in her own, holding it firmly. "Do not fear to touch me. Your touch is a comfort."

Īset looked at the linen that covered the window, stained with the morning sun. "I do not offend Pharaoh, yet my very presence offends him. I remind him of all he has lost and all he could yet lose. I remind him of sons he has never had and daughters he has no longer.

"When I am with him, he cannot put aside his sadness and disappointment, nor can he share it. To whom does a god confess his suffering? Who can heal his heart?"

"You can, my Lady," said Tchefeṭ-t, her luminous emerald eyes glowing with conviction. "We will help you."

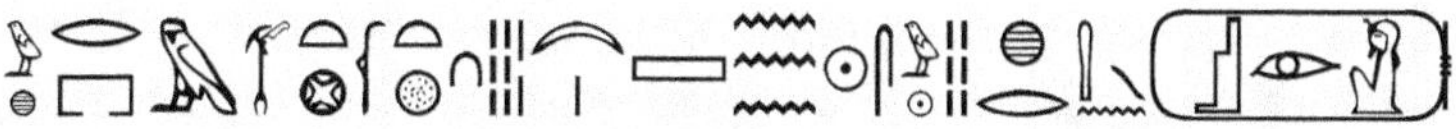

wḫrpr m wꜣst ḥsbt 18 ꜣbd 1 šm sw 6 ḫr ḥm n wsỉr

The Docks in Uas

Year 18, Month 1 of Shemu, Day 6 under the Majesty of Ạsạr

"Master."

The boat master looked up at the single, simple word spoken from the ramp leading to the dock. She was a thin wisp of a woman, nearly as unsubstantial as the gods that were rumored to speak to her.

"Priestess Neb-t-ḥe-t," he said with a smile and a welcoming gesture. "Please come aboard."

She lifted the hem of her skirt above her ankles and glided up the remainder of the ramp.

A handsome woman, not regarded to be as beautiful as her sister the Queen, she had a round face, smooth skin, and almond-shaped eyes. She did not have the fanatical look and carriage of those who spent too much time in the sun and claimed to see gods and hear their voices. Neb-t·ḥe-t had a quiet, shy manner and could go unnoticed in a crowd.

Some said Set never wanted her. They had no children. Shortly after their marriage he began to spend evenings in the company of temple dancers. Some of them, too many to be a coincidence, too few to be a scandal, swelling with child, stole away in the night and never returned.

What she might have said to her husband in private was never repeated. She said nothing about it in public. One day, fifteen inundations ago, she led a train of boxes containing her things from their home to the temple. After that, the two had little to do with one another.

Set continued to enjoy the company of young, pretty women who gave themselves willingly and completely into his hands. Neb-t·ḥe-t buried the dead and consoled the living, bringing dignity and ceremony to the transition from one life to another. She gave herself to this cause as if it might bring closure and meaning to her own unhappy past.

"Can I offer you some wine with honey or some fruit and bread?" the boat master asked.

Neb-t·ḥe-t nodded. A crinkle about the eyes, a curl of her lips, the smile made her look younger, revealing a glimpse of the child that once lived beneath the cares of life.

"Come sit with me beneath the awning," he said. "The day is already warm. Tell me what a priestess seeks from a man of the River."

Neb-t·ḥe-t smiled shyly and blushed, looking down at the polished wood deck. "It has been some time since anyone was happy to see me."

The royal boat master rose and rubbed his hands together in agitation and dipped his head. "My apologies, priestess. They are the words of a foolish old man. I meant nothing by them."

"It is nothing you need apologize for," she said, watching him. "To most, I am death. They welcome me as they would some calamity in their family. All I want to do is help them through the sorrow. They fear me for what they suppose I bring. But not you. You have never been afraid or angry with me. You do not hide or turn away at my approach. You smile when you see me. Why?"

He sighed, wiping his hand across his brow, then settled back in his seat. He picked up a tool and a bit of wood from which he had so far carved half a scarab. "You are special, Neb-t·ḥe-t. I have always thought so."

"Special. I like that."

"I wish Set had never been a part of your life. You carry the scars from the wounds he gave you—though you hide them well. I think half the tears you shed at funerals are secretly for yourself. There you can cry and people will not think you weak or silly or ungrateful."

Neb-t·ḥe-t said nothing, but the boat master looked up from his carving to see the first glistening beads welling up in the corners of her eyes and knew it was time to stop.

"But you didn't come here to hear the ramblings of a bored, lonely boat man. Tell me what you wish of me."

Neb-t·ḥe-t nodded and looked away, blinking and catching her breath. "Queen Īset will need to leave Uas suddenly, perhaps in the middle of the night. You must be ready."

Another slice of wood curled from the back of the scarab. "Is this to be a journey that will require provisions for a departure and return or is this an escape?"

"The latter, I fear. Set is returning."

Neb-t·ḥe-t let her words hang between them, squinting at the reflections off the River, rubbing her forehead and pushing the hair back. The boat master continued his strong, rhythmic strokes across the wood.

"Stock what you need for the rowers," Neb-t·ḥe-t continued. "Load what you can of Īset's possessions, her wealth may be useful, but it is important for the boat to be light and fast. We are to head toward the Great Sea."

"I serve this boat at Pharaoh's pleasure. He will join us?"

"No," Neb-t·ḥe-t said, "I think not."

She saw the boat master look up. But then the tears that had already threatened finally stung her eyes and washed away the sight of the deck, the River, and him. She did not see him get up or approach, but she felt as he lifted her and surrounded her with his arms.

"I love him too," she cried. "The gods tell me Pharaoh's time is almost over, not because he failed, but because he succeeded. Another must take his place."

"Set? The gods want Set to take his place?"

"They will not say."

"But you think Set will win?" he asked.

"I think Set may prevail. And even if he doesn't, he will send someone after Īset. That's how Set is."

"Gods preserve us."

Neb-t·ḥe-t nodded her head against his shoulder. "That is my hope."

He leaned back to look at her but she could see only the outline of his face. "We know Set is coming. We could save Pharaoh," he said.

"We could get ourselves and Īset killed. The gods want us away from here."

"I took an oath," the boat master said. "I must do something."

Neb-t·ḥe-t tightened her arms about him. "Then save the one he values most. Save Īset. She must live."

pr-zfhr mhꜣw šdšr
ḥsbt 18 ꜣbd 1 šm sw 7 ḫr ḥm n wsỉr

Sefher's House Near Shedesher
Year 18, Month 1 of Shemu, Day 7 under the Majesty of Ạsạr

The voice of a child was what Ṭeḥuti remembered first: a soft, melodic girl's voice speaking from close by. His eyes were not yet open, but the timbre and cadence of her voice soothed him as did the sunshine on his bandaged face, the smells that drifted on the soft breeze that touched and tickled his nose: straw, cooking, sand and salt, animals.

A girl telling a story, he realized after some time. She recited a tale that was old when Ṭeḥuti was young about a nomad wandering from adventure to adventure as he traveled the length of the River. Some of the adventures were familiar to Ṭeḥuti, others were new, added in the years since he last remembered hearing it.

She stopped in mid-sentence. Ṭeḥuti had opened his eyes to see her, dark hair falling over and around her eyes, staring at him.

"You're awake," she squeaked. Then she slid off the stool she had been perched on and bolted from the room.

Ṭeḥuti thought that his heart would break. He closed his eyes again, squeezing out tears.

She returned excitedly, leading a woman by the hand. Ṭeḥuti opened his eyes again but could not lift his head to see them.

"Do what I told you," the woman said.

The girl leaned over him and tipped a pitcher to his lips.

The water was cool and sweet, with a bit of honey in it. He drank for a moment and groaned. Water dribbled across his lips and down his cheeks before she drew the pitcher away.

The woman appeared next with another pitcher.

"Wine—for the pain," she said softly, lowering it to his lips, giving him a moment to savor the fruity aroma.

Ṭeḥuti tried to nod, tried to speak, and failing at both tried to thank her with his eyes. Then he opened his mouth to accept as much of the heavy, strong liquid as he could before closing his eyes again.

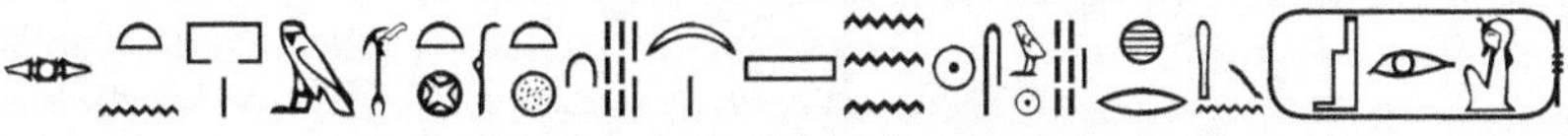

pr-nswt m wꜣst ḥsbt 18 ꜣbd 1 šm sw 7 ḫr ḥm n wsỉr

The House of Pharaoh in Uas
Year 18, Month 1 of Shemu, Day 7 under the Majesty of Ạsạr

It wasn't something Īset would have planned on her own. Dressed as a temple dancer, she prepared to bring Pharaoh his evening meal, intending to seduce him with a dance and draw him from his isolation, ending the string of days during which he answered her questions with silence and the nights when he did not summon her from the Queen's house to share his bed.

She found the skirt to be too tight, too short, too thin. It held her like a second skin and looked as insubstantial as a coating of dust on her naked body, framing each muscle movement in her legs and hips. It wrapped her once and fastened at the waist, extending only to her knees. She had to take short, fluid steps so it would not come apart. In the light, it was nearly invisible, revealing the variations in her skin tone between her tanned ankles and her waist, her pubic hair a dark patch hiding behind a linen mist.

"This is a bad idea. I am not a temple dancer. I haven't spent my youth learning how to walk or stand, tilt my head, lower my eyes and lick my lips in a way that brings a man to instant attention.

"I'm not tall and thin with every muscle under my individual control. I've born two daughters. I'm a woman pretending to be a temple dancer."

"He will not notice. Men never do. He wants the image and will see you as you were the first time he took you. Once the lust rises, he will not think and he will see only what he wishes to see," Kefa·ạb said.

Īset shook her head. "I have been his wife for twenty inundations. He has never asked me to dress or dance for him."

"Yet he no longer calls you," Kefa·ạb said.

"No man can resist a temple dancer. That is what they say," Steppu said.

"I am *not* a temple dancer."

"You need not be. You need only startle him from his silence so he can see you again," Kefa·ạb said.

Īset sighed. Her servants had convinced her yet she remained unconvinced. Smooth little servant tongues and flattering words and for a moment she saw herself as sixteen inundations, smooth, unblemished skin, narrow hips, flat belly, small, high breasts. But once they wrapped her in the tight, gauzy skirt she saw the marks where the skin had stretched as she carried Ḥaāmer and then Āakhu, the small roll that fell over the skirt's waist, breasts larger and lower now, like two old water skins half-empty.

At thirty-six inundations, she felt old. She should be witnessing the births of her daughter's first children now, not seeking to bear more children herself. But Pharaoh needed a son so badly.

The temple dancers wore a top that sometimes covered both breasts, sometimes only one. Īset wore no top at all. Instead, for a pectoral collar, she wore two looping necklaces of lotus blooms harvested from the River. The flowers reminded her of the day she and Ạsạr first met along the River bank near her summer tent on a warm, magical afternoon. *Ạsạr waded into the water and picked a lotus blossom I wanted for my hair. I kissed him, and knew . . .*

Her thoughts flowed and twisted like currents on the River. She felt silly and beneath her station. *Pharaoh loves me for my wisdom and grace, for my beauty and the daughters I have given him. He loves me because I make him smile, because I can show him the side of an argument he never sees. He loves me for my kiss, for the feel of me in his arms, the sound of my sigh. Why would he now want me only for my body wrapped in gaudy display like a common entertainer? But what else can reach him? If I go to him this way maybe he will see and remember all that he really loves about me. Is that wrong?*

So much at stake, she reminded herself. One of them had to reach out to the other. He would not and had never been able to. Pharaoh did not offer a hand and did not always take the hand that was offered him.

If he laughed at her, if he saw past the costume to a graying middle-aged woman trying to imitate something she could never be, she did not think she could bear it. And if he did not laugh, if he welcomed her, she did not think she could believe it.

"Do I really look right?" she asked again of the maidservants hovering about her.

Kefa·ạb rose from the hem of Īset's skirt. Her weathered face wrinkled like dry mud, lit with a smile. Worn, flat teeth peeked from between her parted lips. "You are all the goddesses come to visit us this night. I have never seen you look so beautiful."

Steppu applied a final touch of oil to Īset's neck and shoulders. "You are beautiful."

The finest kohl spread around her warm, brown eyes, making them large and luminous. They sparkled above and below with flakes of mica and gold.

Mica and gold also infused the perfumed oil, myrrh, broom, frankincense, and crushed flower petals that Steppu had applied to her shoulders and neck, her belly and back, covering her with countless tiny stars. Īset shimmered, a vision, a dream, every bit a goddess catching and transforming the amber flames from the oil pots.

A crown of beads, strings of lapis, jade, and ivory, blended into the ebony strands of hair that hung straight to her shoulders. The halo of tiny moons whispered with each turn of her head, the rare, exquisite sound of rain on the sand, or the River stirring in the warmth of a summer evening.

The maidservants watched. Kefa·ạb spoke for them all, her cloudy old eyes bright again, as they had been in Īset's childhood: "You are ready, my lady. It is your night."

Īset studied her reflection in a bronze mirror, her face flushed. "He has not summoned me. I want him to desire me, not *this.*"

Kefa·ạb touched a calloused, trembling hand to each of Īset's cheeks and lowered the queen's face enough that she could see into her eyes. "Each day has become the same for you and Pharaoh—no one moment distinguishable from another. There is nothing in this world that is so constant, not the River, not the seasons, not even life. Nor should it be. Husband and wife should not be so long alone. It is overdue that one of you do something to break this isolation that has drained the joy for living from you both."

The two woman stared at one another for several heartbeats. Kefa·ạb snorted and continued: "Don't look at me as if I am too forward and rising above my place. I changed your soiled linens. You took my nipples in your mouth and received life from me. Listen to me now: If it is the shock of coming to him as a temple dancer that finally wakes him up and brings him back to you, so be it."

"We are with you, Lady," said Steppu, her soft voice filled with emotion. "All women are with you tonight. Men boast of their strength and independence. They talk of victories and courage. But there is a force as old as man that they have not conquered, nor controlled. You are the mother goddess who will show Pharaoh the feminine that no man can control or resist."

"Go, Lady," said Ạaātchṭạ-t, holding out to her the tray with Pharaoh's meal. "May the moon smile upon you, may the waters rise to renew you, and may a gentle breeze guide you to paradise."

They had become like sisters, as unlikely as their origins and cultures and social class made that seem. The generation-old belief that Pharaoh was divine had not become so commonly accepted into their lives that the class barrier between them could not be breached or broken down by familiarity and time. Different ages, different lives, brought by fate from villages distant along the River, the five women found themselves together for an evening outside the rooms of Pharaoh, excited and frightened, five hearts bound together in a common purpose.

Kefa·ạb lifted the door tapestry. Īset slipped inside the first of Pharaoh's rooms. Many of the oil pots were extinguished, casting the room in semi-darkness. Statues of gold and stone and ivory, gods and animals, peered from shadows and corners. Īset started forward with soft steps, looking for her husband.

"I bring nourishment and refreshment for Pharaoh," she said, hesitant, recalling the exact words used by his servants.

There was no reply. She went to the next of Pharaoh's private rooms and the next after that. In each, she stood on the threshold and called again: "I bring—"

His silhouette rested on a terrace beyond the open doorway, the familiar profile painted against the cloudless sunset sky. He reclined on a magnificent chair of wood and ivory, the arms and back carved with charms and spells for his protection and well-being. A small, private garden stretched before him, beyond which lay fields of ripening grain extending down to the dark path of the Nile and the western lands beyond.

He might have been sleeping, except for a trace of sunset glowing in the corner of his eye.

Īset held out the tray. "I bring nourishment and refreshment for Pharaoh."

"I made no request for food," he said.

Īset answered in a low, suggestive voice: "I offer much more than food."

"I did not call for a woman."

"Sometimes a request is made with other than the lips."

He turned at the whispering sound of her steps. "Who are you?"

She sought a place to rest the tray but found no table on the terrace, only Pharaoh and his chair facing off to the west where the dead rested in their quiet graves.

"Have I become a stranger?" she asked, kneeling to place the tray on the ground. The skirt tinkled and clung to her legs.

"Īset?" Pharaoh asked, his gaze focused on her, traveling the length of her body. "What is the meaning of this?"

Īset came to him. "Are you happy to see me?"

She smiled and reached a hand toward his skirt, stumbling over a stool she had not seen in the deepening twilight. The palm of her hand went hard into his groin. Pharaoh's breath came out in a painful grunt. The arms that lifted to catch Īset pushed her away.

Īset stumbled backward, almost regaining her balance, when her heel hit the tray holding Pharaoh's meal. Her left foot upset the jug of wine. Her right foot overturned a fruit bowl. Īset landed with an undignified thud.

Pharaoh bent over his chair, his breathing fast and ragged. The last of the wine trickled from the jug and faded into the sand. The fruit lay scattered in an arc about her.

Īset wept, silent at first, and then with soft, plaintive sobs. The hours of preparation, the work and patience her maidservants had put into making her a living goddess—all come to this. She had shamed and humiliated herself. A clumsy child would have done better. The hopes for the night toppled and scattered as surely as Pharaoh's meal.

"Go back to the Queen's house," Pharaoh said.

"No."

He looked at her. "I could have you put away. Banished."

She wiped at her tears. "How would that be worse than what you have done already, leaving me alone and unwanted? My children are gone, one daughter buried, sent to the gods, the other far down the River, given to a man she did not love. You are all I have. But your spirit is far from me."

Pharaoh looked away, to the river again, and beyond to the land of the dead. "I am the most powerful and most powerless man in all Egypt. I can bring neither of them back to you."

"I would be happy if you came back to me," Īset said, gathering her feet beneath her and standing.

Frogs and insects sang in squeaks and chatters in the garden beyond the terrace. Traces of smoke from cook fires wafted up from the narrow city streets. Īset filled the air about Pharaoh with the lush scents of lotus, frankincense, and delicate flowers that bloomed along the River.

The sun's light extinguished in the West. But the milky white of the moon brightened over the landscape. Scattered torch and cook fires sent bursts of light into the evening sky.

"I will dance for you," she said, poised, bathed in lamp and moonlight. "My maidservants wait outside with instruments and song."

"No," he said. "Come here."

She took a step forward, then stopped. Ashamed, she shrugged out of the lotus collar, touched the clasp of her skirt and let it flutter to her feet. She came and settled gently into his lap, naked, her clothes in a useless puddle behind her.

He placed his arms about her gently, clasped his hands together. He did not hold her like a lover, a wife, the woman to whom he had given two children. He held her like a stranger or a child, careful to not brush against her breasts, his hands locked high around the curve of her waist rather than lower, across her hip or thigh. Īset choked back another lonely tear.

"All I ever wanted to do was sail the River and the sea beyond," he said, his eyes, his thoughts far away. "I did not want to be Pharaoh, I did not want to sit in judgment every day of my life of other peoples desires and faults and transgressions. I did not want to protect the weak, restrain the strong. I wanted the sound of the water in my ears, not the nasty, self-placating whispers, the gasps, the mutterings of those who had no divine inspiration but always thought they knew better. I wanted to bathe in the River every day and sleep on the deck, listening, rocked to sleep by it each night."

"I know," she said, reaching out to touch his cheek and then to kiss his forehead. "I saw it every time we traveled, every time you took Ḥaāmer and went off to see one of Ṭeḥuti's water projects. I saw it in the way you wore the River mud with honor. I could see it even here, those nights you held my hand and caressed my fingers while watching the sails trailing along the River. I could never compete with that."

She leaned into him to draw his warmth against the chill. She looked up at the Aih and cast a prayer its way. "Don't shut me out," Īset said. "When you miss the River, when you are sad because it calls to you and you cannot answer, let me be there to miss it with you. Let me cry the tears that you cannot. I love you, I love your joy and your sadness; I love your godliness and your humanity. Do not deny me, do not make me someone who can only approach you in the Hall of Balance. Keep me by your side, You are part of me as you are part of our daughter. Let me be part of you, never separated, never put away."

Leaves rustled in the garden, stirring though there was no breeze. Baka emerged, tail pointed, and walked across the stones of the terrace. He stopped at Īset's clothing, sniffed at the withering lotus blooms, and came to sit before them, silent, eyes glowing green in the dark like the perfect, inscrutable god.

"Set is coming back. Soon I think. Neb-t·ḥe-t said he would find me."

"Shhh," she said, leaning forward to kiss him again. "I don't want to hear about your brother tonight. You have a naked woman in your lap. What will you do?"

"There is a land and a people out there expecting me to protect them. What will I to do about them?"

"You have tomorrow and the day after and all the days ahead to worry about the land and its people and what you should do. But you have this night, this moon, these stars, and me only once. This moment will be gone and will never come again. I want to be with you tonight, I want to lie with you and see the Aten rise from the warmth of your arms."

And then she was sad again, at his silence and hesitation, at similar words Neb-t·ḥe-t said to her short months that seemed a lifetime ago. *You will have the rest your days to miss her, but only a precious few in which to say good-bye.* Each day was one day less in her life. Each night with Pharaoh was one fewer that she would spend with him. Each was precious because one day they would be gone.

"Say yes to me," she whispered. "Let us lose ourselves, our problems, our cares, all the things that keep us apart and distracted, in each other tonight."

He closed his eyes a moment, she watched the reflections disappear as the lids covered them. His hands broke apart and caressed her belly. "Yes," he said. "Too many things have made me forget you and all you mean to me."

Īset rose from him and went to the tray. She picked among the bowls and plates, the mess of fruit pieces. She found a small, sealed jar. Baka, still, dark, green eyes unblinking, the tip of his tail waving ever so slightly in the night, turned his head to watch her.

"What of your maid servants? Your music?" Pharaoh asked, standing now.

"When I do not return, they will know they are not needed. They will return to the house happy for me."

"And your costume?"

She pushed at it with a toe then left it behind. "I never liked it," she said. "Close your eyes and I will be whatever you desire. I will be a temple dancer. I will be young and eager, I will be gentle like the moon and the night. I will be relentless like the wind. I will cry out for you, and will make you cry out in return. I can be eternal. Let me be the River you so desire and miss. Rise and fall on my waves, let my breath be the wind for your sails, dip your oar and navigate my waters."

"Be Īset," he replied. "That is all I need."

She smiled at last and came to him, her steps light as they had not been in many days. She felt the cares, the sorrows, fading away, as day fades into night. They would be there again tomorrow, but not tonight. Tonight was for dreams, for possibilities, for love and comfort and communion, two hearts beating as one, two souls shining in the darkness, two lives healed. She twisted and broke the seal from the pot, lifting the lid.

"What is that?" Pharaoh asked.

"Honey."

Īset dipped a finger into the pot and drew it across her lips and again, touching behind each ear and at the hollow of her throat. "It sweetens each place you are to kiss me."

Pharaoh nodded. He dipped his fingers into the pot and gently coated each of her nipples. Then, sticky fingers, he took her hand and led her to the darkness of his bed chamber.

Chapter 21

ABYDOS, EGYPT, THE ARCHAEOLOGICAL TRAILER, JULY 12TH, 12:50 P.M.:

"I feel guilty about what happened. I caused the digger's death," said Lisa.

Lisa had told Bill all the details leading to the digger's execution.

"You don't know that. You can't take the captain's guilt. I doubt that you could have stopped him once he thought the digger was an artifact thief."

"I don't understand how he equates artifact theft with terrorism," said Lisa, shaking her head.

Anwar pounded on the trailer door. Letting him in, the men regarded each other with scorn. Bill felt contempt deep in his gut.

"Tell Anwar that we're going to contact the authorities via our channel through Dr. Tu'hut," said Bill.

Lisa nodded. Anwar responded after Lisa had passed on Bill's statement.

"He says he's in charge of this site and is handling the situation."

"Fine job he's doing," snorted Bill. Lisa didn't translate his statement. A flash of anger appeared on Anwar's face followed by indifference. Some expressions have meaning in any language. "Ask him this."

"Was your purpose for taking the digger out of camp to eliminate him?"

Anwar registered surprise, but after a few seconds, he stared at the floor unable to hold Lisa's gaze. He mumbled a few words then his face changed to a vile cast with bared teeth. He shouted a vicious remark, thrusting his hand upward followed by a spate of growled invective sentences.

Bill waited for Lisa's shocked translation.

"He says he is not happy with losing the digger, but he says he was one of the terrorists. His ugly remarks were directed against them. He said he was doing his job catching and interrogating terrorists."

"I still don't see how he can equate artifact theft with terrorism. Why does he think that the digger was a terrorist?"

Lisa asked Anwar who nodded at the computer console.

"He swears that proof is in the computer. He says the digger was the man who murdered the ambassador's wife. He believes the digger received what he deserved. We need to see his proof."

"Right now, I would prefer that he didn't touch the computer, Lisa. I don't want anything to 'accidentally' disappear."

After several exchanges, the scientists were able to view the dossiers that Anwar had prepared. Shocked, Bill scanned each of the twenty-five people that Anwar identified as the terrorist band. Lisa became agitated.

"Those are the two terrorists who attacked me in the trailer and on the ministry steps."

By scanning up and down, they were finally able to locate the pictures of the digger.

"Now I know how he was using all the computer time," Bill said. Lisa nodded her agreement.

The scientists could tell that one of the group acted as the leader although he never appeared entirely on the screen. He always appeared just off screen. Lisa asked Anwar who the terrorist leader was.

"I've never been able to identify him."

"Something about him is vaguely familiar," said Lisa. The men looked at her, waiting. She shook her head raising her shoulders and hands. "I don't know. I'll have think about it."

Bill scanned through the digger's dossier. Lisa continued.

"He claims the tattoo on the digger's wrist is the final proof of his guilt that he murdered the ambassador's wife. He says any court would agree with him that the digger's a terrorist who would've been executed."

Bill expanded a view of his wrist.

"We need to go to the camp and verify the tattoo to see if he's telling the truth."

Anwar started addressing them again. His statement left Lisa shaken. Lisa began to cry, tears running down her cheeks her face contorted in agony.. Her hands covered her mouth as she gasped.

"Oh, no! Oh, no."

"What did he say? What's happening?" Bill demanded his upset with Lisa's reaction obvious.

"During their search for the sniper," she said between heaving breaths. "Anwar found, a place where the terrorists have been hiding their victim's corpses. He has contacted his superiors. They have directed him to clean out the remains as his final job here. Bill, they're closing us down."

"Oh, my God! Human remains here?" gasped Bill. "Closing us down?"

"Yes, he told me that many of the victims on the DVDs are crammed there," she said between sobs.

"Khidr may be here. This gets worse and worse."

* * *

The lieutenant took Bill and Lisa to the army infirmary to see the dead man.

"He is over there."

The digger, unshaven, hair a tangled mess, looked more like a wild beast than a terrorist or murderer.

"I'd like to see his right wrist," Bill told the lieutenant.

The lieutenant caught the digger's right arm and pulled it up for Bill to examine. The Arabic crescent and star emblazoned his skin, but more importantly two purple and yellow snake eyes peered at the Americans from under the crescent. Neither had ever seen that particular juxtaposition of the symbols except on the recording. Additionally a natural mole marked the digger's arm slightly to the left and below the snake's eyes. This combination uniquely identified the digger's arm just as Anwar said. Both remembered the mole in Anwar's pictorial dossier for the man. They both remembered this man shooting a woman, identified as the Kuwaiti ambassador's wife, in one of the videos.

Lisa photographed the digger and his right arm.

"Let's talk," she said walking from the tent. "Thank you, lieutenant."

"Yes, thank you, lieutenant," chimed Bill.

"Yes, ma'am, sir."

"He was a murderer," expressed Lisa. "I believe Anwar's telling the truth."

"Yes, it appears that way. I suspect that we must believe what he says."

The expression on Lisa's face changed to an ah-ha look.

"I know when the digger stole the bowl. The diggers were moving back and forth 'helping' me set up the x-ray equipment in Ḥaāmer's room bringing the blocks. He probably stuffed it in his robe on one of his trips out. We weren't searching them when they were making those short trips. He could have easily stashed the artifact in the rocks outside to be picked up later."

"That hardly matters now," said Bill.

"I wanted to solve how he avoided our security."

"I understand. I'm going with the captain to view the bodies."

"Why are you doing that?"

"The boy may be there."

"Oh," she said, a catch in her voice. "Yes, sorry, I wasn't thinking about that. I'll go with you."

"There's no need for you to subject yourself to that," he said.

Lisa shook her head negatively. "I'll be there for you."

"Thank you. I appreciate that, he hugged her.

"This whole thing's very dark. I understand why the terrorists have been lurking in this area. They were protecting their burial hiding place."

"Damn! The government's shutting us down."

As he said this, tears ran down her cheeks. He shifted her in his arms holding her tightly to his chest, caressing the back of her head and neck.

"We know why Anwar was using so much computer time," he repeated his earlier remark. "He's been analyzing the DVDs and building the dossiers."

"He did many things. He's quite sharp. I'm sorry that it's turned out this way. We don't have our ancient proof."

"I know, but people are dead. It isn't Anwar's fault either."

"No, it isn't. We were too slow."

He shook his head negatively.

"No, we were working hard."

ABYDOS, EGYPT, THE MASS GRAVE, JULY 13TH, 5:19 A.M. DAWN:

Anwar requested two hundred body bags. Command sent them, repeating their order for him to clean it up. Military Headquarters gathered the necessary equipment to handle the dead. The funeral convoy drove through the night to bring Captain Jagardii the cleanup material. 1'iHe began the gruesome work at dawn.

Anwar posted guards on the cliffs above them so there would be no more sniper attacks. The soldiers worked under the rock outcropping, lifting and bagging the stacked bodies. It was a grizzly task, working with the bodies bloating from the heat. The stench hung heavily in the air and penetrated everything. Their clothing reeked of human destruction. Anwar changed the soldiers every forty-five minutes, starting with those requiring disciplinary action. He instructed them to shower and change uniforms when they returned to the camp. The soldiers required no goading to follow that order. They wanted to wash the memories of the horror from their skin even if they couldn't wash them from their minds.

They pulled each body from the stack, stuffing them into the bags. They carried them three hundred yards to the road, loading them into trucks for transport back to Cairo. The government would attempt to identify the bodies and contact the next of kin. Anwar was sure he'd seen the Kuwaiti ambassador's wife.

Wishing to reduce the transfer of stories from one group to the next, he isolated the new troops coming on shift from those returning to camp. He knew their imagination worked more devious attacks on their minds than the terrible physical work.

The American archeologists came to see the remains. Sanders positioned himself on a rock where he could see each body as it was placed in a body-bag. Lisa, kept vigil with him. If a particular corpse interested Sanders, he would walk to the body to have a closer look. Anwar did not understand his curiosity.

With the heavy reporting of the terrorist activity on the internet, little time would pass before this latest governmental impotency would come to light. Some among the military would like to see the government embarrassed. Anwar would be blamed for not performing his duty. His agony made his hatred for the terrorists well up inside of him again even as the bile welled up into his throat. He'd seen the dead, never the stinking, putrefying corpses of innocents.

As the soldiers progressed, loading the bagged bodies into the back of a military truck, Anwar was at his lowest point of depression. The destruction the terrorists were working upon his country was staggering. He accepted the job stoically knowing that his career would end with this fiasco. The government would blame him for the discovery of one more embarrassment, an atrocity that they would be unwilling to recognize, or for that matter, to take responsibility. His feelings were oppressive and almost more than he could bear. He shuddered under his onerous thoughts. As the despair settled over him, the nausea almost overwhelmed him, his stomach refluxing into his throat. Anwar swallowed an acidic chunk that had welled up from his stomach as he paced back and forth. The lieutenant positioned himself before him, looking into his eyes, trying to steady him.

"Get away from me!"

Anwar would have none of that weak-kneed help yet the lieutenant had calmed him. Two soldiers dropped a corpse and foul liquid gushed from the bag. The two vomitted.

"Stick to your duty and be more careful. Get working you two," he said angrily.

His thoughts circled to his hatred of the terrorists. He remembered the flush of pleasure he felt as he struck the digger. Even this memory, made him despondent. As a professional soldier, he could handle death, but not meaningless death. He had killed in combat before, but the digger at the time had not seemed like a combatant no matter how many times he told himself that he was. He saw on the recording the digger murder the ambassador's wife. He certainly deserved to die, but Anwar had only been getting information from him. Most likely this is why the sniper shot him. The courts would have determined the digger's fate.

Now, within his psyche, he discovered that beating the digger felt just as bad as killing a non-combatant. The defenseless digger was weak. Aching, he remembered how Nefri warned him that his insatiable lust for revenge would not bring him pleasure, but rather destruction. He despaired from these thoughts for he understood what had hurt her. His continued aggressive pursuit of the terrorists troubled her. He must stop.

How am I going to turn this around?

He straightened his back. Surveying the carnage, he saw that only a few bodies remained. Looking at his watch, he decided no one else would be introduced to the sight or the smell. He would remember those who had worked and would commend them this evening. He would tell them this was the work of the terrorists they were pursuing. He would avoid the Americans for the time being, but he would make sure that no harm came to either of them. That would be the final nail in his coffin. His nerves steadied; his resolve returned. He wondered at doubting himself. He would continue his campaign. He would make his visitation into the desert tonight. Things were coming to a focal point and he needed to plan. He eyed the lieutenant.

"Lieutenant! This job is done. Get those final bodies out of here."

The lieutenant's expression showed that he marveled at his captain.

So be it.

"Yes, sir."

"I want a double guard posted on the American trailer from now on. At no time will either of the doctors go unescorted. Neither of them is to leave the camp without my knowledge. Do you understand?"

"Yes, sir. They won't like their authority over their project being challenged."

"I have authority over their safety and security. They will *conform* to our assistance. This site will be closed."

"Yes, sir."

"You two," Anwar pointed at the scientists "Fall in."

The Americans stood to follow him.

Anwar came to attention as the last body passed him. He saluted the former resting place of the dead, did an about-face and marched after the last body.

*   *   *

"Khidr wasn't among the remains," Bill told Lisa. "Nor was he in the terrorist dossiers that the captain developed."

"Then he must have escaped from them," said Lisa.

"We can only hope."

*   *   *

When the infidels discovered the hiding place, the terrorist sniper had watched. His job was to guard the grave site, making sure no one or animal found it. Allah protected him from capture by the enemy. He shot the weak one to keep him from giving up the village. After their initial search for him, their attention riveted on the discovered bodies. They had not noticed him. He withdrew to watch the soldier's work, but with all of the sentries, he was unable to shoot any of them. He would report their handiwork to his superiors. He no longer cared about the leader's cause.

ABYDOS, EGYPT, THE ARCHAEOLOGICAL TRAILER, JULY 14TH, 7:35 A.M.

"'Ugh, morning," Lisa grumbled, rubbing the sleep from her eyes as she walked to the front of the trailer. Bill already sat at the table for their ritual 'Breakfast meeting' in which they talked and planned their day. She didn't eat anything and Bill ate avidly as always. His sweat and grime indicated that he'd been out running.

He's such a morning person.

"So how was your run?" she asked.

"Didn't happen. Captain Jagardii has clamped down on our leaving the site. I climbed the cliff-face instead."

"You be careful. I don't need you falling."

"Oh, you care?"

Her mouth twisted in a sardonic grimace. "Yes."

"His security measures are really hampering our exploration."

"I know and I'm sorry about that," she agreed. "How can you eat like that after seeing all those bodies?"

Lisa never ate Breakfast and Bill was aware of that. Even so his face registered genuine surprise by her comment.

"Guy's got'ta eat."

She wrinkled her nose at him.

"This whole thing is taking on such a frantic pace," she moaned.

"I know. I don't like the speed we're traveling. I prefer slow speculation."

"Do you think we're jeopardizing the archaeology?"

"No, but I'd like to take the time to make sure your theory covers all of the facts. This speed doesn't allow us to think."

"Right. Let's focus and figure out what we're looking for," she said.

"I think I'll explore the foyer," Bill told her. "We may not have seen all of the artifacts that are located in front of the tomb seal. There may be another entry to a complex. Why does this tomb have two entrances? That still doesn't make total sense."

Lisa nodded soberly.

"Yeah, we haven't been back there. Of all the information that we've gathered, the foyer is the one area that doesn't fit our theories very well," she agreed.

"We haven't returned to the cave since your initial exploration. There might be more data if not artifacts," he said between bites. "I'll have to widen the hole to get in."

"I squeezed in," she grinned. "Then again, I don't stuff my face."

"Hey, no more food comments."

"We need to discuss how long this exploration is going to take. The Egyptian government is shutting us down soon. What information can we gather before that happens?"

"Right. We may not get a second chance. That does happen here," he concluded. She nodded sadly.

"I'm going to continue cataloging Āakhu's chamber." They still called it that. "I'm trying to get to the back to see if there's another door."

"Good idea. Plenty to do then," agreed Bill. He stood smiling at her. "I'd better get going. You take care."

"You too."

They kissed.

He gathered excavation tools to widen the hole in the cave and departed, leaving Lisa to pick up the dishes. She walked to the door and watched his retreating back. Scowling, Lisa decided she needed to talk with him about casting her in the role of kitchen help. She had definite thoughts about that guy. Their professional interaction had taken on a deeper personal meaning.

Bill had raised the issue of leaving the artifacts in situ with Dr. Tu'hut. He had to retreat before the Secretary General's wrath—mean old bugger.

She would give the good doctor another dose of her opinions. That would be a harangue.

Her thoughts retraced to the previous evening she spent reminiscing with Bill.

Enough of that girl!

She left the dishes on the table.

He came clean up his own mess.

She forced her thoughts to focus on how she would process through the chamber. The throbbing of a helicopter assaulted her ears and drove her thoughts wandering again. Who could be leaving or coming now? No one was scheduled to leave or enter the camp. Bill wasn't leaving.

Must be the military.

She picked up her tools, heading out the door. She looked up for the chopper, but it was landing behind the trailer on the road. A flash of light glinted off the cliff top to her right drawing her attention. She saw a soldier being taken down by another soldier, being hit, maybe stabbed. Alarms went off in her head. The sentinels were stationed around the cliff tops to protect them from snipers. She saw the lieutenant heading toward the road in the jeep. She waved her arms trying to get his attention, but he was in a hurry and ignored her.

Damn! What was that?

She needed to have it investigated. Remembering Bill's lesson, Lisa re-entered the trailer, running to the computer console. She swiped the mouse, removing the screen saver. Three taps on the horn icon brought three blasts from the horn atop the trailer. She paused and tapped the icon three more times and then again. She ran to the bedroom retrieving the captured terrorist pistol. Her hands began to shake.

Steady! she commanded.

By the numbers, from her training, she checked the chamber and the magazine. She chambered a round and released the safety. She peered around the edge of the trailer door. Bill, at the cliff wall facing her, waved, lifting his shoulders as a sign of 'what's going on?' She signaled palm down for him to get down. A squad of soldiers ran across the open area toward the trailer.

Where are the sentinels that Anwar posted by the trailer?

The lieutenant driving the jeep pulled next to the trailer with Dr. Tu'hut, as Lisa descended the steps. Lisa and Secretary General's eyes met at the same instant. Both had the same reaction, shock followed by anger. Dr. Tu'hut's face formed into a snarl, his yellow teeth showed as he spoke.

"You! You!" He bellowed. "What are you doing here?"

"Not now," she responded in a quiet level tone, her right hand holding the gun down by her thigh, her free left hand motioning for him to stop his verbal barrage. She looked wildly around to see the sentinels. She did not find them.

"You are always where you are not supposed to be. You are supposed to be gone. Out of the country," continued Tu'hut unabated.

"Stop!" Lisa commanded in Arabic.

"You are always doing what you want to do, not what you should be doing, throwing your opinion around. Interfering. I will...I will...."

Tu'hut couldn't get out his exasperation. The lieutenant was looking agog from the Secretary General to Lisa. His eyes shifted from them to his right. Lisa followed them.

A soldier stepped from behind the corner of the trailer, pointed his pistol at the lieutenant, and shot him through the forehead, dead. He shifted his aim to Dr. Tu'hut who threw up his hands in shock. The man seemed to have trouble articulating his hand. Tu'hut screeched. Lisa screamed. He jerked, missing Tu'hut and whirling to face Lisa. Surprise, then recognition registered on his face. A look of hate began to form. The bombing terrorist, whose hand Lisa had smashed, raised his gun.

Lisa, crouching in the bent knee, two handed stance that she had been taught, drilled three holes in his chest. The terrorist flung back with a sharp jerk, sprawling on the jeep hood. Tu'hut screamed again. Suddenly, the sound from the tomb site roared in on her. It sounded like a war.

Dammit, Lisa! It is a war!

She certainly didn't need the Secretary General, screeching at her. She ran to the side of the jeep, grabbing his shirt front, wrenching him from the jeep. Bodily dragging him toward the trailer, Lisa thrust him underneath.

"Get under there," she ordered and when two bullets, punctuating her statement, peppering the side of the trailer beside her head, she followed. Tu'hut wailed.

"Be quiet!" she said, giving him a look to silence him.

The dead sentinels were with them. She leaned out and looked toward the cave to see if she could see Bill. Bullets whizzed around the vehicle, forcing Lisa to keep back from the edge. There was a lot of dust flying around inside the cliffs.

I can't see.

She leaned forward again and saw Bill at the entrance of the cave. Suddenly, he was hit and went down. She raised to go to him, but Tu'hut restrained her.

"No!" She screamed at him. She tried to wrench out of his grasp.

"It's too dangerous out there. Stay here," he told her in Arabic. He shoved her down pinning her so she couldn't move. When she quit struggling, he released her. It looked like Anwar's company wasn't doing well. She saw a lot of dead soldiers. She had to get to Bill. She saw Anwar running away from the battle. She suddenly wondered whether they had lost.

What is going to happen? My stomach feels like lead. I may be killed.

Frightened, the awful truth that she had killed a man began to seep into her consciousness. Her hands shook. She felt ill. She knew she was going to throw-up. She dropped the gun. The constant tapping of automatic weapons created a horrific din that reverberated off the cliffs.

I need to get to Bill.

She was up and running, avoiding Dr. Tu'hut's outthrust hand. She ran across the field, bullets trailing her, splatting at her feet. She tripped and was up again. The beat of the helicopter props rose behind her in a swirl of dust. The helicopter retreated going away from the enclosed space. She knew Anwar had made his escape.

Damn him!

The pitch changed and the machine seemed to swoop down upon her. She looked up again. The small arms fire was now directed at the helicopter. The chopper lifted high, well above the cliffs. Instantly, it plunged and seemed to charge at them. The rattle of the chopper's heavy Gatling Gun pierced the air. Tracers showed the path of fire even in the morning light. Anwar was picking the terrorists off the cliffs.

Of course! The terrorists had taken the high ground and Anwar was winning it back.

Once the surrounding cliff top was clear, the helicopter shifted to the ground terrorists. The battle changed. The small arms rattle gave way to the sound of the circling helicopter. The battle had stopped. There were very few captives. Soldiers rounded up the isolated groups of terrorists, disarming them, forcing their hands to the backs of their heads, shoving them down on the ground with their rifle butts. The terrorists had not amounted to much of an armed force.

Hadn't Anwar said there was only twenty-five?

The only advantage they had over the trained soldiers was the cliff top and the element of surprise. Once Anwar cleared the high areas, the ground force had no chance. A group of soldiers trotted toward the trailer.

When she got to the cave entrance, she could see where Bill fell. There was a lot of blood. He had to be inside the cave. She had no idea whether there were any terrorists inside, but she felt Bill needed her help.

"Bill!"

She listened. She heard nothing, her heart sinking.

"Bill!" She screamed at silence.

Terrified, Lisa entered the cave. Soldiers turned, but no one challenged her. Maybe he wasn't dead, her gut told her. Maybe he was wounded and she could help him.

ABYDOS, EGYPT, THE CAVE ABOVE THE FIRST TOMB SEAL, JULY 14TH, 8:15 A.M.

Lisa didn't think. She crawled along the passage. Bill lay on the floor. Lisa's examination found a shoulder wound. She put her head to his back and heard the low thump of his still beating heart. He was unconscious, not dead.

Should she turn him over?

She decided to leave him still. Tears welled to her eyes and ran down her cheeks. He moaned and she put her arms around his neck supporting him. She thrust her finger into the wound, pinching the artery to stop the bleeding.

"Live!" she ordered him. "You must live."

His eyes fluttered then closed.

"Bill! You have to stay with me. Dammit! You can't die on me. Not now. I love you Bill. Dammit! Stay with me."

Chapter 22

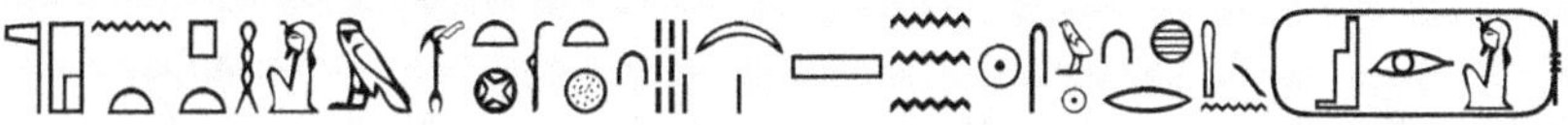

ḥwt-nṯr nt ptḥ m wꜣst ḥsbt 18 ꜣbd 1 šm sw 10 ḫr ḥm n wsỉr

The Temple of Ptah is Uas,
Year 18, Month 1 of Shemu, Day 10 under the Majesty of Ạsạr

"Welcome," Temu called in a voice too loud, his eyes bright with the wine he had already consumed, his breath sour with its taste. "Such a special evening. The entertainment and feasting have commenced. Come in!"

Temu welcomed Pharaoh inside. He frowned and put out a hand when Pharaoh's guard followed.

"Not your men, not tonight. This is a place of celebration. Let me be your devoted guardian tonight."

Pharaoh hesitated, studying Temu's face.

"Please," Temu smiled.

Pharaoh turned to his captain. "Wait for me here. Come if I call."

"Let my boldness be on my own head," said the captain, going to one knee. "One of us should be with you. It was your command at Meḥ."

"We are your friends and servants," Temu said. "There is no threat here. Be it on my head and the heads of each of my fellows here in the temple if you are not as safe in this hall as in your private rooms. Please, noble Pharaoh, let them wait here. The presence of armed men will inhibit the celebration."

People moved beyond the open doorway. The sounds of music and singing, people laughing and calling to one another spilled out to Pharaoh, as well as the scents of incense and food. The light inside was warm and bright, beckoning. Pharaoh looked past Temu a moment, his senses drawn to the excitement beyond that doorway. He turned to his captain and said: "Wait here."

The captain frowned but nodded. "As you command."

The guard retreated and temple servants let the heavy tapestries close on them. Temu ushered Pharaoh deeper into the room.

So many torches and oil pots burned, it was bright as day and smokey, the ceiling high above nearly lost in cloud. The music was overwhelming, the sound a breeze, a pressure against Pharaoh's ears. Musicians filled every corner, playing in unison.

Dancers jumped and pranced about, whirling like dust storms across the floor. Women clad only in skirts or in girdles with wisps of linen and feathers hanging from them, catapulting, leaping, twirling, providing a beat for the musicians to follow. It was a jarring mixture of formal temple dances, joyous, free-motion celebratory dances, slow, humble worship dances, suggestive courtship dances, all without any particular theme or progression.

"What is this vulgar display?" Pharaoh growled. "I came here to—"

There was a trace of something in Temu's face, just for a moment. Insult taken, anger, a need to retaliate, until his smile chased it away. "No frowns tonight, this is a celebration! How seldom we get to entertain you. Relax, enjoy yourself. I promise you will get what you came here for before the evening ends."

Temu led Pharaoh to a pile of pillows and short, decorated tables. One held several jugs of wine and drinking bowls. Another displayed trays of fire-roasted meats, clumps of garlic, young, boiled onions, and fruits soaked in honey and sweet spices.

A young woman with the easy, unpracticed grace of a dancer, filled a plate with samples and approached.

"This is Merit," Temu smiled. "She will serve you tonight."

The woman smiled and dipped her head, offering the plate for Pharaoh's inspection. Her dress covered one breast. The other hung like a firm, tawny fruit, nipple erect, an arm's length from him. Pharaoh stared and his face warmed at the realization that his first thoughts were not of Īset waiting in the Queen's House or the inviting smells of the food Merit held for his choice, but to reach out and pluck that fruit.

Temu smiled. "Delicious, is she not? For tonight, she is yours."

Merit took a date soaked in honey between thumb and forefinger and held it out. Pharaoh opened his mouth and she set it on his tongue so gently that he did not feel it until she had withdrawn her fingers and was reaching for another.

He closed his mouth and chewed, savoring the sweet, subtle taste.

Temu lifted a hand. "Bring us some wine. That jar from Set's personal stock. Pharaoh's mood is not yet lightened."

Pharaoh had no time to frown. Merit already had another morsel poised before his lips.

* * *

Pharaoh's guards remained alert outside the hall, listening to sounds of laughter and strains of music coming from inside. They did not hear the sound of sandals approaching from a dim, torch lit corridor.

Four temple women with trays of food and drink, the trays concealing more than their wispy, gauzy gowns.

"Pharaoh sent this for you," said the first, smiling and lowering her eyes. She settled the tray so her breasts peeked over the top.

"He did not want you to pass the evening alone," said another.

Their eyes were painted with kohl, glowing like jewels above cinnamon-colored cheeks. Their lips, stained red, enticed and invited. They floated more than walked, their bodies fluid after the years of practice.

"You are a temple dancer," the captain said, half question, half revelation.

"I am," she replied.

"I have heard of you, but never seen one of you before," he said.

"They say you are beautiful as sunrise, gentle as moonlight," another added.

The men relaxed and looked to their captain. "Pharaoh sent you?" He asked with a frown. But his hand opened, the fingers uncurling, and dropped away from the bronze knife secured to his girdle. The frown melted as he answered the young woman's smile.

"Yes," she said, drawing the word out into a song. "And when you have eaten, we will dance for you."

The scent of herbs and spices made the mouth water. Surrounding it, caressing it, the scent of oils, perfumes, and soaps from soft feminine skin stirred its own form of hunger.

The captain turned his head toward the hall. The music continued. The women seemed to sway to its rhythm, languid and hypnotic. He nodded and they flowed, each to a man, their hips accentuating the slow, suggestive sounds from the hall. Each executed a short, smooth knee flex, lowering long lashes, tilting the head forward then smiling, bright, sudden, like sunrise.

The youngest of the guards reached for the tray held before him. The young woman drew it away. "Let me serve you," she said.

She shifted the tray to one arm. Like a signal, each of the others did the same. This, too, was a dance. She dipped her fingers in a pot of honey and raised them, dripping, to his lips. Its taste was not as sweet as her smile, her cheeks, the smokey torchlight burning bright and deep in her eyes.

They ate as if they had never eaten before, fed piece by delicate piece from the honeyed tips of slender, graceful fingers.

Sleep settled quickly on the unsuspecting men. There was a moment of wrongness, when cloudy, distant thoughts that this was not right, this was not the time to slumber, bubbled up to consciousness. Numb hands reached for impossibly distant weapons and could not find them. The women, their deft fluid hands, inviting smiles and longing eyes blurred and faded away.

Pharaoh's guard tumbled quietly to the floor and lay still. The four temple dancers stood over them, motionless, like statues. They suddenly had nothing to do, no one to serve or entice. Their gowns stirred to the gentle breath of air creeping through the dark temple corridor, quivering to the beat of each young, passionate heart.

They waited and seeing nothing, the woman who led turned. They left the way they had come, still dancing, unable to stop, beautiful and serene as Peret mist drifting across the River at dawn.

No sooner had the whisper of their sandals died away, their shadows dwindling and lost in the torchlight, that Set's men came with their bronze swords to make sure Pharaoh's guards would never wake again.

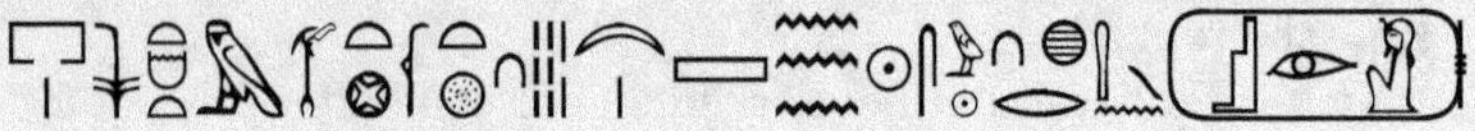

pr ḥmt nswt m wꜣst ḥsbt 18 ꜣbd 1 šm sw 8 ḫr ḥm n wsỉr

The House of Pharaoh's Wife in Uas
Year 18, Month 1 of Shemu, Day 10 under the Majesty of Ạsạr

"Go," shouted a voice in the temple.

Neb-t·ḥe-t jerked in surprise, raising her head and looking around. No one else moved. She was the only one who heard. She saw a flicker of motion in a dark corner and nodded. There was no time to question or worry or hesitate.

She left the private, most holy area of the temple, quiet, sparse with worshipers once night had settled, hurried across the common area, between the carved and decorated pillars. On the street, the cool night air greeted her. She wrapped her cloak more tightly and hurried among and past those going to or from the evening's entertainments.

Men and women with sweet, pure voices that carried along on the night air like delicious scents called out, inviting her to join them in food or drink, to watch graceful, soaring dancers, to come listen to soothing voices and beguiling musicians, to come as a couple or come as one and find another for the evening.

Past the evening revelers the way led to the House of Pharaoh and beside it, the Queen's house.

The guards recognized her but did not step aside and allow her to pass. "She has retired for the evening," their captain said.

"Something has happened. I must see my sister," Neb-t·ḥe-t said.

She saw him glance past her to the Temple of Ptah and the hall beyond it, brightly lit, flags unfurled at this late hour, stirring in the hushed evening breeze, the voices of the celebration carrying as a murmur even to this distance. Neb-t·ḥe-t could feel it behind her, like a change in wind direction or the up-welling of cold water in the warm River.

"What?" he asked, more alert, eyes large and uneasy in the torch light.

No time to think. "If Īset is to see the Aten tomorrow, she must leave Uas tonight. Pharaoh's boat waits for her at the Ukher. I am here to take her there. Help me or stay here."

He looked to the Temple of Ptah again. "Pharaoh has not returned from his celebration."

Neb-t·ḥe-t put a hand on his shoulder. "We can no longer help him. We must save Īset."

He looked down into her eyes. She could see the lights from the temple reflected in them. She did not know what it was he saw in her, but it was enough. "I believe you," he said, moving from before the doorway. "Tell me what to do."

"Come," she called, plunging into the darkened passage.

They encountered another set of guards at the entrance to Īset's common room and two maidservants, Steppu and Ạaātchṭạ-t, waiting at the door to her private chambers. The guard with Īset got them by the two at the common room, one of the two joining them. "Where are Tchefeṭ-t and Rāmạtet?" Neb-t·ḥe-t asked.

"I sent them to the Ukher," Steppu said, holding out a candle to Neb-t·-ḥe-t.

Neb-t·ḥe-t nodded and pushed through the tapestry. Steppu and Ạaātchṭạ-t followed, lighting oil pots in Īset's bedroom.

"What is this?" Īset called out, throwing an arm across her eyes and rolling onto her side.

"We must go," Neb-t·ḥe-t said. "Get up and get dressed."

"Neb-t·ḥe-t? How late is it?"

"Perhaps too late."

Steppu had a dress draped over her arm, Ạaātchṭạ-t had a cloak and sandals. Neb-t·ḥe-t pulled Īset upright and transferred the dress to her lap.

"What's happened?" Īset asked. She was more awake now, her eyes focused on Neb-t·ḥe-t.

"Set has returned to the temple."

Steppu helped Īset with her sleep shift, slipping the straps off her shoulders and stripping her bare to the waist.

"Lift your arms," Neb-t·ḥe-t said. She shook the dress loose and pulled it over her sister's head.

"Is Pharaoh still at his celebration?"

"Yes," Neb-t·ḥe-t said.

Ạaātchṭạ-t knelt and arranged the sandals before Īset. She stood, the sleep shift dropping to the floor at her feet and the dress over her head, arms through the sleeves, unfurling down to her ankles. She slipped her feet into the sandals. "We must go to him."

"It's too late for that. We must leave Uas."

"I won't!" Īset cried.

"Think of your child, Īset. He must live."

Steppu and Ạaātchṭạ-t stopped frantically gathering and looked up. Īset touched her belly with trembling fingers.

"Yes, he's there," Neb-t·ḥe-t said, "though it's too early for you to know for sure. You must protect Ạsạr's heir."

"I thought, maybe," Īset said, stumbling over the words, "but I wasn't sure."

Neb-t·ḥe-t nodded. "The gods have graced you at last."

"We must do something for Ạsạr."

Neb-t·ḥe-t took her sister's hand and drew her towards the door. "Everything that could be done has been. The gods sent me to you—you and your son. Pharaoh will join us at the boat if he can. Come."

"No," Īset shouted. "I won't go without him."

The servants looked up. From the shadows a lion as tall at the shoulder as Īset padded forward and growled, tail twitching, eyes large and golden and angry, focused on Īset.

Īset shrank back towards her bed, a small strangled cry escaping her. The servants frowned and returned to their gathering, seeing only Baka, tail curled into a sickle shape, standing before Īset and Neb-t·ḥe-t.

"If you do not go, Akeru will eat you and carry you to the boat in his belly," Neb-t·ḥe-t said.

"Will the gods bring Ạsạr?"

Akeru growled again.

"If they can save him, that is where he will go. You must be there for him," Neb-t·ḥe-t translated.

Īset looked into the cold, inscrutable feline face. "Please," she pleaded.

Akeru stepped forward and snarled.

Neb-t·ḥe-t took her sister's arm. "We must go now."

Steppu and Ạaātchṭạ-t closed their bags and boxes and tossed them on a sled outside Īset's bedroom. The guards lifted the sled by handles and carried it through the common room behind Neb-t·ḥe-t and Īset. The servants trailed behind them.

Baka waited as the sights and sounds and odors of the others diminished in the distance. He turned his head, hissed, and watched each candle and oil pot in turn smolder into a final thread of smoke and go out. He followed the others from the queen's house, doors closing silently behind him, lights going out, extinguished by invisible breaths, leaving the house ready in case any of them ever returned.

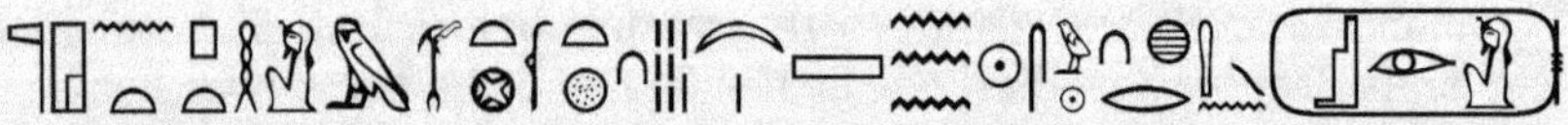

ḥwt-nṯr nt ptḥ m wȝst ḥsbt 18 ȝbd 1 šm sw 10 ḫr ḥm n wsỉr

The Temple of Ptah is Uas,
Year 18, Month 1 of Shemu, Day 10 under the Majesty of Ạsạr

Pharaoh turned his head as Merit bent low over him to refill his wine bowl, her breath a warm, fragrant kiss against his cheek.

"I grow weary of this, Temu. Bring me the men behind this conspiracy."

"One more guest," Temu smiled.

"No," Pharaoh shouted and started to rise, but Merit still hovered above him. He stumbled sideways away from her and fell over a stack of pillows. Merit reached to steady him, her hands soft on his forearm and shoulder, and with a startled cry tumbled on top of him.

"Here he is," Temu announced.

Ạsạr looked around Merit's head and the long hair that had fanned out across his face, "Set!"

Ạsạr struggled to get up but Merit was relaxed and spread out over him like a blanket. He tried to push her gently aside, then felt the warm blood and lifted his head to see the knife sticking from her back. She was dead.

Set smiled. "Sampling the delicacies. I prefer them alive, myself."

This was the Set Pharaoh had seen far too often through the years: slouching beside a dead, bloodied pet, vague as to what happened; standing before the tall grass, perplexed, as a sobbing maiden gathered the tatters of her clothing and ran off; puzzled, examining a rock that had mysteriously come loose and crushed the leg of a rival. Set, always present, never involved. Set, who could run through the inundation and never have mud stick to him.

The musicians snatched up their instruments and fled the room, the dancers racing along behind them in billowing clouds of gauzy linen, panting and glowing with sweat.

Pharaoh struggled out from under the dead temple dancer and looked about the nearly empty room. Set and the other priests and ministers from the Uas temple stared back at him, no one speaking or moving.

"Not what you were expecting, was it?" Set asked.

Pharaoh looked at his brother. "I had hoped it would not be you."

"Yet you don't seem surprised," Set said.

"Why do you want to kill me?" Pharaoh asked. "I've supported and encouraged you, helped you when you needed it. I've overlooked your mistakes and poor judgments. I did not choose to become Pharaoh in your stead. I did not take Īset from you."

"You claim these things were done against your will?"

"I had no will," Pharaoh said. "Neither did you. While our father lived there was only his will. He made these decisions for both of us."

"Nothing that goes wrong is ever your fault, is it, brother?"

"You did nothing to change his mind. Or mine. Now why do you want to kill me?"

"I want what's mine."

"You've been given that and more."

"I want my birthright."

"No," Pharaoh said. "You lost that."

"Then we have nothing more to discuss," Set said.

"Guards," Pharaoh called.

Set shook his head. "They will not be answering. They are dead as you shall soon be."

Set pulled the knife from Merit's back and drove it deep into Pharaoh's belly, cutting upward before pulling it out again.

Ạsạr stumbled to his feet and was suddenly cold. He watched his entrails bulge through the wound and unfold to the floor. Then he was far away and knew the gods were leaving him, fleeing, abandoning him to his fate.

"Is this all I ever meant to you?" Ạsạr asked as he fell.

* * *

Set stabbed and stabbed at his brother, he didn't know how many times. Finally exhaustion overcame anger and he slowed and stopped.

His breathing was difficult, he couldn't get any air, only the coppery smell of blood. His brother's face was still recognizable but his body was a mass of cuts and gouges. There was blood everywhere.

"Help me," Set said to the stunned men about him.

"Gods," one said.

Another leaned over and vomited.

It was Temu who finally broke through the shock and stillness. "It's done."

"We must hide the body," Set said.

"That will be easier if we divide it into pieces," Temu said.

Set looked down at his brother's body. His breathing slowed. He nodded and looked at Temu. "Bring jars and urns—large ones."

"It will stink unless we cover it with sand. We should also reseal the lids. There should be empty wine and oil jars in the back rooms where the feast was prepared. Go fetch them," Temu said to get the others moving.

They scattered, relieved to be away from the gruesome sight. Pharaoh, chosen of the gods, dead by his brother's hand. How angry would the gods be when they discovered that?

Temu reached to take the sword from Set's shaking hand.

"No," Set said, "I will finish what I started, Tell me where to cut."

Temu nodded. "Separate the head."

The wet, crunching sound of the sword slicing through the neck and spine sent a sudden shiver through those still in the hall, it pierced all attempts at distraction, and caused those gathering the empty oil and wine pots to pause, close their eyes, and shake away a chill.

Set was a meat cutter performing each instruction: separate each limb and divide it at the joint. Cut the body into four pieces. Strike hard to break through both breast and spine.

It did not seem possible Pharaoh had contained so much blood. Set stopped after each cut to wipe the blade and hilt on the linen decorations. The smell grew worse, blood, bile, urine, feces, all the smells mingled and fought with one another and with the very air in the room as Pharaoh's body was divided.

"Cover his head. Put it in the first jar. I'm tired of him staring at me."

Pharaoh's eyes were still open, but cloudy and unfocused. Blood dotted his gray cheeks, nose, and forehead. His face grayed further as the last of his blood dripped from the stub of a neck that still remained beneath his chin.

Weariness made Set's strokes clumsy but he would not pass the sword to Temu or one of his guards. Set did as complete a job crushing Pharaoh's body as he did dividing it into small pieces.

Temu gripped Set's shoulders. "That's good enough. We've sealed all the pieces away."

Set looked up and saw the line of jars starting behind him and stretching back towards the kitchens. "Now we must hide them. Far from each other. Far from here."

Chapter 23

ABYDOS, EGYPT, THE FEATURE, JULY 14TH, 8:48 A.M.:

Bodies were spread over the field below the cliffs. Soldiers tended the living and covered the dead. Bill was critical—not expected to live. He had taken a bullet through the shoulder and his blood loss had put him in jeopardy. Even with Lisa screaming, the army took several minutes to find her in the cave. Bill made incoherent noises. The medic found his blood pressure nearly absent.

Soldiers pried her away from Bill so the medic could treat him, giving him plasma. The helicopter landed to transport him and the other wounded to the military hospital in Cairo. Nearly in hysterics, Lisa insisting on traveling with him. While they flew, she couldn't see him breathing. His gray color looked horrible even as the medics gave him oxygen. Bill did not regain consciousness during the flight.

Waiting in surgical reception, Lisa was reduced to raw terror. The male military triage nurse gave Lisa no hope, shaking his head, telling her to expect the worst because her man had lost too much blood.

My man.

Helicopters arrived, transporting more wounded and the dead—soldiers and terrorists. Additional Egyptian soldiers came to guard the four captured terrorists. Military families arrived to find their relatives. The room was turmoil. Lisa wanted to run away from the noise, run away to Bill, but that was not possible so she rocked back and forth, gripping her shoulders, sobbing through the bedlam. She prayed and she wept.

Lisa was vaguely aware Dr. Tu'hut arrived. They did not speak, but he did look sadly at her, murmuring something as he left.

Time began to stretch. Two hours passed. Periodically, the doctors would wade into the morass of bodies calling the name of a soldier. The family would follow the doctor with screams of anguish if their loved one had not survived, while others followed with the joy of relief. The room was slowly emptying.

"Dr. Hampton?" a voice said in Arabic.

Lisa, her senses dull, looked at an Egyptian woman dressed in a robe standing beside her.

"Have you heard something?" she whispered.

"No."

Lisa sank back into her tormented thoughts and began to weep again. The woman touched Lisa's shoulder, startling Lisa who refocused on the native woman shocked by her touch.

"My name is Nefri," she said. When Lisa did not respond, she continued. "Omar was my husband. He came here a few weeks ago."

Lisa recognized the name.

"Oh my, I'm so sorry," gasped Lisa having made the connection. Nefri nodded her eyes distant, vacant, looking back to another time.

"There has been too much death," Nefri said. Lisa took several gulps of air to control her emotions. "Anwar said your warning saved his company. He thanks you. He said you needed help."

"Is he OK? Is he here?"

"Anwar's all right, but he isn't here. He's at your tomb."

The idiomatic mistake jolted Lisa.

"I appreciate your coming to the hospital," she eventually replied. Nefri nodded.

"Anwar sent word your man's badly injured, near death that I should come."

"Oh," gasped Lisa tears welling to the surface again. "Anwar is a good man."

"Yes, he is. Sometimes he thinks too much about war, but he's a good man. He loves everything that's Egypt."

"Yes, he does," Lisa agreed. She saw a doctor enter the room. He was searching. When he saw her, he walked to her.

"You're here with the American scientist?"

"Yes!"

"I've just completed surgery and he's been moved to recovery. He's survived this first step. It'll be several days before we can tell whether he'll survive the trauma. When he arrived, he had lost a lot of blood and was in shock. I gave him blood and treated his wounds. The bullet has been removed. He was lucky it only scratched the artery. I assume your pinching the blood vessel saved his life." He pointed at her bloody hands. "Wash those and change your clothes. Now we must fight shock and infection. He's a lucky man. Let's hope his luck continues."

The air rushed out of Lisa in a huge whoosh.

"Oh, thank you, doctor. Thank you."

"As I said, he's in recovery, but you may wait in his room."

"Oh, thank you again."

The doctor nodded and left.

"I'm happy for you," said Nefri who'd remained beside Lisa to hear her news.

"I must go to his room. Please, stay with me."

CAIRO, EGYPT, THE MILITARY HOSPITAL, JULY 16TH, 9:23 A.M.:

Lisa never left the hospital. Lisa realized for the first time her independence depended on everyone around her. For the past two days she had relied on Omar's wife. Nefri brought her food while she held vigil over Bill.

Her lack of sleep was taking its toll, but she would not allow comfort for herself with him in jeopardy. She would have time to think and she did not wish to think of losing Bill. Nor did she want to think of killing the terrorist.

She discovered she needed Bill. At first, he'd been there to bounce her ideas. He had been a familiar, daily professional colleague. They had lived closely, working interactively. She realized she had deep feelings for Bill. She realized she had fallen in love with Bill. She had fallen in love again, amazing just after a month and a half. Now he hung near death.

Why do my relationships always go south?

He supported her theory, working with her to prove its truth. In an instant, she understood they had not proven their theory. They had not found the necessary evidence before the battle took place. The site was closed. Lisa did not wish to remember the feature. It was her great failure. It was the source of her pain.

We didn't have enough time. Not enough time.

Eventually, she understood she had to get her feelings out. She needed to keep her sanity by working through her emotions. When her desire to speak finally came, it rushed in a torrent.

"The rooms are beautiful, decorated for a queen. The walls appeared blank, but Anwar made a great discovery. They were covered with beautiful pictures and stories faded with age."

"I recognize Anwar," said Nefri with a warm smile. "His passion."

"The rooms are stacked with belongings, floor to ceiling, wall to wall. Ḥaāmer had a loving sister, Āakhu, who wrote her love for her in poetry. Wonderful!"

CAIRO, EGYPT, BILL'S ROOM AT THE MILITARY HOSPITAL, JULY 17TH, 9:17 A.M.:

His throat dry and swollen, a result of his being on oxygen, would hardly swallow. Lisa lay against his side. Her head down so he couldn't see her face.

She is here.

"I love you too," he rasped the first words he'd spoken since the day he'd been shot.

She jumped at the sound of his voice.

"Oh!" she gasped. "You're awake."

Apparently, she had not heard him.

"I said...."

"I heard you," she said quickly. Her face was serious and he wondered if he had made a mistake. Suddenly she was in his face, pressing her lips hard against his. "I love you too. Bill Sanders, you scared me to death. I thought I'd lost you."

"So I did hear you in the tomb?" his voice grated surprising him. She nodded as she brought the flask of water and the straw to his lips, her shy eyes downcast. She allowed him to rinse his mouth and swallow the wonderful fluid. "Thank you."

"You're welcome. Yes, you heard me."

"Lisa...."

"Rest. You need your strength," she insisted. He thought she was avoiding the conversation.

"I want to say something."

"I want to talk too, but you need to rest."

He sighed, relaxed and fell asleep.

CAIRO, EGYPT, BILL'S ROOM AT THE MILITARY HOSPITAL, JULY 17TH, 12:30 P.M.:

He awoke, he had no idea how much later, but the shadows had shifted across the room. Lisa was still there. This time she was holding his hand. He lay still trying to sense what was happening, but she felt his presence. She looked at him seeing him looking at her. She blushed smiling at him, squeezing his hand. A native woman stood walking from the room.

"You're back again," she smiled and squeezed his hand.

"Among all your accomplishments, I didn't realize you were a nurse too."

"Oh, my clothes. Mine were soiled," she said. "With...."

Her face went pale.

...my blood? he thought. When she did not continue, he had his answer.

"How long was I out?" he asked.

"This last time or when they brought you in?"

He considered her question.

"Both I guess."

"After your surgery, you were out three days. You awoke this morning for the first time, three hours ago."

"I guess I've been sleeping a lot on the job," he croaked. She laughed, giving him more water.

"I'm sure glad to have you around."

He nodded at her. He was beginning to feel better, stronger with the liquid.

"Who was the woman who left?"

"Nefri, Omar's wife."

"Oh," he was surprised. Then sadly he continued. "So she was sitting with you? That's a sobering thought."

"Yes," she said. "I was terribly worried about you."

"So...we need to talk about us," he said his thoughts turning serious.

"I think so," she agreed with a smile.

"Before this happened. At the feature. Things had changed for me," he said.

She nodded at him.

"Yes, me too. That evening on the cliff when you kissed me, I was shocked. I didn't know what to do."

"I thought I had offended you."

"You surprised me. I wasn't offended."

"You recovered nicely," he grinned.

She blushed.

"Yes, that was good," she said. "Before that, I considered myself to be strictly professional, but I recognize I was fooling myself."

"Yeah, me too."

"When I thought I'd lost you, it sucked the life out of me. I thought I couldn't go on. I couldn't live," she said her emotions etched on her face.

"I'm glad you're here with me."

"I won't be leaving."

"I thought you might go to the feature."

"Oh, Bill, I'm never going to leave you."

He smiled at her.

"I feel that way too," he said sighing a deep breath. Tugging her arm, he pulled her face to his, kissing her for a long time. After a deep breath he continued. "Wonderful. So what has the government done with the feature?"

"It's closed. Dr. Tu'hut came by several times to see you."

"You're kidding. That's amazing."

"I think he appreciates my saving his neck at the feature," she told Bill. When he frowned she explained to him the full story. She concluded with, "and he even seems to accept me now."

He shook his head.

"I'm sorry to hear about the lieutenant, but saving Dr. Tu'hut, Lisa, as always you're incredibly skilled."

"I'd rather not remember what happened because of my skill. I find the loss of the lieutenant devastating. He and I interacted on so many occasions. We walked the tomb corridor together during the first viewing. I liked him. I will miss him."

"Well, I for one am glad Dr. Tu'hut knows your part in the exploration," said Bill, changing to a happier subject. "I'm glad you two are getting along better. But we didn't get our proof."

"That's not important," she assured him.

"It is too! You know it is. I want you to talk with Dr. Tu'hut and explain how important it is for both of us to go there."

"I don't know how soon you can do that."

He nodded. "Not this second, but soon. I think there is a wonderful thing to be discovered. I want to prove you right."

CAIRO, EGYPT, MINISTER TU'HUT'S OFFICE, JULY 19TH 10:15 A.M.:

"Ah, Dr. Hampton. Please come in. Ali, would you please bring tea for Dr. Hampton and me."

Lisa didn't expect that form of reception.

"Thank you, Minister Tu'hut."

"I prefer Doctor. Please sit here. I'm happy you weren't harmed in these most recent unpleasant incidents. I grieve the losses for our army, removing our country's vermin. It's certainly unfortunate that several were killed, but it's their job. The military's paid to protect us."

Lisa nodded. Tu'hut looked steadily at her for several seconds.

"But it's most unfortunate Dr. Sanders' condition. I don't wish any harm to a distinguished scientist who's come to help us in the study of our country. How is his healing? I pray for his survival and recovery."

Lisa was moved. "He is gaining strength. We are hopeful that he will make a full recovery."

"Good. And you Dr. Hampton. I appreciate what you did for me. Are you recovering?"

She nodded. Once again Lisa was shocked. She didn't think he had a sensitive bone in his body. He was concerned about her feelings, having shot a man.

He's appreciative of my saving him.

"I will be fine," she said.

"Good. You said you had something to discuss. Now what can I do for you?"

"I came to request being allowed back to the site."

Dr. Tu'hut's head jerked back with surprise.

"I'm shocked that you'd want to return there, seeing that it was only an investigation."

"Our investigation is not complete." Her statement seemed cold and detached under the circumstances. It seemed to be coming from someone else's mouth. "Oh my, I did not want that to come out as coldly as it seemed to."

"I had no idea that you're so dedicated to this exploration. I'm greatly surprised."

"Now that Bill is recovering, we, *both,* would like to continue our exploration. We wish to open this tomb."

"Dr. Sanders wishes to return as well?" asked an amazed Dr. Tu'hut.

"More than ever. He is the one actually making the request."

He sat looking at her his eyes blinking rapidly.

"Are we sure the evil ones are finished?"

"Well as soon as that can be cleared up."

Their tea arrived and their conversation dwindled while they waited for their cups. Ali handed Dr. Tu'hut his cup first and Jabar handed the cup to Lisa. She smiled at him. Jabar accepted the second cup and spent time preparing his tea. He added a large amount of sugar. They both sipped. Lisa wondered if he were being a gracious host or if he had actually offered a woman his cup of tea. She settled on the former. Lisa's tea was scalding hot. They sipped for several minutes neither speaking. Dr. Tu'hut set his cup on the small table in front of him, leaning back, he interlaced his fingers across his chest. He looked into her eyes for several seconds studying her, thinking.

"I'm sorry to inform you that it isn't possible to go to the feature. I always seem to be giving you bad news; however, in this case the government causes it. Not me. The government."

"The government?" Lisa responded.

"Yes, I'd like to go there personally, but even I'm forbidden. They've sealed the tomb. The army still guards it to keep looters away, but everyone associated with the tomb has been forbidden to return. Even the army officer who was guarding the site has been reassigned."

Jabar Tu'hut was watching her face intently as he spoke. Tears formed in her eyes. She seemed to be crying a lot recently now that her tough facade had vanished. Jabar didn't seem disturbed by her emotional response. He reached into the pocket of his western suit coat offering her his handkerchief. She took the cloth and dabbed her eyes. Lisa tried to calm herself before she responded.

"Is this prohibition temporary or permanent?"

"I wished that I could give you that answer. I'm not even being informed and I'm supposed to manage all of our antiquities. I understand this decree comes from the highest order. I believe the president."

Lisa was heart sick, but she understood. If Jabar was telling her the truth, his hands were tied the same as hers.

"Can you tell me why you two are so driven in this exploration?" he asked.

Lisa studied Dr. Tu'hut intently for several seconds, not knowing whether to tell him or not. He would think that she was crazy. She sighed. She must make this decision.

"What were the dates from the latest materials we sent you?"

He nodded then smiled.

"Until this moment, I've never thought of your being the source of the items that I received for dating. Now I realize you're deeply involved and of course interested, fascinated?" he smiled warmly at her. "Five thousand three hundred three years with an error of fifteen years."

"Within the same timeframe as the previous material that we sent you," Lisa mused.

"Yes, amazingly close."

"That puts the site near the time of Menes reign," Lisa speculated.

"Yes, I know that Dr. Sanders and you've been careful in selecting a representative group of items for dating."

"Yes. I believe the mummy's tissue is the most demonstrative. Did we capture her DNA?"

"Ah, yes, the mummy. Yes, we have her DNA. This find is truly important."

"I agree. Much more than you can imagine."

"What do you mean, Dr. Hampton?"

"We have found Osiris," she said simply.

"Of course you have. He's everywhere or are you saying you have found God?" snorted Dr. Tu'hut tickled by his little joke.

"The later, the real Osiris and Isis," she thrust her annoyance aside for she needed this man's support. It dawned on her that she must explain her theory to him because he was not following her thought process. "The god, Osiris, and the goddess, Isis, are buried in this tomb."

Dr. Tu'hut's mouth fell open with shock, and when he finally recovered, he threw back his head laughing heartily.

"You cannot be serious," he said, putting his hand to his mouth to stifle his laughter.

"Quite."

He understood that she was crazy. The stress of the last few days must have indeed unhinged her.

"Dr. Sanders and I have found numerous artifacts that corroborate our theory. Many of the artifacts are completely wrong in the timeframe of this tomb, out of place in this time, Osiris and Isis had not been invented, yet your dating indicates the correctness of our timeline."

"I'm confident the dating is correct."

"I agree. Dr. Sanders and I both believe we have discovered the legendary Osiris and Isis or more preciously in the ancient Egyptian language, Ạsạr and Īset. That is what kept confusing us. The two were always referred to as Ạsạr and Īset which we immediately translated to Osiris and Isis."

"You really are serious. Please let me understand what you're saying." Dr. Tu'hut's heavy eyebrows knit together. "You believe Osiris and Isis are buried in this tomb yet it's my understanding that two women, ah...ah... Ḥaāmer and...and Āakhu were buried in this feature."

"At least one woman, Ḥaāmer. Does this fact in itself seem strange? Our very first mystery when we looked through the ceiling into the tomb was Ḥaāmer's name appeared in a serekh. A serekh without a Horus falcon. There was no falcon because Horus had not ascended to a god. Or perhaps he was their younger brother so he had not even been born at the time of Ḥaāmer's death. Here are mentioned two women of ancient importance, the undocumented daughters of Ạsạr and Īset, Osiris and Isis."

"Osiris and Isis had no daughters."

"In the legend that is true. They had a son named Horus, Heru, who avenged his father's death at the hands of his uncle, Seth, Set. We have found inscriptions from Heru written to his sisters."

Tu'hut stared at her in shock.

"Heru?"

"Yes, we have found evidence of each of these characters, but we had not locked down our proof. We believe that Osiris and Isis are buried in an undiscovered room at the feature."

"So you really haven't found Osiris or Isis?"

"True, that is why we must return and finish the project."

"Dr. Hampton! This isn't possible. It is too unbelievable."

"True. It must seem very unbelievable. Dr. Sanders was as skeptical as you about the explanation at first, but now he has thrown his entire energy into proving or disproving this theory. He has brought you all of the evidence we have been able to develop. Please study the information and help us to return to the site."

Dr. Tu'hut twisted his mustache looking skeptically at Lisa. He was becoming interested.

"Your statements are truly amazing. You really believe this?"

"Yes."

Tu'hut gazed at the ceiling continuing to twist his mustache in concentration. After a moment, he said.

"There's a significant body of knowledge that does indeed point to a mortal beginning for Osiris and Isis. Most scientists ignore this, but many scientists believe it. You think you've discovered their tomb?"

He was putting his thoughts into words now.

"Yes."

"Oh, my. What an startling thought."

Lisa could tell that he was truly intrigued. If this were true, he would be famous forever. His eyes were unfocused. He played the deep thoughts around in his mind, thoughts based on what he had seen in the pictures they had sent.

"You realize the archaeological community won't agree with this unless you can show direct proof?"

"Which is why Bill and I wish to go to the feature again."

"I understand. I'll work at getting all of us to the tomb again, but I don't recommend your sneaking there."

Lisa gave Jabar a wry smile. "Right. Not like before?"

Dr. Tu'hut nodded. "By the way Dr. Hampton, we believe that Ḥaāmer was poisoned."

"What!"

"The tissue samples you sent us had lethal amounts of arsenic poison in them."

"We thought she died of tuberculosis."

"We found evidence that she had severe tuberculosis as well; however, maybe she was helped from this world. I'll study your findings. If I agree with your analysis from the artifacts, I'll put every effort into convincing my government in the importance of our continuing our exploration. I've found you to be a most enterprising young woman, Dr. Hampton. I wish you success in your theory."

"You are most kind. Thank you, Dr. Tu'hut. I certainly hope that we will be able to work together in the future."

Lisa was fishing with this comment, taking a chance with that statement, but she wanted to know.

"That would be a great pleasure, doctor. I look forward to it."

Lisa was amazed how far he'd come.

CAIRO, EGYPT, MILITARY HEADQUARTERS, GENERAL FADI'S OFFICE, JULY 19TH 10:18 A.M.:

Captain Anwar Jagardii stood at rigid attention precisely one pace, the army prescribed distance, away from and in the center of General Fadi's desk. The general stood leaning over his desk, his hands gripping the back edge, ripping the captain. The cords on his neck stood out. His purple, apoplectic face contorted with his rage. Anwar did not move a muscle nor twitch, as the general tongue-lashed him. The captain already had learned two new meanings to words previously unknown to him and certainly not repeatable by him.

"I'll expect a full accounting of your actions at the Abydos site, captain. You'll explain your lack of preparedness in the regard to the terrorist attack. You'll explain all use of military equipment. It's my understanding that you appropriated a helicopter that now has many holes bored through it. I understand that you lost ten men in this fiasco with no clear determination of the results. How many of these slimy bastards have slithered away into the desert only to erupt again on our streets?"

The general seemed to run out of steam with the interrogative.

"May I respond to your questions, sir? I'll provide you with a written report of all my activities as you've requested, sir."

General Fadi fixed Captain Jagardii with a deadly stare.

"If you think you're prepared for my wrath."

So he did expect me to respond, but he also indicates that he's prepared to burn me.

Anwar swallowed.

"I'm sure, sir, that we've routed out this nest of snakes."

"Oh? And how are you so confident?"

"I've used the American technology to determine the faces of each of the terrorists, sir. I believe I can tell you that I know each and every one of the bastards."

The general deflated. Genuine shock appeared on his face.

"You never mentioned any of this to me."

"I had no proof then, sir."

"Continue," Fadi prompted, his inflated body sagging.

"I ran the American photo-enhancing software against all of the recorded incidents to prove that I knew all terrorists involved in every incidence, sir. I've built a dossier on every one of them. If you'll permit me, sir, I'll show you photographs of the work."

"Proceed."

Anwar bent to a brief case that stood next to his right foot. He popped the clasps on the case and extracted a stack of 8 x 10 photographs and a DVD, placing them on the desk in front of the general. Marked on each photograph was the deposition of each person: DEAD, CAPTURED or AT LARGE.

"You contend that these are all of the terrorists? How are you sure?'"

"Each of the incidences on the internet was recorded for me, sir. When I evaluated the recordings, only the individuals in those photographs were there. As you will remember, I went to each of these places. I discovered that the local residents and authorities had no knowledge of the incident. I felt at the time that this was most peculiar, sir."

"I recall your reports," said the general, his manner leaving Anwar with the impression that he wasn't pleased with the results of these investigations.

Justifiably so, thought Anwar.

"Using the enhancement software, sir, I determined that each of the supposed villages was in reality a single place recorded from many different angles. Sir, the DVD recording will demonstrate this fact."

"Just continue your narrative, captain."

"Yes, sir. I can prove that the village landmarks included in the recordings were added afterward. It's very obvious in the enhanced views, sir."

The general drew a deep breath. Anwar believed that he saw the general relax at that instant. He realized that he may have just saved the general's ass. Obviously, Fadi was under a lot of heat—probably from the president and the ministry.

The general sat down, reaching forward and lifting the pile of photographs. He slowly leafed through each one stopping briefly to study each picture.

"You indicate we only captured four of the terrorists and the rest are dead?"

"Yes, sir, with the exception of the leader of the terrorists, who never fully appears on screen and the reporter who tells the story at each location. They are marked 'AT LARGE' on the photographs. Otherwise, every one of the combatants has been identified and contained, sir."

"So you haven't captured everyone?"

"No, sir," Anwar held his breath concerned that the general would throw out all of his explanation and work. The general regarded Anwar for several seconds.

"Colonel!" roared the general. Colonel Mohieddin entered the office from a side door a moment later. Anwar came to attention again.

"At ease, captain," waved the general. Addressing Mohieddin, he said, "The captain has provided us with a DVD of the entire mob of terrorists. Play it on my television."

"Yes, sir."

Fadi handed the disk to Colonel Mohieddin. Anwar looked at Mohieddin whose look and expression indicated Mohieddin loathed him. The colonel put the DVD into the player.

"You may leave, colonel," said Fadi.

Anwar played the video for the general. Each terrorist appeared on the screen. Each appeared first in full face as in the photographs with their deposition, DEAD or CAPTURED. Then as if by magic each pirouetted like puppets on a string to show all angles of each man. The reporter appeared with the caption, AT LARGE. A set of legs appeared that were the only view of the last person shown on the disk. The caption was marked 'AT LARGE.' Each person was shown where they appeared in the original disks with short segments showing their movements.

The execution village appeared from different angles overlaid with prominent landmarks from the multiple villages. As Anwar indicated, the subterfuge was obvious in the enhanced version.

"I have rotated the village after stripping away the added features. I made an aerial view. With satellite imagery, I believe we will be able to find the village."

"Thank you, captain. I'm amazed by your work. I believe you've done a great service for our country. I'll review your results. In the meantime, please prepare your statements as I requested."

"Yes, sir."

Anwar had anticipated the general's request. He had already completed his report.

CAIRO, EGYPT, MILITARY HOSPITAL, JULY 19TH 12:04 P.M.:

"Lisa!" A voice boomed through the lobby as she entered the hospital.

"Robert! What are you doing here?"

"I was at the university. I heard the most extraordinary story about your exploits in the south. I heard that a battle had been fought, and your site closed."

"Yes." Her eyes began to smart.

"I heard that your project leader had been shot and was here at the hospital so I came to find you."

"Yes, Bill was shot, but is recovering. I thought we'd lost him. Thank you for coming."

"What happened?"

"The terrorists attacked, but the army was able to stop them. The army captain in charge of our site believes he's put an end to the terrorist problem."

"That would be great! I heard you saved Tu'hut's neck?"

"I really don't want to talk about that. It's a little too fresh in my mind." Her emotions cleared.

"Eventually, I want to hear the whole story."

"Probably not."

She led Robert to Bill's room.

CAIRO, EGYPT, MILITARY HOSPITAL, BILL'S ROOM, JULY 19TH 12:38 P.M.:

"Bill, they're not letting us return to the feature," Lisa told him after Robert had left, her eyes filling with tears again.

"Was Dr. Tu'hut uncooperative?"

"No, just the opposite, he had me for tea and listened politely to everything that I said."

Bill lifted a questioning eyebrow. Lisa continued.

"He laughed at me when I expressed our theory, but when I told him that we both wanted to prove it, he became interested. He told me that the site closure came from as high as the president. He had no idea when the site would be reopened."

"So this is more of a political situation than Dr. Tu'hut's lack of cooperation."

"Right. By the end of our conversation, he was suggesting that Osiris might have been human."

"Hmm, it sounds as if there's a chance he may come onboard. That's important if we want to get back there. After all, he does run the place."

"We need to find out what is stopping the president. He should be happy to divert attention to other areas away from the terrorists." said Lisa.

"We need to go through channels and discover what's happening," he suggested.

"I think Dr. Tu'hut's doing that for us. He is committed. We need to let him convince his government to proceed. By the way, Dr. Tu'hut has discovered that Ḥaāmer was poisoned—perhaps euthanized."

"Really? Now I'm more than itching to get going again. I'd like to unravel their story."

"Bill Sanders! This doesn't sound like my all business, professional project manager speaking."

"You've captured my imagination, girl."

Lisa smiled at him appreciating the double meaning of his statement.

CAIRO, EGYPT, THE POLICE INVESTIGATION, JULY 21ST 9:50 A.M.:

The terrorist investigation was continued by the police. When they went to interrogate the captured the terrorists, they found the four, dead in their cells. A professional had slit their throats killing all of their witnesses even in the state prison.

They investigated the backgrounds of every terrorist that Captain Jagardii had identified in his dossiers. The bodies from the site were examined. The evidence from each was eliminated one at a time. Their histories, families and connections were followed. Their investigation found all to be mercenaries and murderers.

Following up on cell phone calls to an apartment, the police found the reporter who led each incident on television. He'd been dead in his apartment for three days. A thorough search of his apartment was conducted using intense forensic techniques, fingerprints, foreign substance tracing and blood traces. No information led away from the dead reporter. All calls had been made into his apartment from burner cell phones held by two terrorists. He had made no outgoing calls. His murderer was presumed to be the same professional who had killed the terrorists in the prison.

Using satellite imagery and Jagardii's rotated village photograph, the military located the village used to carry out the executions. It was located within two miles of the Abydos site. When the police arrived at the village, intensive, forensic analysis was made. Video equipment was discovered lending credence that this was the terrorists' village. Serial numbers from the equipment were checked. All appeared to have been obtained through the black market. Nothing led away from the the village.

The prime leader had covered his tracks remaining unknown and at large.

CAIRO, EGYPT, THE PRESIDENTIAL PALACE, AUGUST 6TH 11:00 A.M.:

General Fadi requested an audience with the president. Field Marshal Aaliyah was skeptical of Fadi's claim of success, but was willing to watch Fadi fail. Fadi's staff and he had made minute inspection of Captain Jagardii's data. With the lack of further terrorist activity, they concluded that the captain had indeed eradicated the terrorists. General Fadi was now prepared to propose the idea to the president.

Field Marshal Aaliyah and Fadi arrived at the Presidential Palace at Fadi's appointed time, presenting themselves to the president's secretary. Satisfied that Fadi had an appointment, the assistant buzzed the president announcing the generals. Fadi puffed out his chest and adjusted his uniform. All metal on his uniform as well as his shoes gleamed. He was magnificent.

What he hadn't expected was to find Saladin Aboud standing with the president. Fadi stiffened.

"Ah, Aaliyah, come," said the president wiggling his fingers for the field marshal to approach. He continued, "Fadi, you indicated in your request that you have been successful in solving our disgusting, mutual problem."

"Yes, Mr. President."

Fadi noted that Aboud was sipping tea from a silver service on the sideboard. Aaliyah went to the sideboard to pour himself some tea. The president didn't offer Fadi anything. The general knew this was a political statement. He concluded that he was still outside his leader's pale. He was about to change that.

"I believe we can make the statement that I have solved the terrorist problem," Fadi explained. He saw the president's eyebrows lift. Fadi glanced at Minister Aboud. His expression was grim as he turned to Aaliyah. Aaliyah shrugged. Fadi knew how the Field Marshal felt about him. Fadi was sure that would soon change. He had overlooked showing the FM the DVD.

"Really? You have proof?"

"Yes, as you know, Mr. President, I have been working to eradicate this nest of snakes. I have brought with me a most enlightening DVD. I would like to play it for you."

The president expression changed to surprise. He rang for his aide.

"The recording contains a collection of all terrorist incidents sent to us," Fadi continued. "I apologize for having to subject you to all of the gruesome details one more time."

The president waved his hand in a derisive manner indicating for Fadi to get on with it. Fadi pressed the PLAY button. The screen showed the first incident.

"Using computer technology, we have isolated individuals. All victims were removed from the recording. Each victim has been identified. We are moving to contact their families."

The president grunted his approval.

Fadi went forward with his narrative.

"Using this technique, we reduced the terrorist's complex movements into a set of individual simple actions. Almost like choreographing dancers in a ballet."

Fadi noted that the president appeared rather fascinated by the slow-motion tracking of a false colored selected terrorist.

"If we knew that we had killed or captured him, we removed this individual from consideration."

Following his narrative, Fadi felt he had demonstrated his success to the president.

"As you can see, Mr. President, all individuals have been identified and compared against the group of people we know are dead."

"This was done with American technology?" asked the president.

"Yes, Mr. President."

Fadi saw that the president was completely absorbed in the process. He glanced at Minister Aboud and was shocked at how sick he appeared. His skin had taken on an ashen paler. Field Marshal Aaliyah appeared angry. Fadi was satisfied he had out maneuvered the field marshal at least for the moment; however, this could cause future political ramifications.

"And all of the monsters have been identified?" the president asked.

"Yes, Mr. President, with the exception of this person who through his actions appears to be directing the activities of the others. He is the leader, but is not a combatant. We're in the deepest pursuit of this person."

The president smiled for the first time.

"Good. You have chopped up the body of the snake. You are pursuing the head. It has been three weeks since you reported success. I have been watching. There have been no incidences. I am sure you will capture the leader. You've done an excellent job, general. The fact we know that you've eradicated this scourge eases my mind and all the minds of our people. Gentlemen, the general's done a wonderful service. Don't you agree?" he turned to the other two.

"Yes, Mr. President. A wonderful service, sir. Congratulations general on your success," said Aboud.

Field Marshal Aaliyah echoed Aboud's praise though it was obvious he was angry with being left out of the final resolution.

Fadi bowed. He saw that Minister Aboud had regained his stomach.

"General, do you have time for some tea?"

"Thank you. You are most gracious, Mr. President."

CAIRO, EGYPT, MILITARY HEADQUARTERS, GENERAL FADI'S OFFICE, AUGUST 6TH 3:12 P.M.:

"My congratulation on your successful mission," the ambassador spoke to Fadi by telephone upon Fadi's return from the Presidential Palace. "May my country have the opportunity to question the mercenaries?"

"Unfortunately none have survived, Your Excellency."

"Then they've escaped my vengeance and are lucky. Have you located the source?"

"No my most talented officer has determined that each of the mercenaries has been killed, but unfortunately even though the source has been partially identified, we've insufficient information to determine who he is, Your Excellency."

"A grave concern to me. This monster may rise from the ashes again. My intelligence service is most impressed with your Captain Jagardii. He is a resourceful and talented man."

"Yes, we agree, Your Excellency. It is Colonel Jagardii."

"Ah, yes, a good move. Could we suggest another sharing of information?"

"What is that, Your Excellency?"

"We would like to have your *Colonel* Jagardii lecture our service."
"An intriguing thought, sir. We will consider it."

CAIRO, EGYPT, THE PRESIDENTIAL PALACE, AUGUST 13TH 10:00 A.M.:

The press assembled in the presidential briefing room to hear the announcement advertised as the terrorist resolution. The president stepped to the podium.

"Let us begin," said the president. "I'm happy to announce that through the heroic efforts of our army, the terrorist problem has been removed. We're confident that these monsters have been eliminated. We're sad to report that several of our soldiers were killed in this final cleaning out. We'd like to commend the brave men who gave their lives in protecting our country. We grieve with their families.

"Turning to a related topic, today, I would like to announce the appointment of our new Prime Minister. His dedicated service for our country and his support of me has earned Saladin Aboud my greatest appreciation. He'll assume command of the Ministry immediately. He will begin to rebuild our country's confidence in its government. His former post, that of Ministry of the Interior, will be filled by Minister Abdul Fadi whose energy has brought this page in our history to an end. I'd like to turn this news conference over to our new Prime Minister to answer any questions that you might present.

"Minister Aboud...."

Chapter 24

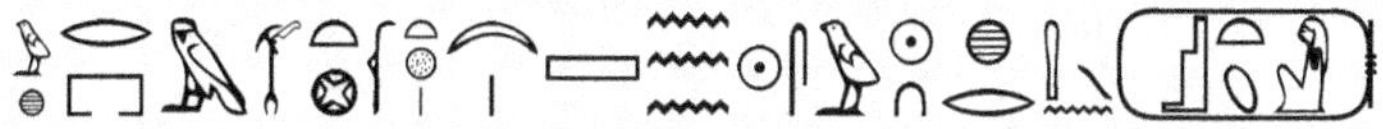

wḫrpr m wꜣst ḥsbt 1 ꜣbd 1 šm sw 10 ḫr ḥm n ꜣst

The Docks in Uas

Year 1, Month 1 of Shemu, Day 10 under the Majesty of Īset

Īset's handmaids arrived with the last of her possessions when the line of torches appeared from the direction of the Temple of Ptah. Steppu paused in unloading a cart and frowned as she watched it.

"They know," said Kefa·ạb beside her.

"I am afraid they do," Steppu replied already turning her thoughts to their options.

"What will we do? We cannot let them take Īset."

Steppu looked to the Royal Boat, then back to the torches bobbing along the crooked streets. She called to Neb-t·ḥe-t who had also turned to watch them. "Time to go."

"Yes," Neb-t·ḥe-t said. She looked at Steppu and frowned. "You're not coming, are you."

Steppu's voice was as calm as an afternoon at the ovens. But her expression was serious. "There is no time. I would that it might be different, but it isn't. Take the others and go. I will delay Set as long as I am able. Ptah will see that it is enough."

Neb-t·ḥe-t looked at Tchefeṭ-t, her green eyes flashing over the top of the cart. "I stay with Steppu."

"Our hearts have made us sisters," said Ạaātchṭạ-t beside Tchefeṭ-t, looking at Steppu and following her gaze off toward the temple. "We go with you Steppu. You will need us."

Rāmạtet, her eyes large with the first chill of fear, nevertheless answered with brave formality. "Tell Lady Īset we love her and will see her again."

Neb-t·ḥe-t nodded. "You can do nothing here Kefa·ạb. Surely you will come. Īset still needs you."

Kefa·ạb shook her head, her eyes filled with tears. "I am old now, I cannot go with either of you. Īset doesn't need me, she has you now. And I would only slow you down, Steppu. I will disappear into the city and await your return."

"Go, both of you," Steppu said.

Neb-t·ḥe-t kissed her and whispered. "Let Set see how pretty you are. Don't let him see how smart you are until you escape."

Neb-t·ḥe-t hurried down the pier and up the ramp. Each of the servants gave Kefa·ạb a hug. Steppu, the last, gave her a gentle push back along the pier toward the city streets. To the others she said: "Come. We need to reach Set quickly."

*   *   *

Īset paused at the door to her cabin to see Neb-t·ḥe-t stumbling onto the boat. "Set is coming. Go," she said to the boat master.

The boat master looked up, following the direction Neb-t·ḥe-t pointed, and saw torches halfway along the path from the Temple of Ptah. He immediately barked orders and the ropes that held the boat were cast off.

The rowers dropped oars into the water and pulled, an echoing, rhythmic, song starting among them to provide a cadence for their motions.

Īset saw the torches coming down the hillside and pointed. "Pharaoh is coming. We must wait."

"That isn't Pharaoh. It's Set coming for you," Neb-t·ḥe-t replied.

Boxes of Īset's possessions remained on the dock. "We should send someone to see. Where are my handmaids?"

She started to the side of the boat nearest the dock. "We can't leave, they're still ashore!"

Īset was intercepted by one of the guards. "My Lady, you need to be out of view."

"No," Īset said, struggling to get around him. "My husband and handmaids are not aboard."

Neb-t·ḥe-t joined them and hugged Īset, tears in her tired eyes. She sobbed: "Your handmaids have stayed behind to slow Set down. They are risking their lives that we might get away."

Not risk, oh dark Ptah in Amennt: not risk. They are additional sacrifices on the dark altars of you who claim to love us.

"Oh gods," Īset moaned.

*   *   *

Steppu took a look back before the Ukher was lost from view. The royal boat had left the dock and was moving out into the River. *Will it be enough?*

The others had stopped behind her. She looked at each in turn. "Follow my lead. Let me do the talking."

Three pairs of large, somber eyes watched her without blinking. Three heads nodded.

Steppu plunged around a corner onto the most likely street. Halfway along it she paused at another intersection to look both ways. She nodded and hurried off, the others in tow. Little Rāmạtet, still young enough to have nearly boundless childhood energy, ran to keep up with the others, her hand still held firmly in Ạaātchtạ-t's.

They ran into Set's party moments later.

"It's a ruse," Steppu called. "Īset is not on the boat. She sent some of her servants on the Nile to trick us. She's going by land to Kush. If we hurry, we might still catch her."

The party of priests came to a confused halt, never expecting to be met by three young women and a child who knew where they were going.

wꜣst ḥsbt 1 ꜣbd 1 šm sw 10 ḫr ḥm n ꜣst

Uas

Year 1, Month 1 of Shemu, Day 10 under the Majesty of Īset

"What is this?" Set asked, as he and Shepses reached the front of the party.

"Lord Set," The oldest of the four women said, bowing. Her voice had soft, almost beguiling harmonics. "Īset is not on the royal boat."

"Why not?"

A second woman, with unusual eyes that Set found both disturbing and strangely compelling in the amber torchlight, sneered: "She sent us to take the royal boat towards the sea, giving her time to slip southward. She left us at your mercy to save her own skin. I've served her and her daughters my whole life, and *this* is how she rewards me. When I catch up to her I will carve a little justice from her hide."

She fingered the handle of a small, bronze kitchen knife that was tucked in the girdle of her skirt.

"If we hurry, we could catch her by dawn," Steppu added.

Set looked at Shepses.

"I think we should go after the boat," Shepses said.

"Well fine," huffed the second woman, motioning to her companions, facing a crooked street that wandered southward. "When we catch her we'll tell her that her simple ploy fooled you. Come, sisters, we are losing time here."

"Hold," shouted Set, his pride unexpectedly stung by her goading. He looked at each of the four, the two youngest silent to this point. "What about you two?"

The third of the young beauties, barely a woman in age, looked sadly at Set. "My sisters speak truly."

A tear spilled down the cheek of the youngest. Her eyes were large and frightened. She trembled, and clung to the third woman, who dropped a hand to smooth back her tussled hair. She cried in her child's voice, "Our Lady has left us!"

Set quickly ran through a number of thoughts, in an attempt to determine truth from this unexpected encounter. *Īset is certainly capable of such a plan, but would she? Would one who places so much importance in loyalty desert so many? But they are just servants. And how would mere servants concoct such a story?*

Around and around the thoughts chased themselves, leaving Set no clear answer. The priests watched him. Shepses watched him. He looked toward the Ukher, searched the inscrutable faces of each of the sisters, and glanced at the twisted path that led southward.

If she is heading north, the Royal Boat and all the people aboard it will be an easy prey to follow and find. But if Īset is moving south with a small party, she will be able to fade away much too easily. Each moment I wait gives her a better chance of eluding me.

Set looked at Steppu. "You will go south with us."

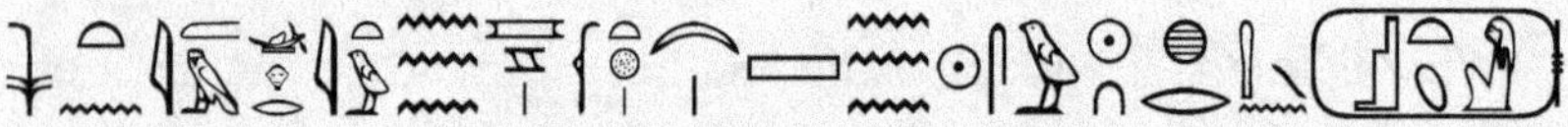

jmw-nswt ḥr jtrw ḥsbt 1 ꜣbd 1 šm sw 10 ḫr ḥm n ꜣst

Pharaoh's Boat on the River
Year 1, Month 1 of Shemu, Day 10 under the Majesty of Īset

Neb-t·ḥe-t watched the soft glow of the city and the temple fade in the distance. She frowned and sought the boat master. "Bring the strong wine."

"Wine now?" Īset scoffed.

"Everyone is busy except us. We must stay calm and out of the way."

"We must turn back and look for Ạsạr," Īset demanded.

The boat master brought a jar and two bowls, bowing and setting the jar at Neb-t·ḥe-t's feet. "No pursuit yet," he said, passing the bowls into her hands.

"See," Īset said, grasping Neb-t·ḥe-t's arm. "Pharaoh has prevailed. He has his guards with him. Master, turn the boat around."

"Pharaoh and his guards are dead," Neb-t·ḥe-t said.

Īset said and did nothing for a moment, not even to take a breath. The boat master, eyes large and glistening, slid back a step before turning and seeking the furthest point of the deck.

"Curse him," Īset said at last, in a low, dangerous whisper, like the first innocent stirring of the air that presages the sand storm. "Curse the stupid idiot for letting his brother kill him in spite of the warnings. Curse him for giving Maaạ my last child. Curse him for leaving me alone."

Her voice rose in pitch and volume, swirling higher and higher in the night air. Tears filled her eyes and spilled down her cheeks in the cold, gray light of Aih. She trembled.

Neb-t·ḥe-t poured the wine into a bowl and pulled a piece of papyrus from her girdle, unfolding it in her fingers and sprinkling the powder into the wine. She pushed the bowl to Īset's lips. "Drink this."

"Curse the gods! Curse you!" Īset wailed.

"I have been cursed all the days of my life," Neb-t·ḥe-t said and tipped the bowl so Īset could either drink or dribble the wine down her chin and the front of her dress.

Īset drank and choked and cried and beat at Neb-t·ḥe-t with her fists. Her finger nails sought Neb-t·ḥe-t's face and throat, her arms. She screamed out her pain and loss in vile oaths. But not for long. Her voice thickened and grew quiet. Her arms became heavy, her attacks more feeble.

Her eyes widened and lost focus. Her fists relaxed and fell to her side. Her breathing slowed. "The wine," she said.

"It makes you sleep," Neb-t·ḥe-t said. "Let me help you to your bed."

She guided Īset with an arm about her waist into the room to the bed she and Pharaoh shared when they traveled the River. Īset sat heavily and fell backward onto a pillow. Neb-t·ḥe-t lifted her feet and removed her sandals before pulling a linen sheet over her.

"Is it worth it?" Īset whispered. "Is *anything* worth the lives that have been given?"

Neb-t·ḥe-t soothed her. "You and the son you carry will determine that. Make the days to come worth their lives. Think of them, remember who they were in the days ahead, let their courage and bravery strengthen your own, let their acts of compassion and wisdom guide you each day as you raise this child—Pharaoh's child."

"Is there any hope for my maid servants?"

"There is always hope." Neb-t·ḥe-t said. "Steppu is not foolish. When Set looks at a woman he sees an evening's pleasure. He is quite unprepared for women with minds as nimble and quick as Steppu and Tchefeṭ-t. If there is safe passage along the dangerous path they have taken, those two will find it."

"Tell me again what Ạaātchṭạ-t said at the dock."

Neb-t·ḥe-t sighed. "She said that our hearts have made us sisters."

Īset nodded and closed her eyes and fell into a deep sleep. Neb-t·ḥe-t watched her for awhile as a candle burned low and then left her to the care of the gods.

The boat master was waiting by the door as she emerged. "What you said about Pharaoh . . . "

"Set killed him," Neb-t·ḥe-t said.

"Then Īset is Pharaoh."

"In name only. Set rules in Uas."

"Maybe we should send men back for his body that we might give him a proper burial."

Neb-t·ḥe-t reached out and took the boat master by the hand. "A worthy thought, but Set has dismembered Pharaoh and will soon scatter the parts that he might never be reunited and buried. He thinks that in so doing Ạsạr can never return or seek revenge."

"So Set wins?"

"No, Set's defeat has only begun. We will recover the pieces and rejoin them. Pharaoh will have a funeral as befits the gods. But not tonight. Tonight we flee for our lives."

"Yes, priestess," he said and frowned, bending to peer at her. "You're bleeding. May I?" he asked, pointing at her cheek.

Neb-t·ḥe-t nodded.

He took a linen cloth from his girdle and brushed beneath her eye. She winced but did not pull away from him. "It could use some ointment," he said.

"My sister is a better fighter than she looks. Maybe I deserved it. I didn't deliver the news with any gentleness."

"There is no gentle way to deliver such sad, horrible news. What can I do for you?"

"Nothing."

"The night gets cold. Take my cloak," he said, shrugging out of it and wrapping it about her shoulders.

With a bow he walked forward, to the rowers, to the lookouts, to encourage them, to change them out for rest as they tired, to look back uneasily at Neb-t·ḥe-t and beyond her to the glow that was Uas dwindling in the distance.

Neb-t·ḥe-t thought in a weak moment that she might run forward and fall into his arms, tell him that it would be alright, that he would see Uas again and live a long and happy life and father many fine sons. But there would be that question in his eyes and she would have to admit that it would not be her with whom he found that happiness and fathered those sons, much as she might wish and pray for it at this moment. She was her sister's shadow, now and always, and shadows could not have lives of their own.

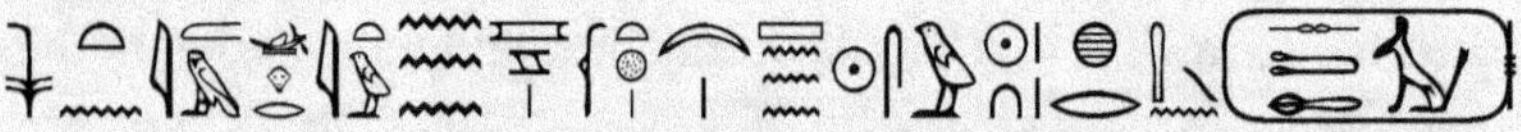

jmw-nswt ḥr jtrw ḥsbt 1 ꜣbd 1 šm sw 12 ḫr ḥm n sth

Pharaoh's Boat on the River

Year 1, Month 1 of Shemu, Day 12 under the Majesty of Set

Īset watched the people pointing at the royal boat from the banks of the River. "I must go."

"If he pursues, he will have no trouble following you," Neb-t·ḥe-t said beside her.

"Where are we?"

"The boat master said that we should reach Meḥ by tomorrow at midday," Neb-t·ḥe-t replied.

Īset sighed. "Tonight, then."

"We should tell the boat master."

Īset remained at the stern of the boat, watching the East and West banks slip past, composing her thoughts.

The season of Semut was nearly half over. The fields and hills up to the desert were brown. Most of the crops had been or were now being harvested. In the coming weeks, the River would begin to rise again. With hope, it would be a large and long inundation, bringing the rich, black soil from the south and depositing it where it would be used to grow the coming year's crop.

Where will I be? Īset wondered. *Where will the child that is growing within me be?*

Īset heard her sister and the boat master returning. She turned from the view of the River valley passing behind the stern and out of sight to see the boat master, Neb-t·ḥe-t and those few who had accompanied her, puzzlement on their faces. For some reason, they had all come.

"We must disperse if we are to survive," Īset said.

"No," they muttered, "Never."

She held up her hand. "Yes."

Her gaze settled for a moment on one before moving on to another. "Set wants me—Set needs me—to legitimize this false claim he makes on the throne of the fourteen provinces. But he doesn't need you. In joining this exodus, Set considers you unreliable at best. More likely, you have been proclaimed traitors."

"So be it," the boat master said. There were murmurs of agreement.

"Too many people have watched the royal boat pass and have recognized it. Set will have no trouble following us.

"The boat will reach Meḥ tomorrow at midday. There or soon after, dock the boat and sell it."

Īset gestured for quiet and waited. "Split the money among yourselves and start new lives, either under the eyes of prince Maaạ in Meḥ or somewhere else. Do not call attention to yourselves and don't give Set and his men a trail that they can follow to you."

"Why would Set be concerned with us?" asked Teqer, the house guard. He still stood straight and proud, the bronze knife belted at his side gleaming in the late afternoon sun.

"Because you might know of my whereabouts, and because you know the truth of what happened in Uas."

Īset again focused on the group, small as it was, her gaze moving from face to face. "The truth of the evil that Set committed against Pharaoh Ạsạr and the people of Egypt can still hurt him. Set fears that truth enough to kill every one of you.

"If you cannot sell the boat, strip it and sell everything you can. But do it quickly—and disappear. Forget your service to me, forget your service to Pharaoh Ạsạr. For the sake of your lives, forget that you ever knew me."

She stopped, seeing shock and sadness. She felt it reflected back to her. She swallowed the lump in her throat, putting a hand to her chest.

"I will never forget any of you. You have become as precious to me as my own daughters. I want you to live and be happy. You must leave me in order to do that."

"You are not coming with us?"

"No," said Īset sadly. "I am going ashore tonight."

"Why?"

Īset gestured for quiet once more.

"If I stay with you, you will know where I am. Set will get that information from you before he takes your lives. And if he finds me first, and I am with you, then he will kill all of you to bury the truth of how he came to power.

"I know how it hurts to hear this, almost as much as it does to say it and know the truth of it. We must scatter, like sand on the wind. Until you know that Set has stopped looking, if you encounter each other on the street, pass by without acknowledgment. Remember that the local priests, for a time, may be his eyes and ears. Do not speak of me. Do not remember me—except in your hearts and in your dreams."

She watched them, the few members of the royal staff that had come with her. She knew them, their wives and husbands, their lovers, their children. She had lost her family. Now she was losing another, larger family. Nobody moved. They stood silently, some with mouths open, their dark, wounded eyes watching.

"Please," Īset pleaded. "The only thing worse than sending you away like this would be to watch each of you die at Set's command, knowing it could have been avoided."

Īset's throat tightened again. Too much death in too short a time. She turned back to the boat's stern and the ripples on the water in the boat's wake without saying another word.

Distantly she heard the people disperse again, some on their own, and others sent off with a word or gesture from Neb-t·ḥe-t. She noted the silence, then heard the scuff of sandals on wood, and sensed that Neb-t·ḥe-t was again standing beside her.

"I must pack," Īset said, as much to herself as to her sister.

Neb-t·ḥe-t placed a hand on her shoulder and squeezed it sympathetically. "You are no longer a queen and cannot travel as one. Choose only what you can carry."

Īset's room was full of clothing and jewelry. It suddenly seemed like another life—one that had not ended well. From the clutter she selected a plain bag and laid it on her bed. She gathered a few simple mementos, items given to her by Ạsạr and her daughters. She found a couple of pairs of traveling sandals and cut the jewels off the straps to make them less conspicuous.

She folded two simple dresses and a cloak. By that time, the bag was almost full. She selected her favorite writing stick.

She took a last look at herself in a mirror of polished bronze. She removed the gold earrings and a gold and lapis collar from around her neck, and placed them carefully in her jewelry box. From her bag she removed two scarab earrings of lapis, and an ankh carved from wood and fixed to a leather strip.

Ạsạr had carved it himself and had given it to her as a child. He had teased her about it many times during their marriage, wondering why she would cling to such a plain, simple necklace when she had others that were much more elegant. She had smiled and shrugged and said "It was the first."

The ankh settled comfortably in the hollow between her breasts. Īset pulled the pack up over her shoulder and headed out to the deck.

The boat master stood at the front of the boat looking ahead. The River here was wide and quiet. He dropped to one knee when she approached.

"Get up," she said. "I am no longer a queen and you no longer serve me."

"You will always be my queen."

He studied her for a moment, his thoughts inscrutable.

"Ask," he said softly, "and I would accompany you. My life is yours."

She shook her head. "I could not command such a sacrifice. My best chance lies in retiring to one of the smaller villages where with a bit of dirt on my face, and a few tangles in my hair, I can be just another poor widow depending on the good will of my neighbors."

"I would like to think you are right," he said.

"So would I."

The day was nearly done. The sun was fading into the West, the light falling on the boat and the water was orange. Īset lifted a hand to her brow and scanned the River ahead. Seeing what she desired, she dropped the hand away from her face and pointed.

"Just before that bend I would like to be put ashore. See the rocks there that lead up into the hills?"

The boat master looked, and nodded. "I will not be able to take the boat all the way to shore. I can take you there in one of the skiffs."

"Your place is with the boat. Until you have sold it and divided the shares, all the others are your responsibility. Let one of the crew take me across. Can you do this without anchoring?"

"Yes, but we're going to have to anchor for the night anyway."

"Wait as long as you can. Put some space between us."

The boat master started to bow, caught himself, and nodded instead. "As you wish."

He gestured to one of the crew. Īset turned to look for Neb-t·ḥe-t and saw her alone, kneeling by the edge of the boat, praying, gesturing with her hands almost as if she were talking to someone.

Īset felt badly for what she was about to do, but she could not bear another good-bye.

The boat master appeared once more at her side. "We are ready."

"Treat her well," Īset said, watching her sister. "I have seen how you look at her, how you see to her comfort and how she comes to life when you are close. Take care of her. Do not let her follow me. Tie her to the mast if you must."

A momentary surprise crossed his face as he nodded.

Īset followed him aft. The boat master helped her down into the skiff. He touched her hand. "Ptah be with you, Īset."

"And you. Perhaps we will meet again one day, on this side or the other."

He nodded, wiped something from his eye, and strode off to resume his watch. A young man assigned to the skiff pushed off and rowed hard for the shore.

To look back towards the boat, or ahead towards the shore, thought Īset. *Past or future?*

If I could go back, if I could live each day over, if I could savor each tender moment with Ạsạr and Āakhu and Ḥaāmer to the fullest, it still would not be enough. The past, with all its tender moments, is still the path to longing and regret.

To the future then, with all its uncertainty. To the future and the child that rests within me. To new love and new hope.

Īset focused on the approaching bank, studying the paths that wandered up into the hills and the cliffs and desert beyond.

The young man coasted the skiff gently to a stop at the shore. He jumped out and steadied the skiff while Īset stepped out. He lifted her sack and helped settle it on her shoulder.

"Thank you," she said.

He smiled quite self-consciously in return. She watched him push the skiff back into the water and climb aboard. He waved just before he grasped the oars and pulled for the retreating boat.

Īset waved in return and started up the nearest path.

The light was deepening from orange to red. The air was still warm. The way before her had been smoothed by the passage of many feet, probably animal herds, and ascended at a comfortable grade. She knew there would be a small village nearby where she could find food and shelter for the evening.

Reaching the crest, Īset paused to take a last look before she disappeared into the safety of the rocks. Rounding a bend in the River, the royal boat slipped from view, several sad faces still visible from the stern. Closer, she saw a shadowed figure stumbling up the broken path below her.

Īset smiled, and at the same time a tear welled up in her eye. She retraced her steps down the rocky hill, meeting her sister halfway. They embraced, the tears in both their eyes the first communication to pass between them.

"Did you think you could go without your shadow?"

Īset cried. "Why would you spend your remaining days with the disgraced and pregnant widow of a fallen god?"

"You saw them; you know why," Neb-t-ḥe-t replied. "We each have our purpose for the gods. They have promised me I will see your son and he will someday avenge us both on Set."

"Let it be as you say," Īset nodded.

Hand in hand, they reclaimed the hill and began their journey, constant as water, invisible as wind, persistent as sand, concealed by the rocks from the River's view, two shadows fading into evening with the last rays of the Aten.

ABOUT THIS BOOK

This book is typeset and produced in Portable Document Format (PDF) using the MiKTeX typesetting system and the TeXmaker LaTeX editor. MiKTeX is developed by Chrisitan Schenk an is available under the "several free" license. TeXmaker is developed by Pascal Brachet and Joël Ambland and is available under the GNU General Public License (GPL). For more information, see the following web sites:

- MiKTeX project page: http://miktex.org
- TeXmaker home page: http://www.xm1math.net/texmaker/

LaTeX is a document markup language and document preparation system for the TeX typesetting program. LaTeX was authored by Leslie Lamport. TeX was developed by Donald Knuth.

This novel uses Bitstream Charter, an original design by Matthew Carter and implemented in the LaTeX PostScript New Font Selection scheme (PNFSS) by Sebastian Rahatz.

Hieroglyphics and transliterations use the HieroTeX package created by Serge Rosmordue. The hieroglyphic characters are based on classifications developed by Sir Alan Gardiner and first published in his "*Egyptian Grammar*" in 1927.

Ancient Egyptian people, places, and things use a transliteration alphabet created by Sir E. A. Wallis Budge and were developed using his two-volume "*An Egyptian Hieroglyphic Dictionary*," published by John Murray, London, in 1920 and republished by Dover Publications, Inc., New York, in 1978.

The image **Isis, Osiris, and Horus** that appears on the title page is permission-free clip art image 113 from the CD-ROM and book "*Egyptian Designs*," © 1999 by Dover Publications, Inc.

ABOUT THE AUTHORS

Dean Martin Herr

Born in Battle Creek, Michigan, Dean is named after his grandfather and father—not the famous singer. He received degrees in Mathematics and Physics from Michigan Technological University and has since worked as a technical writer and occasional application developer for the computer industry. I DIG MURDER is his first novel and his first collaboration with Roger Stacy. He lives in Houston, Texas, with his wife and very best friend, Connie Stein, and their cats.

Roger A. Stacy

Roger grew up in Illinois where he attended the University of Illinois, Champaign / Urbana. He received a degree in Civil Engineering with electives in Computer Science. He has worked as a Computer Software Product Author and a Project Manager (PMP). I DIG MURDER is his first novel. He lives in Houston, Texas, with his wife. He has two children and three grandchildren.

www.ingramcontent.com/pod-product-compliance
Lightning Source LLC
Chambersburg PA
CBHW060138260626
47160CB00001B/28
* 9 7 8 0 6 1 5 7 7 8 9 7 6 *